THE DECAMERON

GIOVANNI BOCCACCIO

Translated by
JOHN PAYNE

CONTENTS

DAY THE THIRD

DAY THE FOURTH

DAY THE FIFTH

DAY THE SIXTH

DAY THE SEVENTH

DAY THE EIGHTH

DAY THE NINTH

DAY THE TENTH

PROEM

HERE BEGINNETH THE BOOK CALLED DECAMERON
AND SURNAMED PRINCE GALAHALT WHEREIN ARE
CONTAINED AN HUNDRED STORIES IN TEN DAYS
TOLD BY SEVEN LADIES AND THREE YOUNG MEN

A KINDLY THING it is to have compassion of the afflicted and albeit it well beseemeth every one, yet of those is it more particularly required who have erst had need of comfort and have found it in any, amongst whom, if ever any had need thereof or held it dear or took pleasure therein aforetimes, certes, I am one of these. For that, having from my first youth unto this present been beyond measure inflamed with a very high and noble passion (higher and nobler, perchance, than might appear, were I to relate it, to sort with my low estate) albeit by persons of discretion who had intelligence thereof I was commended therefor and accounted so much the more worth, natheless a passing sore travail it was to me to bear it, not, certes, by reason of the cruelty of the beloved lady, but because of the exceeding ardour begotten in my breast of an ill-ordered appetite, for which, for that it suffered me not to stand content at any reasonable bounds, caused me ofttimes feel more chagrin than I had occasion for. In this my affliction the pleasant discourse of a certain friend of mine and his admirable consolations afforded me such refreshment that I firmly believe of these it came that I died not. But, as it pleased Him who, being Himself infinite, hath for immutable law appointed unto all things mundane that they shall have an end, my love,—beyond every other fervent and which nor stress of reasoning nor counsel, no, nor yet manifest shame nor peril that might ensue thereof, had availed either to break or to bend,—of its own motion, in process of time, on such wise abated that of itself at this present it hath left me only that pleasance which it is used to afford unto whoso adventureth himself not too far in the navigation of its profounder oceans; by reason whereof, all chagrin being done away, I feel it grown delightsome, whereas it used to be grievous. Yet, albeit the pain hath ceased, not, therefore, is the memory fled of the benefits whilom received and the kindnesses bestowed on me by those to whom, of the goodwill they bore me, my troubles were grievous; nor, as I deem, will it ever pass away, save for death. And for that gratitude, to my thinking, is, among the other virtues, especially commendable and its contrary blameworthy, I have, that I may not appear ungrateful, bethought myself, now that I can call myself free, to endeavour, in that little which is possible to me, to afford some relief, in requital of that which I received aforetime,—if not to those who succoured me and who, belike, by reason of their good sense or of their fortune, have no occasion therefor,—to those, at least, who stand in need thereof. And albeit my support, or rather I should say my comfort, may be and indeed is of little enough avail to the afflicted, natheless meseemeth it should rather be proffered whereas the need appeareth greater, as well because it will there do more service as for that it will still be there the liefer had. And who will deny that this [comfort], whatsoever [worth] it be, it behoveth much more to give unto lovesick ladies than unto men? For that these within their tender bosoms, fearful and shamefast, hold hid the fires of love (which those who have proved know how much more puissance they have than those which are manifest), and constrained by the wishes, the pleasures, the commandments of fathers, mothers, brothers and husbands, abide most time enmewed in the narrow compass of their chambers and sitting in a manner idle, willing and willing not in one breath, revolve in themselves various thoughts which it is not possible should still be merry. By reason whereof if there arise in their minds any melancholy, bred of ardent desire, needs must it with grievous annoy abide therein, except it be done away by new discourse; more by token that they are far less strong than men to endure. With men in love it happeneth not on this wise, as we may manifestly see. They, if any melancholy or heaviness of thought oppress them, have many means of easing it or doing it away, for that to them, an they have a mind thereto, there lacketh not commodity of going about hearing and seeing many things, fowling, hunting, fishing, riding, gaming and trafficking; each of which means hath, altogether or in part, power to draw the mind unto itself and to divert it from troublous thought, at least for some space of time, whereafter, one way or another, either solacement superveneth or else the annoy groweth less. Wherefore, to the end that the unright of Fortune may by me in part be amended, which, where there is the less strength to endure, as we see it in delicate ladies, hath there been the more niggard of support, I purpose, for the succour and solace of ladies in love (unto others[1] the needle and the spindle and the reel suffice) to recount an hundred stories or fables or parables or histories or whatever you like to style them, in ten days' time related by an honourable company of seven ladies and three young men made in the days of the late deadly pestilence, together with sundry canzonets sung by the aforesaid ladies for their diversion. In these stories will be found love-chances,[2] both gladsome and grievous, and other accidents of fortune befallen as well in times present as in days of old, whereof the ladies aforesaid, who shall read them, may at once take solace from the delectable things therein shown forth and useful counsel, inasmuch as they may learn thereby what is to be eschewed and what is on like wise to be ensued,—the which methinketh cannot betide without cease of chagrin. If it happen thus (as God grant it may) let them render thanks therefor to Love, who, by loosing me from his bonds, hath vouchsafed me the power of applying myself to the service of their pleasures.

---

1. *i.e.* those not in love.
2. Syn. adventures (*casi*).

DAY THE FIRST

Here Beginneth the First Day of the Decameron
Wherein (After Demonstration Made by the Author
of the Manner in Which it Came to Pass That the
Persons Who Are Hereinafter Presented
Foregathered for the Purpose of Devising Together)
Under the Governance of Pampinea Is Discoursed
of That Which Is Most Agreeable Unto Each

As often, most gracious ladies, as, taking thought in myself, I mind me how very pitiful you are all by nature, so often do I recognize that this present work will, to your thinking, have a grievous and a weariful beginning, inasmuch as the dolorous remembrance of the late pestiferous mortality, which it beareth on its forefront, is universally irksome to all who saw or otherwise knew it. But I would not therefore have this affright you from reading further, as if in the reading you were still to fare among sighs and tears. Let this grisly beginning be none other to you than is to wayfarers a rugged and steep mountain, beyond which is situate a most fair and delightful plain, which latter cometh so much the pleasanter to them as the greater was the hardship of the ascent and the descent; for, like as dolour occupieth the extreme of gladness, even so are miseries determined by imminent joyance. This brief annoy (I say brief, inasmuch as it is contained in few pages) is straightway succeeded by the pleasance and delight which I have already promised you and which, belike, were it not aforesaid, might not be looked for from such a beginning. And in truth, could I fairly have availed to bring you to my desire otherwise than by so rugged a path as this will be I had gladly done it; but being in a manner constrained thereto, for that, without this reminiscence of our past miseries, it might not be shown what was the occasion of the coming about of the things that will hereafter be read, I have brought myself to write them.[1]

I say, then, that the years [of the era] of the fruitful Incarnation of the Son of God had attained to the number of one thousand three hundred and forty-eight, when into the notable city of Florence, fair over every other of Italy, there came the death-dealing pestilence, which, through the operation of the heavenly bodies or of our own iniquitous dealings, being sent down upon mankind for our correction by the just wrath of God, had some years before appeared in the parts of the East and after having bereft these latter of an innumerable number of inhabitants, extending without cease from one place to another, had now unhappily spread towards the West. And thereagainst no wisdom availing nor human foresight (whereby the city was purged of many impurities by officers deputed to that end and it was forbidden unto any sick person to enter therein and many were the counsels given[2] for the preservation of health) nor yet humble supplications, not once but many times both in ordered processions and on other wise made unto God by devout persons,—about the coming in of the Spring of the aforesaid year, it began on horrible and miraculous wise to show forth its dolorous effects. Yet not as it had done in the East, where, if any bled at the nose, it was a manifest sign of inevitable death; nay, but in men and women alike there appeared, at the beginning of the malady, certain swellings, either on the groin or under the armpits, whereof some waxed of the bigness of a common apple, others like unto an egg, some more and some less, and these the vulgar named plague-boils. From these two parts the aforesaid death-bearing plague-boils proceeded, in brief space, to appear and come indifferently in every part of the body; wherefrom, after awhile, the fashion of the contagion began to change into black or livid blotches, which showed themselves in many [first] on the arms and about the thighs and [after spread to] every other part of the person, in some large and sparse and in others small and thick-sown; and like as the plague-boils had been first (and yet were) a very certain token of coming death, even so were these for every one to whom they came.

To the cure of these maladies nor counsel[3] of physician nor virtue of any medicine appeared to avail or profit aught; on the contrary,—whether it was that the nature of the infection suffered it not or that the ignorance of the physicians (of whom, over and above the men of art, the number, both men and women, who had never had any teaching of medicine, was become exceeding great,) availed not to know whence it arose and consequently took not due measures thereagainst,—not only did few recover thereof, but well nigh all died within the third day from the appearance of the aforesaid signs, this sooner and that later, and for the most part without fever or other accident.[4] And this pestilence was the more virulent for that, by communication with those who were sick thereof, it gat hold upon the sound, no otherwise than fire upon things dry or greasy, whenas they are brought very near thereunto. Nay, the mischief was yet greater; for that not only did converse and consortion with the sick give to the sound infection of cause of common death, but the mere touching of the clothes or of whatsoever other thing had been touched or used of the sick appeared of itself to communicate the malady to the toucher. A marvellous thing to hear is that which I have to tell and one which, had it not been seen of many men's eyes and of mine own, I had scarce dared credit, much less set down in writing, though I had heard it from one worthy of belief. I say, then, that of such efficience was the nature of the pestilence in question in communicating itself from one to another, that, not only did it pass from man to man, but this, which is much more, it many times visibly did;—to wit, a thing which had pertained to a man sick or dead of the aforesaid sickness, being touched by an animal foreign to the human species, not only infected this latter with the plague, but in a very brief space of time killed it. Of this mine own eyes (as hath a little before been said) had one day, among others, experience on this wise; to wit, that the rags of a poor man, who had died of the plague, being cast out into the public way, two hogs came up to them and having first, after their wont, rooted amain among them with their snouts, took them in their mouths and tossed them about their jaws; then, in a little while, after turning round and round, they both, as if they had taken poison, fell down dead upon the rags with which they had in an ill hour intermeddled.

From these things and many others like unto them or yet stranger divers fears and conceits were begotten in those who abode alive, which well nigh all tended to a very barbarous conclusion, namely, to shun and flee from the sick and all that pertained to them, and thus doing, each thought to secure immunity for himself. Some there were who conceived that to live moderately and keep oneself from all excess was the best defence against such a danger; wherefore, making up their company, they lived removed from every other and shut themselves up in those houses where none had been sick and where living was best; and there, using very temperately of the most delicate viands and the finest wines and eschewing all incontinence, they abode with music and such other diversions as they might have, never suffering themselves to speak with any nor choosing to hear any news from without of death or sick folk. Others, inclining to the contrary opinion, maintained that to carouse and make merry and go about singing and frolicking and satisfy the appetite in everything possible and laugh and scoff at whatsoever befell was a very certain remedy for such an ill. That which they said they put in practice as best they might, going about day and night, now to this tavern, now to that, drinking without stint or measure; and on this wise they did yet more freely in other folk's houses, so but they scented there aught that liked or tempted them, as they might lightly do, for that every one—as he were to live no longer—had abandoned all care of his possessions, as of himself, wherefore the most part of the houses were become common good and strangers used them, whenas they happened upon them, like as the very owner might have done; and with all this bestial preoccupation, they still shunned the sick to the best of their power.

In this sore affliction and misery of our city, the reverend authority of the laws, both human and divine, was all in a manner dissolved and fallen into decay, for [lack of] the ministers and executors thereof, who, like other men, were all either dead or sick or else left so destitute of followers that they were unable to exercise any office, wherefore every one had license to do whatsoever pleased him. Many others held a middle course between the two aforesaid, not straitening themselves so exactly in the matter of diet as the first neither allowing themselves such license in drinking and other debauchery as the second, but using things in sufficiency, according to their appetites; nor did they seclude themselves, but went about, carrying in their hands, some flowers, some odoriferous herbs and other some divers kinds of spiceries,[5] which they set often to their noses, accounting it an excellent thing to fortify the brain with such odours, more by token that the air seemed all heavy and attainted with the stench of the dead bodies and that of the sick and of the remedies used.

Some were of a more barbarous, though, peradventure, a surer way of thinking, avouching that there was no remedy against pestilences better than—no, nor any so good as—to flee before them; wherefore, moved by this reasoning and recking of nought but themselves, very many, both men and women, abandoned their own city, their own houses and homes, their kinsfolk and possessions, and sought the country seats of others, or, at the least, their own, as if the wrath of God, being moved to punish the iniquity of mankind, would not proceed to do so wheresoever they might be, but would content itself with afflicting those only who were found within the walls of their city, or as if they were persuaded that no person was to remain therein and that its last hour was come. And albeit these, who opined thus variously, died not all, yet neither did they all escape; nay, many of each way of thinking and in every place sickened of the plague and languished on all sides, well nigh abandoned, having themselves, what while they were whole, set the example to those who abode in health.

Indeed, leaving be that townsman avoided townsman and that well nigh no neighbour took thought unto other and that kinsfolk seldom or never visited one another and held no converse together save from afar, this tribulation had stricken such terror to the hearts of all, men and women alike, that brother forsook brother, uncle nephew and sister brother and oftentimes wife husband; nay (what is yet more extraordinary and well nigh incredible) fathers and mothers refused to visit or tend their very children, as they had not been theirs. By reason whereof there remained unto those (and the number of them, both males and females, was incalculable) who fell sick, none other succour than that which they owed either to the charity of friends (and of these there were few) or the greed of servants, who tended them, allured by high and extravagant wage; albeit, for all this, these latter were not grown many, and those men and women of mean understanding and for the most part unused to such offices, who served for well nigh nought but to reach things called for by the sick or to note when they died; and in the doing of these services many of them perished with their gain.

Of this abandonment of the sick by neighbours, kinsfolk and friends and of the scarcity of servants arose an usage before well nigh unheard, to wit, that no woman, how fair or lovesome or well-born soever she might be, once fallen sick, recked aught of having a man to tend her, whatever he might be, or young or old, and without any shame discovered to him every part of her body, no otherwise than she would have done to a woman, so but the necessity of her sickness required it; the which belike, in those who recovered, was the occasion of lesser modesty in time to come. Moreover, there ensued of this abandonment the death of many who peradventure, had they been succoured, would have escaped alive; wherefore, as well for the lack of the opportune services which the sick availed not to have as for the virulence of the plague, such was the multitude of those who died in the city by day and by night that it was an astonishment to hear tell thereof, much more to see it; and thence, as it were of necessity, there sprang up among those who abode alive things contrary to the pristine manners of the townsfolk.

It was then (even as we yet see it used) a custom that the kinswomen and she-neighbours of the dead should assemble in his house and there condole with those who more nearly pertained unto him, whilst his neighbours and many other citizens foregathered with his next of kin before his house, whither, according to the dead man's quality, came the clergy, and he with funeral pomp of chants and candles was borne on the shoulders of his peers to the church chosen by himself before his death; which usages, after the virulence of the plague began to increase, were either altogether or for the most part laid aside, and other and strange customs sprang up in their stead. For that, not only did folk die without having a multitude of women about them, but many there were who departed this life without witness and few indeed were they to whom the pious plaints and bitter tears of their kinsfolk were vouchsafed; nay, in lieu of these things there obtained, for the most part, laughter and jests and gibes and feasting and merrymaking in company; which usance women, laying aside womanly pitifulness, had right well learned for their own safety.

Few, again, were they whose bodies were accompanied to the church by more than half a score or a dozen of their neighbours, and of these no worshipful and illustrious citizens, but a sort of blood-suckers, sprung from the dregs of the people, who styled themselves *pickmen*[6] and did such offices for hire, shouldered the bier and bore it with hurried steps, not to that church which the dead man had chosen before his death, but most times to the nearest, behind five or six[7] priests, with little light[8] and whiles none at all, which latter, with the aid of the said pickmen, thrust him into what grave soever they first found unoccupied, without troubling themselves with too long or too formal a service.

The condition of the common people (and belike, in great part, of the middle class also) was yet more pitiable to behold, for that these, for the most part retained by hope[9] or poverty in their houses and abiding in their own quarters, sickened by the thousand daily and being altogether untended and unsuccoured, died well nigh all without recourse. Many breathed their last in the open street, whilst other many, for all they died in their houses, made it known to the neighbours that they were dead rather by the stench of their rotting bodies than otherwise; and of these and others who died all about the whole city was full. For the most part one same usance was observed by the neighbours, moved more by fear lest the corruption of the dead bodies should imperil themselves than by any charity they had for the departed; to wit, that either with their own hands or with the aid of certain bearers, whenas they might have any, they brought the bodies of those who had died forth of their houses and laid them before their doors, where, especially in the morning, those who went about might see corpses without number; then they fetched biers and some, in default thereof, they laid upon some board or other. Nor was it only one bier that carried two or three corpses, nor did this happen but once; nay, many might have been counted which contained husband and wife, two or three brothers, father and son or the like. And an infinite number of times it befell that, two priests going with one cross for some one, three or four biers, borne by bearers, ranged themselves behind the latter,[10] and whereas the priests thought to have but one dead man to bury, they had six or eight, and whiles more. Nor therefore were the dead honoured with aught of tears or candles or funeral train; nay, the thing was come to such a pass that folk recked no more of men that died than nowadays they would of goats; whereby it very manifestly appeared that that which the natural course of things had not availed, by dint of small and infrequent harms, to teach the wise to endure with patience, the very greatness of their ills had brought even the simple to expect and make no account of. The consecrated ground sufficing not to the burial of the vast multitude of corpses aforesaid, which daily and well nigh hourly came carried in crowds to every church,—especially if it were sought to give each his own place, according to ancient usance,—there were made throughout the churchyards, after every other part was full, vast trenches, wherein those who came after were laid by the hundred and being heaped up therein by layers, as goods are stowed aboard ship, were covered with a little earth, till such time as they reached the top of the trench.

Moreover,—not to go longer searching out and recalling every particular of our past miseries, as they befell throughout the city,—I say that, whilst so sinister a time prevailed in the latter, on no wise therefor was the surrounding country spared, wherein, (letting be the castles,[11] which in their littleness[12] were like unto the city,) throughout the scattered villages and in the fields, the poor and miserable husbandmen and their families, without succour of physician or aid of servitor, died, not like men, but well nigh like beasts, by the ways or in their tillages or about the houses, indifferently by day and night. By reason whereof, growing lax like the townsfolk in their manners and customs, they recked not of any thing or business of theirs; nay, all, as if they looked for death that very day, studied with all their wit, not to help to maturity the future produce of their cattle and their fields and the fruits of their own past toils, but to consume those which were ready to hand. Thus it came to pass that the oxen, the asses, the sheep, the goats, the swine, the fowls, nay, the very dogs, so faithful to mankind, being driven forth of their own houses, went straying at their pleasure about the fields, where the very corn was abandoned, without being cut, much less gathered in; and many, well nigh like reasonable creatures, after grazing all day, returned at night, glutted, to their houses, without the constraint of any herdsman.

To leave the country and return to the city, what more can be said save that such and so great was the cruelty of heaven (and in part, peradventure, that of men) that, between March and the following July, what with the virulence of that pestiferous sickness and the number of sick folk ill tended or forsaken in their need, through the fearfulness of those who were whole, it is believed for certain that upward of an hundred thousand human beings perished within the walls of the city of Florence, which, peradventure, before the advent of that death-dealing calamity, had not been accounted to hold so many? Alas, how many great palaces, how many goodly houses, how many noble mansions, once full of families, of lords and of ladies, abode empty even to the meanest servant! How many memorable families, how many ample heritages, how many famous fortunes were seen to remain without lawful heir! How many valiant men, how many fair ladies, how many sprightly youths, whom, not others only, but Galen, Hippocrates or Æsculapius themselves would have judged most hale, breakfasted in the morning with their kinsfolk, comrades and friends and that same night supped with their ancestors in the other world!

I am myself weary of going wandering so long among such miseries; wherefore, purposing henceforth to leave such part thereof as I can fitly, I say that,—our city being at this pass, well nigh void of inhabitants,—it chanced (as I afterward heard from a person worthy of credit) that there foregathered in the venerable church of Santa Maria Novella, one Tuesday morning when there was well nigh none else there, seven young ladies, all knit one to another by friendship or neighbourhood or kinship, who had heard divine service in mourning attire, as sorted with such a season. Not one of them had passed her eight-and-twentieth year nor was less than eighteen years old, and each was discreet and of noble blood, fair of favour and well-mannered and full of honest sprightliness. The names of these ladies I would in proper terms set out, did not just cause forbid me, to wit, that I would not have it possible that, in time to come, any of them should take shame by reason of the things hereinafter related as being told or hearkened by them, the laws of disport being nowadays somewhat straitened, which at that time, for the reasons above shown, were of the largest, not only for persons of their years, but for those of a much riper age; nor yet would I give occasion to the envious, who are still ready to carp at every praiseworthy life, on anywise to disparage the fair fame of these honourable ladies with unseemly talk. Wherefore, so that which each saith may hereafterward be apprehended without confusion, I purpose to denominate them by names altogether or in part sorting with each one's quality.[13] The first of them and her of ripest age I shall call Pampinea, the second Fiammetta, the third Filomena and the fourth Emilia. To the fifth we will give the name of Lauretta, to the sixth that of Neifile and the last, not without cause, we will style Elisa.[14] These, then, not drawn of any set purpose, but foregathering by chance in a corner of the church, having seated themselves in a ring, after divers sighs, let be the saying of paternosters and fell to devising with one another many and various things of the nature of the time. After awhile, the others being silent, Pampinea proceeded to speak thus:

"Dear my ladies, you may, like myself, have many times heard that whoso honestly useth his right doth no one wrong; and it is the natural right of every one who is born here below to succour, keep and defend his own life as best he may, and in so far is this allowed that it hath happened whiles that, for the preservation thereof, men have been slain without any fault. If this much be conceded of the laws, which have in view the well-being of all mortals, how much more is it lawful for us and whatsoever other, without offence unto any, to take such means as we may for the preservation of our lives? As often as I consider our fashions of this morning and those of many other mornings past and bethink me what and what manner discourses are ours, I feel, and you likewise must feel, that each of us is in fear for herself. Nor do I anywise wonder at this; but I wonder exceedingly, considering that we all have a woman's wit, that we take no steps to provide ourselves against that which each of us justly feareth. We abide here, to my seeming, no otherwise than as if we would or should be witness of how many dead bodies are brought hither for burial or to hearken if the friars of the place, whose number is come well nigh to nought, chant their offices at the due hours or by our apparel to show forth unto whosoever appeareth here the nature and extent of our distresses. If we depart hence, we either see dead bodies or sick persons carried about or those, whom for their misdeeds the authority of the public laws whilere condemned to exile, overrun the whole place with unseemly excesses, as if scoffing at the laws, for that they know the executors thereof to be either dead or sick; whilst the dregs of our city, fattened with our blood, style themselves *pickmen* and ruffle it everywhere in mockery of us, riding and running all about and flouting us with our distresses in ribald songs. We hear nothing here but 'Such an one is dead' or 'Such an one is at the point of death'; and were there any to make them, we should hear dolorous lamentations on all sides. And if we return to our houses, I know not if it is with you as with me, but, for my part, when I find none left therein of a great household, save my serving-maid, I wax fearful and feel every hair of my body stand on end; and wherever I go or abide about the house, meseemeth I see the shades of those who are departed and who wear not those countenances that I was used to see, but terrify me with a horrid aspect, I know not whence newly come to them.

By reason of these things I feel myself alike ill at ease here and abroad and at home, more by token that meseemeth none, who hath, as we have, the power and whither to go, is left here, other than ourselves; or if any such there be, I have many a time both heard and perceived that, without making any distinction between things lawful and unlawful, so but appetite move them, whether alone or in company, both day and night, they do that which affordeth them most delight. Nor is it the laity alone who do thus; nay, even those who are shut in the monasteries, persuading themselves that what befitteth and is lawful to others alike sortable and unforbidden unto them,[15] have broken the laws of obedience and giving themselves to carnal delights, thinking thus to escape, are grown lewd and dissolute. If thus, then, it be, as is manifestly to be seen, what do we here? What look we for? What dream we? Why are we more sluggish and slower to provide for our safety than all the rest of the townsfolk? Deem we ourselves of less price than others, or do we hold our life to be bounden in our bodies with a stronger chain than is theirs and that therefore we need reck nothing of aught that hath power to harm it? We err, we are deceived; what folly is ours, if we think thus! As often as we choose to call to mind the number and quality of the youths and ladies overborne of this cruel pestilence, we may see a most manifest proof thereof.

Wherefore, in order that we may not, through wilfulness or nonchalance, fall into that wherefrom we may, peradventure, an we but will, by some means or other escape, I know not if it seem to you as it doth to me, but methinketh it were excellently well done that we, such as we are, depart this city, as many have done before us, and eschewing, as we would death, the dishonourable example of others, betake ourselves quietly to our places in the country, whereof each of us hath great plenty, and there take such diversion, such delight and such pleasance as we may, without anywise overpassing the bounds of reason. There may we hear the small birds sing, there may we see the hills and plains clad all in green and the fields full of corn wave even as doth the sea; there may we see trees, a thousand sorts, and there is the face of heaven more open to view, the which, angered against us though it be, nevertheless denieth not unto us its eternal beauties, far goodlier to look upon than the empty walls of our city. Moreover, there is the air far fresher[16] and there at this season is more plenty of that which behoveth unto life and less is the sum of annoys, for that, albeit the husbandmen die there, even as do the townsfolk here, the displeasance is there the less, insomuch as houses and inhabitants are rarer than in the city.

Here, on the other hand, if I deem aright, we abandon no one; nay, we may far rather say with truth that we ourselves are abandoned, seeing that our kinsfolk, either dying or fleeing from death, have left us alone in this great tribulation, as it were we pertained not unto them. No blame can therefore befall the ensuing of this counsel; nay, dolour and chagrin and belike death may betide us, an we ensue it not. Wherefore, an it please you, methinketh we should do well to take our maids and letting follow after us with the necessary gear, sojourn to-day in this place and to-morrow in that, taking such pleasure and diversion as the season may afford, and on this wise abide till such time (an we be not earlier overtaken of death) as we shall see what issue Heaven reserveth unto these things. And I would remind you that it is no more forbidden unto us honourably to depart than it is unto many others of our sex to abide in dishonour."

The other ladies, having hearkened to Pampinea, not only commended her counsel, but, eager to follow it, had already begun to devise more particularly among themselves of the manner, as if, arising from their session there, they were to set off out of hand. But Filomena, who was exceeding discreet, said, "Ladies, albeit that which Pampinea allegeth is excellently well said, yet is there no occasion for running, as meseemeth you would do. Remember that we are all women and none of us is child enough not to know how [little] reasonable women are among themselves and how [ill], without some man's guidance, they know how to order themselves. We are fickle, wilful, suspicious, faint-hearted and timorous, for which reasons I misdoubt me sore, an we take not some other guidance than our own, that our company will be far too soon dissolved and with less honour to ourselves than were seemly; wherefore we should do well to provide ourselves, ere we begin."

"Verily," answered Elisa, "men are the head of women, and without their ordinance seldom cometh any emprise of ours to good end; but how may we come by these men? There is none of us but knoweth that of her kinsmen the most part are dead and those who abide alive are all gone fleeing that which we seek to flee, in divers companies, some here and some there, without our knowing where, and to invite strangers would not be seemly, seeing that, if we would endeavour after our welfare, it behoveth us find a means of so ordering ourselves that, wherever we go for diversion and repose, scandal nor annoy may ensue thereof."

Whilst such discourse was toward between the ladies, behold, there entered the church three young men,—yet not so young that the age of the youngest of them was less than five-and-twenty years,—in whom neither the perversity of the time nor loss of friends and kinsfolk, no, nor fear for themselves had availed to cool, much less to quench, the fire of love. Of these one was called Pamfilo,[17] another Filostrato[18] and the third Dioneo,[19] all very agreeable and well-bred, and they went seeking, for their supreme solace, in such a perturbation of things, to see their mistresses, who, as it chanced, were all three among the seven aforesaid; whilst certain of the other ladies were near kinswomen of one or other of the young men.

No sooner had their eyes fallen on the ladies than they were themselves espied of them; whereupon quoth Pampinea, smiling, "See, fortune is favourable to our beginnings and hath thrown in our way young men of worth and discretion, who will gladly be to us both guides and servitors, an we disdain not to accept of them in that capacity." But Neifile, whose face was grown all vermeil for shamefastness, for that it was she who was beloved of one of the young men, said, "For God's sake, Pampinea, look what thou sayest! I acknowledge most frankly that there can be nought but all good said of which one soever of them and I hold them sufficient unto a much greater thing than this, even as I opine that they would bear, not only ourselves, but far fairer and nobler dames than we, good and honourable company. But, for that it is a very manifest thing that they are enamoured of certain of us who are here, I fear lest, without our fault or theirs, scandal and blame ensue thereof, if we carry them with us." Quoth Filomena, "That skilleth nought; so but I live honestly and conscience prick me not of aught, let who will speak to the contrary; God and the truth will take up arms for me. Wherefore, if they be disposed to come, verily we may say with Pampinea that fortune is favourable to our going."

The other ladies, hearing her speak thus absolutely, not only held their peace, but all with one accord agreed that the young men should be called and acquainted with their project and bidden to be pleased bear them company in their expedition. Accordingly, without more words, Pampinea, who was knit by kinship to one of them, rising to her feet, made for the three young men, who stood fast, looking upon them, and saluting them with a cheerful countenance, discovered to them their intent and prayed them, on behalf of herself and her companions, that they would be pleased to bear them company in a pure and brotherly spirit. The young men at the first thought themselves bantered, but, seeing that the lady spoke in good earnest, they made answer joyfully that they were ready, and without losing time about the matter, forthright took order for that which they had to do against departure.

On the following morning, Wednesday to wit, towards break of day, having let orderly make ready all things needful and despatched them in advance whereas they purposed to go,[20] the ladies, with certain of their waiting-women, and the three young men, with as many of their serving-men, departing Florence, set out upon their way; nor had they gone more than two short miles from the city, when they came to the place fore-appointed of them, which was situate on a little hill, somewhat withdrawn on every side from the high way and full of various shrubs and plants, all green of leafage and pleasant to behold. On the summit of this hill was a palace, with a goodly and great courtyard in its midst and galleries[21] and saloons and bedchambers, each in itself most fair and adorned and notable with jocund paintings, with lawns and grassplots round about and wonder-goodly gardens and wells of very cold water and cellars full of wines of price, things more apt unto curious drinkers than unto sober and modest ladies. The new comers, to their no little pleasure, found the place all swept and the beds made in the chambers and every thing full of such flowers as might be had at that season and strewn with rushes.

As soon as they had seated themselves, Dioneo, who was the merriest springald in the world and full of quips and cranks, said, "Ladies, your wit, rather than our foresight, hath guided us hither, and I know not what you purpose to do with your cares; as for my own, I left them within the city gates, whenas I issued thence with you awhile agone; wherefore, do you either address yourselves to make merry and laugh and sing together with me (in so far, I mean, as pertaineth to your dignity) or give me leave to go back for my cares and abide in the afflicted city." Whereto Pampinea, no otherwise than as if in like manner she had banished all her own cares, answered blithely, "Dioneo, thou sayst well; it behoveth us live merrily, nor hath any other occasion caused us flee from yonder miseries. But, for that things which are without measure may not long endure, I, who began the discourse wherethrough this so goodly company came to be made, taking thought for the continuance of our gladness, hold it of necessity that we appoint some one to be principal among us, whom we may honour and obey as chief and whose especial care it shall be to dispose us to live joyously. And in order that each in turn may prove the burden of solicitude, together with the pleasure of headship; and that, the chief being thus drawn, in turn, from one and the other sex, there may be no cause for jealousy, as might happen, were any excluded from the sovranty, I say that unto each be attributed the burden and the honour for one day. Let who is to be our first chief be at the election of us all. For who shall follow, be it he or she whom it shall please the governor of the day to appoint, whenas the hour of vespers draweth near, and let each in turn, at his or her discretion, order and dispose of the place and manner wherein we are to live, for such time as his or her seignory shall endure."

Pampinea's words pleased mightily, and with one voice they elected her chief of the first day; whereupon Filomena, running nimbly to a laurel-tree—for that she had many a time heard speak of the honour due to the leaves of this plant and how worship-worth they made whoso was deservedly crowned withal—and plucking divers sprays therefrom, made her thereof a goodly and honourable wreath, which, being set upon her head, was thenceforth, what while their company lasted, a manifest sign unto every other of the royal office and seignory.

Pampinea, being made queen, commanded that every one should be silent; then, calling the serving-men of the three young gentlemen and her own and the other ladies' women, who were four in number, before herself and all being silent, she spoke thus: "In order that I may set you a first example, by which, proceeding from good to better, our company may live and last in order and pleasance and without reproach so long as it is agreeable to us, I constitute, firstly, Parmeno, Dioneo's servant, my seneschal and commit unto him the care and ordinance of all our household and [especially] that which pertaineth to the service of the saloon. Sirisco, Pamfilo's servant, I will shall be our purveyor and treasurer and ensue the commandments of

Parmeno. Tindaro shall look to the service of Filostrato and the other two gentlemen in their bed chambers, what time the others, being occupied about their respective offices, cannot attend thereto. Misia, my woman, and Filomena's Licisca shall still abide in the kitchen and there diligently prepare such viands as shall be appointed them of Parmeno. Lauretta's Chimera and Fiammetta's Stratilia it is our pleasure shall occupy themselves with the ordinance of the ladies' chambers and the cleanliness of the places where we shall abide; and we will and command all and several, as they hold our favour dear, to have a care that, whithersoever they go or whencesoever they return and whatsoever they hear or see, they bring us from without no news other than joyous." These orders summarily given and commended of all, Pampinea, rising blithely to her feet, said, "Here be gardens, here be meadows, here be store of other delectable places, wherein let each go a-pleasuring at will; and when tierce[22] soundeth, let all be here, so we may eat in the cool."

The merry company, being thus dismissed by the new queen, went straying with slow steps, young men and fair ladies together, about a garden, devising blithely and diverting themselves with weaving goodly garlands of various leaves and carolling amorously. After they had abidden there such time as had been appointed them of the queen, they returned to the house, where they found that Parmeno had made a diligent beginning with his office, for that, entering a saloon on the ground floor, they saw there the tables laid with the whitest of cloths and beakers that seemed of silver and everything covered with the flowers of the broom; whereupon, having washed their hands, they all, by command of the queen, seated themselves according to Parmeno's ordinance. Then came viands delicately drest and choicest wines were proffered and the three serving-men, without more, quietly tended the tables. All, being gladdened by these things, for that they were fair and orderly done, ate joyously and with store of merry talk, and the tables being cleared away,[23] the queen bade bring instruments of music, for that all the ladies knew how to dance, as also the young men, and some of them could both play and sing excellent well. Accordingly, by her commandment, Dioneo took a lute and Fiammetta a viol and began softly to sound a dance; whereupon the queen and the other ladies, together with the other two young men, having sent the serving-men to eat, struck up a round and began with a slow pace to dance a brawl; which ended, they fell to singing quaint and merry ditties. On this wise they abode till it seemed to the queen time to go to sleep,[24] and she accordingly dismissed them all; whereupon the young men retired to their chambers, which were withdrawn from the ladies' lodging, and finding them with the beds well made and as full of flowers as the saloon, put off their clothes and betook themselves to rest, whilst the ladies, on their part, did likewise.

None[25] had not long sounded when the queen, arising, made all the other ladies arise, and on like wise the three young men, alleging overmuch sleep to be harmful by day; and so they betook themselves to a little meadow, where the grass grew green and high nor there had the sun power on any side. There, feeling the waftings of a gentle breeze, they all, as their queen willed it, seated themselves in a ring on the green grass; while she bespoke them thus, "As ye see, the sun is high and the heat great, nor is aught heard save the crickets yonder among the olives; wherefore it were doubtless folly to go anywhither at this present. Here is the sojourn fair and cool, and here, as you see, are chess and tables,[26] and each can divert himself as is most to his mind. But, an my counsel be followed in this, we shall pass away this sultry part of the day, not in gaming,—wherein the mind of one of the players must of necessity be troubled, without any great pleasure of the other or of those who look on,—but in telling stories, which, one telling, may afford diversion to all the company who hearken; nor shall we have made an end of telling each his story but the sun will have declined and the heat be abated, and we can then go a-pleasuring whereas it may be most agreeable to us. Wherefore, if this that I say please you, (for I am disposed to follow your pleasure therein,) let us do it; and if it please you not, let each until the hour of vespers do what most liketh him." Ladies and men alike all approved the story-telling, whereupon, "Then," said the queen, "since this pleaseth you, I will that this first day each be free to tell of such matters as are most to his liking." Then, turning to Pamfilo, who sat on her right hand, she smilingly bade him give beginning to the story-telling with one of his; and he, hearing the commandment, forthright began thus, whilst all gave ear to him.

---

1. *i.e.* the few pages of which he speaks above.
2. Syn. provisions made or means taken (*consigli dati*). Boccaccio constantly uses *consiglio* in this latter sense.
3. Syn. help, remedy.
4. *Accidente*, what a modern physician would call "complication." "Symptom" does not express the whole meaning of the Italian word.
5. *i.e.* aromatic drugs.
6. *i.e.* gravediggers (*becchini*).
7. Lit. *four* or six. This is the equivalent Italian idiom.
8. *i.e.* but few tapers.
9. *i.e.* expectation of gain from acting as tenders of the sick, gravediggers, etc. The word *speranza* is, however, constantly used by Dante and his follower Boccaccio in the contrary sense of "fear," and may be so meant in the present instance.
10. *i.e.* the cross.
11. *i.e.* walled burghs.
12. *i.e.* in miniature.
13. Or character (*qualità*).
14. I know of no explanation of these names by the commentators, who seem, indeed, after the manner of their kind, to have generally confined themselves to the elaborate illustration and elucidation (or rather, alas! too often, obscuration) of passages already perfectly plain, leaving the difficult passages for the most part untouched. The following is the best I can make of them. *Pampinea* appears to be formed from the Greek πᾶν, all, and πινύω, I advise, admonish or inform, and to mean all-advising or admonishing, which would agree well enough with the character of Pampinea, who is represented as the eldest and sagest of the female personages of the Decameron and as taking the lead in everything. *Fiammetta* is the name by which Boccaccio designates his mistress, the Princess Maria of Naples (the lady for whom he cherished "the very high and noble passion" of which he speaks in his Proem), in his earlier opuscule, the "Elégia di Madonna Fiammetta," describing, in her name, the torments of separation from the beloved. In this work he speaks of himself under the name of Pamfilo (Gr. πᾶν, all, and φιλέω, I love, *i.e.* the all-loving or the passionate lover), and it is probable, therefore, that under these names he intended to introduce his royal ladylove and himself in the present work. *Filomena* (Italian form of Philomela, a nightingale, Greek φίλος loving, and μελός, melody, song, *i.e.* song-loving) is perhaps so styled for her love of music, and *Emilia's* character, as it appears in the course of the work, justifies the derivation of her name from the Greek αἱμύλιος, pleasing, engaging in manners and behaviour, cajoling. *Lauretta* Boccaccio probably intends us to look upon as a learned lady, if, as we may suppose, her name is a corruption of *laureata*, laurel-crowned; whilst *Neifile's* name (Greek νεῖος [νεός] new, and φιλέω, I love, *i.e.* novelty-loving) stamps her as being of a somewhat curious disposition, eager "to tell or to hear some new thing." The name *Elisa* is not so easily to be explained as the others; possibly it was intended by the author as a reminiscence of Dido, to whom the name (which is by some authorities explained to mean "Godlike," from a Hebrew root) is said to have been given "quòd plurima supra animi muliebris fortitudinem gesserit." It does not, however, appear that there was in Elisa's character or life anything to justify the implied comparison.
15. This phrase may also be read "persuading themselves that that (*i.e.* their breach of the laws of obedience, etc.) beseemeth them and is forbidden only to others" (*faccendosi a credere che quello a lor si convenga e non si disdica che all' altre*); but the reading in the text appears more in harmony with the general sense and is indeed indicated by the punctuation of the Giunta Edition of 1527, which I generally follow in case of doubt.
16. Syn. cooler.
17. See ante, n. 15.
18. *Filostrato*, Greek φίλος, loving, and στρατός, army, *met.* strife, war, *i.e.* one who loves strife. This name appears to be a reminiscence of Boccaccio's poem (*Il Filostrato*, well known through its translation by Chaucer and the Senechal d'Anjou) upon the subject of the loves of Troilus and Cressida and to be in this instance used by him as a synonym for an unhappy lover, whom no rebuffs, no treachery can divert from his ill-starred passion. Such a lover may well be said to be in love with strife, and that the Filostrato of the Decameron sufficiently answers to this description we learn later on from his own lips.
19. *Dioneo*, a name probably coined from the Greek Διωνη, one of the *agnomina* of Venus (properly her mother's

name) and intended to denote the amorous temperament of his personage, to which, indeed, the erotic character of most of the stories told by him bears sufficient witness.

20. *e prima mandato là dove*, etc. This passage is obscure and may be read to mean "and having first despatched [a messenger] (or sent [word]) whereas," etc. I think, however, that *mandato* is a copyist's error for *mandata*, in which case the meaning would be as in the text.

21. Or balconies (*loggie*).

22. *i.e.* Nine o'clock a.m. Boccaccio's habit of measuring time by the canonical hours has been a sore stumbling-block to the ordinary English and French translator, who is generally terribly at sea as to his meaning, inclining to render *tierce* three, *sexte* six o'clock and *none* noon and making shots of the same wild kind at the other hours. The monasterial rule (which before the general introduction of clocks was commonly followed by the mediæval public in the computation of time) divided the twenty-four hours of the day and night into seven parts (six of three hours each and one of six), the inception of which was denoted by the sound of the bells that summoned the clergy to the performance of the seven canonical offices *i.e. Matins* at 3 a.m., *Prime* at 6 a.m., *Tierce* at 9 a.m., *Sexte* or Noonsong at noon, *None* at 3 p.m., *Vespers* or Evensong at 6 p.m. and *Complines* or Nightsong at 9 p.m., and at the same time served the laity as a clock.

23. The table of Boccaccio's time was a mere board upon trestles, which when not in actual use, was stowed away, for room's sake, against the wall.

24. *i.e.* to take the siesta or midday nap common in hot countries.

25. *i.e.* three o'clock p.m.

26. *i.e.* backgammon.

❧ I ❧

THE FIRST STORY

MASTER CIAPPELLETTO DUPETH A HOLY FRIAR WITH
A FALSE CONFESSION AND DIETH; AND HAVING BEEN
IN HIS LIFETIME THE WORST OF MEN, HE IS, AFTER
HIS DEATH, REPUTED A SAINT AND CALLED SAINT
CIAPPELLETTO.

"IT IS A SEEMLY THING, dearest ladies, that whatsoever a man doth, he give it beginning from the holy and admirable name of Him who is the maker of all things. Wherefore, it behoving me, as the first, to give commencement to our story-telling, I purpose to begin with one of His marvels, to the end that, this being heard, our hope in Him, as in a thing immutable, may be confirmed and His name be ever praised of us. It is manifest that, like as things temporal are all transitory and mortal, even so both within and without are they full of annoy and anguish and travail and subject to infinite perils, against which it is indubitable that we, who live enmingled therein and who are indeed part and parcel thereof, might avail neither to endure nor to defend ourselves, except God's especial grace lent us strength and foresight; which latter, it is not to be believed, descendeth unto us and upon us by any merit of our own, but of the proper motion of His own benignity and the efficacy of the prayers of those who were mortals even as we are and having diligently ensued His commandments, what while they were on life, are now with Him become eternal and blessed and unto whom we,—belike not daring to address ourselves unto the proper presence of so august a judge,—proffer our petitions of the things which we deem needful unto ourselves, as unto advocates[1] informed by experience of our frailty. And this more we discern in Him, full as He is of compassionate liberality towards us, that, whereas it chanceth whiles (the keenness of mortal eyes availing not in any wise to penetrate the secrets of the Divine intent), that we peradventure, beguiled by report, make such an one our advocate unto His majesty, who is outcast from His presence with an eternal banishment,—nevertheless He, from whom nothing is hidden, having regard rather to the purity of the suppliant's intent than to his ignorance or to the reprobate estate of him whose intercession be invoketh, giveth ear unto those who pray unto the latter, as if he were in very deed blessed in His aspect. The which will manifestly appear from the story which I purpose to relate; I say manifestly, ensuing, not the judgment of God, but that of men.

It is told, then, that Musciatto Franzesi,[2] being from a very rich and considerable merchant in France become a knight and it behoving him thereupon go into Tuscany with Messire Charles Sansterre,[3] brother to the king of France,[4] who had been required and bidden thither by

Pope Boniface,[5] found his affairs in one part and another sore embroiled, (as those of merchants most times are,) and was unable lightly or promptly to disentangle them; wherefore he bethought himself to commit them unto divers persons and made shift for all, save only he abode in doubt whom he might leave sufficient to the recovery of the credits he had given to certain Burgundians. The cause of his doubt was that he knew the Burgundians to be litigious, quarrelsome fellows, ill-conditioned and disloyal, and could not call one to mind, in whom he might put any trust, curst enough to cope with their perversity. After long consideration of the matter, there came to his memory a certain Master Ciapperello da Prato, who came often to his house in Paris and whom, for that he was little of person and mighty nice in his dress, the French, knowing not what Cepparello[6] meant and thinking it be the same with Cappello, to wit, in their vernacular, Chaplet, called him, not Cappello, but Ciappelletto,[7] and accordingly as Ciappelletto he was known everywhere, whilst few knew him for Master Ciapperello.

Now this said Ciappelletto was of this manner life, that, being a scrivener, he thought very great shame whenas any of his instrument was found (and indeed he drew few such) other than false; whilst of the latter[8] he would have drawn as many as might be required of him and these with a better will by way of gift than any other for a great wage. False witness he bore with especial delight, required or not required, and the greatest regard being in those times paid to oaths in France, as he recked nothing of forswearing himself, he knavishly gained all the suits concerning which he was called upon to tell the truth upon his faith. He took inordinate pleasure and was mighty diligent in stirring up troubles and enmities and scandals between friends and kinsfolk and whomsoever else, and the greater the mischiefs he saw ensue thereof, the more he rejoiced. If bidden to manslaughter or whatsoever other naughty deed, he went about it with a will, without ever saying nay thereto; and many a time of his proper choice he had been known to wound men and do them to death with his own hand. He was a terrible blasphemer of God and the saints, and that for every trifle, being the most choleric man alive. To church he went never and all the sacraments thereof he flouted in abominable terms, as things of no account; whilst, on the other hand, he was still fain to haunt and use taverns and other lewd places. Of women he was as fond as dogs of the stick; but in the contrary he delighted more than any filthy fellow alive. He robbed and pillaged with as much conscience as a godly man would make oblation to God; he was a very glutton and a great wine bibber, insomuch that bytimes it wrought him shameful mischief, and to boot, he was a notorious gamester and a caster of cogged dice. But why should I enlarge in so many words? He was belike the worst man that ever was born.[9] His wickedness had long been upheld by the power and interest of Messer Musciatto, who had many a time safeguarded him as well from private persons, to whom he often did a mischief, as from the law, against which he was a perpetual offender.

This Master Ciappelletto then, coming to Musciatto's mind, the latter, who was very well acquainted with his way of life, bethought himself that he should be such an one as the perversity of the Burgundians required and accordingly, sending for him, he bespoke him thus: 'Master Ciappelletto, I am, as thou knowest, about altogether to withdraw hence, and having to do, amongst others, with certain Burgundians, men full of guile, I know none whom I may leave to recover my due from them more fitting than thyself, more by token that thou dost nothing at this present; wherefore, an thou wilt undertake this, I will e'en procure thee the favour of the Court and give thee such part as shall be meet of that which thou shalt recover.'

Don Ciappelletto, who was then out of employ and ill provided with the goods of the world, seeing him who had long been his stay and his refuge about to depart thence, lost no time in deliberation, but, as of necessity constrained, replied that he would well. They being come to an accord, Musciatto departed and Ciappelletto, having gotten his patron's procuration and letters commendatory from the king, betook himself into Burgundy, where well nigh none knew him, and there, contrary to his nature, began courteously and blandly to seek to get in his payments and do that wherefor he was come thither, as if reserving choler and violence for a last resort. Dealing thus and lodging in the house of two Florentines, brothers, who there lent at usance and who entertained him with great honour for the love of Messer Musciatto, it chanced that he fell sick, whereupon the two brothers promptly fetched physicians and servants to tend him and furnished him with all that behoved unto the recovery of his health. But every succour was in vain, for that, by the physicians' report, the good man, who was now old and had lived disorderly, grew daily worse, as one who had a mortal sickness; wherefore the two brothers were sore concerned and one day, being pretty near the chamber where he lay sick, they began to take counsel together, saying one to the other, 'How shall we do with yonder fellow? We have a sorry bargain on our hands of his affair, for that to send him forth of our house, thus sick, were a sore reproach to us and a manifest sign of little wit on our part, if the folk, who have seen us first receive him and after let tend and medicine him with such solicitude, should now see him suddenly put out of our house, sick unto death as he is, without it being possible for him to have done aught that should displease us. On the other hand, he hath been so wicked a man that he will never consent to confess or take any sacrament of the church; and he dying without confession, no church will receive his body; nay, he will be cast into a ditch, like a dog. Again, even if he do confess, his sins are so many and so horrible that the like will come of it, for that there is nor priest nor friar who can or will absolve him thereof; wherefore, being unshriven, he will still be cast into the ditches. Should it happen thus, the people of the city, as well on account of our trade, which appeareth to them most iniquitous and of which they missay all day, as of their itch to plunder us, seeing this, will rise up in riot and cry out, "These Lombard dogs, whom the church refuseth to receive, are to be suffered here no longer";—and they will run to our houses and despoil us not only of our good, but may be of our lives, to boot; wherefore in any case it will go ill with us, if yonder fellow die.'

Master Ciappelletto, who, as we have said, lay near the place where the two brothers were in discourse, being quick of hearing, as is most times the case with the sick, heard what they said of him and calling them to him, bespoke them thus: 'I will not have you anywise misdoubt of me nor fear to take any hurt by me. I have heard what you say of me and am well assured that it would happen even as you say, should matters pass as you expect; but it shall go otherwise. I have in my lifetime done God the Lord so many an affront that it will make neither more nor less, an I do Him yet another at the point of death; wherefore do you make shift to bring me the holiest and worthiest friar you may avail to have, if any such there be,[10] and leave the rest to me, for that I will assuredly order your affairs and mine own on such wise that all shall go well and you shall have good cause to be satisfied.'

The two brothers, albeit they conceived no great hope of this, nevertheless betook themselves to a brotherhood of monks and demanded some holy and learned man to hear the confession of a Lombard who lay sick in their house. There was given them a venerable brother of holy and good life and a past master in Holy Writ, a very reverend man, for whom all the townsfolk had a very great and special regard, and they carried him to their house; where, coming to the chamber where Master Ciappelletto lay and seating himself by his side, he began first tenderly to comfort him and after asked him how long it was since he had confessed last; whereto Master Ciappelletto, who had never confessed in his life, answered, 'Father, it hath been my usance to confess every week once at the least and often more; it is true that, since I fell sick, to wit, these eight days past, I have not confessed, such is the annoy that my sickness hath given me.' Quoth the friar, 'My son, thou hast done well and so must thou do henceforward. I see, since thou confessest so often, that I shall be at little pains either of hearing or questioning.' 'Sir,' answered Master Ciappelletto, 'say not so; I have never confessed so much nor so often but I would still fain make a general confession of all my sins that I could call to mind from the day of my birth to that of my confession; wherefore I pray you, good my father, question me as punctually of everything, nay, everything, as if I had never confessed; and consider me not because I am sick, for that I had far liefer displease this my flesh than, in consulting its ease, do aught that might be the perdition of my soul, which my Saviour redeemed with His precious blood.'

These words much pleased the holy man and seemed to him to argue a well-disposed mind; wherefore, after he had much commended Master Ciappelletto for that his usance, he asked him if he had ever sinned by way of lust with any woman. 'Father,' replied Master Ciappelletto, sighing, 'on this point I am ashamed to tell you the truth, fearing to sin by way of vainglory.' Quoth the friar, 'Speak in all security, for never did one sin by telling the truth, whether in confession or otherwise.' 'Then,' said Master Ciappelletto, 'since you certify me of this, I will tell you; I am yet a virgin, even as I came forth of my mother's body.' 'O blessed be thou of God!' cried the monk. 'How well hast thou done! And doing thus, thou hast the more deserved, inasmuch as, an thou wouldst, thou hadst more leisure to do the contrary than we and whatsoever others are limited by any rule.'

After this he asked him if he had ever offended against God in the sin of gluttony; whereto Master Ciappelletto answered, sighing, Ay had he, and that many a time; for that, albeit, over and above the Lenten fasts that are yearly observed of the devout, he had been wont to fast on bread and water three days at the least in every week,—he had oftentimes (and especially whenas he had endured any fatigue, either praying or going a-pilgrimage) drunken the water with as much appetite and as keen a relish as great drinkers do wine. And many a time he had longed to have such homely salads of potherbs as women make when they go into the country; and whiles eating had given him more pleasure than himseemed it should do to one who fasteth for devotion, as did he. 'My son,' said the friar, 'these sins are natural and very slight and I would not therefore have thee burden thy conscience withal more than behoveth. It happeneth to every man, how devout soever he be, that, after long fasting, meat seemeth good to him, and after travail, drink.'

'Alack, father mine,' rejoined Ciappelletto, 'tell me not this to comfort me; you must know I know that things done for the service of God should be done sincerely and with an ungrudging mind; and whoso doth otherwise sinneth.' Quoth the friar, exceeding well pleased, 'I am content that thou shouldst thus apprehend it and thy pure and good conscience therein pleaseth me exceedingly. But, tell me, hast thou sinned by way of avarice, desiring more than befitted or withholding that which it behoved thee not to withhold?' 'Father mine,' replied Ciappelletto, 'I would not have you look to my being in the house of these usurers; I have nought to do here; nay, I came hither to admonish and chasten them and turn them from this their abominable way of gain; and methinketh I should have made shift to do so, had not God thus visited me. But you must know that I was left a rich man by my father, of whose good, when he was dead, I bestowed the most part in alms, and after, to sustain my life and that I might be able to succour Christ's poor, I have done my little traffickings, and in these I have desired to gain; but still with God's poor have I shared that which I gained, converting my own half to my occasion and giving them the other, and in this so well hath my Creator prospered me that my affairs have still gone from good to better.'

'Well hast thou done,' said the friar; 'but hast thou often been angered?' 'Oh,' cried Master Ciappelletto, 'that I must tell you I have very often been! And who could keep himself therefrom, seeing men do unseemly things all day long, keeping not the commandments of God neither fearing His judgment? Many times a day I had liefer been dead than alive, seeing young men follow after vanities and hearing them curse and forswear themselves, haunting the taverns, visiting not the churches and ensuing rather the ways of the world than that of God.' 'My son,' said the friar, 'this is a righteous anger, nor for my part might I enjoin thee any penance therefor. But hath anger at any time availed to move thee to do any manslaughter or to bespeak any one unseemly or do any other unright?' 'Alack, sir,' answered the sick man, 'you, who seem to me a man of God, how can you say such words? Had I ever had the least thought of doing any one of the things whereof you speak, think you I believe that God would so long have forborne me? These be the doings of outlaws and men of nought, whereof I never saw any but I said still, "Go, may God amend thee!"'

Then said the friar, 'Now tell me, my son (blessed be thou of God), hast thou never borne false witness against any or missaid of another, or taken others' good, without leave of him to whom it pertained?' 'Ay, indeed, sir,' replied Master Ciappelletto; 'I have missaid of others; for that I had a neighbour aforetime, who, with the greatest unright in the world, did nought but beat his wife, insomuch that I once spoke ill of him to her kinsfolk, so great was the compassion that overcame me for the poor woman, whom he used as God alone can tell, whenassoever he had drunken overmuch.' Quoth the friar, 'Thou tellest me thou hast been a merchant. Hast thou never cheated any one, as merchants do whiles!' 'I' faith, yes, sir,' answered Master Ciappelletto; 'but I know not whom, except it were a certain man, who once brought me monies which he owed me for cloth I had sold him and which I threw into a chest, without counting. A good month after, I found that they were four farthings more than they should have been; wherefore, not seeing him again and having kept them by me a full year, that I might restore them to him, I gave them away in alms.' Quoth the friar, 'This was a small matter, and thou didst well to deal with it as thou didst.'

Then he questioned him of many other things, of all which he answered after the same fashion, and the holy father offering to proceed to absolution, Master Ciappelletto said, 'Sir, I have yet sundry sins that I have not told you.' The friar asked him what they were, and he answered, 'I mind me that one Saturday, after none, I caused my servant sweep out the house and had not that reverence for the Lord's holy day which it behoved me have.' 'Oh,' said the friar, 'that is a light matter, my son.' 'Nay,' rejoined Master Ciappelletto, 'call it not a light matter, for that the Lord's Day is greatly to be honoured, seeing that on such a day our Lord rose from the dead.' Then said the friar, 'Well, hast thou done aught else?' 'Ay, sir,' answered Master Ciappelletto; 'once, unthinking what I did, I spat in the church of God.' Thereupon the friar fell a-smiling, and said, 'My son, that is no thing to be recked of; we who are of the clergy, we spit there all day long.' 'And you do very ill,' rejoined Master Ciappelletto; 'for that there is nought which it so straitly behoveth to keep clean as the holy temple wherein is rendered sacrifice to God.'

Brief, he told him great plenty of such like things and presently fell a-sighing and after weeping sore, as he knew full well to do, whenas he would. Quoth the holy friar, 'What aileth thee, my son?' 'Alas, sir,' replied Master Ciappelletto, 'I have one sin left, whereof I never yet confessed me, such shame have I to tell it; and every time I call it to mind, I weep, even as you see, and meseemeth very certain that God will never pardon it me.' 'Go to, son,' rejoined the friar; 'what is this thou sayest? If all the sins that were ever wrought or are yet to be wrought of all mankind, what while the world endureth, were all in one man and he repented him thereof and were contrite therefor, as I see thee, such is the mercy and loving-kindness of God that, upon confession, He would freely pardon them to him. Wherefore do thou tell it in all assurance.' Quoth Master Ciappelletto, still weeping sore, 'Alack, father mine, mine is too great a sin, and I can scarce believe that it will ever be forgiven me of God, except your prayers strive for me.' Then said the friar, 'Tell it me in all assurance, for I promise thee to pray God for thee.'

Master Ciappelletto, however, still wept and said nought; but, after he had thus held the friar a great while in suspense, he heaved a deep sigh and said, 'Father mine, since you promise me to pray God for me, I will e'en tell it you. Know, then, that, when I was little, I once cursed my mother.' So saying, he fell again to weeping sore. 'O my son,' quoth the friar, 'seemeth this to thee so heinous a sin? Why, men blaspheme God all day long and He freely pardoneth whoso repenteth him of having blasphemed Him; and deemest thou not He will pardon thee this? Weep not, but comfort thyself; for, certes, wert thou one of those who set Him on the cross, He would pardon thee, in favour of such contrition as I see in thee.' 'Alack, father mine, what say you?' replied Ciappelletto. 'My kind mother, who bore me nine months in her body, day and night, and carried me on her neck an hundred times and more, I did passing ill to curse her and it was an exceeding great sin; and except you pray God for me, it will not be forgiven me.'

The friar, then, seeing that Master Ciappelletto had no more to say, gave him absolution and bestowed on him his benison, holding him a very holy man and devoutly believing all that he had told him to be true. And who would not have believed it, hearing a man at the point of death speak thus? Then, after all this, he said to him, 'Master Ciappelletto, with God's help you will speedily be whole; but, should it come to pass that God call your blessed and well-disposed soul to Himself, would it please you that your body be buried in our convent?' 'Ay, would it, sir,' replied Master Ciappelletto. 'Nay, I would fain no be buried otherwhere, since you have promised to pray God for me; more by token that I have ever had a special regard for your order. Wherefore I pray you that whenas you return to your lodging, you must cause bring me that most veritable body of Christ, which you consecrate a-mornings upon the altar, for that, with your leave, I purpose (all unworthy as I am) to take it and after, holy and extreme unction, to the intent that, if I have lived as a sinner, I may at the least die like a Christian.' The good friar replied that it pleased him much and that he said well and promised to see it presently brought him; and so was it done.

Meanwhile, the two brothers, misdoubting them sore lest Master Ciappelletto should play them false, had posted themselves behind a wainscot, that divided the chamber where he lay from another, and listening, easily heard and apprehended that which he said to the friar and had whiles so great a mind to laugh, hearing the things which he confessed to having done, that they were like to burst and said, one to other, 'What manner of man is this, whom neither old age nor sickness nor fear of death, whereunto he seeth himself near, nor yet of God, before whose judgment-seat he looketh to be ere long, have availed to turn from his wickedness nor hinder him from choosing to die as he hath lived?' However, seeing that he had so spoken that he should be admitted to burial in a church, they recked nought of the rest.

Master Ciappelletto presently took the sacrament and, growing rapidly worse, received extreme unction, and a little after evensong of the day he had made his fine confession, he died; whereupon the two brothers, having, of his proper monies, taken order for his honourable burial, sent to the convent to acquaint the friars therewith, bidding them come thither that night to hold vigil, according to usance, and fetch away the body in the morning, and meanwhile made ready all that was needful thereunto.

The holy friar, who had shriven him, hearing that he had departed this life, betook himself to the prior of the convent and, letting ring to chapter, gave out to the brethren therein assembled that Master Ciappelletto had been a holy man, according to that which he had gathered from his confession, and persuaded them to receive his body with the utmost reverence and devotion, in the hope that God should show forth many miracles through him. To this the prior and brethren credulously consented and that same evening, coming all whereas Master Ciappelletto lay dead, they held high and solemn vigil over him and on the morrow, clad all in albs and copes, book in hand and crosses before them, they went, chanting the while, for his body and brought it with the utmost pomp and solemnity to their church, followed by well nigh all the people of the city, men and women.

As soon as they had set the body down in the church, the holy friar, who had confessed him, mounted the pulpit and fell a-preaching marvellous things of the dead man and of his life, his fasts, his virginity, his simplicity and innocence and sanctity, recounting, amongst other things, that which he had confessed to him as his greatest sin and how he had hardly availed to persuade him that God would forgive it him; thence passing on to reprove the folk who hearkened, 'And you, accursed that you are,' quoth he, 'for every waif of straw that stirreth between your feet, you blaspheme God and the Virgin and all the host of heaven.' Moreover, he told them many other things of his loyalty and purity of heart; brief, with his speech, whereto entire faith was yielded of the people of the city, he so established the dead man in the reverent consideration of all who were present that, no sooner was the service at an end, than they all with the utmost eagerness flocked to kiss his hands and feet and the clothes were torn off his back, he holding himself blessed who might avail to have never so little thereof; and needs must they leave him thus all that day, so he might be seen and visited of all.

The following night he was honourably buried in a marble tomb in one of the chapels of the church and on the morrow the folk began incontinent to come and burn candles and offer up prayers and make vows to him and hang images of wax[11] at his shrine, according to the promise made. Nay, on such wise waxed the frame of his sanctity and men's devotion to him that there was scarce any who, being in adversity, would vow himself to another saint than him; and they styled and yet style him Saint Ciappelletto and avouch that God through him hath wrought many miracles and yet worketh, them every day for whoso devoutly commendeth himself unto him.

Thus, then, lived and died Master Cepperello[12] da Prato and became a saint, as you have heard; nor would I deny it to be possible that he is beatified in God's presence, for that, albeit his life was wicked and perverse, he may at his last extremity have shown such contrition that peradventure God had mercy on him and received him into His kingdom; but, for that this is hidden from us, I reason according to that which, is apparent and say that he should rather be in the hands of the devil in perdition than in Paradise. And if so it be, we may know from this how great is God's loving-kindness towards us, which, having regard not to our error, but to the purity of our faith, whenas we thus make an enemy (deeming him a friend) of His our intermediary, giveth ear unto us, even as if we had recourse unto one truly holy, as intercessor for His favour. Wherefore, to the end that by His grace we may be preserved safe and sound in this present adversity and in this so joyous company, let us, magnifying His name, in which we have begun our diversion, and holding Him in reverence, commend ourselves to Him in our necessities, well assured of being heard." And with this he was silent.

---

1. Or procurators.
2. A Florentine merchant settled in France; he had great influence over Philippe le Bel and made use of the royal favour to enrich himself by means of monopolies granted at the expense of his compatriots.
3. Charles, Comte de Valois et d'Alençon.
4. Philippe le Bel, a.d. 1268-1314.
5. The Eighth.
6. Sic. *Cepparello* means a log or stump. Ciapperello is apparently a dialectic variant of the same word.
7. Diminutive of Cappello. This passage is obscure and most likely corrupt. Boccaccio probably meant to write "hat" instead of "chaplet" (*ghirlanda*), as the meaning of *cappello*, chaplet (diminutive of Old English *chapel*, a hat,) being the meaning of *ciappelletto* (properly *cappelletto*).
8. *i.e.* false instruments.

9. A "twopence-coloured" sketch of an impossible villain, drawn with a crudeness unusual in Boccaccio.
10. *i.e.* if there be such a thing as a holy and worthy friar.
11. *i.e.* ex voto.
12. It will be noted that this is Boccaccio's third variant of his hero's name (the others being Ciapperello and Cepparello) and the edition of 1527 furnishes us with a fourth and a fifth form, *i.e.* Ciepparello and Ciepperello.

❧ 2 ❧

THE SECOND STORY

ABRAHAM THE JEW, AT THE INSTIGATION OF JEHANNOT DE CHEVIGNÉ, GOETH TO THE COURT OF ROME AND SEEING THE DEPRAVITY OF THE CLERGY, RETURNETH TO PARIS AND THERE BECOMETH A CHRISTIAN

PAMFILO'S STORY was in part laughed at and altogether commended by the ladies, and it being come to its end, after being diligently hearkened, the queen bade Neifile, who sat next him, ensue the ordinance of the commenced diversion by telling one[1] of her fashion. Neifile, who was distinguished no less by courteous manners than by beauty, answered blithely that she would well and began on this wise: "Pamfilo hath shown us in his story that God's benignness regardeth not our errors, when they proceed from that which is beyond our ken; and I, in mine, purpose to show you how this same benignness,—patiently suffering the defaults of those who, being especially bounden both with words and deeds to bear true witness thereof[2] yet practise the contrary,—exhibiteth unto us an infallible proof of itself, to the intent that we may, with the more constancy of mind, ensue that which we believe.

As I have heard tell, gracious ladies, there was once in Paris a great merchant and a very loyal and upright man, whose name was Jehannot de Chevigné and who was of great traffic in silks and stuffs. He had particular friendship for a very rich Jew called Abraham, who was also a merchant and a very honest and trusty man, and seeing the latter's worth and loyalty, it began to irk him sore that the soul of so worthy and discreet and good a man should go to perdition for default of faith; wherefore he fell to beseeching him on friendly wise leave the errors of the Jewish faith and turn to the Christian verity, which he might see still wax and prosper, as being holy and good, whereas his own faith, on the contrary, was manifestly on the wane and dwindling to nought. The Jew made answer that he held no faith holy or good save only the Jewish, that in this latter he was born and therein meant to live and die, nor should aught ever make him remove therefrom.

Jehannot for all that desisted not from him, but some days after returned to the attack with similar words, showing him, on rude enough wise (for that merchants for the most part can no better), for what reasons our religion is better than the Jewish; and albeit the Jew was a past master in their law, nevertheless, whether it was the great friendship he bore Jehannot that moved him or peradventure words wrought it that the Holy Ghost put into the good simple man's mouth, the latter's arguments began greatly to please him; but yet, persisting in his own belief, he would not suffer himself to be converted. Like as he abode obstinate, even so

23

Jehannot never gave over importuning him, till at last the Jew, overcome by such continual insistence, said, 'Look you, Jehannot, thou wouldst have me become a Christian and I am disposed to do it; insomuch, indeed, that I mean, in the first place, to go to Rome and there see him who, thou sayest, is God's Vicar upon earth and consider his manners and fashions and likewise those of his chief brethren.[3] If these appear to me such that I may, by them, as well as by your words, apprehend that your faith is better than mine, even as thou hast studied to show me, I will do as I have said; and if it be not so, I will remain a Jew as I am.'

When Jehannot heard this, he was beyond measure chagrined and said in himself, 'I have lost my pains, which meseemed I had right well bestowed, thinking to have converted this man; for that, an he go to the court of Rome and see the lewd and wicked life of the clergy, not only will he never become a Christian, but, were he already a Christian, he would infallibly turn Jew again.' Then, turning to Abraham, he said to him, 'Alack, my friend, why wilt thou undertake this travail and so great a charge as it will be to thee to go from here to Rome? More by token that, both by sea and by land, the road is full of perils for a rich man such as thou art. Thinkest thou not to find here who shall give thee baptism? Or, if peradventure thou have any doubts concerning the faith which I have propounded to thee, where are there greater doctors and men more learned in the matter than are here or better able to resolve thee of that which thou wilt know or ask? Wherefore, to my thinking, this thy going is superfluous. Bethink thee that the prelates there are even such as those thou mayst have seen here, and indeed so much the better as they are nearer unto the Chief Pastor. Wherefore, an thou wilt be counselled by me, thou wilt reserve this travail unto another time against some jubilee or other, whereunto it may be I will bear thee company.' To this the Jew made answer, 'I doubt not, Jehannot, but it is as thou tellest me; but, to sum up many words in one, I am altogether determined, an thou wouldst have me do that whereof thou hast so instantly besought me, to go thither; else will I never do aught thereof.' Jehannot, seeing his determination, said, 'Go and good luck go with thee!' And inwardly assured that he would never become a Christian, when once he should have seen the court of Rome, but availing[4] nothing in the matter, he desisted.

The Jew mounted to horse and as quickliest he might betook himself to the court of Rome, he was honourably entertained of his brethren, and there abiding, without telling any the reason of his coming, he began diligently to enquire into the manners and fashions of the Pope and Cardinals and other prelates and of all the members of his court, and what with that which he himself noted, being a mighty quick-witted man, and that which he gathered from others, he found all, from the highest to the lowest, most shamefully given to the sin of lust, and that not only in the way of nature, but after the Sodomitical fashion, without any restraint of remorse or shamefastness, insomuch that the interest of courtezans and catamites was of no small avail there in obtaining any considerable thing.

Moreover, he manifestly perceived them to be universally gluttons, wine-bibbers, drunkards and slaves to their bellies, brute-beast fashion, more than to aught else after lust. And looking farther, he saw them all covetous and greedy after money, insomuch that human, nay, Christian blood, no less than things sacred, whatsoever they might be, whether pertaining to the sacrifices of the altar or to the benefices of the church, they sold and bought indifferently for a price, making a greater traffic and having more brokers thereof than folk at Paris of silks and stuffs or what not else. Manifest simony they had christened 'procuration' and gluttony 'sustentation,' as if God apprehended not,—let be the meaning of words but,—the intention of depraved minds and would suffer Himself, after the fashion of men, to be duped by the names of things. All this, together with much else which must be left unsaid, was supremely displeasing to the Jew, who was a sober and modest man, and himseeming he had seen enough, he determined to return to Paris and did so.

As soon as Jehannot knew of his return, he betook himself to him, hoping nothing less than that he should become a Christian, and they greeted each other with the utmost joy. Then, after Abraham had rested some days, Jehannot asked him how himseemed of the Holy Father and of the cardinals and others of his court. Whereto the Jew promptly answered, 'Meseemeth, God give them ill one and all! And I say this for that, if I was able to observe aright, no piety, no devoutness, no good work or example of life or otherwhat did I see there in any who was a churchman; nay, but lust, covetise, gluttony and the like and worse (if worse can be) meseemed to be there in such favour with all that I hold it for a forgingplace of things diabolical rather than divine. And as far as I can judge, meseemeth your chief pastor and consequently all the others endeavour with all diligence and all their wit and every art to bring to nought and banish from the world the Christian religion, whereas they should be its foundation and support. And for that I see that this whereafter they strive cometh not to pass, but that your religion continually increaseth and waxeth still brighter and more glorious, meseemeth I manifestly discern that the Holy Spirit is verily the foundation and support thereof, as of that which is true and holy over any other. Wherefore, whereas, aforetime I abode obdurate and insensible to thine exhortations and would not be persuaded to embrace thy faith, I now tell thee frankly that for nothing in the world would I forbear to become a Christian. Let us, then, to church and there have me baptized, according to the rite and ordinance of your holy faith.'

Jehannot, who looked for a directly contrary conclusion to this, was the joyfullest man that might be, when he heard him speak thus, and repairing with him to our Lady's Church of Paris, required the clergy there to give Abraham baptism. They, hearing that the Jew himself demanded it, straightway proceeded to baptize him, whilst Jehannot raised him from the sacred font[5] and named him Giovanni. After this, he had him thoroughly lessoned by men of great worth and learning in the tenets of our holy faith, which he speedily apprehended and thenceforward was a good man and a worthy and one of a devout life."

---

1. *i.e.* a story.
2. *i.e.* of God's benignness.
3. Lit. cardinal brethren (*fratelli cardinali*).
4. Lit. losing (*perdendo*), but this is probably some copyist's mistake for *podendo*, the old form of *potendo*, availing.
5. *i.e.* stood sponsor for him.

❦ 3 ❧

THE THIRD STORY

MELCHIZEDEK THE JEW, WITH A STORY OF THREE RINGS, ESCAPETH A PARLOUS SNARE SET FOR HIM BY SALADIN

NEIFILE HAVING MADE an end of her story, which was commended of all, Filomena, by the queen's good pleasure, proceeded to speak thus: "The story told by Neifile bringeth to my mind a parlous case the once betided a Jew; and for that, it having already been excellent well spoken both of God and of the verity of our faith, it should not henceforth be forbidden us to descend to the doings of mankind and the events that have befallen them, I will now proceed to relate to you the case aforesaid, which having heard, you will peradventure become more wary in answering the questions that may be put to you. You must know, lovesome[1] companions[2] mine, that, like as folly ofttimes draweth folk forth of happy estate and casteth them into the utmost misery, even so doth good sense extricate the wise man from the greatest perils and place him in assurance and tranquillity. How true it is that folly bringeth many an one from fair estate unto misery is seen by multitude of examples, with the recounting whereof we have no present concern, considering that a thousand instances thereof do every day manifestly appear to us; but that good sense is a cause of solacement I will, as I promised, briefly show you by a little story.

Saladin,—whose valour was such that not only from a man of little account it made him Soldan of Babylon, but gained him many victories over kings Saracen and Christian,—having in divers wars and in the exercise of his extraordinary munificences expended his whole treasure and having an urgent occasion for a good sum of money nor seeing whence he might avail to have it as promptly as it behoved him, called to mind a rich Jew, by name Melchizedek, who lent at usance in Alexandria, and bethought himself that this latter had the wherewithal to oblige him, and he would; but he was so miserly that he would never have done it of his freewill and Saladin was loath to use force with him; wherefore, need constraining him, he set his every wit awork to find a means how the Jew might be brought to serve him in this and presently concluded to do him a violence coloured by some show of reason.

Accordingly he sent for Melchizedek and receiving him familiarly, seated him by himself, then said to him, 'Honest man, I have understood from divers persons that thou art a very learned man and deeply versed in matters of divinity; wherefore I would fain know of thee whether of the three Laws thou reputest the true, the Jewish, the Saracen or the Christian.' The

Jew, who was in truth a man of learning and understanding, perceived but too well that Saladin looked to entrap him in words, so he might fasten a quarrel on him, and bethought himself that he could not praise any of the three more than the others without giving him the occasion he sought. Accordingly, sharpening his wits, as became one who felt himself in need of an answer by which he might not be taken at a vantage, there speedily occurred to him that which it behoved him reply and he said, 'My lord, the question that you propound to me is a nice one and to acquaint you with that which I think of the matter, it behoveth me tell you a little story, which you shall hear.

An I mistake not, I mind me to have many a time heard tell that there was once a great man and a rich, who among other very precious jewels in his treasury, had a very goodly and costly ring, whereunto being minded, for its worth and beauty, to do honour and wishing to leave it in perpetuity to his descendants, he declared that whichsoever of his sons should, at his death, be found in possession thereof, by his bequest unto him, should be recognized as his heir and be held of all the others in honour and reverence as chief and head. He to whom the ring was left by him held a like course with his own descendants and did even as his father had done. In brief the ring passed from hand to hand, through many generations, and came at last into the possession of a man who had three goodly and virtuous sons, all very obedient to their father wherefore he loved them all three alike. The young men, knowing the usance of the ring, each for himself, desiring to be the most honoured among his folk, as best he might, besought his father, who was now an old man, to leave him the ring, whenas he came to die. The worthy man, who loved them all alike and knew not himself how to choose to which he had liefer leave the ring, bethought himself, having promised it to each, to seek to satisfy all three and privily let make by a good craftsman other two rings, which were so like unto the first that he himself scarce knew which was the true. When he came to die, he secretly gave each one of his sons his ring, wherefore each of them, seeking after their father's death, to occupy the inheritance and the honour and denying it to the others, produced his ring, in witness of his right, and the three rings being found so like unto one another that the true might not be known, the question which was the father's very heir abode pending and yet pendeth. And so say I to you, my lord, of the three Laws to the three peoples given of God the Father, whereof you question me; each people deemeth itself to have his inheritance, His true Law and His commandments; but of which in very deed hath them, even as of the rings, the question yet pendeth.'

Saladin perceived that the Jew had excellently well contrived to escape the snare which he had spread before his feet; wherefore he concluded to discover to him his need and see if he were willing to serve him; and so accordingly he did, confessing to him that which he had it in mind to do, had he not answered him on such discreet wise. The Jew freely furnished him with all that he required, and the Soldan after satisfied him in full; moreover, he gave him very great gifts and still had him to friend and maintained him about his own person in high and honourable estate."

---

1. Lit. amorous (*amorose*), but Boccaccio frequently uses *amoroso, vago*, and other adjectives, which are now understood in an active or transitive sense only, in their ancient passive or intransitive sense of lovesome, desirable, etc.
2. *Compagne, i.e.* she-companions. Filomena is addressing the female part of the company.

✤ 4 ✤

THE FOURTH STORY

A MONK, HAVING FALLEN INTO A SIN DESERVING OF VERY GRIEVOUS PUNISHMENT, ADROITLY REPROACHING THE SAME FAULT TO HIS ABBOT, QUITTETH HIMSELF OF THE PENALTY

FILOMENA, having despatched her story, was now silent, whereupon Dioneo, who sat next her, knowing already, by the ordinance begun, that it fell to his turn to tell, proceeded, without awaiting farther commandment from the queen, to speak on this wise: "Lovesome ladies, if I have rightly apprehended the intention of you all, we are here to divert ourselves with story-telling; wherefore, so but it be not done contrary to this our purpose, I hold it lawful unto each (even as our queen told us a while agone) to tell such story as he deemeth may afford most entertainment. Accordingly having heard how, by the good counsels of Jehannot de Chevigné, Abraham had his soul saved and how Melchizedek, by his good sense, defended his riches from Saladin's ambushes, I purpose, without looking for reprehension from you, briefly to relate with what address a monk delivered his body from a very grievous punishment.

There was in Lunigiana, a country not very far hence, a monastery whilere more abounding in sanctity and monks than it is nowadays, and therein, among others, was a young monk, whose vigour and lustiness neither fasts nor vigils availed to mortify. It chanced one day, towards noontide, when all the other monks slept, that, as he went all alone round about the convent,[1] which stood in a very solitary place, he espied a very well-favoured lass, belike some husbandman's daughter of the country, who went about the fields culling certain herbs, and no sooner had he set eyes on her than he was violently assailed by carnal appetite. Wherefore, accosting her, he entered into parley with her and so led on from one thing to another that he came to an accord with her and brought her to his cell, unperceived of any; but whilst, carried away by overmuch ardour, he disported himself with her less cautiously than was prudent, it chanced that the abbot arose from sleep and softly passing by the monk's cell, heard the racket that the twain made together; whereupon he came stealthily up to the door to listen, that he might the better recognize the voices, and manifestly perceiving that there was a woman in the cell, was at first minded to cause open to him, but after bethought himself to hold another course in the matter and, returning to his chamber, awaited the monk's coming forth.

The latter, all taken up as he was with the wench and his exceeding pleasure and delight in her company, was none the less on his guard and himseeming he heard some scuffling of feet in the dormitory, he set his eye to a crevice and plainly saw the abbot stand hearkening unto him;

whereby he understood but too well that the latter must have gotten wind of the wench's presence in his cell and knowing that sore punishment would ensue to him thereof, he was beyond measure chagrined. However, without discovering aught of his concern to the girl, he hastily revolved many things in himself, seeking to find some means of escape, and presently hit upon a rare device, which went straight to the mark he aimed at. Accordingly, making a show of thinking he had abidden long enough with the damsel, he said to her, 'I must go cast about for a means how thou mayest win forth hence, without being seen; wherefore do thou abide quietly until my return.'

Then, going forth and locking the cell door on her, he betook himself straight to the abbot's chamber and presenting him with the key, according as each monk did, whenas he went abroad, said to him, with a good countenance, 'Sir, I was unable to make an end this morning of bringing off all the faggots I had cut; wherefore with your leave I will presently go to the wood and fetch them away.' The abbot, deeming the monk unaware that he had been seen of him, was glad of such an opportunity to inform himself more fully of the offence committed by him and accordingly took the key and gave him the leave he sought. Then, as soon as he saw him gone, he fell to considering which he should rather do, whether open his cell in the presence of all the other monks and cause them to see his default, so they might after have no occasion to murmur against himself, whenas he should punish the offender, or seek first to learn from the girl herself how the thing had passed; and bethinking himself that she might perchance be the wife or daughter of such a man that he would be loath to have done her the shame of showing her to all the monks, he determined first to see her and after come to a conclusion; wherefore, betaking himself to the cell, he opened it and, entering, shut the door after him.

The girl, seeing the abbot enter, was all aghast and fell a-weeping for fear of shame; but my lord abbot, casting his eyes upon her and seeing her young and handsome, old as he was, suddenly felt the pricks of the flesh no less importunate than his young monk had done and fell a-saying in himself, 'Marry, why should I not take somewhat of pleasure, whenas I may, more by token that displeasance and annoy are still at hand, whenever I have a mind to them? This is a handsome wench and is here unknown of any in the world. If I can bring her to do my pleasure, I know not why I should not do it. Who will know it? No one will ever know it and a sin that's hidden is half forgiven. Maybe this chance will never occur again. I hold it great sense to avail ourselves of a good, whenas God the Lord sendeth us thereof.'

So saying and having altogether changed purpose from that wherewith he came, he drew near to the girl and began gently to comfort her, praying her not to weep, and passing from one word to another, he ended by discovering to her his desire. The girl, who was neither iron nor adamant, readily enough lent herself to the pleasure of the abbot, who, after he had clipped and kissed her again and again, mounted upon the monk's pallet and having belike regard to the grave burden of his dignity and the girl's tender age and fearful of irking her for overmuch heaviness, bestrode not her breast, but set her upon his own and so a great while disported himself with her.

Meanwhile, the monk, who had only made believe to go to the wood and had hidden himself in the dormitory, was altogether reassured, whenas he saw the abbot enter his cell alone, doubting not but his device should have effect, and when he saw him lock the door from within, he held it for certain. Accordingly, coming forth of his hiding-place, he stealthily betook himself to a crevice, through which he both heard and saw all that the abbot did and said. When it seemed to the latter that he had tarried long enough with the damsel, he locked her in the cell and returned to his own chamber, whence, after awhile, he heard the monk stirring and deeming him returned from the wood, thought to rebuke him severely and cast him into prison, so himself might alone possess the prey he had gotten; wherefore, sending for him, he very grievously rebuked him and with a stern countenance and commanded that he should be put in prison.

The monk very readily answered, 'Sir, I have not yet pertained long enough to the order of St. Benedict to have been able to learn every particular thereof, and you had not yet shown me that monks should make of women a means of mortification,[2] as of fasts and vigils; but, now that you have shown it me, I promise you, so you will pardon me this default, never again to offend therein, but still to do as I have seen you do.' The abbot, who was a quick-witted man, readily understood that the monk not only knew more than himself, but had seen what he did; wherefore, his conscience pricking him for his own default, he was ashamed to inflict on the monk a punishment which he himself had merited even as he. Accordingly, pardoning him and charging him keep silence of that which he had seen, they privily put the girl out of doors and it is believed that they caused her return thither more than once thereafterward."

---

1. Lit. his church (*sua chiesa*); but the context seems to indicate that the monastery itself is meant.
2. Lit. a pressure or oppression (*priemere*, hod. *premere*, to press or oppress, indicative used as a noun). The monk of course refers to the posture in which he had seen the abbot have to do with the girl, pretending to believe that he placed her on his own breast (instead of mounting on hers) out of a sentiment of humility and a desire to mortify his flesh *ipsâ in voluptate*.

𝕾 5 𝕾

THE FIFTH STORY

THE MARCHIONESS OF MONFERRATO, WITH A DINNER OF HENS AND CERTAIN SPRIGHTLY WORDS, CURBETH THE EXTRAVAGANT PASSION OF THE KING OF FRANCE

THE STORY TOLD by Dioneo at first pricked the hearts of the listening ladies with somewhat of shamefastness, whereof a modest redness appearing in their faces gave token; but after, looking one at other and being scarce able to keep their countenance, they listened, laughing in their sleeves. The end thereof being come, after they had gently chidden him, giving him to understand that such tales were not fit to be told among ladies, the queen, turning to Fiammetta, who sat next him on the grass, bade her follow on the ordinance. Accordingly, she began with a good grace and a cheerful countenance, "It hath occurred to my mind, fair my ladies,—at once because it pleaseth me that we have entered upon showing by stories how great is the efficacy of prompt and goodly answers and because, like as in men it is great good sense to seek still to love a lady of higher lineage than themselves,[1] so in women it is great discretion to know how to keep themselves from being taken with the love of men of greater condition than they,—to set forth to you, in the story which it falleth to me to tell, how both with deeds and words a noble lady guarded herself against this and diverted another therefrom.

The Marquis of Monferrato, a man of high worth and gonfalonier[2] of the church, had passed beyond seas on the occasion of a general crusade undertaken by the Christians, arms in hand, and it being one day discoursed of his merit at the court of King Phillippe le Borgne,[3] who was then making ready to depart France upon the same crusade, it was avouched by a gentleman present that there was not under the stars a couple to match with the marquis and his lady, for that, even as he was renowned among knights for every virtue, so was she the fairest and noblest of all the ladies in the world. These words took such hold upon the mind of the King of France that, without having seen the marchioness, he fell of a sudden ardently in love with her and determined to take ship for the crusade, on which he was to go, no otherwhere than at Genoa, in order that, journeying thither by land, he might have an honourable occasion of visiting the marchioness, doubting not but that, the marquis being absent, he might avail to give effect to his desire.

As he had bethought himself, so he put his thought into execution; for, having sent forward all his power, he set out, attended only by some few gentlemen, and coming within a day's journey of the marquis's domains, despatched a vauntcourier to bid the lady expect him the following morning to dinner. The marchioness, who was well advised and discreet, replied blithely that in this he did her the greatest of favours and that he would be welcome and after bethought herself what this might mean that such a king should come to visit her in her husband's absence, nor was she deceived in the conclusion to which she came, to wit, that the report of her beauty drew him thither. Nevertheless, like a brave lady as she was, she determined to receive him with honour and summoning to her counsels sundry gentlemen of those who remained there, with their help, she let provide for everything needful. The ordinance of the repast and of the viands she reserved to herself alone and having forthright caused collect as many hens as were in the country, she bade her cooks dress various dishes of these alone for the royal table.

The king came at the appointed time and was received by the lady with great honour and rejoicing. When he beheld her, she seemed to him fair and noble and well-bred beyond that which he had conceived from the courtier's words, whereat he marvelled exceedingly and commended her amain, waxing so much the hotter in his desire as he found the lady overpassing his foregone conceit of her. After he had taken somewhat of rest in chambers adorned to the utmost with all that pertaineth to the entertainment of such a king, the dinner hour being come, the king and the marchioness seated themselves at one table, whilst the rest, according to their quality, were honourably entertained at others. The king, being served with many dishes in succession, as well as with wines of the best and costliest, and to boot gazing with delight the while upon the lovely marchioness, was mightily pleased with his entertainment; but, after awhile, as the viands followed one upon another, he began somewhat to marvel, perceiving that, for all the diversity of the dishes, they were nevertheless of nought other than hens, and this although he knew the part where he was to be such as should abound in game of various kinds and although he had, by advising the lady in advance of his coming, given her time to send a-hunting. However, much as he might marvel at this, he chose not to take occasion of engaging her in parley thereof, otherwise than in the matter of her hens, and accordingly, turning to her with a merry air, 'Madam,' quoth he, 'are hens only born in these parts, without ever a cock?' The marchioness, who understood the king's question excellent well, herseeming God had vouchsafed her, according to her wish, an opportune occasion of discovering her mind, turned to him and answered boldly, 'Nay, my lord; but women, albeit in apparel and dignities they may differ somewhat from others, are natheless all of the same fashion here as elsewhere.'

The King, hearing this, right well apprehended the meaning of the banquet of hens and the virtue hidden in her speech and perceived that words would be wasted upon such a lady and that violence was out of the question; wherefore, even as he had ill-advisedly taken fire for her, so now it behoved him sagely, for his own honour's sake, stifle his ill-conceived passion. Accordingly, without making any more words with her, for fear of her replies, he dined, out of all hope; and the meal ended, thanking her for the honourable entertainment he had received from her and commending her to God, he set out for Genoa, so by his prompt departure he might make amends for his unseemly visit."

---

1. An evident allusion to Boccaccio's passion for the Princess Maria, *i.e.* Fiammetta herself.
2. Or standard-bearer.
3. *i.e.* the One-eyed (syn. le myope, the short-sighted, the Italian word [*Il Bornio*] having both meanings), *i.e.* Philip II. of France, better known as Philip Augustus.

❧ 6 ❧

THE SIXTH STORY

AN HONEST MAN, WITH A CHANCE PLEASANTRY, PUTTETH TO SHAME THE PERVERSE HYPOCRISY OF THE RELIGIOUS ORDERS

EMILIA, who sat next after Fiammetta,—the courage of the marchioness and the quaint rebuke administered by her to the King of France having been commended of all the ladies,—began, by the queen's pleasure, boldly to speak as follows: "I also, I will not keep silence of a biting reproof given by an honest layman to a covetous monk with a speech no less laughable than commendable.

There was, then, dear lasses, no great while agone, in our city, a Minor friar and inquisitor of heretical pravity, who, for all he studied hard to appear a devout and tender lover of the Christian religion, as do they all, was no less diligent in enquiring of who had a well-filled purse than of whom he might find wanting in the things of the Faith. Thanks to this his diligence, he lit by chance upon a good simple man, richer, by far in coin than in wit, who, of no lack of religion, but speaking thoughtlessly and belike overheated with wine or excess of mirth, chanced one day to say to a company of his friends that he had a wine so good that Christ himself might drink thereof. This being reported to the inquisitor and he understanding that the man's means were large and his purse well filled, ran in a violent hurry *cum gladiis et fustibus*[1] to clap up a right grievous suit against him, looking not for an amendment of misbelief in the defendant, but for the filling of his own hand with florins to ensue thereof (as indeed it did,) and causing him to be cited, asked him if that which had been alleged against him were true.

The good man replied that it was and told him how it chanced; whereupon quoth the most holy inquisitor, who was a devotee of St. John Goldenbeard,[2] 'Then hast thou made Christ a wine-bibber and curious in wines of choice, as if he were Cinciglione[3] or what not other of your drunken sots and tavern-haunters; and now thou speakest lowly and wouldst feign this to be a very light matter! It is not as thou deemest; thou hast merited the fire therefor, an we were minded to deal with thee as we ought.' With these and many other words he bespoke him, with as menacing a countenance as if the poor wretch had been Epicurus denying the immortality of the soul, and in brief so terrified him that the good simple soul, by means of certain intermediaries, let grease his palm with a good dose of St. John Goldenmouth's ointment[4] (the which is a sovereign remedy for the pestilential covetise of the clergy and especially of the Minor Brethren, who dare not touch money), so he should deal mercifully with him.

This unguent, being of great virtue (albeit Galen speaketh not thereof in any part of his Medicines), wrought to such purpose that the fire denounced against him was by favour commuted into [the wearing, by way of penance, of] a cross, and to make the finer banner, as he were to go a crusading beyond seas, the inquisitor imposed it him yellow upon black. Moreover, whenas he had gotten the money, he detained him about himself some days, enjoining him, by way of penance, hear a mass every morning at Santa Croce and present himself before him at dinner-time, and after that he might do what most pleased him the rest of the day; all which he diligently performed.

One morning, amongst others, it chanced that at the Mass he heard a Gospel, wherein these words were chanted, 'For every one ye shall receive an hundred and shall possess eternal life.'[5] This he laid fast up in his memory and according to the commandment given him, presented him at the eating hour before the inquisitor, whom he found at dinner. The friar asked him if he had heard mass that morning, whereto he promptly answered, 'Ay have I, sir.' Quoth the inquisitor, 'Heardest thou aught therein whereof thou doubtest or would question?' 'Certes,' replied the good man, 'I doubt not of aught that I heard, but do firmly believe all to be true. I did indeed hear something which caused and yet causeth me have the greatest compassion of you and your brother friars, bethinking me of the ill case wherein you will find yourselves over yonder in the next life.' 'And what was it that moved thee to such compassion of us?' asked the inquisitor. 'Sir,' answered the other, 'it was that verse of the Evangel, which saith, "For every one ye shall receive an hundred." 'That is true,' rejoined the inquisitor; 'but why did these words move thee thus?' 'Sir,' replied the good man, 'I will tell you. Since I have been used to resort hither, I have seen give out every day to a multitude of poor folk now one and now two vast great cauldrons of broth, which had been taken away from before yourself and the other brethren of this convent, as superfluous; wherefore, if for each one of these cauldrons of broth there be rendered you an hundred in the world to come, you will have so much thereof that you will assuredly all be drowned therein.'

All who were at the inquisitor's table fell a-laughing; but the latter, feeling the hit at the broth-swilling[6] hypocrisy of himself and his brethren, was mightily incensed, and but that he had gotten blame for that which he had already done, he would have saddled him with another prosecution, for that with a laughable speech he had rebuked him and his brother good-for-noughts; wherefore, of his despite, he bade him thenceforward do what most pleased him and not come before him again."

---

1. *i.e.* with sword and whips, a technical term of ecclesiastical procedure, about equivalent to our "with the strong arm of the law."
2. *i.e.* a lover of money.
3. A notorious drinker of the time.
4. *i.e.* money.
5. "And every one that hath forsaken houses or brethren or sisters or father or mother or wife or children or lands for my name's sake shall receive an hundredfold and shall inherit everlasting life."—Matthew xix. 29. Boccaccio has garbled the passage for the sake of his point.
6. Syn. gluttonous (*brodajuola*).

THE SEVENTH STORY

BERGAMINO, WITH A STORY OF PRIMASSO AND THE ABBOT OF CLUNY, COURTEOUSLY REBUKETH A FIT OF PARSIMONY NEWLY COME TO MESSER CANE DELLA SCALA

EMILIA'S PLEASANTNESS and her story moved the queen and all the rest to laugh and applaud the rare conceit of this new-fangled crusader. Then, after the laughter had subsided and all were silent again, Filostrato, whose turn it was to tell, began to speak on this wise: "It is a fine thing, noble ladies, to hit a mark that never stirreth; but it is well-nigh miraculous if, when some unwonted thing appeareth of a sudden, it be forthright stricken of an archer. The lewd and filthy life of the clergy, in many things as it were a constant mark for malice, giveth without much difficulty occasion to all who have a mind to speak of, to gird at and rebuke it; wherefore, albeit the worthy man, who pierced the inquisitor to the quick touching the hypocritical charity of the friars, who give to the poor that which it should behove them cast to the swine or throw away, did well, I hold him much more to be commended of whom, the foregoing tale moving me thereto, I am to speak and who with a quaint story rebuked Messer Cane della Scala, a magnificent nobleman, of a sudden and unaccustomed niggardliness newly appeared in him, figuring, in the person of another, that which he purposed to say to him concerning themselves; the which was on this wise.

As very manifest renown proclaimeth well nigh throughout the whole world, Messer Cane della Scala, to whom in many things fortune was favourable, was one of the most notable and most magnificent gentlemen that have been known in Italy since the days of the Emperor Frederick the Second. Being minded to make a notable and wonder-goodly entertainment in Verona, whereunto many folk should have come from divers parts and especially men of art[1] of all kinds, he of a sudden (whatever might have been the cause) withdrew therefrom and having in a measure requited those who were come thither, dismissed them all, save only one, Bergamino by name, a man ready of speech and accomplished beyond the credence of whoso had not heard him, who, having received neither largesse nor dismissal, abode behind, in the hope that his stay might prove to his future advantage. But Messer Cane had taken it into his mind that what thing soever he might give him were far worse bestowed than if it had been thrown into the fire, nor of this did he bespeak him or let tell him aught.

Bergamino, after some days, finding himself neither called upon nor required unto aught that pertained to his craft and wasting his substance, to boot, in the hostelry with his horses and his servants, began to be sore concerned, but waited yet, himseeming he would not do well to depart. Now he had brought with him three goodly and rich suits of apparel, which had been given him of other noblemen, that he might make a brave appearance at the festival, and his host pressing for payment, he gave one thereof to him. After this, tarrying yet longer, it behoved him give the host the second suit, an he would abide longer with him, and withal he began to live upon the third, resolved to abide in expectation so long as this should last and then depart. Whilst he thus fed upon the third suit, he chanced one day, Messer Cane being at dinner, to present himself before him with a rueful countenance, and Messer Cane, seeing this, more by way of rallying him than of intent to divert himself with any of his speech, said to him, 'What aileth thee, Bergamino, to stand thus disconsolate? Tell us somewhat.'[2] Whereupon Bergamino, without a moment's hesitation, forthright, as if he had long considered it, related the following story to the purpose of his own affairs.

'My lord,' said he, 'you must know that Primasso was a very learned grammarian[3] and a skilful and ready verse-maker above all others, which things rendered him so notable and so famous that, albeit he might not everywhere be known by sight, there was well nigh none who knew him not by name and by report. It chanced that, finding himself once at Paris in poor case, as indeed he abode most times, for that worth is[4] little prized of those who can most,[5] he heard speak of the Abbot of Cluny, who is believed to be, barring the Pope, the richest prelate of his revenues that the Church of God possesseth, and of him he heard tell marvellous and magnificent things, in that he still held open house nor were meat and drink ever denied to any who went whereas he might be, so but he sought it what time the Abbot was at meat. Primasso, hearing this and being one who delighted in looking upon men of worth and nobility, determined to go see the magnificence of this Abbot and enquired how near he then abode to Paris. It was answered him that he was then at a place of his maybe half a dozen miles thence; wherefore Primasso thought to be there at dinner-time, by starting in the morning betimes.

Accordingly, he enquired the way, but, finding none bound thither, he feared lest he might go astray by mischance and happen on a part where there might be no victual so readily to be found; wherefore, in order that, if this should betide, he might not suffer for lack of food, he bethought himself to carry with him three cakes of bread, judging that water (albeit it was little to his taste) he should find everywhere. The bread he put in his bosom and setting out, was fortunate enough to reach the Abbot's residence before the eating-hour. He entered and went spying all about and seeing the great multitude of tables set and the mighty preparations making in the kitchen and what not else provided against dinner, said in himself, "Of a truth this Abbot is as magnificent as folk say." After he had abidden awhile intent upon these things, the Abbot's seneschal, eating-time being come, bade bring water for the hands; which being done, he seated each man at table, and it chanced that Primasso was set right over against the door of the chamber, whence the Abbot should come forth into the eating-hall.

Now it was the usance in that house that neither wine nor bread nor aught else of meat or drink should ever be set on the tables, except the Abbot were first came to sit at his own table. Accordingly, the seneschal, having set the tables, let tell the Abbot that, whenas it pleased him, the meat was ready. The Abbot let open the chamber-door, that he might pass into the saloon, and looking before him as he came, as chance would have it, the first who met his eyes was Primasso, who was very ill accoutred and whom he knew not by sight. When he saw him, incontinent there came into his mind an ill thought and one that had never yet been there, and he said in himself, "See to whom I give my substance to eat!" Then, turning back, he bade shut the chamber-door and enquired of those who were about him if any knew yonder losel who sat at table over against his chamber-door; but all answered no.

Meanwhile Primasso, who had a mind to eat, having come a journey and being unused to fast, waited awhile and seeing that the Abbot came not, pulled out of his bosom one of the three cakes of bread he had brought with him and fell to eating. The Abbot, after he had waited awhile, bade one of his serving-men look if Primasso were gone, and the man answered, "No, my lord; nay, he eateth bread, which it seemeth he hath brought with him." Quoth the Abbot, "Well, let him eat of his own, an he have thereof; for of ours he shall not eat to-day." Now he would fain have had Primasso depart of his own motion, himseeming it were not well done to turn him away; but the latter, having eaten one cake of bread and the Abbot coming not, began upon the second; the which was likewise reported to the Abbot, who had caused look if he were gone.

At last, the Abbot still tarrying, Primasso, having eaten the second cake, began upon the third, and this again was reported to the Abbot, who fell a-pondering in himself and saying, "Alack, what new maggot is this that is come into my head to-day? What avarice! What despite! And for whom? This many a year have I given my substance to eat to whosoever had a mind thereto, without regarding if he were gentle or simple, poor or rich, merchant or huckster, and have seen it with mine own eyes squandered by a multitude of ribald knaves; nor ever yet came there to my mind the thought that hath entered into me for yonder man. Of a surety avarice cannot have assailed me for a man of little account; needs must this who seemeth to me a losel be some great matter, since my soul hath thus repugned to do him honour."

So saying, he desired to know who he was and finding that it was Primasso, whom he had long known by report for a man of merit, come thither to see with his own eyes that which he had heard of his magnificence, was ashamed and eager to make him amends, studied in many ways to do him honour. Moreover, after eating, he caused clothe him sumptuously, as befitted his quality, and giving him money and a palfrey, left it to his own choice to go or stay; whereupon Primasso, well pleased with his entertainment, rendered him the best thanks in his power and returned on horseback to Paris, whence he had set out afoot.

Messer Cane, who was a gentleman of understanding, right well apprehended Bergamino's meaning, without further exposition, and said to him, smiling, 'Bergamino, thou hast very aptly set forth to me thy wrongs and merit and my niggardliness, as well as that which thou wouldst have of me; and in good sooth, never, save now on thine account, have I been assailed of parsimony; but I will drive it away with that same stick which thou thyself hast shown me.' Then, letting pay Bergamino's host and clothing himself most sumptuously in a suit of his own apparel, he gave him money and a palfrey and committed to his choice for the nonce to go or stay."

---

1. *i.e.* gleemen, minstrels, story-tellers, jugglers and the like, lit. men of court (*uomini di corte*).
2. *Dinne alcuna cosa.* If we take the affix *ne* (thereof, of it), in its other meaning (as dative of *noi*, we), of "to us," this phrase will read "Tell somewhat thereof," *i.e.* of the cause of thy melancholy.
3. *i.e.* Latinist.
4. Lit. was (*era*); but as Boccaccio puts "can" (*possono*) in the present tense we must either read *è* and *possono* or *era* and *potevano*. The first reading seems the more probable.
5. *i.e.* have most power or means of requiting it.

✣ 8 ✣

THE EIGHTH STORY

GUGLIELMO BORSIERE WITH SOME QUAINT WORDS REBUKETH THE NIGGARDLINESS OF MESSER ERMINO DE' GRIMALDI

NEXT FILOSTRATO SAT LAURETTA, who, after she had heard Bergamino's address commended, perceiving that it behoved her tell somewhat, began, without awaiting any commandment, blithely to speak thus: "The foregoing story, dear companions,[1] bringeth me in mind to tell how an honest minstrel on like wise and not without fruit rebuked the covetise of a very rich merchant, the which, albeit in effect it resembleth the last story, should not therefore be less agreeable to you, considering that good came thereof in the end.

There was, then, in Genoa, a good while agone, a gentleman called Messer Ermino de' Grimaldi, who (according to general belief) far overpassed in wealth of lands and monies the riches of whatsoever other richest citizen was then known in Italy; and like as he excelled all other Italians in wealth, even so in avarice and sordidness he outwent beyond compare every other miser and curmudgeon in the world; for not only did he keep a strait purse in the matter of hospitality, but, contrary to the general usance of the Genoese, who are wont to dress sumptuously, he suffered the greatest privations in things necessary to his own person, no less than in meat and in drink, rather than be at any expense; by reason whereof the surname de' Grimaldi had fallen away from him and he was deservedly called of all only Messer Ermino Avarizia.

It chanced that, whilst, by dint of spending not, he multiplied his wealth, there came to Genoa a worthy minstrel,[2] both well-bred and well-spoken, by name Guglielmo Borsiere, a man no whit like those[3] of the present day, who (to the no small reproach of the corrupt and blameworthy usances of those[4] who nowadays would fain be called and reputed gentlefolk and seigniors) are rather to be styled asses, reared in all the beastliness and depravity of the basest of mankind, than [minstrels, bred] in the courts [of kings and princes]. In those times it used to be a minstrel's office and his wont to expend his pains in negotiating treaties of peace, where feuds or despites had befallen between noblemen, or transacting marriages, alliances and friendships, in solacing the minds of the weary and diverting courts with quaint and pleasant sayings, ay, and with sharp reproofs, father-like, rebuking the misdeeds of the froward,—and this for slight enough reward; but nowadays they study to spend their time in hawking evil reports from one to another, in sowing discord, in speaking naughtiness and obscenity and

38

(what is worse) doing them in all men's presence, in imputing evil doings, lewdnesses and knaveries, true or false, one to other, and in prompting men of condition with treacherous allurements to base and shameful actions; and he is most cherished and honoured and most munificently entertained and rewarded of the sorry unmannerly noblemen of our time who saith and doth the most abominable words and deeds; a sore and shameful reproach to the present age and a very manifest proof that the virtues have departed this lower world and left us wretched mortals to wallow in the slough of the vices.

But to return to my story, from which a just indignation hath carried me somewhat farther astray than I purposed,—I say that the aforesaid Guglielmo was honoured by all the gentlemen of Genoa and gladly seen of them, and having sojourned some days in the city and hearing many tales of Messer Ermino's avarice and sordidness, he desired to see him. Messer Ermino having already heard how worthy a man was this Guglielmo Borsiere and having yet, all miser as he was, some tincture of gentle breeding, received him with very amicable words and blithe aspect and entered with him into many and various discourses. Devising thus, he carried him, together with other Genoese who were in his company, into a fine new house of his which he had lately built and after having shown it all to him, said, 'Pray, Messer Guglielmo, you who have seen and heard many things, can you tell me of something that was never yet seen, which I may have depictured in the saloon of this my house?' Guglielmo, hearing this his preposterous question, answered, 'Sir, I doubt me I cannot undertake to tell you of aught that was never yet seen, except it were sneezings or the like; but, an it like you, I will tell you of somewhat which me thinketh you never yet beheld.' Quoth Messer Ermino, not looking for such an answer as he got, 'I pray you tell me what it is.' Whereto Guglielmo promptly replied, 'Cause Liberality to be here depictured.'

When Messer Ermino heard this speech, there took him incontinent such a shame that it availed in a manner to change his disposition altogether to the contrary of that which it had been and he said, 'Messer Guglielmo, I will have it here depictured after such a fashion that neither you nor any other shall ever again have cause to tell me that I have never seen nor known it.' And from that time forth (such was the virtue of Guglielmo's words) he was the most liberal and the most courteous gentleman of his day in Genoa and he who most hospitably entreated both strangers and citizens."

---

1. Fem.
2. *Uomo di corte.* This word has been another grievous stumbling block to the French and English translators of Boccaccio, who render it literally "courtier." The reader need hardly be reminded that the minstrel of the middle ages was commonly jester, gleeman and story-teller all in one and in these several capacities was allowed the utmost license of speech. He was generally attached to the court of some king or sovereign prince, but, in default of some such permanent appointment, passed his time in visiting the courts and mansions of princes and men of wealth and liberty, where his talents were likely to be appreciated and rewarded; hence the name *uomo di corte*, "man of court" (not "courtier," which is *cortigiano*).
3. *i.e.* those minstrels.
4. *i.e.* the noblemen their patrons.

9

THE NINTH STORY

THE KING OF CYPRUS, TOUCHED TO THE QUICK BY A GASCON LADY, FROM A MEAN-SPIRITED PRINCE BECOMETH A MAN OF WORTH AND VALIANCE

THE QUEEN'S last commandment rested with Elisa, who, without awaiting it, began all blithely, "Young ladies, it hath often chanced that what all manner reproofs and many pains[1] bestowed upon a man have not availed to bring about in him hath been effected by a word more often spoken at hazard than of purpose aforethought. This is very well shown in the story related by Lauretta and I, in my turn, purpose to prove to you the same thing by means of another and a very short one; for that, since good things may still serve, they should be received with a mind attent, whoever be the sayer thereof.

I say, then, that in the days of the first King of Cyprus, after the conquest of the Holy Land by Godefroi de Bouillon, it chanced that a gentlewoman of Gascony went on a pilgrimage to the Holy Sepulchre and returning thence, came to Cyprus, where she was shamefully abused of certain lewd fellows; whereof having complained, without getting any satisfaction, she thought to appeal to the King for redress, but was told that she would lose her pains, for that he was of so abject a composition and so little of worth that, far from justifying others of their wrongs, he endured with shameful pusillanimity innumerable affronts offered to himself, insomuch that whose had any grudge [against him] was wont to vent his despite by doing him some shame or insult.

The lady, hearing this and despairing of redress, bethought herself, by way of some small solacement of her chagrin, to seek to rebuke the king's pusillanimity; wherefore, presenting herself in tears before him, she said to him, 'My lord, I come not into thy presence for any redress that I expect of the wrong that hath been done me; but in satisfaction thereof, I prithee teach me how thou dost to suffer those affronts which I understand are offered unto thyself, so haply I may learn of thee patiently to endure mine own, the which God knoweth, an I might, I would gladly bestow on thee, since thou art so excellent a supporter thereof.'

The King, who till then had been sluggish and supine, awoke as if from sleep and beginning with the wrong done to the lady, which he cruelly avenged, thenceforth became a very rigorous prosecutor of all who committed aught against the honour of his crown."

---

1. Syn. penalties, punishments (*pene*).

10

THE TENTH STORY

MASTER ALBERTO OF BOLOGNA CIVILLY PUTTETH A LADY TO THE BLUSH WHO THOUGHT TO HAVE SHAMED HIM OF BEING ENAMOURED OF HER

ELISA BEING NOW SILENT, the last burden of the story-telling rested with the queen, who, with womanly grace beginning to speak, said, "Noble damsels, like as in the lucid nights the stars are the ornament of the sky and as in Spring-time the flowers of the green meadows, even so are commendable manners and pleasing discourse adorned by witty sallies, which latter, for that they are brief, are yet more beseeming to women than to men, inasmuch as much and long speech, whenas it may be dispensed with, is straitlier forbidden unto women than to men, albeit nowadays there are few or no women left who understand a sprightly saying or, if they understand it, know how to answer it, to the general shame be it said of ourselves and of all women alive. For that virtue,[1] which was erst in the minds of the women of times past, those of our day have diverted to the adornment of the body, and she on whose back are to be seen the most motley garments and the most gaudily laced and garded and garnished with the greatest plenty of fringes and purflings and broidery deemeth herself worthy to be held of far more account than her fellows and to be honoured above them, considering not that, were it a question of who should load her back and shoulders with bravery, an ass would carry much more thereof than any of them nor would therefore be honoured for more than an ass.

I blush to avow it, for that I cannot say aught against other women but I say it against myself; these women that are so laced and purfled and painted and parti-coloured abide either mute and senseless, like marble statues, or, an they be questioned, answer after such a fashion that it were far better to have kept silence. And they would have you believe that their unableness to converse among ladies and men of parts proceedeth from purity of mind, and to their witlessness they give the name of modesty, as if forsooth no woman were modest but she who talketh with her chamberwoman or her laundress or her bake-wench; the which had Nature willed, as they would have it believed, she had assuredly limited unto them their prattle on other wise. It is true that in this, as in other things, it behoveth to have regard to time and place and with whom one talketh; for that it chanceth bytimes that women or men, thinking with some pleasantry or other to put another to the blush and not having well measured their own powers with those of the latter, find that confusion, which they thought to cast upon another, recoil upon themselves. Wherefore, so you may know how to keep yourselves and that, to boot, you may not serve as a text for the proverb which is current everywhere, to wit, that women in everything still take the worst, I would have you learn a lesson from the last of to-day's stories, which falleth to me to tell, to the intent that, even as you are by nobility of mind distinguished from other women, so likewise you may show yourselves no less removed from them by excellence of manners.

It is not many years since there lived (and belike yet liveth) at Bologna a very great and famous physician, known by manifest renown to well nigh all the world. His name was Master Alberto and such was the vivacity of his spirit that, albeit he was an old man of hard upon seventy years of age and well nigh all natural heat had departed his body, he scrupled not to expose himself to the flames of love; for that, having seen at an entertainment a very beautiful widow lady, called, as some say, Madam Malgherida[2] de' Ghisolieri, and being vastly taken with her, he received into his mature bosom, no otherwise than if he had been a young gallant, the amorous fire, insomuch that himseemed he rested not well by night, except the day foregone he had looked upon the delicate and lovesome countenance of the fair lady. Wherefore he fell to passing continually before her house, now afoot and now on horseback, as the occasion served him, insomuch that she and many other ladies got wind of the cause of his constant passings to and fro and oftentimes made merry among themselves to see a man thus ripe of years and wit in love, as if they deemed that that most pleasant passion of love took root and flourished only in the silly minds of the young and not otherwhere.

What while he continued to pass back and forth, it chanced one holiday that, the lady being seated with many others before her door and espying Master Alberto making towards them from afar, they one and all took counsel together to entertain him and do him honour and after to rally him on that his passion. Accordingly, they all rose to receive him and inviting him [to enter,] carried him into a shady courtyard, whither they let bring the choicest of wines and sweetmeats and presently enquired of him, in very civil and pleasant terms, how it might be that he was fallen enamoured of that fair lady, knowing her to be loved of many handsome, young and sprightly gentlemen. The physician, finding himself thus courteously attacked, put on a blithe countenance and answered, 'Madam, that I love should be no marvel to any understanding person, and especially that I love yourself, for that you deserve it; and albeit old men are by operation of nature bereft of the vigour that behoveth unto amorous exercises, yet not for all that are they bereft of the will nor of the wit to apprehend that which is worthy to be loved; nay, this latter is naturally the better valued of them, inasmuch as they have more knowledge and experience than the young. As for the hope that moveth me, who am an old man, to love you who are courted of many young gallants, it is on this wise: I have been many a time where I have seen ladies lunch and eat lupins and leeks. Now, although in the leek no part is good, yet is the head[3] thereof less hurtful and more agreeable to the taste; but you ladies, moved by a perverse appetite, commonly hold the head in your hand and munch the leaves, which are not only naught, but of an ill savour. How know I, madam, but you do the like in the election of your lovers? In which case, I should be the one chosen of you and the others would be turned away.'

The gentlewoman and her companions were somewhat abashed and said, 'Doctor, you have right well and courteously chastised our presumptuous emprise; algates, your love is dear to me, as should be that of a man of worth and learning; wherefore, you may in all assurance command me, as your creature, of your every pleasure, saving only mine honour.' The physician, rising with his companions, thanked the lady and taking leave of her with laughter and merriment, departed thence. Thus the lady, looking not whom she rallied and thinking to discomfit another, was herself discomfited; wherefrom, an you be wise, you will diligently guard yourselves."

. . .

THE SUN HAD BEGUN to decline towards the evening, and the heat was in great part abated, when the stories of the young ladies and of the three young men came to an end; whereupon quoth the queen blithesomely, "Henceforth, dear companions, there remaineth nought more to do in the matter of my governance for the present day, save to give you a new queen, who shall, according to her judgment, order her life and ours, for that[4] which is to come, unto honest pleasance. And albeit the day may be held to endure from now until nightfall, yet,—for that whoso taketh not somewhat of time in advance cannot, meseemeth, so well provide for the future and in order that what the new queen shall deem needful for the morrow may be prepared,—methinketh the ensuing days should commence at this hour. Wherefore, in reverence of Him unto whom all things live and for our own solacement, Filomena, a right discreet damsel, shall, as queen, govern our kingdom for the coming day." So saying, she rose to her feet and putting off the laurel-wreath, set it reverently on the head of Filomena, whom first herself and after all the other ladies and the young men likewise saluted as queen, cheerfully submitting themselves to her governance.

Filomena blushed somewhat to find herself invested with the queendom, but, calling to mind the words a little before spoken by Pampinea,[5]—in order that she might not appear witless, she resumed her assurance and in the first place confirmed all the offices given by Pampinea; then, having declared that they should abide whereas they were, she appointed that which was to do against the ensuing morning, as well as for that night's supper, and after proceeded to speak thus:

"Dearest companions, albeit Pampinea, more of her courtesy than for any worth of mine, hath made me queen of you all, I am not therefore disposed to follow my judgment alone in the manner of our living, but yours together with mine; and that you may know that which meseemeth is to do and consequently at your pleasure add thereto or abate thereof, I purpose briefly to declare it to you.

If I have well noted the course this day held by Pampinea, meseemeth I have found it alike praiseworthy and delectable; wherefore till such time as, for overlong continuance or other reason, it grow irksome to us, I judge it not to be changed. Order, then, being taken for [the continuance of] that which we have already begun to do, we will, arising hence, go awhile a-pleasuring, and whenas the sun shall be for going under, we will sup in the cool of the evening, and after sundry canzonets and other pastimes, we shall do well to betake ourselves to sleep. To-morrow, rising in the cool of the morning, we will on like wise go somewhither a-pleasuring, as shall be most agreeable to every one; and as we have done to-day, we will at the due hour come back to eat; after which we will dance and when we arise from sleep, as to-day we have done, we will return hither to our story-telling, wherein meseemeth a very great measure to consist alike of pleasance and of profit. Moreover, that which Pampinea had indeed no opportunity of doing, by reason of her late election to the governance, I purpose now to enter upon, to wit, to limit within some bound that whereof we are to tell and to declare it[6] to you beforehand, so each of you may have leisure to think of some goodly story to relate upon the theme proposed, the which, an it please you, shall be on this wise; namely, seeing that since the beginning of the world men have been and will be, until the end thereof, bandied about by various shifts of fortune, each shall be holden to tell OF THOSE WHO AFTER BEING BAFFLED BY DIVERS CHANCES HAVE WON AT LAST TO A JOYFUL ISSUE BEYOND THEIR HOPE."

Ladies and men alike all commended this ordinance and declared themselves ready to ensue it. Only Dioneo, the others all being silent, said, "Madam, as all the rest have said, so say

I, to wit that the ordinance given by you is exceeding pleasant and commendable; but of especial favour I crave you a boon, which I would have confirmed to me for such time as our company shall endure, to wit, that I may not be constrained by this your law to tell a story upon the given theme, an it like me not, but shall be free to tell that which shall most please me. And that none may think I seek this favour as one who hath not stories, in hand, from this time forth I am content to be still the last to tell."

The queen,—who knew him for a merry man and a gamesome and was well assured that he asked this but that he might cheer the company with some laughable story, whenas they should be weary of discoursing,—with the others' consent, cheerfully accorded him the favour he sought. Then, arising from session, with slow steps they took their way towards a rill of very clear water, that ran down from a little hill, amid great rocks and green herbage, into a valley overshaded with many trees and there, going about in the water, bare-armed and shoeless, they fell to taking various diversions among themselves, till supper-time drew near, when they returned to the palace and there supped merrily. Supper ended, the queen called for instruments of music and bade Lauretta lead up a dance, whilst Emilia sang a song, to the accompaniment of Dioneo's lute. Accordingly, Lauretta promptly set up a dance and led it off, whilst Emilia amorously warbled the following song:

> *I burn for mine own charms with such a fire,*
> *Methinketh that I ne'er*
> *Of other love shall reck or have desire.*
>
> *Whene'er I mirror me, I see therein[7]*
> *That good which still contenteth heart and spright;*
> *Nor fortune new nor thought of old can win*
> *To dispossess me of such dear delight.*
> *What other object, then, could fill my sight,*
> *Enough of pleasance e'er*
> *To kindle in my breast a new desire?*
>
> *This good flees not, what time soe'er I'm fain*
> *Afresh to view it for my solacement;*
> *Nay, at my pleasure, ever and again*
> *With such a grace it doth itself present*
> *Speech cannot tell it nor its full intent*
> *Be known of mortal e'er,*
> *Except indeed he burn with like desire.*
>
> *And I, grown more enamoured every hour,*
> *The straitlier fixed mine eyes upon it be,*
> *Give all myself and yield me to its power,*
> *E'en tasting now of that it promised me,*
> *And greater joyance yet I hope to see,*
> *Of such a strain as ne'er*
> *Was proven here below of love-desire.*

Lauretta having thus made an end of her ballad,[8]—in the burden of which all had blithely joined, albeit the words thereof gave some much matter for thought,—divers other rounds were danced and a part of the short night being now spent, it pleased the queen to give an end to the first day; wherefore, letting kindle the flambeaux, she commanded that all should betake themselves to rest until the ensuing morning, and all, accordingly, returning to their several chambers, did so.

---

1. *Virtù*, in the old Roman sense of strength, vigour, energy.
2. Old form of Margherita.
3. *i.e.* the base or eatable part of the stem.
4. *i.e.* that day.
5. See ante, n. 16.
6. *i.e.* the terms of the limitation aforesaid.
7. *i.e.* in the mirrored presentment of her own beauty.
8. *Ballatella*, lit. little dancing song or song made to be sung as an accompaniment to a dance (from *ballare*, to dance). This is the origin of our word ballad.

DAY THE SECOND

Here Beginneth the Second Day of the Decameron
Wherein Under the Governance of Filomena Is
Discoursed of Those Who After Being Baffled by
Divers Chances Have Won at Last to a Joyful Issue
Beyond Their Hope

The sun had already everywhere brought on the new day with its light and the birds, carolling blithely among the green branches, bore witness thereof unto the ear with their merry songs, when the ladies and the three young men, arising all, entered the gardens and pressing the dewy grass with slow step, went wandering hither and thither, weaving goodly garlands and disporting themselves, a great while. And like as they had done the day foregone, even so did they at present; to wit, having eaten in the cool and danced awhile, they betook them to repose and arising thence after none, came all, by command of their queen, into the fresh meadows, where they seated themselves round about her. Then she, who was fair of favour and exceeding pleasant of aspect, having sat awhile, crowned with her laurel wreath, and looked all her company in the face, bade Neifile give beginning to the day's stories by telling one of her fashion; whereupon the latter, without making any excuse, blithely began to speak thus:

THE FIRST STORY

MARTELLINO FEIGNETH HIMSELF A CRIPPLE AND MAKETH BELIEVE TO WAX WHOLE UPON THE BODY OF ST. ARRIGO. HIS IMPOSTURE BEING DISCOVERED, HE IS BEATEN AND BEING AFTER TAKEN [FOR A THIEF,] GOETH IN PERIL OF BEING HANGED BY THE NECK, BUT ULTIMATELY ESCAPETH

"IT CHANGETH OFT, dearest ladies, that he who studieth to befool others, and especially in things reverend, findeth himself with nothing for his pains but flouts and whiles cometh not off scathless. Wherefore, that I may obey the queen's commandment and give beginning to the appointed theme with a story of mine, I purpose to relate to you that which, first misfortunately and after happily, beyond his every thought, betided a townsman of ours.

No great while agone there was at Treviso a German called Arrigo, who, being a poor man, served whoso required him to carry burdens for hire; and withal he was held of all a man of very holy and good life. Wherefore, be it true or untrue, when he died, it befell, according to that which the Trevisans avouch, that, in the hour of his death, the bells of the great church of Treviso began to ring, without being pulled of any. The people of the city, accounting this a miracle, proclaimed this Arrigo a saint and running all to the house where he lay, bore his body, for that of a saint, to the Cathedral, whither they fell to bringing the halt, the impotent and the blind and others afflicted with whatsoever defect or infirmity, as if they should all be made whole by the touch of the body.

In the midst of this great turmoil and concourse of folk, it chanced that there arrived at Treviso three of our townsmen, whereof one was called Stecchi, another Martellino and the third Marchese, men who visited the courts of princes and lords and diverted the beholders by travestying themselves and counterfeiting whatsoever other man with rare motions and grimaces. Never having been there before and seeing all the folk run, they marvelled and hearing the cause, were for going to see what was toward; wherefore they laid up their baggage at an inn and Marchese said, 'We would fain go look upon this saint; but, for my part, I see not how we may avail to win thither, for that I understand the Cathedral place is full of German and other men-at-arms, whom the lord of this city hath stationed there, so no riot may betide; more by token that they say the church is so full of folk that well nigh none else might enter there.' 'Let not that hinder you,' quoth Martellino, who was all agog to see the show; 'I warrant you I will find a means of winning to the holy body.' 'How so?' asked Marchese, and Martellino answered, 'I will tell thee. I will counterfeit myself a cripple and thou on one side and Stecchi on the other shall go upholding me, as it were I could not walk of myself, making as if you

49

would fain bring me to the saint, so he may heal me. There will be none but, seeing us, will make way for us and let us pass.'

The device pleased Marchese and Stecchi and they went forth of the inn without delay, all three. Whenas they came to a solitary place, Martellino writhed his hands and fingers and arms and legs and eke his mouth and eyes and all his visnomy on such wise that it was a frightful thing to look upon, nor was there any saw him but would have avouched him to be verily all fordone and palsied of his person. Marchese and Stecchi, taking him up, counterfeited as he was, made straight for the church, with a show of the utmost compunction, humbly beseeching all who came in their way for the love of God to make room for them, the which was lightly yielded them. Brief, every one gazing on them and crying well nigh all, 'Make way! Make way!' they came whereas Saint Arrigo's body lay and Martellino was forthright taken up by certain gentlemen who stood around and laid upon the body, so he might thereby regain the benefit of health. Martellino, having lain awhile, whilst all the folk were on the stretch to see what should come of him, began, as right well he knew how, to make a show of opening first one finger, then a hand and after putting forth an arm and so at last coming to stretch himself out altogether. Which when the people saw, they set up such an outcry in praise of Saint Arrigo as would have drowned the very thunder.

Now, as chance would have it, there was therenigh a certain Florentine, who knew Martellino very well, but had not recognized him, counterfeited as he was, whenas he was brought thither. However, when he saw him grown straight again, he knew him and straightway fell a-laughing and saying, 'God confound him! Who that saw him come had not deemed him palsied in good earnest?' His words were overheard of sundry Trevisans, who asked him incontinent, 'How! Was he not palsied?' 'God forbid!' answered the Florentine. 'He hath ever been as straight as any one of us; but he knoweth better than any man in the world how to play off tricks of this kind and counterfeit what shape soever he will.'

When the others heard this, there needed nothing farther; but they pushed forward by main force and fell a-crying out and saying, 'Seize yonder traitor and scoffer at God and His saints, who, being whole of his body, hath come hither, in the guise of a cripple, to make mock of us and of our saint!' So saying, they laid hold of Martellino and pulled him down from the place where he lay. Then, taking him by the hair of his head and tearing all the clothes off his back, they fell upon him with cuffs and kicks; nor himseemed was there a man in the place but ran to do likewise. Martellino roared out, 'Mercy, for God's sake!' and fended himself as best he might, but to no avail; for the crowd redoubled upon him momently. Stecchi and Marchese, seeing this, began to say one to the other that things stood ill, but, fearing for themselves, dared not come to his aid; nay, they cried out with the rest to put him to death, bethinking them the while how they might avail to fetch him out of the hands of the people, who would certainly have slain him, but for a means promptly taken by Marchese; to wit, all the officers of the Seignory being without the church, he betook himself as quickliest he might, to him who commanded for the Provost and said, 'Help, for God's sake! There is a lewd fellow within who hath cut my purse, with a good hundred gold florins. I pray you take him, so I may have mine own again.'

Hearing this, a round dozen of sergeants ran straightway whereas the wretched Martellino was being carded without a comb and having with the greatest pains in the world broken through the crowd, dragged him out of the people's hands, all bruised and tumbled as he was, and haled him off to the palace, whither many followed him who held themselves affronted of him and hearing that he had been taken for a cutpurse and themseeming they had no better occasion[1] of doing him an ill turn,[2] began each on like wise to say that he had cut his purse. The Provost's judge, who was a crabbed, ill-conditioned fellow, hearing this, forthright took him apart and began to examine him of the matter; but Martellino answered jestingly, as if he made light of his arrest; whereat the judge, incensed, caused truss him up and give him two or three good bouts of the strappado, with intent to make him confess that which they laid to his charge, so he might after have him strung up by the neck.

When he was let down again, the judge asked him once more if that were true which the folk avouched against him, and Martellino, seeing that it availed him not to deny, answered, 'My lord, I am ready to confess the truth to you; but first make each who accuseth me say when and where I cut his purse, and I will tell you what I did and what not.' Quoth the judge, 'I will well,' and calling some of his accusers, put the question to them; whereupon one said that he had cut his purse eight, another six and a third four days agone, whilst some said that very day. Martellino, hearing this, said, 'My lord, these all lie in their throats and I can give you this proof that I tell you the truth, inasmuch as would God it were as sure that I had never come hither as it is that I was never in this place till a few hours agone; and as soon as I arrived, I went, of my ill fortune, to see yonder holy body in the church, where I was carded as you may see; and that this I say is true, the Prince's officer who keepeth the register of strangers can certify you, he and his book, as also can my host. If, therefore, you find it as I tell you, I beseech you torture me not neither put me to death at the instance of these wicked, men.'

Whilst things were at this pass, Marchese and Stecchi, hearing that the judge of the Provostry was proceeding rigorously against Martellino and had already given him the strappado, were sore affeared and said in themselves, 'We have gone the wrong way to work; we have brought him forth of the frying-pan and cast him into the fire.' Wherefore they went with all diligence in quest of their host and having found him, related to him how the case stood. He laughed and carried them to one Sandro Agolanti, who abode in Treviso and had great interest with the Prince, and telling him everything in order, joined with them in beseeching him to occupy himself with Martellino's affairs. Sandro, after many a laugh, repaired to the Prince and prevailed upon him to send for Martellino.

The Prince's messengers found Martellino still in his shirt before the judge, all confounded and sore adread, for that the judge would hear nothing in his excuse; nay, having, by chance, some spite against the people of Florence, he was altogether determined to hang him by the neck and would on no wise render him up to the Prince till such time as he was constrained thereto in his despite. Martellino, being brought before the lord of the city and having told him everything in order, besought him, by way of special favour, to let him go about his business, for that, until he should be in Florence again, it would still seem to him he had the rope about his neck. The Prince laughed heartily at his mischance and let give each of the three a suit of apparel, wherewith they returned home safe and sound, having, beyond all their hope, escaped so great a peril."

---

1. Or pretext (*titolo*).
2. Or "having him punished," lit. "causing give him ill luck" (*fargli dar la mala ventura*). This passage, like so many others of the Decameron, is ambiguous and may also be read "themseeming none other had a juster title to do him an ill turn."

❦ 2 ❦

THE SECOND STORY

RINALDO D'ASTI, HAVING BEEN ROBBED, MAKETH HIS
WAY TO CASTEL GUGLIELMO, WHERE HE IS
HOSPITABLY ENTERTAINED BY A WIDOW LADY AND
HAVING MADE GOOD HIS LOSS, RETURNETH TO HIS
OWN HOUSE, SAFE AND SOUND

THE LADIES LAUGHED IMMODERATELY at Martellino's misfortunes narrated by Neifile, as did also the young men and especially Filostrato, whom, for that he sat next Neifile, the queen bade follow her in story-telling. Accordingly he began without delay, "Fair ladies, needs must I tell you a story[1] of things Catholic,[2] in part mingled with misadventures and love-matters, which belike will not be other than profitable to hear, especially to those who are wayfarers in the perilous lands of love, wherein whoso hath not said St. Julian his Paternoster is oftentimes ill lodged, for all he have a good bed.

In the days, then, of the Marquis Azzo of Ferrara, there came a merchant called Rinaldo d'Asti to Bologna on his occasions, which having despatched and returning homeward, it chanced that, as he issued forth of Ferrara and rode towards Verona, he fell in with certain folk who seemed merchants, but were in truth highwaymen and men of lewd life and condition, with whom he unwarily joined company and entered into discourse. They, seeing him to be a merchant and judging him to have monies about him, took counsel together to rob him, at the first opportunity that should offer; wherefore, that he might take no suspicion, they went devising with him, like decent peaceable folk, of things honest and seemly and of loyalty, ordering themselves toward him, in so far as they knew and could, with respect and complaisance, so that he deemed himself in great luck to have met with them, for that he was alone with a serving-man of his on horseback.

Thus faring on and passing from one thing to another, as it chanceth in discourse, they presently fell to talking of the orisons that men offer up to God, and one of the highwaymen, who were three in number, said to Rinaldo, 'And you, fair sir, what orison do you use to say on a journey?' Whereto he answered, 'Sooth to say, I am but a plain man and little versed in these matters and have few orisons in hand; I live after the old fashion and let a couple of shillings pass for four-and-twenty pence.[3] Nevertheless, I have still been wont, when on a journey, to say of a morning, what time I come forth of the inn, a Pater and an Ave for the soul of St. Julian's father and mother, after which I pray God and the saint to grant me a good lodging for the ensuing night. Many a time in my day have I, in the course of my journeyings, been in great perils, from all of which I have escaped and have still found myself at night, to boot, in a place of safety and well lodged. Wherefore I firmly believe that St. Julian, in whose honour I say it, hath gotten me this favour of God; nor meseemeth should I fare well by day nor come to good harbourage at night, except I had said it in the morning.' 'And did you say it[4] this morning?' asked he who had put the question to him. 'Ay did I,' answered Rinaldo; whereupon quoth the other in himself, knowing well how the thing was to go, 'May it stand thee in stead![5] For, an no hindrance betide us, methinketh thou art e'en like to lodge ill.' Then, to Rinaldo, 'I likewise,' quoth he, 'have travelled much and have never said this orison, albeit I have heard it greatly commended, nor ever hath it befallen me to lodge other than well; and this evening maybe you shall chance to see which will lodge the better, you who have said it or I who have not. True, I use, instead thereof, the *Dirupisti* or the *Intemerata* or the *De Profundis*, the which, according to that which a grandmother of mine used to tell me, are of singular virtue.'

Discoursing thus of various matters and faring on their way, on the look out the while for time and place apt unto their knavish purpose, they came, late in the day, to a place a little beyond Castel Guglielmo, where, at the fording of a river, the three rogues, seeing the hour advanced and the spot solitary and close shut in, fell upon Rinaldo and robbed him of money, clothes and horse. Then, leaving him afoot and in his shirt, they departed, saying, 'Go see if thy St. Julian will give thee a good lodging this night, even as ours[6] will assuredly do for us.' And passing the stream, they went their ways. Rinaldo's servant, seeing him attacked, like a cowardly knave as he was, did nought to help him, but turning his horse's head, never drew bridle till he came to Castel Guglielmo and entering the town, took up his lodging there, without giving himself farther concern.

Rinaldo, left in his shirt and barefoot, it being very cold and snowing hard, knew not what to do and seeing the night already at hand, looked about him, trembling and chattering the while with his teeth, if there were any shelter to be seen therenigh, where he might pass the night, so he should not perish of cold; but, seeing none, for that a little before there had been war in those parts and everything had been burnt, set off at a run, spurred by the cold, towards Castel Guglielmo, knowing not withal if his servant were fled thither or otherwise and thinking that, so he might but avail to enter therein, God would send him some relief. But darkness overtook him near a mile from the town, wherefore he arrived there so late that, the gates being shut and the draw-bridges raised, he could get no admission. Thereupon, despairing and disconsolate, he looked about, weeping, for a place where he might shelter, so at the least it should not snow upon him, and chancing to espy a house that projected somewhat beyond the walls of the town, he determined to go bide thereunder till day. Accordingly, betaking himself thither, he found there a door, albeit it was shut, and gathering at foot thereof somewhat of straw that was therenigh, he laid himself down there, tristful and woebegone, complaining sore to St. Julian and saying that this was not of the faith he had in him.

However, the saint had not lost sight of him and was not long in providing him with a good lodging. There was in the town a widow lady, as fair of favour as any woman living, whom the Marquis Azzo loved as his life and there kept at his disposition, and she abode in that same house, beneath the projection whereof Rinaldo had taken shelter. Now, as chance would have it, the Marquis had come to the town that day, thinking to lie the night with her, and had privily let make ready in her house a bath and a sumptuous supper. Everything being ready and nought awaited by the lady but the coming of the Marquis, it chanced that there came a serving-man to the gate, who brought him news, which obliged him to take horse forthright; wherefore, sending to tell his mistress not to expect him, he departed in haste. The lady, somewhat disconsolate at this, knowing not what to do, determined to enter the bath prepared for the Marquis and after sup and go to bed.

Accordingly she entered the bath, which was near the door, against which the wretched merchant was crouched without the city-wall; wherefore she, being therein, heard the weeping and trembling kept up by Rinaldo, who seemed as he were grown a stork,[7] and calling her maid, said to her, 'Go up and look over the wall who is at the postern-foot and what he doth there.' The maid went thither and aided by the clearness of the air, saw Rinaldo in his shirt and barefoot, sitting there, as hath been said, and trembling sore; whereupon she asked him who he was. He told her, as briefliest he might, who he was and how and why he was there, trembling the while on such wise that he could scarce form the words, and after fell to beseeching her piteously not to leave him there all night to perish of cold, [but to succour him,] an it might be. The maid was moved to pity of him and returning to her mistress, told her all. The lady, on like wise taking compassion on him and remembering that she had the key of the door aforesaid, which served whiles for the privy entrances of the Marquis, said, 'Go softly and open to him; here is this supper and none to eat it and we have commodity enough for his lodging.'

The maid, having greatly commended her mistress for this her humanity, went and opening to Rinaldo, brought him in; whereupon the lady, seeing him well nigh palsied with cold, said to him, 'Quick, good man, enter this bath, which is yet warm.' Rinaldo, without awaiting farther invitation, gladly obeyed and was so recomforted with the warmth of the bath that himseemed he was come back from death to life. The lady let fetch him a suit of clothes that had pertained to her husband, then lately dead, which when he had donned, they seemed made to his measure, and whilst awaiting what she should command him, he fell to thanking God and St. Julian for that they had delivered him from the scurvy night he had in prospect and had, as he deemed, brought him to good harbourage.

Presently, the lady, being somewhat rested,[8] let make a great fire in her dining-hall and betaking herself thither, asked how it was with the poor man; whereto the maid answered, 'Madam, he hath clad himself and is a handsome man and appeareth a person of good condition and very well-mannered.' Quoth the lady, 'Go, call him and bid him come to the fire and sup, for I know he is fasting.' Accordingly, Rinaldo entered the hall and seeing the gentlewoman, who appeared to him a lady of quality, saluted her respectfully and rendered her the best thanks in his power for the kindness done him. The lady, having seen and heard him and finding him even as her maid had said, received him graciously and making him sit familiarly with her by the fire, questioned him of the chance that had brought him thither; whereupon he related everything to her in order. Now she had heard somewhat of this at the time of his servant's coming into the town, wherefore she gave entire belief to all he said and told him, in turn, what she knew of his servant and how he might lightly find him again on the morrow. Then, the table being laid, Rinaldo, at the lady's instance, washed his hands and sat down with her to supper. Now he was tall of his person and comely and pleasant of favour and very engaging and agreeable of manners and a man in the prime of life; wherefore the lady had several times cast her eyes on him and found him much to her liking, and her desires being already aroused for the Marquis, who was to have come to lie with her, she had taken a mind to him. Accordingly, after supper, whenas they were risen from table, she took counsel with her maid whether herseemed she would do well, the Marquis having left her in the lurch, to use the good which fortune had sent her. The maid, seeing her mistress's drift, encouraged her as best she might to ensue it; whereupon the lady, returning to the fireside, where she had left Rinaldo alone, fell to gazing amorously upon him and said to him, 'How now, Rinaldo, why bide you thus melancholy? Think you you cannot be requited the loss of a horse and of some small matter of clothes? Take comfort and be of good cheer; you are in your own house. Nay, I will e'en tell you more, that, seeing you with those clothes on your back, which were my late husband's, and meseeming you were himself, there hath taken me belike an hundred times to-night a longing to embrace you and kiss you: and but that I feared to displease you, I had certainly done it.'

Rinaldo, who was no simpleton, hearing these words and seeing the lady's eyes sparkle, advanced towards her with open arms, saying, 'Madam, considering that I owe it to you to say that I am now alive and having regard to that from which you delivered me, it were great unmannerliness in me, did I not study to do everything that may be agreeable to you; wherefore do you embrace me and kiss me to your heart's content, and I will kiss and clip you more than willingly.' There needed no more words. The lady, who was all afire with amorous longing, straightway threw herself into his arms and after she had strained him desirefully to her bosom and bussed him a thousand times and had of him been kissed as often, they went off to her chamber, and there without delay betaking themselves to bed, they fully and many a time, before the day should come, satisfied their desires one of the other. Whenas the day began to appear, they arose,—it being her pleasure, so the thing might not be suspected of any,—and she, having given him some sorry clothes and a purse full of money and shown him how he should go about to enter the town and find his servant, put him forth at the postern whereby he had entered, praying him keep the matter secret.

As soon as it was broad day and the gates were opened, he entered the town, feigning to come from afar, and found his servant. Therewithal he donned the clothes that were in the saddle-bags and was about to mount the man's horse and depart, when, as by a miracle, it befell that the three highwaymen, who had robbed him overnight, having been a little after taken for some other misdeed of them committed, were brought into the town and on their confession, his horse and clothes and money were restored to him, nor did he lose aught save a pair of garters, with which the robbers knew not what they had done. Rinaldo accordingly gave thanks to God and St. Julian and taking horse, returned home, safe and sound, leaving the three rogues to go kick on the morrow against the wind."[9]

---

1. Lit. a story striveth in (draweth) me to be told or to tell itself (*a raccontarsi mi tira una novella*).
2. *i.e.* religious matters (*cose cattoliche*).
3. *i.e.* take things by the first intention, without seeking to refine upon them, or, in English popular phrase, "I do not pretend to see farther through a stone wall than my neighbours."
4. *i.e.* the aforesaid orison.
5. Or "'Iwill have been opportunely done of thee."
6. *i.e.* our patron saint.
7. *i.e.* whose teeth chattered as it were the clapping of a stork's beak.
8. *i.e.* after her bath.
9. *i.e.* to be hanged or, in the equivalent English idiom, to dance upon nothing.

3

THE THIRD STORY

THREE YOUNG MEN SQUANDER THEIR SUBSTANCE
AND BECOME POOR; BUT A NEPHEW OF THEIRS,
RETURNING HOME IN DESPERATION, FALLETH IN
WITH AN ABBOT AND FINDETH HIM TO BE THE
KING'S DAUGHTER OF ENGLAND, WHO TAKETH HIM
TO HUSBAND AND MAKETH GOOD ALL HIS UNCLES'
LOSSES, RESTORING THEM TO GOOD ESTATE

THE ADVENTURES of Rinaldo d'Asti were hearkened with admiration and his devoutness commended by the ladies, who returned thanks to God and St. Julian for that they had succoured him in his utmost need. Nor yet (though this was said half aside) was the lady reputed foolish, who had known how to take the good God had sent her in her own house. But, whilst they discoursed, laughing in their sleeves, of the pleasant night she had had, Pampinea, seeing herself beside Filostrato and deeming, as indeed it befell, that the next turn would rest with her, began to collect her thoughts and take counsel with herself what she should say; after which, having received the queen's commandment, she proceeded to speak thus, no less resolutely than blithely, "Noble ladies, the more it is discoursed of the doings of Fortune, the more, to whoso is fain to consider her dealings aright, remaineth to be said thereof; and at this none should marvel, an he consider advisedly that all the things, which we foolishly style ours, are in her hands and are consequently, according to her hidden ordinance, transmuted by her without cease from one to another and back again, without any method known unto us. Wherefore, albeit this truth is conclusively demonstrated in everything and all day long and hath already been shown forth in divers of the foregoing stories, nevertheless, since it is our queen's pleasure that we discourse upon this theme, I will, not belike without profit for the listeners, add to the stories aforesaid one of my own, which methinketh should please.

There was once in our city a gentleman, by name Messer Tedaldo, who, as some will have it, was of the Lamberti family, albeit others avouch that he was of the Agolanti, arguing more, belike, from the craft after followed by his sons,[1] which was like unto that which the Agolanti have ever practised and yet practise, than from aught else. But, leaving be of which of these two houses he was, I say that he was, in his time, a very rich gentleman and had three sons, whereof the eldest was named Lamberto, the second Tedaldo and the third Agolante, all handsome and sprightly youths, the eldest of whom had not reached his eighteenth year when it befell that the aforesaid Messer Tedaldo died very rich and left all his possessions, both moveable and immoveable, to them, as his legitimate heirs. The young men, seeing themselves left very rich both in lands and monies, began to spend without check or reserve or other governance than that of their own pleasure, keeping a vast household and many and goodly horses and dogs

56

and hawks, still holding open house and giving largesse and making tilts and tournaments and doing not only that which pertaineth unto men of condition, but all, to boot, that it occurred to their youthful appetite to will.

They had not long led this manner of life before the treasure left by their father melted away and their revenues alone sufficing not unto their current expenses, they proceeded to sell and mortgage their estates, and selling one to-day and another to-morrow, they found themselves well nigh to nought, without perceiving it, and poverty opened their eyes, which wealth had kept closed. Whereupon Lamberto, one day, calling the other two, reminded them how great had been their father's magnificence and how great their own and setting before them what wealth had been theirs and the poverty to which they were come through their inordinate expenditure, exhorted them, as best he knew, ere their distress should become more apparent, to sell what little was left them and get them gone, together with himself. They did as he counselled them and departing Florence, without leavetaking or ceremony, stayed not till they came to England, where, taking a little house in London and spending very little, they addressed themselves with the utmost diligence to lend money at usance. In this fortune was so favourable to them that in a few years they amassed a vast sum of money, wherewith, returning to Florence, one after another, they bought back great part of their estates and purchased others to boot and took unto themselves wives.

Nevertheless, they still continued to lend money in England and sent thither, to look to their affairs, a young man, a nephew of theirs, Alessandro by name, whilst themselves all three at Florence, for all they were become fathers of families, forgetting to what a pass inordinate expenditure had aforetime brought them, began to spend more extravagantly than ever and were high in credit with all the merchants, who trusted them for any sum of money, however great. The monies remitted them by Alessandro, who had fallen to lending to the barons upon their castles and other their possessions, which brought him great profit, helped them for some years to support these expenses; but, presently, what while the three brothers spent thus freely and lacking money, borrowed, still reckoning with all assurance upon England, it chanced that, contrary to all expectation, there broke out war in England between the king and his son, through which the whole island was divided into two parties, some holding with the one and some with the other; and by reason thereof all the barons' castles were taken from Alessandro nor was there any other source of revenue that answered him aught. Hoping that from day to day peace should be made between father and son and consequently everything restored to him, both interest and capital, Alessandro departed not the island and the three brothers in Florence no wise abated their extravagant expenditure, borrowing more and more every day. But, when, after several years, no effect was seen to follow upon their expectation, the three brothers not only lost their credit, but, their creditors seeking to be paid their due, they were suddenly arrested and their possessions sufficing not unto payment, they abode in prison for the residue, whilst their wives and little ones betook themselves, some into the country, some hither and some thither, in very ill plight, unknowing what to expect but misery for the rest of their lives.

Meanwhile, Alessandro, after waiting several years in England for peace, seeing that it came not and himseeming that not only was his tarrying there in vain, but that he went in danger of his life, determined to return to Italy. Accordingly, he set out all alone and as chance would have it, coming out of Bruges, he saw an abbot of white friars likewise issuing thence, accompanied by many monks and with a numerous household and a great baggage-train in his van. After him came two old knights, kinsmen of the King, whom Alessandro accosted as acquaintances and was gladly admitted into their company. As he journeyed with them, he asked them softly who were the monks that rode in front with so great a train and whither they were bound; and one of them answered, 'He who rideth yonder is a young gentleman of our kindred, who hath been newly elected abbot of one of the most considerable abbeys of England, and for that he is younger than is suffered by the laws for such a dignity, we go with him to Rome to obtain of the Holy Father that he dispense him of his defect of overmuch youthfulness and confirm him in the dignity aforesaid; but this must not be spoken of with any.'

The new abbot, faring on thus, now in advance of his retinue and now in their rear, as daily we see it happen with noblemen on a journey, chanced by the way to see near him Alessandro, who was a young man exceedingly goodly of person and favour, well-bred, agreeable and fair of fashion as any might be, and who at first sight pleased him marvellously, as nought had ever done, and calling him to his side, fell a-discoursing pleasantly with him, asking him who he was and whence he came and whither he was bound; whereupon Alessandro frankly discovered to him his whole case and satisfied his questions, offering himself to his service in what little he might. The abbot, hearing his goodly and well-ordered speech, took more particular note of his manners and inwardly judging him to be a man of gentle breeding, for all his business had been mean, grew yet more enamoured of his pleasantness and full of compassion for his mishaps, comforted him on very friendly wise, bidding him be of good hope, for that, an he were a man of worth, God would yet replace him in that estate whence fortune had cast him down, nay, in a yet higher. Moreover, he prayed him, since he was bound for Tuscany, that it would please him bear him company, inasmuch as himself was likewise on the way thitherward; whereupon Alessandro returned him thanks for his encouragement and declared himself ready to his every commandment.

The abbot, in whose breast new feelings had been aroused by the sight of Alessandro, continuing his journey, it chanced that, after some days, they came to a village not overwell furnished with hostelries, and the abbot having a mind to pass the night there, Alessandro caused him alight at the house of an innkeeper, who was his familiar acquaintance, and let prepare him his sleeping-chamber in the least incommodious place of the house; and being now, like an expert man as he was, grown well nigh a master of the household to the abbot, he lodged all his company, as best he might, about the village, some here and some there. After the abbot had supped, the night being now well advanced and every one gone to bed, Alessandro asked the host where he himself could lie; whereto he answered, 'In truth, I know not; thou seest that every place is full and I and my household must needs sleep upon the benches. Algates, in the abbot's chamber there be certain grain-sacks, whereto I can bring thee and spread thee thereon some small matter of bed, and there, an it please thee, thou shalt lie this night, as best thou mayst.' Quoth Alessandro, 'How shall I go into the abbot's chamber, seeing thou knowest it is little and of its straitness none of his monks might lie there? Had I bethought me of this, ere the curtains were drawn, I would have let his monks lie on the grain-sacks and have lodged myself where they sleep.' 'Nay,' answered the host, 'the case standeth thus;[2] but, an thou wilt, thou mayst lie whereas I tell thee with all the ease in the world. The abbot is asleep and his curtains are drawn; I will quickly lay thee a pallet-bed there, and do thou sleep on it.' Alessandro, seeing that this might be done without giving the abbot any annoy, consented thereto and settled himself on the grain-sacks as softliest he might.

The abbot, who slept not, nay, whose thoughts were ardently occupied with his new desires, heard what passed between Alessandro and the host and noted where the former laid himself to sleep, and well pleased with this, began to say in himself, 'God hath sent an occasion unto my desires; an I take it not, it may be long ere the like recur to me.' Accordingly, being altogether resolved to take the opportunity and himseeming all was quiet in the inn, he called to Alessandro in a low voice and bade him come couch with him. Alessandro, after many excuses, put off his clothes and laid himself beside the abbot, who put his hand on his breast and fell to touching him no otherwise than amorous damsels use to do with their lovers; whereat Alessandro marvelled exceedingly and misdoubted him the abbot was moved by unnatural love to handle him on that wise; but the latter promptly divined his suspicions, whether of presumption or through some gesture of his, and smiled; then, suddenly putting off a shirt that he wore, he took Alessandro's hand and laying it on his own breast, said, 'Alessandro, put away thy foolish thought and searching here, know that which I conceal.'

Alessandro accordingly put his hand to the abbot's bosom and found there two little breasts, round and firm and delicate, no otherwise than as they were of ivory, whereby perceiving that the supposed prelate was a woman, without awaiting farther bidding, he straightway took her in his arms and would have kissed her; but she said to him, 'Ere thou draw nearer to me, hearken to that which I have to say to thee. As thou mayst see, I am a woman and not a man, and having left home a maid, I was on my way to the Pope, that he might marry me. Be it thy good fortune or my mishap, no sooner did I see thee the other day than love so fired me for thee, that never yet was woman who so loved man. Wherefore, I am resolved to take thee, before any other, to husband; but, an thou wilt not have me to wife, begone hence forthright and return to thy place.'

Alessandro, albeit he knew her not, having regard to her company and retinue, judged her to be of necessity noble and rich and saw that she was very fair; wherefore, without overlong thought, he replied that, if this pleased her, it was mighty agreeable to him. Accordingly, sitting up with him in bed, she put a ring into his hand and made him espouse her[3] before a picture wherein our Lord was portrayed, after which they embraced each other and solaced themselves with amorous dalliance, to the exceeding pleasure of both parties, for so much as remained of the night.

When the day came, after they had taken order together concerning their affairs, Alessandro arose and departed the chamber by the way he had entered, without any knowing where he had passed the night. Then, glad beyond measure, he took to the road again with the abbot and his company and came after many days to Rome. There they abode some days, after which the abbot, with the two knights and Alessandro and no more, went in to the Pope and having done him due reverence, bespoke him thus, 'Holy Father, as you should know better than any other, whoso is minded to live well and honestly should, inasmuch as he may, eschew every occasion that may lead him to do otherwise; the which that I, who would fain live honestly, may throughly do, having fled privily with a great part of the treasures of the King of England my father, (who would have given me to wife to the King of Scotland, a very old prince, I being, as you see, a young maid), I set out, habited as you see me, to come hither, so your Holiness might marry me. Nor was it so much the age of the King of Scotland that made me flee as the fear, if I were married to him, lest I should, for the frailty of my youth, be led to do aught that might be contrary to the Divine laws and the honour of the royal blood of my father. As I came, thus disposed, God, who alone knoweth aright that which behoveth unto every one, set before mine eyes (as I believe, of His mercy) him whom it pleased Him should be my husband, to wit, this young man,' showing Alessandro, 'whom you see here beside me and whose fashions and desert are worthy of however great a lady, although belike the nobility of his blood is not so illustrious as the blood-royal. Him, then, have I taken and him I desire, nor will I ever have any other than he, however it may seem to my father or to other folk. Thus, the principal occasion of my coming is done away; but it pleased me to make an end of my journey, at once that I might visit the holy and reverential places, whereof this city is full, and your Holiness and that through you I might make manifest, in your presence and consequently in that of the rest of mankind, the marriage contracted between Alessandro and myself in the presence of God alone. Wherefore I humbly pray you that this which hath pleased God and me may find favour with you and that you will vouchsafe us your benison, in order that with this, as with more assurance of His approof whose Vicar you are, we may live and ultimately die together.'

Alessandro marvelled to hear that the damsel was the King's daughter of England and was inwardly filled with exceeding great gladness; but the two knights marvelled yet more and were so incensed, that, had they been otherwhere than in the Pope's presence, they had done Alessandro a mischief and belike the lady also. The Pope also, on his part, marvelled exceedingly both at the habit of the lady and at her choice; but, seeing that there was no going back on that which was done, he consented to satisfy her of her prayer. Accordingly, having first appeased the two knights, whom he knew to be angered, and made them well at one again with the lady and Alessandro, he took order for that which was to do, and the day appointed by him being come, before all the cardinals and many other men of great worship, come, at his bidding, to a magnificent bride-feast prepared by him, he produced the lady, royally apparelled, who showed so fair and so agreeable that she was worthily commended of all, and on like wise Alessandro splendidly attired, in bearing and appearance no whit like a youth who had lent at usury, but rather one of royal blood, and now much honoured of the two knights. There he caused solemnly celebrate the marriage afresh and after goodly and magnificent nuptials made, he dismissed them with his benison.

It pleased Alessandro, and likewise the lady, departing Rome, to betake themselves to Florence, whither report had already carried the news. There they were received by the townsfolk with the utmost honour and the lady caused liberate the three brothers, having first paid every man [his due]. Moreover, she reinstated them and their ladies in their possessions and with every one's goodwill, because of this, she and her husband departed Florence, carrying Agolante with them, and coming to Paris, were honourably entertained by the King. Thence the two knights passed into England and so wrought with the King that the latter restored to his daughter his good graces and with exceeding great rejoicing received her and his son-in-law, whom he a little after made a knight with the utmost honour and gave him the Earldom of Cornwall. In this capacity he approved himself a man of such parts and made shift to do on such wise that he reconciled the son with his father, whereof there ensued great good to the island, and thereby he gained the love and favour of all the people of the country.

Moreover, Agolante thoroughly recovered all that was there due to him and his brethren and returned to Florence, rich beyond measure, having first been knighted by Count Alessandro. The latter lived long and gloriously with his lady, and according as some avouch, what with his wit and valour and the aid of his father-in-law, he after conquered Scotland and was crowned King thereof."

---

1. *i.e.* usury? See post. One of the commentators ridiculously suggests that they were needlemakers, from *ago*, a needle.
2. *i.e.* the thing is done and cannot be undone; there is no help for it.
3. *i.e.* make her a solemn promise of marriage, formally plight her his troth. The ceremony of betrothal was formerly (and still is in certain countries) the most essential part of the marriage rite.

❦ 4 ❧

THE FOURTH STORY

LANDOLFO RUFFOLO, GROWN POOR, TURNETH CORSAIR AND BEING TAKEN BY THE GENOESE, IS WRECKED AT SEA, BUT SAVETH HIMSELF UPON A COFFER FULL OF JEWELS OF PRICE AND BEING ENTERTAINED IN CORFU BY A WOMAN, RETURNETH HOME RICH

LAURETTA, who sat next Pampinea, seeing her come to the glorious ending of her story, began, without awaiting more, to speak on this wise: "Most gracious ladies, there can, to my judgment, be seen no greater feat of fortune than when we behold one raised from the lowest misery to royal estate, even as Pampinea's story hath shown it to have betided her Alessandro. And for that from this time forth whosoever relateth of the appointed matter must of necessity speak within these limits,[1] I shall think no shame to tell a story, which, albeit it compriseth in itself yet greater distresses hath not withal so splendid an issue. I know well, indeed, that, having regard unto that, my story will be hearkened with less diligence; but, as I can no otherwise, I shall be excused.

The sea-coast from Reggio to Gaeta is commonly believed to be well nigh the most delightful part of Italy, and therein, pretty near Salerno, is a hillside overlooking the sea, which the countryfolk call Amalfi Side, full of little towns and gardens and springs and of men as rich and stirring in the matter of trade as any in the world. Among the said cities is one called Ravello and therein, albeit nowadays there are rich men there, there was aforetime one, Landolfo Ruffolo by name, who was exceeding rich and who, his wealth sufficing him not, came nigh, in seeking to double it, to lose it all and himself withal. This man, then, having, after the usance of merchants, laid his plans, bought a great ship and freighting it all of his own monies with divers merchandise, repaired therewith to Cyprus. There he found sundry other ships come with the same kind and quality of merchandise as he had brought, by reason of which not only was he constrained to make great good cheap of his own venture, but it behoved him, an he would dispose of his goods, well nigh to throw them away, whereby he was brought near unto ruin.

Sore chagrined at this mischance and knowing not what to do, seeing himself thus from a very rich man in brief space grown in a manner poor, he determined either to die or repair his losses by pillage, so he might not return thither poor, whence he had departed rich. Accordingly, having found a purchaser for his great ship, with the price thereof and that which he had gotten of his wares, he bought a little vessel, light and apt for cruising and arming and garnishing it excellent well with everything needful unto such a service, addressed himself to

61

make his purchase of other men's goods and especially of those of the Turks. In this trade fortune was far kinder to him than she had been in that of a merchant, for that, in some year's space, he plundered and took so many Turkish vessels that he found he had not only gotten him his own again that he had lost in trade, but had more than doubled his former substance. Whereupon, schooled by the chagrin of his former loss and deeming he had enough, he persuaded himself, rather than risk a second mischance, to rest content with that which he had, without seeking more. Accordingly he resolved to return therewith to his own country and being fearful of trade, concerned not himself to employ his money otherwise, but, thrusting his oars into the water, set out homeward in that same little vessel wherewith he had gained it.

He had already reached the Archipelago when there arose one evening a violent south-east wind, which was not only contrary to his course, but raised so great a sea that his little vessel could not endure it; wherefore he took refuge in a bight of the sea, made by a little island, and there abode sheltered from the wind and purposing there to await better weather. He had not lain there long when two great Genoese carracks, coming from Constantinople, made their way with great difficulty into the little harbour, to avoid that from which himself had fled. The newcomers espied the little ship and hearing that it pertained to Landolfo, whom they already knew by report to be very rich, blocked against it the way by which it might depart and addressed themselves, like men by nature rapacious and greedy of gain,[2] to make prize of it. Accordingly, they landed part of their men well harnessed and armed with crossbows and posted them on such wise that none might come down from the bark, an he would not be shot; whilst the rest, warping themselves in with small boats and aided by the current, laid Landolfo's little ship aboard and took it out of hand, crew and all, without missing a man. Landolfo they carried aboard one of the carracks, leaving him but a sorry doublet; then, taking everything out of the ship, they scuttled her.

On the morrow, the wind having shifted, the carracks made sail westward and fared on their voyage prosperously all that day; but towards evening there arose a tempestuous wind which made the waves run mountains high and parted the two carracks one from the other. Moreover, from stress of wind it befell that that wherein was the wretched and unfortunate Landolfo smote with great violence upon a shoal over against the island of Cephalonia and parting amidships, broke all in sunder no otherwise than a glass dashed against a wall. The sea was in a moment all full of bales of merchandise and chests and planks, that floated on the surface, as is wont to happen in such cases, and the poor wretches on board, swimming, those who knew how, albeit it was a very dark night and the sea was exceeding great and swollen, fell to laying hold of such things as came within their reach. Among the rest the unfortunate Landolfo, albeit many a time that day he had called for death, (choosing rather to die than return home poor as he found himself,) seeing it near at hand, was fearful thereof and like the others, laid hold of a plank that came to his hand, so haply, an he put off drowning awhile, God might send him some means of escape.

Bestriding this, he kept himself afloat as best he might, driven hither and thither of the sea and the wind, till daylight, when he looked about him and saw nothing but clouds and sea and a chest floating on the waves, which bytimes, to his sore affright, drew nigh unto him, for that he feared lest peradventure it should dash against him on such wise as to do him a mischief; wherefore, as often as it came near him, he put it away from him as best he might with his hand, albeit he had little strength thereof. But presently there issued a sudden flaw of wind out of the air and falling on the sea, smote upon the chest and drove it with such violence against Landolfo's plank that the latter was overset and he himself perforce went under water. However, he struck out and rising to the surface, aided more by fear than by strength, saw the plank far removed from him, wherefore, fearing he might be unable to reach it again, he made for the chest, which was pretty near him, and laying himself flat with his breast on the lid thereof, guided it with his arms as best he might.[3]

On this wise, tossed about by the sea now hither and now thither, without eating, as one indeed who had not the wherewithal, but drinking more than he could have wished, he abode all that day and the ensuing night, unknowing where he was and descrying nought but sea; but, on the following day, whether it was God's pleasure or stress of wind that wrought it, he came, grown well nigh a sponge and clinging fast with both hands to the marges of the chest, even as we see those do who are like to drown, to the coast of the island of Corfu, where a poor woman chanced to be scouring her pots and pans and making them bright with sand and salt water. Seeing Landolfo draw near and discerning in him no [human] shape, she drew back, affrighted and crying out. He could not speak and scarce saw, wherefore he said nothing; but presently, the sea carrying him landward, the woman descried the shape of the chest and looking straitlier, perceived first the arms outspread upon it and then the face and guessed it for that which it was.

Accordingly, moved with compassion, she entered somedele into the sea, which was now calm, and seizing Landolfo by the hair, dragged him ashore, chest and all. There having with difficulty unclasped his hands from the chest, she set the latter on the head of a young daughter of hers, who was with her, and carried him off, as he were a little child, to her hut, where she put him in a bagnio and so chafed and bathed him with warm water that the strayed heat returned to him, together with somewhat of his lost strength. Then, taking him up out of the bath, whenas it seemed good to her, she comforted him with somewhat of good wine and confections and tended him some days, as best she might, till he had recovered his strength and knew where he was, when she judged it time to restore him his chest, which she had kept safe for him, and to tell him that he might now prosecute his fortune.

Landolfo, who had no recollection of the chest, yet took it, when the good woman presented it to him, thinking it could not be so little worth but that it might defray his expenses for some days, but, finding it very light, was sore abated of his hopes. Nevertheless, what while his hostess was abroad, he broke it open, to see what it contained, and found therein store of precious stones, both set and unset. He had some knowledge of these matters and seeing them, knew them to be of great value; wherefore he praised God, who had not yet forsaken him, and was altogether comforted. However, as one who had in brief space been twice cruelly baffled by fortune, fearing a third misadventure, he bethought himself that it behoved him use great wariness and he would bring those things home; wherefore, wrapping them, as best he might, in some rags, he told the good woman that he had no more occasion for the chest, but that, an it pleased her, she should give him a bag and take the chest herself. This she willingly did and he, having rendered her the best thanks in his power for the kindness received from her, shouldered his bag and going aboard a bark, passed over to Brindisi and thence made his way, along the coast, to Trani.

Here he found certain townsmen of his, who were drapers and clad him for the love of God,[4] after he had related to them all his adventures, except that of the chest; nay more, they lent him a horse and sent him, under escort, to Ravello, whither he said he would fain return. There, deeming himself in safety and thanking God who had conducted him thither, he opened his bag and examining everything more diligently than he had yet done, found he had so many and such stones that, supposing he sold them at a fair price or even less, he was twice as rich again as when he departed thence. Then, finding means to dispose of his jewels, he sent a good sum of money to Corfu to the good woman who had brought him forth of the sea, in requital of the service received, and the like to Trani to those who had reclothed him. The rest he kept for himself and lived in honour and worship to the end of his days, without seeking to trade any more."

---

1. *i.e.* cannot hope to tell a story presenting more extraordinary shifts from one to the other extreme of human fortune than that of Pampinea.
2. The Genoese have the reputation in Italy of being thieves by nature.
3. It seems doubtful whether *la reggeva diritta* should not rather be rendered "kept it upright." Boccaccio has a knack, very trying to the translator, of constantly using words in an obscure or strained sense.
4. *i.e.* for nothing.

✿ 5 ✿

THE FIFTH STORY

ANDREUCCIO OF PERUGIA, COMING TO NAPLES TO BUY HORSES, IS IN ONE NIGHT OVERTAKEN WITH THREE GRIEVOUS ACCIDENTS, BUT ESCAPETH THEM ALL AND RETURNETH HOME WITH A RUBY

"The stones found by Landolfo," began Fiammetta, to whose turn it came to tell, "have brought to my mind a story scarce less full of perilous scapes than that related by Lauretta, but differing therefrom inasmuch as the adventures comprised in the latter befell in the course of belike several years and these of which I have to tell in the space of a single night, as you shall hear.

There was once in Perugia, as I have heard tell aforetime, a young man, a horse-courser, by name Andreuccio di Pietro,[1] who, hearing that horses were good cheap at Naples, put five hundred gold florins in his purse and betook himself thither with other merchants, having never before been away from home. He arrived there one Sunday evening, towards vespers, and having taken counsel with his host, sallied forth next morning to the market, where he saw great plenty of horses. Many of them pleased him and he cheapened one and another, but could not come to an accord concerning any. Meanwhile, to show that he was for buying, he now and again, like a raw unwary clown as he was, pulled out the purse of florins he had with him, in the presence of those who came and went. As he was thus engaged, with his purse displayed, it chanced that a Sicilian damsel, who was very handsome, but disposed for a small matter to do any man's pleasure, passed near him, without his seeing her, and catching sight of the purse, said straightway in herself, 'Who would fare better than I, if yonder money were mine!' And passed on.

Now there was with her an old woman, likewise a Sicilian, who, seeing Andreuccio, let her companion pass on and running to him, embraced him affectionately, which when the damsel saw, she stepped aside to wait for her, without saying aught. Andreuccio, turning to the old woman and recognizing her, gave her a hearty greeting and she, having promised to visit him at his inn, took leave, without holding overlong parley there, whilst he fell again to chaffering, but bought nothing that morning. The damsel, who had noted first Andreuccio's purse and after her old woman's acquaintance with him, began cautiously to enquire of the latter, by way of casting about for a means of coming at the whole or part of the money, who and whence he was and what he did there and how she came to know him. The old woman told her every particular of Andreuccio's affairs well nigh as fully as he himself could have done, having long abidden with his father, first in Sicily and after at Perugia, and acquainted her, to boot, where he lodged and wherefore he was come thither.

The damsel, being thus fully informed both of his name and parentage, thereby with subtle craft laid her plans for giving effect to her desire and returning home, set the old woman awork for the rest of the day, so she might not avail to return to Andreuccio. Then, calling a maid of hers, whom she had right well lessoned unto such offices, she despatched her, towards evensong, to the inn where Andreuccio lodged. As chance would have it, she found him alone at the door and enquired at him of himself. He answered that he was the man she sought, whereupon she drew him aside and said to him, 'Sir, an it please you, a gentlewoman of this city would fain speak with you.' Andreuccio, hearing this, considered himself from head to foot and himseeming he was a handsome varlet of his person, he concluded (as if there were no other well-looking young fellow to be found in Naples,) that the lady in question must have fallen in love with him. Accordingly, he answered without further deliberation that he was ready and asked the girl when and where the lady would speak with him; whereto she answered, 'Sir, whenas it pleaseth you to come, she awaiteth you in her house'; and Andreuccio forthwith rejoined, without saying aught to the people of the inn, 'Go thou on before; I will come after thee.'

Thereupon the girl carried him to the house of her mistress, who dwelt in a street called Malpertugio,[2] the very name whereof denoteth how reputable a quarter it is. But he, unknowing neither suspecting aught thereof and thinking to go to most honourable place and to a lady of quality, entered the house without hesitation,—preceded by the serving-maid, who called her mistress and said, 'Here is Andreuccio,'—and mounting the stair, saw the damsel come to the stairhead to receive him. Now she was yet in the prime of youth, tall of person, with a very fair face and very handsomely dressed and adorned. As he drew near her, she came down three steps to meet him with open arms and clasping him round the neck, abode awhile without speaking, as if hindered by excess of tenderness; then kissed him on the forehead, weeping, and said, in a somewhat broken voice, 'O my Andreuccio, thou art indeed welcome.'

He was amazed at such tender caresses and answered, all confounded, 'Madam, you are well met.' Thereupon, taking him by the hand, she carried him up into her saloon and thence, without saying another word to him, she brought him into her chamber, which was all redolent of roses and orange flowers and other perfumes. Here he saw a very fine bed, hung round with curtains, and store of dresses upon the pegs and other very goodly and rich gear, after the usance of those parts; by reason whereof, like a freshman as he was, he firmly believed her to be no less than a great lady. She made him sit with her on a chest that stood at the foot of the bed and bespoke him thus, 'Andreuccio, I am very certain thou marvellest at these caresses that I bestow on thee and at my tears, as he may well do who knoweth me not and hath maybe never heard speak of me; but I have that to tell thee which is like to amaze thee yet more, namely, that I am thy sister; and I tell thee that, since God hath vouchsafed me to look upon one of my brothers, (though fain would I see you all,) before my death, henceforth I shall not die disconsolate; and as perchance thou has never heard of this, I will tell it thee.

Pietro, my father and thine, as I doubt not thou knowest, abode long in Palermo and there for his good humour and pleasant composition was and yet is greatly beloved of those who knew him; but, among all his lovers, my mother, who was a lady of gentle birth and then a widow, was she who most affected him, insomuch that, laying aside the fear of her father and brethren, as well as the care of her own honour, she became so private with him that I was born thereof and grew up as thou seest me. Presently, having occasion to depart Palermo and return to Perugia, he left me a little maid with my mother nor ever after, for all that I could hear, remembered him of me or her; whereof, were he not my father, I should blame him sore, having regard to the ingratitude shown by him to my mother (to say nothing of the love it behoved him bear me, as his daughter, born of no serving-wench nor woman of mean extraction) who had, moved by very faithful love, without anywise knowing who he might be, committed into his hands her possessions and herself no less. But what [skilleth it]? Things ill done and long time passed are easier blamed than mended; algates, so it was.

He left me a little child in Palermo, where being grown well nigh as I am now, my mother, who was a rich lady, gave me to wife to a worthy gentleman of Girgenti, who, for her love and mine, came to abide at Palermo and there, being a great Guelph,[3] he entered into treaty with our King Charles,[4] which, being discovered by King Frederick,[5] ere effect could be given to it, was the occasion of our being enforced to flee from Sicily, whenas I looked to be the greatest lady was ever in the island; wherefore, taking such few things as we might (I say few, in respect of the many we had) and leaving our lands and palaces, we took refuge in this city, where we found King Charles so mindful of our services that he hath in part made good to us the losses we had sustained for him, bestowing on us both lands and houses, and still maketh my husband, thy kinsman that is, a goodly provision, as thou shalt hereafter see. On this wise come I in this city, where, Godamercy and no thanks to thee, sweet my brother, I now behold thee.' So saying, she embraced him over again and kissed him on the forehead, still weeping for tenderness.

Andreuccio, hearing this fable so orderly, so artfully delivered by the damsel, without ever stammering or faltering for a word, and remembering it to be true that his father had been in Palermo, knowing, moreover, by himself the fashions of young men and how lightly they fall in love in their youth and seeing the affectionate tears and embraces and the chaste kisses that she lavished on him, held all she told him for more than true; wherefore, as soon as she was silent, he answered her, saying, 'Madam, it should seem to you no very great matter if I marvel, for that in truth, whether it be that my father, for whatsoever reason, never spoke of your mother nor of yourself, or that if he did, it came not to my notice, I had no more knowledge of you than if you had never been, and so much the dearer is it to me to find you my sister here, as I am alone in this city and the less expected this. Indeed, I know no man of so high a condition that you should not be dear to him, to say nothing of myself, who am but a petty trader. But I pray you make me clear of one thing; how knew you that I was here?' Whereto she made answer, 'A poor woman, who much frequenteth me, gave me this morning to know of thy coming, for that, as she telleth me, she abode long with our father both at Palermo and at Perugia; and but that meseemed it was a more reputable thing that thou shouldst visit me in my own house than I thee in that of another, I had come to thee this great while agone.' After this, she proceeded to enquire more particularly of all his kinsfolk by name, and he answered her of all, giving the more credence, by reason of this, to that which it the less behoved him to believe.

The talk being long and the heat great, she called for Greek wine and confections and let give Andreuccio to drink, after which he would have taken leave, for that it was supper-time; but she would on no wise suffer it and making a show of being sore vexed, embraced him and said, 'Ah, woe is me! I see but too clearly how little dear I am to thee! Who would believe that thou couldst be with a sister of thine, whom thou hast never yet seen and in whose house thou shouldst have lighted down, whenas thou earnest hither, and offer to leave her, to go sup at the inn? Indeed, thou shalt sup with me, and albeit my husband is abroad, which grieveth me mightily, I shall know well how to do thee some little honour, such as a woman may.' To which Andreuccio, unknowing what else he should say, answered, 'I hold you as dear as a sister should be held; but, an I go not, I shall be expected to supper all the evening and shall do an unmannerliness.' 'Praised be God!' cried she. 'One would think I had no one in the house to send to tell them not to expect thee; albeit thou wouldst do much greater courtesy and indeed but thy duty an thou sentest to bid thy companions come hither to supper; and after, am thou must e'en begone, you might all go away together.'

Andreuccio replied that he had no desire for his companions that evening; but that, since it was agreeable to her, she might do her pleasure of him. Accordingly, she made a show of sending to the inn to say that he was not to be expected to supper, and after much other discourse, they sat down to supper and were sumptuously served with various meats, whilst she adroitly contrived to prolong the repast till it was dark night. Then, when they rose from table and Andreuccio would have taken his leave, she declared that she would on no wise suffer this, for that Naples was no place to go about in by night especially for a stranger, and that, whenas she sent to the inn to say that he was not to be expected to supper, she had at the same time given notice that he would lie abroad. Andreuccio, believing this and taking pleasure in being with her, beguiled as he was by false credence, abode where he was, and after supper they held much and long discourse, not without reason,[6] till a part of the night was past, when she withdrew with her women into another room, leaving Andreuccio in her own chamber, with a little lad to wait upon him, if he should lack aught.

The heat being great, Andreuccio, as soon as he found himself alone, stripped to his doublet and putting off his hosen, laid them at the bedhead; after which, natural use soliciting him to rid himself of the overmuch burden of his stomach, he asked the boy where this might be done, who showed him a door in one corner of the room and said, 'Go in there.' Accordingly he opened the door and passing through in all assurance, chanced to set foot on a plank, which, being broken loose from the joist at the opposite end, [flew up] and down they went, plank and man together. God so favoured him that he did himself no hurt in the fall, albeit he fell from some height; but he was all bemired with the ordure whereof the place was full; and in order that you may the better apprehend both that which hath been said and that which ensueth, I will show you how the place lay. There were in a narrow alley, such as we often see between two houses, a pair of rafters laid from one house to another, and thereon sundry boards nailed and the place of session set up; of which boards that which gave way with Andreuccio was one.

Finding himself, then, at the bottom of the alley and sore chagrined at the mishap, he fell a-bawling for the boy; but the latter, as soon as he heard him fall, had run to tell his mistress, who hastened to his chamber and searching hurriedly if his clothes were there, found them and with them the money, which, in his mistrust, he still foolishly carried about him. Having now gotten that for which, feigning herself of Palermo and sister to a Perugian, she had set her snare, she took no more reck of him, but hastened to shut the door whereby he had gone out when he fell.

Andreuccio, getting no answer from the boy, proceeded to call loudlier, but to no purpose; whereupon, his suspicions being now aroused, he began too late to smoke the cheat. Accordingly, he scrambled over a low wall that shut off the alley from the street, and letting himself down into the road, went up to the door of the house, which he knew very well, and there called long and loud and shook and beat upon it amain, but all in vain. Wherefore, bewailing himself, as one who was now fully aware of his mischance, 'Ah, woe is me!' cried he. 'In how little time have I lost five hundred florins and a sister!' Then, after many other words, he fell again to battering the door and crying out and this he did so long and so lustily that many of the neighbours, being awakened and unable to brook the annoy, arose and one of the courtezan's waiting-women, coming to the window, apparently all sleepy-eyed, said peevishly, 'Who knocketh below there?'

'What?' cried Andreuccio. 'Dost thou not know me? I am Andreuccio, brother to Madam Fiordaliso.' Whereto quoth she, 'Good man, an thou have drunken overmuch, go sleep and come back to-morrow morning. I know no Andreuccio nor what be these idle tales thou tellest. Begone in peace and let us sleep, so it please thee.' 'How?' replied Andreuccio. 'Thou knowest not what I mean? Certes, thou knowest; but, if Sicilian kinships be of such a fashion that they are forgotten in so short a time, at least give me back my clothes and I will begone with all my heart.' 'Good man,' rejoined she, as if laughing, 'methinketh thou dreamest'; and to say this and to draw in her head and shut the window were one and the same thing. Whereat Andreuccio, now fully certified of his loss, was like for chagrin to turn his exceeding anger into madness and bethought himself to seek to recover by violence that which he might not have again with words; wherefore, taking up a great stone, he began anew to batter the door more furiously than ever.

At this many of the neighbours, who had already been awakened and had arisen, deeming him some pestilent fellow who had trumped up this story to spite the woman of the house and provoked at the knocking he kept up, came to the windows and began to say, no otherwise than as all the dogs of a quarter bark after a strange dog, "Tis a villainous shame to come at this hour to decent women's houses and tell these cock-and-bull stories. For God's sake, good man, please you begone in peace and let us sleep. An thou have aught to mell with her, come back to-morrow and spare us this annoy to-night.' Taking assurance, perchance, by these words, there came to the window one who was within the house, a bully of the gentlewoman's, whom Andreuccio had as yet neither heard nor seen, and said, in a terrible big rough voice, 'Who is below there?'

Andreuccio, hearing this, raised his eyes and saw at the window one who, by what little he could make out, himseemed should be a very masterful fellow, with a bushy black beard on his face, and who yawned and rubbed his eyes, as he had arisen from bed or deep sleep; whereupon, not without fear, he answered, 'I am a brother of the lady of the house.' The other waited not for him to make an end of his reply, but said, more fiercely than before, 'I know not what hindereth me from coming down and cudgelling thee what while I see thee stir, for a pestilent drunken ass as thou must be, who will not let us sleep this night.' Then, drawing back into the house, he shut the window; whereupon certain of the neighbours, who were better acquainted with the fellow's quality, said softly to Andreuccio, 'For God's sake, good man, begone in peace and abide not there to-night to be slain; get thee gone for thine own good.'

Andreuccio, terrified at the fellow's voice and aspect and moved by the exhortations of the neighbours, who seemed to him to speak out of charity, set out to return to his inn, in the direction of the quarter whence he had followed the maid, without knowing whither to go, despairing of his money and woebegone as ever man was. Being loathsome to himself, for the stench that came from him, and thinking to repair to the sea to wash himself, he turned to the left and followed a street called Ruga Catalana,[7] that led towards the upper part of the city. Presently, he espied two men coming towards him with a lantern and fearing they might be officers of the watch or other ill-disposed folk, he stealthily took refuge, to avoid them, in a hovel, that he saw hard by. But they, as of malice aforethought, made straight for the same place and entering in, began to examine certain irons which one of them laid from off his shoulder, discoursing various things thereof the while.

Presently, 'What meaneth this?' quoth one. 'I smell the worst stench meseemeth I ever smelt.' So saying, he raised the lantern and seeing the wretched Andreuccio, enquired, in amazement. 'Who is there?' Andreuccio made no answer, but they came up to him with the light and asked him what he did there in such a pickle; whereupon he related to them all that had befallen him, and they, conceiving where this might have happened, said, one to the other, 'Verily, this must have been in the house of Scarabone Buttafuocco.' Then, turning to him, 'Good man,' quoth one, 'albeit thou hast lost thy money, thou hast much reason to praise God that this mischance betided thee, so that thou fellest nor couldst after avail to enter the house again; for, hadst thou not fallen, thou mayst be assured that, when once thou wast fallen asleep, thou hadst been knocked on the head and hadst lost thy life as well as thy money. But what booteth it now to repine? Thou mayst as well look to have the stars out of the sky as to recover a farthing of thy money; nay, thou art like to be murdered, should yonder fellow hear that thou makest any words thereof.' Then they consulted together awhile and presently said to him, 'Look you, we are moved to pity for thee; wherefore, an thou wilt join with us in somewhat we go about to do, it seemeth to us certain that there will fall to thee for thy share much more than the value of that which thou hast lost.' Whereupon Andreuccio, in his desperation, answered that he was ready.

Now there had been that day buried an archbishop of Naples, by name Messer Filippo Minutolo, and he had been interred in his richest ornaments and with a ruby on his finger worth more than five hundred florins of gold. Him they were minded to despoil and this their intent they discovered to Andreuccio, who, more covetous than well-advised, set out with them for the cathedral. As they went, Andreuccio still stinking amain, one of the thieves said, 'Can we not find means for this fellow to wash himself a little, be it where it may, so he may not stink so terribly?' 'Ay can we,' answered the other. 'We are here near a well, where there useth to be a rope and pulley and a great bucket; let us go thither and we will wash him in a trice.' Accordingly they made for the well in question and found the rope there, but the bucket had been taken away; wherefore they took counsel together to tie him to the rope and let him down into the well, so he might wash himself there, charging him shake the rope as soon as he was clean, and they would pull him up.

Hardly had they let him down when, as chance would have it, certain of the watch, being athirst for the heat and with running after some rogue or another, came to the well to drink, and the two rogues, setting eyes on them, made off incontinent, before the officers saw them. Presently, Andreuccio, having washed himself at the bottom of the well, shook the rope, and the thirsty officers, laying by their targets and arms and surcoats, began to haul upon the rope, thinking the bucket full of water at the other end. As soon as Andreuccio found himself near the top, he let go the rope and laid hold of the marge with both hands; which when the officers saw, overcome with sudden affright, they dropped the rope, without saying a word, and took to their heels as quickliest they might. At this Andreuccio marvelled sore, and but that he had fast hold of the marge, would have fallen to the bottom, to his no little hurt or maybe death. However, he made his way out and finding the arms, which he knew were none of his companions' bringing, he was yet more amazed; but, knowing not what to make of it and misdoubting [some snare], he determined to begone without touching aught and accordingly made off he knew not whither, bewailing his ill-luck.

As he went, he met his two comrades, who came to draw him forth of the well; and when they saw him, they marvelled exceedingly and asked him who had drawn him up. Andreuccio replied that he knew not and told them orderly how it had happened and what he had found by the wellside, whereupon the others, perceiving how the case stood, told him, laughing, why they had fled and who these were that had pulled him up. Then, without farther parley, it being now middle night, they repaired to the cathedral and making their way thereinto lightly enough, went straight to the archbishop's tomb, which was of marble and very large. With their irons they raised the lid, which was very heavy, and propped it up so as a man might enter; which being done, quoth one, 'Who shall go in?' 'Not I,' answered the other. 'Nor I,' rejoined his fellow; 'let Andreuccio enter.' 'That will I not,' said the latter; whereupon the two rogues turned upon him and said, 'How! Thou wilt not? Cock's faith, an thou enter not, we will clout thee over the costard with one of these iron bars till thou fall dead.'

Andreuccio, affrighted, crept into the tomb, saying in himself the while, 'These fellows will have me go in here so they may cheat me, for that, when I shall have given them everything, they will begone about their business, whilst I am labouring to win out of the tomb, and I shall abide empty-handed.' Accordingly, he determined to make sure of his share beforehand; wherefore, as soon as he came to the bottom, calling to mind the precious ring whereof he had heard them speak, he drew it from the archbishop's finger and set it on his own. Then he passed them the crozier and mitre and gloves and stripping the dead man to his shirt, gave them everything, saying that there was nothing more. The others declared that the ring must be there and bade him seek everywhere; but he replied that he found it not and making a show of seeking it, kept them in play awhile. At last, the two rogues, who were no less wily than himself, bidding him seek well the while, took occasion to pull away the prop that held up the lid and made off, leaving him shut in the tomb.

What became of Andreuccio, when he found himself in this plight, you may all imagine for yourselves. He strove again and again to heave up the lid with his head and shoulders, but only wearied himself in vain; wherefore, overcome with chagrin and despair, he fell down in a swoon upon the archbishop's dead body; and whoso saw him there had hardly known which was the deader, the prelate or he. Presently, coming to himself, he fell into a passion of weeping, seeing he must there without fail come to one of two ends, to wit, either he must, if none came thither to open the tomb again, die of hunger and stench, among the worms of the dead body, or, if any came and found him there, he would certainly be hanged for a thief.

As he abode in this mind, exceeding woebegone, he heard folk stirring in the Church and many persons speaking and presently perceived that they came to do that which he and his comrades had already done; whereat fear redoubled upon him. But, after the newcomers had forced open the tomb and propped up the lid, they fell into dispute of who should go in, and none was willing to do it. However, after long parley, a priest said, 'What fear ye? Think you he will eat you? The dead eat not men. I will go in myself.' So saying, he set his breast to the marge of the tomb and turning his head outward, put in his legs, thinking to let himself drop. Andreuccio, seeing this, started up and catching the priest by one of his legs, made a show of offering to pull him down into the tomb. The other, feeling this, gave a terrible screech and flung precipitately out of the tomb; whereupon all the others fled in terror, as they were pursued by an hundred thousand devils, leaving the tomb open.

Andreuccio, seeing this, scrambled hastily out of the tomb, rejoiced beyond all hope, and made off out of the church by the way he had entered in. The day now drawing near, he fared on at a venture, with the ring on his finger, till he came to the sea-shore and thence made his way back to his inn, where he found his comrades and the host, who had been in concern for him all that night. He told them what had betided him and themseemed, by the host's counsel, that he were best depart Naples incontinent. Accordingly, he set out forthright and returned to Perugia, having invested his money in a ring, whereas he came to buy horses."

---

1. *i.e.* son of Pietro, as they still say in Lancashire and other northern provinces, "Tom o' Dick" for "Thomas, son of Richard," etc.
2. *i.e.* ill hole.
3. *i.e.* a member of the Guelph party, as against the Ghibellines or partisans of the Pope.
4. Charles d'Anjou, afterwards King of Sicily.
5. *i.e.* Frederick II. of Germany.
6. The reason was that she wished to keep him in play till late into the night, when all the folk should be asleep and she might the lightlier deal with him.
7. *i.e.* Catalan Street.

❧ 6 ❧

THE SIXTH STORY

MADAM BERITOLA, HAVING LOST HER TWO SONS, IS
FOUND ON A DESERT ISLAND WITH TWO KIDS AND
GOETH THENCE INTO LUNIGIANA, WHERE ONE OF
HER SONS, TAKING SERVICE WITH THE LORD OF THE
COUNTRY, LIETH WITH HIS DAUGHTER AND IS CAST
INTO PRISON. SICILY AFTER REBELLING AGAINST
KING CHARLES AND THE YOUTH BEING RECOGNIZED
BY HIS MOTHER, HE ESPOUSETH HIS LORD'S
DAUGHTER, AND HIS BROTHER BEING LIKEWISE
FOUND, THEY ARE ALL THREE RESTORED TO HIGH
ESTATE

LADIES and young men alike laughed heartily at Andreuccio's adventures, as related by Fiammetta, and Emilia, seeing the story ended, began, by the queen's commandment, to speak thus: "Grievous things and woeful are the various shifts of Fortune, whereof,—for that, whenassoever it is discoursed of them, it is an awakenment for our minds, which lightly fall asleep under her blandishments,—methinketh it should never be irksome either to the happy or the unhappy to hear tell, inasmuch as it rendereth the former wary and consoleth the latter. Wherefore, albeit great things have already been recounted upon this subject, I purpose to tell you thereanent a story no less true than pitiful, whereof, for all it had a joyful ending, so great and so longsome was the bitterness that I can scarce believe it to have been assuaged by any subsequent gladness.

You must know, dearest ladies, that, after the death of the Emperor Frederick the Second, Manfred was crowned King of Sicily, in very high estate with whom was a gentleman of Naples called Arrighetto Capece, who had to wife a fair and noble lady, also of Naples, by name Madam Beritola Caracciola. The said Arrighetto, who had the governance of the island in his hands, hearing that King Charles the First[1] had overcome and slain Manfred at Benevento and that all the realm had revolted to him and having scant assurance of the short-lived fidelity of the Sicilians, prepared for flight, misliking to become a subject of his lord's enemy; but, his intent being known of the Sicilians, he and many other friends and servants of King Manfred were suddenly made prisoners and delivered to King Charles, together with possession of the island.

Madam Beritola, in this grievous change of affairs, knowing not what was come of Arrighetto and sore adread of that which had befallen, abandoned all her possessions for fear of shame and poor and pregnant as she was, embarked, with a son of hers and maybe eight years of age, Giusfredi by name, in a little boat and fled to Lipari, where she gave birth to another male child, whom she named Scacciato,[2] and getting her a nurse, took ship with all three to return to her kinsfolk at Naples. But it befell otherwise than as she purposed; for that the ship, which should have gone to Naples, was carried by stress of wind to the island of Ponza,[3] where they entered a little bight of the sea and there awaited an occasion for continuing their voyage. Madam Beritola, going up, like the rest, into the island and finding a remote and solitary place, addressed herself to make moan for her Arrighetto, all alone there.

This being her daily usance, it chanced one day that, as she was occupied in bewailing herself, there came up a pirate galley, unobserved of any, sailor or other, and taking them all at unawares, made off with her prize. Madam Beritola, having made an end of her diurnal lamentation, returned to the sea-shore, as she was used to do, to visit her children, but found none there; whereat she first marvelled and after, suddenly misdoubting her of that which had happened, cast her eyes out to sea and saw the galley at no great distance, towing the little ship after it; whereby she knew but too well that she had lost her children, as well as her husband, and seeing herself there poor and desolate and forsaken, unknowing where she should ever again find any of them, she fell down aswoon upon the strand, calling upon her husband and her children. There was none there to recall her distracted spirits with cold water or other remedy, wherefore they might at their leisure go wandering whither it pleased them; but, after awhile, the lost senses returning to her wretched body, in company with tears and lamentations, she called long upon her children and went a great while seeking them in every cavern. At last, finding all her labour in vain and seeing the night coming on, she began, hoping and knowing not what, to be careful for herself and departing the sea-shore, returned to the cavern where she was wont to weep and bemoan herself.

She passed the night in great fear and inexpressible dolour and the new day being come and the hour of tierce past, she was fain, constrained by hunger, for that she had not supped overnight, to browse upon herbs; and having fed as best she might, she gave herself, weeping, to various thoughts of her future life. Pondering thus, she saw a she-goat enter a cavern hard by and presently issue thence and betake herself into the wood; whereupon she arose and entering whereas the goat had come forth, found there two little kidlings, born belike that same day, which seemed to her the quaintest and prettiest things in the world. Her milk being yet undried from her recent delivery, she tenderly took up the kids and set them to her breast. They refused not the service, but sucked her as if she had been their dam and thenceforth made no distinction between the one and the other. Wherefore, herseeming she had found some company in that desert place, and growing no less familiar with the old goat than with her little ones, she resigned herself to live and die there and abode eating of herbs and drinking water and weeping as often as she remembered her of her husband and children and of her past life.

The gentle lady, thus grown a wild creature, abiding on this wise, it befell, after some months, that there came on like wise to the place whither she had aforetime been driven by stress of weather, a little vessel from Pisa and there abode some days. On broad this bark was a gentleman named Currado [of the family] of the Marquises of Malespina, who, with his wife, a lady of worth and piety, was on his return home from a pilgrimage to all the holy places that be in the kingdom of Apulia. To pass away the time, Currado set out one day, with his lady and certain of his servants and his dogs, to go about the island, and not far from Madam Beritola's place of harbourage, the dogs started the two kids, which were now grown pretty big, as they went grazing. The latter, chased by the dogs, fled to no other place but into the cavern where was Madam Beritola, who, seeing this, started to her feet and catching up a staff, beat off the dogs. Currado and his wife, who came after them, seeing the lady, who was grown swart and lean and hairy, marvelled, and she yet more at them. But after Currado had, at her instance, called off his dogs, they prevailed with her, by dint of much entreaty, to tell them who she was and what she did there; whereupon she fully discovered to them her whole condition and all that had befallen her, together with her firm resolution [to abide alone in the island].

Currado, who had know Arrighetto Capece very well, hearing this, wept for pity, and did his utmost to divert her with words from so barbarous a purpose, offering to carry her back to her own house or to keep her with himself, holding her in such honour as his sister, until God should send her happier fortune. The lady not yielding to these proffers, Currado left his wife with her, bidding the latter cause bring thither to eat and clothe the lady, who was all in rags, with some of her own apparel, and charging her contrive, by whatsoever means, to bring her away with her. Accordingly, the gentle lady, being left with Madam Beritola, after condoling with her amain of her misfortunes, sent for raiment and victual and prevailed on her, with all the pains in the world, to don the one and eat the other.

Ultimately, after many prayers, Madam Beritola protesting that she would never consent to go whereas she might be known, she persuaded her to go with her into Lunigiana, together with the two kids and their dam, which latter were meantime returned and had greeted her with the utmost fondness, to the no small wonderment of the gentlewoman. Accordingly, as soon as fair weather was come, Madam Beritola embarked with Currado and his lady in their vessel, carrying with her the two kids and the she-goat (on whose account, her name being everywhere unknown, she was styled Cavriuola[4]) and setting sail with a fair wind, came speedily to the mouth of the Magra,[5] where they landed and went up to Currado's castle. There Madam Beritola abode, in a widow's habit, about the person of Currado's lady, as one of her waiting-women, humble, modest and obedient, still cherishing her kids and letting nourish them.

Meanwhile, the corsairs, who had taken the ship wherein Madam Beritola came to Ponza, but had left herself, as being unseen of them, betook themselves with all the other folk to Genoa, where, the booty coming to be shared among the owners of the galley, it chanced that the nurse and the two children fell, amongst other things, to the lot of a certain Messer Guasparrino d'Oria,[6] who sent them all three to his mansion, to be there employed as slaves about the service of the house. The nurse, afflicted beyond measure at the loss of her mistress and at the wretched condition where into she found herself and the two children fallen, wept long and sore; but, for that, albeit a poor woman, she was discreet and well-advised, when she saw that tears availed nothing and that she was become a slave together with them, she first comforted herself as best she might and after, considering whither they were come, she bethought herself that, should the two children be known, they might lightly chance to suffer hindrance; wherefore, hoping withal that, sooner or later fortune might change and they, an they lived, regain their lost estate, she resolved to discover to no one who they were, until she should see occasion therefor, and told all who asked her thereof that they were her sons. The elder she named, not Giusfredi, but Giannotto di Procida (the name of the younger she cared not to change), and explained to him, with the utmost diligence, why she had changed his name, showing him in what peril he might be, an he were known. This she set out to him not once, but many and many a time, and the boy, who was quick of wit, punctually obeyed the enjoinment of his discreet nurse.

Accordingly, the two boys and their nurse abode patiently in Messer Guasparrino's house several years, ill-clad and worse shod and employed about the meanest offices. But Giannotto, who was now sixteen years of age, and had more spirit than pertained to a slave, scorning the baseness of a menial condition, embarked on board certain galleys bound for Alexandria and taking leave of Messer Guasparrino's service, journeyed to divers parts, without any wise availing to advance himself. At last some three or four years after his departure from Genoa, being grown a handsome youth and tall of his person and hearing that his father, whom he thought dead, was yet alive, but was kept by King Charles in prison and duresse, he went wandering at a venture, well nigh despairing of fortune, till he came to Lunigiana and there, as chance would have it, took service with Currado Malespina, whom he served with great aptitude and acceptance. And albeit he now and again saw his mother, who was with Currado's lady, he never recognized her nor she him, so much had time changed the one and the other from that which they were used to be, whenas they last set eyes on each other.

Giannotto being, then, in Currado's service, it befell that a daughter of the latter, by name Spina, being left the widow of one Niccolo da Grignano, returned to her father's house and being very fair and agreeable and a girl of little more than sixteen years of age, chanced to cast eyes on Giannotto and he on her, and they became passionately enamoured of each other. Their love was not long without effect and lasted several months ere any was ware thereof. Wherefore, taking overmuch assurance, they began to order themselves with less discretion than behoveth unto matters of this kind, and one day, as they went, the young lady and Giannotto together, through a fair and thickset wood, they pushed on among the trees, leaving the rest of the company behind. Presently, themseeming they had far foregone the others, they laid themselves down to rest in a pleasant place, full of grass and flowers and shut in with trees, and there fell to taking amorous delight one of the other.

In this occupation, the greatness of their delight making the time seem brief to them, albeit they had been there a great while, they were surprised, first by the girl's mother and after by Currado, who, chagrined beyond measure at this sight, without saying aught of the cause, had them both seized by three of his serving-men and carried in bonds to a castle of his and went off, boiling with rage and despite and resolved to put them both to a shameful death. The girl's mother, although sore incensed and holding her daughter worthy of the severest punishment for her default, having by certain words of Currado apprehended his intent towards the culprits and unable to brook this, hastened after her enraged husband and began to beseech him that it would please him not run madly to make himself in his old age the murderer of his own daughter and to soil his hands with the blood of one of his servants, but to find other means of satisfying his wrath, such as to clap them in prison and there let them pine and bewail the fault committed. With these and many other words the pious lady so wrought upon him that she turned his mind from putting them to death and he bade imprison them, each in a place apart, where they should be well guarded and kept with scant victual and much unease, till such time as he should determine farther of them. As he bade, so was it done, and what their life was in duresse and continual tears and in fasts longer than might have behoved unto them, each may picture to himself.

What while Giannotto and Spina abode in this doleful case and had therein already abidden a year's space, unremembered of Currado, it came to pass that King Pedro of Arragon, by the procurement of Messer Gian di Procida, raised the island of Sicily against King Charles and took it from him, whereat Currado, being a Ghibelline,[7] rejoiced exceedingly, Giannotto, hearing of this from one of those who had him in guard, heaved a great sigh and said, 'Ah, woe is me! These fourteen years have I gone ranging beggarlike about the world, looking for nought other than this, which, now that it is come, so I may never again hope for weal, hath found me in a prison whence I have no hope ever to come forth, save dead.' 'How so?' asked the gaoler. 'What doth that concern thee which great kings do to one another? What hast thou to do in Sicily?' Quoth Giannotto, 'My heart is like to burst when I remember me of that which my father erst had to do there, whom, albeit I was but a little child, when I fled thence, yet do I mind me to have been lord thereof, in the lifetime of King Manfred.' 'And who was thy father?' asked the gaoler. 'My father's name,' answered Giannotto, 'I may now safely make known, since I find myself in the peril whereof I was in fear, an I discovered it. He was and is yet, an he live, called Arrighetto Capece, and my name is, not Giannotto, but Giusfredi, and I doubt not a jot, an I were quit of this prison, but I might yet, by returning to Sicily, have very high place there.'

The honest man, without asking farther, reported Giannotto's words, as first he had occasion, to Currado, who, hearing this,—albeit he feigned to the gaoler to make light of it,—betook himself to Madam Beritola and courteously asked her if she had had by Arrighetto a son named Giusfredi. The lady answered, weeping, that, if the elder of her two sons were alive, he would so be called and would be two-and-twenty years old. Currado, hearing this, concluded that this must be he and bethought himself that, were it so, he might at once do a great mercy and take away his own and his daughter's shame by giving her to Giannotto to wife; wherefore, sending privily for the latter, he particularly examined him touching all his past life and finding, by very manifest tokens, that he was indeed Giusfredi, son of Arrighetto Capece, he said to him, 'Giannotto, thou knowest what and how great is the wrong thou hast done me in the person of my daughter, whereas, I having ever well and friendly entreated thee, it behoved thee, as a servant should, still to study and do for my honour and interest; and many there be who, hadst thou used them like as thou hast used me, would have put thee to a shameful death, the which my clemency brooked not. Now, if it be as thou tellest me, to wit, that thou art the son of a man of condition and of a noble lady, I purpose, an thou thyself be willing, to put an end to thy tribulations and relieving thee from the misery and duresse wherein thou abidest, to reinstate at once thine honour and mine own in their due stead. As thou knowest, Spina, whom thou hast, though after a fashion misbeseeming both thyself and her, taken with love-liking, is a widow and her dowry is both great and good; as for her manners and her father and mother, thou knowest them, and of thy present state I say nothing. Wherefore, an thou will, I purpose that, whereas she hath unlawfully been thy mistress, she shall now lawfully become thy wife and that thou shalt abide here with me and with her, as my very son, so long as it shall please thee.'

Now prison had mortified Giannotto's flesh, but had nothing abated the generous spirit, which he derived from his noble birth, nor yet the entire affection he bore his mistress; and albeit he ardently desired that which Currado proffered him and saw himself in the latter's power, yet no whit did he dissemble of that which the greatness of his soul prompted him to say; wherefore he answered, 'Currado, neither lust of lordship nor greed of gain nor other cause whatever hath ever made me lay snares, traitor-wise, for thy life or thy good. I loved and love thy daughter and still shall love her, for that I hold her worthy of my love, and if I dealt with her less than honourably, in the opinion of the vulgar, my sin was one which still goeth hand in hand with youth and which an you would do away, it behoveth you first do away with youth. Moreover, it is an offence which, would the old but remember them of having been young and measure the defaults of others by their own and their own by those of others, would show less grievous than thou and many others make it; and as a friend, and not as an enemy, I committed it. This that thou profferest me I have still desired and had I thought it should be vouchsafed me, I had long since sought it; and so much the dearer will it now be to me, as my hope thereof was less. If, then, thou have not that intent which thy words denote, feed me not with vain hope; but restore me to prison and there torment me as thou wilt, for, so long as I love Spina, even so, for the love of her, shall I still love thee, whatsoever thou dost with me, and have thee in reverence.'

Currado, hearing this, marvelled and held him great of soul and his love fervent and tendered him therefore the dearer; wherefore, rising to his feet, he embraced him and kissed him and without more delay bade privily bring Spina thither. Accordingly, the lady—who was grown lean and pale and weakly in prison and showed well nigh another than she was wont to be, as on like wise Giannotto another man—being come, the two lovers in Currado's presence with one consent contracted marriage according to our usance. Then, after some days, during which he had let furnish the newly-married pair with all that was necessary or agreeable to them, he deemed it time to gladden their mothers with the good news and accordingly calling his lady and Cavriuola, he said to the latter, 'What would you say, madam, an I should cause you have again your elder son as the husband of one of my daughters?' Whereto she answered, 'Of that I can say to you no otherwhat than that, could I be more beholden to you than I am, I should be so much the more so as you would have restored to me that which is dearer to me than mine own self; and restoring it to me on such wise as you say, you would in some measure re-awaken in me my lost hope.' With this, she held her peace, weeping, and Currado said to his lady, 'And thou, mistress, how wouldst thou take it, were I to present thee with such a son-in-law?' The lady replied, 'Even a common churl, so he pleased you, would please me, let alone one of these,[8] who are men of gentle birth.' 'Then,' said Currado, 'I hope, ere many days, to make you happy women in this.'

Accordingly, seeing the two young folk now restored to their former cheer, he clad them sumptuously and said to Giusfredi, 'Were it not dear to thee, over and above thy present joyance, an thou sawest thy mother here?' Whereto he answered, 'I dare not flatter myself that the chagrin of her unhappy chances can have left her so long alive; but, were it indeed so, it were dear to me above all, more by token that methinketh I might yet, by her counsel, avail to recover great part of my estate in Sicily.' Thereupon Currado sent for both the ladies, who came and made much of the newly-wedded wife, no little wondering what happy inspiration it could have been that prompted Currado to such exceeding complaisance as he had shown in joining Giannotto with her in marriage. Madam Beritola, by reason of the words she had heard from Currado, began to consider Giannotto and some remembrance of the boyish lineaments of her son's countenance being by occult virtue awakened in her, without awaiting farther explanation, she ran, open-armed, to cast herself upon his neck, nor did overabounding emotion and maternal joy suffer her to say a word; nay, they so locked up all her senses that she fell into her son's arms, as if dead.

The latter, albeit he was sore amazed, remembering to have many times before seen her in that same castle and never recognized her, nevertheless knew incontinent the maternal odour and blaming himself for his past heedlessness, received her, weeping, in his arms and kissed her tenderly. After awhile, Madam Beritola, being affectionately tended by Currado's lady and Spina and plied both with cold water and other remedies, recalled her strayed senses and embracing her son anew, full of maternal tenderness, with many tears and many tender words, kissed him a thousand times, whilst he all reverently beheld and entreated her. After these joyful and honourable greetings had been thrice or four times repeated, to the no small contentment of the bystanders, and they had related unto each other all that had befallen them, Currado now, to the exceeding satisfaction of all, signified to his friends the new alliance made by him and gave ordinance for a goodly and magnificent entertainment.

Then said Giusfredi to him, 'Currado, you have made me glad of many things and have long honourably entertained my mother; and now, that no whit may remain undone of that which it is in your power to do, I pray you gladden my mother and bride-feast and myself with the presence of my brother, whom Messer Guasparrino d'Oria holdeth in servitude in his house and whom, as I have already told you, he took with me in one of his cruises. Moreover, I would have you send into Sicily one who shall thoroughly inform himself of the state and condition of the country and study to learn what is come of Arrighetto, my father, an he be alive or dead, and if he be alive, in what estate; of all which having fully certified himself, let him return to us.' Giusfredi's request was pleasing to Currado, and without any delay he despatched very discreet persons both to Genoa and to Sicily.

He who went to Genoa there sought out Messer Guasparrino and instantly besought him, on Currado's part, to send him Scacciato and his nurse, orderly recounting to him all his lord's dealings with Giusfredi and his mother. Messer Guasparrino marvelled exceedingly to hear this and said, 'True is it I would do all I may to pleasure Currado, and I have, indeed, these fourteen years had in my house the boy thou seekest and one his mother, both of whom I will gladly send him; but do thou bid him, on my part, beware of lending overmuch credence to the fables of Giannotto, who nowadays styleth himself Giusfredi, for that he is a far greater knave than he deemeth.' So saying, he caused honourably entertain the gentleman and sending privily for the nurse, questioned her shrewdly touching the matter. Now she had heard of the Sicilian revolt and understood Arrighetto to be alive, wherefore, casting off her former fears, she told him everything in order and showed him the reasons that had moved her to do as she had done.

Messer Guasparrino, finding her tale to accord perfectly with that of Currado's messenger, began to give credit to the latter's words and having by one means and another, like a very astute man as he was, made enquiry of the matter and happening hourly upon things that gave him more and more assurance of the fact, took shame to himself of his mean usage of the lad, in amends whereof, knowing what Arrighetto had been and was, he gave him to wife a fair young daughter of his, eleven years of age, with a great dowry. Then, after making a great bride-feast thereon, he embarked with the boy and girl and Currado's messenger and the nurse in a well-armed galliot and betook himself to Lerici, where he was received by Currado and went up, with all his company, to one of the latter's castles, not far removed thence, where there was a great banquet toward.

The mother's joy at seeing her son again and that of the two brothers in each other and of all three in the faithful nurse, the honour done of all to Messer Guasparrino and his daughter and of him to all and the rejoicing of all together with Currado and his lady and children and friends, no words might avail to express; wherefore, ladies, I leave it to you to imagine. Thereunto,[9] that it might be complete, it pleased God the Most High, a most abundant giver, whenas He beginneth, to add the glad news of the life and well-being of Arrighetto Capece; for that, the feast being at its height and the guests, both ladies and men, yet at table for the first service, there came he who had been sent into Sicily and amongst other things, reported of Arrighetto that he, being kept in captivity by King Charles, whenas the revolt against the latter broke out in the land, the folk ran in a fury to the prison and slaying his guards, delivered himself and as a capital enemy of King Charles, made him their captain and followed him to expel and slay the French: wherefore he was become in especial favour with King Pedro,[10] who had reinstated him in all his honours and possessions, and was now in great good case. The messenger added that he had received himself with the utmost honour and had rejoiced with inexpressible joy in the recovery of his wife and son, of whom he had heard nothing since his capture; moreover, he had sent a brigantine for them, with divers gentlemen aboard, who came after him.

The messenger was received and hearkened with great gladness and rejoicing, whilst Currado, with certain of his friends, set out incontinent to meet the gentlemen who came for Madam Beritola and Giusfredi and welcoming them joyously, introduced them into his banquet, which was not yet half ended. There both the lady and Giusfredi, no less than all the others, beheld them with such joyance that never was heard the like; and the gentlemen, ere they sat down to meat, saluted Currado and his lady on the part of Arrighetto, thanking them, as best they knew and might, for the honour done both to his wife and his son and offering himself to their pleasure,[11] in all that lay in his power. Then, turning to Messer Guasparrino, whose kindness was unlooked for, they avouched themselves most certain that, whenas that which he had done for Scacciato should be known of Arrighetto, the like thanks and yet greater would be rendered him.

Thereafter they banqueted right joyously with the new-made bridegrooms at the bride-feast of the two newly-wedded wives; nor that day alone did Currado entertain his son-in-law and other his kinsmen and friends, but many others. As soon as the rejoicings were somewhat abated, it appearing to Madam Beritola and to Giusfredi and the others that it was time to depart, they took leave with many tears of Currado and his lady and Messer Guasparrino and embarked on board the brigantine, carrying Spina with them; then, setting sail with a fair wind, they came speedily to Sicily, where all alike, both sons and daughters-in-law, were received by Arrighetto in Palermo with such rejoicing as might never be told; and there it is believed that they all lived happily a great while after, in love and thankfulness to God the Most High, as mindful of the benefits received."

---

1. Charles d'Anjou.
2. *i.e.* the Banished or the Expelled One.
3. An island in the Gulf of Gaeta, about 70 miles from Naples. It is now inhabited, but appears in Boccaccio's time to have been desert.
4. *i.e.* wild she-goat.
5. A river falling into the Gulf of Genoa between Carrara and Spezzia.
6. More familiar to modern ears as Doria.
7. The Ghibellines were the supporters of the Papal faction against the Guelphs or adherents of the Emperor Frederick II. of Germany. The cardinal struggle between the two factions took place over the succession to the throne of Naples and Sicily, to which the Pope appointed Charles of Anjou, who overcame and killed the reigning sovereign Manfred, but was himself, through the machinations of the Ghibellines, expelled from Sicily by the celebrated popular rising known as the Sicilian Vespers.
8. *i.e.* Beritola's sons.
9. *i.e.* to which general joy.
10. Pedro of Arragon, son-in-law of Manfred, who, in consequence of the Sicilian Vespers, succeeded Charles d'Anjou as King of Sicily.
11. Or (in modern phrase) putting himself at their disposition.

❦ 7 ❦

THE SEVENTH STORY

THE SOLDAN OF BABYLON SENDETH A DAUGHTER OF HIS TO BE MARRIED TO THE KING OF ALGARVE, AND SHE, BY DIVERS CHANCES, IN THE SPACE OF FOUR YEARS COMETH TO THE HANDS OF NINE MEN IN VARIOUS PLACES. ULTIMATELY, BEING RESTORED TO HER FATHER FOR A MAID, SHE GOETH TO THE KING OF ALGARVE TO WIFE, AS FIRST SHE DID

HAD Emilia's story been much longer protracted, it is like the compassion had by the young ladies on the misfortunes of Madam Beritola would have brought them to tears; but, an end being now made thereof, it pleased the queen that Pamfilo should follow on with his story, and accordingly he, who was very obedient, began thus, "Uneath, charming ladies, is it for us to know that which is meet for us, for that, as may oftentimes have been seen, many, imagining that, were they but rich, they might avail to live without care and secure, have not only with prayers sought riches of God, but have diligently studied to acquire them, grudging no toil and no peril in the quest, and who,—whereas, before they became enriched, they loved their lives,—once having gotten their desire, have found folk to slay them, for greed of so ample an inheritance. Others of low estate, having, through a thousand perilous battles and the blood of their brethren and their friends, mounted to the summit of kingdoms, thinking in the royal estate to enjoy supreme felicity, without the innumerable cares and alarms whereof they see and feel it full, have learned, at the cost of their lives, that poison is drunken at royal tables in cups of gold. Many there be who have with most ardent appetite desired bodily strength and beauty and divers personal adornments and perceived not that they had desired ill till they found these very gifts a cause to them of death or dolorous life. In fine, not to speak particularly of all the objects of human desire, I dare say that there is not one which can, with entire assurance, be chosen by mortal men as secure from the vicissitudes of fortune; wherefore, an we would do aright, needs must we resign ourselves to take and possess that which is appointed us of Him who alone knoweth that which behoveth unto us and is able to give it to us. But for that, whereas men sin in desiring various things, you, gracious ladies, sin, above all, in one, to wit, in wishing to be fair,—insomuch that, not content with the charms vouchsafed you by nature, you still with marvellous art study to augment them,—it pleaseth me to recount to you how ill-fortunedly fair was a Saracen lady, whom it befell, for her beauty, to be in some four years' space nine times wedded anew.

It is now a pretty while since there was a certain Soldan of Babylon,[1] by name Berminedab, to whom in his day many things happened in accordance with his pleasure.[2] Amongst many other children, both male and female, he had a daughter called Alatiel, who, by report of all who saw her, was the fairest woman to be seen in the world in those days, and having, in a great defeat he had inflicted upon a vast multitude of Arabs who were come upon him, been wonder-well seconded by the King of Algarve,[3] had, at his request, given her to him to wife, of especial favour; wherefore, embarking her aboard a ship well armed and equipped, with an honourable company of men and ladies and store of rich and sumptuous gear and furniture, he despatched her to him, commending her to God.

The sailors, seeing the weather favourable, gave their sails to the wind and departing the port of Alexandria, fared on prosperously many days, and having now passed Sardinia, deemed themselves near the end of their voyage, when there arose one day of a sudden divers contrary winds, which, being each beyond measure boisterous, so harassed the ship, wherein was the lady, and the sailors, that the latter more than once gave themselves over for lost. However, like valiant men, using every art and means in their power, they rode it out two days, though buffeted by a terrible sea; but, at nightfall of the third day, the tempest abating not, nay, waxing momently, they felt the ship open, being then not far off Majorca, but knowing not where they were neither availing to apprehend it either by nautical reckoning or by sight, for that the sky was altogether obscured by clouds and dark night; wherefore, seeing no other way of escape and having each himself in mind and not others, they lowered a shallop into the water, into which the officers cast themselves, choosing rather to trust themselves thereto than to the leaking ship. The rest of the men in the ship crowded after them into the boat, albeit those who had first embarked therein opposed it, knife in hand,—and thinking thus to flee from death, ran straight into it, for that the boat, availing not, for the intemperance of the weather, to hold so many, foundered and they perished one and all.

As for the ship, being driven by a furious wind and running very swiftly, albeit it was now well nigh water-logged, (none being left on board save the princess and her women, who all, overcome by the tempestuous sea and by fear, lay about the decks as they were dead,) it stranded upon a beach of the island of Majorca and such and so great was the shock that it well nigh buried itself in the sand some stone's cast from the shore, where it abode the night, beaten by the waves, nor might the wind avail to stir it more. Broad day came and the tempest somewhat abating, the princess, who was half dead, raised her head and weak as she was, fell to calling now one, now another of her household, but to no purpose, for that those she called were too far distant. Finding herself unanswered of any and seeing no one, she marvelled exceedingly and began to be sore afraid; then, rising up, as best she might, she saw the ladies who were in her company and the other women lying all about and trying now one and now another, found few who gave any signs of life, the most of them being dead what with sore travail of the stomach and what with affright; wherefore fear redoubled upon her.

Nevertheless, necessity constraining her, for that she saw herself alone there and had neither knowledge nor inkling where she was, she so goaded those who were yet alive that she made them arise and finding them unknowing whither the men were gone and seeing the ship stranded and full of water, she fell to weeping piteously, together with them. It was noon ere they saw any about the shore or elsewhere, whom they might move to pity and succour them; but about that hour there passed by a gentleman, by name Pericone da Visalgo, returning by chance from a place of his, with sundry of his servants on horseback. He saw the ship and forthright conceiving what it was, bade one of the servants board it without delay and tell him what he found there. The man, though with difficulty, made his way on board and found the young lady, with what little company she had, crouched, all adread, under the heel of the bowsprit. When they saw him, they besought him, weeping, of mercy again and again; but, perceiving that he understood them not nor they him, they made shift to make known to him their misadventure by signs.

The servant having examined everything as best he might, reported to Pericone that which was on board; whereupon the latter promptly caused to bring the ladies ashore, together with the most precious things that were in the ship and might be gotten, and carried them off to a castle of his, where, the women being refreshed with food and rest, he perceived, from the richness of her apparel, that the lady whom he had found must needs be some great gentlewoman, and of this he was speedily certified by the honour that he saw the others do her and her alone; and although she was pale and sore disordered of her person, for the fatigues of the voyage, her features seemed to him exceeding fair; wherefore he forthright took counsel with himself, an she had no husband, to seek to have her to wife, and if he might not have her in marriage, to make shift to have her favours.

He was a man of commanding presence and exceeding robust and having for some days let tend the lady excellently well and she being thereby altogether restored, he saw her lovely past all conception and was grieved beyond measure that he could not understand her nor she him and so he might not learn who she was. Nevertheless, being inordinately inflamed by her charms, he studied, with pleasing and amorous gestures, to engage her to do his pleasure without contention; but to no avail; she altogether rejected his advances and so much the more waxed Pericone's ardour. The lady, seeing this and having now abidden there some days, perceived, by the usances of the folk, that she was among Christians and in a country where, even if she could, it had little profited her to make herself known and foresaw that, in the end, either perforce or for love, needs must she resign herself to do Pericone's pleasure, but resolved nevertheless by dint of magnanimity to override the wretchedness of her fortune; wherefore she commanded her women, of whom but three were left her, that they should never discover to any who she was, except they found themselves whereas they might look for manifest furtherance in the regaining of their liberty, and urgently exhorted them, moreover, to preserve their chastity, avouching herself determined that none, save her husband, should ever enjoy her. They commended her for this and promised to observe her commandment to the best of their power.

Meanwhile Pericone, waxing daily more inflamed, insomuch as he saw the thing desired so near and yet so straitly denied, and seeing that his blandishments availed him nothing, resolved to employ craft and artifice, reserving force unto the last. Wherefore, having observed bytimes that wine was pleasing to the lady, as being unused to drink thereof, for that her law forbade it, he bethought himself that he might avail to take her with this, as with a minister of enus. Accordingly, feigning to reck no more of that whereof she showed herself so chary, he made one night by way of special festival a goodly supper, whereto he bade the lady, and therein, the repast being gladdened with many things, he took order with him who served her that he should give her to drink of various wines mingled. The cupbearer did his bidding punctually and she, being nowise on her guard against this and allured by the pleasantness of the drink, took more thereof than consisted with her modesty; whereupon, forgetting all her past troubles, she waxed merry and seeing some women dance after the fashion of Majorca, herself danced in the Alexandrian manner.

Pericone, seeing this, deemed himself on the high road to that which he desired and continuing the supper with great plenty of meats and wines, protracted it far into the night. Ultimately, the guests having departed, he entered with the lady alone into her chamber, where she, more heated with wine than restrained by modesty, without any reserve of shamefastness, undid herself in his presence, as he had been one of her women, and betook herself to bed. Pericone was not slow to follow her, but, putting out all the lights, promptly hid himself beside her and catching her in his arms, proceeded, without any gainsayal on her part, amorously to solace himself with her; which when once she had felt,—having never theretofore known with what manner horn men butt,—as if repenting her of not having yielded to Pericone's solicitations, thenceforth, without waiting to be bidden to such agreeable nights, she oftentimes invited herself thereto, not by words, which she knew not how to make understood, but by deeds.

But, in the midst of this great pleasance of Pericone and herself, fortune, not content with having reduced her from a king's bride to be the mistress of a country gentleman, had foreordained unto her a more barbarous alliance. Pericone had a brother by name Marato, five-and-twenty years of age and fair and fresh as a rose, who saw her and she pleased him mightily. Himseemed, moreover, according to that which he could apprehend from her gestures, that he was very well seen of her and conceiving that nought hindered him of that which he craved of her save the strait watch kept on her by Pericone, he fell into a barbarous thought, whereon the nefarious effect followed without delay.

There was then, by chance, in the harbour of the city a vessel laden with merchandise and bound for Chiarenza[4] in Roumelia; whereof two young Genoese were masters, who had already hoisted sail to depart as soon as the wind should be fair. Marato, having agreed with them, took order how he should on the ensuing night be received aboard their ship with the lady; and this done, as soon as it was dark, having inwardly determined what he should do, he secretly betook himself, with certain of his trustiest friends, whom he had enlisted for the purpose, to the house of Pericone, who nowise mistrusted him. There he hid himself, according to the ordinance appointed between them, and after a part of the night had passed, he admitted his companions and repaired with them to the chamber where Pericone lay with the lady. Having opened the door, they slew Pericone, as he slept, and took the lady, who was now awake and in tears, threatening her with death, if she made any outcry; after which they made off, unobserved, with great part of Pericone's most precious things and betook themselves in haste to the sea-shore, where Marato and the lady embarked without delay on board the ship, whilst his companions returned whence they came.

The sailors, having a fair wind and a fresh, made sail and set out on their voyage, whilst the princess sore and bitterly bewailed both her former and that her second misadventure; but Marato, with that Saint Waxeth-in-hand, which God hath given us [men,] proceeded to comfort her after such a fashion that she soon grew familiar with him and forgetting Pericone, began to feel at her ease, when fortune, as if not content with the past tribulations wherewith it had visited her, prepared her a new affliction; for that, she being, as we have already more than once said, exceeding fair of favour and of very engaging manners, the two young men, the masters of the ship, became so passionately enamoured of her that, forgetting all else, they studied only to serve and pleasure her, being still on their guard lest Marato should get wind of the cause. Each becoming aware of the other's passion, they privily took counsel together thereof, and agreed to join in getting the lady for themselves and enjoy her in common, as if love should suffer this, as do merchandise and gain.

Seeing her straitly guarded by Marato and being thereby hindered of their purpose, one day, as the ship fared on at full speed under sail and Marato stood at the poop, looking out on the sea and nowise on his guard against them, they went of one accord and laying hold of him suddenly from behind, cast him into the sea, nor was it till they had sailed more than a mile farther that any perceived Marato to be fallen overboard. Alatiel, hearing this and seeing no possible way of recovering him, began anew to make moan for herself; whereupon the two lovers came incontinent to her succour and with soft words and very good promises, whereof she understood but little, studied to soothe and console the lady, who lamented not so much her lost husband as her own ill fortune. After holding much discourse with her at one time and another, themseeming after awhile they had well nigh comforted her, they came to words with one another which should first take her to lie with him. Each would fain be the first and being unable to come to any accord upon this, they first with words began a sore and hot dispute and thereby kindled into rage, they clapped hands to their knives and falling furiously on one another, before those on board could part them, dealt each other several blows, whereof one incontinent fell dead, whilst the other abode on life, though grievously wounded in many places.

This new mishap was sore unpleasing to the lady, who saw herself alone, without aid or counsel of any, and feared lest the anger of the two masters' kinsfolk and friends should revert upon herself; but the prayers of the wounded man and their speedy arrival at Chiarenza delivered her from danger of death. There she went ashore with the wounded man and took up her abode with him in an inn, where the report of her great beauty soon spread through the city and came to the ears of the Prince of the Morea, who was then at Chiarenza and was fain to see her. Having gotten sight of her and himseeming she was fairer than report gave out, he straightway became so sore enamoured of her that he could think of nothing else and hearing how she came thither, doubted not to be able to get her for himself. As he cast about for a means of effecting his purpose, the wounded man's kinsfolk got wind of his desire and without awaiting more, sent her to him forthright, which was mighty agreeable to the prince and to the lady also, for that herseemed she was quit of a great peril. The prince, seeing her graced, over and above her beauty, with royal manners and unable otherwise to learn who she was, concluded her to be some noble lady, wherefore he redoubled in his love for her and holding her in exceeding honour, entreated her not as a mistress, but as his very wife.

The lady, accordingly, having regard to her past troubles and herseeming she was well enough bestowed, was altogether comforted and waxing blithe again, her beauties flourished on such wise that it seemed all Roumelia could talk of nothing else. The report of her loveliness reaching the Duke of Athens, who was young and handsome and doughty of his person and a friend and kinsman of the prince, he was taken with a desire to see her and making a show of paying him a visit, as he was wont bytimes to do, repaired, with a fair and worshipful company, to Chiarenza, where he was honourably received and sumptuously entertained. Some days after, the two kinsmen coming to discourse together of the lady's charms, the duke asked if she were indeed so admirable a creature as was reported; to which the prince answered, 'Much more so; but thereof I will have not my words, but thine own eyes certify thee.' Accordingly, at the duke's solicitation, they betook themselves together to the princess's lodging, who, having had notice of their coming, received them very courteously and with a cheerful favour, and they seated her between them, but might not have the pleasure of conversing with her, for that she understood little or nothing of their language; wherefore each contented himself with gazing upon her, as upon a marvel, and especially the duke, who could scarce bring himself to believe that she was a mortal creature and thinking to satisfy his desire with her sight, heedless of the amorous poison he drank in at his eyes, beholding her, he miserably ensnared himself, becoming most ardently enamoured of her.

After he had departed her presence with the prince and had leisure to bethink himself, he esteemed his kinsman happy beyond all others in having so fair a creature at his pleasure, and after many and various thoughts, his unruly passion weighing more with him than his honour, he resolved, come thereof what might, to do his utmost endeavour to despoil the prince of that felicity and bless himself therewith. Accordingly, being minded to make a quick despatch of the matter and setting aside all reason and all equity, he turned his every thought to the devising of means for the attainment of his wishes, and one day, in accordance with the nefarious ordinance taken by him with a privy chamberlain of the prince's, by name Ciuriaci, he let make ready in secret his horses and baggage for a sudden departure.

The night come, he was, with a companion, both armed, stealthily introduced by the aforesaid Ciuriaci into the prince's chamber and saw the latter (the lady being asleep) standing, all naked for the great heat, at a window overlooking the sea-shore, to take a little breeze that came from that quarter; whereupon, having beforehand informed his companion of that which he had to do, he went softly up to the window and striking the prince with a knife, stabbed him, through and through the small of his back; then, taking him up in haste, he cast him forth of the window. The palace stood over against the sea and was very lofty and the window in question looked upon certain houses that had been undermined by the beating of the waves and where seldom or never any came; wherefore it happened, as the duke had foreseen, that the fall of the prince's body was not nor might be heard of any. The duke's companion, seeing this done, pulled out a halter he had brought with him to that end and making a show of caressing Ciuriaci, cast it adroitly about his neck and drew it so that he could make no outcry; then, the duke coming up, they strangled him and cast him whereas they had cast the prince.

This done and they being manifestly certified that they had been unheard of the lady or of any other, the duke took a light in his hand and carrying it to the bedside, softly uncovered the princess, who slept fast. He considered her from head to foot and mightily commended her; for, if she was to his liking, being clothed, she pleased him, naked, beyond all compare. Wherefore, fired with hotter desire and unawed by his new-committed crime, he couched himself by her side, with hands yet bloody, and lay with her, all sleepy-eyed as she was and thinking him to be the prince. After he had abidden with her awhile in the utmost pleasure, he arose and summoning certain of his companions, caused take up the lady on such wise that she could make no outcry and carry her forth by a privy door, whereat he had entered; then, setting her on horseback, he took to the road with all his men, as softliest he might, and returned to his own dominions. However (for that he had a wife) he carried the lady, who was the most distressful of women, not to Athens, but to a very goodly place he had by the sea, a little without the city, and there entertained her in secret, causing honourably furnish her with all that was needful.

The prince's courtiers on the morrow awaited his rising till none, when, hearing nothing, they opened the chamber-doors, which were but closed, and finding no one, concluded that he was gone somewhither privily, to pass some days there at his ease with his fair lady, and gave themselves no farther concern. Things being thus, it chanced next day that an idiot, entering the ruins where lay the bodies of the prince and Ciuriaci, dragged the latter forth by the halter and went haling him after him. The body was, with no little wonderment, recognized by many, who, coaxing the idiot to bring them to the place whence he had dragged it, there, to the exceeding grief of the whole city, found the prince's corpse and gave it honourable burial. Then, enquiring for the authors of so heinous a crime and finding that the Duke of Athens was no longer there, but had departed by stealth, they concluded, even as was the case, that it must be he who had done this and carried off the lady; whereupon they straightway substituted a brother of the dead man to their prince and incited him with all their might to vengeance. The new prince, being presently certified by various other circumstances that it was as they had surmised, summoned his friends and kinsmen and servants from divers parts and promptly levying a great and goodly and powerful army, set out to make war upon the Duke of Athens.

The latter, hearing of this, on like wise mustered all his forces for his own defence, and to his aid came many lords, amongst whom the Emperor of Constantinople sent Constantine his son and Manual his nephew, with a great and goodly following. The two princes were honourably received by the duke and yet more so by the duchess, for that she was their sister,[5] and matters drawing thus daily nearer unto war, taking her occasion, she sent for them both one day to her chamber and there, with tears galore and many words, related to them the whole story, acquainting them with the causes of the war. Moreover, she discovered to them the affront done her by the duke in the matter of the woman whom it was believed he privily entertained, and complaining sore thereof, besought them to apply to the matter such remedy as best they might, for the honour of the duke and her own solacement.

The young men already knew all the facts as it had been; wherefore, without enquiring farther, they comforted the duchess, as best they might, and filled her with good hope. Then, having learned from her where the lady abode, they took their leave and having a mind to see the latter, for that they had oftentimes heard her commended for marvellous beauty, they besought the duke to show her to them. He, unmindful of that which had befallen the Prince of the Morea for having shown her to himself, promised to do this and accordingly next morning, having let prepare a magnificent collation in a very goodly garden that pertained to the lady's place of abode, he carried them and a few others thither to eat with her. Constantine, sitting with Alatiel, fell a-gazing upon her, full of wonderment, avouching in himself that he had never seen aught so lovely and that certes the duke must needs be held excused, ay, and whatsoever other, to have so fair a creature, should do treason or other foul thing, and looking on her again and again and each time admiring her more, it betided him no otherwise than it had betided the duke; wherefore, taking his leave, enamoured of her, he abandoned all thought of the war and occupied himself with considering how he might take her from the duke, carefully concealing his passion the while from every one.

Whilst he yet burnt in this fire, the time came to go out against the new prince, who now drew near to the duke's territories; wherefore the latter and Constantine and all the others, sallied forth of Athens according to the given ordinance and betook themselves to the defence of certain frontiers, so the prince might not avail to advance farther. When they had lain there some days, Constantine having his mind and thought still intent upon the lady and conceiving that, now the duke was no longer near her, he might very well avail to accomplish his pleasure, feigned himself sore indisposed of his person, to have an occasion of returning to Athens; wherefore, with the duke's leave, committing his whole power to Manuel, he returned to Athens to his sister, and there, after some days, putting her upon talk of the affront which herseemed she suffered from the duke by reason of the lady whom he entertained, he told her that, an it liked her, he would soon ease her thereof by causing take the lady from whereas she was and carry her off. The duchess, conceiving that he did this of regard for herself and not for love of the lady, answered that it liked her exceeding well so but it might be done on such wise that the duke should never know that she had been party thereto, which Constantine fully promised her, and thereupon she consented that he should do as seemed best to him.

Constantine, accordingly, let secretly equip a light vessel and sent it one evening to the neighbourhood of the garden where the lady abode; then, having taught certain of his men who were on board what they had to do, he repaired with others to the lady's pavilion, where he was cheerfully received by those in her service and indeed by the lady herself, who, at his instance, betook herself with him to the garden, attended by her servitors and his companions. There, making as he would speak with her on the duke's part, he went with her alone towards a gate, which gave upon the sea and had already been opened by one of his men, and calling the bark thither with the given signal, he caused suddenly seize the lady and carry her aboard; then, turning to her people, he said to them, 'Let none stir or utter a word, an he would not die; for that I purpose not to rob the duke of his wench, but to do away the affront which he putteth upon my sister.'

To this none dared make answer; whereupon Constantine, embarking with his people and seating himself by the side of the weeping lady, bade thrust the oars into the water and make off. Accordingly, they put out to sea and not hieing, but flying,[6] came, after a little after daybreak on the morrow, to Egina, where they landed and took rest, whilst Constantine solaced himself awhile with the lady, who bemoaned her ill-fated beauty. Thence, going aboard the bark again, they made their way, in a few days, to Chios, where it pleased Constantine to take up his sojourn, as in a place of safety, for fear of his father's resentment and lest the stolen lady should be taken from him. There the fair lady bewailed her ill fate some days, but, being presently comforted by Constantine, she began, as she had done otherwhiles, to take her pleasure of that which fortune had foreordained to her.

Things being at this pass, Osbech, King of the Turks, who abode in continual war with the Emperor, came by chance to Smyrna, where hearing how Constantine abode in Chios, without any precaution, leading a wanton life with a mistress of his, whom he had stolen away, he repaired thither one night with some light-armed ships and entering the city by stealth with some of his people, took many in their beds, ere they knew of the enemy's coming. Some, who, taking the alert, had run to arms, he slew and having burnt the whole place, carried the booty and captives on board the ships and returned to Smyrna. When they arrived there, Osbech, who was a young man, passing his prisoners in review, found the fair lady among them and knowing her for her who had been taken with Constantine asleep in bed, was mightily rejoiced at sight of her. Accordingly, he made her his wife without delay, and celebrating the nuptials forthright, lay with her some months in all joyance.

Meanwhile, the Emperor, who had, before these things came to pass, been in treaty with Bassano, King of Cappadocia, to the end that he should come down upon Osbech from one side with his power, whilst himself assailed him on the other, but had not yet been able to come to a full accord with him, for that he was unwilling to grant certain things which Bassano demanded and which he deemed unreasonable, hearing what had betided his son and chagrined beyond measure thereat, without hesitating farther, did that which the King of Cappadocia asked and pressed him as most he might to fall upon Osbech, whilst himself made ready to come down upon him from another quarter. Osbech, hearing this, assembled his army, ere he should be straitened between two such puissant princes, and marched against Bassano, leaving his fair lady at Smyrna, in charge of a trusty servant and friend of his. After some time he encountered the King of Cappadocia and giving him battle, was slain in the mellay and his army discomfited and dispersed; whereupon Bassano advanced in triumph towards Smyrna, unopposed, and all the folk submitted to him by the way, as to a conqueror.

Meanwhile, Osbech's servant, Antiochus by name, in whose charge the lady had been left, seeing her so fair, forgot his plighted faith to his friend and master and became enamoured of her, for all he was a man in years. Urged by love and knowing her tongue (the which was mighty agreeable to her, as well as it might be to one whom it had behoved for some years live as she were deaf and dumb, for that she understood none neither was understood of any) he began, in a few days, to be so familiar with her that, ere long, having no regard to their lord and master who was absent in the field, they passed from friendly commerce to amorous privacy, taking marvellous pleasure one of the other between the sheets. When they heard that Osbech was defeated and slain and that Bassano came carrying all before him, they took counsel together not to await him there and laying hands on great part of the things of most price that were there pertaining to Osbech, gat them privily to Rhodes, where they had not long abidden ere Antiochus sickened unto death.

As chance would have it, there was then in lodging with him a merchant of Cyprus, who was much loved of him and his fast friend, and Antiochus, feeling himself draw to his end, bethought himself to leave him both his possessions and his beloved lady; wherefore, being now nigh upon death, he called them both to him and bespoke them thus, 'I feel myself, without a doubt, passing away, which grieveth me, for that never had I such delight in life as I presently have. Of one thing, indeed, I die most content, in that, since I must e'en die, I see myself die in the arms of those twain whom I love over all others that be in the world, to wit, in thine, dearest friend, and in those of this lady, whom I have loved more than mine own self, since first I knew her. True, it grieveth me to feel that, when I am dead, she will abide here a stranger, without aid or counsel; and it were yet more grievous to me, did I not know thee here, who wilt, I trust, have that same care of her, for the love of me, which thou wouldst have had of myself. Wherefore, I entreat thee, as most I may, if it come to pass that I die, that thou take my goods and her into thy charge and do with them and her that which thou deemest may be for the solacement of my soul. And thou, dearest lady, I prithee forget me not after my death, so I may vaunt me, in the other world, of being beloved here below of the fairest lady ever nature formed; of which two things an you will give me entire assurance, I shall depart without misgiving and comforted.'

The merchant his friend and the lady, hearing these words, wept, and when he had made an end of his speech, they comforted him and promised him upon their troth to do that which he asked, if it came to pass that he died. He tarried not long, but presently departed this life and was honourably interred of them. A few days after, the merchant having despatched all his business in Rhodes and purposing to return to Cyprus on board a Catalan carrack that was there, asked the fair lady what she had a mind to do, for that it behoved him return to Cyprus. She answered that, an it pleased him, she would gladly go with him, hoping for Antiochus his love to be of him entreated and regarded as a sister. The merchant replied that he was content to do her every pleasure, and the better to defend her from any affront that might be offered her, ere they came to Cyprus, he avouched that she was his wife. Accordingly, they embarked on board the ship and were given a little cabin on the poop, where, that the fact might not belie his words, he lay with her in one very small bed. Whereby there came about that which was not intended of the one or the other of them at departing Rhodes, to wit, that—darkness and commodity and the heat of the bed, matters of no small potency, inciting them,—drawn by equal appetite and forgetting both the friendship and the love of Antiochus dead, they fell to dallying with each other and before they reached Baffa, whence the Cypriot came, they had clapped up an alliance together.

At Baffa she abode some time with the merchant till, as chance would have it, there came thither, for his occasions, a gentleman by name Antigonus, great of years and greater yet of wit, but little of wealth, for that, intermeddling in the affairs of the King of Cyprus, fortune had in many things been contrary to him. Chancing one day to pass by the house where the fair lady dwelt with the merchant, who was then gone with his merchandise into Armenia, he espied her at a window and seeing her very beautiful, fell to gazing fixedly upon her and presently began to recollect that he must have seen her otherwhere, but where he could on no wise call to mind. As for the lady, who had long been the sport of fortune, but the term of whose ills was now drawing near, she no sooner set eyes on Antigonus than she remembered to have seen him at Alexandria in no mean station in her father's service; wherefore, conceiving a sudden hope of yet by his aid regaining her royal estate, and knowing her merchant to be abroad, she let call him to her as quickliest she might and asked him, blushing, an he were not, as she supposed, Antigonus of Famagosta. He answered that he was and added, 'Madam, meseemeth I know you, but on no wise can I remember me where I have seen you; wherefore I pray you, an it mislike you not, put me in mind who you are.'

The lady hearing that it was indeed he, to his great amazement, cast her arms about his neck, weeping sore, and presently asked him if he had never seen her in Alexandria. Antigonus, hearing this, incontinent knew her for the Soldan's daughter Alatiel, who was thought to have perished at sea, and would fain have paid her the homage due to her quality;

but she would on no wise suffer it and besought him to sit with her awhile. Accordingly, seating himself beside her, he asked her respectfully how and when and whence she came thither, seeing that it was had for certain, through all the land of Egypt, that she had been drowned at sea years agone. 'Would God,' replied she, 'it had been so, rather than that I should have had the life I have had; and I doubt not but my father would wish the like, if ever he came to know it.'

So saying, she fell anew to weeping wonder-sore; whereupon quoth Antigonus to her, 'Madam, despair not ere it behove you; but, an it please you, relate to me your adventures and what manner of life yours hath been; it may be the matter hath gone on such wise that, with God's aid, we may avail to find an effectual remedy.' 'Antigonus,' answered the fair lady, 'when I beheld thee, meseemed I saw my father, and moved by that love and tenderness, which I am bounden to bear him, I discovered myself to thee, having it in my power to conceal myself from thee, and few persons could it have befallen me to look upon in whom I could have been so well-pleased as I am to have seen and known thee before any other; wherefore that which in my ill fortune I have still kept hidden, to thee, as to a father, I will discover. If, after thou hast heard it, thou see any means of restoring me to my pristine estate, prithee use it; but, if thou see none, I beseech thee never tell any that thou hast seen me or heard aught of me.'

This said, she recounted to him, still weeping, that which had befallen her from the time of her shipwreck on Majorca up to that moment; whereupon he fell a-weeping for pity and after considering awhile, 'Madam,' said he, 'since in your misfortunes it hath been hidden who you are, I will, without fail, restore you, dearer than ever, to your father and after to the King of Algarve to wife.' Being questioned of her of the means, he showed her orderly that which was to do, and lest any hindrance should betide through delay, he presently returned to Famagosta and going in to the king, said to him, 'My lord, an it like you, you have it in your power at once to do yourself exceeding honour and me, who am poor through you, a great service, at no great cost of yours.' The king asked how and Antigonus replied, 'There is come to Baffa the Soldan's fair young daughter, who hath so long been reputed drowned and who, to save her honour, hath long suffered very great unease and is presently in poor case and would fain return to her father. An it pleased you send her to him under my guard, it would be much to your honour and to my weal, nor do I believe that such a service would ever be forgotten of the Soldan.'

The king, moved by a royal generosity of mind, answered forthright that he would well and sending for Alatiel, brought her with all honour and worship to Famagosta, where she was received by himself and the queen with inexpressible rejoicing and entertained with magnificent hospitality. Being presently questioned of the king and queen of her adventures, she answered according to the instructions given her by Antigonus and related everything;[7] and a few days after, at her request, the king sent her, under the governance of Antigonus, with a goodly and worshipful company of men and women, back to the Soldan, of whom let none ask if she was received with rejoicing, as also was Antigonus and all her company.

As soon as she was somewhat rested, the Soldan desired to know how it chanced that she was yet alive and where she had so long abidden, without having ever let him know aught of her condition; whereupon the lady, who had kept Antigonus his instructions perfectly in mind, bespoke him thus, 'Father mine, belike the twentieth day after my departure from you, our ship, having sprung a leak in a terrible storm, struck in the night upon certain coasts yonder in the West,[8] near a place called Aguamorta, and what became of the men who were aboard I know not nor could ever learn; this much only do I remember that, the day come and I arisen as it were from death to life, the shattered vessel was espied of the country people, who ran from all the parts around to plunder it. I and two of my women were first set ashore and the latter were incontinent seized by certain of the young men, who fled with them, one this way and the other that, and what came of them I never knew.

As for myself, I was taken, despite my resistance, by two young men, and haled along by the hair, weeping sore the while; but, as they crossed over a road, to enter a great wood, there passed by four men on horseback, whom when my ravishers saw, they loosed me forthwith and took to flight. The new comers, who seemed to me persons of great authority, seeing this, ran where I was and asked me many questions; whereto I answered much, but neither understood nor was understood of them. However, after long consultation they set me on one of their horses and carried me to a convent of women vowed to religion, according to their law, where, whatever they said, I was of all the ladies kindly received and still entreated with honour, and there with great devotion I joined them in serving Saint Waxeth-in-Deepdene, a saint for whom the women of that country have a vast regard.

After I had abidden with them awhile and learned somewhat of their language, they questioned me of who I was and fearing, an I told the truth, to be expelled from amongst them, as an enemy of their faith, I answered that I was the daughter of a great gentleman of Cyprus, who was sending me to be married in Crete, when, as ill-luck would have it, we had run thither and suffered shipwreck. Moreover, many a time and in many things I observed their customs, for fear of worse, and being asked by the chief of the ladies, her whom they call abbess, if I wished to return thence to Cyprus, I answered that I desired nothing so much; but she, tender of my honour, would never consent to trust me to any person who was bound for Cyprus, till some two months agone, when there came thither certain gentlemen of France with their ladies. One of the latter being a kinswoman of the abbess and she hearing that they were bound for Jerusalem, to visit the Sepulchre where He whom they hold God was buried, after He had been slain by the Jews, she commended me to their care and besought them to deliver me to my father in Cyprus.

With what honour these gentlemen entreated me and how cheerfully they received me together with their ladies, it were a long story to tell; suffice it to say that we took ship and came, after some days, to Baffa, where finding myself arrived and knowing none in the place, I knew not what to say to the gentlemen, who would fain have delivered me to my father, according to that which had been enjoined them of the reverend lady; but God, taking pity belike on my affliction, brought me Antigonus upon the beach what time we disembarked at Baffa, whom I straightway hailed and in our tongue, so as not to be understood of the gentlemen and their ladies, bade him receive me as a daughter. He promptly apprehended me and receiving me with a great show of joy, entertained the gentlemen and their ladies with such honour as his poverty permitted and carried me to the King of Cyprus, who received me with such hospitality and hath sent me back to you [with such courtesy] as might never be told of me. If aught remain to be said, let Antigonus, who hath ofttimes heard from me these adventures, recount it.'

Accordingly Antigonus, turning to the Soldan, said, 'My lord, even as she hath many a time told me and as the gentlemen and ladies, with whom she came, said to me, so hath she recounted unto you. Only one part hath she forborne to tell you, the which methinketh she left unsaid for that it beseemeth her not to tell it, to wit, how much the gentlemen and ladies, with whom she came, said of the chaste and modest life which she led with the religious ladies and of her virtue and commendable manners and the tears and lamentations of her companions, both men and women, when, having restored her to me, they took leave of her. Of which things were I fain to tell in full that which they said to me, not only this present day, but the ensuing night would not suffice unto us; be it enough to say only that (according to that which their words attested and that also which I have been able to see thereof,) you may vaunt yourself of having the fairest daughter and the chastest and most virtuous of any prince that nowadays weareth a crown.'

The Soldan was beyond measure rejoiced at these things and besought God again and again to vouchsafe him of His grace the power of worthily requiting all who had succoured his daughter and especially the King of Cyprus, by whom she had been sent back to him with honour. After some days, having caused prepare great gifts for Antigonus, he gave him leave to return to Cyprus and rendered, both by letters and by special ambassadors, the utmost thanks to the king for that which he had done with his daughter. Then desiring that that which was begun should have effect, to wit, that she should be the wife of the King of Algarve, he acquainted the latter with the whole matter and wrote to him to boot, that, an it pleased him have her, he should send for her. The King of Algarve was mightily rejoiced at this news and sending for her in state, received her joyfully; and she, who had lain with eight men belike ten thousand times, was put to bed to him for a maid and making him believe that she was so, lived happily with him as his queen awhile after; wherefore it was said, 'Lips for kissing forfeit no favour; nay, they renew as the moon doth ever.'"

---

1. *i.e.* Egypt, Cairo was known in the middle ages by the name of "Babylon of Egypt." It need hardly be noted that the Babylon of the Bible was the city of that name on the Euphrates, the ancient capital of Chaldæa (Irak Babili). The names Beminedab and Alatiel are purely imaginary.
2. *i.e.* to his wish, to whom fortune was mostly favourable in his enterprises.
3. *Il Garbo*, Arabic El Gherb or Gharb, الغرب, the West, a name given by the Arabs to several parts of the Muslim empire, but by which Boccaccio apparently means Algarve, the southernmost province of Portugal and the last part of that kingdom to succumb to the wave of Christian reconquest, it having remained in the hands of the Muslims till the second half of the thirteenth century. This supposition is confirmed by the course taken by Alatiel's ship, which would naturally pass Sardinia and the Balearic Islands on its way from Alexandria to Portugal.
4. The modern Klarentza in the north-west of the Morea, which latter province formed part of Roumelia under the Turkish domination.
5. *i.e.* sister to the one and cousin to the other.
6. *Non vogando, ma volando.*
7. Sic (*contò tutto*); but this is an oversight of the author's, as it is evident from what follows that she did *not* relate everything.
8. Lit. Ponant (*Ponente*), *i.e.* the Western coasts of the Mediterranean, as opposed to the Eastern or Levant.

❧ 8 ❧

THE EIGHTH STORY

THE COUNT OF ANTWERP, BEING FALSELY ACCUSED, GOETH INTO EXILE AND LEAVETH HIS TWO CHILDREN IN DIFFERENT PLACES IN ENGLAND, WHITHER, AFTER AWHILE, RETURNING IN DISGUISE AND FINDING THEM IN GOOD CASE, HE TAKETH SERVICE AS A HORSEBOY IN THE SERVICE OF THE KING OF FRANCE AND BEING APPROVED INNOCENT, IS RESTORED TO HIS FORMER ESTATE

THE LADIES SIGHED amain over the fortunes of the fair Saracen; but who knoweth what gave rise to those sighs? Maybe there were some of them who sighed no less for envy of such frequent nuptials than for pity of Alatiel. But, leaving that be for the present, after they had laughed at Pamfilo's last words, the queen, seeing his story ended, turned to Elisa and bade her follow on with one of hers. Elisa cheerfully obeyed and began as follows: "A most ample field is that wherein we go to-day a-ranging, nor is there any of us but could lightly enough run, not one, but half a score courses there, so abounding hath Fortune made it in her strange and grievous chances; wherefore, to come to tell of one of these latter, which are innumerable, I say that:

When the Roman Empire was transferred from the French to the Germans,[1] there arose between the one and the other nation an exceeding great enmity and a grievous and continual war, by reason whereof, as well for the defence of their own country as for the offence of that of others, the King of France and a son of his, with all the power of their realm and of such friends and kinsfolk as they could command, levied a mighty army to go forth upon the foe; and ere they proceeded thereunto,—not to leave the realm without governance,—knowing Gautier, Count of Antwerp,[2] for a noble and discreet gentleman and their very faithful friend and servant, and for that (albeit he was well versed in the art of war) he seemed to them more apt unto things delicate than unto martial toils, they left him vicar general in their stead over all the governance of the realm of France and went on their way. Gautier accordingly addressed himself with both order and discretion to the office committed unto him, still conferring of everything with the queen and her daughter-in-law, whom, for all they were left under his custody and jurisdiction, he honoured none the less as his liege ladies and mistresses.

Now this Gautier was exceedingly goodly of his body, being maybe forty years old and as agreeable and well-mannered a gentleman as might be; and withal, he was the sprightliest and daintiest cavalier known in those days and he who went most adorned of his person. His countess was dead, leaving him two little children, a boy and a girl, without more, and it befell that, the King of France and his son being at the war aforesaid and Gautier using much at the court of the aforesaid ladies and speaking often with them of the affairs of the kingdom, the wife of the king's son cast her eyes on him and considering his person and his manners with very great affection, was secretly fired with a fervent love for him. Feeling herself young and lusty and knowing him wifeless, she doubted not but her desire might lightly be accomplished unto her and thinking nought hindered her thereof but shamefastness, she bethought herself altogether to put that away and discover to him her passion. Accordingly, being one day alone and it seeming to her time, she sent for him into her chamber, as though she would discourse with him of other matters.

The count, whose thought was far from that of the lady, betook himself to her without any delay and at her bidding, seated himself by her side on a couch; then, they being alone together, he twice asked her the occasion for which she had caused him come thither; but she made him no reply. At last, urged by love and grown all vermeil for shame, well nigh in tears and all trembling, with broken speech she thus began to say: 'Dearest and sweet friend and my lord, you may easily as a man of understanding apprehend how great is the frailty both of men and of women, and that more, for divers reasons, in one than in another; wherefore, at the hands of a just judge, the same sin in diverse kinds of qualities of persons should not in equity receive one same punishment. And who is there will deny that a poor man or a poor woman, whom it behoveth gain with their toil that which is needful for their livelihood, would, an they were stricken with Love's smart and followed after him, be far more blameworthy than a lady who is rich and idle and to whom nothing is lacking that can flatter her desires? Certes, I believe, no one. For which reason methinketh the things aforesaid [to wit, wealth and leisure and luxurious living] should furnish forth a very great measure of excuse on behalf of her who possesseth them, if, peradventure, she suffer herself lapse into loving, and the having made choice of a lover of worth and discretion should stand for the rest,[3] if she who loveth hath done that. These circumstances being both, to my seeming, in myself (beside several others which should move me to love, such as my youth and the absence of my husband), it behoveth now that they rise up in my behalf for the defence of my ardent love in your sight, wherein if they avail that which they should avail in the eyes of men of understanding, I pray you afford me counsel and succour in that which I shall ask of you. True is it, that availing not, for the absence of my husband, to withstand the pricks of the flesh nor the might of love-liking, the which are of such potency that they have erst many a time overcome and yet all days long overcome the strongest men, to say nothing of weak women,—and enjoying the commodities and the leisures wherein you see me, I have suffered myself lapse into ensuing Love his pleasures and becoming enamoured; the which,—albeit, were it known, I acknowledge it would not be seemly, yet,— being and abiding hidden, I hold[4] well nigh nothing unseemly; more by token that Love hath been insomuch gracious to me that not only hath he not bereft me of due discernment in the choice of a lover, but hath lent me great plenty thereof[5] to that end, showing me yourself worthy to be loved of a lady such as I,—you whom, if my fancy beguile me not, I hold the goodliest, the most agreeable, the sprightliest and the most accomplished cavalier that may be found in all the realm of France; and even as I may say that I find myself without a husband, so likewise are you without a wife. Wherefore, I pray you, by the great love which I bear you, that you deny me not your love in return, but have compassion on my youth, the which, in very deed, consumeth for you, as ice before the fire.'

With these words her tears welled up in such abundance that, albeit she would fain have proffered him yet other prayers, she had no power to speak farther, but, bowing her face, as if overcome, she let herself fall, weeping, her head on the count's bosom. The latter, who was a very loyal gentleman, began with the gravest reproofs to rebuke so fond a passion and to repel the princess, who would fain have cast herself on his neck, avouching to her with oaths that he had liefer be torn limb from limb than consent unto such an offence against his lord's honour, whether in himself or in another. The lady, hearing this, forthright forgot her love and kindling into a furious rage, said, 'Felon knight that you are, shall I be this wise flouted by you of my desire? Now God forbid, since you would have me die, but I have you put to death or driven from the world!' So saying, she set her hands to her tresses and altogether disordered and tore them; then, rending her raiment at the breast, she fell to crying aloud and saying, 'Help! Help! The Count of Antwerp would do me violence.' The count, seeing this, misdoubting far more the courtiers' envy than his own conscience and fearful lest, by reason of this same envy, more credence should be given to the lady's malice than to his own innocence, started up and departing the chamber and the palace as quickliest he might, fled to his own house, where, without taking other counsel, he set his children on horseback and mounting himself to horse, made off with them, as most he might, towards Calais.

Meanwhile, many ran to the princess's clamour and seeing her in that plight and hearing [her account of] the cause of her outcry, not only gave credence to her words, but added[6] that the count's gallant bearing and debonair address had long been used by him to win to that end. Accordingly, they ran in a fury to his houses to arrest him, but finding him not, first plundered them all and after razed them to the foundations. The news, in its perverted shape, came presently to the army to the king and his son, who, sore incensed, doomed Gautier and his descendants to perpetual banishment, promising very great guerdons to whoso should deliver him to them alive or dead.

The count, woeful for that by his flight he had, innocent as he was, approved himself guilty, having, without making himself known or being recognized, reached Calais with his children, passed hastily over into England and betook himself in mean apparel to London, wherein ere he entered, with many words he lessoned his two little children, and especially in two things; first, that they should brook with patience the poor estate, whereunto, without their fault, fortune had brought them, together with himself,—and after, that with all wariness they should keep themselves from ever discovering unto any whence or whose children they were, as they held life dear. The boy, Louis by name, who was some nine and the girl, who was called Violante and was some seven years old, both, as far as their tender age comported, very well apprehended their father's lessons and showed it thereafter by deed. That this might be the better done,[7] he deemed it well to change their names; wherefore he named the boy Perrot and the girl Jeannette and all three, entering London, meanly clad, addressed themselves to go about asking alms, like as we see yonder French vagabonds do.

They being on this account one morning at a church door, it chanced that a certain great lady, the wife of one of the king's marshals of England, coming forth of the church, saw the count and his two little ones asking alms and questioned him whence he was and if the children were his, to which he replied that he was from Picardy and that, by reason of the misfeasance of a rakehelly elder son of his, it had behoved him depart the country with these two, who were his. The lady, who was pitiful, cast her eyes on the girl and being much taken with her, for that she was handsome, well-mannered and engaging, said, 'Honest man, an thou be content to leave thy daughter with me, I will willingly take her, for that she hath a good favour, and if she prove an honest woman, I will in due time marry her on such wise that she shall fare well.' This offer was very pleasing to the count, who promptly answered, 'Yes,' and with tears gave up the girl to the lady, urgently commending her to her care.

Having thus disposed of his daughter, well knowing to whom, he resolved to abide there no longer and accordingly, begging his way across the island, came, not without sore fatigue, as one who was unused to go afoot, into Wales. Here dwelt another of the king's marshals, who held great state and entertained a numerous household, and to his court both the count and his son whiles much resorted to get food. Certain sons of the said marshal and other gentlemen's children being there engaged in such boyish exercises as running and leaping, Perrot began to mingle with them and to do as dextrously as any of the rest, or more so, each feat that was practised among them. The marshal, chancing whiles to see this and being much taken with the manners and fashion of the boy, asked who he was and was told that he was the son of a poor man who came there bytimes for alms; whereupon he caused require him of the count, and the latter, who indeed besought God of nought else, freely resigned the boy to him, grievous as it was to him to be parted from him. Having thus provided his son and daughter, he determined to abide no longer in England and passing over into Ireland, made his way, as best he might, to Stamford, where he took service with a knight belonging to an earl of the country, doing all such things as pertain unto a lackey or a horseboy, and there, without being known of any, he abode a great while in unease and travail galore.

Meanwhile Violante, called Jeannette, went waxing with the gentlewoman in London in years and person and beauty and was in such favour both with the lady and her husband and with every other of the house and whoso else knew her, that it was a marvellous thing to see; nor was there any who noted her manners and fashions but avouched her worthy of every greatest good and honour. Wherefore the noble lady who had received her from her father, without having ever availed to learn who he was, otherwise than as she had heard from himself, was purposed to marry her honourably according to that condition whereof she deemed her. But God, who is a just observer of folk's deserts, knowing her to be of noble birth and to bear, without fault, the penalty of another's sin, ordained otherwise, and fain must we believe that He of His benignity permitted that which came to pass to the end that the gentle damsel might not fall into the hands of a man of low estate.

The noble lady with whom Jeannette dwelt had of her husband one only son, whom both she and his father loved with an exceeding love, both for that he was their child and that he deserved it by reason of his worth and virtues. He, being some six years older than Jeannette and seeing her exceeding fair and graceful, became so sore enamoured of her that he saw nought beyond her; yet, for that he deemed her to be of mean extraction, not only dared he not demand her of his father and mother to wife, but, fearing to be blamed for having set himself to love unworthily, he held his love, as most he might, hidden; wherefore it tormented him far more than if he had discovered it; and thus it came to pass that, for excess of chagrin, he fell sick and that grievously. Divers physicians were called in to medicine him, who, having noted one and another symptom of his case and being nevertheless unable to discover what ailed him, all with one accord despaired of his recovery; whereat the young man's father and mother suffered dolour and melancholy so great that greater might not be brooked, and many a time, with piteous prayers, they questioned him of the cause of his malady, whereto or sighs he gave for answer or replied that he felt himself all wasting away.

It chanced one day that, what while a doctor, young enough, but exceedingly deeply versed in science, sat by him and held him by the arm in that part where leaches use to seek the pulse, Jeannette, who, of regard for his mother, tended him solicitously, entered, on some occasion or another, the chamber where the young man lay. When the latter saw her, without word said or gesture made, he felt the amorous ardour redouble in his heart, wherefore his pulse began to beat stronglier than of wont; the which the leach incontinent noted and marvelling, abode still to see how long this should last. As soon as Jeannette left the chamber, the beating abated, wherefore it seemed to the physician he had gotten impartment of the cause of the young man's ailment, and after waiting awhile, he let call Jeannette to him, as he would question her of somewhat, still holding the sick man by the arm. She came to him incontinent and no sooner did she enter than the beating of the youth's pulse returned and she being gone again, ceased. Thereupon, it seeming to the physician that he had full enough assurance, he rose and taking the young man's father and mother apart, said to them, 'The healing of your son is not in the succour of physicians, but abideth in the hands of Jeannette, whom, as I have by sure signs manifestly recognized, the young man ardently loveth, albeit, for all I can see, she is unaware thereof. You know now what you have to do, if his life be dear to you.'

The gentleman and his lady, hearing this, were well pleased, inasmuch as some means was found for his recoverance, albeit it irked them sore that the means in question should be that whereof they misdoubted them, to wit, that they should give Jeannette to their son to wife. Accordingly, the physician being gone, they went into the sick man and the lady bespoke him thus: 'Son mine, I could never have believed that thou wouldst keep from me any desire of thine, especially seeing thyself pine away for lack thereof; for that thou shouldst have been and shouldst be assured that there is nought I can for thy contentment, were it even less than seemly, which I would not do as for myself. But, since thou hast e'en done this, God the Lord hath been more pitiful over thee than thou thyself and that thou mayst not die of this sickness, hath shown me the cause of thine ill, which is no otherwhat than excess of love for some damsel or other, whoever she may be; and this, indeed, thou needest not have thought shame to discover, for that thine age requireth it, and wert thou not enamoured, I should hold thee of very little account. Wherefore, my son, dissemble not with me, but in all security discover to me thine every desire and put away from thee the melancholy and the thought-taking which be upon thee and from which proceedeth this thy sickness and take comfort and be assured that there is nothing of that which thou mayst impose on me for thy satisfaction but I will do it to the best of my power, as she who loveth thee more than her life. Banish shamefastness and fearfulness and tell me if I can do aught to further thy passion; and if thou find me not diligent therein or if I bring it not to effect for thee, account me the cruellest mother that ever bore son.'

The young man, hearing his mother's words, was at first abashed, but presently, bethinking himself that none was better able than she to satisfy his wishes, he put away shamefastness and said thus to her: 'Madam, nothing hath wrought so effectually with me to keep my love hidden as my having noted of most folk that, once they are grown in years, they choose not to remember them of having themselves been young. But, since in this I find you reasonable, not only will I not deny that to be true which you say you have observed, but I will, to boot, discover to you of whom [I am enamoured], on condition that you will, to the best of your power, give effect to your promise; and thus may you have me whole again.' Whereto the lady (trusting overmuch in that which was not to come to pass for her on such wise as she deemed in herself) answered freely that he might in all assurance discover to her his every desire, for that she would without any delay address herself to contrive that he should have his pleasure. 'Madam,' then said the youth, 'the exceeding beauty and commendable fashions of our Jeannette and my unableness to make her even sensible, still less to move her to pity, of my love and the having never dared to discover it unto any have brought me whereas you see me; and if that which you have promised me come not, one way or another, to pass, you may be assured that my life will be brief.'

The lady, to whom it appeared more a time for comfort than for reproof, said, smilingly, 'Alack, my son, hast thou then for this suffered thyself to languish thus? Take comfort and leave me do, once thou shalt be recovered.' The youth, full of good hope, in a very short time showed signs of great amendment, whereas the lady, being much rejoiced, began to cast about how she might perform that which she had promised him. Accordingly, calling Jeannette to her one day, she asked her very civilly, as by way of a jest, if she had a lover; whereupon she waxed all red and answered, 'Madam, it concerneth not neither were it seemly in a poor damsel like myself, banished from house and home and abiding in others' service, to think of love.' Quoth the lady, 'An you have no lover, we mean to give you one, in whom you may rejoice and live merry and have more delight of your beauty, for it behoveth not that so handsome a girl as you are abide without a lover.' To this Jeannette made answer, 'Madam, you took me from my father's poverty and have reared me as a daughter, wherefore it behoveth me to do your every pleasure; but in this I will nowise comply with you, and therein methinketh I do well. If it please you give me a husband, him do I purpose to love, but none other; for that, since of the inheritance of my ancestors nought is left me save only honour, this latter I mean to keep and preserve as long as life shall endure to me.'

This speech seemed to the lady very contrary to that whereto she thought to come for the keeping of her promise to her son,—albeit, like a discreet woman as she was, she inwardly much commended the damsel therefor,—and she said, 'How now, Jeannette? If our lord the king, who is a young cavalier, as thou art a very fair damsel, would fain have some easance of thy love, wouldst thou deny it to him?' Whereto she answered forthright, 'The king might do me violence, but of my consent he should never avail to have aught of me save what was honourable.' The lady, seeing how she was minded, left parleying with her and bethought herself to put her to the proof; wherefore she told her son that, whenas he should be recovered, she would contrive to get her alone with him in a chamber, so he might make shift to have his pleasure of her, saying that it appeared to her unseemly that she should, procuress-wise, plead for her son and solicit her own maid.

With this the young man was nowise content and presently waxed grievously worse, which when his mother saw, she opened her mind to Jeannette, but, finding her more constant than ever, recounted what she had done to her husband, and he and she resolved of one accord, grievous though it seemed to them, to give her to him to wife, choosing rather to have their son alive with a wife unsorted to his quality than dead without any; and so, after much parley, they did; whereat Jeannette was exceeding content and with a devout heart rendered thanks to God, who had not forgotten her; but for all that she never avouched herself other than the daughter of a Picard. As for the young man, he presently recovered and celebrating his nuptials, the gladdest man alive, proceeded to lead a merry life with his bride.

Meanwhile, Perrot, who had been left in Wales with the King of England's marshal, waxed likewise in favour with his lord and grew up very goodly of his person and doughty as any man in the island, insomuch that neither in tourneying nor jousting nor in any other act of arms was there any in the land who could cope with him; wherefore he was everywhere known and famous under the name of Perrot the Picard. And even as God had not forgotten his sister, so on like wise He showed that He had him also in mind; for that a pestilential sickness, being come into those parts, carried off well nigh half the people thereof, besides that most part of those who survived fled for fear into other lands; wherefore the whole country appeared desert. In this mortality, the marshal his lord and his lady and only son, together with many others, brothers and nephews and kinsmen, all died, nor was any left of all his house save a daughter, just husband-ripe, and Perrot, with sundry other serving folk. The pestilence being somewhat abated, the young lady, with the approof and by the counsel of some few gentlemen of the country[8] left alive, took Perrot, for that he was a man of worth and prowess, to husband and made him lord of all that had fallen to her by inheritance; nor was it long ere the King of England, hearing the marshal to be dead and knowing the worth of Perrot the Picard, substituted him in the dead man's room and made him his marshal. This, in brief, is what came of the two innocent children of the Count of Antwerp, left by him for lost.

Eighteen years were now passed since the count's flight from Paris, when, as he abode in Ireland, having suffered many things in a very sorry way of life, there took him a desire to learn, as he might, what was come of his children. Wherefore, seeing himself altogether changed of favour from that which he was wont to be and feeling himself, for long exercise, grown more robust of his person than he had been when young and abiding in ease and idlesse, he took leave of him with whom he had so long abidden and came, poor and ill enough in case, to England. Thence he betook himself whereas he had left Perrot and found him a marshal and a great lord and saw him robust and goodly of person; the which was mighty pleasing unto him, but he would not make himself known to him till he should have learned how it was with Jeannette. Accordingly, he set out and stayed not till he came to London, where, cautiously enquiring of the lady with whom he had left his daughter and of her condition, he found Jeannette married to her son, which greatly rejoiced him and he counted all his past adversity a little thing, since he had found his children again alive and in good case.

Then, desirous of seeing Jeannette, he began beggarwise, to haunt the neighbourhood of her house, where one day Jamy Lamiens, (for so was Jeannette's husband called,) espying him and having compassion on him, for that he saw him old and poor, bade one of his servants bring him in and give him to eat for the love of God, which the man readily did. Now Jeannette had had several children by Jamy, whereof the eldest was no more than eight years old, and they were the handsomest and sprightliest children in the world. When they saw the count eat, they came one and all about him and began to caress him, as if, moved by some occult virtue, they divined him to be their grandfather. He, knowing them for his grandchildren, fell to fondling and making much of them, wherefore the children would not leave him, albeit he who had charge of their governance called them. Jeannette, hearing this, issued forth of a chamber therenigh and coming whereas the count was, chid them amain and threatened to beat them, an they did not what their governor willed. The children began to weep and say that they would fain abide with that honest man, who loved them better than their governor, whereat both the lady and the count laughed. Now the latter had risen, nowise as a father, but as a poor man, to do honour to his daughter, as to a mistress, and seeing her, felt a marvellous pleasure at his heart. But she nor then nor after knew him any whit, for that he was beyond measure changed from what he was used to be, being grown old and hoar and bearded and lean and swart, and appeared altogether another man than the count.

The lady then, seeing that the children were unwilling to leave him and wept, when she would have them go away, bade their governor let them be awhile and the children thus being with the good man, it chanced that Jamy's father returned and heard from their governor what had passed, whereupon quoth the marshal, who held Jeannette in despite, 'Let them be, God give them ill-luck! They do but hark back to that whence they sprang. They come by their mother of a vagabond and therefore it is no wonder if they are fain to herd with vagabonds.' The count heard these words and was mightily chagrined thereat; nevertheless, he shrugged his shoulders and put up with the affront, even as he had put up with many others. Jamy, hearing how the children had welcomed the honest man, to wit, the count, albeit it misliked him, nevertheless so loved them that, rather than see them weep, he commanded that, if the good man chose to abide there in any capacity, he should be received into his service. The count answered that he would gladly abide there, but he knew not to do aught other than tend horses, whereto he had been used all his lifetime. A horse was accordingly assigned to him and when he had cared for it, he busied himself with making sport for the children.

Whilst fortune handled the Count of Antwerp and his children on such wise as hath been set out, it befell that the King of France, after many truces made with the Germans, died and his son, whose wife was she through whom the count had been banished, was crowned in his place; and no sooner was the current truce expired than he again began a very fierce war. To his aid the King of England, as a new-made kinsman, despatched much people, under the commandment of Perrot his marshal and Jamy Lamiens, son of the other marshal, and with them went the good man, to wit, the count, who, without being recognized of any, abode a pretty while with the army in the guise of a horseboy, and there, like a man of mettle as he was, wrought good galore, more than was required of him, both with counsels and with deeds.

During the war, it came to pass that the Queen of France fell grievously sick and feeling herself nigh unto death, contrite for all her sins, confessed herself unto the Archbishop of Rouen, who was held of all a very holy and good man. Amongst her other sins, she related to him that which the Count of Antwerp had most wrongfully suffered through her; nor was she content to tell it to him alone, nay, but before many other men of worth she recounted all as it had passed, beseeching them so to do with the king that the count, an he were on life, or, if not, one of his children, should be restored to his estate; after which she lingered not long, but, departing this life, was honourably buried. Her confession, being reported to the king, moved him, after he had heaved divers sighs of regret for the wrong done to the nobleman, to let cry throughout all the army and in many other parts, that whoso should give him news of the Count of Antwerp or of either of his children should for each be wonder-well guerdoned of him, for that he held him, upon the queen's confession, innocent of that for which he had gone into exile and was minded to restore him to his first estate and more.

The count, in his guise of a horseboy, hearing this and being assured that it was the truth,[9] betook himself forthright to Jamy Lamiens and prayed him go with him to Perrot, for that he had a mind to discover to them that which the king went seeking. All three being then met together, quoth the count to Perrot, who had it already in mind to discover himself, 'Perrot, Jamy here hath thy sister to wife nor ever had any dowry with her; wherefore, that thy sister may not go undowered, I purpose that he and none other shall, by making thee known as the son of the Count of Antwerp, have this great reward that the king promiseth for thee and for Violante, thy sister and his wife, and myself, who am the Count of Antwerp and your father.' Perrot, hearing this and looking steadfastly upon him, presently knew him and cast himself, weeping, at his feet and embraced him, saying, 'Father mine, you are dearly welcome.' Jamy, hearing first what the count said and after seeing what Perrot did, was overcome at once with such wonderment and such gladness that he scarce knew what he should do. However, after awhile, giving credence to the former's speech and sore ashamed for the injurious words he had whiles used to the hostler-count, he let himself fall, weeping, at his feet and humbly besought him pardon of every past affront, the which the count, having raised him to his feet, graciously accorded him.

Then, after they had all three discoursed awhile of each one's various adventures and wept and rejoiced together amain, Perrot and Jamy would have reclad the count, who would on nowise suffer it, but willed that Jamy, having first assured himself of the promised guerdon, should, the more to shame the king, present him to the latter in that his then plight and in his groom's habit. Accordingly, Jamy, followed by the count and Perrot, presented himself before the king, and offered, provided he would guerdon him according to the proclamation made, to produce to him the count and his children. The king promptly let bring for all three a guerdon marvellous in Jamy's eyes and commanded that he should be free to carry it off, whenas he should in very deed produce the count and his children, as he promised. Jamy, then, turning himself about and putting forward the count his horseboy and Perrot, said, 'My lord, here be the father and the son; the daughter, who is my wife and who is not here, with God's aid you shall soon see.'

The king, hearing this, looked at the count and albeit he was sore changed from that which he was used to be, yet, after he had awhile considered him, he knew him and well nigh with tears in his eyes raised him—for that he was on his knees before him—to his feet and kissed and embraced him. Perrot, also, he graciously received and commanded that the count should incontinent be furnished anew with clothes and servants and horses and harness, according as his quality required, which was straightway done. Moreover, he entreated Jamy with exceeding honour and would fain know every particular of his[10] past adventures. Then, Jamy being about to receive the magnificent guerdons appointed him for having discovered the count and his children, the former said to him, 'Take these of the munificence of our lord the king and remember to tell thy father that thy children, his grandchildren and mine, are not by their mother born of a vagabond.' Jamy, accordingly, took the gifts and sent for his wife and mother to Paris, whither came also Perrot's wife; and there they all foregathered in the utmost joyance with the count, whom the king had reinstated in all his good and made greater than he ever was. Then all, with Gautier's leave, returned to their several homes and he until his death abode in Paris more worshipfully than ever."

---

1. *i.e.* a.d. 912, when, upon the death of Louis III, the last prince of the Carlovingian race, Conrad, Duke of Franconia, was elected Emperor and the Empire, which had till then been hereditary in the descendants of Charlemagne, became elective and remained thenceforth in German hands.
2. *Anguersa*, the old form of *Anversa*, Antwerp. All versions that I have seen call Gautier Comte d'*Angers* or *Angiers*, the translators, who forgot or were unaware that Antwerp, as part of Flanders, was then a fief of the French crown, apparently taking it for granted that the mention of the latter city was in error and substituting the name of the ancient capital of Anjou on their own responsibility.
3. *i.e.* of her excuse.
4. Lit. Thou holdest (or judges); but *giudichi* in the text is apparently a mistake for *giudico*.
5. *i.e.* of discernment.
6. Sic (*aggiunsero*); but *semble* should mean "believed, in addition."
7. *i.e.* That the secret might be the better kept.
8. *Paesani*, lit., countrymen; but Boccaccio evidently uses the word in the sense of "vassals."
9. *i.e.* that it was not a snare.
10. *Quære*, the Count's?

⚜ 9 ⚜

THE NINTH STORY

BERNABO OF GENOA, DUPED BY AMBROGIUOLO,
LOSETH HIS GOOD AND COMMANDETH THAT HIS
INNOCENT WIFE BE PUT TO DEATH. SHE ESCAPETH
AND SERVETH THE SOLDAN IN A MAN'S HABIT. HERE
SHE LIGHTETH UPON THE DECEIVER OF HER
HUSBAND AND BRINGETH THE LATTER TO
ALEXANDRIA, WHERE, HER TRADUCER BEING
PUNISHED, SHE RESUMETH WOMAN'S APPAREL AND
RETURNETH TO GENOA WITH HER HUSBAND, RICH

ELISA HAVING FURNISHED her due with her pitiful story, Filomena the queen, who was tall and goodly of person and smiling and agreeable of aspect beyond any other of her sex, collecting herself, said, "Needs must the covenant with Dioneo be observed, wherefore, there remaining none other to tell than he and I, I will tell my story first, and he, for that he asked it as a favour, shall be the last to speak." So saying, she began thus, "There is a proverb oftentimes cited among the common folk to the effect that the deceiver abideth[1] at the feet of the deceived; the which meseemeth may by no reasoning be shown to be true, an it approve not itself by actual occurrences. Wherefore, whilst ensuing the appointed theme, it hath occurred to me, dearest ladies, to show you, at the same time, that this is true, even as it is said; nor should it mislike you to hear it, so you may know how to keep yourselves from deceivers.

There were once at Paris in an inn certain very considerable Italian merchants, who were come thither, according to their usance, some on one occasion and some on another, and having one evening among others supped all together merrily, they fell to devising of divers matters, and passing from one discourse to another, they came at last to speak of their wives, whom they had left at home, and one said jestingly, 'I know not how mine doth; but this I know well, that, whenas there cometh to my hand here any lass that pleaseth me, I leave on one side the love I bear my wife and take of the other such pleasure as I may.' 'And I,' quoth another, 'do likewise, for that if I believe that my wife pusheth her fortunes [in my absence,] she doth it, and if I believe it not, still she doth it; wherefore tit for tat be it; an ass still getteth as good as he giveth.'[2] A third, following on, came well nigh to the same conclusion, and in brief all seemed agreed upon this point, that the wives they left behind had no mind to lose time in their husbands' absence. One only, who hight Bernabo Lomellini of Genoa, maintained the contrary, avouching that he, by special grace of God, had a lady to wife who was belike the most accomplished woman of all Italy in all those qualities which a lady, nay, even (in great part) in those which a knight or an esquire, should have; for that she was fair of favour and yet in her first youth and adroit and robust of her person; nor was there aught that pertaineth unto a woman, such as works of broidery in silk and the like, but she did it better than any other of her sex. Moreover, said he, there was no sewer, or in other words, no serving-man, alive who served better or more deftly at a nobleman's table than did she, for that she was very well bred and exceeding wise and discreet. He after went on to extol her as knowing better how to ride a horse and fly a hawk, to read and write and cast a reckoning than if she were a merchant; and thence, after many other commendations, coming to that whereof it had been discoursed among them, he avouched with an oath that there could be found no honester nor chaster woman than she; wherefore he firmly believed that, should he abide half a score years, or even always, from home, she would never incline to the least levity with another man. Among the merchants who discoursed thus was a young man called Ambrogiuolo of Piacenza, who fell to making the greatest mock in the world of this last commendation bestowed by Bernabo upon his wife and asked him scoffingly if the emperor had granted him that privilege over and above all other men. Bernabo, some little nettled, replied that not the emperor, but God, who could somewhat more than the emperor, had vouchsafed him the favour in question. Whereupon quoth Ambrogiuolo, 'Bernabo, I doubt not a whit but that thou thinkest to say sooth; but meseemeth thou hast paid little regard to the nature of things; for that, hadst thou taken heed thereunto, I deem thee not so dull of wit but thou wouldst have noted therein certain matters which had made thee speak more circumspectly on this subject. And that thou mayst not think that we, who have spoken much at large of our wives, believe that we have wives other or otherwise made than thine, but mayst see that we spoke thus, moved by natural perception, I will e'en reason with thee a little on this matter. I have always understood man to be the noblest animal created of God among mortals, and after him, woman; but man, as is commonly believed and as is seen by works, is the more perfect and having more perfection, must without fail have more of firmness and constancy, for that women universally are more changeable; the reason whereof might be shown by many natural arguments, which for the present I purpose to leave be. If then man be of more stability and yet cannot keep himself, let alone from complying with a woman who soliciteth him, but even from desiring one who pleaseth him, nay more, from doing what he can, so he may avail to be with her,—and if this betide him not once a month, but a thousand times a day,—what canst thou expect a woman, naturally unstable, to avail against the prayers, the blandishments, the gifts and a thousand other means which an adroit man, who loveth her, will use? Thinkest thou she can hold out? Certes, how much soever thou mayst affirm it, I believe not that thou believest it; and thou thyself sayst that thy wife is a woman and that she is of flesh and blood, as are other women. If this be so, those same desires must be hers and the same powers that are in other women to resist these natural appetites; wherefore, however honest she be, it is possible she may do that which other women do; and nothing that is possible she be so peremptorily denied nor the contrary thereof affirmed with such rigour as thou dost.' To which Bernabo made answer, saying, 'I am a merchant, and not a philosopher, and as a merchant I will answer; and I say that I acknowledge that what thou sayst may happen to foolish women in whom there is no shame; but those who are discreet are so careful of their honour that for the guarding thereof they become stronger than men, who reck not of this; and of those thus fashioned is my wife.' 'Indeed,' rejoined Ambrogiuolo, 'if, for every time they occupy themselves with toys of this kind, there sprouted from their foreheads a horn to bear witness of that which they have done, there be few, I believe, who would incline thereto; but, far from the horn sprouting, there appeareth neither trace nor token thereof in those who are discreet, and shame and soil of honour consist not but in things discovered; wherefore, whenas they may secretly, they do it, or, if they forebear, it is for stupidity. And have thou this for certain that she alone is chaste, who hath either never been solicited of any or who, having herself solicited, hath not been hearkened. And although I know by natural and true reasons that it is e'en as I say, yet should I not speak thereof with so full an assurance, had I not many a time and with many women made essay thereof. And this I tell thee, that, were I near this most sanctified wife of thine, I warrant me I would in brief space of time bring her to that which I have already gotten of other women.' Whereupon quoth Bernabo, 'Disputing with words might be prolonged without end; thou wouldst say and I should say, and in the end it would all amount to nothing. But, since thou wilt have it that all women are so compliant and that thine address is such, I am content, so I may certify thee of my wife's honesty, to have my head cut off, and thou canst anywise avail to bring her to do thy pleasure in aught of the kind; and if thou fail thereof, I will have thee lose no otherwhat than a thousand gold florins.' 'Bernabo,' replied Ambrogiuolo, who was now grown heated over the dispute, 'I know not what I should do with thy blood, if I won the wager; but, an thou have a mind to see proof of that which I have advanced, do thou stake five thousand gold florins of thy monies, which should be less dear to thee than thy head, against a thousand of mine, and whereas thou settest no limit [of time,] I will e'en bind myself to go to Genoa and within three months from the day of my departure hence to have done my will of thy wife and to bring back with me, in proof thereof, sundry of her most precious things and such and so many tokens that thou shalt thyself confess it to be truth, so verily thou wilt pledge me thy faith not to come to Genoa within that term nor write her aught of the matter.' Bernabo said that it liked him well and albeit the other merchants endeavoured to hinder the affair, foreseeing that sore mischief might come thereof, the two merchants' minds were so inflamed that, in despite of the rest, they bound themselves one to other by express writings under their hands. This done, Bernabo abode behind, whilst Ambrogiuolo, as quickliest he might, betook himself to Genoa. There he abode some days and informing himself with the utmost precaution of the name of the street where the lady dwelt and of her manner of life, understood of her that and more than that which he had heard of her from Bernabo, wherefore himseemed he was come on a fool's errand. However, he presently clapped up an acquaintance with a poor woman, who was much about the house and whose great well-wisher the lady was, and availing not to induce her to aught else, he debauched her with money and prevailed with her to bring him, in a chest wroughten after a fashion of his own, not only into the house, but into the gentlewoman's very bedchamber, where, according to the ordinance given her of him, the good woman commended it to her care for some days, as if she had a mind to go somewhither. The chest, then being left in the chamber and the night come, Ambrogiuolo, what time he judged the lady to be asleep, opened the chest with certain engines of his and came softly out into the chamber, where there was a light burning, with whose aid he proceeded to observe the ordinance of the place, the paintings and every other notable thing that was therein and fixed them in his memory. Then, drawing near the bed and perceiving that the lady and a little girl, who was with her, were fast asleep, he softly altogether uncovered the former and found that she was as fair, naked, as clad, but saw no sign about her that he might carry away, save one, to wit, a mole which she had under the left pap and about which were sundry little hairs as red as gold. This noted he covered her softly up again, albeit, seeing her so fair, he was tempted to adventure his life and lay himself by her side; however, for that he had heard her to be so obdurate and uncomplying in matters of this kind, he hazarded not himself, but, abiding at his leisure in the chamber the most part of the night, took from one of her coffers a purse and a night-rail, together with sundry rings and girdles, and laying them all in his chest, returned thither himself and shut himself up therein as before; and on this wise he did two nights, without the lady being ware of aught. On the third day the good woman came back for the chest, according to the given ordinance, and carried it off whence she had taken it, whereupon Ambrogiuolo came out and having rewarded her according to promise, returned, as quickliest he might, with the things aforesaid, to Paris, where he arrived before the term appointed. There he summoned the merchants who had been present at the dispute and the laying of the wager and declared, in Bernabo's presence, that he had won the wager laid between them, for that he had accomplished that whereof he had vaunted himself; and to prove this to be true, he first described the fashion of the chamber and the paintings thereof and after showed the things he had brought with him thence, avouching that he had them of herself. Bernabo confessed the chamber to be as he had said and owned, moreover, that he recognized the things in question as being in truth his wife's; but said that he might have learned from one of the servants of the house the fashion of the chamber and have gotten the things in like manner; wherefore, an he had nought else to say, himseemed not that this should suffice to prove him to have won. Whereupon quoth Ambrogiuolo, 'In sooth this should suffice, but, since thou wilt have me say more, I will say it. I tell thee that Madam Ginevra thy wife hath under her left pap a pretty big mole, about which are maybe half a dozen little hairs as red as gold.' When Bernabo heard this, it was as if he had gotten a knife-thrust in the heart, such anguish did he feel, and though he had said not a word, his countenance, being all changed, gave very manifest token that what Ambrogiuolo said was true. Then, after awhile, 'Gentlemen,' quoth he, 'that which Ambrogiuolo saith is true; wherefore, he having won, let him come whenassoever it pleaseth him and he shall be paid.' Accordingly, on the ensuing day Ambrogiuolo was paid in full and Bernabo, departing Paris, betook himself to Genoa with fell intent against the lady. When he drew near the city, he would not enter therein, but lighted down a good score miles away at a country house of his and despatched one of his servants, in whom he much trusted, to Genoa with two horses and letters under his hand, advising his wife that he had returned and bidding her come to him; and he privily charged the man, whenas he should be with the lady in such place as should seem best to him, to put her to death without pity and return to him. The servant accordingly repaired to Genoa and delivering the letters and doing his errand, was received with great rejoicing by the lady, who on the morrow took horse with him and set out for their country house. As they fared on together, discoursing of one thing and another, they came to a very deep and lonely valley, beset with high rocks and trees, which seeming to the servant a place wherein he might, with assurance for himself, do his lord's commandment, he pulled out his knife and taking the lady by the arm, said, 'Madam, commend your soul to God, for needs must you die, without faring farther.' The lady, seeing the knife and hearing these words, was all dismayed and said, 'Mercy, for God's sake! Ere thou slay me, tell me wherein I have offended thee, that thou wouldst put me to death.' 'Madam,' answered the man, 'me you have nowise offended; but wherein you have offended your husband I know not, save that he hath commanded me slay you by the way, without having any pity upon you, threatening me, an I did it not, to have me hanged by the neck. You know well how much I am beholden to him and how I may not gainsay him in aught that he may impose upon me; God knoweth it irketh me for you, but I can no otherwise.' Whereupon quoth the lady, weeping, 'Alack, for God's sake, consent not to become the murderer of one who hath never wronged thee, to serve another! God who knoweth all knoweth that I never did aught for which I should receive such a recompense from my husband. But let that be; thou mayst, an thou wilt, at once content God and thy master and me, on this wise; to wit, that thou take these my clothes and give me but thy doublet and a hood and with the former return to my lord and thine and tell him that thou hast slain me; and I swear to thee, by that life which thou wilt have bestowed on me, that I will remove hence and get me gone into a country whence never shall any news of me win either to him or to thee or into these parts.' The servant, who was loath to slay her, was lightly moved to compassion; wherefore he took her clothes and give her a sorry doublet of his and a hood, leaving her sundry monies she had with her. Then praying her depart the country, he left her in the valley and afoot and betook himself to his master, to whom he avouched that not only was his commandment accomplished, but that he had left the lady's dead body among a pack of wolves, and Bernabo presently returned to Genoa, where the thing becoming known, he was much blamed. As for the lady, she abode alone and disconsolate till nightfall, when she disguised herself as most she might and repaired to a village hard by, where, having gotten from an old woman that which she needed, she fitted the doublet to her shape and shortening it, made a pair of linen breeches of her shift; then, having cut her hair and altogether transformed herself in the guise of a sailor, she betook herself to the sea-shore, where, as chance would have it, she found a Catalan gentleman, by name Senor Encararch, who had landed at Alba from a ship he had in the offing, to refresh himself at a spring there. With him she entered into parley and engaging with him as a servant, embarked on board the ship, under the name of Sicurano da Finale. There, being furnished by the gentleman with better clothes, she proceeded to serve him so well and so aptly that she became in the utmost favour with him. No great while after it befell that the Catalan made a voyage to Alexandria with a lading of his and carrying thither certain peregrine falcons for the Soldan, presented them to him. The Soldan, having once and again entertained him at meat and noting with approof the fashions of Sicurano, who still went serving him, begged him[3] of his master, who yielded him to him, although it irked him to do it, and Sicurano, in a little while, by his good behaviour, gained the love and favour of the Soldan, even as he had gained that of the Catalan. Wherefore, in process of time, it befell that,—the time coming for a great assemblage, in the guise of a fair, of merchants, both Christian and Saracen, which was wont at a certain season of the year to be held in Acre, a town under the seignory of the Soldan, and to which, in order that the merchants and their merchandise might rest secure, the latter was still used to despatch, besides other his officers, some one of his chief men, with troops, to look to the guard,—he bethought himself to send Sicurano, who was by this well versed in the language of the country, on this service; and so he did. Sicurano accordingly came to Acre as governor and captain of the guard of the merchants and their merchandise and there well and diligently doing that which pertained to his office and going round looking about him, saw many merchants there, Sicilians and Pisans and Genoese and Venetians and other Italians, with whom he was fain to make acquaintance, in remembrance of his country. It befell, one time amongst others, that, having lighted down at the shop of certain Venetian merchants, he espied among other trinkets, a purse and a girdle, which he straightway knew for having been his and marvelled thereat; but, without making any sign, he carelessly asked to whom they pertained and if they were for sale. Now Ambrogiuolo of Piacenza was come thither with much merchandise on board a Venetian ship and hearing the captain of the guard ask whose the trinkets were, came forward and said, laughing, 'Sir, the things are mine and I do not sell them; but, if they please you, I will gladly give them to you.' Sicurano, seeing him laugh, misdoubted he had recognized him by some gesture of his; but yet, keeping a steady countenance, he said, 'Belike thou laughest to see me, a soldier, go questioning of these women's toys?' 'Sir,' answered Ambrogiuolo, 'I laugh not at that; nay, but at the way I came by them.' 'Marry, then,' said Sicurano, 'an it be not unspeakable, tell me how thou gottest them, so God give thee good luck.' Quoth Ambrogiuolo, 'Sir, a gentlewoman of Genoa, hight Madam Ginevra, wife of Bernabo Lomellini, gave me these things, with certain others, one night that I lay with her, and prayed me keep them for the love of her. Now I laugh for that I mind me of the simplicity of Bernabo, who was fool enough to lay five thousand florins to one that I would not bring his wife to do my pleasure; the which I did and won the wager; whereupon he, who should rather have punished himself for his stupidity than her for doing that which all women do, returned from Paris to Genoa and there, by what I have since heard, caused her put to death.' Sicurano, hearing this, understood forthwith what was the cause of Bernabo's anger against his wife[4] and manifestly perceiving this fellow to have been the occasion of all her ills, determined not to let him go unpunished therefor. Accordingly he feigned to be greatly diverted with the story and artfully clapped up a strait acquaintance with him, insomuch that, the fair being ended, Ambrogiuolo, at his instance, accompanied him, with all his good, to Alexandria. Here Sicurano let build him a warehouse and lodged in his hands store of his own monies; and Ambrogiuolo, foreseeing great advantage to himself, willingly took up his abode there. Meanwhile, Sicurano, careful to make Bernabo clear of his[5] innocence, rested not till, by means of certain great Genoese merchants who were then in Alexandria, he had, on some plausible occasion of his[6] own devising, caused him come thither, where finding him in poor enough case, he had him privily entertained by a friend of his[7] against it should seem to him[8] time to do that which he purposed. Now he had already made Ambrogiuolo recount his story before the Soldan for the latter's diversion; but seeing Bernabo there and thinking there was no need to use farther delay in the matter, he took occasion to procure the Soldan to have Ambrogiuolo and Bernabo brought before him and in the latter's presence, to extort from the former, by dint of severity, an it might not easily be done [by other means,] the truth of that whereof he vaunted himself concerning Bernabo's wife. Accordingly, they both being come, the Soldan, in the presence of many, with a stern countenance commanded Ambrogiuolo to tell the truth how he had won of Bernabo the five thousand gold florins; and Sicurano himself, in whom he most trusted, with a yet angrier aspect, threatened him with the most grievous torments, an he told it not; whereupon Ambrogiuolo, affrighted on one side and another and in a measure constrained, in the presence of Bernabo and many others, plainly related everything, even as it passed, expecting no worse punishment therefor than the restitution of the five thousand gold florins and of the stolen trinkets. He having spoken, Sicurano, as he were the Soldan's minister in the matter, turned to Bernabo and said to him, 'And thou, what didst thou to thy lady for this lie?' Whereto Bernabo replied, 'Overcome with wrath for the loss of my money and with resentment for the shame which meseemed I had gotten from my wife, I caused a servant of mine put her to death, and according to that which he reported to me, she was straightway devoured by a multitude of wolves,' These things said in the presence of the Soldan and all heard and apprehended of him, albeit he knew not yet to what end Sicurano, who had sought and ordered this, would fain come, the latter said to him, 'My lord, you may very clearly see how much reason yonder poor lady had to vaunt herself of her gallant and her husband, for that the former at once bereaved her of honour, marring her fair fame with lies, and despoiled her husband, whilst the latter more credulous of others' falsehoods than of the truth which he might by long experience have known, caused her to be slain and eaten of wolves; and moreover, such is the goodwill and the love borne her by the one and the other that, having long abidden with her, neither of them knoweth her. But that you may the better apprehend that which each of these hath deserved, I will,—so but you vouchsafe me, of special favour to punish the deceiver and pardon the dupe,—e'en cause her come hither into your and their presence.' The Soldan, disposed in the matter altogether to comply with Sicurano's wishes, answered that he would well and bade him produce the lady; whereat Bernabo marvelled exceedingly, for that he firmly believed her to be dead, whilst Ambrogiuolo, now divining his danger, began to be in fear of worse than paying of monies and knew not whether more to hope or to fear from the coming of the lady, but awaited her appearance with the utmost amazement. The Soldan, then, having accorded Sicurano his wish, the latter threw himself, weeping, on his knees before him and putting off, as it were at one and the same time, his manly voice and masculine demeanour, said, 'My lord, I am the wretched misfortunate Ginevra, who have these six years gone wandering in man's disguise about the world, having been foully and wickedly aspersed by this traitor Ambrogiuolo and given by yonder cruel and unjust man to one of his servants to be slain and eaten of wolves.' Then, tearing open the fore part of her clothes and showing her breast, she discovered herself to the Soldan and all else who were present and after, turning to Ambrogiuolo, indignantly demanded of him when he had ever lain with her, according as he had aforetime boasted; but he, now knowing her and fallen well nigh dumb for shame, said nothing. The Soldan, who had always held her a man, seeing and hearing this, fell into such a wonderment that he more than once misdoubted that which he saw and heard to be rather a dream than true. However, after his amazement had abated, apprehending the truth of the matter, he lauded to the utmost the life and fashions of Ginevra, till then called Sicurano, and extolled her constancy and virtue; and letting bring her very sumptuous woman's apparel and women to attend her, he pardoned Bernabo, in accordance with her request, the death he had merited, whilst the latter, recognizing her, cast himself at her feet, weeping and craving forgiveness, which she, ill worthy as he was thereof, graciously accorded him and raising him to his feet, embraced him tenderly, as her husband. Then the Soldan commanded that Ambrogiuolo should incontinent be bound to a stake and smeared with honey and exposed to the sun in some high place of the city, nor should ever be loosed thence till such time as he should fall of himself; and so was it done. After this he commanded that all that had belonged to him should be given to the lady, the which was not so little but that it outvalued ten thousand doubloons. Moreover, he let make a very goodly banquet, wherein he entertained Bernabo with honour, as Madam Ginevra's husband, and herself as a very valiant lady and gave her, in jewels and vessels of gold and silver and monies, that which amounted to better[9] than other ten thousand doubloons. Then, the banquet over, he caused equip them a ship and gave them leave to return at their pleasure to Genoa, whither accordingly they returned with great joyance and exceeding rich; and there they were received with the utmost honour, especially Madam Ginevra, who was of all believed to be dead and who, while she lived, was still reputed of great worth and virtue. As for Ambrogiuolo, being that same day bounded to the stake and anointed with honey, he was, to his exceeding torment, not only slain, but devoured, of the flies and wasps and gadflies, wherewith that country aboundeth, even to the bones, which latter, waxed white and hanging by the sinews, being left unremoved, long bore witness of his villainy to all who saw them. And on this wise did the deceiver abide at the feet of the deceived."

---

1. *Rimane.* The verb *rimanere* is constantly used by the old Italian writers in the sense of "to become," so that the proverb cited in the text may be read "The deceiver becometh (*i.e.* findeth himself in the end) at the feet (*i.e.* at the mercy) of the person deceived."
2. Lit. Whatsoever an ass giveth against a wall, such he receiveth (*Quale asino da in parete, tal riceve*). I cannot find any satisfactory explanation of this proverbial saying, which may be rendered in two ways, according as *quale* and *tale* are taken as relative to a thing or a person. The probable reference seems to be to the circumstance of an ass making water against a wall, so that his urine returns to him.
3. From this point until the final discovery of her true sex, the heroine is spoken of in the masculine gender, as became her assumed name and habit.
4. Here Boccaccio uses the feminine pronoun, immediately afterward resuming the masculine form in speaking of Sicurano.
5. *i.e.* her.
6. *i.e.* her.
7. *i.e.* her.
8. *i.e.* her.
9. Sic (*meglio*).

🙰 10 🙰

THE TENTH STORY

PAGANINO OF MONACO STEALETH AWAY THE WIFE OF
MESSER RICCIARDO DI CHINZICA, WHO, LEARNING
WHERE SHE IS, GOETH THITHER AND MAKING
FRIENDS WITH PAGANINO, DEMANDETH HER AGAIN
OF HIM. THE LATTER CONCEDETH HER TO HIM, AN
SHE WILL; BUT SHE REFUSETH TO RETURN WITH
HIM AND MESSER RICCIARDO DYING, SHE BECOMETH
THE WIFE OF PAGANINO

EACH OF THE honourable company highly commended for goodly the story told by their queen, especially Dioneo, with whom alone for that present day it now rested to tell, and who, after many praises bestowed upon the preceding tale, said, "Fair ladies, one part of the queen's story hath caused me change counsel of telling you one that was in my mind, and determine to tell you another,—and that is the stupidity of Bernabo (albeit good betided him thereof) and of all others who give themselves to believe that which he made a show of believing and who, to wit, whilst going about the world, diverting themselves now with this woman and now with that, imagine that the ladies left at home abide with their hands in their girdles, as if we knew not, we who are born and reared among the latter, unto what they are fain. In telling you this story, I shall at once show you how great is the folly of these folk and how greater yet is that of those who, deeming themselves more potent than nature herself, think by dint of sophistical inventions[1] to avail unto that which is beyond their power and study to bring others to that which they themselves are, whenas the complexion of those on whom they practise brooketh it not.

There was, then, in Pisa a judge, by name Messer Ricciardo di Chinzica, more gifted with wit than with bodily strength, who, thinking belike to satisfy a wife by the same means which served him to despatch his studies and being very rich, sought with no little diligence to have a fair and young lady to wife; whereas, had he but known to counsel himself as he counselled others, he should have shunned both the one and the other. The thing came to pass according to his wish, for Messer Lotto Gualandi gave him to wife a daughter of his, Bartolomea by name, one of the fairest and handsomest young ladies of Pisa, albeit there be few there that are not very lizards to look upon. The judge accordingly brought her home with the utmost pomp and having held a magnificent wedding, made shift the first night to hand her one venue for the consummation of the marriage, but came within an ace of making a stalemate of it, whereafter, lean and dry and scant of wind as he was, it behoved him on the morrow bring himself back to life with malmsey and restorative confections and other remedies. Thenceforward, being now a better judge of his own powers than he was, he fell to teaching his wife a calendar fit for children learning to read and belike made aforetime at Ravenna,[2] for that, according to what he feigned to her, there was no day in the year but was sacred not to one saint only, but to many, in reverence of whom he showed by divers reasons that man and wife should abstain from carnal conversation; and to these be added, to boot, fast days and Emberdays and the vigils of the Apostles and of a thousand other saints and Fridays and Saturdays and Lord's Day and all Lent and certain seasons of the moon and store of other exceptions, conceiving belike that it behoved to keep holiday with women in bed like as he did bytimes whilst pleading in the courts of civil law. This fashion (to the no small chagrin of the lady, whom he handled maybe once a month, and hardly that) he followed a great while, still keeping strait watch over her, lest peradventure some other should teach her to know working-days, even as he had taught her holidays. Things standing thus, it chanced that, the heat being great and Messer Ricciardo having a mind to go a-pleasuring to a very fair country-seat he had, near Monte Nero, and there abide some days to take the air, he betook himself thither, carrying with him his fair lady. There sojourning, to give her some diversion, he caused one day fish and they went out to sea in two boats, he in one with the fishermen, and she in another with other ladies. The sport luring them on, they drifted some miles out to sea, well nigh without perceiving it, and whilst they were intent upon their diversion, there came up of a sudden a galliot belonging to Paganino da Mare, a famous corsair of those days. The latter, espying the boats, made for them, nor could they flee so fast but he overtook that in which were the women and seeing therein the judge's fair lady, he carried her aboard the galliot, in full sight of Messer Ricciardo, who was now come to land, and made off without recking of aught else. When my lord judge, who was so jealous that he misdoubted of the very air, saw this, it booteth not to ask if he was chagrined; and in vain, both at Pisa and otherwhere, did he complain of the villainy of the corsairs, for that he knew not who had taken his wife from him nor whither he had carried her. As for Paganino, finding her so fair, he deemed himself in luck and having no wife, resolved to keep her for himself. Accordingly, seeing her weeping sore, he studied to comfort her with soft words till nightfall, when, his calendar having dropped from his girdle and saints' days and holidays gone clean out of his head, he fell to comforting her with deeds, himseeming that words had availed little by day; and after such a fashion did he console her that, ere they came to Monaco, the judge and his ordinances had altogether escaped her mind and she began to lead the merriest of lives with Paganino. The latter carried her to Monaco and there, over and above the consolations with which he plied her night and day, he entreated her honourably as his wife. After awhile it came to Messer Ricciardo's ears where his wife was and he, being possessed with the most ardent desire to have her again and bethinking himself that none other might thoroughly suffice to do what was needful to that end, resolved to go thither himself, determined to spend any quantity of money for her ransom. Accordingly he set out by sea and coming to Monaco, there both saw and was seen of the lady, who told it to Paganino that same evening and acquainted him with her intent. Next morning Messer Ricciardo, seeing Paganino, accosted him and quickly clapped up a great familiarity and friendship with him, whilst the other feigned not to know him and waited to see at what he aimed. Accordingly, whenas it seemed to him time, Messer Ricciardo discovered to him, as best and most civilly he knew, the occasion of his coming and prayed him take what he pleased and restore him the lady. To which Paganino made answer with a cheerful countenance, 'Sir, you are welcome, and to answer you briefly, I say thus; it is true I have a young lady in my house, if she be your wife or another's I know not, for that I know you not nor indeed her, save in so much as she hath abidden awhile with me. If you be, as you say, her husband, I will, since you seem to me a civil gentleman, carry you to her and I am assured that she will know you right well. If she say it is as you avouch and be willing to go with you, you shall, for the sake of your civility, give me what you yourself will to her ransom; but, an it be not so, you would do ill to seek to take her from me, for that I am a young man and can entertain a woman as well as another, and especially such an one as she, who is the most pleasing I ever saw.' Quoth Messer Ricciardo, 'For certain she is my wife, an thou bring me where she is, thou shalt soon see it; for she will incontinent throw herself on my neck; wherefore I ask no better than that it be as thou proposest.' 'Then,' said Paganino, 'let us be going.' Accordingly they betook themselves to the corsair's house, where he brought the judge into a saloon of his and let call the lady, who issued forth of a chamber, all dressed and tired, and came whereas they were, but accosted Messer Ricciardo no otherwise than as she would any other stranger who might have come home with Paganino. The judge, who looked to have been received by her with the utmost joy, marvelled sore at this and fell a-saying in himself, 'Belike the chagrin and long grief I have suffered, since I lost her, have so changed me that she knoweth me not.' Wherefore he said to her, 'Wife, it hath cost me dear to carry thee a-fishing, for that never was grief felt like that which I have suffered since I lost thee, and now meseemeth thou knowest me not, so distantly dost thou greet me. Seest thou not that I am thine own Messer Ricciardo, come hither to pay that which this gentleman, in whose house we are, shall require to thy ransom and to carry thee away? And he, of his favour, restoreth thee to me for what I will.' The lady turned to him and said, smiling somewhat, 'Speak you to me, sir? Look you mistake me not, for, for my part, I mind me not ever to have seen you.' Quoth Ricciardo, 'Look what thou sayest; consider me well; an thou wilt but recollect thyself, thou wilt see that I am thine own Ricciardo di Chinzica.' 'Sir,' answered the lady, 'you will pardon me; belike it is not so seemly a thing as you imagine for me to look much on you. Nevertheless I have seen enough of you to know that I never before set eyes on you.' Ricciardo, concluding that she did this for fear of Paganino and chose not to confess to knowing him in the latter's presence, besought him of his favour that he might speak with her in a room alone. Paganino replied that he would well, so but he would not kiss her against her will, and bade the lady go with him into a chamber and there hear what he had to say and answer him as it should please her. Accordingly the lady and Messer Ricciardo went into a room apart and as soon as they were seated, the latter began to say, 'Alack, heart of my body, sweet my soul and my hope, knowest thou not thy Ricciardo, who loveth thee more than himself? How can this be? Am I so changed? Prithee, fair mine eye, do but look on me a little.' The lady began to laugh and without letting him say more, replied, 'You may be assured that I am not so scatterbrained but that I know well enough you are Messer Ricciardo di Chinzica, my husband; but, what time I was with you, you showed that you knew me very ill, for that you should have had the sense to see that I was young and lusty and gamesome and should consequently have known that which behoveth unto young ladies, over and above clothes and meat, albeit for shamefastness they name it not; the which how you performed, you know. If the study of the laws was more agreeable to you than your wife, you should not have taken her, albeit it never appeared to me that you were a judge; nay, you seemed to me rather a common crier of saints' days and sacraments and fasts and vigils, so well you knew them. And I tell you this, that, had you suffered the husbandmen who till your lands keep as many holidays as you allowed him who had the tilling of my poor little field, you would never have reaped the least grain of corn. However, as God, having compassion on my youth, hath willed it, I have happened on yonder man, with whom I abide in this chamber, wherein it is unknown what manner of thing is a holiday (I speak of those holidays which you, more assiduous in the service of God than in that of the ladies, did so diligently celebrate) nor ever yet entered in at this door Saturday nor Friday nor vigil nor Emberday nor Lent, that is so long; nay, here swink we day and night and thump our wool; and this very night after matinsong, I know right well how the thing went, once he was up. Wherefore I mean to abide with him and work; whilst I am young, and leave saints' days and jubilees and fasts for my keeping when I am old; so get you gone about your business as quickliest you may, good luck go with you, and keep as many holidays as you please, without me.' Messer Ricciardo, hearing these words, was distressed beyond endurance and said, whenas he saw she had made an end of speaking. 'Alack, sweet my soul, what is this thou sayest? Hast thou no regard for thy kinsfolk's honour and thine own? Wilt thou rather abide here for this man's whore and in mortal sin than at Pisa as my wife? He, when he is weary of thee, will turn thee away to thine own exceeding reproach, whilst I will still hold thee dear and still (e'en though I willed it not) thou shalt be mistress of my house. Wilt thou for the sake of a lewd and disorderly appetite, forsake thine honour and me, who love thee more than my life? For God's sake, dear my hope, speak no more thus, but consent to come with me; henceforth, since I know thy desire, I will enforce myself [to content it;] wherefore, sweet my treasure, change counsel and come away with me, who have never known weal since thou wast taken from me.' Whereto answered the lady, 'I have no mind that any, now that it availeth not, should be more tender of my honour than I myself; would my kinsfolk had had regard thereto, whenas they gave me to you! But, as they had then no care for my honour, I am under no present concern to be careful of theirs; and if I am herein *mortar*[3] sin, I shall abide though it be in pestle sin. And let me tell you that here meseemeth I am Paganino's wife, whereas at Pisa meseemed I was your whore, seeing that there, by season of the moon and quadratures of geometry, needs must be planets concur to couple betwixt you and me, whereas here Paganino holdeth me all night in his arms and straineth me and biteth me, and how he serveth me, let God tell you for me. You say forsooth you will enforce yourself; to what? To do it in three casts and cause it stand by dint of cudgelling? I warrant me you are grown a doughty cavalier since I saw you last! Begone and enforce yourself to live, for methinketh indeed you do but sojourn here below upon sufferance, so peaked and scant o' wind you show to me. And yet more I tell you, that, should he leave me (albeit meseemeth he is nowise inclined thereto, so I choose to stay,) I purpose not therefor ever to return to you, of whom squeeze you as I might, there were no making a porringer of sauce; for that I abode with you once to my grievous hurt and loss, wherefore in such a case I should seek my vantage elsewhere. Nay, once again I tell you, here be neither saints' days nor vigils; wherefore here I mean to abide; so get you gone in God's name as quickliest you may, or I will cry out that you would fain force me.' Messer Ricciardo, seeing himself in ill case and now recognizing his folly in taking a young wife, whenas he was himself forspent, went forth the chamber tristful and woebegone, and bespoke Paganino with many words, that skilled not a jot. Ultimately, leaving the lady, he returned to Pisa, without having accomplished aught, and there for chagrin fell into such dotage that, as he went about Pisa, to whoso greeted him or asked him of anywhat, he answered nought but 'The ill hole[4] will have no holidays;'[5] and there, no great while after, he died. Paganino, hearing this and knowing the love the lady bore himself, espoused her to his lawful wife and thereafter, without ever observing saints' day or vigil or keeping Lent, they wrought what while their legs would carry them and led a jolly life of it. Wherefore, dear my ladies, meseemeth Bernabo, in his dispute with Ambrogiuolo, rode the she-goat down the steep."[6]

THIS STORY GAVE such occasion for laughter to all the company that there was none whose jaws ached not therefor, and all the ladies avouched with one accord that Dioneo spoke sooth and that Bernabo had been an ass. But, after the story was ended and the laughter abated, the queen, observing that the hour was now late and that all had told and seeing that the end of her seignory was come, according to the ordinance commenced, took the wreath from her own head and set it on that of Neifile, saying, with a blithe aspect, "Henceforth, companion dear, be thine the governance of this little people"; and reseated herself. Neifile blushed a little at the honour received and became in countenance like as showeth a new-blown rose of April or of May in the breaking of the day, with lovesome eyes some little downcast, sparkling no otherwise than the morning-star. But, after the courteous murmur of the bystanders, whereby they gladsomely approved their goodwill towards the new-made queen, had abated and she had taken heart again, she seated herself somewhat higher than of wont and said, "Since I am to be your queen, I will, departing not from the manner holden of those who have foregone me and whose governance you have by your obedience commended, make manifest to you in few words my opinion, which, an it be approved by your counsel, we will ensue. To-morrow, as you know, is Friday and the next day is Saturday, days which, by reason of the viands that are used therein,[7] are somewhat irksome to most folk, more by token that Friday, considering that He who died for our life on that day suffered passion, is worthy of reverence; wherefore I hold it a just thing and a seemly that, in honour of the Divinity, we apply ourselves rather to orisons than to story-telling. As for Saturday, it is the usance of ladies on that day to wash their heads and do away all dust and all uncleanliness befallen them for the labours of the past week; and many, likewise, use, in reverence of the Virgin Mother of the Son of God, to fast and rest from all manner of work in honour of the ensuing Sunday. Wherefore, we being unable fully to ensue the order of living taken by us, on like wise methinketh we were well to rest from story-telling on that day also; after which, for that we shall then have sojourned here four days, I hold it opportune, an we would give no occasion for newcomers to intrude upon us, that we remove hence and get us gone elsewhither; where I have already considered and provided. There when we shall be assembled together on Sunday, after sleeping,—we having to-day had leisure enough for discoursing at large,[8]—I have bethought myself,—at once that you may have more time to consider and because it will be yet goodlier that the license of our story-telling be somewhat straitened and that we devise of one of the many fashions of fortune,—that our discourse shall be OF SUCH AS HAVE, BY DINT OF DILIGENCE,[9] ACQUIRED SOME MUCH DESIRED THING OR RECOVERED SOME LOST GOOD. Whereupon let each think to tell somewhat that may be useful or at least entertaining to the company, saving always Dioneo his privilege." All commended the speech and disposition of the queen and ordained that it should be as she had said. Then, calling for her seneschal, she particularly instructed him where he should set the tables that evening and after of what he should do during all the time of her seignory; and this done, rising to her feet, she gave the company leave to do that which was most pleasing unto each. Accordingly, ladies and men betook themselves to a little garden and there, after they had disported themselves awhile, the hour of supper being come, they supped with mirth and pleasance; then, all arising thence and Emilia, by the queen's commandment, leading the round, the ditty following was sung by Pampinea, whilst the other ladies responded:

What lady aye should sing, and if not I,
Who'm blest with all for which a maid can sigh?
Come then, O Love, thou source of all my weal,
All hope and every issue glad and bright
Sing ye awhile yfere
Of sighs nor bitter pains I erst did feel,
That now but sweeten to me thy delight,
Nay, but of that fire clear,
Wherein I, burning, live in joy and cheer,
And as my God, thy name do magnify.

Thou settest, Love, before these eyes of mine
Whenas thy fire I entered the first day,
A youngling so beseen
With valour, worth and loveliness divine,
That never might one find a goodlier, nay,
Nor yet his match, I ween.
So sore I burnt for him I still must e'en
Sing, blithe, of him with thee, my lord most high.

And that in him which crowneth my liesse
Is that I please him, as he pleaseth me,
Thanks to Love debonair;
Thus in this world my wish I do possess
And in the next I trust at peace to be,
Through that fast faith I bear
To him; sure God, who seeth this, will ne'er
The kingdom of His bliss to us deny.

After this they sang sundry other songs and danced sundry dances and played upon divers instruments of music. Then, the queen deeming it time to go to rest, each betook himself, with torches before him, to his chamber, and all on the two following days, whilst applying themselves to those things whereof the queen had spoken, looked longingly for Sunday.

---

1. Lit. fabulous demonstrations (*dimostrazioni favolose*), casuistical arguments, founded upon premises of their own invention.
2. According to one of the commentators of the Decameron, there are as many churches at Ravenna as days in the year and each day is there celebrated as that of some saint or other.
3. A trifling jingle upon the similarity in sound of the words *mortale* (mortal), *mortaio* (mortar), *pestello* (pestle), and *pestilente* (pestilential). The same word-play occurs at least once more in the Decameron.
4. *Il mal foro*, a woman's commodity (Florio).
5. *i.e. Cunnus nonvult feriari.* Some commentators propose to read *il mal furo*, the ill thief, supposing Ricciardo to allude to Paganino, but this seems far-fetched.
6. *i.e. semble* ran headlong to destruction. The commentators explain this proverbial expression by saying that a she-goat is in any case a hazardous mount, and *a fortiori* when ridden down a precipice; but this seems a somewhat "sporting" kind of interpretation.
7. *i.e.* Friday being a fast day and Saturday a *jour maigre*.
8. *i.e.* generally upon the vicissitudes of Fortune and not upon any particular feature.
9. *Industria*, syn. address, skilful contrivance.

DAY THE THIRD

Here Beginneth the Third Day of the Decameron
wherein Under the Governance of Neifile Is
Discoursed of Such as Have by Dint of Diligence
Acquired Some Much Desired Thing or Recovered
Some Lost Good

THE dawn from vermeil began to grow orange-tawny, at the approach of the sun, when on the Sunday the queen arose and caused all her company rise also. The seneschal had a great while before despatched to the place whither they were to go store of things needful and folk who should there make ready that which behoved, and seeing the queen now on the way, straightway let load everything else, as if the camp were raised thence, and with the household stuff and such of the servants as remained set out in rear of the ladies and gentlemen. The queen, then, with slow step, accompanied and followed by her ladies and the three young men and guided by the song of some score nightingales and other birds, took her way westward, by a little-used footpath, full of green herbs and flowers, which latter now all began to open for the coming sun, and chatting, jesting and laughing with her company, brought them a while before half tierce,[1] without having gone over two thousand paces, to a very fair and rich palace, somewhat upraised above the plain upon a little knoll. Here they entered and having gone all about and viewed the great saloons and the quaint and elegant chambers all throughly furnished with that which pertaineth thereunto, they mightily commended the place and accounted its lord magnificent. Then, going below and seeing the very spacious and cheerful court thereof, the cellars full of choicest wines and the very cool water that welled there in great abundance, they praised it yet more. Thence, as if desirous of repose, they betook themselves to sit in a gallery which commanded all the courtyard and was all full of flowers, such as the season afforded, and leafage, whereupon there came the careful seneschal and entertained and refreshed them with costliest confections and wines of choice. Thereafter, letting open to them a garden, all walled about, which coasted the palace, they entered therein and it seeming to them, at their entering, altogether[2] wonder-goodly, they addressed themselves more intently to view the particulars thereof. It had about it and athwart the middle very spacious alleys, all straight as arrows and embowered with trellises of vines, which made great show of bearing abundance of grapes that year and being then all in blossom, yielded so rare a savour about the garden, that, as it blent with the fragrance of many another sweet-smelling plant that there gave scent, themseemed they were among all the spiceries that ever grew in the Orient. The sides of these alleys were all in a manner walled about with roses, red and white, and jessamine, wherefore not only of a morning, but what while the sun was highest, one might go all about, untouched thereby, neath odoriferous and delightsome shade. What and how many and how orderly disposed were the plants that grew in that place, it were tedious to recount; suffice it that there is none goodly of those which may brook our air but was there in abundance. Amiddleward the garden (what was not less, but yet more commendable than aught else there) was a plat of very fine grass, so green that it seemed well nigh black, enamelled all with belike a thousand kinds of flowers and closed about with the greenest and lustiest of orange and citron trees, the which, bearing at once old fruits and new and flowers, not only afforded the eyes a pleasant shade, but were no less grateful to the smell. Midmost the grass-plat was a fountain of the whitest marble, enchased with wonder-goodly sculptures, and thence,—whether I know not from a natural or an artificial source,—there sprang, by a figure that stood on a column in its midst, so great a jet of water and so high towards the sky, whence not without a delectable sound it fell back into the wonder-limpid fount, that a mill might have wrought with less; the which after (I mean the water which overflowed the full basin) issued forth of the lawn by a hidden way, and coming to light therewithout, encompassed it all about by very goodly and curiously wroughten channels. Thence by like channels it ran through well nigh every part of the pleasance and was gathered again at the last in a place whereby it had issue from the fair garden and whence it descended, in the clearest of streams, towards the plain; but, ere it won thither, it turned two mills with exceeding power and to the no small vantage of the lord. The sight of this garden and its fair ordinance and the plants and the fountain, with the rivulets proceeding therefrom, so pleased the ladies and the three young men that they all of one accord avouched that, an Paradise might be created upon earth, they could not avail to conceive what form, other than that of this garden, might be given it nor what farther beauty might possibly be added thereunto. However, as they went most gladsomely thereabout, weaving them the goodliest garlands of the various leafage of the trees and hearkening the while to the carols of belike a score of different kinds of birds, that sang as if in rivalry one of other, they became aware of a delectable beauty, which, wonderstricken as they were with the other charms of the place, they had not yet noted; to wit, they found the garden full of maybe an hundred kinds of goodly creatures, and one showing them to other, they saw on one side rabbits issue, on another hares run; here lay kids and there fawns went grazing, and there was many another kind of harmless animal, each going about his pastime at his pleasure, as if tame; the which added unto them a yet greater pleasure than the others. After they had gone about their fill, viewing now this thing and now that, the queen let set the tables around the fair fountain and at her commandment, having first sung half a dozen canzonets and danced sundry dances, they sat down to meat. There, being right well and orderly served, after a very fair and sumptuous and tranquil fashion, with goodly and delicate viands, they waxed yet blither and arising thence, gave themselves anew to music-making and singing and dancing till it seemed good to the queen that those whom it pleased should betake themselves to sleep. Accordingly some went thither, whilst others, overcome with the beauty of the place, willed not to leave it, but, abiding there, addressed themselves, some to reading romances and some to playing chess or tables, whilst the others slept. But presently, the hour of none being past and the sleepers having arisen and refreshed their faces with cold water, they came all, at the queen's commandment, to the lawn hard by the fountain and there seating themselves, after the wonted fashion, waited to fall to story-telling upon the subject proposed by her. The first upon whom she laid this charge was Filostrato, who began on this wise:

1. *i.e.* half *before* (not half *after*) tierce or 7.30 a.m. *Cf.* the equivalent German idiom, *halb acht*, 7.30 (not 8.30) a.m.
2. *i.e.* as a whole (*tutto insieme*).

❦ I ❦

THE FIRST STORY

MASETTO OF LAMPORECCHIO FEIGNETH HIMSELF DUMB AND BECOMETH GARDENER TO A CONVENT OF WOMEN, WHO ALL FLOCK TO LIE WITH HIM

"Fairest ladies, there be many men and women foolish enough to believe that, whenas the white fillet is bound about a girl's head and the black cowl clapped upon her back, she is no longer a woman and is no longer sensible of feminine appetites, as if the making her a nun had changed her to stone; and if perchance they hear aught contrary to this their belief, they are as much incensed as if a very great and heinous misdeed had been committed against nature, considering not neither having regard to themselves, whom full license to do that which they will availeth not to sate, nor yet to the much potency of idlesse and thought-taking.[1] On like wise there are but too many who believe that spade and mattock and coarse victuals and hard living do altogether purge away carnal appetites from the tillers of the earth and render them exceeding dull of wit and judgment. But how much all who believe thus are deluded, I purpose, since the queen hath commanded it to me, to make plain to you in a little story, without departing from the theme by her appointed.

There was (and is yet) in these our parts a convent of women, very famous for sanctity (the which, that I may not anywise abate its repute, I will not name), wherein no great while agone, there being then no more than eight nuns and an abbess, all young, in the nunnery, a poor silly dolt of a fellow was gardener of a very goodly garden of theirs, who, being miscontent with his wage, settled his accounts with the ladies' bailiff and returned to Lamporecchio, whence he came. There, amongst others who welcomed him home, was a young labouring man, stout and robust and (for a countryman) a well-favoured fellow, by name of Masetto, who asked him where he had been so long. The good man, whose name was Nuto, told him, whereupon Masetto asked him in what he had served the convent, and he, 'I tended a great and goodly garden of theirs, and moreover I went while to the coppice for faggots and drew water and did other such small matters of service; but the nuns gave me so little wage that I could scarce find me in shoon withal. Besides, they are all young and methinketh they are possessed of the devil, for there was no doing anything to their liking; nay, when I was at work whiles in the hortyard,[2] quoth one, "Set this here," and another, "Set that here," and a third snatched the spade from my hand, saying, "That is naught"; brief, they gave me so much vexation that I would leave work be and begone out of the hortyard; insomuch that, what with one thing and what with another, I would abide there no longer and took myself off. When I came away, their bailiff besought me, an I could lay my hand on any one apt unto that service, to send the man to him, and I promised it him; but may God make him sound of the loins as he whom I shall get him, else will I send him none at all!' Masetto, hearing this, was taken with so great a desire to be with these nuns that he was all consumed therewith, judging from Nuto's words that he might avail to compass somewhat of that which he desired. However, foreseeing that he would fail of his purpose, if he discovered aught thereof to Nuto, he said to the latter, 'Egad, thou didst well to come away. How is a man to live with women? He were better abide with devils. Six times out of seven they know not what they would have themselves.' But, after they had made an end of their talk, Masetto began to cast about what means he should take to be with them and feeling himself well able to do the offices of which Nuto had spoken, he had no fear of being refused on that head, but misdoubted him he might not be received, for that he was young and well-looked. Wherefore, after pondering many things in himself, he bethought himself thus: 'The place is far hence and none knoweth me there, an I can but make a show of being dumb, I shall for certain be received there.' Having fixed upon this device, he set out with an axe he had about his neck, without telling any whither he was bound, and betook himself, in the guise of a beggarman, to the convent, where being come, he entered in and as luck would have it, found the bailiff in the courtyard. Him he accosted with signs such as dumb folk use and made a show of asking food of him for the love of God and that in return he would, an it were needed, cleave wood for him. The bailiff willingly gave him to eat and after set before him divers logs that Nuto had not availed to cleave, but of all which Masetto, who was very strong, made a speedy despatch. By and by, the bailiff, having occasion to go to the coppice, carried him thither and put him to cutting faggots; after which, setting the ass before him, he gave him to understand by signs that he was to bring them home. This he did very well; wherefore the bailiff kept him there some days, so he might have him do certain things for which he had occasion. One day it chanced that the abbess saw him and asked the bailiff who he was. 'Madam,' answered he, 'this is a poor deaf and dumb man, who came hither the other day to ask an alms; so I took him in out of charity and have made him do sundry things of which we had need. If he knew how to till the hortyard and chose to abide with us, I believe we should get good service of him; for that we lack such an one and he is strong and we could make what we would of him; more by token that you would have no occasion to fear his playing the fool with yonder lasses of yours.' 'I' faith,' rejoined the abbess, 'thou sayst sooth. Learn if he knoweth how to till and study to keep him here; give him a pair of shoes and some old hood or other and make much of him, caress him, give him plenty to eat.' Which the bailiff promised to do. Masetto was not so far distant but he heard all this, making a show the while of sweeping the courtyard, and said merrily in himself, 'An you put me therein, I will till you your hortyard as it was never tilled yet.' Accordingly, the bailiff, seeing that he knew right well how to work, asked him by signs if he had a mind to abide there and he replied on like wise that he would do whatsoever he wished; whereupon the bailiff engaged him and charged him till the hortyard, showing him what he was to do; after which he went about other business of the convent and left him. Presently, as Masetto went working one day after another, the nuns fell to plaguing him and making mock of him, as ofttimes it betideth that folk do with mutes, and bespoke him the naughtiest words in the world, thinking he understood them not; whereof the abbess, mayhap supposing him to be tailless as well as tongueless, recked little or nothing. It chanced one day, however, that, as he rested himself after a hard morning's work, two young nuns, who went about the garden,[3] drew near the place where he lay and fell to looking upon him, whilst he made a show of sleeping. Presently quoth one who was somewhat the bolder of the twain to the other, 'If I thought thou wouldst keep my counsel, I would tell thee a thought which I have once and again had and which might perchance profit thee also.' 'Speak in all assurance,' answered the other, 'for certes I will never tell it to any.' Then said the forward wench, 'I know not if thou have ever considered how straitly we are kept and how no man dare ever enter here, save the bailiff, who is old, and yonder dumb fellow; and I have again and again heard ladies, who come to visit us, say that all other delights in the world are but toys in comparison with that which a woman enjoyeth, whenas she hath to do with a man. Wherefore I have often had it in mind to make trial with this mute, since with others I may not, if it be so. And indeed he is the best in the world to that end, for that, e'en if he would, he could not nor might tell it again. Thou seest he is a poor silly lout of a lad, who hath overgrown his wit, and I would fain hear how thou deemest of the thing.' 'Alack!' rejoined the other, 'what is this thou sayest? Knowest thou not that we have promised our virginity to God?' 'Oh, as for that,' answered the first, 'how many things are promised Him all day long, whereof not one is fulfilled unto Him! An we have promised it Him, let Him find Himself another or others to perform it to Him.' 'Or if,' went on her fellow, 'we should prove with child, how would it go then?' Quoth the other, 'Thou beginnest to take thought unto ill ere it cometh; when that betideth, then will we look to it; there will be a thousand ways for us of doing so that it shall never be known, provided we ourselves tell it not.' The other, hearing this and having now a greater itch than her companion to prove what manner beast a man was, said, 'Well, then, how shall we do?' Quoth the first, 'Thou seest it is nigh upon none and methinketh the sisters are all asleep, save only ourselves; let us look about the hortyard if there be any there, and if there be none, what have we to do but to take him by the hand and carry him into yonder hut, whereas he harboureth against the rain, and there let one of us abide with him, whilst the other keepeth watch? He is so simple that he will do whatever we will.' Masetto heard all this talk and disposed to compliance, waited but to be taken by one of the nuns. The latter having looked well all about and satisfied themselves that they could be seen from nowhere, she who had broached the matter came up to Masetto and aroused him, whereupon he rose incontinent to his feet. The nun took him coaxingly by the hand and led him, grinning like an idiot, to the hut, where, without overmuch pressing, he did what she would. Then, like a loyal comrade, having had her will, she gave place to her fellow, and Masetto, still feigning himself a simpleton, did their pleasure. Before they departed thence, each of the girls must needs once more prove how the mute could horse it, and after devising with each other, they agreed that the thing was as delectable as they had heard, nay, more so. Accordingly, watching their opportunity, they went oftentimes at fitting seasons to divert themselves with the mute, till one day it chanced that one of their sisters, espying them in the act from the lattice of her cell, showed it to other twain. At first they talked of denouncing the culprits to the abbess, but, after, changing counsel and coming to an accord with the first two, they became sharers with them in Masetto's services, and to them the other three nuns were at divers times and by divers chances added as associates. Ultimately, the abbess, who had not yet gotten wind of these doings, walking one day alone in the garden, the heat being great, found Masetto (who had enough of a little fatigue by day, because of overmuch posting it by night) stretched out asleep under the shade of an almond-tree, and the wind lifting the forepart of his clothes, all abode discovered. The lady, beholding this and seeing herself alone, fell into that same appetite which had gotten hold of her nuns, and arousing Masetto, carried him to her chamber, where, to the no small miscontent of the others, who complained loudly that the gardener came not to till the hortyard, she kept him several days, proving and reproving that delight which she had erst been wont to blame in others. At last she sent him back to his own lodging, but was fain to have him often again and as, moreover, she required of him more than her share, Masetto, unable to satisfy so many, bethought himself that his playing the mute might, an it endured longer, result in his exceeding great hurt. Wherefore, being one night with the abbess, he gave loose to[4] his tongue and bespoke her thus: 'Madam, I have heard say that one cock sufficeth unto half a score hens, but that half a score men can ill or hardly satisfy one woman; whereas needs must I serve nine, and to this I can no wise endure; nay, for that which I have done up to now, I am come to such a pass that I can do neither little nor much; wherefore do ye either let me go in God's name or find a remedy for the matter.' The abbess, hearing him speak whom she held dumb, was all amazed and said, 'What is this? Methought thou wast dumb.' 'Madam,' answered Masetto, 'I was indeed dumb, not by nature, but by reason of a malady which bereft me of speech, and only this very night for the first time do I feel it restored to me, wherefore I praise God as most I may.' The lady believed this and asked him what he meant by saying that he had to serve nine. Masetto told her how the case stood, whereby she perceived that she had no nun but was far wiser than herself; but, like a discreet woman as she was, she resolved to take counsel with her nuns to find some means of arranging the matter, without letting Masetto go, so the convent might not be defamed by him. Accordingly, having openly confessed to one another that which had been secretly done of each, they all of one accord, with Masetto's consent, so ordered it that the people round about believed speech to have been restored to him, after he had long been mute, through their prayers and by the merits of the saint in whose name the convent was intituled, and their bailiff being lately dead, they made Masetto bailiff in his stead and apportioned his toils on such wise that he could endure them. Thereafter, albeit he began upon them monikins galore, the thing was so discreetly ordered that nothing took vent thereof till after the death of the abbess, when Masetto began to grow old and had a mind to return home rich. The thing becoming known, enabled him lightly to accomplish his desire, and thus Masetto, having by his foresight contrived to employ his youth to good purpose, returned in his old age, rich and a father, without being at the pains or expense of rearing children, to the place whence he had set out with an axe about his neck, avouching that thus did Christ entreat whoso set horns to his cap."

---

1. *Sollecitudine.* The commentators will have it that this is an error for *solitudine,* solitude, but I see no necessity for the substitution, the text being perfectly acceptable as it stands.
2. Hortyard (*orto*) is the old form of orchard, properly an enclosed tract of land in which fruit, vegetables and potherbs are cultivated for use, *i.e.* the modern kitchen garden and orchard in one, as distinguished from the pleasaunce or flower garden (*giardino*).
3. *Giardino, i.e.* flower-garden.
4. Lit. broke the string of.

⚜ 2 ⚜

THE SECOND STORY

A HORSEKEEPER LIETH WITH THE WIFE OF KING AGILULF, WHO, BECOMING AWARE THEREOF, WITHOUT WORD SAID, FINDETH HIM OUT AND POLLETH HIM; BUT THE POLLED MAN POLLETH ALL HIS FELLOWS ON LIKE WISE AND SO ESCAPETH ILL HAP

THE END of Filostrato's story, whereat whiles the ladies had some little blushed and other whiles laughed, being come, it pleased the queen that Pampinea should follow on with a story, and she accordingly, beginning with a smiling countenance, said, "Some are so little discreet in seeking at all hazards to show that they know and apprehend that which it concerneth them not to know, that whiles, rebuking to this end unperceived defects in others, they think to lessen their own shame, whereas they do infinitely augment it; and that this is so I purpose, lovesome ladies, to prove to you by the contrary thereof, showing you the astuteness of one who, in the judgment of a king of worth and valour, was held belike of less account than Masetto himself.

Agilulf, King of the Lombards, as his predecessors had done, fixed the seat of his kingship at Pavia, a city of Lombardy, and took to wife Theodolinda[1] the widow of Autari, likewise King of the Lombards, a very fair lady and exceeding discreet and virtuous, but ill fortuned in a lover.[2] The affairs of the Lombards having, thanks to the valour and judgment of King Agilulf, been for some time prosperous and in quiet, it befell that one of the said queen's horse-keepers, a man of very low condition, in respect of birth, but otherwise of worth far above so mean a station, and comely of person and tall as he were the king, became beyond measure enamoured of his mistress. His mean estate hindered him not from being sensible that this love of his was out of all reason, wherefore, like a discreet man as he was, he discovered it unto none, nor dared he make it known to her even with his eyes. But, albeit he lived without any hope of ever winning her favour, yet inwardly he gloried in that he had bestowed his thoughts in such high place, and being all aflame with amorous fire, he studied, beyond every other of his fellows, to do whatsoever he deemed might pleasure the queen; whereby it befell that, whenas she had occasion to ride abroad, she liefer mounted the palfrey of which he had charge than any other; and when this happened, he reckoned it a passing great favour to himself nor ever stirred from her stirrup, accounting himself happy what time he might but touch her clothes. But, as often enough we see it happen that, even as hope groweth less, so love waxeth greater, so did it betide this poor groom, insomuch that sore uneath it was to him to avail to brook his great desire, keeping it, as he did, hidden and being upheld by no hope; and many a time, unable to rid himself of that his love, he determined in himself to die. And considering inwardly of the

123

manner, he resolved to seek his death on such wise that it should be manifest he died for the love he bore the queen, to which end he bethought himself to try his fortune in an enterprise of such a sort as should afford him a chance of having or all or part of his desire. He set not himself to seek to say aught to the queen nor to make her sensible of his love by letters, knowing he should speak and write in vain, but chose rather to essay an he might by practice avail to lie with her; nor was there any other shift for it but to find a means how he might, in the person of the king, who, he knew, lay not with her continually, contrive to make his way to her and enter her bedchamber. Accordingly, that he might see on what wise and in what habit the king went, whenas he visited her, he hid himself several times by night in a great saloon of the palace, which lay between the king's bedchamber and that of the queen, and one night, amongst others, he saw the king come forth of his chamber, wrapped in a great mantle, with a lighted taper in one hand and a little wand in the other, and making for the queen's chamber, strike once or twice upon the door with the wand, without saying aught, whereupon it was incontinent opened to him and the taper taken from his hand. Noting this and having seen the king return after the same fashion, he bethought himself to do likewise. Accordingly, finding means to have a cloak like that which he had seen the king wear, together with a taper and a wand, and having first well washed himself in a bagnio, lest haply the smell of the muck should offend the queen or cause her smoke the cheat, he hid himself in the great saloon, as of wont. Whenas he knew that all were asleep and it seemed to him time either to give effect to his desire or to make his way by high emprise[3] to the wished-for death, he struck a light with a flint and steel he had brought with him and kindling the taper, wrapped himself fast in the mantle, then, going up to the chamber-door, smote twice upon it with the wand. The door was opened by a bedchamber-woman, all sleepy-eyed, who took the light and covered it; whereupon, without saying aught, he passed within the curtain, put off his mantle and entered the bed where the queen slept. Then, taking her desirefully in his arms and feigning himself troubled (for that he knew the king's wont to be that, whenas he was troubled, he cared not to hear aught), without speaking or being spoken to, he several times carnally knew the queen; after which, grievous as it seemed to him to depart, yet, fearing lest his too long stay should be the occasion of turning the gotten delight into dolour, he arose and taking up the mantle and the light, withdrew, without word said, and returned, as quickliest he might, to his own bed. He could scarce yet have been therein when the king arose and repaired to the queen's chamber, whereat she marvelled exceedingly; and as he entered the bed and greeted her blithely, she took courage by his cheerfulness and said, 'O my lord, what new fashion is this of to-night? You left me but now, after having taken pleasure of me beyond your wont, and do you return so soon? Have a care what you do.' The king, hearing these words, at once concluded that the queen had been deceived by likeness of manners and person, but, like a wise man, bethought himself forthright, seeing that neither she nor any else had perceived the cheat, not to make her aware thereof; which many simpletons would not have done, but would have said, 'I have not been here, I. Who is it hath been here? How did it happen? Who came hither?' Whence many things might have arisen, whereby he would needlessly have afflicted the lady and given her ground for desiring another time that which she had already tasted; more by token that, an he kept silence of the matter, no shame might revert to him, whereas, by speaking, he would have brought dishonour upon himself. The king, then, more troubled at heart than in looks or speech, answered, saying, 'Wife, seem I not to you man enough to have been here a first time and to come yet again after that?' 'Ay, my lord,' answered she. 'Nevertheless, I beseech you have regard to your health.' Quoth Agilulf, 'And it pleaseth me to follow your counsel, wherefore for the nonce I will get me gone again, without giving you more annoy.' This said, taking up his mantle, he departed the chamber, with a heart full of wrath and despite for the affront that he saw had been done him, and bethought himself quietly to seek to discover the culprit, concluding that he must be of the household and could not, whoever he might be, have issued forth of the palace. Accordingly, taking a very small light in a little lantern, he betook himself to a very long gallery that was over the stables of his palace and where all his household slept in different beds, and judging that, whoever he might be that had done what the queen said, his pulse and the beating of his heart for the swink endured could not yet have had time to abate, he silently, beginning at one end of the gallery, fell to feeling each one's breast, to know if his heart beat high. Although every other slept fast, he who had been with the queen was not yet asleep, but, seeing the king come and guessing what he went seeking, fell into such a fright that to the beating of the heart caused by the late-had fatigue, fear added yet a greater and he doubted not but the king, if he became aware of this, would put him to death without delay, and many things passed through his thought that he should do. However, seeing him all unarmed, he resolved to feign sleep and await what he should do. Agilulf, then, having examined many and found none whom he judged to be he of whom he was in quest, came presently to the horsekeeper and feeling his heart beat high, said in himself, 'This is the man.' Nevertheless, an he would have nought be known of that which he purposed to do, he did nought to him but poll, with a pair of scissors he had brought with him, somewhat on one side of his hair, which they then wore very long, so by that token he might know him again on the morrow; and this done, he withdrew and returned to his own chamber. The culprit, who had felt all this, like a shrewd fellow as he was, understood plainly enough why he had been thus marked; wherefore he arose without delay and finding a pair of shears, whereof it chanced there were several about the stables for the service of the horses, went softly up to all who lay in the gallery and clipped each one's hair on like wise over the ear; which having done without being observed, he returned to sleep. When the king arose in the morning, he commanded that all his household should present themselves before him, or ever the palace-doors were opened; and it was done as he said. Then, as they all stood before him with uncovered heads, he began to look that he might know him whom he had polled; but, seeing the most part of them with their hair clipped after one and the same fashion, he marvelled and said in himself, 'He whom I seek, for all he may be of mean estate, showeth right well he is of no mean wit.' Then, seeing that he could not, without making a stir, avail to have him whom he sought, and having no mind to incur a great shame for the sake of a paltry revenge, it pleased him with one sole word to admonish the culprit and show him that he was ware of the matter; wherefore, turning to all who were present, he said, 'Let him who did it do it no more and get you gone in peace.' Another would have been for giving them the strappado, for torturing, examining and questioning, and doing this, would have published that which every one should go about to conceal; and having thus discovered himself, though he should have taken entire revenge for the affront suffered, his shame had not been minished, nay, were rather much enhanced therefor and his lady's honour sullied. Those who heard the king's words marvelled and long debated amongst themselves what he meant by this speech; but none understood it, save he whom it concerned, and he, like a wise man, never, during Agilulf's lifetime, discovered the matter nor ever again committed his life to the hazard of such a venture."

---

1. Boccaccio calls her *Teudelinga*; but I know of no authority for this form of the name of the famous Longobardian queen.
2. Referring apparently to the adventure related in the present story.
3. Lit. with high (*i.e.* worthy) cause (*con alta cagione*).

⚜ 3 ⚜

DAY THE THIRD

UNDER COLOUR OF CONFESSION AND OF
EXCEEDING NICENESS OF CONSCIENCE, A LADY,
BEING ENAMOURED OF A YOUNG MAN, BRINGETH A
GRAVE FRIAR, WITHOUT HIS MISDOUBTING HIM
THEREOF, TO AFFORD A MEANS OF GIVING ENTIRE
EFFECT TO HER PLEASURE

PAMPINEA BEING NOW silent and the daring and subtlety of the horsekeeper having been extolled by several of the company, as also the king's good sense, the queen, turning to Filomena, charged her follow on; whereupon she blithely began to speak thus, "I purpose to recount to you a cheat which was in very deed put by a fair lady upon a grave friar and which should be so much the more pleasing to every layman as these [—friars, to wit—], albeit for the most part very dull fools and men of strange manners and usances, hold themselves to be in everything both better worth and wiser than others, whereas they are of far less account than the rest of mankind, being men who, lacking, of the meanness of their spirit, the ability to provide themselves, take refuge, like swine, whereas they may have what to eat. And this story, charming ladies, I shall tell you, not only for the ensuing of the order imposed, but to give you to know withal that even the clergy, to whom we women, beyond measure credulous as we are, yield overmuch faith, can be and are whiles adroitly befooled, and that not by men only, but even by certain of our own sex.

In our city, the which is fuller of cozenage than of love or faith, there was, not many years agone, a gentlewoman adorned with beauty and charms and as richly endowed by nature as any of her sex with engaging manners and loftiness of spirit and subtle wit, whose name albeit I know, I purpose not to discover it, no, nor any other that pertaineth unto the present story, for that there be folk yet alive who would take it in despite, whereas it should be passed over with a laugh. This lady, then, seeing herself, though of high lineage, married to a wool-monger and unable, for that he was a craftsman, to put off the haughtiness of her spirit, whereby she deemed no man of mean condition, how rich soever he might be, worthy of a gentlewoman and seeing him moreover, for all his wealth, to be apt unto nothing of more moment than to lay a warp for a piece of motley or let weave a cloth or chaffer with a spinster anent her yarn, resolved on no wise to admit of his embraces, save in so far as she might not deny him, but to seek, for her own satisfaction, to find some one who should be worthier of her favours than the wool-monger appeared to her to be, and accordingly fell so fervently in love with a man of very good quality and middle age, that, whenas she saw him not by day, she could not pass the ensuing night without unease. The gentleman, perceiving not how the case stood, took no heed of her, and she, being very circumspect, dared not make the matter known to him by sending of women nor by letter, fearing the possible perils that might betide. However, observing that he companied much with a churchman, who, albeit a dull lump of a fellow, was nevertheless, for that he was a man of very devout life, reputed of well nigh all a most worthy friar, she bethought herself that this latter would make an excellent go-between herself and her lover and having considered what means she should use, she repaired, at a fitting season, to the church where he abode, and letting call him to her, told him that, an he pleased, she would fain confess herself to him. The friar seeing her and judging her to be a woman of condition, willingly gave ear to her, and she, after confession, said to him, 'Father mine, it behoveth me have recourse to you for aid and counsel anent that which you shall hear. I know, as having myself told you, that you know my kinsfolk and my husband, who loveth me more than his life, nor is there aught I desire but I have it of him incontinent, he being a very rich man and one who can well afford it; wherefore I love him more than mine own self and should I but think, let alone do, aught that might be contrary to his honour and pleasure, there were no woman more wicked or more deserving of the fire than I. Now one, whose name in truth I know not, but who is, meseemeth, a man of condition, and is, if I mistake not, much in your company,—a well-favoured man and tall of his person and clad in very decent sad-coloured raiment,—unaware belike of the constancy of my purpose, appeareth to have laid siege to me, nor can I show myself at door or window nor go without the house, but he incontinent presenteth himself before me, and I marvel that he is not here now; whereat I am sore concerned, for that such fashions as these often bring virtuous women into reproach, without their fault. I have whiles had it in mind to have him told of this by my brothers; but then I have bethought me that men oftentimes do messages on such wise that ill answers ensue, which give rise to words and from words they come to deeds; wherefore, lest mischief spring therefrom and scandal, I have kept silence of the matter and have determined to discover it to yourself rather than to another, at once because meseemeth you are his friend and for that it beseemeth you to rebuke not only friends, but strangers, of such things. I beseech you, therefore, for the one God's sake, that you rebuke him of this and pray him leave these his fashions. There be women enough, who incline belike to these toys and would take pleasure in being dogged and courted by him, whereas to me, who have no manner of mind to such matters, it is a very grievous annoy.' So saying, she bowed her head as she would weep. The holy friar understood incontinent of whom she spoke and firmly believing what she said to be true, greatly commended her righteous intent and promised her to do on such wise that she should have no farther annoy from the person in question; and knowing her to be very rich, he commended to her works of charity and almsdeeds, recounting to her his own need. Quoth the lady, 'I beseech you thereof for God's sake, and should he deny, prithee scruple not to tell him that it was I who told you this and complained to you thereof.' Then, having made her confession and gotten her penance, recalling the friar's exhortations to works of almsgiving, she stealthily filled his hand with money, praying him to say masses for the souls of her dead kinsfolk; after which she rose from his feet and taking leave of him, returned home. Not long after up came the gentleman, according to his wont, and after they had talked awhile of one thing and another, the friar, drawing his friend aside, very civilly rebuked him of the manner in which, as he believed, he pursued and spied upon the lady aforesaid, according to that which she had given him to understand. The other marvelled, as well he might, having never set eyes upon her and being used very rarely to pass before her house, and would have excused himself; but the friar suffered him not to speak, saying, 'Now make no show of wonderment nor waste words in denying it, for it will avail thee nothing; I learnt not these matters from the neighbours; nay, she herself told them to me, complaining sore of thee. And besides that such toys beseem not a man of thine age, I may tell thee this much of her, that if ever I saw a woman averse to these follies, it is she; wherefore, for thine own credit and her comfort, I prithee desist therefrom and let her be in peace.' The gentleman, quicker of wit than the friar, was not slow to apprehend the lady's device and feigning to be somewhat abashed, promised to meddle no more with her thenceforward; then, taking leave of the friar, he betook himself to the house of the lady, who still abode await at a little window, so she might see him, should he pass that way. When she saw him come, she showed herself so rejoiced and so gracious to him, that he might very well understand that he had gathered the truth from the friar's words, and thenceforward, under colour of other business, he began with the utmost precaution to pass continually through the street, to his own pleasure and to the exceeding delight and solace of the lady. After awhile, perceiving that she pleased him even as he pleased her and wishful to inflame him yet more and to certify him of the love she bore him, she betook herself again, choosing her time and place, to the holy friar and seating herself at his feet in the church, fell a-weeping. The friar, seeing this, asked her affectionately what was to do with her anew. 'Alack, father mine,' answered she, 'that which aileth me is none other than yonder God-accursed friend of yours, of whom I complained to you the other day, for that methinketh he was born for my especial torment and to make me do a thing, such that I should never be glad again nor ever after dare to seat myself at your feet.' 'How?' cried the friar. 'Hath he not given over annoying thee?' 'No, indeed,' answered she; 'nay, since I complained to you of him, as if of despite, maybe taking it ill that I should have done so, for every once he used to pass before my house, I verily believe he hath passed seven times. And would to God he were content with passing and spying upon me! Nay, he is grown so bold and so malapert that but yesterday he despatched a woman to me at home with his idle tales and toys and sent me a purse and a girdle, as if I had not purses and girdles galore; the which I took and take so ill that I believe, but for my having regard to the sin of it and after for the love of you, I had played the devil. However, I contained myself and would not do or say aught whereof I should not first have let you know. Nay, I had already returned the purse and the girdle to the baggage who brought them, that she might carry them back to him, and had given her a rough dismissal, but after, fearing she might keep them for herself and tell him that I had accepted them, as I hear women of her fashion do whiles, I called her back and took them, full of despite, from her hands and have brought them to you, so you may return them to him and tell him I want none of his trash, for that, thanks to God and my husband, I have purses and girdles enough to smother him withal. Moreover, if hereafter he desist not from this, I tell you, as a father, you must excuse me, but I will tell it, come what may, to my husband and my brothers; for I had far liefer he should brook an affront, if needs he must, than that I should suffer blame for him; wherefore let him look to himself.' So saying, still weeping sore, she pulled out from under her surcoat a very handsome and rich purse and a quaint and costly girdle and threw them into the lap of the friar, who, fully crediting that which she told him and incensed beyond measure, took them and said to her, 'Daughter, I marvel not that thou art provoked at these doings, nor can I blame thee therefor; but I much commend thee for following my counsel in the matter. I rebuked him the other day and he hath ill performed that which he promised me; wherefore, as well for that as for this that he hath newly done, I mean to warm his ears[1] for him after such a fashion that methinketh he will give thee no farther concern; but do thou, God's benison on thee, suffer not thyself to be so overcome with anger that thou tell it to any of thy folk, for that overmuch harm might ensue thereof unto him. Neither fear thou lest this blame anywise ensue to thee, for I shall still, before both God and men, be a most constant witness to thy virtue.' The lady made believe to be somewhat comforted and leaving that talk, said, as one who knew his greed and that of his fellow-churchmen, 'Sir, these some nights past there have appeared to me sundry of my kinsfolk, who ask nought but almsdeeds, and meseemeth they are indeed in exceeding great torment, especially my mother, who appeareth to me in such ill case and affliction that it is pity to behold. Methinketh she suffereth exceeding distress to see me in this tribulation with yonder enemy of God; wherefore I would have you say me forty masses of Saint Gregory for her and their souls, together with certain of your own prayers, so God may deliver them from that penitential fire.' So saying, she put a florin into his hand, which the holy father blithely received and confirming her devoutness with fair words and store of pious instances, gave her his benison and let her go. The lady being gone, the friar, never thinking how he was gulled, sent for his friend, who, coming and finding him troubled, at once divined that he was to have news of the lady and awaited what the friar should say. The latter repeated that which he had before said to him and bespeaking him anew angrily and reproachfully, rebuked him severely of that which, according to the lady's report, he had done. The gentleman, not yet perceiving the friar's drift, faintly enough denied having sent her the purse and the girdle, so as not to undeceive the friar, in case the lady should have given him to believe that he had done this; whereat the good man was sore incensed and said, 'How canst thou deny it, wicked man that thou art? See, here they are, for she herself brought them to me, weeping; look if thou knowest them.' The gentleman feigned to be sore abashed and answered, 'Yes, I do indeed know them and I confess to you that I did ill; but I swear to you, since I see her thus disposed, that you shall never more hear a word of this.' Brief, after many words, the numskull of a friar gave his friend the purse and the girdle and dismissed him, after rating him amain and beseeching him occupy himself no more with these follies, the which he promised him. The gentleman, overjoyed both at the assurance that himseemed he had of the lady's love and at the goodly gift, was no sooner quit of the friar than he betook himself to a place where he made shift to let his mistress see that he had the one and the other thing; whereat she was mightily rejoiced, more by token that herseemed her device went from good to better. She now awaited nought but her husband's going abroad to give completion to the work, and it befell not long after that it behoved him repair to Genoa on some occasion or other. No sooner had he mounted to horse in the morning and gone his way, than the lady betook herself to the holy man and after many lamentations, said to him, weeping, 'Father mine, I tell you now plainly that I can brook no more; but, for that I promised you the other day to do nought, without first telling you, I am come to excuse myself to you; and that you may believe I have good reason both to weep and to complain, I will tell you what your friend, or rather devil incarnate, did to me this very morning, a little before matins. I know not what ill chance gave him to know that my husband was to go to Genoa yestermorn; algates, this morning, at the time I tell you, he came into a garden of mine and climbing up by a tree to the window of my bedchamber, which giveth upon the garden, had already opened the lattice and was for entering, when I of a sudden awoke and starting up, offered to cry out, nay, would assuredly have cried out, but that he, who was not yet within, besought me of mercy in God's name and yours, telling me who he was; which when I heard, I held my peace for the love of you and naked as I was born, ran and shut the window in his face; whereupon I suppose he took himself off (ill-luck go with him!), for I heard no more of him. Look you now if this be a goodly thing and to be endured. For my part I mean to bear with him no more; nay, I have already forborne him overmuch for the love of you.' The friar, hearing this, was the wrathfullest man alive and knew not what to say, except to ask again and again if she had well certified herself that it was indeed he and not another; to which she answered, 'Praised be God! As if I did not yet know him from another! I tell you it was himself, and although he should deny it, credit him not.' Then said the friar, 'Daughter, there is nothing to be said for it but that this was exceeding effrontery and a thing exceeding ill done, and in sending him off, as thou didst, thou didst that which it behoved thee to do. But I beseech thee, since God hath preserved thee from shame, that, like as thou hast twice followed my counsel, even so do thou yet this once; to wit, without complaining to any kinsman of thine, leave it to me to see an I can bridle yonder devil broke loose, whom I believed a saint. If I can make shift to turn him from this lewdness, well and good; if not, I give thee leave henceforth to do with him that which thy soul shall judge best, and my benison go with thee.' 'Well, then,' answered the lady, 'for this once I will well not to vex or disobey you; but look you do on such wise that he be ware of annoying me again, for I promise you I will never again return to you for this cause.' Thereupon, without saying more, she took leave of the friar and went away, as if in anger. Hardly was she out of the church when up came the gentleman and was called by the friar, who, taking him apart, gave him the soundest rating ever man had, calling him disloyal and forsworn and traitor. The other, who had already twice had occasion to know to what the monk's reprimands amounted, abode expectant and studied with embarrassed answers to make him speak out, saying, at the first, 'Why all this passion, Sir? Have I crucified Christ?' Whereupon, 'Mark this shameless fellow!' cried the friar. 'Hear what he saith! He speaketh as if a year or two were passed and he had for lapse of time forgotten his misdeeds and his lewdness! Hath it then escaped thy mind between this and matinsong that thou hast outraged some one this very morning? Where wast thou this morning a little before day?' 'I know not,' answered the gentleman; 'but wherever it was, the news thereof hath reached you mighty early.' Quoth the friar, 'Certes, the news hath reached me. Doubtless thou supposedst because her husband was abroad, that needs must the gentlewoman receive thee incontinent in her arms. A fine thing, indeed! Here's a pretty fellow! Here's an honourable man! He's grown a nighthawk, a garden-breaker, a tree-climber! Thinkest thou by importunity to overcome this lady's chastity, that thou climbest up to her windows anights by the trees? There is nought in the world so displeasing to her as thou; yet must thou e'en go essaying it again and again. Truly, thou hast profited finely by my admonitions, let alone that she hath shown thee her aversion in many ways. But this I have to say to thee; she hath up to now, not for any love she beareth thee, but at my instant entreaty, kept silence of that which thou hast done; but she will do so no more; I have given her leave to do what seemeth good to her, an thou annoy her again in aught. What wilt thou do, an she tell her brothers?' The gentleman having now gathered enough of that which it concerned him to know, appeased the friar, as best he knew and might, with many and ample promises, and taking leave of him, waited till matinsong[2] of the ensuing night, when he made his way into the garden and climbed up by the tree to the window. He found the lattice open and entering the chamber as quickliest he might, threw himself into the arms of his fair mistress, who, having awaited him with the utmost impatience, received him joyfully, saying, 'Gramercy to my lord the friar for that he so well taught thee the way hither!' Then, taking their pleasure one of the other, they solaced themselves together with great delight, devising and laughing amain anent the simplicity of the dolt of a friar and gibing at wool-hanks and teasels and carding-combs. Moreover, having taken order for their future converse, they did on such wise that, without having to resort anew to my lord the friar, they foregathered in equal joyance many another night, to the like whereof I pray God, of His holy mercy, speedily to conduct me and all Christian souls who have a mind thereto."

---

1. Lit. (*riscaldare gli orecchi*).
2. *i.e.* three a.m. next morning.

☙ 4 ☙

THE FOURTH STORY

DOM FELICE TEACHETH FRA PUCCIO HOW HE MAY BECOME BEATIFIED BY PERFORMING A CERTAIN PENANCE OF HIS FASHION, WHICH THE OTHER DOTH, AND DOM FELICE MEANWHILE LEADETH A MERRY LIFE OF IT WITH THE GOOD MAN'S WIFE

FILOMENA, having made an end of her story, was silent and Dioneo having with dulcet speech mightily commended the lady's shrewdness and eke the prayer with which Filomena had concluded, the queen turned with a smile to Pamfilo and said, "Come, Pamfilo, continue our diversion with some pleasant trifle." Pamfilo promptly answered that he would well and began thus: "Madam, there are many persons who, what while they study to enter Paradise, unwittingly send others thither; the which happened, no great while since, to a neighbour of ours, as you shall hear.

According to that which I have heard tell, there abode near San Pancrazio an honest man and a rich, called Puccio di Rinieri, who, devoting himself in his latter days altogether to religious practices, became a tertiary[1] of the order of St. Francis, whence he was styled Fra Puccio, and ensuing this his devout life, much frequented the church, for that he had no family other than a wife and one maid and consequently, it behoved him not apply himself to any craft. Being an ignorant, clod-pated fellow, he said his paternosters, went to preachments and attended mass, nor ever failed to be at the Lauds chanted by the seculars,[2] and fasted and mortified himself; nay, it was buzzed about that he was of the Flagellants.[3] His wife, whose name was Mistress Isabetta,[4] a woman, yet young, of eight-and-twenty to thirty years of age, fresh and fair and plump as a lady-apple, kept, by reason of the piety and belike of the age of her husband, much longer and more frequent fasts than she could have wished, and when she would have slept or maybe frolicked with him, he recounted to her the life of Christ and the preachments of Fra Nastagio or the Complaint of Mary Magdalene or the like. Meantime there returned home from Paris a monk hight Dom[5] Felice, Conventual[6] of San Pancrazio, who was young and comely enough of person, keen of wit and a profound scholar, and with him Fra Puccio contracted a strait friendship. And for that this Dom Felice right well resolved him his every doubt and knowing his pious turn of mind, made him a show of exceeding devoutness, Fra Puccio fell to carrying him home bytimes and giving him to dine and sup, as the occasion offered; and the lady also, for her husband's sake, became familiar with him and willingly did him honour. The monk, then, continuing to frequent Fra Puccio's house and seeing the latter's wife so fresh and plump, guessed what should be the thing whereof she suffered the most default and bethought himself, an he might, to go about to furnish her withal himself, and so spare Fra Puccio fatigue. Accordingly, craftily casting his eyes on her, at one time and another, he made shift to kindle in her breast that same desire which he had himself, which when he saw, he bespoke her of his wishes as first occasion betided him. But, albeit he found her well disposed to give effect to the work, he could find no means thereunto, for that she would on nowise trust herself to be with him in any place in the world save her own house, and there it might not be, seeing that Fra Puccio never went without the town. At this the monk was sore chagrined; but, after much consideration, he hit upon a device whereby he might avail to foregather with the lady in her own house, without suspect, for all Fra Puccio should be at home. Accordingly, the latter coming one day to visit him, he bespoke him thus, 'I have many a time understood, Fra Puccio, that all thy desire is to become a saint and to this end meseemeth thou goest about by a long road, whereas there is another and a very short one, which the Pope and the other great prelates, who know and practise it, will not have made known, for that the clergy, who for the most part live by alms, would incontinent be undone, inasmuch as the laity would no longer trouble themselves to propitiate them with alms or otherwhat. But, for that thou art my friend and hast very honourably entertained me, I would teach it thee, so I were assured thou wouldst practise it and wouldst not discover it to any living soul.' Fra Puccio, eager to know the thing, began straightway to entreat him with the utmost instancy that he would teach it him and then to swear that never, save in so far as it should please him, would he tell it to any, engaging, an if it were such as he might avail to follow, to address himself thereunto. Whereupon quoth the monk, 'Since thou promisest me this, I will e'en discover it to thee. Thou must know that the doctors of the church hold that it behoveth whoso would become blessed to perform the penance which thou shalt hear; but understand me aright; I do not say that, after the penance, thou wilt not be a sinner like as thou presently art; but this will betide, that the sins which thou hast committed up to the time of the penance will all by virtue thereof be purged and pardoned unto thee, and those which thou shalt commit thereafterward will not be written to thy prejudice, but will pass away with the holy water, as venial sins do now. It behoveth a man, then, in the first place, whenas he cometh to begin the penance, to confess himself with the utmost diligence of his sins, and after this he must keep a fast and a very strict abstinence for the space of forty days, during which time thou[7] must abstain from touching, not to say other women, but even thine own wife. Moreover, thou must have in thine own house some place whence thou mayst see the sky by night, whither thou must betake thyself towards the hour of complines,[8] and there thou must have a wide plank set up, on such wise that, standing upright, thou mayst lean thy loins against it and keeping thy feet on the ground, stretch out thine arms, crucifix fashion. An thou wouldst rest them upon some peg or other, thou mayst do it, and on this wise thou must abide gazing upon the sky, without budging a jot, till matins. Wert thou a scholar, thou wouldst do well to repeat certain orisons I would give thee; but, as thou art it not, thou must say three hundred Paternosters and as many Ave Marys, in honour of the Trinity, and looking upon heaven, still have in remembrance that God is the Creator of heaven and earth and the passion of Christ, abiding on such wise as He abode on the cross. When the bell ringeth to matins, thou mayst, an thou wilt, go and cast thyself, clad as thou art, on thy bed and sleep, and after, in the forenoon, betake thyself to church and there hear at least three masses and repeat fifty Paternosters and as many Aves; after which thou shalt with a single heart do all and sundry thine occasions, if thou have any to do, and dine and at evensong be in church again and there say certain orisons which I will give thee by writ and without which it cannot be done. Then, towards complines, do thou return to the fashion aforesaid, and thus doing, even as I have myself done aforetime, I doubt not but, ere thou come to the end of the penance, thou wilt, (provided thou shalt have performed it with devoutness and compunction,) feel somewhat marvellous of eternal beatitude.' Quoth Fra Puccio, 'This is no very burdensome matter, nor yet overlong, and may very well be done; wherefore I purpose in God's name to begin on Sunday.' Then, taking leave of him and returning home, he related everything in due order to his wife, having the other's permission therefor. The lady understood very well what the monk meant by bidding him stand fast without stirring till matins; wherefore, the device seeming to her excellent, she replied that she was well pleased therewith and with every other good work that he did for the health of his soul and that, so God might make the penance profitable to him, she would e'en fast with him, but do no more. They being thus of accord and Sunday come, Fra Puccio began his penance and my lord monk, having agreed with the lady, came most evenings to sup with her, bringing with him store of good things to eat and drink, and after lay with her till matinsong, when he arose and took himself off, whilst Fra Puccio returned to bed. Now the place which Fra Puccio had chosen for his penance adjoined the chamber where the lady lay and was parted therefrom but by a very slight wall, wherefore, Master Monk wantoning it one night overfreely with the lady and she with him, it seemed to Fra Puccio that he felt a shaking of the floor of the house. Accordingly, having by this said an hundred of his Paternosters, he made a stop there and without moving, called to his wife to know what she did. The lady, who was of a waggish turn and was then belike astride of San Benedetto his beast or that of San Giovanni Gualberto, answered, 'I' faith, husband mine, I toss as most I may.' 'How?' quoth Fra Puccio. 'Thou tossest? What meaneth this tossing?' The lady, laughing, for that she was a frolicsome dame and doubtless had cause to laugh, answered merrily; 'How? You know not what it meaneth? Why, I have heard you say a thousand times, "Who suppeth not by night must toss till morning light."' Fra Puccio doubted not but that the fasting was the cause of her unableness to sleep and it was for this she tossed thus about the bed; wherefore, in the simplicity of his heart, 'Wife,' said he, 'I told thee not to fast; but, since thou wouldst e'en do it, think not of that, but address thyself to rest; thou givest such vaults about the bed that thou makest all in the place shake.' 'Have no care for that,' answered the lady; 'I know what I am about; do you but well, you, and I will do as well as I may.' Fra Puccio, accordingly, held his peace and betook himself anew to his Paternosters; and after that night my lord monk and the lady let make a bed in another part of the house, wherein they abode in the utmost joyance what while Fra Puccio's penance lasted. At one and the same hour the monk took himself off and the lady returned to her own bed, whereto a little after came Fra Puccio from his penance; and on this wise the latter continued to do penance, whilst his wife did her delight with the monk, to whom quoth she merrily, now and again, 'Thou hast put Fra Puccio upon performing a penance, whereby we have gotten Paradise.' Indeed, the lady, finding herself in good case, took such a liking to the monk's fare, having been long kept on low diet by her husband, that, whenas Fra Puccio's penance was accomplished, she still found means to feed her fill with him elsewhere and using discretion, long took her pleasure thereof. Thus, then, that my last words may not be out of accord with my first, it came to pass that, whereas Fra Puccio, by doing penance, thought to win Paradise for himself, he put therein the monk, who had shown him the speedy way thither, and his wife, who lived with him in great lack of that whereof Dom Felice, like a charitable man as he was, vouchsafed her great plenty."

---

1. *i.e.* a lay brother or affiliate.
2. *i.e.* the canticles of praise chanted by certain lay confraternities, established for that purpose and answering to our præ-Reformation Laudsingers.
3. An order of lay penitents, who were wont at certain times to go masked about the streets, scourging themselves

in expiation of the sins of the people. This expiatory practice was particularly prevalent in Italy in the middle of the thirteenth century.

4. Contraction of Elisabetta.

5. *Dom*, contraction of Dominus (lord), the title commonly given to the beneficed clergy in the middle ages, answering to our *Sir* as used by Shakespeare (*e.g.* Sir Hugh Evans the Welsh Parson, Sir Topas the Curate, etc.). The expression survives in the title *Dominie* (*i.e.* Domine, voc. of Dominus) still familiarly applied to schoolmasters, who were of course originally invariably clergymen.

6. A Conventual is a member of some monastic order attached to the regular service of a church, or (as would nowadays be said) a "beneficed" monk.

7. *Sic.* This confusion of persons constantly occurs in Boccaccio, especially in the conversational parts of the Decameron, in which he makes the freest use of the various forms of enallage and of other rhetorical figures, such as hyperbaton, synecdoche, etc., to the no small detriment of his style in the matter of clearness.

8. *i.e.* nine o'clock p.m.

❧ 5 ❧

THE FIFTH STORY

RICCIARDO, SURNAMED IL ZIMA, GIVETH MESSER FRANCESCO VERGELLESI A PALFREY OF HIS AND HATH THEREFOR HIS LEAVE TO SPEAK WITH HIS WIFE. SHE KEEPING SILENCE, HE IN HER PERSON REPLIETH UNTO HIMSELF, AND THE EFFECT AFTER ENSUETH IN ACCORDANCE WITH HIS ANSWER

PAMFILO HAVING MADE AN END, not without laughter on the part of the ladies, of the story of Fra Puccio, the queen with a commanding air bade Elisa follow on. She, rather tartly than otherwise, not out of malice, but of old habit, began to speak thus, "Many folk, knowing much, imagine that others know nothing, and so ofttimes, what while they think to overreach others, find, after the event, that they themselves have been outwitted of them; wherefore I hold his folly great who setteth himself without occasion to test the strength of another's wit. But, for that maybe all are not of my opinion, it pleaseth me, whilst following on the given order of the discourse, to relate to you that which befell a Pistolese gentleman[1] by reason thereof.

There was in Pistoia a gentleman of the Vergellesi family, by name Messer Francesco, a man of great wealth and understanding and well advised in all else, but covetous beyond measure. Being made provost of Milan, he had furnished himself with everything necessary for his honourable going thither, except only with a palfrey handsome enough for him, and finding none to his liking, he abode in concern thereof. Now there was then in the same town a young man called Ricciardo, of little family, but very rich, who still went so quaintly clad and so brave of his person that he was commonly known as Il Zima,[2] and he had long in vain loved and courted Messer Francesco's wife, who was exceeding fair and very virtuous. Now he had one of the handsomest palfreys in all Tuscany and set great store by it for its beauty and it being public to every one that he was enamoured of Messer Francesco's wife, there were those who told the latter that, should he ask it, he might have the horse for the love Il Zima bore his lady. Accordingly, moved by covetise, Messer Francesco let call Il Zima to him and sought of him his palfrey by way of sale, so he should proffer it to him as a gift. The other, hearing this, was well pleased and made answer to him, saying, "Sir, though you gave me all you have in the world, you might not avail to have my palfrey by way of sale, but by way of gift you may have it, whenas it pleaseth you, on condition that, ere you take it, I may have leave to speak some words with your lady in your presence, but so far removed from every one that I may be heard of none other than herself.' The gentleman, urged by avarice and looking to outwit the other, answered that it liked him well and [that he might speak with her] as much as he would; then, leaving him in the saloon of his palace, he betook himself to the lady's chamber and telling her

135

how easily he might acquire the palfrey, bade her come hearken to Il Zima, but charged her take good care to answer neither little or much to aught that he should say. To this the lady much demurred, but, it behoving her ensue her husband's pleasure, she promised to do his bidding and followed him to the saloon, to hear what Il Zima should say. The latter, having renewed his covenant with the gentleman, seated himself with the lady in a part of the saloon at a great distance from every one and began to say thus, 'Noble lady, meseemeth certain that you have too much wit not to have long since perceived how great a love I have been brought to bear you by your beauty, which far transcendeth that of any woman whom methinketh I ever beheld, to say nothing of the engaging manners and the peerless virtues which be in you and which might well avail to take the loftiest spirits of mankind; wherefore it were needless to declare to you in words that this [my love] is the greatest and most fervent that ever man bore woman; and thus, without fail, will I do[3] so long as my wretched life shall sustain these limbs, nay, longer; for that, if in the other world folk love as they do here below, I shall love you to all eternity. Wherefore you may rest assured that you have nothing, be it much or little worth, that you may hold so wholly yours and whereon you may in every wise so surely reckon as myself, such as I am, and that likewise which is mine. And that of this you may take assurance by very certain argument, I tell you that I should count myself more graced, did you command me somewhat that I might do and that would pleasure you, than if, I commanding, all the world should promptliest obey me. Since, then, I am yours, even as you have heard, it is not without reason that I dare to offer up my prayers to your nobility, wherefrom alone can all peace, all health and all well-being derive for me, and no otherwhence; yea, as the humblest of your servants, I beseech you, dear my good and only hope of my soul, which, midmost the fire of love, feedeth upon its hope in you,—that your benignity may be so great and your past rigour shown unto me, who am yours, on such wise be mollified that I, recomforted by your kindness, may say that, like as by your beauty I was stricken with love, even so by your pity have I life, which latter, an your haughty soul incline not to my prayers, will without fail come to nought and I shall perish and you may be said to be my murderer. Letting be that my death will do you no honour, I doubt not eke but that, conscience bytimes pricking you therefor, you will regret having wrought it[4] and whiles, better disposed, will say in yourself, "Alack, how ill I did not to have compassion upon my poor Zima!" and this repentance, being of no avail, will cause you the great annoy. Wherefore, so this may not betide, now that you have it in your power to succour me, bethink yourself and ere I die, be moved to pity on me, for that with you alone it resteth to make me the happiest or the most miserable man alive. I trust your courtesy will be such that you will not suffer me to receive death in guerdon of such and so great a love, but will with a glad response and full of favour quicken my fainting spirits, which flutter, all dismayed, in your presence.' Therewith he held his peace and heaving the deepest of sighs, followed up with sundry tears, proceeded to await the lady's answer. The latter,—whom the long court he had paid her, the joustings held and the serenades given in her honour and other like things done of him for the love of her had not availed to move,—was moved by the passionate speech of this most ardent lover and began to be sensible of that which she had never yet felt, to wit, what manner of thing love was; and albeit, in ensuance of the commandment laid upon her by her husband, she kept silence, she could not withal hinder sundry gentle sighs from discovering that which, in answer to Il Zima, she would gladly have made manifest. Il Zima, having waited awhile and seeing that no response ensued, was wondered and presently began to divine the husband's device; but yet, looking her in the face and observing certain flashes of her eyes towards him now and again and noting, moreover, the sighs which she suffered not to escape her bosom with all her strength, conceived fresh hope and heartened thereby, took new counsel[5] and proceeded to answer himself after the following fashion, she hearkening the while: 'Zima mine, this long time, in good sooth, have I perceived thy love for me to be most great and perfect, and now by thy words I know it yet better and am well pleased therewith, as indeed I should be. Algates, an I have seemed to thee harsh and cruel, I will not have thee believe that I have at heart been that which I have shown myself in countenance; nay, I have ever loved thee and held thee dear above all other men; but thus hath it behoved me do, both for fear of others and for the preserving of my fair fame. But now is the time at hand when I may show thee clearly that I love thee and guerdon thee of the love that thou hast borne and bearest me. Take comfort, therefore, and be of good hope, for that a few days hence Messer Francesco is to go to Milan for provost, as indeed thou knowest, who hast for the love of me given him thy goodly palfrey; and whenas he shall be gone, I promise thee by my troth and of the true love I bear thee, that, before many days, thou shalt without fail foregather with me and we will give gladsome and entire accomplishment to our love. And that I may not have to bespeak thee otherwhiles of the matter, I tell thee presently that, whenas thou shalt see two napkins displayed at the window of my chamber, which giveth upon our garden, do thou that same evening at nightfall make shift to come to me by the garden door, taking good care that thou be not seen. Thou wilt find me awaiting thee and we will all night long have delight and pleasance one of another, to our hearts' content.' Having thus spoken for the lady, he began again to speak in his own person and rejoined on this wise, 'Dearest lady, my every sense is so transported with excessive joy for your gracious reply that I can scarce avail to make response, much less to render you due thanks; nay, could I e'en speak as I desire, there is no term so long that it might suffice me fully to thank you as I would fain do and as it behoveth me; wherefore I leave it to your discreet consideration to imagine that which, for all my will, I am unable to express in words. This much only I tell you that I will without fail bethink myself to do as you have charged me, and being then, peradventure, better certified of so great a grace as that which you have vouchsafed me, I will, as best I may, study to render you the utmost thanks in my power. For the nonce there abideth no more to say; wherefore, dearest lady mine, God give you that gladness and that weal which you most desire, and so to Him I commend you.' For all this the lady said not a word; whereupon Il Zima arose and turned towards the husband, who, seeing him risen, came up to him and said, laughing 'How deemest thou? Have I well performed my promise to thee?' 'Nay, sir' answered Il Zima; 'for you promised to let me speak with your lady and you have caused me speak with a marble statue.' These words were mighty pleasing to the husband, who, for all he had a good opinion of the lady, conceived of her a yet better and said, 'Now is thy palfrey fairly mine.' 'Ay is it, sir,' replied Il Zima, 'but, had I thought to reap of this favour received of you such fruit as I have gotten, I had given you the palfrey, without asking it[6] of you; and would God I had done it, for that now you have bought the palfrey and I have not sold it.' The other laughed at this and being now provided with a palfrey, set out upon his way a few days after and betook himself to Milan, to enter upon the Provostship. The lady, left free in her house, called to mind Il Zima's words and the love he bore her and the palfrey given for her sake and seeing him pass often by the house, said in herself, 'What do I? Why waste I my youth? Yonder man is gone to Milan and will not return these six months. When will he ever render me them[7] again? When I am old? Moreover, when shall I ever find such a lover as Il Zima? I am alone and have no one to fear. I know not why I should not take this good opportunity what while I may; I shall not always have such leisure as I presently have. None will know the thing, and even were it to be known, it is better to do and repent, than to abstain and repent.' Having thus taken counsel with herself, she one day set two napkins in the garden window, even as Il Zima had said, which when he saw, he was greatly rejoiced and no sooner was the night come than he betook himself, secretly and alone, to the gate of the lady's garden and finding it open, passed on to another door that opened into the house, where he found his mistress awaiting him. She, seeing him come, started up to meet him and received him with the utmost joy, whilst he clipped and kissed her an hundred thousand times and followed her up the stair to her chamber, where, getting them to bed without a moment's delay, they knew the utmost term of amorous delight. Nor was this first time the last, for that, what while the gentleman abode at Milan and even after his coming back, Il Zima returned thither many another time, to the exceeding satisfaction of both parties."

---

1. *i.e.* a gentleman of Pistoia.
2. Lit. "The summit," or in modern slang "The tiptop," *i.e.* the pink of fashion.
3. *i.e.* this love shall I bear you. This is a flagrant instance of the misuse of ellipsis, which so frequently disfigures Boccaccio's dialogue.
4. *i.e.* my death.
5. Syn. a rare or strange means (*nuovo consiglio*). The word *nuovo* is constantly used by Boccaccio in the latter sense, as is *consiglio* in its remoter signification of means, remedy, etc.
6. *i.e.* the favour.
7. *i.e.* the lost six months.

❦ 6 ❦

THE SIXTH STORY

RICCIARDO MINUTOLO, BEING ENAMOURED OF THE WIFE OF FILIPPELLO FIGHINOLFI AND KNOWING HER JEALOUSY OF HER HUSBAND, CONTRIVETH, BY REPRESENTING THAT FILIPPELLO WAS ON THE ENSUING DAY TO BE WITH HIS OWN WIFE IN A BAGNIO, TO BRING HER TO THE LATTER PLACE, WHERE, THINKING TO BE WITH HER HUSBAND, SHE FINDETH THAT SHE HATH ABIDDEN WITH RICCIARDO

ELISA HAVING NO MORE to say, the queen, after commending the sagacity of Il Zima, bade Fiammetta proceed with a story, who answered, all smilingly, "Willingly, Madam," and began thus: "It behoveth somedele to depart our city (which, like as it aboundeth in all things else, is fruitful in instances of every subject) and as Elisa hath done, to recount somewhat of the things that have befallen in other parts of the world; wherefore, passing over to Naples, I shall tell how one of those she-saints, who feign themselves so shy of love, was by the ingenuity of a lover of hers brought to taste the fruits of love, ere she had known its flowers; the which will at once teach you circumspection in the things that may hap and afford you diversion of those already befallen.

In Naples, a very ancient city and as delightful as any in Italy or maybe more so, there was once a young man, illustrious for nobility of blood and noted for his much wealth, whose name was Ricciardo Minutolo. Albeit he had to wife a very fair and lovesome young lady, he fell in love with one who, according to general opinion, far overpassed in beauty all the other ladies of Naples. Her name was Catella and she was the wife of another young gentleman of like condition, hight Filippello Fighinolfi, whom, like a very virtuous woman as she was, she loved and cherished over all. Ricciardo, then, loving this Catella and doing all those things whereby the love and favour of a lady are commonly to be won, yet for all that availing not to compass aught of his desire, was like to despair; and unknowing or unable to rid him of his passion, he neither knew how to die nor did it profit him to live.

Abiding in this mind, it befell that he was one day urgently exhorted by certain ladies of his kinsfolk to renounce this passion of his, seeing he did but weary himself in vain, for that Catella had none other good than Filippello, of whom she lived in such jealousy that she fancied every bird that flew through the air would take him from her. Ricciardo, hearing of Catella's jealousy, forthright bethought himself how he might compass his wishes and accordingly proceeded to feign himself in despair of her love and to have therefore set his mind upon another lady, for whose love he began to make a show of jousting and tourneying and doing all those things which he had been used to do for Catella; nor did he do this long before well nigh all the Neapolitans, and among the rest the lady herself, were persuaded that he no longer loved

Catella, but was ardently enamoured of this second lady; and on this wise he persisted until it was so firmly believed not only of others, but of Catella herself, that the latter laid aside a certain reserve with which she was wont to entreat him, by reason of the love he bore her, and coming and going, saluted him familiarly, neighbourwise, as she did others.

It presently befell that, the weather being warm, many companies of ladies and gentlemen went, according to the usance of the Neapolitans, to divert themselves on the banks of the sea and there to dine and sup, and Ricciardo, knowing Catella to be gone thither with her company, betook himself to the same place with his friends and was received into Catella's party of ladies, after allowing himself to be much pressed, as if he had no great mind to abide there. The ladies and Catella fell to rallying him upon his new love, and he, feigning himself sore inflamed therewith, gave them the more occasion for discourse. Presently, one lady going hither and thither, as commonly happeneth in such places, and Catella being left with a few whereas Ricciardo was, the latter cast at her a hint of a certain amour of Filippello her husband, whereupon she fell into a sudden passion of jealousy and began to be inwardly all afire with impatience to know what he meant. At last, having contained herself awhile and being unable to hold out longer, she besought Ricciardo, for that lady's sake whom he most loved, to be pleased to make her clear[1] of that which he had said of Filippello; whereupon quoth he, 'You conjure me by such a person that I dare not deny aught you ask me; wherefore I am ready to tell it you, so but you promise me that you will never say a word thereof either to him or to any other, save whenas you shall by experience have seen that which I shall tell you to be true; for that, when you please, I will teach you how you may see it.'

The lady consented to that which he asked and swore to him never to repeat that which he should tell her, believing it the more to be true. Then, withdrawing apart with her, so they might not be overheard of any, he proceeded to say thus: 'Madam, an I loved you as once I loved, I should not dare tell you aught which I thought might vex you; but, since that love is passed away, I shall be less chary of discovering to you the whole truth. I know not if Filippello have ever taken umbrage at the love I bore you or have believed that I was ever loved of you. Be this as it may, he hath never personally shown me aught thereof; but now, having peradventure awaited a time whenas he deemed I should be less suspicious, it seemeth he would fain do unto me that which I misdoubt me he feareth I have done unto him, to wit, [he seeketh] to have my wife at his pleasure. As I find, he hath for some little time past secretly solicited her with sundry messages, all of which I have known from herself, and she hath made answer thereunto according as I have enjoined her. This very day, however, ere I came hither, I found in the house, in close conference with my wife, a woman whom I set down incontinent for that which she was, wherefore I called my wife and asked her what the woman wanted. Quoth she, "She is the agent of Filippello, with whom thou hast saddled me, by dint of making me answer him and give him hopes, and she saith that he will e'en know once for all what I mean to do and that, an I will, he would contrive for me to be privily at a bagnio in this city; nay, of this he prayeth and importuneth me; and hadst thou not, I know not why, caused me keep this traffic with him, I would have rid myself of him after such a fashion that he should never more have looked whereas I might be." Thereupon meseemed this was going too far and that it was no longer to be borne; and I bethought myself to tell it to you, so you might know how he requiteth that entire fidelity of yours, whereby aforetime I was nigh upon death. And so you shall not believe this that I tell you to be words and fables, but may, whenas you have a mind thereto, openly both see and touch it, I caused my wife make this answer to her who awaited it, that she was ready to be at the bagnio in question to-morrow at none, whenas the folk sleep; with which the woman took leave of her, very well pleased. Now methinketh not you believe that I will send my wife thither; but, were I in your place, I would contrive that he should find me there in the room of her he thinketh to meet, and whenas I had abidden with him awhile, I would give him to know with whom he had been and render him such honour thereof as should beseem him; by which means methinketh you would do him such a shame that the affront he would fain put upon yourself and upon me would at one blow be avenged.'

Catella, hearing this, without anywise considering who it was that said it to her or suspecting his design, forthright, after the wont of jealous folk, gave credence to his words and fell a-fitting to his story certain things that had already befallen; then, fired with sudden anger, she answered that she would certainly do as he counselled,—it was no such great matter,—and that assuredly, if Filippello came thither, she would do him such a shame that it should still recur to his mind, as often as he saw a woman. Ricciardo, well pleased at this and himseeming his device was a good one and in a fair way of success, confirmed her in her purpose with many other words and strengthened her belief in his story, praying her, natheless, never to say that she had heard it from him, the which she promised him on her troth.

Next morning, Ricciardo betook himself to a good woman, who kept the bagnio he had named to Catella, and telling her what he purposed to do, prayed her to further him therein as most she might. The good woman, who was much beholden to him, answered that she would well and agreed with him what she should do and say. Now in the house where the bagnio was she had a very dark chamber, for that no window gave thereon by which the light might enter. This chamber she made ready and spread a bed there, as best she might, wherein Ricciardo, as soon as he had dined, laid himself and proceeded to await Catella. The latter, having heard Ricciardo's words and giving more credence thereto than behoved her, returned in the evening, full of despite, to her house, whither Filippello also returned and being by chance full of other thought, maybe did not show her his usual fondness. When she saw this, her suspicions rose yet higher and she said in herself, 'Forsooth, his mind is occupied with yonder lady with whom he thinketh to take his pleasure to-morrow; but of a surety this shall not come to pass.' An in this thought she abode well nigh all that night, considering how she should bespeak him, whenas she should be with him [in the bagnio].

What more [need I say?] The hour of none come, she took her waiting-woman and without anywise changing counsel, repaired to the bagnio that Ricciardo had named to her, and there finding the good woman, asked her if Filippello had been there that day, whereupon quoth the other, who had been duly lessoned by Ricciardo, 'Are you the lady that should come to speak with him?' 'Ay am I,' answered Catella. 'Then,' said the woman, 'get you in to him.' Catella, who went seeking that which she would fain not have found, caused herself to be brought to the chamber where Ricciardo was and entering with covered head, locked herself in. Ricciardo, seeing her enter, rose joyfully to his feet and catching her in his arms, said softly, 'Welcome, my soul!' Whilst she, the better to feign herself other than she was, clipped him and kissed him and made much of him, without saying a word, fearing to be known of him if she should speak. The chamber was very dark, wherewith each of them was well pleased, nor for long abiding there did the eyes recover more power. Ricciardo carried her to the bed and there, without speaking, lest their voices should betray them, they abode a long while, to the greater delight and pleasance of the one party than the other.

But presently, it seeming to Catella time to vent the resentment she felt, she began, all afire with rage and despite, to speak thus, 'Alas, how wretched is women's lot and how ill bestowed the love that many of them bear their husbands! I, unhappy that I am, these eight years have I loved thee more than my life, and thou, as I have felt, art all afire and all consumed with love of a strange woman, wicked and perverse man that thou art! Now with whom thinkest thou to have been? Thou hast been with her whom thou hast too long beguiled with thy false blandishments, making a show of love to her and being enamoured elsewhere. I am Catella, not

Ricciardo's wife, disloyal traitor that thou art! Hearken if thou know my voice; it is indeed I; and it seemeth to me a thousand years till we be in the light, so I may shame thee as thou deservest, scurvy discredited cur that thou art! Alack, woe is me! To whom have I borne so much love these many years? To this disloyal dog, who, thinking to have a strange woman in his arms, hath lavished on me more caresses and more fondnesses in this little while I have been here with him than in all the rest of the time I have been his. Thou hast been brisk enough to-day, renegade cur that thou art, that usest at home to show thyself so feeble and forspent and impotent; but, praised be God, thou hast tilled thine own field and not, as thou thoughtest, that of another. No wonder thou camest not anigh me yesternight; thou lookedst to discharge thee of thy lading elsewhere and wouldst fain come fresh to the battle; but, thanks to God and my own foresight, the stream hath e'en run in its due channel. Why answerest thou not, wicked man? Why sayst thou not somewhat? Art thou grown dumb, hearing me? Cock's faith, I know not what hindereth me from thrusting my hands into thine eyes and tearing them out for thee. Thou thoughtest to do this treason very secretly; but, perdie, one knoweth as much as another; thou hast not availed to compass thine end; I have had better beagles at thy heels than thou thoughtest.'

Ricciardo inwardly rejoiced at these words and without making any reply, clipped her and kissed her and fondled her more than ever; whereupon quoth she, following on her speech, 'Ay, thou thinkest to cajole me with thy feigned caresses, fashious dog that thou art, and to appease and console me; but thou art mistaken; I shall never be comforted for this till I have put thee to shame therefor in the presence of all our friends and kinsmen and neighbours. Am I not as fair as Ricciardo's wife, thou villain? Am I not as good a gentlewoman? Why dost thou not answer, thou sorry dog? What hath she more than I? Keep thy distance; touch me not; thou hast done enough feats of arms for to-day. Now thou knowest who I am, I am well assured that all thou couldst do would be perforce; but, so God grant me grace, I will yet cause thee suffer want thereof, and I know not what hindereth me from sending for Ricciardo, who hath loved me more than himself and could never boast that I once even looked at him; nor know I what harm it were to do it. Thou thoughtest to have his wife here and it is as if thou hadst had her, inasmuch as it is none of thy fault that the thing hath miscarried; wherefore, were I to have himself, thou couldst not with reason blame me.'

Brief, many were the lady's words and sore her complaining. However, at last, Ricciardo, bethinking himself that, an he let her go in that belief, much ill might ensue thereof, determined to discover himself and undeceive her; wherefore, catching her in his arms and holding her fast, so she might not get away, he said, 'Sweet my soul, be not angered; that which I could not have of you by simply loving you, Love hath taught me to obtain by practice; and I am your Ricciardo.' Catella, hearing this and knowing him by the voice, would have thrown herself incontinent out of bed, but could not; whereupon she offered to cry out; but Ricciardo stopped her mouth with one hand and said, 'Madam, this that hath been may henceforth on nowise be undone, though you should cry all the days of your life; and if you cry out or cause this ever anywise to be known of any one, two things will come thereof; the one (which should no little concern you) will be that your honour and fair fame will be marred, for that, albeit you may avouch that I brought you hither by practice, I shall say that it is not true, nay, that I caused you come hither for monies and gifts that I promised you, whereof for that I gave you not so largely as you hoped, you waxed angry and made all this talk and this outcry; and you know that folk are more apt to credit ill than good, wherefore I shall more readily be believed than you. Secondly, there will ensue thereof a mortal enmity between your husband and myself, and it may as well happen that I shall kill him as he me, in which case you are never after like to be happy or content. Wherefore, heart of my body, go not about at once to dishonour yourself and to cast your husband and myself into strife and peril. You are not the first woman, nor will you be the last, who hath been deceived, nor have I in this practised upon you to bereave you of your own, but for the exceeding love that I bear you and am minded ever to bear you and to be your most humble servant. And although it is long since I and all that I possess or can or am worth have been yours and at your service, henceforward I purpose that they shall be more than ever so. Now, you are well advised in other things and so I am certain you will be in this.'

Catella, what while Ricciardo spoke thus, wept sore, but, albeit she was sore provoked and complained grievously, nevertheless, her reason allowed so much force to his true words that she knew it to be possible that it should happen as he said; wherefore quoth she, 'Ricciardo, I know not how God will vouchsafe me strength to suffer the affront and the cheat thou hast put upon me; I will well to make no outcry here whither my simplicity and overmuch jealousy have brought me; but of this be assured that I shall never be content till one way or another I see myself avenged of this thou hast done to me. Wherefore, leave me, hold me no longer; thou hast had that which thou desiredst and hast tumbled me to thy heart's content; it is time to leave me; let me go, I prithee.'

Ricciardo, seeing her mind yet overmuch disordered, had laid it to heart never to leave her till he had gotten his pardon of her; wherefore, studying with the softest words to appease her, he so bespoke and so entreated and so conjured her that she was prevailed upon to make peace with him, and of like accord they abode together a great while thereafter in the utmost delight. Moreover, Catella, having thus learned how much more savoury were the lover's kisses than those of the husband and her former rigour being changed into kind love-liking for Ricciardo, from that day forth she loved him very tenderly and thereafter, ordering themselves with the utmost discretion, they many a time had joyance of their loves. God grant us to enjoy ours!"

---

1. Or, in modern parlance, to enlighten her.

✣ 7 ✣

THE SEVENTH STORY

TEDALDO ELISEI, HAVING FALLEN OUT WITH HIS
MISTRESS, DEPARTETH FLORENCE AND RETURNING
THITHER, AFTER AWHILE, IN A PILGRIM'S FAVOUR,
SPEAKETH WITH THE LADY AND MAKETH HER
COGNISANT OF HER ERROR; AFTER WHICH HE
DELIVERETH HER HUSBAND, WHO HAD BEEN
CONVICTED OF MURDERING HIM, FROM DEATH AND
RECONCILING HIM WITH HIS BRETHREN,
THENCEFORWARD DISCREETLY ENJOYETH HIMSELF
WITH HIS MISTRESS

FAIMMETTA BEING NOW SILENT, commended of all, the queen, to lose no time, forthright committed the burden of discourse to Emilia, who began thus: "It pleaseth me to return to our city, whence it pleased the last two speakers to depart, and to show you how a townsman of ours regained his lost mistress.

There was, then, in Florence a noble youth, whose name was Tedaldo Elisei and who, being beyond measure enamoured of a lady called Madam Ermellina, the wife of one Aldobrandino Palermini, deserved for his praiseworthy fashions, to enjoy his desire. However, Fortune, the enemy of the happy, denied him this solace, for that, whatever might have been the cause, the lady, after complying awhile with Tedaldo's wishes, suddenly altogether withdrew her good graces from him and not only refused to hearken to any message of his, but would on no wise see him; wherefore he fell into a dire and cruel melancholy; but his love for her had been so hidden that none guessed it to be the cause of his chagrin. After he had in divers ways studied amain to recover the love himseemed he had lost without his fault and finding all his labour vain, he resolved to withdraw from the world, that he might not afford her who was the cause of his ill the pleasure of seeing him pine away; wherefore, without saying aught to friend or kinsman, save to a comrade of his, who knew all, he took such monies as he might avail to have and departing secretly, came to Ancona, where, under the name of Filippo di Sanlodeccio, he made acquaintance with a rich merchant and taking service with him, accompanied him to Cyprus on board a ship of his.

His manners and behaviour so pleased the merchant that he not only assigned him a good wage, but made him in part his associate and put into his hands a great part of his affairs, which he ordered so well and so diligently that in a few years he himself became a rich and famous and considerable merchant; and albeit, in the midst of these his dealings, he oft remembered him of his cruel mistress and was grievously tormented of love and yearned sore to look on her again, such was his constancy that seven years long he got the better of the battle. But, chancing one day to hear sing in Cyprus a song that himself had made aforetime and wherein was recounted the love he bore his mistress and she him and the pleasure he had of her, and thinking it could not be she had forgotten him, he flamed up into such a passion of desire to see her again that, unable to endure longer, he resolved to return to Florence.

Accordingly, having set all his affairs in order, he betook himself with one only servant to Ancona and transporting all his good thither, despatched it to Florence to a friend of the Anconese his partner, whilst he himself, in the disguise of a pilgrim returning from the Holy Sepulchre, followed secretly after with his servant and coming to Florence, put up at a little hostelry kept by two brothers, in the neighbourhood of his mistress's house, whereto he repaired first of all, to see her, an he might. However, he found the windows and doors and all else closed, wherefore his heart misgave him she was dead or had removed thence and he betook himself, in great concern, to the house of his brethren, before which he saw four of the latter clad all in black. At this he marvelled exceedingly and knowing himself so changed both in habit and person from that which he was used to be, whenas he departed thence, that he might not lightly be recognized, he boldly accosted a cordwainer hard by and asked him why they were clad in black; whereto he answered, 'Yonder men are clad in black for that it is not yet a fortnight since a brother of theirs, who had not been here this great while, was murdered, and I understand they have proved to the court that one Aldobrandino Palermini, who is in prison, slew him, for that he was a well-wisher of his wife and had returned hither unknown to be with her.'

Tedaldo marvelled exceedingly that any one should so resemble him as to be taken for him and was grieved for Aldobrandino's ill fortune. Then, having learned that the lady was alive and well and it being now night, he returned, full of various thoughts, to the inn and having supped with his servant, was put to sleep well nigh at the top of the house. There, what with the many thoughts that stirred him and the badness of the bed and peradventure also by reason of the supper, which had been meagre, half the night passed whilst he had not yet been able to fall asleep; wherefore, being awake, himseemed about midnight he heard folk come down into the house from the roof, and after through the chinks of the chamber-door he saw a light come up thither. Thereupon he stole softly to the door and putting his eye to the chink, fell a-spying what this might mean and saw a comely enough lass who held the light, whilst three men, who had come down from the roof, made towards her; and after some greetings had passed between them, one of them said to the girl, 'Henceforth, praised be God, we may abide secure, since we know now for certain that the death of Tedaldo Elisei hath been proved by his brethren against Aldobrandino Palermini, who hath confessed thereto, and judgment is now recorded; nevertheless, it behoveth to keep strict silence, for that, should it ever become known that it was we [who slew him], we shall be in the same danger as is Aldobrandino.' Having thus bespoken the woman, who showed herself much rejoiced thereat, they left her and going below, betook themselves to bed.

Tedaldo, hearing this, fell a-considering how many and how great are the errors which may befall the minds of men, bethinking him first of his brothers who had bewept and buried a stranger in his stead and after of the innocent man accused on false suspicion and brought by untrue witness to the point of death, no less than of the blind severity of laws and rulers, who ofttimes, under cover of diligent investigation of the truth, cause, by their cruelties, prove that which is false and style themselves ministers of justice and of God, whereas indeed they are executors of iniquity and of the devil; after which he turned his thought to the deliverance of Aldobrandino and determined in himself what he should do. Accordingly, arising in the morning, he left his servant at the inn and betook himself alone, whenas it seemed to him time, to the house of his mistress, where, chancing to find the door open, he entered in and saw the lady seated, all full of tears and bitterness of soul, in a little ground floor room that was there.

At this sight he was like to weep for compassion of her and drawing near to her, said, 'Madam, afflict not yourself; your peace is at hand.' The lady, hearing this, lifted her eyes and said, weeping, 'Good man, thou seemest to me a stranger pilgrim; what knowest thou of my peace or of my affliction?' 'Madam,' answered Tedaldo, 'I am of Constantinople and am but now come hither, being sent of God to turn your tears into laughter and to deliver your husband from death.' Quoth she, 'An thou be of Constantinople and newly come hither, how knowest thou who I am or who is my husband?' Thereupon, the pilgrim beginning from the beginning, recounted to her the whole history of Aldobrandino's troubles and told her who she was and how long she had been married and other things which he very well knew of her affairs; whereat she marvelled exceedingly and holding him for a prophet, fell on her knees at his feet, beseeching him for God's sake, an he were come for Aldobrandino's salvation, to despatch, for that the time was short.

The pilgrim, feigning himself a very holy man, said, 'Madam, arise and weep not, but hearken well to that which I shall say to you and take good care never to tell it to any. According to that which God hath revealed unto me, the tribulation wherein you now are hath betided you because of a sin committed by you aforetime, which God the Lord hath chosen in part to purge with this present annoy and will have altogether amended of you; else will you fall into far greater affliction.' 'Sir,' answered the lady, 'I have many sins and know not which one, more than another, God the Lord would have me amend; wherefore, an you know it, tell me and I will do what I may to amend it.' 'Madam,' rejoined the pilgrim, 'I know well enough what it is, nor do I question you thereof the better to know it, but to the intent that, telling it yourself, you may have the more remorse thereof. But let us come to the fact; tell me, do you remember, ever to have had a lover?'

The lady, hearing this, heaved a deep sigh and marvelled sore, supposing none had ever known it, albeit, in the days when he was slain who had been buried for Tedaldo, there had been some whispering thereof, for certain words not very discreetly used by Tedaldo's confidant, who knew it; then answered, 'I see that God discovereth unto you all men's secrets, wherefore I am resolved not to hide mine own from you. True it is that in my youth I loved over all the ill-fortuned youth whose death is laid to my husband's charge, which death I have bewept as sore as it was grievous to me, for that, albeit I showed myself harsh and cruel to him before his departure, yet neither his long absence nor his unhappy death hath availed to tear him from my heart.' Quoth the pilgrim, 'The hapless youth who is dead you never loved, but Tedaldo Elisei ay.[1] But tell me, what was the occasion of your falling out with him? Did he ever give you any offence?' 'Certes, no,' replied she; 'he never offended against me; the cause of the breach was the prate of an accursed friar, to whom I once confessed me and who, when I told him of the love I bore Tedaldo and the privacy I had with him, made such a racket about my ears that I tremble yet to think of it, telling me that, an I desisted not therefrom, I should go in the devil's mouth to the deepest deep of hell and there be cast into everlasting fire; whereupon there entered into me such a fear that I altogether determined to forswear all further converse with him, and that I might have no occasion therefor, I would no longer receive his letters or messages; albeit I believe, had he persevered awhile, instead of getting him gone (as I presume) in despair, that, seeing him, as I did, waste away like snow in the sun, my harsh resolve would have yielded, for that I had no greater desire in the world.'

'Madam,' rejoined the pilgrim, 'it is this sin alone that now afflicteth you. I know for certain that Tedaldo did you no manner of violence; whenas you fell in love with him, you did it of your own free will, for that he pleased you; and as you yourself would have it, he came to you and enjoyed your privacy, wherein both with words and deeds you showed him such complaisance that, if he loved you before, you caused his love redouble a thousandfold. And this being so (as I know it was) what cause should have availed to move you so harshly to withdraw yourself from him? These things should be pondered awhile beforehand and if you think you may presently have cause to repent thereof, as of ill doing, you ought not to do them. You might, at your pleasure, have ordained of him, as of that which belonged to you, that he should no longer be yours; but to go about to deprive him of yourself, you who were his, was a theft and an unseemly thing, whenas it was not his will. Now you must know that I am a friar and am therefore well acquainted with all their usances; and if I speak somewhat at large of them for your profit, it is not forbidden me, as it were to another; nay, and it pleaseth me to speak of them, so you may henceforward know them better than you appear to have done in the past.

Friars of old were very pious and worthy men, but those who nowadays style themselves friars and would be held such have nothing of the monk but the gown; nor is this latter even that of a true friar, for that,—whereas of the founders of the monastic orders they[2] were ordained strait and poor and of coarse stuff and demonstrative[3] of the spirit of the wearers, who testified that they held things temporal in contempt whenas they wrapped their bodies in so mean a habit,—those of our time have them made full and double and glossy and of the finest cloth and have brought them to a quaint pontifical cut, insomuch that they think it no shame to flaunt it withal peacock-wise, in the churches and public places, even as do the laity with their apparel; and like as with the sweep-net the fisher goeth about to take many fishes in the river at one cast, even so these, wrapping themselves about with the amplest of skirts, study to entangle therein great store of prudish maids and widows and many other silly women and men, and this is their chief concern over any other exercise; wherefore, to speak more plainly, they have not the friar's gown, but only the colours thereof.

Moreover, whereas the ancients[4] desired the salvation of mankind, those of our day covet women and riches and turn their every thought to terrifying the minds of the foolish with clamours and depicturements[5] and to making believe that sins may be purged with almsdeeds and masses, to the intent that unto themselves (who, of poltroonery, not of devoutness, and that they may not suffer fatigue,[6] have, as a last resort, turned friars) one may bring bread, another send wine and a third give them a dole of money for the souls of their departed friends. Certes, it is true that almsdeeds and prayers purge away sins; but, if those who give alms knew on what manner folks they bestow them, they would or keep them for themselves or cast them before as many hogs. And for that these[7] know that, the fewer the possessors of a great treasure, the more they live at ease, every one of them studieth with clamours and bugbears to detach others from that whereof he would fain abide sole possessor. They decry lust in men, in order that, they who are chidden desisting from women, the latter may be left to the chiders; they condemn usury and unjust gains, to the intent that, it being entrusted to them to make restitution thereof, they may, with that which they declare must bring to perdition him who hath it, make wide their gowns and purchase bishopricks and other great benefices.

And when they are taken to task of these and many other unseemly things that they do, they think that to answer, "Do as we say and not as we do," is a sufficient discharge of every grave burden, as if it were possible for the sheep to be more constant and stouter to resist temptation[8] than the shepherds. And how many there be of those to whom they make such a reply who apprehend it not after the fashion[9] in which they say it, the most part of them know. The monks of our day would have you do as they say, to wit, fill their purses with money, trust your secrets to them, observe chastity, practise patience and forgiveness of injuries and keep yourselves from evil speaking,—all things good, seemly and righteous; but why would they have this? So they may do that, which if the laity did, themselves could not do. Who knoweth not that without money idleness may not endure? An thou expend thy monies in thy pleasures, the friar will not be able to idle it in the monastery; an thou follow after women, there will be no room for him, and except thou be patient or a forgiver of injuries, he will not dare to come to thy house to corrupt thy family. But why should I hark back after every particular? They condemn themselves in the eyes of the understanding as often as they make this excuse. An they believe not themselves able to abstain and lead a devout life, why do they not rather abide at home? Or, if they will e'en give themselves unto this,[10] why do they not ensue that other holy saying of the Gospel, "Christ began to do and to teach?"[11] Let them first do and after teach others. I have in my time seen a thousand of them wooers, lovers and haunters, not of lay women alone, but of nuns; ay, and of those that make the greatest outcry in the pulpit. Shall we, then, follow after these who are thus fashioned? Whoso doth it doth that which he will, but God knoweth if he do wisely.

But, granted even we are to allow that which the friar who chid you said to you, to wit, that it is a grievous sin to break the marriage vow, is it not a far greater sin to rob a man and a greater yet to slay him or drive him into exile, to wander miserably about the world? Every one must allow this. For a woman to have converse with a man is a sin of nature; but to rob him or slay him or drive him into exile proceedeth from malignity of mind. That you robbed Tedaldo I have already shown you, in despoiling him of yourself, who had become his of your spontaneous will, and I say also that, so far as in you lay, you slew him, for that it was none of your fault,—showing yourself, as you did, hourly more cruel,—that he slew not himself with his own hand; and the law willeth that whoso is the cause of the ill that is done be held alike guilty with him who doth it. And that you were the cause of his exile and of his going wandering seven years about the world cannot be denied. So that in whichever one of these three things aforesaid you have committed a far greater sin than in your converse with him.

But, let us see; maybe Tedaldo deserved this usage? Certes, he did not; you yourself have already confessed it, more by token that I know he loveth[12] you more than himself. No woman was ever so honoured, so exalted, so magnified over every other of her sex as were you by him, whenas he found himself where he might fairly speak of you, without engendering suspicion. His every good, his every honour, his every liberty were all committed by him into your hands. Was he not noble and young? Was he not handsome among all his townsmen? Was he not accomplished in such things as pertain unto young men? Was he not loved, cherished and well seen of every one? You will not say nay to this either. Then how, at the bidding of a scurvy, envious numskull of a friar, could you take such a cruel resolve against him? I know not what error is that of women who eschew men and hold them in little esteem, whenas, considering what themselves are and what and how great is the nobility, beyond every other animal, given of God to man, they should rather glory whenas they are loved of any and prize him over all and study with all diligence to please him, so he may never desist from loving them. This how you did, moved by the prate of a friar, who must for certain have been some broth-swilling pasty-gorger, you yourself know; and most like he had a mind to put himself in the place whence he studied to expel others.

This, then, is the sin that Divine justice, the which with a just balance bringeth all its operations to effect, hath willed not to leave unpunished; and even as you without reason studied to withdraw yourself from Tedaldo, so on like wise hath your husband been and is yet, without reason, in peril for Tedaldo, and you in tribulation. Wherefrom an you would be delivered, that which it behoveth you to promise, and yet more to do, is this; that, should it ever chance that Tedaldo return hither from his long banishment, you will render him again your favour, your love, your goodwill and your privacy and reinstate him in that condition wherein he was, ere you foolishly hearkened to yonder crack-brained friar.'

The pilgrim having thus made an end of his discourse, the lady, who had hearkened thereto with the utmost attention, for that his arguments appeared to her most true and that, hearing him say, she accounted herself of a certainty afflicted for the sin of which he spoke, said, 'Friend of God, I know full well that the things you allege are true, and in great part by your showing do I perceive what manner of folk are these friars, whom till now I have held all saints. Moreover, I acknowledge my default without doubt to have been great in that which I wrought against Tedaldo; and an I might, I would gladly amend it on such wise as you have said; but how may this be done? Tedaldo can never more return hither; he is dead; wherefore I know not why it should behove me promise that which may not be performed.' 'Madam,' replied the pilgrim, 'according to that which God hath revealed unto me, Tedaldo is nowise dead, but alive and well and in good case, so but he had your favour.' Quoth the lady, 'Look what you say; I saw him dead before my door of several knife-thrusts and had him in these arms and bathed his dead face with many tears, the which it may be gave occasion for that which hath been spoken thereof unseemly.' 'Madam,' replied the pilgrim, 'whatever you may say, I certify you that Tedaldo is alive, and if you will e'en promise me that [which I ask,] with intent to fulfil your promise, I hope you shall soon see him.' Quoth she, 'That do I promise and will gladly perform; nor could aught betide that would afford me such content as to see my husband free and unharmed and Tedaldo alive.'

Thereupon it seemed to Tedaldo time to discover himself and to comfort the lady with more certain hope of her husband, and accordingly he said, 'Madam, in order that I may comfort you for your husband, it behoveth me reveal to you a secret, which look you discover not unto any, as you value your life.' Now they were in a very retired place and alone, the lady having conceived the utmost confidence of the sanctity which herseemed was in the pilgrim; wherefore Tedaldo, pulling out a ring, which she had given him the last night he had been with her and which he had kept with the utmost diligence, and showing it to her, said, 'Madam, know you this?' As soon as she saw it, she recognized it and answered, 'Ay, sir; I gave it to Tedaldo aforetime.' Whereupon the pilgrim, rising to his feet, hastily cast off his palmer's gown and hat and speaking Florence-fashion, said, 'And know you me?'

When the lady saw this, she knew him to be Tedaldo and was all aghast, fearing him as one feareth the dead, an they be seen after death to go as if alive; wherefore she made not towards him to welcome him as Tedaldo returned from Cyprus, but would have fled from him in affright, as he were Tedaldo come back from the tomb. Whereupon, 'Madam,' quoth he, 'fear not; I am your Tedaldo, alive and well, and have never died nor been slain, whatsoever you and my brothers may believe.' The lady, somewhat reassured and knowing his voice, considered him awhile longer and avouched in herself that he was certainly Tedaldo; wherefore she threw herself, weeping, on his neck and kissed him, saying, 'Welcome back, sweet my Tedaldo.'

Tedaldo, having kissed and embraced her, said, 'Madam, it is no time now for closer greetings; I must e'en go take order that Aldobrandino may be restored to you safe and sound; whereof I hope that, ere to-morrow come eventide, you shall hear news that will please you; nay, if, as I expect, I have good news of his safety, I trust this night to be able to come to you and report them to you at more leisure than I can at this present.' Then, donning his gown and hat again, he kissed the lady once more and bidding her be of good hope, took leave of her and repaired whereas Aldobrandino lay in prison, occupied more with fear of imminent death than with hopes of deliverance to come. Tedaldo, with the gaoler's consent, went in to him, in the guise of a ghostly comforter, and seating himself by his side, said to him, 'Aldobrandino, I am a friend of thine, sent thee for thy deliverance by God, who hath taken pity on thee because of thine innocence; wherefore, if, in reverence to Him, thou wilt grant me a little boon that I shall ask of thee, thou shalt without fail, ere to-morrow be night, whereas thou lookest for sentence of death, hear that of thine acquittance.'

'Honest man,' replied the prisoner, 'since thou art solicitous of my deliverance, albeit I know thee not nor mind me ever to have seen thee, needs must thou be a friend, as thou sayst. In truth, the sin, for which they say I am to be doomed to death, I never committed; though others enough have I committed aforetime, which, it may be, have brought me to this pass. But this I say to thee, of reverence to God; an He presently have compassion on me, I will not only promise, but gladly do any thing, however great, to say nothing of a little one; wherefore ask that which pleaseth thee, for without fail, if it come to pass that I escape with life, I will punctually perform it.' Then said the pilgrim, 'What I would have of thee is that thou pardon Tedaldo's four brothers the having brought thee to this pass, believing thee guilty of their brother's death, and have them again for brethren and for friends, whenas they crave thee pardon thereof.' Whereto quoth Aldobrandino, 'None knoweth but he who hath suffered the affront how sweet a thing is vengeance and with what ardour it is desired; nevertheless, so God may apply Himself to my deliverance, I will freely pardon them; nay, I pardon them now, and if I come off hence alive and escape, I will in this hold such course as shall be to thy liking.'

This pleased the pilgrim and without concerning himself to say more to him, he exhorted him to be of good heart, for that, ere the ensuing day came to an end, he should without fail hear very certain news of his safety. Then, taking leave of him, he repaired to the Seignory and said privily to a gentleman who was in session there, 'My lord, every one should gladly labour to bring to light the truth of things, and especially those who hold such a room as this of yours, to the end that those may not suffer the penalty who have not committed the crime and that the guilty may be punished; that which may be brought about, to your honour and the bane of those who have merited it, I am come hither to you. As you know, you have rigorously proceeded against Aldobrandino Palermini and thinking you have found for truth that it was he who slew Tedaldo Elisei, are minded to condemn him; but this is most certainly false, as I doubt not to show you, ere midnight betide, by giving into your hands the murderers of the young man in question.'

The worthy gentleman, who was in concern for Aldobrandino, willingly gave ear to the pilgrim's words and having conferred at large with him upon the matter, on his information, took the two innkeeper brothers and their servant, without resistance, in their first sleep. He would have put them to the question, to discover how the case stood; but they brooked it not and each first for himself, and after all together, openly confessed that it was they who had slain Tedaldo Elisei, knowing him not. Being questioned of the case, they said [that it was] for that he had given the wife of one of them sore annoy, what while they were abroad, and would fain have enforced her to do his will.

The pilgrim, having heard this, with the magistrate's consent took his leave and repairing privily to the house of Madam Ermellina, found her alone and awaiting him, (all else in the house being gone to sleep,) alike desirous of having good news of her husband and of fully reconciling herself with her Tedaldo. He accosted her with a joyful countenance and said, 'Dearest lady mine, be of good cheer, for to-morrow thou shalt certainly have thine Aldobrandino here again safe and sound'; and to give her more entire assurance thereof, he fully recounted to her that which he had done. Whereupon she, glad as ever woman was of two so sudden and so happy chances, to wit, the having her lover alive again, whom she verily believed to have bewept dead, and the seeing Aldobrandino free from peril, whose death she looked ere many days to have to mourn, affectionately embraced and kissed Tedaldo; then, getting them to bed together, with one accord they made a glad and gracious peace, taking delight and joyance one of the other. Whenas the day drew near, Tedaldo arose, after showing the lady that which he purposed to do and praying her anew to keep it a close secret, and went forth, even in his pilgrim's habit, to attend, whenas it should be time, to Aldobrandino's affairs.

The day come, it appearing to the Seignory that they had full information of the matter, they straightway discharged Aldobrandino and a few days after let strike off the murderers' heads whereas they had committed the crime.

Aldobrandino being now, to the great joy of himself and his wife and of all his friends and kinsfolk, free and manifestly acknowledging that he owed his deliverance to the good offices of the pilgrim, carried the latter to his house for such time as it pleased him to sojourn in the city; and there they could not sate themselves of doing him honour and worship, especially the lady, who knew with whom she had to do. After awhile, deeming it time to bring his brothers to an accord with Aldobrandino and knowing that they were not only put to shame by the latter's acquittance, but went armed for fear [of his resentment,] he demanded of his host the fulfilment of his promise. Aldobrandino freely answered that he was ready, whereupon the pilgrim caused him prepare against the morrow a goodly banquet, whereat he told him he would have him and his kinsmen and kinswomen entertain the four brothers and their ladies, adding that he himself would go incontinent and bid the latter on his part to peace and his banquet. Aldobrandino consenting to all that liked the pilgrim, the latter forthright betook himself to the four brothers and plying them with store of such words as behoved unto the matter, in fine, with irrepugnable arguments, brought them easily enough to consent to regain Aldobrandino's friendship by asking pardon; which done, he invited them and their ladies to dinner with Aldobrandino next morning, and they, being certified of his good faith, frankly accepted the invitation.

Accordingly, on the morrow, towards dinner-time, Tedaldo's four brothers, clad all in black as they were, came, with sundry of their friends, to the house of Aldobrandino, who stayed for them, and there, in the presence of all who had been bidden of him to bear them company, cast down their arms and committed themselves to his mercy, craving forgiveness of that which they had wrought against him. Aldobrandino, weeping, received them affectionately, and kissing them all on the mouth, despatched the matter in a few words, remitting unto them every injury received. After them came their wives and sisters, clad all in sad-coloured raiment, and were graciously received by Madam Ermellina and the other ladies. Then were all, ladies and men alike, magnificently entertained at the banquet, nor was there aught in the entertainment other than commendable, except it were the taciturnity occasioned by the yet fresh sorrow expressed in the sombre raiment of Tedaldo's kinsfolk. Now on this account the pilgrim's device of the banquet had been blamed of some and he had observed it; wherefore, the time being come to do away with the constraint aforesaid, he rose to his feet, according as he had foreordained in himself, what while the rest still ate of the fruits, and said, 'Nothing hath lacked to this entertainment that should make it joyful, save only Tedaldo himself; whom (since having had him continually with you, you have not known him) I will e'en discover to you.'

So saying, he cast off his palmer's gown and all other his pilgrim's weeds and abiding in a jerkin of green sendal, was with no little amazement, long eyed and considered of all, ere any would venture to believe it was indeed he. Tedaldo, seeing this, recounted many particulars of the relations and things betided between them, as well as of his own adventures; whereupon his brethren and the other gentlemen present ran all to embrace him, with eyes full of joyful tears, as after did the ladies on like wise, as well strangers as kinswomen, except only Madam Ermellina. Which Aldobrandino seeing, 'What is this, Ermellina?' quoth he. 'Why dost thou not welcome Tedaldo, as do the other ladies?' Whereto she answered, in the hearing of all, 'There is none who had more gladly welcomed and would yet welcome him than myself, who am more beholden to him than any other woman, seeing that by his means I have gotten thee again; but the unseemly words spoken in the days when we mourned him whom we deemed Tedaldo

made me refrain therefrom.' Quoth her husband, 'Go to; thinkest thou I believe in the howlers?
[13] He hath right well shown their prate to be false by procuring my deliverance; more by token
that I never believed it. Quick, rise and go and embrace him.'

The lady, who desired nothing better, was not slow to obey her husband in this and
accordingly, arising, embraced Tedaldo, as the other ladies had done, and gave him joyous
welcome. This liberality of Aldobrandino was mighty pleasing to Tedaldo's brothers and to
every man and woman there, and thereby all suspect[14] that had been aroused in the minds of
some by the words aforesaid was done away. Then, every one having given Tedaldo joy, he
with his own hands rent the black clothes on his brothers' backs and the sad-coloured on those
of his sisters and kinswomen and would have them send after other apparel, which whenas
they had donned, they gave themselves to singing and dancing and other diversions galore;
wherefore the banquet, which had had a silent beginning had a loud-resounding ending.
Thereafter, with the utmost mirth, they one and all repaired, even as they were, to Tedaldo's
house, where they supped that night, and on this wise they continued to feast several days
longer.

The Florentines awhile regarded Tedaldo with amazement, as a man risen from the dead;
nay, in many an one's mind, and even in that of his brethren, there abode a certain faint doubt
an he were indeed himself and they did not yet thoroughly believe it, nor belike had they
believed it for a long time to come but for a chance which made them clear who the murdered
man was which was on this wise. There passed one day before their house certain footmen[15] of
Lunigiana, who, seeing Tedaldo, made towards him and said, 'Give you good day, Faziuolo.'
Whereto Tedaldo in his brothers' presence answered, 'You mistake me.' The others, hearing him
speak, were abashed and cried him pardon, saying, 'Forsooth you resemble, more than ever we
saw one man favour another, a comrade of ours called Faziuolo of Pontremoli, who came hither
some fortnight or more agone, nor could we ever since learn what is come of him. Indeed, we
marvelled at the dress, for that he was a soldier, even as we are.' Tedaldo's elder brother,
hearing this, came forward and enquired how this Faziuolo had been clad. They told him and it
was found to have been punctually as they said; wherefore, what with these and what with
other tokens, it was known for certain that he who had been slain was Faziuolo and not
Tedaldo, and all doubt of the latter[16] accordingly departed [the minds of] his brothers and of
every other. Tedaldo, then, being returned very rich, persevered in his love and the lady falling
out with him no more, they long, discreetly dealing, had enjoyment of their love. God grant us
to enjoy ours!"

---

1. *i.e.* It was not the dead man, but Tedaldo Elisei whom you loved. (*Lo sventurato giovane che fu morto non amasti voi mai, ma Tedaldo Elisei si.*)
2. *i.e.* friars' gowns. Boccaccio constantly uses this irregular form of enallage, especially in dialogue.
3. Or, as we should nowadays say, "typical."
4. *i.e.* the founders of the monastic orders.
5. Lit. pictures, paintings (*dipinture*), but evidently here used in a tropical sense, Boccaccio's apparent meaning being that the hypocritical friars used to terrify their devotees by picturing to them, in vivid colours, the horrors of the punishment reserved for sinners.
6. *i.e.* may not have to labour for their living.
7. *i.e.* the false friars.
8. Lit. more of iron (*più di ferro*).
9. Sic (*per lo modo*); but *quære* not rather "in the sense."
10. *i.e.* if they must enter upon this way of life, to wit, that of the friar.
11. The reference is apparently to the opening verse of the Acts of the Apostles, where Luke says, "The former treatise have I made, O Theophilus, of all that Jesus began to do and to teach." It need hardly be remarked that the passage in question does not bear the interpretation Boccaccio would put upon it.
12. Sic; but the past tense "loved" is probably intended, as the pretended pilgrim had not yet discovered Tedaldo to be alive.

13. Lit. barkers (*abbajatori*), *i.e.* slanderers.
14. Lit. despite, rancour (*rugginuzza*), but the phrase appears to refer to the suspicions excited by the whispers that had been current, as above mentioned, of the connection between Ermellina and Tedaldo.
15. *i.e.* foot-soldiers.
16. *i.e.* of his identity.

🜚 8 🜚

THE EIGHTH STORY

FERONDO, HAVING SWALLOWED A CERTAIN POWDER,
IS ENTOMBED FOR DEAD AND BEING TAKEN FORTH
OF THE SEPULCHRE BY THE ABBOT, WHO ENJOYETH
HIS WIFE THE WHILE, IS PUT IN PRISON AND GIVEN
TO BELIEVE THAT HE IS IN PURGATORY; AFTER
WHICH, BEING RAISED UP AGAIN, HE REARETH FOR
HIS OWN A CHILD BEGOTTEN OF THE ABBOT ON
HIS WIFE

THE END BEING COME of Emilia's long story,—which had not withal for its length been unpleasing to any of the company, nay, but was held of all the ladies to have been briefly narrated, having regard to the number and diversity of the incidents therein recounted,—the queen, having with a mere sign intimated her pleasure to Lauretta, gave her occasion to begin thus: "Dearest ladies, there occurreth to me to tell you a true story which hath much more semblance of falsehood than of that which it indeed is and which hath been recalled to my mind by hearing one to have been bewept and buried for another. I purpose then, to tell you how a live man was entombed for dead and how after he and many other folk believed himself to have come forth of the sepulchre as one raised from the dead, by reason whereof he[1] was adored as a saint who should rather have been condemned as a criminal.

There was, then, and yet is, in Tuscany, an abbey situate, like as we see many thereof, in a place not overmuch frequented of men, whereof a monk was made abbot, who was a very holy man in everything, save in the matter of women, and in this he contrived to do so warily that well nigh none, not to say knew, but even suspected him thereof, for that he was holden exceeding godly and just in everything. It chanced that a very wealthy farmer, by name Ferondo, contracted a great intimacy with him, a heavy, clodpate fellow and dull-witted beyond measure, whose commerce pleased the abbot but for that his simplicity whiles afforded him some diversion, and in the course of their acquaintance, the latter perceived that Ferondo had a very handsome woman to wife, of whom he became so passionately enamoured that he thought of nothing else day or night; but, hearing that, simple and shallow-witted as Ferondo was in everything else, he was shrewd enough in the matter of loving and guarding his wife, he well nigh despaired of her.

However, like a very adroit man as he was, he wrought on such wise with Ferondo that he came whiles, with his wife, to take his pleasance in the abbey-garden, and there he very demurely entertained them with discourse of the beatitude of the life eternal and of the pious works of many men and women of times past, insomuch that the lady was taken with a desire to confess herself to him and asked and had Ferondo's leave thereof. Accordingly, to the abbot's exceeding pleasure, she came to confess to him and seating herself at his feet, before she proceeded to say otherwhat, began thus: 'Sir, if God had given me a right husband or had given me none, it would belike be easy to me, with the help of your exhortations, to enter upon the road which you say leadeth folk unto life eternal; but I, having regard to what Ferondo is and to his witlessness, may style myself a widow, and yet I am married, inasmuch as, he living, I can have no other husband; and dolt as he is, he is without any cause, so out of all measure jealous of me that by reason thereof I cannot live with him otherwise than in tribulation and misery; wherefore, ere I come to other confession, I humbly beseech you, as most I may, that it may please you give me some counsel concerning this, for that, an the occasion of my well-doing begin not therefrom, confession or other good work will profit me little.'

This speech gave the abbot great satisfaction and himseemed fortune had opened him the way to his chief desire; wherefore, 'Daughter,' quoth he, 'I can well believe that it must be a sore annoy for a fair and dainty dame such as you are to have a blockhead to husband, but a much greater meseemeth to have a jealous man; wherefore, you having both the one and the other, I can lightly credit that which you avouch of your tribulation. But for this, speaking briefly, I see neither counsel nor remedy save one, the which is that Ferondo be cured of this jealousy. The medicine that will cure him I know very well how to make, provided you have the heart to keep secret that which I shall tell you.' 'Father mine,' answered the lady, 'have no fear of that, for I would liefer suffer death than tell any that which you bid me not repeat; but how may this be done?' Quoth the abbot, 'An we would have him cured, it behoveth of necessity that he go to purgatory.' 'But how,' asked she, 'can he go thither alive?' 'Needs must he die,' replied the abbot, 'and so go thither; and whenas he shall have suffered such penance as shall suffice to purge him of his jealousy, we will pray God, with certain orisons that he restore him to this life, and He will do it.' 'Then,' said the lady, 'I am to become a widow?' 'Ay,' answered the abbot, 'for a certain time, wherein you must look well you suffer not yourself to be married again, for that God would take it in ill part, and whenas Ferondo returned hither, it would behove you return to him and he would then be more jealous than ever.' Quoth she, 'Provided he be but cured of this calamity, so it may not behove me abide in prison all my life, I am content; do as it pleaseth you.' 'And I will do it,'[2] rejoined he; 'but what guerdon am I to have of you for such a service?' 'Father,' answered the lady, 'you shall have whatsoever pleaseth you, so but it be in my power; but what can the like of me that may befit such a man as yourself?' 'Madam,' replied the abbot 'you can do no less for me than that which I undertake to do for you; for that, like as I am disposed to do that which is to be your weal and your solacement, even so can you do that which will be the saving and assainment of my life.' Quoth she, 'An it be so, I am ready.' 'Then,' said the abbot, 'you must give me your love and vouchsafe me satisfaction of yourself, for whom I am all afire with love and languishment.'

The lady, hearing this, was all aghast and answered, 'Alack, father mine, what is this you ask? Methought you were a saint. Doth it beseem holy men to require women, who come to them for counsel, of such things?' 'Fair my soul,' rejoined the abbot, 'marvel not, for that sanctity nowise abateth by this, seeing it hath its seat in the soul and that which I ask of you is a sin of the body. But, be that as it may, your ravishing beauty hath had such might that love constraineth me to do thus; and I tell you that you may glory in your charms over all other women, considering that they please holy men, who are used to look upon the beauties of heaven. Moreover, abbot though I be, I am a man like another and am, as you see, not yet old. Nor should this that I ask be grievous to you to do; nay, you should rather desire it, for that, what while Ferondo sojourneth in purgatory, I will bear you company by night and render you that solacement which he should give you; nor shall any ever come to know of this, for that every one believeth of me that, and more than that, which you but now believed of me. Reject not the grace that God sendeth you, for there be women enough who covet that which you may have and shall have, if, like a wise woman, you hearken to my counsel. Moreover, I have fair and precious jewels, which I purpose shall belong to none other than yourself. Do, then, for me, sweet my hope, that which I willingly do for you.'

The lady hung her head, knowing not how to deny him, whilst herseemed it were ill done to grant him what he asked; but the abbot, seeing that she hearkened and hesitated to reply and himseeming he had already half converted her, followed up his first words with many others and stayed not till he had persuaded her that she would do well to comply with him. Accordingly, she said, blushing, that she was ready to do his every commandment, but might not avail thereto till such time as Ferondo should be gone to purgatory; whereupon quoth the abbot, exceeding well pleased, 'And we will make shift to send him thither incontinent; do you but contrive that he come hither to-morrow or next day to sojourn with me.' So saying, he privily put a very handsome ring into her hand and dismissed her. The lady rejoiced at the gift and looking to have others, rejoined her companions, to whom she fell to relating marvellous things of the abbot's sanctity, and presently returned home with them.

A few days after Ferondo repaired to the abbey, whom, whenas the abbot saw, he cast about to send him to purgatory. Accordingly, he sought out a powder of marvellous virtue, which he had gotten in the parts of the Levant of a great prince who avouched it to be that which was wont to be used of the Old Man of the Mountain,[3] whenas he would fain send any one, sleeping, into his paradise or bring him forth thereof, and that, according as more or less thereof was given, without doing any hurt, it made him who took it sleep more or less [time] on such wise that, whilst its virtue lasted, none would say he had life in him. Of this he took as much as might suffice to make a man sleep three days and putting it in a beaker of wine, that was not yet well cleared, gave it to Ferondo to drink in his cell, without the latter suspecting aught; after which he carried him into the cloister and there with some of his monks fell to making sport of him and his dunceries; nor was it long before, the powder working, Ferondo was taken with so sudden and overpowering a drowsiness, that he slumbered as yet he stood afoot and presently fell down fast asleep.

The abbot made a show of being concerned at this accident and letting untruss him, caused fetch cold water and cast it in his face and essay many other remedies of his fashion, as if he would recall the strayed life and senses from [the oppression of] some fumosity of the stomach or what not like affection that had usurped them. The monks, seeing that for all this he came not to himself and feeling his pulse, but finding no sign of life in him, all held it for certain that he was dead. Accordingly, they sent to tell his wife and his kinsfolk, who all came thither forthright, and the lady having bewept him awhile with her kinswomen, the abbot caused lay him, clad as he was, in a tomb; whilst the lady returned to her house and giving out that she meant never to part from a little son, whom she had had by her husband, abode at home and occupied herself with the governance of the child and of the wealth which had been Ferondo's. Meanwhile, the abbot arose stealthily in the night and with the aid of a Bolognese monk, in whom he much trusted and who was that day come thither from Bologna, took up Ferondo out of the tomb and carried him into a vault, in which there was no light to be seen and which had been made for prison of such of the monks as should make default in aught. There they pulled off his garments and clothing him monk-fashion, laid him on a truss of straw and there left him against he should recover his senses, whilst the Bolognese monk, having been instructed by the abbot of that which he had to do, without any else knowing aught thereof, proceeded to await his coming to himself.

On the morrow, the abbot, accompanied by sundry of his monks, betook himself, by way of visitation, to the house of the lady, whom he found clad in black and in great tribulation, and having comforted her awhile, he softly required her of her promise. The lady, finding herself free and unhindered of Ferondo or any other and seeing on his finger another fine ring, replied that she was ready and appointed him to come to her that same night. Accordingly, night come, the abbot, disguised in Ferondo's clothes and accompanied by the monk his confidant, repaired thither and lay with her in the utmost delight and pleasance till the morning, when he returned to the abbey. After this he very often made the same journey on a like errand and being whiles encountered, coming or going, of one or another of the villagers, it was believed he was Ferondo who went about those parts, doing penance; by reason whereof many strange stories were after bruited about among the simple countryfolk, and this was more than once reported to Ferondo's wife, who well knew what it was.

As for Ferondo, when he recovered his senses and found himself he knew not where, the Bolognese monk came in to him with a horrible noise and laying hold of him, gave him a sound drubbing with a rod he had in his hand. Ferondo, weeping and crying out, did nought but ask, 'Where am I?' To which the monk answered, 'Thou art in purgatory.' 'How?' cried Ferondo. 'Am I then dead?' 'Ay, certes,' replied the other; whereupon Ferondo fell to bemoaning himself and his wife and child, saying the oddest things in the world. Presently the monk brought him somewhat of meat and drink, which Ferondo seeing, 'What!' cried he. 'Do the dead eat?' 'Ay do they,' answered the monk. 'This that I bring thee is what the woman, thy wife that was, sent this morning to the church to let say masses for thy soul, and God the Lord willeth that it be made over to thee.' Quoth Ferondo, 'God grant her a good year! I still cherished her ere I died, insomuch that I held her all night in mine arms and did nought but kiss her, and t' other thing also I did, when I had a mind thereto.' Then, being very sharp-set, he fell to eating and drinking and himseeming the wine was not overgood, 'Lord confound her!' quoth he. 'Why did not she give the priest wine of the cask against the wall?'

After he had eaten, the monk laid hold of him anew and gave him another sound beating with the same rod; whereat Ferondo roared out lustily and said, 'Alack, why dost thou this to me?' Quoth the monk, 'Because thus hath God the Lord ordained that it be done unto thee twice every day.' 'And for what cause?' asked Ferondo. 'Because,' answered the monk, 'thou wast jealous, having the best woman in the country to wife.' 'Alas!' said Ferondo. 'Thou sayst sooth, ay, and the kindest creature; she was sweeter than syrup; but I knew not that God the Lord held it for ill that a man should be jealous; else had I not been so.' Quoth the monk, 'Thou shouldst have bethought thyself of that, whenas thou wast there below,[4] and have amended thee thereof; and should it betide that thou ever return thither, look thou so have in mind that which I do unto thee at this present that thou be nevermore jealous.' 'What?' said Ferondo. 'Do the dead ever return thither?' 'Ay,' answered the monk; 'whom God willeth.' 'Marry,' cried Ferondo, 'and I ever return thither, I will be the best husband in the world; I will never beat her nor give her an ill word, except it be anent the wine she sent hither this morning and for that she sent no candles, so it behoved me to eat in the dark.' 'Nay,' said the monk, 'she sent candles enough, but they were all burnt for the masses.' 'True,' rejoined Ferondo; 'and assuredly, an I return thither, I will let her do what she will. But tell me, who art thou that usest me thus?' Quoth the monk, 'I also am dead. I was of Sardinia and for that aforetime I much commended a master of mine of being jealous, I have been doomed of God to this punishment, that I must give thee to eat and drink and beat thee thus, till such time as God shall ordain otherwhat of thee and of me.' Then said Ferondo, 'Is there none here other than we twain?' 'Ay,' answered the monk, 'there be folk by the thousands; but thou canst neither see nor hear them, nor they thee.' Quoth Ferondo, 'And how far are we from our own countries?' 'Ecod,' replied the other, 'we are distant thence more miles than we can well cack at a bout.' 'Faith,' rejoined the farmer, 'that is far enough; meseemeth we must be out of the world, an it be so much as all that.'

In such and the like discourse was Ferondo entertained half a score months with eating and drinking and beating, what while the abbot assiduously visited the fair lady, without miscarriage, and gave himself the goodliest time in the world with her. At last, as ill-luck would have it, the lady found herself with child and straightway acquainted the abbot therewith, wherefore it seemed well to them both that Ferondo should without delay be recalled from purgatory to life and return to her, so she might avouch herself with child by him. Accordingly, the abbot that same night caused call to Ferondo in prison with a counterfeit voice, saying, 'Ferondo, take comfort, for it is God's pleasure that thou return to the world, where thou shalt have a son by thy wife, whom look thou name Benedict, for that by the prayers of thy holy abbot and of thy wife and for the love of St. Benedict He doth thee this favour.' Ferondo, hearing this, was exceedingly rejoiced and said, 'It liketh me well, Lord grant a good year to Seignior God Almighty and to the abbot and St. Benedict and my cheesy[5] sweet honey wife.' The abbot let give him, in the wine that he sent him, so much of the powder aforesaid as should cause him sleep maybe four hours and with the aid of his monk, having put his own clothes on him, restored him privily to the tomb wherein he had been buried.

Next morning, at break of day, Ferondo came to himself and espying light,—a thing which he had not seen for good ten months,—through some crevice of the tomb, doubted not but he was alive again. Accordingly, he fell to bawling out, 'Open to me! Open to me!' and heaving so lustily at the lid of the tomb with his head that he stirred it, for that it was eath to move, and had begun to move it away, when the monks, having now made an end of saying matins, ran thither and knew Ferondo's voice and saw him in act to come forth of the sepulchre; whereupon, all aghast for the strangeness of the case, they took to their heels and ran to the abbot, who made a show of rising from prayer and said, 'My sons, have no fear; take the cross and the holy water and follow after me, so we may see that which God willeth to show forth to us of His might'; and as he said, so he did.

Now Ferondo was come forth of the sepulchre all pale, as well might he be who had so long abidden without seeing the sky. As soon as he saw the abbot, he ran to cast himself at his feet and said, 'Father mine, according to that which hath been revealed to me, your prayers and those of St. Benedict and my wife have delivered me from the pains of purgatory and restored me to life, wherefore I pray God to give you a good year and good calends now and always.' Quoth the abbot, 'Praised be God His might! Go, my son, since He hath sent thee back hither; comfort thy wife, who hath been still in tears, since thou departedst this life, and henceforth be a friend and servant of God.' 'Sir,' replied Ferondo, 'so hath it indeed been said to me; only leave me do; for, as soon as I find her, I shall buss her, such goodwill do I bear her.'

The abbot, left alone with his monks, made a great show of wonderment at this miracle and caused devoutly sing Miserere therefor. As for Ferondo, he returned to his village, where all who saw him fled, as men use to do from things frightful; but he called them back and avouched himself to be raised up again. His wife on like wise feigned to be adread of him; but, after the folk were somewhat reassured anent him and saw that he was indeed alive, they questioned him of many things, and he, as it were he had returned wise, made answer to all and gave them news of the souls of their kinsfolk, making up, of his own motion, the finest fables in the world of the affairs of purgatory and recounting in full assembly the revelation made him by the mouth of the Rangel Bragiel[6] ere he was raised up again. Then, returning to his house and entering again into possession of his goods, he got his wife, as he thought, with child, and by chance it befell that, in due time,—to the thinking of the fools who believe that women go just nine months with child,—the lady gave birth to a boy, who was called Benedict Ferondi.[7]

. . .

FERONDO'S RETURN and his talk, well nigh every one believing him to have risen from the dead, added infinitely to the renown of the abbot's sanctity, and he himself, as if cured of his jealousy by the many beatings he had received therefor, thenceforward, according to the promise made by the abbot to the lady, was no more jealous; whereat she was well pleased and lived honestly with him, as of her wont, save indeed that, whenas she conveniently might, she willingly foregathered with the holy abbot, who had so well and diligently served her in her greatest needs."

---

1. *i.e.* the abbot who played the trick upon Ferondo. See post.
2. *i.e.* I will cure your husband of his jealousy.
3. The well-known chief of the Assassins (properly *Heshashin, i.e.* hashish or hemp eaters). The powder in question is apparently a preparation of hashish or hemp. Boccaccio seems to have taken his idea of the Old Man of the Mountain from Marco Polo, whose travels, published in the early part of the fourteenth century, give a most romantic account of that chieftain and his followers.
4. *i.e.* in the sublunary world.
5. *Sic (casciata)*; meaning that he loves her as well as he loves cheese, for which it is well known that the lower-class Italian has a romantic passion. According to Alexandre Dumas, the Italian loves cheese so well that he has succeeded in introducing it into everything he eats or drinks, with the one exception of coffee.
6. *i.e.* the Angel Gabriel.
7. The plural of a surname is, in strictness, always used by the Italians in speaking of a man by his full name, *dei* being understood between the Christian and surname, as *Benedetto (dei) Ferondi,* Benedict of the Ferondos or Ferondo family, whilst, when he is denominated by the surname alone, it is used in the singular, *il* (the) being understood, *e.g.* (Il) Boccaccio, (Il) Ferondo, *i.e.* the particular Boccaccio or Ferondo in question for the nonce.

❧ 9 ❧

THE NINTH STORY

GILLETTE DE NARBONNE RECOVERETH THE KING
OF FRANCE OF A FISTULA AND DEMANDETH FOR HER
HUSBAND BERTRAND DE ROUSSILLON, WHO
MARRIETH HER AGAINST HIS WILL AND BETAKETH
HIM FOR DESPITE TO FLORENCE, WHERE, HE PAYING
COURT TO A YOUNG LADY, GILLETTE, IN THE
PERSON OF THE LATTER, LIETH WITH HIM AND HATH
BY HIM TWO SONS; WHEREFORE AFTER, HOLDING
HER DEAR, HE ENTERTAINETH HER FOR HIS WIFE

LAURETTA'S STORY being now ended, it rested but with the queen to tell, an she would not infringe upon Dioneo's privilege; wherefore, without waiting to be solicited by her companions, she began all blithesomely to speak thus: "Who shall tell a story that may appear goodly, now we have heard that of Lauretta? Certes, it was well for us that hers was not the first, for that few of the others would have pleased after it, as I misdoubt me[1] will betide of those which are yet to tell this day. Natheless, be that as it may, I will e'en recount to you that which occurreth to me upon the proposed theme.

There was in the kingdom of France a gentleman called Isnard, Count of Roussillon, who, for that he was scant of health, still entertained about his person a physician, by name Master Gerard de Narbonne. The said count had one little son, and no more, hight Bertrand, who was exceeding handsome and agreeable, and with him other children of his own age were brought up. Among these latter was a daughter of the aforesaid physician, by name Gillette, who vowed to the said Bertrand an infinite love and fervent more than pertained unto her tender years. The count dying and leaving his son in the hands of the king, it behoved him betake himself to Paris, whereof the damsel abode sore disconsolate, and her own father dying no great while after, she would fain, an she might have had a seemly occasion, have gone to Paris to see Bertrand: but, being straitly guarded, for that she was left rich and alone, she saw no honourable way thereto; and being now of age for a husband and having never been able to forget Bertrand, she had, without reason assigned, refused many to whom her kinsfolk would have married her.

Now it befell that, what while she burned more than ever for love of Bertrand, for that she heard he was grown a very goodly gentleman, news came to her how the King of France, by an imposthume which he had had in his breast and which had been ill tended, had gotten a fistula, which occasioned him the utmost anguish and annoy, nor had he yet been able to find a physician who might avail to recover him thereof, albeit many had essayed it, but all had aggravated the ill; wherefore the king, despairing of cure, would have no more counsel nor aid of any. Hereof the young lady was beyond measure content and bethought herself that not only would this furnish her with a legitimate occasion of going to Paris, but that, should the king's ailment be such as she believed, she might lightly avail to have Bertrand to husband. Accordingly, having aforetime learned many things of her father, she made a powder of certain simples useful for such an infirmity as she conceived the king's to be and taking horse, repaired to Paris.

Before aught else she studied to see Bertrand and next, presenting herself before the king, she prayed him of his favour to show her his ailment. The king, seeing her a fair and engaging damsel, knew not how to deny her and showed her that which ailed him. Whenas she saw it, she was certified incontinent that she could heal it and accordingly said, 'My lord, an it please you, I hope in God to make you whole of this your infirmity in eight days' time, without annoy or fatigue on your part.' The king scoffed in himself at her words, saying, 'That which the best physicians in the world have availed not neither known to do, how shall a young woman know?' Accordingly, he thanked her for her good will and answered that he was resolved no more to follow the counsel of physicians. Whereupon quoth the damsel, 'My lord, you make light of my skill, for that I am young and a woman; but I would have you bear in mind that I medicine not of mine own science, but with the aid of God and the science of Master Gerard de Narbonne, who was my father and a famous physician whilst he lived.'

The king, hearing this, said in himself, 'It may be this woman is sent me of God; why should I not make proof of her knowledge, since she saith she will, without annoy of mine, cure me in little time?' Accordingly, being resolved to essay her, he said, 'Damsel, and if you cure us not, after causing us break our resolution, what will you have ensue to you therefor?' 'My lord,' answered she, 'set a guard upon me and if I cure you not within eight days, let burn me alive; but, if I cure you, what reward shall I have?' Quoth the king, 'You seem as yet unhusbanded; if you do this, we will marry you well and worshipfully.' 'My lord,' replied the young lady, 'I am well pleased that you should marry me, but I will have a husband such as I shall ask of you, excepting always any one of your sons or of the royal house.' He readily promised her that which she sought, whereupon she began her cure and in brief, before the term limited, she brought him back to health.

The king, feeling himself healed, said, 'Damsel, you have well earned your husband'; whereto she answered, 'Then, my lord, I have earned Bertrand de Roussillon, whom I began to love even in the days of my childhood and have ever since loved over all.' The king deemed it a grave matter to give him to her; nevertheless, having promised her and unwilling to fail of his faith, he let call the count to himself and bespoke him thus: 'Bertrand, you are now of age and accomplished [in all that behoveth unto man's estate];[2] wherefore it is our pleasure that you return to govern your county and carry with you a damsel, whom we have given you to wife.' 'And who is the damsel, my lord?' asked Bertrand; to which the king answered, 'It is she who hath with her medicines restored to us our health.'

Bertrand, who had seen and recognized Gillette, knowing her (albeit she seemed to him very fair) to be of no such lineage as sorted with his quality, said all disdainfully, 'My lord, will you then marry me to a she-leach? Now God forbid I should ever take such an one to wife!' 'Then,' said the king, 'will you have us fail of our faith, the which, to have our health again, we pledged to the damsel, who in guerdon thereof demanded you to husband?' 'My lord,' answered Bertrand, 'you may, an you will, take from me whatsoever I possess or, as your liegeman, bestow me upon whoso pleaseth you; but of this I certify you, that I will never be a consenting party unto such a marriage.' 'Nay,' rejoined the king, 'but you shall, for that the damsel is fair and wise and loveth you dear; wherefore we doubt not but you will have a far happier life with her than with a lady of higher lineage.' Bertrand held his peace and the king let make great preparations for the celebration of the marriage.

The appointed day being come, Bertrand, sore against his will, in the presence of the king, espoused the damsel, who loved him more than herself. This done, having already determined in himself what he should do, he sought leave of the king to depart, saying he would fain return to his county and there consummate the marriage; then, taking horse, he repaired not thither, but betook himself into Tuscany, where, hearing that the Florentines were at war with those of Sienna, he determined to join himself to the former, by whom he was joyfully received and made captain over a certain number of men-at-arms; and there, being well provided[3] of them, he abode a pretty while in their service.

The newly-made wife, ill content with such a lot, but hoping by her fair dealing to recall him to his county, betook herself to Roussillon, where she was received of all as their liege lady. There, finding everything waste and disordered for the long time that the land had been without a lord, with great diligence and solicitude, like a discreet lady as she was, she set all in order again, whereof the count's vassals were mightily content and held her exceeding dear, vowing her a great love and blaming the count sore for that he accepted not of her. The lady, having thoroughly ordered the county, notified the count thereof by two knights, whom she despatched to him, praying him that, an it were on her account he forbore to come to his county, he should signify it to her and she, to pleasure him, would depart thence; but he answered them very harshly, saying, 'For that, let her do her pleasure; I, for my part, will return thither to abide with her, whenas she shall have this my ring on her finger and in her arms a son by me begotten.' Now the ring in question he held very dear and never parted with it, by reason of a certain virtue which it had been given him to understand that it had.

The knights understood the hardship of the condition implied in these two well nigh impossible requirements, but, seeing that they might not by their words avail to move him from his purpose, they returned to the lady and reported to her his reply; whereat she was sore afflicted and determined, after long consideration, to seek to learn if and where the two things aforesaid might be compassed, to the intent that she might, in consequence, have her husband again. Accordingly, having bethought herself what she should do, she assembled certain of the best and chiefest men of the county and with plaintive speech very orderly recounted to them that which she had already done for love of the count and showed them what had ensued thereof, adding that it was not her intent that, through her sojourn there, the count should abide in perpetual exile; nay, rather she purposed to spend the rest of her life in pilgrimages and works of mercy and charity for her soul's health; wherefore she prayed them take the ward and governance of the county and notify the count that she had left him free and vacant possession and had departed the country, intending nevermore to return to Roussillon. Many were the tears shed by the good folk, whilst she spoke, and many the prayers addressed to her that it would please her change counsel and abide there; but they availed nought. Then, commending them to God, she set out upon her way, without telling any whither she was bound, well furnished with monies and jewels of price and accompanied by a cousin of hers and a chamberwoman, all in pilgrims' habits, and stayed not till she came to Florence, where, chancing upon a little inn, kept by a decent widow woman, she there took up her abode and lived quietly, after the fashion of a poor pilgrim, impatient to hear news of her lord.

It befell, then, that on the morrow of her arrival she saw Bertrand pass before her lodging, a-horseback with his company, and albeit she knew him full well, natheless she asked the good woman of the inn who he was. The hostess answered, 'That is a stranger gentleman, who calleth himself Count Bertrand, a pleasant man and a courteous and much loved in this city; and he is the most enamoured man in the world of a she-neighbour of ours, who is a gentlewoman, but poor. Sooth to say, she is a very virtuous damsel and abideth, being yet unmarried for poverty, with her mother, a very good and discreet lady, but for whom, maybe, she had already done the count's pleasure.' The countess took good note of what she heard and having more closely enquired into every particular and apprehended all aright, determined in herself how she should do.

Accordingly, having learned the house and name of the lady whose daughter the count loved, she one day repaired privily thither in her pilgrim's habit and finding the mother and daughter in very poor case, saluted them and told the former that, an it pleased her, she would fain speak with her alone. The gentlewoman, rising, replied that she was ready to hearken to her and accordingly carried her into a chamber of hers, where they seated themselves and the countess began thus, 'Madam, meseemeth you are of the enemies of Fortune, even as I am; but, an you will, belike you may be able to relieve both yourself and me.' The lady answered that she desired nothing better than to relieve herself by any honest means; and the countess went on, 'Needs must you pledge me your faith, whereto an I commit myself and you deceive me, you will mar your own affairs and mine.' 'Tell me anything you will in all assurance,' replied the gentlewoman; 'for never shall you find yourself deceived of me.'

Thereupon the countess, beginning with her first enamourment, recounted to her who she was and all that had betided her to that day after such a fashion that the gentlewoman, putting faith in her words and having, indeed, already in part heard her story from others, began to have compassion of her. The countess, having related her adventures, went on to say, 'You have now, amongst my other troubles, heard what are the two things which it behoveth me have, an I would have my husband, and to which I know none who can help me, save only yourself, if that be true which I hear, to wit, that the count my husband is passionately enamoured of your daughter.' 'Madam,' answered the gentlewoman, 'if the count love my daughter I know not; indeed he maketh a great show thereof. But, an it be so, what can I do in this that you desire?' 'Madam,' rejoined the countess, 'I will tell you; but first I will e'en show you what I purpose shall ensue thereof to you, an you serve me. I see your daughter fair and of age for a husband and according to what I have heard, meseemeth I understand the lack of good to marry her withal it is that causeth you keep her at home. Now I purpose, in requital of the service you shall do me, to give her forthright of mine own monies such a dowry as you yourself shall deem necessary to marry her honorably.'

The mother, being needy, was pleased with the offer; algates, having the spirit of a gentlewoman, she said, 'Madam, tell me what I can do for you; if it consist with my honour, I will willingly do it, and you shall after do that which shall please you.' Then said the countess, 'It behoveth me that you let tell the count my husband by some one in whom you trust, that your daughter is ready to do his every pleasure, so she may but be certified that he loveth her as he pretendeth, the which she will never believe, except he send her the ring which he carrieth on his finger and by which she hath heard he setteth such store. An he send you the ring, you must give it to me and after send to him to say that your daughter is ready do his pleasure; then bring him hither in secret and privily put me to bed to him in the stead of your daughter. It may be God will vouchsafe me to conceive and on this wise, having his ring on my finger and a child in mine arms of him begotten, I shall presently regain him and abide with him, as a wife should abide with her husband, and you will have been the cause thereof.'

This seemed a grave matter to the gentlewoman, who feared lest blame should haply ensue thereof to her daughter; nevertheless, bethinking her it were honourably done to help the poor lady recover her husband and that she went about to do this to a worthy end and trusting in the good and honest intention of the countess, she not only promised her to do it, but, before many days, dealing with prudence and secrecy, in accordance with the latter's instructions, she both got the ring (albeit this seemed somewhat grievous to the count) and adroitly put her to bed with her husband, in the place of her own daughter. In these first embracements, most ardently sought of the count, the lady, by God's pleasure, became with child of two sons, as her delivery in due time made manifest. Nor once only, but many times, did the gentlewoman gratify the countess with her husband's embraces, contriving so secretly that never was a word known of the matter, whilst the count still believed himself to have been, not with his wife, but with her whom he loved; and whenas he came to take leave of a morning, he gave her, at one time and another, divers goodly and precious jewels, which the countess laid up with all diligence.

Then, feeling herself with child and unwilling to burden the gentlewoman farther with such an office, she said to her, 'Madam, thanks to God and you, I have gotten that which I desired, wherefore it is time that I do that which shall content you and after get me gone hence.' The gentlewoman answered that, if she had gotten that which contented her, she was well pleased, but that she had not done this of any hope of reward, nay, for that herseemed it behoved her to do it, an she would do well. 'Madam,' rejoined the countess, 'that which you say liketh me well and so on my part I purpose not to give you that which you shall ask of me by way of reward, but to do well, for that meseemeth behoveful so to do.' The gentlewoman, then, constrained by necessity, with the utmost shamefastness, asked her an hundred pounds to marry her daughter withal; but the countess, seeing her confusion and hearing her modest demand, gave her five hundred and so many rare and precious jewels as were worth maybe as much more. With this the gentlewoman was far more than satisfied and rendered the countess the best thanks in her power; whereupon the latter, taking leave of her, returned to the inn, whilst the other, to deprive Bertrand of all farther occasion of coming or sending to her house, removed with her daughter into the country to the house of one of her kinsfolk, and he, being a little after recalled by his vassals and hearing that the countess had departed the country, returned to his own house.

The countess, hearing that he had departed Florence and returned to his county, was mightily rejoiced and abode at Florence till her time came to be delivered, when she gave birth to two male children, most like their father, and let rear them with all diligence. Whenas it seemed to her time, she set out and came, without being known of any, to Montpellier, where having rested some days and made enquiry of the count and where he was, she learned that he was to hold a great entertainment of knights and ladies at Roussillon on All Saints' Day and betook herself thither, still in her pilgrim's habit that she was wont to wear. Finding the knights and ladies assembled in the count's palace and about to sit down to table, she went up, with her children in her arms and without changing her dress, into the banqueting hall and making her way between man and man whereas she saw the count, cast herself at his feet and said, weeping, 'I am thine unhappy wife, who, to let thee return and abide in thy house, have long gone wandering miserably about the world. I conjure thee, in the name of God, to accomplish unto me thy promise upon the condition appointed me by the two knights I sent thee; for, behold, here in mine arms is not only one son of thine, but two, and here is thy ring. It is time, then, that I be received of thee as a wife, according to thy promise.'

The count, hearing this, was all confounded and recognized the ring and the children also, so like were they to him; but yet he said, 'How can this have come to pass?' The countess, then, to his exceeding wonderment and that of all others who were present, orderly recounted that which had passed and how it had happened; whereupon the count, feeling that she spoke sooth and seeing her constancy and wit and moreover two such goodly children, as well for the observance of his promise as to pleasure all his liegemen and the ladies, who all besought him thenceforth to receive and honour her as his lawful wife, put off his obstinate despite and raising the countess to her feet, embraced her and kissing her, acknowledged her for his lawful wife and those for his children. Then, letting clothe her in apparel such as beseemed her quality, to the exceeding joyance of as many as were there and of all other his vassals who heard the news, he held high festival, not only all that day, but sundry others, and from that day forth still honoured her as his bride and his wife and loved and tendered her over all."

---

1. Lit. and so I hope (*spero*), a curious instance of the ancient Dantesque use of the word *spero*, I hope, in its contrary sense of fear.
2. *Fornito*, a notable example of what the illustrious Lewis Carroll Dodgson, Waywode of Wonderland, calls a "portmanteau-word," a species that abounds in mediæval Italian, for the confusion of translators.
3. *i.e.* getting good pay and allowances (*avendo buona provisione*).

❧ 1 0 ❧

THE TENTH STORY

ALIBECH, TURNING HERMIT, IS TAUGHT BY RUSTICO, A MONK, TO PUT THE DEVIL IN HELL, AND BEING AFTER BROUGHT AWAY THENCE, BECOMETH NEERBALE HIS WIFE

DIONEO, who had diligently hearkened to the queen's story, seeing that it was ended and that it rested with him alone to tell, without awaiting commandment, smilingly began to speak as follows: "Charming ladies, maybe you have never heard tell how one putteth the devil in hell; wherefore, without much departing from the tenor of that whereof you have discoursed all this day, I will e'en tell it you. Belike, having learned it, you may catch the spirit[1] thereof and come to know that, albeit Love sojourneth liefer in jocund palaces and luxurious chambers than in the hovels of the poor, yet none the less doth he whiles make his power felt midmost thick forests and rugged mountains and in desert caverns; whereby it may be understood that all things are subject to his puissance.

To come, then, to the fact, I say that in the city of Capsa in Barbary there was aforetime a very rich man, who, among his other children, had a fair and winsome young daughter, by name Alibech. She, not being a Christian and hearing many Christians who abode in the town mightily extol the Christian faith and the service of God, one day questioned one of them in what manner one might avail to serve God with the least hindrance. The other answered that they best served God who most strictly eschewed the things of the world, as those did who had betaken them into the solitudes of the deserts of Thebais. The girl, who was maybe fourteen years old and very simple, moved by no ordered desire, but by some childish fancy, set off next morning by stealth and all alone, to go to the desert of Thebais, without letting any know her intent. After some days, her desire persisting, she won, with no little toil, to the deserts in question and seeing a hut afar off, went thither and found at the door a holy man, who marvelled to see her there and asked her what she sought. She replied that, being inspired of God, she went seeking to enter into His service and was now in quest of one who should teach her how it behoved to serve Him.

The worthy man, seeing her young and very fair and fearing lest, an he entertained her, the devil should beguile him, commended her pious intent and giving her somewhat to eat of roots of herbs and wild apples and dates and to drink of water, said to her, 'Daughter mine, not far hence is a holy man, who is a much better master than I of that which thou goest seeking; do thou betake thyself to him'; and put her in the way. However, when she reached the man in question, she had of him the same answer and faring farther, came to the cell of a young hermit, a very devout and good man, whose name was Rustico and to whom she made the same request as she had done to the others. He, having a mind to make a trial of his own constancy, sent her not away, as the others had done, but received her into his cell, and the night being come, he made her a little bed of palm-fronds and bade her lie down to rest thereon. This done, temptations tarried not to give battle to his powers of resistance and he, finding himself grossly deceived by these latter, turned tail, without awaiting many assaults, and confessed himself beaten; then, laying aside devout thoughts and orisons and mortifications, he fell to revolving in his memory the youth and beauty of the damsel and bethinking himself what course he should take with her, so as to win to that which he desired of her, without her taking him for a debauched fellow.

Accordingly, having sounded her with sundry questions, he found that she had never known man and was in truth as simple as she seemed; wherefore he bethought him how, under colour of the service of God, he might bring her to his pleasures. In the first place, he showeth her with many words how great an enemy the devil was of God the Lord and after gave her to understand that the most acceptable service that could be rendered to God was to put back the devil into hell, whereto he had condemned him. The girl asked him how this might be done; and he, 'Thou shalt soon know that; do thou but as thou shalt see me do.' So saying, he proceeded to put off the few garments he had and abode stark naked, as likewise did the girl, whereupon he fell on his knees, as he would pray, and caused her abide over against himself.[2]

E cosí stando, essendo Rustico, piú che mai, nel suo disidero acceso, per lo vederla cosí bella, venue la resurrezion della carne; la quale riguardando Alibech, e maravigliatasti, disse: Rustico, quella che cosa è, che io ti veggio, che cosí si pigne in fuori, e non l' ho io? O figliuola mia, disse Rustico, questo è il diavolo, di che io t'ho parlato, e vedi tu ora: egli mi dà grandissima molestia, tanta, che io appena la posso sofferire. Allora disse la giovane. O lodato sia Iddio, ché io veggio, che io sto meglio, che non stai tu, ché io non ho cotesto diavolo io. Disse Rustico, tu di vero; ma tu hai un' altra cosa, che non l'ho io, et haila in iscambio di questo. Disse Alibech: O che? A cui Rustico disse: Hai l'inferno; e dicoti, che io mi credo, che Dio t'abbia qui mandata per la salute dell' anima mia; perciòche, se questo diavolo pur mi darà questa noia, ove tu cogli aver di me tanta pietà, e sofferire, che io in inferno il rimetta; tu mi darai grandissima consolazione, et a Dio farai grandissimo piacere, e servigio; se tu per quello fare in queste parti venuta se; che tu di. La giovane di buona fede rispose O padre mio, poscia che io ho l'inferno, sia pure quando vi piacerà mettervi il diavolo. Disse allora Rustico: Figliuola mia benedetta sia tu: andiamo dunque, e rimettiamlovi sí, che egli poscia mi lasci stare. E cosí detto, menate la giovane sopra uno de' loro letticelli, le 'nsegnò, come star si dovesse a dover incarcerare quel maladetto da Dio. La giovane, che mai piú non aveva in inferno messo diavolo alcuno, per la prima volta sentí un poco di noia; perché ella disse a Rustico.

Per certo, padre mio, mala cosa dee essere questo diavolo, e veramente nimico di Iddio ché ancora all'inferno, non che altrui duole quando, egli v'è dentro rimesso. Disse Rustico: Figliuola, egli non averrà sempre cosí: e per fare, che questo non avvenisse, da sei volte anziche di su il letticel si movesero, ve 'l rimisero; tantoche per quella volta gli trasser sí la superbia del capo, che egli si stette volentieri in pace. Ma ritornatagli poi nel seguente tempo piú volte, e la giovane ubbidente sempre a trargliela si disponesse, avvenne, che il giuoco le cominciò a piacere; e cominciò a dire a Rustico. Ben veggio, che il ver dicevano que valenti uomini in Capsa, che il servire a Dio era cosí dolce cosa, e per certo io non mi ricordo, che mai alcuna altra ne facessi, che di tanto diletto, e piacere mi fosse, quanto è il rimettere il diavolo in inferno; e perciò giudico ogn' altra persona, che ad altro che a servire a Dio attende, essere una bestia. Per la qual cosa essa spesse volte andava a Rustico, e gli diceva. Padre mio, io son qui venuta per servire a Dio, e non per istare oziosa; andiamo a rimittere il diavolo in inferno. La qual cosa faccendo, diceva ella alcuna volta. Rustico, io non so perché il diavolo si fugga di ninferno, ché s' egli vi stesse cosí volentiere, come l'inferno il riceve, e tiene; agli non sene uscirebbe mai. Cosí adunque invitando spesso la giovane Rustico, et al servigio di Dio confortandolo, se la bambagia del farsetto tratta gli avea, che egli a talora sentiva freddo, che un' altro sarebbe sudato; e perciò egli incominciò a dire alla giovane, che il diavolo non era da gastigare, né da rimettere in inferno, se non quando egli per superbia levasse il capo; e noi, per la grazia, di Dio, l'abbiamo sí sgannato, che egla priega Iddio di starsi in pace: e cosí alquanto impose di silenzio alla giovane. La qual, poiche vide che Rustico non la richiedeva a dovere il diavolo rimettere in inferno, gli disse un giorno. Rustico, se il diavolo tuo è gastigato, e piú non ti dà noia me il mio ninferno non lascia stare: perché tu farai bene, che tu col tuo diavolo aiuti ad attutare la rabbia al mio inferno; come io col mio ninferno ho ajutato a trarre la superbia al tuo diavolo.

Rustico, who lived on roots and water, could ill avail to answer her calls and told her that it would need overmany devils to appease hell, but he would do what he might thereof. Accordingly he satisfied her bytimes, but so seldom it was but casting a bean into the lion's mouth; whereas the girl, herseeming she served not God as diligently as she would fain have done, murmured somewhat. But, whilst this debate was toward between Rustico his devil and Alibech her hell, for overmuch desire on the one part and lack of power on the other, it befell that a fire broke out in Capsa and burnt Alibech's father in his own house, with as many children and other family as he had; by reason whereof she abode heir to all his good. Thereupon, a young man called Neerbale, who had spent all his substance in gallantry, hearing that she was alive, set out in search of her and finding her, before the court[3] had laid hands upon her father's estate, as that of a man dying without heir, to Rustico's great satisfaction, but against her own will, brought her back to Capsa, where he took her to wife and succeeded, in her right, to the ample inheritance of her father.

There, being asked by the women at what she served God in the desert, she answered (Neerbale having not yet lain with her) that she served Him at putting the devil in hell and that Neerbale had done a grievous sin in that he had taken her from such service. The ladies asked, 'How putteth one the devil in hell?' And the girl, what with words and what with gestures, expounded it to them; whereat they set up so great a laughing that they laugh yet and said, 'Give yourself no concern, my child; nay, for that is done here also and Neerbale will serve our Lord full well with thee at this.' Thereafter, telling it from one to another throughout the city, they brought it to a common saying there that the most acceptable service one could render to God was to put the devil in hell, which byword, having passed the sea hither, is yet current here. Wherefore do all you young ladies, who have need of God's grace, learn to put the devil in hell, for that this is highly acceptable to Him and pleasing to both parties and much good may grow and ensue thereof."

A thousand times or more had Dioneo's story moved the modest ladies to laughter, so quaint and comical did his words appear to them; then, whenas he had made an end thereof, the queen, knowing the term of her sovranty to be come, lifted the laurel from her head and set it merrily on that of Filostrato, saying: "We shall presently see if the wolf will know how to govern the ewes better than the ewes have governed the wolves." Filostrato, hearing this, said, laughing, "An I were hearkened to, the wolves had taught the ewes to put the devil in hell, no worse than Rustico taught Alibech; wherefore do ye not style us wolven, since you yourselves have not been ewen. Algates, I will govern the kingdom committed to me to the best of my power." "Harkye, Filostrato," rejoined Neifile, "in seeking to teach us, you might have chanced to learn sense, even as did Masetto of Lamporecchio of the nuns, and find your tongue what time your bones should have learnt to whistle without a master."

Filostrato, finding that he still got a Roland for his Oliver,[4] gave over pleasantry and addressed himself to the governance of the kingdom committed to him. Wherefore, letting call the seneschal, he was fain to know at what point things stood all and after discreetly ordained that which he judged would be well and would content the company for such time as his seignory should endure. Then, turning to the ladies, "Lovesome ladies," quoth he, "since I knew good from evil, I have, for my ill fortune, been still subject unto Love for the charms of one or other of you; nor hath humility neither obedience, no, nor the assiduous ensuing him in all his usances, in so far as it hath been known of me, availed me but that first I have been abandoned for another and after have still gone from bad to worse; and so I believe I shall fare unto my death; wherefore it pleaseth me that it be discoursed to-morrow of none other matter than that which is most conformable to mine own case, to wit, OF THOSE WHOSE LOVES HAVE HAD UNHAPPY ENDING, for that I in the long run look for a most unhappy [issue to mine own]; nor was the name by which you call me conferred on me for otherwhat by such an one who knew well what it meant."[5] So saying, he rose to his feet and dismissed every one until supper-time.

The garden was so goodly and so delightsome that there was none who elected to go forth thereof, in the hope of finding more pleasance elsewhere. Nay, the sun, now grown mild, making it nowise irksome to give chase to the fawns and kids and rabbits and other beasts which were thereabout and which, as they sat, had come maybe an hundred times to disturb them by skipping through their midst, some addressed themselves to pursue them. Dioneo and Fiammetta fell to singing of Messer Guglielmo and the Lady of Vergiu,[6] whilst Filomena and Pamfilo sat down to chess; and so, some doing one thing and some another, the time passed on such wise that the hour of supper came well nigh unlooked for; whereupon, the tables being set round about the fair fountain, they supped there in the evening with the utmost delight.

As soon as the tables were taken away, Filostrato, not to depart from the course holden of those who had been queens before him, commanded Lauretta to lead up a dance and sing a song. "My lord," answered she, "I know none of other folk's songs, nor have I in mind any of mine own which should best beseem so joyous a company; but, an you choose one of those which I have, I will willingly sing it." Quoth the king, "Nothing of thine can be other than goodly and pleasing; wherefore sing us such as thou hast." Lauretta, then, with a sweet voice enough, but in a somewhat plaintive style, began thus, the other ladies answering:

> No maid disconsolate
> Hath cause as I, alack!
> Who sigh for love in vain, to mourn her fate.
>
> He who moves heaven and all the stars in air
> Made me for His delight
> Lovesome and sprightly, kind and debonair,
> E'en here below to give each lofty spright
> Some inkling of that fair
> That still in heaven abideth in His sight;
> But erring men's unright,
> Ill knowing me, my worth

Accepted not, nay, with dispraise did bate.

Erst was there one who held me dear and fain
Took me, a youngling maid,
Into his arms and thought and heart and brain,
Caught fire at my sweet eyes; yea time, unstayed
Of aught, that flits amain
And lightly, all to wooing me he laid.
I, courteous, nought gainsaid
And held[7] him worthy me;
But now, woe's me, of him I'm desolate.

Then unto me there did himself present
A youngling proud and haught,
Renowning him for valorous and gent;
He took and holds me and with erring thought[8]
To jealousy is bent;
Whence I, alack! nigh to despair am wrought,
As knowing myself, —brought
Into this world for good
Of many an one, —engrossed of one sole mate.

The luckless hour I curse, in very deed,
When I, alas! said yea,
Vesture to change, —so fair in that dusk wede
I was and glad, whereas in this more gay
A weary life I lead,
Far less than erst held honest, welaway!
Ah, dolorous bridal day,
Would God I had been dead
Or e'er I proved thee in such ill estate!

O lover dear, with whom well pleased was I
Whilere past all that be, —
Who now before Him sittest in the sky
Who fashioned us, —have pity upon me
Who cannot, though I die,
Forget thee for another; cause me see
The flame that kindled thee
For me lives yet unquenched
And my recall up thither[9] impetrate.

Here Lauretta made an end of her song, wherein, albeit attentively followed of all, she was diversely apprehended of divers persons, and there were those who would e'en understand, Milan-fashion, that a good hog was better than a handsome wench;[10] but others were of a loftier and better and truer apprehension, whereof it booteth not to tell at this present. Thereafter the king let kindle store of flambeaux upon the grass and among the flowers and caused sing divers other songs, until every star began to decline, that was above the horizon, when, deeming it time for sleep, he bade all with a good night betake themselves to their chambers.

---

1. *Guadagnare l'anima,* lit. gain the soul (syn. pith, kernel, substance). This passage is ambiguous and should perhaps be rendered "catch the knack or trick" or "acquire the wish."
2. The translators regret that the disuse into which magic has fallen, makes it impossible to render the technicalities of that mysterious art into tolerable English; they have therefore found it necessary to insert several passages in the original Italian.
3. *i.e.* the government (*corte*).
4. Lit. that scythes were no less plenty that he had arrows (*che falci si trovavano non meno che egli avesse strali*), a proverbial expression the exact bearing of which I do not know, but whose evident sense I have rendered in the equivalent English idiom.
5. Syn. what he said (*che si dire*).
6. Apparently the well-known fabliau of the Dame de Vergy, upon which Marguerite d'Angoulême founded the seventieth story of the Heptameron.
7. Lit. made (*Di me il feci digno*).
8. *i.e.* false suspicion (*falso pensiero*).
9. *i.e.* to heaven (*e costa su m'impetra la tornata*).
10. The pertinence of this allusion, which probably refers to some current Milanese proverbial saying, the word *tosa,* here used by Boccaccio for "wench," belonging to the Lombard dialect, is not very clear. The expression "Milan-fashion" (*alla melanese*) may be supposed to refer to the proverbial materialism of the people of Lombardy.

DAY THE FOURTH

Here Beginneth the Fourth Day of the Decameron
Wherein Under the Governance of Filostrato Is
Discoursed of Those Whose Loves Have Had
Unhappy Endings

Dearest ladies, as well by words of wise men heard as by things many a time both seen and read of myself, I had conceived that the boisterous and burning blast of envy was apt to smite none but lofty towers or the highest summits of the trees; but I find myself mistaken in my conceit, for that, fleeing, as I have still studied to flee, from the cruel onslaught of that raging wind, I have striven to go, not only in the plains, but in the very deepest of the valleys, as many manifestly enough appear to whoso considereth these present stories, the which have been written by me, not only in vulgar Florentine and in prose and without [author's] name, but eke in as humble and sober a style as might be. Yet for all this have I not availed to escape being cruelly shaken, nay, well nigh uprooted, of the aforesaid wind and all torn of the fangs of envy; wherefore I can very manifestly understand that to be true which the wise use to say, to wit, that misery alone in things present is without envy.[1]

There are then, discreet ladies, some who, reading these stories, have said that you please me overmuch and that it is not a seemly thing that I should take so much delight in pleasuring and solacing you; and some have said yet worse of commending you as I do. Others, making a show of wishing to speak more maturely, have said that it sorteth ill with mine age henceforth to follow after things of this kind, to wit, to discourse of women or to study to please them. And many, feigning themselves mighty tender of my repute, avouch that I should do more wisely to abide with the Muses on Parnassus than to busy myself among you with these toys. Again, there be some who, speaking more despitefully than advisedly, have said that I should do more discreetly to consider whence I might get me bread than to go peddling after these baubles, feeding upon wind; and certain others, in disparagement of my pains, study to prove the things recounted by me to have been otherwise than as I present them to you.

With such, then, and so many blusterings,[2] such atrocious backbitings, such needle-pricks, noble ladies, am I, what while I battle in your service, baffled and buffeted and transfixed even to the quick. The which things, God knoweth, I hear and apprehend with an untroubled mind; and albeit my defence in this pertaineth altogether unto you, natheless, I purpose not to spare mine own pains; nay, without answering so much [at large] as it might behove, I mean to rid mine ears of them with some slight rejoinder, and that without delay; for that if even now, I being not yet come to[3] the third part of my travail, they[4] are many and presume amain, I opine that, ere I come to the end thereof, they may, having had no rebuff at the first, on such wise be multiplied that with whatsoever little pains of theirs they might overthrow me, nor might your powers, great though they be, avail to withstand this.

But, ere I come to make answer to any of them, it pleaseth me, in mine own defence, to relate, not an entire story,—lest it should seem I would fain mingle mine own stories with those of so commendable a company as that which I have presented to you,—but a part of one,—that so its very default [of completeness] may attest that it is none of those,—and accordingly, speaking to my assailants, I say that in our city, a good while agone, there was a townsman, by name Filippo Balducci, a man of mean enough extraction, but rich and well addressed and versed in such matters as his condition comported. He had a wife, whom he loved with an exceeding love, as she him, and they lived a peaceful life together, studying nothing so much as wholly to please one another. In course of time it came to pass, as it cometh to pass of all, that the good lady departed this life and left Filippo nought of herself but one only son, begotten of him and maybe two years old. Filippo for the death of his lady abode as disconsolate as ever man might, having lost a beloved one, and seeing himself left alone and forlorn of that company which most he loved, he resolved to be no more of the world, but to give himself altogether to the service of God and do the like with his little son. Wherefore, bestowing all his good for the love of God,[5] he repaired without delay to the top of Mount Asinajo, where he took up his abode with his son in a little hut and there living with him upon alms, in the practice of fasts and prayers, straitly guarded himself from discoursing whereas the boy was, of any temporal thing, neither suffered him see aught thereof, lest this should divert him from the service aforesaid, but still bespoke him of the glories of life eternal and of God and the saints, teaching him nought but pious orisons; and in this way of life he kept him many years, never suffering him go forth of the hermitage nor showing him aught other than himself.

Now the good man was used to come whiles into Florence, where being succoured, according to his occasions, of the friends of God, he returned to his hut, and it chanced one day that, his son being now eighteen years old and Filippo an old man, the lad asked him whither he went. Filippo told him and the boy said, "Father mine, you are now an old man and can ill endure fatigue; why do you not whiles carry me to Florence and bring me to know the friends and devotees of God and yourself, to the end that I, who am young and better able to toil than you, may after, whenas it pleaseth you, go to Florence for our occasions, whilst you abide here?" The worthy man, considering that his son was now grown to man's estate and thinking him so inured to the service of God that the things of this world might thenceforth uneath allure him to themselves, said in himself, "The lad saith well"; and accordingly, having occasion to go thither, he carried him with him. There the youth, seeing the palaces, the houses, the churches and all the other things whereof one seeth all the city full, began, as one who had never to his recollection beheld the like, to marvel amain and questioned his father of many things what they were and how they were called. Filippo told him and he, hearing him, abode content and questioned of somewhat else.

As they went thus, the son asking and the father answering, they encountered by chance a company of pretty and well-dressed young women, coming from a wedding, whom as soon as the young man saw, he asked his father what manner of things these were. "My son," answered Filippo, "cast your eyes on the ground and look not at them, for that they are an ill thing." Quoth the son, "And how are they called?" The father, not to awaken in the lad's mind a carnal appetite less than useful, would not name them by the proper name, to wit, women, but said, "They are called green geese." Whereupon, marvellous to relate, he who have never seen a woman and who recked not of palaces nor oxen nor horses nor asses nor monies nor of aught else he had seen, said suddenly, "Father mine, I prithee get me one of these green geese." "Alack, my son," replied the father, "hold they peace; I tell thee they are an ill thing." "How!" asked the youth. "Are ill things then made after this fashion?" and Filippo answered, "Ay." Then said the son, "I know not what you would say nor why these are an ill thing; for my part, meseemeth I never yet saw aught goodly or pleasing as are these. They are fairer than the painted angels you have shown me whiles. For God's sake, an you reck of me, contrive that we may carry one of yonder green geese back with us up yonder, and I will give it to eat." "Nay," answered the father, "I will not: thou knowest not whereon they feed." And he understood incontinent that nature was stronger than his wit and repented him of having brought the youth to Florence. But I will have it suffice me to have told this much of the present story and return to those for whose behoof I have related it.

Some, then, of my censurers say that I do ill, young ladies, in studying overmuch to please you and that you please me overmuch. Which things I do most openly confess, to wit, that you please me and that I study to please you, and I ask them if they marvel thereat,—considering (let be the having known the dulcet kisses and amorous embracements and delightsome couplings that are of you, most sweet ladies, often gotten) only my having seen and still seeing your dainty manners and lovesome beauty and sprightly grace and above all your womanly courtesy,—whenas he who had been reared and bred on a wild and solitary mountain and within the bounds of a little cell, without other company than his father, no sooner set eyes on you than you alone were desired of him, you alone sought, you alone followed with the eagerness of passion. Will they, then, blame me, back bite me, rend me with their tongues if I, whose body Heaven created all apt to love you, I, who from my childhood vowed my soul to you, feeling the potency of the light of your eyes and the sweetness of your honeyed words and the flame enkindled by your piteous sighs,—if, I say, you please me or if I study to please you, seeing that you over all else pleased a hermitling, a lad without understanding, nay, rather, a wild animal? Certes, it is only those, who, having neither sense nor cognizance of the pleasures and potency of natural affection, love you not nor desire to be loved of you, that chide me thus; and of these I reck little.

As for those who go railing anent mine age, it would seem they know ill that, for all the leek hath a white head, the tail thereof is green. But to these, laying aside pleasantry, I answer that never, no, not to the extreme limit of my life, shall I repute it to myself for shame to seek to please those whom Guido Cavalcanti and Dante Alighieri, when already stricken in years, and Messer Cino da Pistoja, when a very old man, held in honour and whose approof was dear to them. And were it not to depart from the wonted usance of discourse, I would cite history in support and show it to be all full of stories of ancient and noble men who in their ripest years have still above all studied to please the ladies, the which an they know not, let them go learn. That I should abide with the Muses on Parnassus, I confess to be good counsel; but, since we can neither abide for ever with the Muses, nor they with us, it is nothing blameworthy if, whenas it chanceth a man is parted from them, he take delight in seeing that which is like unto them. The muses are women, and albeit women may not avail to match with them, yet at first sight they have a semblance of them; insomuch that, an they pleased me not for aught else, for this they should please me; more by token that women have aforetime been to me the occasion of composing a thousand verses, whereas the Muses never were to me the occasion of making any. They aided me, indeed, and showed me how to compose the verses in question; and peradventure, in the writing of these present things, all lowly though they be, they have come whiles to abide with me, in token maybe and honour of the likeness that women bear to them; wherefore, in inditing these toys, I stray not so far from Mount Parnassus nor from the Muses as many belike conceive.

But what shall we say to those who have such compassion on my hunger that they counsel me provide myself bread? Certes, I know not, save that, whenas I seek to imagine in myself what would be their answer, an I should of necessity beseech them thereof, to wit, of bread, methinketh they would reply, "Go seek it among thy fables." Indeed, aforetime poets have found more thereof among their fables than many a rich man among his treasures, and many, following after their fables, have caused their age to flourish; whereas, on the contrary, many, in seeking to have more bread than they needed, have perished miserably. What more [shall I say?] Let them drive me forth, whenas I ask it of them, not that, Godamercy, I have yet need thereof; and even should need betide, I know with the Apostle Paul both how to abound and suffer need;[6] wherefore let none be more careful of me than I am of myself. For those who say that these things have not been such as I have here set them down, I would fain have them produce the originals, and an these latter accord not with that of which I write, I will confess their objection for just and will study to amend myself; but till otherwhat than words appeareth, I will leave them to their opinion and follow mine own, saying of them that which they say of me.

Wherefore, deeming that for the nonce I have answered enough, I say that, armed, as I hope to be, with God's aid and yours, gentlest ladies, and with fair patience, I will fare on with this that I have begun, turning my back to the wind aforesaid and letting it blow, for that I see not that aught can betide me other than that which betideth thin dust, the which a whirlwind, whenas it bloweth, either stirreth not from the earth, or, an it stir it, carrieth it aloft and leaveth it oftentimes upon the heads of men and upon the crowns of kings and emperors, nay, bytimes upon high palaces and lofty towers, whence an it fall, it cannot go lower than the place wherefrom it was uplifted. And if ever with all my might I vowed myself to seek to please you in aught, now more than ever shall I address myself thereto; for that I know none can with reason say otherwhat than that I and others who love you do according to nature, whose laws to seek to gainstand demandeth overgreat strength, and oftentimes not only in vain, but to the exceeding hurt of whoso striveth to that end, is this strength employed. Such strength I confess I have not nor ever desired in this to have; and an I had it, I had liefer lend it to others than use it for myself. Wherefore, let the carpers be silent and an they avail not to warm themselves, let them live star-stricken[7] and abiding in their delights—or rather their corrupt appetites,—leave me to abide in mine for this brief life that is appointed me. But now, fair ladies, for that we have strayed enough, needs must we return whence we set out and ensue the ordinance commenced.

The sun had already banished every star from the sky and had driven from the earth the humid vapours of the night, when Filostrato, arising, caused all his company arise and with them betook himself to the fair garden, where they all proceeded to disport themselves, and the eating-hour come, they dined whereas they had supped on the foregoing evening. Then, after having slept, what time the sun was at its highest, they seated themselves, after the wonted fashion, hard by the fair fountain, and Filostrato bade Fiammetta give beginning to the storytelling; whereupon, without awaiting further commandment, she began with womanly grace as follows:

---

1. Sic (*senza invidia*); but the meaning is that misery alone is without *enviers*.
2. *i.e.* blasts of calumny.
3. *i.e.* having not yet accomplished.
4. *i.e.* my censors.
5. *i.e.* in alms.
6. "I know both how to be abased and I know how to abound; everywhere and in all things I am instructed both to be full and to be hungry, both to abound and suffer need."—*Philippians* iv. 12.
7. *i.e.* benumbed (*assiderati*).

THE FIRST STORY

TANCRED, PRINCE OF SALERNO, SLAYETH HIS DAUGHTER'S LOVER AND SENDETH HER HIS HEART IN A BOWL OF GOLD; WHEREUPON, POURING POISONED WATER OVER IT, SHE DRINKETH THEREOF AND DIETH

"OUR KING HATH this day appointed us a woeful subject of discourse, considering that, whereas we came hither to make merry, needs must we tell of others' tears, the which may not be recounted without moving both those who tell and those who hearken to compassion thereof. He hath mayhap done this somedele to temper the mirth of the foregoing days; but, whatsoever may have moved him thereto, since it pertaineth not to me to change his pleasure, I will relate a piteous chance, nay, an ill-fortuned and a worthy of your tears.

Tancred, Lord of Salerno, was a humane prince and benign enough of nature, (had he not in his old age imbrued his hands in lover's blood,) who in all the course of his life had but one daughter, and happier had he been if he had none. She was of him as tenderly loved as ever daughter of father, and knowing not, by reason of this his tender love for her, how to part with her, he married her not till she had long overpassed the age when she should have had a husband. At last, he gave her to wife to a son of the Duke of Capua, with whom having abidden a little while, she was left a widow and returned to her father. Now she was most fair of form and favour, as ever was woman, and young and sprightly and learned perchance more than is required of a lady. Abiding, then, with her father in all ease and luxury, like a great lady as she was, and seeing that, for the love he bore her, he recked little of marrying her again, nor did it seem to her a seemly thing to require him thereof, she bethought herself to seek, an it might be, to get her privily a worthy lover. She saw men galore, gentle and simple, frequent her father's court, and considering the manners and fashions of many, a young serving-man of her father's, Guiscardo by name, a man of humble enough extraction, but nobler of worth and manners than whatsoever other, pleased her over all and of him, seeing him often, she became in secret ardently enamoured, approving more and more his fashions every hour; whilst the young man, who was no dullard, perceiving her liking for him, received her into his heart, on such wise that his mind was thereby diverted from well nigh everything other than the love of her.

Each, then, thus secretly tendering the other, the young lady, who desired nothing so much as to foregather with him, but had no mind to make any one a confidant of her passion, bethought herself of a rare device to apprize him of the means; to wit, she wrote him a letter, wherein she showed him how he should do to foregather with her on the ensuing day, and placing it in the hollow of a cane, gave the letter jestingly to Guiscardo, saying, 'Make thee a bellows thereof for thy serving-maid, wherewith she may blow up the fire to-night.' Guiscardo took the cane and bethinking himself that she would not have given it him nor spoken thus, without some cause, took his leave and returned therewith to his lodging. There he examined the cane and seeing it to be cleft, opened it and found therein the letter, which having read and well apprehended that which he had to do, he was the joyfullest man alive and set about taking order how he might go to her, according to the fashion appointed him of her.

There was, beside the prince's palace, a grotto hewn out of the rock and made in days long agone, and to this grotto some little light was given by a tunnel[1] by art wrought in the mountain, which latter, for that the grotto was abandoned, was well nigh blocked at its mouth with briers and weeds that had overgrown it. Into this grotto one might go by a privy stair which was in one of the ground floor rooms of the lady's apartment in the palace and which was shut in by a very strong door. This stair was so out of all folk's minds, for that it had been unused from time immemorial, that well nigh none remembered it to be there; but Love, to whose eyes there is nothing so secret but it winneth, had recalled it to the memory of the enamoured lady, who, that none should get wind of the matter, had laboured sore many days with such tools as she might command, ere she could make shift to open the door; then, going down alone thereby into the grotto and seeing the tunnel, she sent to bid Guiscardo study to come to her thereby and acquainted him with the height which herseemed should be from the mouth thereof to the ground.

To this end Guiscardo promptly made ready a rope with certain knots and loops, whereby he might avail to descend and ascend, and donning a leathern suit, that might defend him from the briers, he on the ensuing night repaired, without letting any know aught of the matter, to the mouth of the tunnel. There making one end of the rope fast to a stout tree-stump that had grown up in the mouth, he let himself down thereby into the grotto and there awaited the lady, who, on the morrow, feigning a desire to sleep, dismissed her women and shut herself up alone in her chamber; then, opening the privy door, she descended into the grotto, where she found Guiscardo. They greeted one another with marvellous joy and betook themselves to her chamber, where they abode great part of the day in the utmost delight; and after they had taken order together for the discreet conduct of their loves, so they might abide secret, Guiscardo returned to the grotto, whilst she shut the privy door and went forth to her women. The night come, Guiscardo climbed up by his rope to the mouth of the tunnel and issuing forth whence he had entered in, returned to his lodging; and having learned this road, he in process of time returned many times thereafter.

But fortune, jealous of so long and so great a delight, with a woeful chance changed the gladness of the two lovers into mourning and sorrow; and it befell on this wise. Tancred was wont to come bytimes all alone into his daughter's chamber and there abide with her and converse awhile and after go away. Accordingly, one day, after dinner, he came thither, what time the lady (whose name was Ghismonda) was in a garden of hers with all her women, and willing not to take her from her diversion, he entered her chamber, without being seen or heard of any. Finding the windows closed and the curtains let down over the bed, he sat down in a corner on a hassock at the bedfoot and leant his head against the bed; then, drawing the curtain over himself, as if he had studied to hide himself there, he fell asleep. As he slept thus, Ghismonda, who, as ill chance would have it, had appointed her lover to come thither that day, softly entered the chamber, leaving her women in the garden, and having shut herself in, without perceiving that there was some one there, opened the secret door to Guiscardo, who awaited her. They straightway betook themselves to bed, as of their wont, and what while they sported and solaced themselves together, it befell that Tancred awoke and heard and saw that which Guiscardo and his daughter did; whereat beyond measure grieved, at first he would have cried out at them, but after bethought himself to keep silence and abide, an he might, hidden, so with more secrecy and less shame to himself he might avail to do that which had already occurred to his mind.

The two lovers abode a great while together, according to their usance, without observing Tancred, and coming down from the bed, whenas it seemed to them time, Guiscardo returned to the grotto and she departed the chamber; whereupon Tancred, for all he was an old man, let himself down into the garden by a window and returned, unseen of any, to his own chamber, sorrowful unto death. That same night, at the time of the first sleep, Guiscardo, by his orders, was seized by two men, as he came forth of the tunnel, and carried secretly, trussed as he was in his suit of leather, to Tancred, who, whenas he saw him, said, well nigh weeping, 'Guiscardo, my kindness to thee merited not the outrage and the shame thou hast done me in mine own flesh and blood, as I have this day seen with my very eyes.' Whereto Guiscardo answered nothing but this, 'Love can far more than either you or I.' Tancred then commanded that he should be kept secretly under guard and in one of the chambers of the palace, and so was it done.

On the morrow, having meanwhile revolved in himself many and divers devices, he betook himself, after eating, as of his wont, to his daughter's chamber and sending for the lady, who as yet knew nothing of these things, shut himself up with her and proceeded, with tears in his eyes, to bespeak her thus: 'Ghismonda, meseemed I knew thy virtue and thine honesty, nor might it ever have occurred to my mind, though it were told me, had I not seen it with mine own eyes, that thou wouldst, even so much as in thought, have abandoned thyself to any man, except he were thy husband; wherefore in this scant remnant of life that my eld reserveth unto me, I shall still abide sorrowful, remembering me of this. Would God, an thou must needs stoop to such wantonness, thou hadst taken a man sortable to thy quality! But, amongst so many who frequent my court, thou hast chosen Guiscardo, a youth of the meanest condition, reared in our court, well nigh of charity, from a little child up to this day; wherefore thou hast put me in sore travail of mind, for that I know not what course to take with thee. With Guiscardo, whom I caused take yesternight, as he issued forth of the tunnel and have in ward, I am already resolved how to deal; but with thee God knoweth I know not what to do. On one side love draweth me, which I still borne thee more than father ever bore daughter, and on the other most just despite, conceived for thine exceeding folly; the one would have me pardon thee, the other would have me, against my nature, deal harshly by thee. But ere I come to a decision, I would fain hear what thou hast to say to this.' So saying, he bowed his head and wept sore as would a beaten child.

Ghismonda, hearing her father's words and seeing that not only was her secret love discovered, but Guiscardo taken, felt an inexpressible chagrin and came many a time near upon showing it with outcry and tears, as women mostly do; nevertheless, her haughty soul overmastering that weakness, with marvellous fortitude she composed her countenance and rather than proffer any prayer for herself, determined inwardly to abide no more on life, doubting not but her Guiscardo was already dead. Wherefore, not as a woman rebuked and woeful for her default, but as one undaunted and valiant, with dry eyes and face open and nowise troubled, she thus bespoke her father: 'Tancred, I purpose neither to deny nor to entreat, for that the one would profit me nothing nor would I have the other avail me; more by token that I am nowise minded to seek to render thy mansuetude and thine affection favourable to me, but rather, confessing the truth, first with true arguments to vindicate mine honour and after with deeds right resolutely to ensue the greatness of my soul. True is it I have loved and love Guiscardo, and what while I live, which will be little, I shall love him, nor, if folk live after death, shall I ever leave loving him; but unto this it was not so much my feminine frailty that moved me as thy little solicitude to remarry me and his own worth.

It should have been manifest to thee, Tancred, being as thou art flesh and blood, that thou hadst begotten a daughter of flesh and blood and not of iron or stone; and thou shouldst have remembered and should still remember, for all thou art old, what and what like are the laws of youth and with what potency they work; nor, albeit thou, being a man, hast in thy best years exercised thyself in part in arms, shouldst thou the less know what ease and leisure and luxury can do in the old, to say nothing of the young. I am, then, as being of thee begotten, of flesh and blood and have lived so little that I am yet young and (for the one and the other reason) full of carnal desire, whereunto the having aforetime, by reason of marriage, known what pleasure it is to give accomplishment to such desire hath added marvellous strength. Unable, therefore, to withstand the strength of my desires, I addressed myself, being young and a woman, to ensue that whereto they prompted me and became enamoured. And certes in this I set my every faculty to the endeavouring that, so far as in me lay, no shame should ensue either to thee or to me through this to which natural frailty moved me. To this end compassionate Love and favouring Fortune found and showed me a very occult way, whereby, unknown of any, I won to my desire, and this, whoever it be discovered it to thee or howsoever thou knowest it, I nowise deny.

Guiscardo I took not at hazard, as many women do; nay, of deliberate counsel I chose him before every other and with advisement prepense drew him to me[2] and by dint of perseverance and discretion on my part and on his, I have long had enjoyment of my desire. Whereof it seemeth that thou, ensuing rather vulgar prejudice than truth, reproachest me with more bitterness than of having sinned by way of love, saying (as if thou shouldst not have been chagrined, had I chosen therefor a man of gentle birth,) that I have committed myself with a man of mean condition. Wherein thou seest not that thou blamest not my default, but that of fortune, which too often advanceth the unworthy to high estate, leaving the worthiest alow.

But now let us leave this and look somewhat to the first principles of things, whereby thou wilt see that we all get our flesh from one same stock and that all souls were by one same Creator created with equal faculties, equal powers and equal virtues. Worth it was that first distinguished between us, who were all and still are born equal; wherefore those who had and used the greatest sum thereof were called noble and the rest abode not noble. And albeit contrary usance hath since obscured this primary law, yet is it nowise done away nor blotted out from nature and good manners; wherefore he who doth worthily manifestly showeth himself a gentleman, and if any call him otherwise, not he who is called, but he who calleth committeth default. Look among all thy gentlemen and examine into their worth, their usances and their manners, and on the other hand consider those of Guiscardo; if thou wilt consent to judge without animosity, thou wilt say that he is most noble and that these thy nobles are all churls. With regard to his worth and virtue, I trusted not to the judgment of any other, but to that of thy words and of mine own eyes. Who ever so commended him as thou didst in all those praiseworthy things wherefor a man of worth should be commended? And certes not without reason; for, if mine eyes deceived me not, there was no praise given him of thee which I saw him not justify by deeds, and that more admirably than thy words availed to express; and even had I suffered any deceit in this, it is by thyself I should have been deceived. An, then, thou say that I have committed myself with a man of mean condition, thou sayst not sooth; but shouldst thou say with a poor man, it might peradventure be conceded thee, to thy shame who hast so ill known to put a servant of thine and a man of worth in good case; yet poverty bereaveth not any of gentilesse; nay, rather, wealth it is that doth this. Many kings, many great princes were once poor and many who delve and tend sheep were once very rich.

The last doubt that thou broachest, to wit, what thou shouldst do with me, drive it away altogether; an thou in thine extreme old age be disposed to do that which thou usedst not, being young, namely, to deal cruelly, wreak thy cruelty upon me, who am minded to proffer no prayer unto thee, as being the prime cause of this sin, if sin it be; for of this I certify thee, that whatsoever thou hast done or shalt do with Guiscardo, an thou do not the like with me, mine own hands shall do it. Now begone; go shed tears with women and waxing cruel, slay him and me with one same blow, an it seem to thee we have deserved it.'

The prince knew the greatness of his daughter's soul, but notwithstanding believed her not altogether so firmly resolved as she said unto that which her words gave out. Wherefore, taking leave of her and having laid aside all intent of using rigour against her person, he thought to cool her fervent love with other's suffering and accordingly bade Guiscardo's two guardians strangle him without noise that same night and taking out his heart, bring it to him. They did even as it was commanded them, and on the morrow the prince let bring a great and goodly bowl of gold and setting therein Guiscardo's heart, despatched it to his daughter by the hands of a very privy servant of his, bidding him say, whenas he gave it her, 'Thy father sendeth thee this, to solace thee of the thing thou most lovest, even as thou hast solaced him of that which he loved most.'

Now Ghismonda, unmoved from her stern purpose, had, after her father's departure, let bring poisonous herbs and roots and distilled and reduced them in water, so she might have it at hand, an that she feared should come to pass. The serving-man coming to her with the prince's present and message, she took the cup with a steadfast countenance and uncovered it. Whenas she saw the heart and apprehended the words of the message, she was throughly certified that this was Guiscardo's heart and turning her eyes upon the messenger, said to him, 'No sepulchre less of worth than one of gold had beseemed a heart such as this; and in this my father hath done discreetly.' So saying, she set the heart to her lips and kissing it, said, 'Still in everything and even to this extreme limit of my life have I found my father's love most tender towards me; but now more than ever; wherefore do thou render him on my part for so great a gift the last thanks I shall ever have to give him.'

Then, bending down over the cup, which she held fast, she said, looking upon the heart, 'Alack, sweetest harbourage of all my pleasures, accursed be his cruelty who maketh me now to see thee with the eyes of the body! Enough was it for me at all hours to behold thee with those of the mind. Thou hast finished thy course and hast acquitted thyself on such wise as was vouchsafed thee of fortune; thou art come to the end whereunto each runneth; thou hast left the toils and miseries of the world, and of thy very enemy thou hast that sepulchre which thy worth hath merited. There lacked nought to thee to make thy funeral rites complete save her tears whom in life thou so lovedst, the which that thou mightest have, God put it into the heart of my unnatural father to send thee to me and I will give them to thee, albeit I had purposed to die with dry eyes and visage undismayed of aught; and having given them to thee, I will without delay so do that my soul, thou working it,[3] shall rejoin that soul which thou erst so dearly guardedst. And in what company could I betake me more contentedly or with better assurance to the regions unknown than with it?[4] Certain am I that it abideth yet herewithin[5] and vieweth the seats of its delights and mine and as that which I am assured still loveth me, awaiteth my soul, whereof it is over all beloved.'

So saying, no otherwise than as she had a fountain of water in her head, bowing herself over the bowl, without making any womanly outcry, she began, lamenting, to shed so many and such tears that they were a marvel to behold, kissing the dead heart the while an infinite number of times. Her women, who stood about her, understood not what this heart was nor what her words meant, but, overcome with compassion, wept all and in vain questioned her affectionately of the cause of her lament and studied yet more, as best they knew and might, to comfort her. The lady, having wept as much as herseemed fit, raised her head and drying her eyes, said, 'O much-loved heart, I have accomplished mine every office towards thee, nor is there left me aught else to do save to come with my soul and bear thine company.' So saying, she called for the vial wherein was the water she had made the day before and poured the latter into the bowl where was the heart bathed with so many of her tears; then, setting her mouth thereto without any fear, she drank it all off and having drunken, mounted, with the cup in her hand, upon the bed, where composing her body as most decently she might, she pressed her dead lover's heart to her own and without saying aught, awaited death.

Her women, seeing and hearing all this, albeit they knew not what water this was she had drunken, had sent to tell Tancred everything, and he, fearing that which came to pass, came quickly down into his daughter's chamber, where he arrived what time she laid herself on her bed and addressed himself too late to comfort her with soft words; but, seeing the extremity wherein she was, he fell a-weeping grievously; whereupon quoth the lady to him, 'Tancred, keep these tears against a less desired fate than this of mine and give them not to me, who desire them not. Who ever saw any, other than thou, lament for that which he himself hath willed? Nevertheless, if aught yet live in thee of the love which once thou borest me, vouchsafe me for a last boon that, since it was not thy pleasure that I should privily and in secret live with Guiscardo, my body may openly abide with his, whereassoever thou hast caused cast him dead.' The agony of his grief suffered not the prince to reply; whereupon the young lady, feeling herself come to her end, strained the dead heart to her breast and said, 'Abide ye with God, for I go hence.' Then, closing her eyes and losing every sense, she departed this life of woe. Such, then, as you have heard, was the sorrowful ending of the loves of Guiscardo and Ghismonda, whose bodies Tancred, after much lamentation, too late repenting him of his cruelty, caused honourably bury in one same sepulchre, amid the general mourning of all the people of Salerno."

---

1. Or airshaft (*spiraglio*).
2. Lit. introduced him to me (*a me lo 'ntrodussi*); but Boccaccio here uses the word *introdurre* in its rarer literal sense to lead, to draw, to bring in.
3. *i.e.* thou being the means of bringing about the conjunction (*adoperandol tu*).
4. *i.e.* Guiscardo's soul.
5. *i.e.* in the heart.

𝔰 2 𝔰

THE SECOND STORY

FRA ALBERTO GIVETH A LADY TO BELIEVE THAT THE
ANGEL GABRIEL IS ENAMOURED OF HER AND IN HIS
SHAPE LIETH WITH HER SUNDRY TIMES; AFTER
WHICH, FOR FEAR OF HER KINSMEN, HE CASTETH
HIMSELF FORTH OF HER WINDOW INTO THE CANAL
AND TAKETH REFUGE IN THE HOUSE OF A POOR MAN,
WHO ON THE MORROW CARRIETH HIM, IN THE GUISE
OF A WILD MAN OF THE WOODS, TO THE PIAZZA,
WHERE, BEING RECOGNIZED, HE IS TAKEN BY HIS
BRETHREN AND PUT IN PRISON

THE STORY TOLD by Fiammetta had more than once brought the tears to the eyes of the ladies her companions; but, it being now finished, the king with a stern countenance said, "My life would seem to me a little price to give for half the delight that Guiscardo had with Ghismonda, nor should any of you ladies marvel thereat, seeing that every hour of my life I suffer a thousand deaths, nor for all that is a single particle of delight vouchsafed me. But, leaving be my affairs for the present, it is my pleasure that Pampinea follow on the order of the discourse with some story of woeful chances and fortunes in part like to mine own; which if she ensue like as Fiammetta hath begun, I shall doubtless begin to feel some dew fallen upon my fire." Pampinea, hearing the order laid upon her, more by her affection apprehended the mind of the ladies her companions than that of Filostrato by his words,[1] wherefore, being more disposed to give them some diversion than to content the king, farther than in the mere letter of his commandment, she bethought herself to tell a story, that should, without departing from the proposed theme, give occasion for laughter, and accordingly began as follows:

"The vulgar have a proverb to the effect that he who is naught and is held good may do ill and it is not believed of him; the which affordeth me ample matter for discourse upon that which hath been proposed to me and at the same time to show what and how great is the hypocrisy of the clergy, who, with garments long and wide and faces paled by art and voices humble and meek to solicit the folk, but exceeding loud and fierce to rebuke in others their own vices, pretend that themselves by taking and others by giving to them come to salvation, and to boot, not as men who have, like ourselves, to purchase paradise, but as in a manner they were possessors and lords thereof, assign unto each who dieth, according to the sum of the monies left them by him, a more or less excellent place there, studying thus to deceive first themselves, an they believe as they say, and after those who put faith for that matter in their words. Anent whom, were it permitted me to discover as much as it behoved, I would quickly make clear to many simple folk that which they keep hidden under those huge wide gowns of theirs. But would God it might betide them all of their cozening tricks, as it betided a certain minor friar, and he no youngling, but held one of the first casuists[2] in Venice; of whom it especially pleaseth me to tell you, so as peradventure somewhat to cheer your hearts, that are full of compassion for the death of Ghismonda, with laughter and pleasance.

There was, then, noble ladies, in Imola, a man of wicked and corrupt life, who was called Berto della Massa and whose lewd fashions, being well known of the Imolese, had brought him into such ill savour with them that there was none in the town who would credit him, even when he said sooth; wherefore, seeing that his shifts might no longer stand him in stead there, he removed in desperation to Venice, the receptacle of every kind of trash, thinking to find there new means of carrying on his wicked practices. There, as if conscience-stricken for the evil deeds done by him in the past, feigning himself overcome with the utmost humility and waxing devouter than any man alive, he went and turned Minor Friar and styled himself Fra Alberta da Imola; in which habit he proceeded to lead, to all appearance, a very austere life, greatly commending abstinence and mortification and never eating flesh nor drinking wine, whenas he had not thereof that which was to his liking. In short, scarce was any ware of him when from a thief, a pimp, a forger, a manslayer, he suddenly became a great preacher, without having for all that forsworn the vices aforesaid, whenas he might secretly put them in practice. Moreover, becoming a priest, he would still, whenas he celebrated mass at the altar, an he were seen of many, beweep our Saviour's passion, as one whom tears cost little, whenas he willed it. Brief, what with his preachings and his tears, he contrived on such wise to inveigle the Venetians that he was trustee and depository of well nigh every will made in the town and guardian of folk's monies, besides being confessor and counsellor of the most part of the men and women of the place; and doing thus, from wolf he was become shepherd and the fame of his sanctity was far greater in those parts than ever was that of St. Francis at Assisi.

It chanced one day that a vain simple young lady, by name Madam Lisetta da Ca[3] Quirino, wife of a great merchant who was gone with the galleys into Flanders, came with other ladies to confess to this same holy friar, at whose feet kneeling and having, like a true daughter of Venice as she was (where the women are all feather-brained), told him part of her affairs, she was asked of him if she had a lover. Whereto she answered, with an offended air, 'Good lack, sir friar, have you no eyes in your head? Seem my charms to you such as those of yonder others? I might have lovers and to spare, an I would; but my beauties are not for this one nor that. How many women do you see whose charms are such as mine, who would be fair in Paradise?' Brief, she said so many things of this beauty of hers that it was a weariness to hear. Fra Alberto incontinent perceived that she savoured of folly and himseeming she was a fit soil for his tools, he fell suddenly and beyond measure in love with her; but, reserving blandishments for a more convenient season, he proceeded, for the nonce, so he might show himself a holy man, to rebuke her and tell her that this was vainglory and so forth. The lady told him he was an ass and knew not what one beauty was more than another, whereupon he, unwilling to vex her overmuch, took her confession and let her go away with the others.

He let some days pass, then, taking with him a trusty companion of his, he repaired to Madam Lisetta's house and withdrawing with her into a room apart, where none might see him, he fell on his knees before her and said, 'Madam, I pray you for God's sake pardon me that which I said to you last Sunday, whenas you bespoke me of your beauty, for that the following night I was so cruelly chastised there that I have not since been able to rise from my bed till to-day.' Quoth Mistress Featherbrain, 'And who chastised you thus?' 'I will tell you,' replied the monk. 'Being that night at my orisons, as I still use to be, I saw of a sudden a great light in my cell and ere I could turn me to see what it might be, I beheld over against me a very fair youth with a stout cudgel in his hand, who took me by the gown and dragging me to my feet, gave me such a drubbing that he broke every bone in my body. I asked him why he used me thus and he answered, "For that thou presumedst to-day, to disparage the celestial charms of Madam Lisetta, whom I love over all things, save only God." "Who, then, are you?" asked I; and he replied that he was the angel Gabriel. "O my lord," said I, "I pray you pardon me"; and he, "So be it; I pardon thee on condition that thou go to her, as first thou mayst, and get her pardon; but if she pardons thee not, I will return to thee and give thee such a bout of it that I will make thee a woeful man for all the time thou shalt live here below." That which he said to me after I dare not tell you, except you first pardon me.'

My Lady Addlepate, who was somewhat scant of wit, was overjoyed to hear this, taking it all for gospel, and said, after a little, 'I told you, Fra Alberto, that my charms were celestial, but, so God be mine aid, it irketh me for you and I will pardon you forthright, so you may come to no more harm, provided you tell me truly that which the angel said to you after.' 'Madam,' replied Fra Alberto, 'since you pardon me, I will gladly tell it you; but I must warn you of one thing, to wit, that whatever I tell you, you must have a care not to repeat it to any one alive, an you would not mar your affairs, for that you are the luckiest lady in the world. The angel Gabriel bade me tell you that you pleased him so much that he had many a time come to pass the night with you, but that he feared to affright you. Now he sendeth to tell you by me that he hath a mind to come to you one night and abide awhile with you and (for that he is an angel and that, if he came in angel-form, you might not avail to touch him,) he purposeth, for your delectation, to come in guise of a man, wherefore he biddeth you send to tell him when you would have him come and in whose form, and he will come hither; whereof you may hold yourself blest over any other lady alive.'

My Lady Conceit answered that it liked her well that the angel Gabriel loved her, seeing she loved him well nor ever failed to light a candle of a groat before him, whereas she saw him depictured, and that what time soever he chose to come to her, he should be dearly welcome and would find her all alone in her chamber, but on this condition, that he should not leave her for the Virgin Mary, whose great well-wisher it was said he was, as indeed appeareth, inasmuch as in every place where she saw him [limned], he was on his knees before her. Moreover, she said it must rest with him to come in whatsoever form he pleased, so but she was not affrighted.

Then said Fra Alberto, 'Madam, you speak sagely and I will without fail take order with him of that which you tell me. But you may do me a great favour, which will cost you nothing; it is this, that you will him come with this my body. And I will tell you in what you will do me a favour; you must know that he will take my soul forth of my body and put it in Paradise, whilst he himself will enter into me; and what while he abideth with you, so long will my soul abide in Paradise.' 'With all my heart,' answered Dame Littlewit. 'I will well that you have this consolation, in requital of the buffets he gave you on my account.' Then said Fra Alberto, 'Look that he find the door of your house open to-night, so he may come in thereat, for that, coming in human form, as he will, he might not enter save by the door.' The lady replied that it should be done, whereupon the monk took his leave and she abode in such a transport of exultation that her breech touched not her shift and herseemed a thousand years till the angel Gabriel should come to her.

Meanwhile, Fra Alberto, bethinking him that it behoved him play the cavalier, not the angel, that night proceeded to fortify himself with confections and other good things, so he might not lightly be unhorsed; then, getting leave, as soon as it was night, he repaired with one of his comrades to the house of a woman, a friend of his, whence he was used whiles to take his start what time he went to course the fillies; and thence, whenas it seemed to him time, having disguised himself, he betook him to the lady's house. There he tricked himself out as an angel with the trappings he had brought with him and going up, entered the chamber of the lady, who, seeing this creature all in white, fell on her knees before him. The angel blessed her and raising her to her feet, signed to her to go to bed, which she, studious to obey, promptly did, and the angel after lay down with his devotee. Now Fra Alberto was a personable man of his body and a lusty and excellent well set up on his legs; wherefore, finding himself in bed with Madam Lisetta, who was young and dainty, he showed himself another guess bedfellow than her husband and many a time that night took flight without wings, whereof she avowed herself exceeding content; and eke he told her many things of the glories of heaven. Then, the day drawing near, after taking order for his return, he made off with his trappings and returned to his comrade, whom the good woman of the house had meanwhile borne amicable company, lest he should get a fright, lying alone.

As for the lady, no sooner had she dined than, taking her waiting-woman with her, she betook herself to Fra Alberto and gave him news of the angel Gabriel, telling him that which she had heard from him of the glories of life eternal and how he was made and adding to boot, marvellous stories of her own invention. 'Madam,' said he, 'I know not how you fared with him; I only know that yesternight, whenas he came to me and I did your message to him, he suddenly transported my soul amongst such a multitude of roses and other flowers that never was the like thereof seen here below, and I abode in one of the most delightsome places that was aye until the morning; but what became of my body meanwhile I know not.' 'Do I not tell you?' answered the lady. 'Your body lay all night in mine arms with the angel Gabriel. If you believe me not, look under your left pap, whereas I gave the angel such a kiss that the marks of it will stay by you for some days to come.' Quoth the friar, 'Say you so? Then will I do to-day a thing I have not done this great while; I will strip myself, to see if you tell truth.' Then, after much prating, the lady returned home and Fra Alberto paid her many visits in angel-form, without suffering any hindrance.

However, it chanced one day that Madam Lisetta, being in dispute with a gossip of hers upon the question of female charms, to set her own above all others, said, like a woman who had little wit in her noddle, 'An you but knew whom my beauty pleaseth, in truth you would hold your peace of other women.' The other, longing to hear, said, as one who knew her well, 'Madam, maybe you say sooth; but knowing not who this may be, one cannot turn about so lightly.' Thereupon quoth Lisetta, who was eath enough to draw, 'Gossip, it must go no farther; but he I mean is the angel Gabriel, who loveth me more than himself, as the fairest lady (for that which he telleth me) who is in the world or the Maremma.'[4] The other had a mind to laugh, but contained herself, so she might make Lisetta speak farther, and said, 'Faith, madam, an the angel Gabriel be your lover and tell you this, needs must it be so; but methought not the angels did these things.' 'Gossip,' answered the lady, 'you are mistaken; zounds, he doth what you wot of better than my husband and telleth me they do it also up yonder; but, for that I seem to him fairer than any she in heaven, he hath fallen in love with me and cometh full oft to lie with me; seestow now?'[5]

The gossip, to whom it seemed a thousand years till she should be whereas she might repeat these things, took her leave of Madam Lisetta and foregathering at an entertainment with a great company of ladies, orderly recounted to them the whole story. They told it again to their husbands and other ladies, and these to yet others, and so in less than two days Venice was all full of it. Among others to whose ears the thing came were Lisetta's brothers-in-law, who, without saying aught to her, bethought themselves to find the angel in question and see if he knew how to fly, and to this end they lay several nights in wait for him. As chance would have it, some inkling of the matter[6] came to the ears of Fra Alberto, who accordingly repaired one night to the lady's house, to reprove her, but hardly had he put off his clothes ere her brothers-in-law, who had seen him come, were at the door of her chamber to open it.

Fra Alberto, hearing this and guessing what was to do, started up and having no other resource, opened a window, which gave upon the Grand Canal, and cast himself thence into the water. The canal was deep there and he could swim well, so that he did himself no hurt, but made his way to the opposite bank and hastily entering a house that stood open there, besought a poor man, whom he found within, to save his life for the love of God, telling him a tale of his own fashion, to explain how he came there at that hour and naked. The good man was moved to pity and it behoving him to go do his occasions, he put him in his own bed and bade him abide there against his return; then, locking him in, he went about his affairs. Meanwhile, the lady's brothers-in-law entered her chamber and found that the angel Gabriel had flown, leaving his wings there; whereupon, seeing themselves baffled, they gave her all manner hard words and ultimately made off to their own house with the angel's trappings, leaving her disconsolate.

Broad day come, the good man with whom Fra Alberto had taken refuge, being on the Rialto, heard how the angel Gabriel had gone that night to lie with Madam Lisetta and being surprised by her kinsmen, had cast himself for fear into the canal, nor was it known what was come of him, and concluded forthright that this was he whom he had at home. Accordingly, he returned thither and recognizing the monk, found means after much parley, to make him fetch him fifty ducats, an he would not have him give him up to the lady's kinsmen. Having gotten the money and Fra Alberto offering to depart thence, the good man said to him, 'There is no way of escape for you, an it be not one that I will tell you. We hold to-day a festival, wherein one bringeth a man clad bear-fashion and another one accoutred as a wild man of the woods and what not else, some one thing and some another, and there is a hunt held in St. Mark's Place, which finished, the festival is at an end and after each goeth whither it pleaseth him with him whom he hath brought. An you will have me lead you thither, after one or other of these fashions, I can after carry you whither you please, ere it be spied out that you are here; else I know not how you are to get away, without being recognized, for the lady's kinsmen, concluding that you must be somewhere hereabout, have set a watch for you on all sides.'

Hard as it seemed to Fra Alberto to go on such wise, nevertheless, of the fear he had of the lady's kinsmen, he resigned himself thereto and told his host whither he would be carried, leaving the manner to him. Accordingly, the other, having smeared him all over with honey and covered him with down, clapped a chain about his neck and a mask on his face; then giving him a great staff in on hand and in the other two great dogs which he had fetched from the shambles he despatched one to the Rialto to make public proclamation that whoso would see the angel Gabriel should repair to St. Mark's Place; and this was Venetian loyalty! This done, after a while, he brought him forth and setting him before himself, went holding him by the chain behind, to the no small clamour of the folk, who said all, 'What be this? What be this?'[7] till he came to the place, where, what with those who had followed after them and those who, hearing the proclamation, were come thither from the Rialto, were folk without end. There he tied his wild man to a column in a raised and high place, making a show of awaiting the hunt, whilst the flies and gads gave the monk exceeding annoy, for that he was besmeared with honey. But, when he saw the place well filled, making as he would unchain his wild man, he pulled off Fra Alberto's mask and said, 'Gentlemen, since the bear cometh not and there is no hunt toward, I purpose, so you may not be come in vain, that you shall see the angel Gabriel, who cometh down from heaven to earth anights, to comfort the Venetian ladies.'

No sooner was the mask off than Fra Alberto was incontinent recognized of all, who raised a general outcry against him, giving him the scurviest words and the soundest rating was ever given a canting knave; moreover, they cast in his face, one this kind of filth and another that, and so they baited him a great while, till the news came by chance to his brethren, whereupon half a dozen of them sallied forth and coming thither, unchained him and threw a gown over him; then, with a general hue and cry behind them, they carried him off to the convent, where it is believed he died in prison, after a wretched life. Thus then did this fellow, held good and doing ill, without it being believed, dare to feign himself the angel Gabriel, and after being turned into a wild man of the woods and put to shame, as he deserved, bewailed, when too late, the sins he had committed. God grant it happen thus to all other knaves of his fashion!"

---

1. *i.e.* was more inclined to consider the wishes of the ladies her companions, which she divined by sympathy, than those of Filostrato, as shown by his words (*più per la sua affezione cognobbe l'animo delle campagne che quello del re per le sue parole*). It is difficult, however, in this instance as in many others, to discover with certainty Boccaccio's exact meaning, owing to his affectation of Ciceronian concision and delight in obscure elliptical forms of construction; whilst his use of words in a remote or unfamiliar sense and the impossibility of deciding, in certain cases, the person of the pronouns and adjectives employed tend still farther to darken counsel. *E.g.*, if we render *affezione* sentiment, *cognobbe* (as *riconobbe*) acknowledged, recognized, and read *le sue parole* as meaning *her* (instead of *his*) words, the whole sense of the passage is changed, and we must read it "more by her sentiment (*i.e.* by the tendency and spirit of her story) recognized the inclination of her companions than that of the king by her [actual] words." I have commented thus at large on this passage, in order to give my readers some idea of the difficulties which at every page beset the translator of the Decameron and which make Boccaccio perhaps the most troublesome of all authors to render into representative English.
2. Lit. of those who *was* held of the greatest casuists (*di quelli che de' maggior cassesi era tenuto*). This is another very obscure passage. The meaning of the word *cassesi* is unknown and we can only guess it to be a dialectic (probably Venetian) corruption of the word *casisti* (casuists). The Giunta edition separates the word thus, *casse si*, making *si* a mere corroborative prefix to *era*, but I do not see how the alteration helps us, the word *casse* (chests, boxes) being apparently meaningless in this connection.
3. Venetian contraction of *Casa*, house. Da Ca Quirino, of the Quirino house or family.
4. *cf.* Artemus Ward's "Natives of the Universe and other parts."
5. *Mo vedi vu*, Venetian for *Or vedi tu*, now dost thou see? I have rendered it by the equivalent old English form.
6. *i.e.* not of the trap laid for him by the lady's brothers-in-law, but of her indiscretion in discovering the secret.
7. *Che xe quel?* Venetian for *che c'e quella cosa*, What is this thing?

❧ 3 ❧

THE THIRD STORY

THREE YOUNG MEN LOVE THREE SISTERS AND FLEE
WITH THEM INTO CRETE, WHERE THE ELDEST
SISTER FOR JEALOUSY SLAYETH HER LOVER. THE
SECOND, YIELDING HERSELF TO THE DUKE OF
CRETE, SAVETH HER SISTER FROM DEATH,
WHEREUPON HER OWN LOVER SLAYETH HER AND
FLEETH WITH THE ELDEST SISTER. MEANWHILE THE
THIRD LOVER AND THE YOUNGEST SISTER ARE
ACCUSED OF THE NEW MURDER AND BEING TAKEN,
CONFESS IT; THEN, FOR FEAR OF DEATH, THEY
CORRUPT THEIR KEEPERS WITH MONEY AND FLEE
TO RHODES, WHERE THEY DIE IN POVERTY

FILOSTRATO, having heard the end of Pampinea's story, bethought himself awhile and presently, turning to her, said, "There was some little that was good and that pleased me in the ending of your story; but there was overmuch before that which gave occasion for laughter and which I would not have had there." Then, turning to Lauretta, "Lady," said he, "ensue you with a better, and it may be." Quoth she, laughing, "You are too cruel towards lovers, an you desire of them only an ill end;[1] but, to obey you, I will tell a story of three who all ended equally ill, having had scant enjoyment of their loves." So saying, she began thus: "Young ladies, as you should manifestly know, every vice may turn to the grievous hurt of whoso practiseth it, and often of other folk also; but of all others that which with the slackest rein carrieth us away to our peril, meseemeth is anger, which is none otherwhat than a sudden and unconsidered emotion, aroused by an affront suffered, and which, banishing all reason and overclouding the eyes of the understanding with darkness, kindleth the soul to the hottest fury. And although this often cometh to pass in men and more in one than in another, yet hath it been seen aforetime to work greater mischiefs in women, for that it is lightlier enkindled in these latter and burneth in them with a fiercer flame and urgeth them with less restraint. Nor is this to be marvelled at, for that, an we choose to consider, we may see that fire, of its nature, catcheth quicklier to light and delicate things than to those which are denser and more ponderous; and we women, indeed,—let men not take it ill,—are more delicately fashioned than they and far more mobile. Wherefore, seeing that we are naturally inclined thereunto[2] and considering after how our mansuetude and our loving kindness are of repose and pleasance to the men with whom we have to do and how big with harm and peril are anger and fury, I purpose, to the intent that we may with a more steadfast, mind keep ourselves from these latter, to show you by my story how the loves of three young men and as many ladies came, as I said before, to an ill end, becoming through the ire of one of the latter, from happy most unhappy.

Marseilles is, as you know, a very ancient and noble city, situate in Provence on the seashore, and was once more abounding in rich and great merchants than it is nowadays. Among the latter was one called Narnald Cluada, a man of mean extraction, but of renowned good faith and a loyal merchant, rich beyond measure in lands and monies, who had by a wife of his several children, whereof the three eldest were daughters. Two of these latter, born at a birth, were fifteen and the third fourteen years old, nor was aught awaited by their kinsfolk to marry them but the return of Narnald, who was gone into Spain with his merchandise. The names of the two elder were the one Ninetta and the other Maddalena and the third called Bertella. Of Ninetta a young man of gentle birth, though poor, called Restagnone, was enamoured as much as man might be, and she of him, and they had contrived to do on such wise that, without any knowing it, they had enjoyment of their loves.

They had already a pretty while enjoyed this satisfaction when it chanced that two young companions, named the one Folco and the other Ughetto, whose fathers were dead, leaving them very rich, fell in love, the one with Maddalena and the other with Bertella. Restagnone, noting this (it having been shown him of Ninetta), bethought himself that he might make shift to supply his own lack by means of the newcomers' love. Accordingly, he clapped up an acquaintance with them, so that now one, now the other of them accompanied him to visit their mistresses and his; and when himseemed he was grown privy enough with them and much their friend, he called them one day into his house and said to them, 'Dearest youths, our commerce should have certified you how great is the love I bear you and that I would do for you that which I would do for myself; and for that I love you greatly, I purpose to discover to you that which hath occurred to my mind, and you and I together will after take such counsel thereof as shall seem to you best. You, an your words lie not and for that to boot which meseemeth I have apprehended by your deeds, both daily and nightly, burn with an exceeding passion for the two young ladies beloved of you, as do I for the third their sister; and to this ardour, an you will consent thereunto,[3] my heart giveth me to find a very sweet and pleasing remedy, the which is as follows. You are both very rich, which I am not; now, if you will agree to bring your riches into a common stock, making me a third sharer with you therein, and determine in which part of the world we shall go lead a merry life with our mistresses, my heart warranteth me I can without fail so do that the three sisters, with a great part of their father's good, will go with, us whithersoever we shall please, and there, each with his wench, like three brothers, we may live the happiest lives of any men in the world. It resteth with you now to determine whether you will go about to solace yourself in this or leave it be.'

The two young men, who were beyond measure inflamed, hearing that they were to have their lasses, were not long in making up their minds, but answered that, so this[4] should ensue, they were ready to do as he said. Restagnone, having gotten this answer from the young men, found means a few days after to foregather with Ninetta, to whom he could not come without great unease, and after he had abidden with her awhile, he told her what he had proposed to the others and with many arguments studied to commend the emprise to her. This was little uneath to him, seeing that she was yet more desirous than himself to be with him without suspect; wherefore she answered him frankly that it liked her well and that her sisters would do whatever she wished, especially in this, and bade him make ready everything needful therefor as quickliest he might. Restagnone accordingly returned to the two young men, who still importuned him amain to do that whereof he had bespoken them, and told them that, so far as concerned their mistresses, the matter was settled. Then, having determined among themselves to go to Crete, they sold certain lands they had, under colour of meaning to go a-trading with the price, and having made money of all their other goods, bought a light brigantine and secretly equipped it to the utmost advantage.

Meanwhile, Ninetta, who well enough knew her sisters' mind, with soft words inflamed them with such a liking for the venture that themseemed they might not live to see the thing accomplished. Accordingly, the night come when they were to go aboard the brigantine, the three sisters opened a great coffer of their father's and taking thence a vast quantity of money and jewels, stole out of the house, according to the given order. They found their gallants awaiting them and going straightway all aboard the brigantine, they thrust the oars into the water and put out to sea nor rested till they came, on the following evening, to Genoa, where the new lovers for the first time took ease and joyance of their loves. There having refreshed themselves with that whereof they had need, they set out again and sailing from port to port, came, ere it was the eighth day, without any hindrance, to Crete, where they bought great and goodly estates near Candia and made them very handsome and delightsome dwelling-houses thereon. Here they fell to living like lords and passed their days in banquets and joyance and merrymaking, the happiest men in the world, they and their mistresses, with great plenty of servants and hounds and hawks and horses.

Abiding on this wise, it befell (even as we see it happen all day long that, how much soever things may please, they grow irksome, an one have overgreat plenty thereof) that Restagnone, who had much loved Ninetta, being now able to have her at his every pleasure, without let or hindrance, began to weary of her, and consequently his love for her began to wane. Having seen at entertainment a damsel of the country, a fair and noble young lady, who pleased him exceedingly, he fell to courting her with all his might, giving marvellous entertainments in her honor and plying her with all manner gallantries; which Ninetta coming to know, she fell into such a jealousy that he could not go a step but she heard of it and after harassed both him and herself with words and reproaches on account thereof. But, like as overabundance of aught begetteth weariness, even so doth the denial of a thing desired redouble the appetite; accordingly, Ninetta's reproaches did but fan the flame of Restagnone's new love and in process of time it came to pass that, whether he had the favours of the lady he loved or not, Ninetta held it for certain, whoever it was reported it to her; wherefore she fell into such a passion of grief and thence passed into such a fit of rage and despite that the love which she bore Restagnone was changed to bitter hatred, and blinded by her wrath, she bethought herself to avenge, by his death, the affront which herseemed she had received.

Accordingly, betaking herself to an old Greek woman, a past mistress in the art of compounding poisons, she induced her with gifts and promises to make her a death-dealing water, which she, without considering farther, gave Restagnone one evening to drink he being heated and misdoubting him not thereof; and such was the potency of the poison that, ere morning came, it had slain him. Folco and Ughetto and their mistresses, hearing of his death and knowing not of what poison he had died,[5] bewept him bitterly, together with Ninetta, and caused bury him honourably. But not many days after it chanced that the old woman, who had compounded the poisoned water for Ninetta, was taken for some other misdeed and being put to the torture, confessed to this amongst her other crimes, fully declaring that which had betided by reason thereof; whereupon the Duke of Crete, without saying aught of the matter, beset Folco's palace by surprise one night and without any noise or gainsayal, carried off Ninetta prisoner, from whom, without putting her to the torture, he readily got what he would know of the death of Restagnone.

Folco and Ughetto (and from them their ladies) had privy notice from the duke why Ninetta had been taken, the which was exceeding grievous to them and they used their every endeavour to save her from the fire, whereto they doubted not she would be condemned, as indeed she richly deserved; but all seemed vain, for that the duke abode firm in willing to do justice upon her. However, Maddalena, who was a beautiful young woman and had long been courted by the duke, but had never yet consented to do aught that might pleasure him, thinking that, by complying with his wishes, she might avail to save her sister from the fire, signified to him by a trusty messenger that she was at his commandment in everything, provided two things should ensue thereof, to wit, that she should have her sister again safe and sound and that the thing should be secret. Her message pleased the duke, and after long debate with himself if he should do as she proposed, he ultimately agreed thereto and said that he was ready. Accordingly, one night, having, with the lady's consent, caused detain Folco and Ughetto, as he would fain examine them of the matter, he went secretly to couch with Maddalena and having first made a show of putting Ninetta in a sack and of purposing to let sink her that night in the sea, he carried her with him to her sister, to whom on the morrow he delivered her at parting, in payment of the night he had passed with her, praying her that this,[6] which had been the first of their loves, might not be the last and charging her send the guilty lady away, lest blame betide himself and it behove him anew proceed against her with rigour.

Next morning, Folco and Ughetto, having heard that Ninetta had been sacked overnight and believing it, were released and returned home to comfort their mistresses for the death of their sister. However, for all Maddalena could do to hide her, Folco soon became aware of Ninetta's presence in the palace, whereat he marvelled exceedingly and suddenly waxing suspicious,—for that he had heard of the duke's passion for Maddalena,—asked the latter how her sister came to be there. Maddalena began a long story, which she had devised to account to him therefor, but was little believed of her lover, who was shrewd and constrained her to confess the truth, which, after long parley, she told him. Folco, overcome with chagrin and inflamed with rage, pulled out a sword and slew her, whilst she in vain besought mercy; then, fearing the wrath and justice of the duke, he left her dead in the chamber and repairing whereas Ninetta was, said to her, with a feigned air of cheerfulness, 'Quick, let us begone whither it hath been appointed of thy sister that I shall carry thee, so thou mayst not fall again into the hands of the duke.' Ninetta, believing this and eager, in her fearfulness, to begone, set out with Folco, it being now night, without seeking to take leave of her sister; whereupon he and she, with such monies (which were but few) as he could lay hands on, betook themselves to the sea-shore and embarked on board a vessel; nor was it ever known whither they went.

On the morrow, Maddalena being found murdered, there were some who, of the envy and hatred they bore to Ughetto, forthright gave notice thereof to the duke, whereupon the latter, who loved Maddalena exceedingly, ran furiously to the house and seizing Ughetto and his lady, who as yet knew nothing of the matter,—to wit, of the departure of Folco and Ninetta,— constrained them to confess themselves guilty, together with Folco, of his mistress's death. They, apprehending with reason death in consequence of this confession, with great pains corrupted those who had them in keeping, giving them a certain sum of money, which they kept hidden in their house against urgent occasions, and embarking with their guards, without having leisure to take any of their goods, fled by night to Rhodes, where they lived no great while after in poverty and distress. To such a pass, then, did Restagnone's mad love and Ninetta's rage bring themselves and others."

---

1. *i.e. semble* "an you would wish them nought but an ill end."
2. *i.e.* to anger.
3. *i.e.* to the proposal I have to make.
4. *i.e.* the possession of their mistresses.
5. Sic (*di che veleno fosse morto*), but this is probably a copyist's error for *che di veleno fosse morto*, *i.e.* that he had died of poison.
6. *i.e.* that night.

4

DAY THE FOURTH

GERBINO, AGAINST THE PLIGHTED FAITH OF HIS GRANDFATHER, KING GUGLIELMO OF SICILY, ATTACKETH A SHIP OF THE KING OF TUNIS, TO CARRY OFF A DAUGHTER OF HIS, WHO BEING PUT TO DEATH OF THOSE ON BOARD, HE SLAYETH THESE LATTER AND IS AFTER HIMSELF BEHEADED

LAURETTA, having made an end of her story, was silent, whilst the company bewailed the illhap of the lovers, some blaming Ninetta's anger and one saying one thing and another another, till presently the king, raising his head, as if aroused from deep thought, signed to Elisa to follow on; whereupon she began modestly, "Charming ladies, there are many who believe that Love launcheth his shafts only when enkindled of the eyes and make mock of those who hold that one may fall in love by hearsay; but that these are mistaken will very manifestly appear in a story that I purpose to relate, wherein you will see that report not only wrought this, without the lovers having ever set eyes on each other, but it will be made manifest to you that it brought both the one and the other to a miserable death.

Guglielmo, the Second, King of Sicily, had (as the Sicilians pretend) two children, a son called Ruggieri and a daughter called Costanza. The former, dying before his father, left a son named Gerbino, who was diligently reared by his grandfather and became a very goodly youth and a renowned for prowess and courtesy. Nor did his fame abide confined within the limits of Sicily, but, resounding in various parts of the world, was nowhere more glorious than in Barbary, which in those days was tributary to the King of Sicily. Amongst the rest to whose ears came the magnificent fame of Gerbino's valour and courtesy was a daughter of the King of Tunis, who, according to the report of all who had seen her, was one of the fairest creatures ever fashioned by nature and the best bred and of a noble and great soul. She, delighting to hear tell of men of valour, with such goodwill received the tales recounted by one and another of the deeds valiantly done of Gerbino and they so pleased her that, picturing to herself the prince's fashion, she became ardently enamoured of him and discoursed more willingly of him than of any other and hearkened to whoso spoke of him.

On the other hand, the great renown of her beauty and worth had won to Sicily, as elsewhither, and not without great delight nor in vain had it reached the ears of Gerbino; nay, it had inflamed him with love of her, no less than that which she herself had conceived for him. Wherefore, desiring beyond measure to see her, against he should find a colourable occasion of having his grandfather's leave to go to Tunis, he charged his every friend who went thither to make known to her, as best he might, his secret and great love and bring him news of her. This was very dexterously done by one of them, who, under pretence of carrying her women's trinkets to view, as do merchants, throughly discovered Gerbino's passion to her and avouched the prince and all that was his to be at her commandment. The princess received the messenger and the message with a glad flavour and answering that she burnt with like love for the prince, sent him one of her most precious jewels in token thereof. This Gerbino received with the utmost joy wherewith one can receive whatsoever precious thing and wrote to her once and again by the same messenger, sending her the most costly gifts and holding certain treaties[1] with her, whereby they should have seen and touched one another, had fortune but allowed it.

But, things going thus and somewhat farther than was expedient, the young lady on the one hand and Gerbino on the other burning with desire, it befell that the King of Tunis gave her in marriage to the King of Granada, whereat she was beyond measure chagrined, bethinking herself that not only should she be separated from her lover by long distance, but was like to be altogether parted from him; and had she seen a means thereto, she would gladly, so this might not betide, have fled from her father and betaken herself to Gerbino. Gerbino, in like manner, hearing of this marriage, was beyond measure sorrowful therefor and often bethought himself to take her by force, if it should chance that she went to her husband by sea. The King of Tunis, getting some inkling of Gerbino's love and purpose and fearing his valour and prowess, sent to King Guglielmo, whenas the time came for despatching her to Granada, advising him of that which he was minded to do and that, having assurance from him that he should not be hindered therein by Gerbino or others, he purposed to do it. The King of Sicily, who was an old man and had heard nothing of Gerbino's passion and consequently suspected not that it was for this that such an assurance was demanded, freely granted it and in token thereof, sent the King of Tunis a glove of his. The latter, having gotten the desired assurance, caused equip a very great and goodly ship in the port of Carthage and furnish it with what was needful for those who were to sail therein and having fitted and adorned it for the sending of his daughter into Granada, awaited nought but weather.

The young lady, who saw and knew all this, despatched one of her servants secretly to Palermo, bidding him salute the gallant Gerbino on her part and tell him that she was to sail in a few days for Granada, wherefore it would now appear if he were as valiant a man as was said and if he loved her as much as he had sundry times declared to her. Her messenger did his errand excellent well and returned to Tunis, whilst Gerbino, hearing this and knowing that his grandfather had given the King of Tunis assurance, knew not what to do. However, urged by love and that he might not appear a craven, he betook himself to Messina, where he hastily armed two light galleys and manning them with men of approved valour, set sail with them for the coast of Sardinia, looking for the lady's ship to pass there. Nor was he far out in his reckoning, for he had been there but a few days when the ship hove in sight with a light wind not far from the place where he lay expecting it.

Gerbino, seeing this, said to his companions, 'Gentlemen, an you be the men of mettle I take you for, methinketh there is none of you but hath either felt or feeleth love, without which, as I take it, no mortal can have aught of valour or worth in himself; and if you have been or are enamoured, it will be an easy thing to you to understand my desire. I love and love hath moved me to give you this present pains; and she whom I love is in the ship which you see becalmed yonder and which, beside that thing which I most desire, is full of very great riches. These latter, an ye be men of valour, we may with little difficulty acquire, fighting manfully; of which victory I desire nothing to my share save one sole lady, for whose love I have taken up arms; everything else shall freely be yours. Come, then, and let us right boldly assail the ship; God is favourable to our emprise and holdeth it here fast, without vouchsafing it a breeze.'

The gallant Gerbino had no need of many words, for that the Messinese, who were with him being eager for plunder, were already disposed to do that unto which he exhorted them. Wherefore, making a great outcry, at the end of his speech, that it should be so, they sounded the trumpets and catching up their arms, thrust the oars into the water and made for the Tunis ship. They who were aboard this latter, seeing the galleys coming afar off and being unable to flee,[2] made ready for defence. The gallant Gerbino accosting the ship, let command that the masters thereof should be sent on board the galleys, an they had no mind to fight; but the Saracens, having certified themselves who they were and what they sought, declared themselves attacked of them against the faith plighted them by King Guglielmo; in token whereof they showed the latter's glove, and altogether refused to surrender themselves, save for stress of battle, or to give them aught that was in the ship.

Gerbino, who saw the lady upon the poop, far fairer than he had pictured her to himself, and was more inflamed than ever, replied to the showing of the glove that there were no falcons there at that present and consequently there needed no gloves; wherefore, an they chose not to give up the lady, they must prepare to receive battle. Accordingly, without further parley, they fell to casting shafts and stones at one another, and on this wise they fought a great while, with loss on either side. At last, Gerbino, seeing that he did little to the purpose, took a little vessel he had brought with him out of Sardinia and setting fire therein, thrust it with both the galleys aboard the ship. The Saracens, seeing this and knowing that they must of necessity surrender or die, fetched the king's daughter, who wept below, on deck and brought her to the ship's prow; then, calling Gerbino, they butchered her before his eyes, what while she called for mercy and succour, and cast her into the sea, saying, 'Take her; we give her to thee, such as we may and such as thine unfaith hath merited.'

Gerbino, seeing their barbarous deed, caused lay himself alongside the ship and recking not of shaft or stone, boarded it, as if courting death, in spite of those who were therein; then,—even as a hungry lion, coming among a herd of oxen, slaughtereth now this, now that, and with teeth and claws sateth rather his fury than his hunger,—sword in hand, hewing now at one, now at another, he cruelly slew many of the Saracens; after which, the fire now waxing in the enkindled ship, he caused the sailors fetch thereout what they might, in payment of their pains, and descended thence, having gotten but a sorry victory over his adversaries. Then, letting take up the fair lady's body from the sea, long and with many tears he bewept it and steering for Sicily, buried it honourably in Ustica, a little island over against Trapani; after which he returned home, the woefullest man alive.

The King of Tunis, hearing the heavy news, sent his ambassadors, clad all in black, to King Guglielmo, complaining of the ill observance of the faith which he had plighted him. They recounted to him how the thing had passed, whereat King Guglielmo was sore incensed and seeing no way to deny them the justice they sought, caused take Gerbino; then himself,—albeit there was none of his barons but strove with prayers to move him from his purpose,—condemned him to death and let strike off his head in his presence, choosing rather to abide without posterity than to be held a faithless king. Thus, then, as I have told you, did these two lovers within a few days[3] die miserably a violent death, without having tasted any fruit of their loves."

---

1. Or, in modern parlance, "laying certain plans."
2. *i.e.* for lack of wind.
3. *i.e.* of each other.

𝓈 5 𝓈

THE FIFTH STORY

LISABETTA'S BROTHERS SLAY HER LOVER, WHO APPEARETH TO HER IN A DREAM AND SHOWETH HER WHERE HE IS BURIED, WHEREUPON SHE PRIVILY DISINTERRETH HIS HEAD AND SETTETH IT IN A POT OF BASIL. THEREOVER MAKING MOAN A GREAT WHILE EVERY DAY, HER BROTHERS TAKE IT FROM HER AND SHE FOR GRIEF DIETH A LITTLE THEREAFTERWARD

ELISA'S TALE being ended and somedele commended of the king, Filomena was bidden to discourse, who, full of compassion for the wretched Gerbino and his mistress, after a piteous sigh, began thus: "My story, gracious ladies, will not treat of folk of so high condition as were those of whom Elisa hath told, yet peradventure it will be no less pitiful; and what brought me in mind of it was the mention, a little before, of Messina, where the case befell.

There were then in Messina three young brothers, merchants and left very rich by their father, who was a man of San Gimignano, and they had an only sister, Lisabetta by name, a right fair and well-mannered maiden, whom, whatever might have been the reason thereof, they had not yet married. Now these brothers had in one of their warehouses a youth of Pisa, called Lorenzo, who did and ordered all their affairs and was very comely and agreeable of person; wherefore, Lisabetta looking sundry times upon him, it befell that he began strangely to please her; of which Lorenzo taking note at one time and another, he in like manner, leaving his other loves, began to turn his thoughts to her; and so went the affair, that, each being alike pleasing to the other, it was no great while before, taking assurance, they did that which each of them most desired.

Continuing on this wise and enjoying great pleasure and delight one of the other, they knew not how to do so secretly but that, one night, Lisabetta, going whereas Lorenzo lay, was, unknown to herself, seen of the eldest of her brothers, who, being a prudent youth, for all the annoy it gave him to know this thing, being yet moved by more honourable counsel, abode without sign or word till the morning, revolving in himself various things anent the matter. The day being come, he recounted to his brothers that which he had seen the past night of Lisabetta and Lorenzo, and after long advisement with them, determined (so that neither to them nor to their sister should any reproach ensue thereof) to pass the thing over in silence and feign to have seen and known nothing thereof till such time as, without hurt or unease to themselves, they might avail to do away this shame from their sight, ere it should go farther. In this mind abiding and devising and laughing with Lorenzo as was their wont, it befell that one day, feigning to go forth the city, all three, a-pleasuring, they carried him with them to a very lonely and remote place; and there, the occasion offering, they slew him, whilst he was off his guard, and buried him on such wise that none had knowledge of it; then, returning to Messina, they gave out that they had despatched him somewhither for their occasions, the which was the lightlier credited that they were often used to send him abroad about their business.

Lorenzo returning not and Lisabetta often and instantly questioning her brothers of him, as one to whom the long delay was grievous, it befell one day, as she very urgently enquired of him, that one of them said to her, 'What meaneth this? What hast thou to do often of him? An thou question of him with Lorenzo, that thou askest thus more, we will make thee such answer as thou deservest.' Wherefore the girl, sad and grieving and fearful she knew not of what, abode without more asking; yet many a time anights she piteously called him and prayed him come to her, and whiles with many tears she complained of his long tarrying; and thus, without a moment's gladness, she abode expecting him alway, till one night, having sore lamented Lorenzo for that he returned not and being at last fallen asleep, weeping, he appeared to her in a dream, pale and all disordered, with clothes all rent and mouldered, and herseemed he bespoke her thus: 'Harkye, Lisabetta; thou dost nought but call upon me, grieving for my long delay and cruelly impeaching me with thy tears. Know, therefore, that I may never more return to thee, for that, the last day thou sawest me, thy brothers slew me.' Then, having discovered to her the place where they had buried him, he charged her no more call him nor expect him and disappeared; whereupon she awoke and giving faith to the vision, wept bitterly.

In the morning, being risen and daring not say aught to her brothers, she determined to go to the place appointed and see if the thing were true, as it had appeared to her in the dream. Accordingly, having leave to go somedele without the city for her disport, she betook herself thither,[1] as quickliest she might, in company of one who had been with them[2] otherwhiles and knew all her affairs; and there, clearing away the dead leaves from the place, she dug whereas herseemed the earth was less hard. She had not dug long before she found the body of her unhappy lover, yet nothing changed nor rotted, and thence knew manifestly that her vision was true, wherefore she was the most distressful of women; yet, knowing that this was no place for lament, she would fain, an she but might, have borne away the whole body, to give it fitter burial; but, seeing that this might not be, she with a knife did off[3] the head from the body, as best she could, and wrapping it in a napkin, laid it in her maid's lap. Then, casting back the earth over the trunk, she departed thence, without being seen of any, and returned home, where, shutting herself in her chamber with her lover's head, she bewept it long and bitterly, insomuch that she bathed it all with her tears, and kissed it a thousand times in every part. Then, taking a great and goodly pot, of those wherein they plant marjoram or sweet basil, she set the head therein, folded in a fair linen cloth, and covered it with earth, in which she planted sundry heads of right fair basil of Salerno; nor did she ever water these with other water than that of her tears or rose or orange-flower water. Moreover she took wont to sit still near the pot and to gaze amorously upon it with all her desire, as upon that which held her Lorenzo hid; and after she had a great while looked thereon, she would bend over it and fall to weeping so sore and so long that her tears bathed all the basil, which, by dint of long and assiduous tending, as well as by reason of the fatness of the earth, proceeding from the rotting head that was therein, waxed passing fair and very sweet of savour.

The damsel, doing without cease after this wise, was sundry times seen of her neighbours, who to her brothers, marvelling at her waste beauty and that her eyes seemed to have fled forth her head [for weeping], related this, saying, 'We have noted that she doth every day after such a fashion.' The brothers, hearing and seeing this and having once and again reproved her therefor, but without avail, let secretly carry away from her the pot, which she, missing, with the utmost instance many a time required, and for that it was not restored to her, stinted not to weep and lament till she fell sick; nor in her sickness did she ask aught other than the pot of basil. The young men marvelled greatly at this continual asking and bethought them therefor to see what was in this pot. Accordingly, turning out the earth, they found the cloth and therein the head, not yet so rotted but they might know it, by the curled hair, to be that of Lorenzo. At this they were mightily amazed and feared lest the thing should get wind; wherefore, burying the head, without word said, they privily departed Messina, having taken order how they should withdraw thence, and betook themselves to Naples. The damsel, ceasing never from lamenting and still demanding her pot, died, weeping; and so her ill-fortuned love had end. But, after a while the thing being grown manifest unto many, there was one who made thereon the song that is yet sung, to wit:

> *Alack! ah, who can the ill Christian be,*
> *That stole my pot away?" etc.*[4]

---

1. *i.e.* to the place shown her in the dream.
2. *i.e.* in their service.
3. Lit. unhung (*spiccò*).
4. The following is a translation of the whole of the song in question, as printed, from a MS. in the Medicean Library, in Fanfani's edition of the Decameron.

    Alack! ah, who can the ill Christian be,
    That stole my pot away,
    My pot of basil of Salern, from me?
    'Twas thriv'n with many a spray
    And I with mine own hand did plant the tree,
    Even on the festal[A] day.
    'Tis felony to waste another's ware.
    'Tis felony to waste another's ware;
    Yea, and right grievous sin.
    And I, poor lass, that sowed myself whilere
    A pot with flowers therein,
    Slept in its shade, so great it was and fair;
    But folk, that envious bin,
    Stole it away even from my very door.
    'Twas stolen away even from my very door.
    Full heavy was my cheer,
    (Ah, luckless maid, would I had died tofore!)
    Who brought[B] it passing dear,
    Yet kept ill ward thereon one day of fear.
    For him I loved so sore,
    I planted it with marjoram about.
    I planted it with marjoram about,
    When May was blithe and new;
    Yea, thrice I watered it, week in, week out,
    And watched how well it grew:
    But now, for sure, away from me 'tis ta'en.
    Ay, now, for sure, away from me 'tis ta'en;
    I may 't no longer hide.
    Had I but known (alas, regret is vain!)
    That which should me betide,
    Before my door on guard I would have lain
    To sleep, my flowers beside.
    Yet might the Great God ease me at His will.
    Yea, God Most High might ease me, at His will,
    If but it liked Him well,
    Of him who wrought me such unright and ill;
    He into pangs of hell
    Cast me who stole my basil-pot, that still
    Was full of such sweet smell,
    Its savour did all dole from me away.
    All dole its savour did from me away;
    It was so redolent,

When, with the risen sun, at early day
To water it I went,
The folk would marvel all at it and say,
"Whence comes the sweetest scent?"
And I for love of it shall surely die.
Yea, I for love of it shall surely die,
For love and grief and pain.
If one would tell me where it is, I'd buy
It willingly again.
Fivescore gold crowns, that in my pouch have I,
I'd proffer him full fain,
And eke a kiss, if so it liked the swain.

[A]
Quære—natal?—perhaps meaning her birthday (*lo giorno della festa*).
[B]
Or "purchased" in the old sense of obtained, acquired (*accattai*).

✣ 6 ✣

THE SIXTH STORY

ANDREVUOLA LOVETH GABRIOTTO AND
RECOUNTETH TO HIM A DREAM SHE HATH HAD,
WHEREUPON HE TELLETH HER ONE OF HIS OWN AND
PRESENTLY DIETH SUDDENLY IN HER ARMS. WHAT
WHILE SHE AND A WAITING WOMAN OF HERS BEAR
HIM TO HIS OWN HOUSE, THEY ARE TAKEN BY THE
OFFICERS OF JUSTICE AND CARRIED BEFORE THE
PROVOST, TO WHOM SHE DISCOVERETH HOW THE
CASE STANDETH. THE PROVOST WOULD FAIN FORCE
HER, BUT SHE SUFFERETH IT NOT AND HER FATHER,
COMING TO HEAR OF THE MATTER, PROCURETH HER
TO BE SET AT LIBERTY, SHE BEING FOUND
INNOCENT; WHEREUPON, ALTOGETHER REFUSING
TO ABIDE LONGER IN THE WORLD, SHE BECOMETH
A NUN

FILOMELA'S STORY was very welcome to the ladies, for that they had many a time heard sing this song, yet could never, for asking, learn the occasion of its making. But the king, having heard the end thereof, charged Pamfilo follow on the ordinance; whereupon quoth he, "The dream in the foregoing story giveth me occasion to recount one wherein is made mention of two dreams, which were of a thing to come, even as the former was of a thing [already] betided, and scarce were they finished telling by those who had dreamt them than the accomplishment followed of both. You must know, then, lovesome ladies, that it is an affection common to all alive to see various things in sleep, whereof,—albeit to the sleeper, what while he sleepeth, they all appear most true and he, awakened, accounteth some true, others probable and yet others out of all likelihood,—many are natheless found to be come to pass. By reason whereof many lend to every dream as much belief as they would to things they should see, waking, and for their proper dreams they sorrow or rejoice, according as by these they hope or fear. And contrariwise, there are those who believe none thereof, save after they find themselves fallen into the peril foreshown. Of these,[1] I approve neither the one nor other, for that dreams are neither always true nor always false. That they are not all true, each one of us must often enough have had occasion to know; and that they are not all false hath been already shown in Filomena her story, and I also purpose, as I said before, to show it in mine. Wherefore I am of opinion that, in the matter of living and doing virtuously, one should have no fear of any dream contrary thereto nor forego good intentions by reason thereof; as for perverse and wicked things, on the other hand, however favourable dreams may appear thereto and how much soever they may hearten him who seeth them with propitious auguries, none of them should be credited, whilst full faith should be accorded unto all that tend to the contrary.[2] But to come to the story.

There was once in the city of Brescia a gentleman called Messer Negro da Ponte Carraro, who amongst sundry other children had a daughter named Andrevuola, young and unmarried and very fair. It chanced she fell in love with a neighbour of hers, Gabriotto by name, a man of mean condition, but full laudable fashions and comely and pleasant of his person, and by the means and with the aid of the serving-maid of the house, she so wrought that not only did Gabriotto know himself beloved of her, but was many and many a time brought, to the delight of both parties, into a goodly garden of her father's. And in order that no cause, other than death, should ever avail to sever those their delightsome loves, they became in secret husband and wife, and so stealthily continuing their foregatherings, it befell that the young lady, being one night asleep, dreamt that she was in her garden with Gabriotto and held him in her arms, to the exceeding pleasure of each; but, as they abode thus, herseemed she saw come forth of his body something dark and frightful, the form whereof she could not discern; the which took Gabriotto and tearing him in her despite with marvellous might from her embrace, made off with him underground, nor ever more might she avail to see either the one or the other.

At this she fell into an inexpressible passion of grief, whereby she awoke, and albeit, awaking, she was rejoiced to find that it was not as she had dreamed, nevertheless fear entered into her by reason of the dream she had seen. Wherefore, Gabriotto presently desiring to visit her that next night, she studied as most she might to prevent his coming; however, seeing his desire and so he might not misdoubt him of otherwhat, she received him in the garden and having gathered great store of roses, white and red (for that it was the season), she went to sit with him at the foot of a very goodly and clear fountain that was there. After they had taken great and long delight together, Gabriotto asked her why she would have forbidden his coming that night; whereupon she told him, recounting to him the dream she had seen the foregoing night and the fear she had gotten therefrom.

He, hearing this, laughed it to scorn and said that it was great folly to put any faith in dreams, for that they arose of excess of food or lack thereof and were daily seen to be all vain, adding, 'Were I minded to follow after dreams, I had not come hither, not so much on account of this of thine as of one I myself dreamt last night; which was that meseemed I was in a fair and delightsome wood, wherein I went hunting and had taken the fairest and loveliest hind was ever seen; for methought she was whiter than snow and was in brief space become so familiar with me that she never left me a moment. Moreover, meseemed I held her so dear that, so she might not depart from me, I had put a collar of gold about her neck and held her in hand with a golden chain. After this medreamed that, once upon a time, what while this hind lay couched with its head in my bosom,[3] there issued I know not whence a greyhound bitch as black as coal, anhungred and passing gruesome of aspect, and made towards me. Methought I offered it no resistance, wherefore meseemed it thrust its muzzle into my breast on the left side and gnawed thereat till it won to my heart, which methought it tore from me, to carry it away. Therewith I felt such a pain that my sleep was broken and awaking, I straightway clapped my hand to my side, to see if I had aught there; but, finding nothing amiss with me, I made mock of myself for having sought. But, after all, what booteth this dream?[4] I have dreamed many such and far more frightful, nor hath aught in the world befallen me by reason thereof; wherefore let it pass and let us think to give ourselves a good time.'

The young lady, already sore adread for her own dream, hearing this, waxed yet more so, but hid her fear, as most she might, not to be the occasion of any unease to Gabriotto. Nevertheless, what while she solaced herself with him, clipping and kissing him again and again and being of him clipped and kissed, she many a time eyed him in the face more than of her wont, misdoubting she knew not what, and whiles she looked about the garden, and she should see aught of black come anywhere. Presently, as they abode thus, Gabriotto heaved a great sigh and embracing her said, 'Alas, my soul, help me, for I die!' So saying, he fell to the ground upon the grass of the lawn. The young lady, seeing this, drew him up into her lap and said, well nigh weeping, 'Alack, sweet my lord, what aileth thee?' He answered not, but, panting sore and sweating all over, no great while after departed this life.

How grievous, how dolorous was this to the young lady, who loved him more than her life, each one of you may conceive for herself. She bewept him sore and many a time called him in vain; but after she had handled him in every part of his body and found him cold in all, perceiving that he was altogether dead and knowing not what to do or to say, she went, all tearful as she was and full of anguish, to call her maid, who was privy to their loves, and discovered to her misery and her grief. Then, after they had awhile made woeful lamentation over Gabriotto's dead face, the young lady said to the maid, 'Since God hath bereft me of him I love, I purpose to abide no longer on life; but, ere I go about to slay myself, I would fain take fitting means to preserve my honour and the secret of the love that hath been between us twain and that the body, wherefrom the gracious spirit is departed, may be buried.'

'Daughter mine,' answered the maid, 'talk not of seeking to slay thyself, for that, if thou have lost him in this world, by slaying thyself thou wouldst lose him in the world to come also, since thou wouldst go to hell, whither I am assured his soul hath not gone; for he was a virtuous youth. It were better far to comfort thyself and think of succouring his soul with prayers and other good works, so haply he have need thereof for any sin committed. The means of burying him are here at hand in this garden and none will ever know of the matter, for none knoweth that he ever came hither. Or, an thou wilt not have it so, let us put him forth of the garden and leave him be; he will be found to-morrow morning and carried to his house, where his kinsfolk will have him buried.' The young lady, albeit she was full of bitter sorrow and wept without ceasing, yet gave ear to her maid's counsels and consenting not to the first part thereof, made answer to the second, saying, 'God forbid that I should suffer so dear a youth and one so beloved of me and my husband to be buried after the fashion of a dog or left to lie in the street! He hath had my tears and inasmuch as I may, he shall have those of his kinsfolk, and I have already bethought me of that which we have to do to that end.'

Therewith she despatched her maid for a piece of cloth of silk, which she had in a coffer of hers, and spreading it on the earth, laid Gabriotto's body thereon, with his head upon a pillow. Then with many tears she closed his eyes and mouth and weaving him a chaplet of roses, covered him with all they had gathered, he and she; after which she said to the maid, 'It is but a little way hence to his house; wherefore we will carry him thither, thou and I, even as we have arrayed him, and lay him before the door. It will not be long ere it be day and he will be taken up; and although this may be no consolation to his friends, yet to me, in whose arms he died, it will be a pleasure.' So saying, once more with most abundant tears she cast herself upon his face and wept a great while. Then, being urged by her maid to despatch, for that the day was at hand, she rose to her feet and drawing from her finger the ring wherewith Gabriotto had espoused her, she set it on his and said, weeping, 'Dear my lord, if thy soul now seeth my tears or if any sense or cognizance abide in the body, after the departure thereof, benignly receive her last gift, whom, living, thou lovedst so well.' This said, she fell down upon him in a swoon, but, presently coming to herself and rising, she took up, together with her maid, the cloth whereon the body lay and going forth the garden therewith, made for his house.

As they went, they were discovered and taken with the dead body by the officers of the provostry, who chanced to be abroad at that hour about some other matter. Andrevuola, more desirous of death than of life, recognizing the officers, said frankly, 'I know who you are and that it would avail me nothing to seek to flee; I am ready to go with you before the Seignory and there declare how the case standeth; but let none of you dare to touch me, provided I am obedient to you, or to remove aught from this body, an he would not be accused of me.' Accordingly, without being touched of any, she repaired, with Gabriotto's body, to the palace, where the Provost, hearing what was to do, arose and sending for her into his chamber, proceeded to enquire of this that had happened. To this end he caused divers physicians look if the dead man had been done to death with poison or otherwise, who all affirmed that it was not so, but that some imposthume had burst near the heart, the which had suffocated him. The magistrate hearing this and feeling her to be guilty in [but] a small matter, studied to make a show of giving her that which he could not sell her and told her that, an she would consent to his pleasures, he would release her; but, these words availing not, he offered, out of all seemliness, to use force. However, Andrevuola, fired with disdain and waxed strong [for indignation], defended herself manfully, rebutting him with proud and scornful words.

Meanwhile, broad day come and these things being recounted to Messer Negro, he betook himself, sorrowful unto death, to the palace, in company with many of his friends, and being there acquainted by the Provost with the whole matter, demanded resentfully[5] that his daughter should be restored to him. The Provost, choosing rather to accuse himself of the violence he would have done her than to be accused of her, first extolled the damsel and her constancy and in proof thereof, proceeded to tell that which he had done; by reason whereof, seeing her of so excellent a firmness, he had vowed her an exceeding love and would gladly, an it were agreeable to him, who was her father, and to herself, espouse her for his lady, notwithstanding she had had a husband of mean condition. Whilst they yet talked, Andrevuola presented herself and weeping, cast herself before her father and said, 'Father mine, methinketh there is no need that I recount to you the story of my boldness and my illhap, for I am assured that you have heard and know it; wherefore, as most I may, I humbly ask pardon of you for my default, to wit, the having without your knowledge taken him who most pleased me to husband. And this boon I ask of you, not for that my life may be spared me, but to die your daughter and not your enemy.' So saying, she fell weeping at his feet.

Messer Negro, who was an old man and kindly and affectionate of his nature, hearing these words, began to weep and with tears in his eyes raised his daughter tenderly to her feet and said, 'Daughter mine, it had better pleased me that thou shouldst have had such a husband as, according to my thinking, behoved unto thee; and that thou shouldst have taken such an one as was pleasing unto thee had also been pleasing to me; but that thou shouldst have concealed him, of thy little confidence in me, grieveth me, and so much the more as I see thee to have lost him, ere I knew it. However, since the case is so, that which had he lived, I had gladly done him, to content thee, to wit, honour, as to my son-in-law, be it done him, now he is dead.' Then, turning to his sons and his kinsfolk, he commanded that great and honourable obsequies should be prepared for Gabriotto.

Meanwhile, the kinsmen and kinswomen of the young man, hearing the news, had flocked thither, and with them well nigh all the men and women in the city. Therewith, the body, being laid out amiddleward the courtyard upon Andrevuola's silken cloth and strewn, with all her roses, was there not only bewept by her and his kinsfolk, but publicly mourned by well nigh all the ladies of the city and by many men, and being brought forth of the courtyard of the Seignory, not as that of a plebeian, but as that of a nobleman, it was with the utmost honour borne to the sepulchre upon the shoulders of the most noble citizens. Some days thereafterward, the Provost ensuing that which he had demanded, Messer Negro propounded it to his daughter, who would hear nought thereof, but, her father being willing to comply with her in this, she and her maid made themselves nuns in a convent very famous for sanctity and there lived honourably a great while after."

1. *i.e.* these two classes of folk.
2. *i.e.* to the encouragement of good and virtuous actions and purposes.
3. Or "lap" (*seno*).
4. Lit. what meaneth this? (*che vuol dire questo?*)
5. Lit. complaining, making complaint (*dolendosi*).

❧ 7 ❧

THE SEVENTH STORY

SIMONA LOVETH PASQUINO AND THEY BEING
TOGETHER IN A GARDEN, THE LATTER RUBBETH A
LEAF OF SAGE AGAINST HIS TEETH AND DIETH. SHE,
BEING TAKEN AND THINKING TO SHOW THE JUDGE
HOW HER LOVER DIED, RUBBETH ONE OF THE SAME
LEAVES AGAINST HER TEETH AND DIETH ON
LIKE WISE

PAMFILO HAVING DELIVERED himself of his story, the king, showing no compassion for Andrevuola, looked at Emilia and signed to her that it was his pleasure she should with a story follow on those who had already told; whereupon she, without delay, began as follows: "Dear companions, the story told by Pamfilo putteth me in mind to tell you one in nothing like unto his save that like as Andrevuola lost her beloved in a garden, even so did she of whom I have to tell, and being taken in like manner as was Andrevuola, freed herself from the court, not by dint of fortitude nor constancy, but by an unlooked-for death. And as hath otherwhile been said amongst us, albeit Love liefer inhabiteth the houses of the great, yet not therefor doth he decline the empery of those of the poor; nay, whiles in these latter he so manifesteth his power that he maketh himself feared, as a most puissant seignior, of the richer sort. This, if not in all, yet in great part, will appear from my story, with which it pleaseth me to re-enter our own city, wherefrom this day, discoursing diversely of divers things and ranging over various parts of the world, we have so far departed.

There was, then, no great while ago, in Florence a damsel very handsome and agreeable, according to her condition, who was the daughter of a poor father and was called Simona; and although it behoved her with her own hands earn the bread she would eat and sustain her life by spinning wool, she was not therefor of so poor a spirit but that she dared to admit into her heart Love, which,—by means of the pleasing words and fashions of a youth of no greater account than herself, who went giving wool to spin for a master of his, a wool-monger,—had long made a show of wishing to enter there. Having, then, received Him into her bosom with the pleasing aspect of the youth who loved her whose name was Pasquino, she heaved a thousand sighs, hotter than fire, at every hank of yarn she wound about the spindle, bethinking her of him who had given it her to spin and ardently desiring, but venturing not to do more. He, on his side, grown exceeding anxious that his master's wool should be well spun, overlooked Simona's spinning more diligently than that of any other, as if the yarn spun by her alone and none other were to furnish forth the whole cloth; wherefore, the one soliciting and the other delighting to be solicited, it befell that, he growing bolder than of his wont and she laying aside much of the timidity and shamefastness she was used to feel, they gave themselves

205

up with a common accord to mutual pleasures, which were so pleasing to both that not only did neither wait to be bidden thereto of the other, but each forewent other in the matter of invitation.

Ensuing this their delight from day to day and waxing ever more enkindled for continuance, it chanced one day that Pasquino told Simona he would fain have her find means to come to a garden, whither he wished to carry her so they might there foregather more at their ease and with less suspect. Simona answered that she would well and accordingly on Sunday, after eating, giving her father to believe that she meant to go a-pardoning to San Gallo,[1] she betook herself, with a friend of hers, called Lagina, to the garden appointed her of Pasquino. There she found him with a comrade of his, whose name was Puccino, but who was commonly called Stramba,[2] and an amorous acquaintance being quickly clapped up between the latter and Lagina, Simona and her lover withdrew to one part of the garden, to do their pleasure, leaving Stramba and Lagina in another.

Now in that part of the garden, whither Pasquino and Simona had betaken themselves, was a very great and goodly bush of sage, at the foot whereof they sat down and solaced themselves together a great while, holding much discourse of a collation they purposed to make there at their leisure. Presently, Pasquino turned to the great sage-bush and plucking a leaf thereof, began to rub his teeth and gums withal, avouching that sage cleaned them excellent well of aught that might be left thereon after eating. After he had thus rubbed them awhile, he returned to the subject of the collation, of which he had already spoken, nor had he long pursued his discourse when he began altogether to change countenance and well nigh immediately after lost sight and speech, and in a little while he died. Simona, seeing this, fell to weeping and crying out and called Stramba and Lagina, who ran thither in haste and seeing Pasquino not only dead, but already grown all swollen and full of dark spots about his face and body, Stramba cried out of a sudden, 'Ah, wicked woman! Thou hast poisoned him.' Making a great outcry, he was heard of many who dwelt near the garden and who, running to the clamour, found Pasquino dead and swollen.

Hearing Stramba lamenting and accusing Simona of having poisoned him of her malice, whilst she, for dolour of the sudden mishap that had carried off her lover, knew not how to excuse herself, being as it were beside herself, they all concluded that it was as he said; and accordingly she was taken and carried off, still weeping sore, to the Provost's palace, where, at the instance of Stramba and other two comrades of Pasquino, by name Atticciato and Malagevole, who had come up meanwhile, a judge addressed himself without delay to examine her of the fact and being unable to discover that she had done malice in the matter or was anywise guilty, he bethought himself, in her presence, to view the dead body and the place and manner of the mishap, as recounted to him by her, for that he apprehended it not very well by her words.

Accordingly, he let bring her, without any stir, whereas Pasquino's body lay yet, swollen as it were a tun, and himself following her thither, marvelled at the dead man and asked her how it had been; whereupon, going up to the sage-bush, she recounted to him all the foregoing story and to give him more fully to understand how the thing had befallen, she did even as Pasquino had done and rubbed one of the sage-leaves against her teeth. Then,—whilst her words were, in the judge's presence, flouted by Stramba and Atticciato and the other friends and comrades of Pasquino as frivolous and vain and they all denounced her wickedness with the more instance, demanding nothing less than that the fire should be the punishment of such perversity,—the wretched girl, who abode all confounded for dolour of her lost lover and fear of the punishment demanded by Stramba fell, for having rubbed the sage against her teeth, into that same mischance, whereinto her lover had fallen [and dropped dead], to the no small wonderment of as many as were present. O happy souls, to whom it fell in one same day to terminate at once your fervent love and your mortal life! Happier yet, an ye went together to one same place! And most happy, if folk love in the other life and ye love there as you loved here below! But happiest beyond compare,—at least in our judgment who abide after her on life,—was Simona's soul, whose innocence fortune suffered not to fall under the testimony of Stramba and Atticciato and Malagevole, wool-carders belike or men of yet meaner condition, finding her a more honourable way, with a death like unto that of her lover, to deliver herself from their calumnies and to follow the soul, so dearly loved of her, of her Pasquino.

The judge, in a manner astonied, as were likewise as many as were there, at this mischance and unknowing what to say, abode long silent; then, recollecting himself, he said, 'It seemeth this sage is poisonous, the which is not wont to happen of sage. But, so it may not avail to offend on this wise against any other, be it cut down even to the roots and cast into the fire.' This the keeper of the garden proceeded to do in the judge's presence, and no sooner had he levelled the great bush with the ground than the cause of the death of the two unfortunate lovers appeared; for thereunder was a toad of marvellous bigness, by whose pestiferous breath they concluded the sage to have become venomous. None daring approach the beast, they made a great hedge of brushwood about it and there burnt it, together with the sage. So ended the judge's inquest upon the death of the unfortunate Pasquino, who, together with his Simona, all swollen as they were, was buried by Stramba and Atticciato and Guccio Imbratta and Malagevole in the church of St. Paul, whereof it chanced they were parishioners."

---

1. *i.e.* to attend the ecclesiastical function called a Pardon, with which word, used in this sense, Meyerbeer's opera of Dinorah (properly Le Pardon de Ploërmel) has familiarized opera-goers. A Pardon is a sort of minor jubilee of the Roman Catholic Church, held in honour of some local saint, at which certain indulgences and remissions of sins (hence the name) are granted to the faithful attending the services of the occasion.

2. *i.e.* Bandy-legs.

🕸 8 🕸

THE EIGHTH STORY

GIROLAMO LOVETH SALVESTRA AND BEING
CONSTRAINED BY HIS MOTHER'S PRAYERS TO GO TO
PARIS, RETURNETH AND FINDETH HIS MISTRESS
MARRIED; WHEREUPON HE ENTERETH HER HOUSE
BY STEALTH AND DIETH BY HER SIDE; AND HE BEING
CARRIED TO A CHURCH, SALVESTRA DIETH
BESIDE HIM

EMILIA'S STORY come to an end, Neifile, by the king's commandment, began thus: "There are some, noble ladies, who believe themselves to know more than other folk, albeit, to my thinking, they know less, and who, by reason thereof, presume to oppose their judgment not only to the counsels of men, but even to set it up against the very nature of things; of which presumption very grave ills have befallen aforetime, nor ever was any good known to come thereof. And for that of all natural things love is that which least brooketh contrary counsel or opposition and whose nature is such that it may lightlier consume of itself than be done away by advisement, it hath come to my mind to narrate to you a story of a lady, who, seeking to be wiser than pertained unto her and than she was, nay, than the matter comported in which she studied to show her wit, thought to tear out from an enamoured heart a love which had belike been set there of the stars, and so doing, succeeded in expelling at once love and life from her son's body.

There was, then, in our city, according to that which the ancients relate, a very great and rich merchant, whose name was Lionardo Sighieri and who had by his wife a son called Girolamo, after whose birth, having duly set his affairs in order, he departed this life. The guardians of the boy, together with his mother, well and loyally ordered his affairs, and he, growing up with his neighbour's children, became familiar with a girl of his own age, the daughter of the tailor, more than with any other of the quarter. As he waxed in age, use turned to love so great and so ardent that he was never easy save what time he saw her, and certes she loved him no less than she was loved of him. The boy's mother, observing this, many a time chid and rebuked him therefor and after, Girolamo availing not to desist therefrom, complained thereof to his guardians, saying to them, as if she thought, thanks to her son's great wealth, to make an orange-tree of a bramble, 'This boy of ours, albeit he is yet scarce fourteen years old, is so enamoured of the daughter of a tailor our neighbour, by name Salvestra, that, except we remove her from his sight, he will peradventure one day take her to wife, without any one's knowledge, and I shall never after be glad; or else he will pine away from her, if he see her married to another; wherefore meseemeth, to avoid this, you were best send him somewhither far from here, about the business of the warehouse; for that, he being removed from seeing her, she will pass out of his mind and we may after avail to give him some well-born damsel to wife.'

The guardians answered that the lady said well and that they would do this to the best of their power; wherefore, calling the boy into the warehouse, one of them began very lovingly to bespeak him thus, 'My son, thou art now somewhat waxen in years and it were well that thou shouldst begin to look for thyself to thine affairs; wherefore it would much content us that thou shouldst go sojourn awhile at Paris, where thou wilt see how great part of thy wealth is employed, more by token that thou wilt there become far better bred and mannered and more of worth than thou couldst here, seeing the lords and barons and gentlemen who are there in plenty and learning their usances; after which thou mayst return hither.' The youth hearkened diligently and answered curtly that he was nowise disposed to do this, for that he believed himself able to fare as well at Florence as another. The worthy men, hearing this, essayed him again with sundry discourse, but, failing to get other answer of him, told his mother, who, sore provoked thereat, gave him a sound rating, not because of his unwillingness to go to Paris, but of his enamourment; after which, she fell to cajoling him with fair words, coaxing him and praying him softly be pleased to do what his guardians wished; brief, she contrived to bespeak him to such purpose that he consented to go to France and there abide a year and no more.

Accordingly, ardently enamoured as he was, he betook himself to Paris and there, being still put off from one day to another, he was kept two years; at the end of which time, returning, more in love than ever, he found his Salvestra married to an honest youth, a tent maker. At this he was beyond measure woebegone; but, seeing no help for it, he studied to console himself therefor and having spied out where she dwelt, began, after the wont of young men in love, to pass before her, expecting she should no more have forgotten him than he her. But the case was otherwise; she had no more remembrance of him than if she had never seen him; or, if indeed she remembered aught of him, she feigned the contrary; and of this, in a very brief space of time, Girolamo became aware, to his no small chagrin. Nevertheless, he did all he might to bring himself to her mind; but, himseeming he wrought nothing, he resolved to speak with her, face to face, though he should die for it.

Accordingly, having learned from a neighbour how her house stood, one evening that she and her husband were gone to keep wake with their neighbours, he entered therein by stealth and hiding himself behind certain tent cloths that were spread there, waited till, the twain having returned and gotten them to bed, he knew her husband to be asleep; whereupon he came whereas he had seen Salvestra lay herself and putting his hand upon her breast, said softly, 'Sleepest thou yet, O my soul?' The girl, who was awake, would have cried out; but he said hastily, 'For God's sake, cry not, for I am thy Girolamo.' She, hearing this, said, all trembling, 'Alack, for God's sake, Girolamo, get thee gone; the time is past when it was not forbidden unto our childishness to be lovers. I am, as thou seest, married and it beseemeth me no more to have regard to any man other than my husband; wherefore I beseech thee, by God the Only, to begone, for that, if my husband heard thee, even should no other harm ensue thereof, yet would it follow that I might never more avail to live with him in peace or quiet, whereas now I am beloved of him and abide with him in weal and in tranquility.'

The youth, hearing these words, was grievously endoloured and recalled to her the time past and his love no whit grown less for absence, mingling many prayers and many great promises, but obtained nothing; wherefore, desiring to die, he prayed her at last that, in requital of so much love, she would suffer him couch by her side, so he might warm himself somewhat, for that he was grown chilled, awaiting her, promising her that he would neither say aught to her nor touch her and would get him gone, so soon as he should be a little warmed. Salvestra, having some little compassion of him, granted him this he asked, upon the conditions aforesaid, and he accordingly lay down beside her, without touching her. Then, collecting into one thought the long love he had borne her and her present cruelty and his lost hope, he resolved to live no longer; wherefore, straitening in himself his vital spirits,[1] he clenched his hands and died by her side, without word or motion.

After a while the young woman, marvelling at his continence and fearing lest her husband should awake, began to say, 'Alack, Girolamo, why dost thou not get thee gone?' Hearing no answer, she concluded that he had fallen asleep and putting out her hand to awaken him, found him cold to the touch as ice, whereat she marvelled sore; then, nudging him more sharply and finding that he stirred not, she felt him again and knew that he was dead; whereat she was beyond measure woebegone and abode a great while, unknowing what she should do. At last she bethought herself to try, in the person of another, what her husband should say was to do [in such a case]; wherefore, awakening him, she told him, as having happened to another, that which had presently betided herself and after asked him what counsel she should take thereof,[2] if it should happen to herself. The good man replied that himseemed the dead man should be quietly carried to his house and there left, without bearing any ill will thereof to the woman, who, it appeared to him, had nowise done amiss. Then said Salvestra, 'And so it behoveth us do'; and taking his hand, made him touch the dead youth; whereupon, all confounded, he arose, without entering into farther parley with his wife, and kindled a light; then, clothing the dead body in its own garments, he took it, without any delay, on his shoulders and carried it, his innocence aiding him, to the door of Girolamo's house, where he set it down and left it.

When the day came and Girolamo was found dead before his own door, great was outcry, especially on the part of his mother, and the physicians having examined him and searched his body everywhere, but finding no wound nor bruise whatsoever on him, it was generally concluded that he had died of grief, as was indeed the case. Then was the body carried into a church and the sad mother, repairing thither with many other ladies, kinswomen and neighbours, began to weep without stint and make sore moan over him, according to our usance. What while the lamentation was at it highest, the good man, in whose house he had died, said to Salvestra, 'Harkye, put some mantlet or other on thy head and get thee to the church whither Girolamo hath been carried and mingle with the women and hearken to that which is discoursed of the matter; and I will do the like among the men, so we may hear if aught be said against us.' The thing pleased the girl, who was too late grown pitiful and would fain look upon him, dead, whom, living, she had not willed to pleasure with one poor kiss, and she went thither. A marvellous thing it is to think how uneath to search out are the ways of love! That heart, which Girolamo's fair fortune had not availed to open, his illhap opened and the old flames reviving all therein, whenas she saw the dead face it[3] melted of a sudden into such compassion that she pressed between the women, veiled as she was in the mantlet, and stayed not till she won to the body, and there, giving a terrible great shriek, she cast herself, face downward, on the dead youth, whom she bathed not with many tears, for that no sooner did she touch him than grief bereaved her of life, even as it had bereft him.

The women would have comforted her and bidden her arise, not yet knowing her; but after they had bespoken her awhile in vain, they sought to lift her and finding her motionless, raised her up and knew her at once for Salvestra and for dead; whereupon all who were there, overcome with double pity, set up a yet greater clamour of lamentation. The news soon spread abroad among the men without the church and came presently to the ears of her husband, who was amongst them and who, without lending ear to consolation or comfort from any, wept a great while; after which he recounted to many of those who were there the story of that which had befallen that night between the dead youth and his wife; and so was the cause of each one's death made everywhere manifest, the which was grievous unto all. Then, taking up the dead girl and decking her, as they use to deck the dead, they laid her beside Girolamo on the same bier and there long bewept her; after which the twain were buried in one same tomb, and so these, whom love had not availed to conjoin on life, death conjoined with an inseparable union."

---

1. *Ristretti in sè gli spiriti.* An obscure passage; perhaps "holding his breath" is meant; but in this case we should read "*lo spirito*" instead of "*gli spiriti.*"
2. *i.e.* what course she should take in the matter, *consiglio* used as before in this special sense.
3. *i.e.* her heart.

🦋 9 🦋

THE NINTH STORY

SIR GUILLAUME DE ROUSSILLON GIVETH HIS WIFE TO EAT THE HEART OF SIR GUILLAUME DE GUARDESTAING BY HIM SLAIN AND LOVED OF HER, WHICH SHE AFTER COMING TO KNOW, CASTETH HERSELF FROM A HIGH CASEMENT TO THE GROUND AND DYING, IS BURIED WITH HER LOVER

NEIFILE HAVING MADE an end of her story, which had awakened no little compassion in all the ladies her companions, the king, who purposed not to infringe Dioneo his privilege, there being none else to tell but they twain, began, "Gentle ladies, since you have such compassion upon ill-fortuned loves, it hath occurred to me to tell you a story whereof it will behove you have no less pity than of the last, for that those to whom that which I shall tell happened were persons of more account than those of whom it hath been spoken and yet more cruel was the mishap that befell them.

You must know, then, that according to that which the Provençals relate, there were aforetime in Provence two noble knights, each of whom had castles and vassals under him, called the one Sir Guillaume de Roussillon and the other Sir Guillaume de Guardestaing, and for that they were both men of great prowess in arms, they loved each other with an exceeding love and were wont to go still together and clad in the same colours to every tournament or jousting or other act of arms. Although they abode each in his own castle and were distant, one from other, a good half score miles, yet it came to pass that, Sir Guillaume de Roussillon having a very fair and lovesome lady to wife, Sir Guillaume de Guardestaing, notwithstanding the friendship and fellowship that was between them, become beyond measure enamoured of her and so wrought, now with one means and now with another, that the lady became aware of his passion and knowing him for a very valiant knight, it pleased her and she began to return his love, insomuch that she desired and tendered nothing more than him nor awaited otherwhat than to be solicited of him; the which was not long in coming to pass and they foregathered once and again.

Loving each other amain and conversing together less discreetly than behoved, it befell that the husband became aware of their familiarity and was mightily incensed thereat, insomuch that the great love he bore to Guardestaing was turned into mortal hatred; but this he knew better to keep hidden than the two lovers had known to conceal their love and was fully resolved in himself to kill him. Roussillon being in this mind, it befell that a great tourneying was proclaimed in France, the which he forthright signified to Guardestaing and sent to bid him come to him, an it pleased him, so they might take counsel together if and how they should

212

go thither; whereto the other very joyously answered that he would without fail come to sup with him on the ensuing day. Roussillon, hearing this, thought the time come whenas he might avail to kill him and accordingly on the morrow he armed himself and mounting to horse with a servant of his, lay at ambush, maybe a mile from his castle, in a wood whereas Guardestaing must pass.

There after he had awaited him a good while, he saw him come, unarmed and followed by two servants in like case, as one who apprehends nothing from him; and when he saw him come whereas he would have him, he rushed out upon him, lance in hand, full of rage and malice, crying, 'Traitor, thou art dead!' And to say thus and to plunge the lance into his breast were one and the same thing. Guardestaing, without being able to make any defence or even to say a word, fell from his horse, transfixed of the lance, and a little after died, whilst his servants, without waiting to learn who had done this, turned their horses' heads and fled as quickliest they might, towards their lord's castle. Roussillon dismounted and opening the dead man's breast with a knife, with his own hands tore out his heart, which he let wrap in the pennon of a lance and gave to one of his men to carry. Then, commanding that none should dare make words of the matter, he remounted, it being now night, and returned to his castle.

The lady, who had heard that Guardestaing was to be there that evening to supper and looked for him with the utmost impatience, seeing him not come, marvelled sore and said to her husband, 'How is it, sir, that Guardestaing is not come?' 'Wife,' answered he, 'I have had [word] from him that he cannot be here till to-morrow'; whereat the lady abode somewhat troubled. Roussillon then dismounted and calling the cook, said to him, 'Take this wild boar's heart and look thou make a dainty dish thereof, the best and most delectable to eat that thou knowest, and when I am at table, send it to me in a silver porringer.' The cook accordingly took the heart and putting all his art thereto and all his diligence, minced it and seasoning it with store of rich spices, made of it a very dainty ragout.

When it was time, Sir Guillaume sat down to table with his wife and the viands came; but he ate little, being hindered in thought for the ill deed he had committed. Presently the cook sent him the ragout, which he caused set before the lady, feigning himself disordered[1] that evening and commending the dish to her amain. The lady, who was nowise squeamish, tasted thereof and finding it good, ate it all; which when the knight saw, he said to her, 'Wife, how deem you of this dish?' 'In good sooth, my lord,' answered she, 'it liketh me exceedingly.' Whereupon, 'So God be mine aid,' quoth Roussillon; 'I do indeed believe it you, nor do I marvel if that please you, dead, which, alive, pleased you more than aught else.' The lady, hearing this, hesitated awhile, then said, 'How? What have you made me eat?' 'This that you have eaten,' answered the knight, 'was in very truth the heart of Sir Guillaume de Guardestaing, whom you, disloyal wife as you are, so loved; and know for certain that it is his very heart, for that I tore it from his breast with these hands a little before my return.'

It needeth not to ask if the lady were woebegone, hearing this of him whom she loved more than aught else; and after awhile she said, 'You have done the deed of a disloyal and base knight, as you are; for, if I, unenforced of him, made him lord of my love and therein offended against you, not he, but I should have borne the penalty thereof. But God forfend that ever other victual should follow upon such noble meat the heart of so valiant and so courteous a gentleman as was Sir Guillaume de Guardestaing!' Then, rising to her feet, without any manner of hesitation, she let herself fall backward through a window which was behind her and which was exceeding high above the ground; wherefore, as she fell, she was not only killed, but well nigh broken in pieces.

Sir Guillaume, seeing this, was sore dismayed and himseemed he had done ill; wherefore, being adread of the country people and of the Count of Provence, he let saddle his horses and made off. On the morrow it was known all over the country how the thing had passed; whereupon the two bodies were, with the utmost grief and lamentation, taken up by Guardestaing's people and those of the lady and laid in one same sepulchre in the chapel of the latter's own castle; and thereover were verses written, signifying who these were that were buried therewithin and the manner and occasion of their death."[2]

---

1. Or surfeited (*svogliato*).
2. This is the well-known story of the Troubadour Guillem de Cabestanh or Cabestaing, whose name Boccaccio alters to Guardastagno or Guardestaing.

❦ 10 ❦

THE TENTH STORY

A PHYSICIAN'S WIFE PUTTETH HER LOVER FOR DEAD
IN A CHEST, WHICH TWO USURERS CARRY OFF TO
THEIR OWN HOUSE, GALLANT AND ALL. THE LATTER,
WHO IS BUT DRUGGED, COMETH PRESENTLY TO
HIMSELF AND BEING DISCOVERED, IS TAKEN FOR A
THIEF; BUT THE LADY'S MAID AVOUCHETH TO THE
SEIGNORY THAT SHE HERSELF HAD PUT HIM INTO
THE CHEST STOLEN BY THE TWO USURERS,
WHEREBY HE ESCAPETH THE GALLOWS AND THE
THIEVES ARE AMERCED IN CERTAIN MONIES

FILOSTRATO HAVING MADE an end of his telling, it rested only with Dioneo to accomplish his task, who, knowing this and it being presently commanded him of the king, began as follows: 'The sorrows that have been this day related of ill fortuned loves have saddened not only your eyes and hearts, ladies, but mine also; wherefore I have ardently longed for an end to be made thereof. Now that, praised be God, they are finished (except I should choose to make an ill addition to such sorry ware, from which God keep me!), I will, without farther ensuing so dolorous a theme, begin with something blither and better, thereby perchance affording a good argument for that which is to be related on the ensuing day.

You must know, then, fairest lasses, that there was in Salerno, no great while since, a very famous doctor in surgery, by name Master Mazzeo della Montagna, who, being already come to extreme old age, took to wife a fair and gentle damsel of his city and kept better furnished with sumptuous and rich apparel and jewels and all that can pleasure a lady than any woman of the place. True it is she went a-cold most of her time, being kept of her husband ill covered abed; for, like as Messer Ricardo di Chinzica (of whom we already told) taught his wife to observe saints' days and holidays, even so the doctor pretended to her that once lying with a woman necessitated I know not how many days' study to recruit the strength and the like toys; whereof she abode exceeding ill content and like a discreet and high-spirited woman as she was, bethought herself, so she might the better husband the household good, to betake herself to the highway and seek to spend others' gear. To this end, considering divers young men, at last she found one to her mind and on him she set all her hope; whereof he becoming aware and she pleasing him mightily, he in like manner turned all his love upon her.

The spark in question was called Ruggieri da Jeroli, a man of noble birth, but of lewd life and blameworthy carriage, insomuch that he had left himself neither friend nor kinsman who wished him well or cared to see him and was defamed throughout all Salerno for thefts and other knaveries of the vilest; but of this the lady recked little, he pleasing her for otherwhat, and with the aid of a maid of hers, she wrought on such wise that they came together. After they had taken some delight, the lady proceeded to blame his past way of life and to pray him, for the love of her, to desist from these ill fashions; and to give him the means of doing this, she fell

215

to succouring him, now with one sum of money and now with another. On this wise they abode together, using the utmost discretion, till it befell that a sick man was put into the doctor's hands, who had a gangrened leg, and Master Mazzeo, having examined the case, told the patient's kinsfolk that, except a decayed bone he had in his leg were taken out, needs must he have the whole limb cut off or die, and that, by taking out the bone, he might recover, but that he would not undertake him otherwise than for a dead man; to which those to whom the sick man pertained agreed and gave the latter into his hands for such. The doctor, judging that the patient might not brook the pain nor would suffer himself to be operated, without an opiate, and having appointed to set about the matter at evensong, let that morning distil a certain water of his composition, which being drunken by the sick man, should make him sleep so long as he deemed necessary for the performing of the operation upon him, and fetching it home, set it in his chamber, without telling any what it was.

The hour of vespers come and the doctor being about to go to the patient in question, there came to him a messenger from certain very great friends of his at Malfi, charging him fail not for anything to repair thither incontinent, for that there had been a great fray there, in which many had been wounded. Master Mazzeo accordingly put off the tending of the leg until the ensuing morning and going aboard a boat, went off to Malfi, whereupon his wife, knowing that he would not return home that night, let fetch Ruggieri, as of her wont, and bringing him into her chamber, locked him therewithin, against certain other persons of the house should be gone to sleep. Ruggieri, then, abiding in the chamber, awaiting his mistress, and being,—whether for fatigue endured that day or salt meat that he had eaten or maybe for usance,—sore, athirst, caught sight of the flagon of water, which the doctor had prepared for the sick man and which stood in the window, and deeming it drinking water, set it to his mouth and drank it all off; nor was it long ere a great drowsiness took him and he fell asleep.

The lady came to the chamber as first she might and finding Ruggieri asleep, nudged him and bade him in a low voice arise, but to no effect, for he replied not neither stirred anywhit; whereat she was somewhat vexed and nudged him more sharply, saying, 'Get up, slugabed! An thou hadst a mind to sleep, thou shouldst have betaken thee to thine own house and not come hither.' Ruggieri, being thus pushed, fell to the ground from a chest whereon he lay and gave no more sign of life than a dead body; whereupon the lady, now somewhat alarmed, began to seek to raise him up and to shake him more roughly, tweaking him by the nose and plucking him by the beard, but all in vain; he had tied his ass to a fast picket.[1] At this she began to fear lest he were dead; nevertheless she proceeded to pinch him sharply and burn his flesh with a lighted taper, but all to no purpose; wherefore, being no doctress, for all her husband was a physician, she doubted not but he was dead in very deed. Loving him over all else as she did, it needeth no asking if she were woebegone for this and daring not make any outcry, she silently fell a-weeping over him and bewailing so sore a mishap.

After awhile, fearing to add shame to her loss, she bethought herself that it behoved her without delay find a means of carrying the dead man forth of the house and knowing not how to contrive this, she softly called her maid and discovering to her her misadventure sought counsel of her. The maid marvelled exceedingly and herself pulled and pinched Ruggieri, but, finding him without sense or motion, agreed with her mistress that he was certainly dead and counselled her put him forth of the house. Quoth the lady, 'And where can we put him, so it may not be suspected, whenas he shall be seen to-morrow morning, that he hath been brought out hence?' 'Madam,' answered the maid, 'I saw, this evening at nightfall, over against the shop of our neighbour yonder the carpenter, a chest not overbig, the which, an the owner have not taken it in again, will come very apt for our affair; for that we can lay him therein, after giving him two or three slashes with a knife, and leave him be. I know no reason why whoso findeth him should suppose him to have been put there from this house rather than otherwhence; nay, it will liefer be believed, seeing he was a young man of lewd life, that he hath been slain by some enemy of his, whilst going about to do some mischief or other, and after clapped in the chest.'

The maid's counsel pleased the lady, save that she would not hear of giving him any wound, saying that for naught in the world would her heart suffer her to do that. Accordingly she sent her to see if the chest were yet whereas she had noted it and she presently returned and said, 'Ay.' Then, being young and lusty, with the aid of her mistress, she took Ruggieri on her shoulders and carrying him out,—whilst the lady forewent her, to look if any came,—clapped him into the chest and shutting down the lid, left him there. Now it chanced that, a day or two before, two young men, who lent at usance, had taken up their abode in a house a little farther and lacking household gear, but having a mind to gain much and spend little, had that day espied the chest in question and had plotted together, if it should abide there the night, to carry it off to their own house. Accordingly, midnight come, they sallied forth and finding the chest still there, without looking farther, they hastily carried it off, for all it seemed to them somewhat heavy, to their own house, where they set it down beside a chamber in which their wives slept and there leaving it, without concerning themselves for the nonce to settle it overnicely, betook them to bed.

Presently, the morning drawing near, Ruggieri, who had slept a great while, having by this time digested the sleeping draught and exhausted its effects, awoke and albeit his sleep was broken and his senses in some measure restored, there abode yet a dizziness in his brain, which held him stupefied, not that night only, but some days after. Opening his eyes and seeing nothing, he put out his hands hither and thither and finding himself in the chest, bethought himself and said, 'What is this? Where am I? Am I asleep or awake? Algates I mind me that I came this evening into my mistress's chamber and now meseemeth I am in a chest. What meaneth this? Can the physician have returned or other accident befallen, by reason whereof the lady hath hidden me here, I being asleep? Methinketh it must have been thus; assuredly it was so.' Accordingly, he addressed himself to abide quiet and hearken if he could hear aught and after he had abidden thus a great while, being somewhat ill at ease in the chest, which was small, and the side whereon he lay irking him, he would have turned over to the other and wrought so dexterously that, thrusting his loins against one of the sides of the chest, which had not been set on a level place, he caused it first to incline to one side and after topple over. In falling, it made a great noise, whereat the women who slept therenigh awoke and being affrighted, were silent for fear. Ruggieri was sore alarmed at the fall of the chest, but, finding that it had opened in the fall, chose rather, if aught else should betide, to be out of it than to abide therewithin. Accordingly, he came forth and what with knowing not where he was and what with one thing and another, he fell to groping about the house, so haply he should find a stair or a door, whereby he might get him gone.

The women, hearing this, began to say, 'Who is there?' But Ruggieri, knowing not the voice, answered not; whereupon they proceeded to call the two young men, who, for that they had overwatched themselves, slept fast and heard nothing of all this. Thereupon the women, waxing more fearful, arose and betaking themselves to the windows, fell a-crying, 'Thieves! Thieves!' At this sundry of the neighbours ran up and made their way, some by the roof and some by one part and some by another, into the house; and the young men also, awaking for the noise, arose and seized Ruggieri, who finding himself there, was in a manner beside himself for wonderment and saw no way of escape. Then they gave him into the hands of the officers of the governor of the city, who had now run thither at the noise and carried him before their chief. The latter, for that he was held of all a very sorry fellow, straightway put him to the question and he confessed to having entered the usurers' house to steal; whereupon the governor thought to let string him up by the neck without delay.

The news was all over Salerno by the morning that Ruggieri had been taken in the act of robbing the money-lenders' house, which the lady and her maid hearing, they were filled with such strange and exceeding wonderment that they were like to persuade themselves that they had not done, but had only dreamed of doing, that which they had done overnight; whilst the lady, to boot, was so concerned at the news of the danger wherein Ruggieri was that she was like to go mad. Soon after half tierce[2] the physician, having returned from Malfi and wishing to medicine his patient, called for his prepared water and finding the flagon empty, made a great outcry, saying that nothing could abide as it was in his house. The lady, who was troubled with another great chagrin, answered angrily, saying 'What wouldst thou say, doctor, of grave matter, whenas thou makest such an outcry anent a flagonlet of water overset? Is there no more water to be found in the world?' 'Wife,' rejoined the physician, 'thou thinkest this was common water; it was not so; nay, it was a water prepared to cause sleep'; and told her for what occasion he had made it. When she heard this, she understood forthright that Ruggieri had drunken the opiate and had therefore appeared to them dead and said to her husband, 'Doctor, we knew it not; wherefore do you make yourself some more'; and the physician, accordingly, seeing he might not do otherwise, let make thereof anew.

A little after, the maid, who had gone by her mistress's commandment to learn what should be reported of Ruggieri, returned and said to her, 'Madam, every one missaith of Ruggieri; nor, for aught I could hear, is there friend or kinsman who hath risen up or thinketh to rise up to assist him, and it is held certain that the prefect of police will have him hanged to-morrow. Moreover, I have a strange thing to tell you, to wit, meseemeth I have discovered how he came into the money-lenders' house, and hear how. You know the carpenter overagainst whose shop was the chest wherein we laid him; he was but now at the hottest words in the world with one to whom it seemeth the chest belonged; for the latter demanded of him the price of his chest, and the carpenter replied that he had not sold it, but that it had that night been stolen from him. Whereto, "Not so," quoth the other, "nay, thou soldest it to the two young men, the money-lenders yonder, as they told me yesternight, when I saw it in their house what time Ruggieri was taken." "They lie," answered the carpenter. "I never sold it to them; but they stole it from me yesternight. Let us go to them." So they went off with one accord to the money-lenders' house, and I came back hither. On this wise, as you may see, I conclude that Ruggieri was transported whereas he was found; but how he came to life again I cannot divine.'

The lady now understood very well how the case stood and telling the maid what she had heard from the physician, besought her help to save Ruggieri, for that she might, an she would, at once save him and preserve her honour. Quoth she, 'Madam, teach me how, and I will gladly do anything.' Whereupon the lady, whose wits were sharpened by the urgency of the case, having promptly bethought herself of that which was to do, particularly acquainted the maid therewith, who first betook herself to the physician and weeping, began to say to him, 'Sir, it behoveth me ask you pardon of a great fault, which I have committed against you.' 'In what?' asked the doctor, and she, never giving over weeping, answered, 'Sir, you know what manner young man is Ruggieri da Jeroli. He took a liking to me awhile agone and partly for fear and partly for love, needs must I become his mistress. Yesternight, knowing that you were abroad, he cajoled me on such wise that I brought him into your house to lie with me in my chamber, and he being athirst and I having no whither more quickly to resort for water or wine, unwilling as I was that your lady, who was in the saloon, should see me, I remembered me to have seen a flagon of water in your chamber. Accordingly, I ran for it and giving him the water to drink, replaced the flagon whence I had taken it, whereof I find you have made a great outcry in the house. And certes I confess I did ill; but who is there doth not ill bytimes? Indeed, I am exceeding grieved to have done it, not so much for the thing itself as for that which hath ensued of it and by reason whereof Ruggieri is like to lose his life. Wherefore I pray you, as most I may, pardon me and give me leave to go succour Ruggieri inasmuch as I can.' The physician, hearing this, for all he was angry, answered jestingly, 'Thou hast given thyself thine own penance therefor, seeing that, whereas thou thoughtest yesternight to have a lusty young fellow who would shake thy skincoats well for thee, thou hadst a sluggard; wherefore go and endeavour for the deliverance of thy lover; but henceforth look thou bring him not into the house again, or I will pay thee for this time and that together.'

The maid, thinking she had fared well for the first venue, betook herself, as quickliest she might, to the prison, where Ruggieri lay and coaxed the gaoler to let her speak with the prisoner, whom after she had instructed what answers he should make to the prefect of police, an he would fain escape, she contrived to gain admission to the magistrate himself. The latter, for that she was young and buxom, would fain, ere he would hearken to her, cast his grapnel aboard the good wench, whereof she, to be the better heard, was no whit chary; then, having quitted herself of the grinding due,[3] 'Sir,' said she, 'you have here Ruggieri da Jeroli taken for a thief; but the truth is not so.' Then, beginning from the beginning, she told him the whole story; how she, being his mistress, had brought him into the physician's house and had given him the drugged water to drink, unknowing what it was, and how she had put him for dead into the chest; after which she told him the talk she had heard between the master carpenter and the owner of the chest, showing him thereby how Ruggieri had come into the money-lenders' house.

The magistrate, seeing it an easy thing to come at the truth of the matter, first questioned the physician if it were true of the water and found that it was as she had said; whereupon he let summon the carpenter and him to whom the chest belonged and the two money-lenders and after much parley, found that the latter had stolen the chest overnight and put it in their house. Ultimately he sent for Ruggieri and questioned him where he had lain that night, whereto he replied that where he had lain he knew not; he remembered indeed having gone to pass the night with Master Mazzeo's maid, in whose chamber he had drunken water for a sore thirst he had; but what became of him after he knew not, save that, when he awoke, he found himself in the money-lenders' house in a chest. The prefect, hearing these things and taking great pleasure therein, caused the maid and Ruggieri and the carpenter and the money-lenders repeat their story again and again; and in the end, seeing Ruggieri to be innocent, he released him and amerced the money-lenders in half a score ounces for that they had stolen the chest. How welcome this was to Ruggieri, none need ask, and it was beyond measure pleasing to his mistress, who together with her lover and the precious maid, who had proposed to give him the slashes with the knife, many a time after laughed and made merry of the matter, still continuing their loves and their disport from good to better; the which I would well might so betide myself, save always the being put in the chest."

If the former stories had saddened the hearts of the lovesome ladies, this last one of Dioneo's made them laugh heartily, especially when he spoke of the prefect casting his grapnel aboard the maid, that they were able thus to recover themselves of the melancholy caused by the others. But the king, seeing that the sun began to grow yellow and that the term of his seignory was come, with very courteous speech excused himself to the fair ladies for that which he had done, to wit, that he had caused discourse of so sorrowful a matter as that of lovers' infelicity; which done, he rose to his feet and taking from his head the laurel wreath, whilst the ladies waited to see on whom he should bestow it, set it daintily on Fiammetta's fair head, saying, "I make over this crown to thee, as to her who will, better than any other, know how with to-morrow's pleasance to console these ladies our companions of to-day's woefulness."

Fiammetta, whose locks were curled and long and golden and fell over her white and delicate shoulders and whose soft-rounded face was all resplendent with white lilies and vermeil roses commingled, with two eyes in her head as they were those of a peregrine falcon and a dainty little mouth, the lips whereof seemed twin rubies, answered, smiling, "And I, Filostrato, I take it willingly, and that thou mayst be the better cognizant of that which thou hast done, I presently will and command that each prepare to discourse to-morrow of THAT WHICH HATH HAPPILY BETIDED LOVERS AFTER SUNDRY CRUEL AND MISFORTUNATE ADVENTURES." Her proposition[4] was pleasing unto all and she, after summoning the seneschal and taking counsel with him of things needful, arising from session, blithely dismissed all the company until supper-time. Accordingly, they all proceeded, according to their various appetites, to take their several pleasures, some wandering about the garden, whose beauties were not such as might lightly tire, and other some betaking themselves towards the mills which wrought therewithout, whilst the rest fared some hither and some thither, until the hour of supper, which being come, they all foregathered, as of their wont, anigh the fair fountain and there supped with exceeding pleasance and well served. Presently, arising thence, they addressed themselves, as of their wont, to dancing and singing, and Filomena leading off the dance, the queen said, "Filostrato, I purpose not to depart from the usance of those who have foregone me in the sovranty, but, like as they have done, so I intend that a song be sung at my commandment; and as I am assured that thy songs are even such as are thy stories, it is our pleasure that, so no more days than this be troubled with thine ill fortunes, thou sing such one thereof as most pleaseth thee." Filostrato replied that he would well and forthright proceeded to sing on this wise:

> Weeping, I demonstrate
> How sore with reason doth my heart complain
> Of love betrayed and plighted faith in vain.
>
> Love, whenas first there was of thee imprest
> Thereon[5] her image for whose sake I sigh,
> Sans hope of succour aye,
> So full of virtue didst thou her pourtray,
> That every torment light accounted I
> That through thee to my breast
> Grown full of drear unrest
> And dole, might come; but now, alack! I'm fain
> To own my error, not withouten pain.
>
> Yea, of the cheat first was I made aware,
> Seeing myself of her forsaken sheer,
> In whom I hoped alone;
> For, when I deemed myself most fairly grown
> Into her favour and her servant dear,
> Without her thought or care
> Of my to-come despair,
> I found she had another's merit ta'en

To heart and put me from her with disdain.

Whenas I knew me banished from my stead,
Straight in my heart a dolorous plaint there grew,
That yet therein hath power,
And oft I curse the day and eke the hour
When first her lovesome visage met my view,
Graced with high goodlihead;
And more enamouréd
Than eye, my soul keeps up its dying strain,
Faith, ardour, hope, blaspheming still amain.
How void my misery is of all relief
Thou mayst e'en feel, so sore I call thee, sire,
With voice all full of woe;
Ay, and I tell thee that it irks me so
That death for lesser torment I desire.
Come, death, then; shear the sheaf
Of this my life of grief
And with thy stroke my madness eke assain;
Go where I may, less dire will be my bane.

No other way than death is left my spright,
Ay, and none other solace for my dole;
Then give it⁶ me straightway,
Love; put an end withal to my dismay:
Ah, do it; since fate's spite
Hath robbed me of delight;
Gladden thou her, lord, with my death, love-slain,
As thou hast cheered her with another swain.

My song, though none to learn thee lend an ear,
I reck the less thereof, indeed, that none
Could sing thee even as I;
One only charge I give thee, ere I die,
That thou find Love and unto him alone
Show fully how undear
This bitter life and drear
Is to me, craving of his might he deign
Some better harbourage I may attain.

Weeping I demonstrate
How sore with reason doth my heart complain
Of love betrayed and plighted faith in vain.

The words of this song clearly enough discovered the state of Filostrato's mind and the cause thereof, the which belike the countenance of a certain lady who was in the dance had yet plainlier declared, had not the shades of the now fallen night hidden the blushes that rose to her face. But, when he had made an end of his song, many others were sung, till such time as the hour of sleep arrived, whereupon, at the queen's commandment, each of the ladies withdrew to her chamber.

---

1. A proverbial way of saying that he was fast asleep.
2. *i.e.* about half-past seven a.m.
3. Or "having risen from the grinding" (*levatasi dal macinio*).
4. *i.e.* the theme proposed by her.
5. *i.e.* on my heart.
6. *i.e.* death.

DAY THE FIFTH

Here Beginneth the Fifth Day of the Decameron
Wherein Under the Governance of Fiammetta Is
Discoursed of That Which Hath Happily Betided
Lovers After Sundry Cruel and Misfortunate
Adventures

The East was already all white and the rays of the rising sun had made it light through all our hemisphere, when Fiammetta, allured by the sweet song of the birds that blithely chanted the first hour of the day upon the branches, arose and let call all the other ladies and the three young men; then, with leisured pace descending into the fields, she went a-pleasuring with her company about the ample plain upon the dewy grasses, discoursing with them of one thing and another, until the sun was somewhat risen, when, feeling that its rays began to grow hot, she turned their steps to their abiding-place. There, with excellent wines and confections, she let restore the light fatigue had and they disported themselves in the delightsome garden until the eating hour, which being come and everything made ready by the discreet seneschal, they sat blithely down to meat, such being the queen's pleasure, after they had sung sundry roundelays and a ballad or two. Having dined orderly and with mirth, not unmindful of their wonted usance of dancing, they danced sundry short dances to the sound of songs and tabrets, after which the queen dismissed them all until the hour of slumber should be past. Accordingly, some betook themselves to sleep, whilst others addressed themselves anew to their diversion about the fair garden; but all, according to the wonted fashion, assembled together again, a little after none, near the fair fountain, whereas it pleased the queen. Then she, having seated herself in the chief room, looked towards Pamfilo and smilingly charged him make a beginning with the fair-fortuned stories; whereto he willingly addressed himself and spoke as follows:

❧ I ❧

THE FIRST STORY

CIMON, LOVING, WAXETH WISE AND CARRIETH OFF TO SEA IPHIGENIA HIS MISTRESS. BEING CAST INTO PRISON AT RHODES, HE IS DELIVERED THENCE BY LYSIMACHUS AND IN CONCERT WITH HIM CARRIETH OFF IPHIGENIA AND CASSANDRA ON THEIR WEDDING-DAY, WITH WHOM THE TWAIN FLEE INTO CRETE, WHERE THE TWO LADIES BECOME THEIR WIVES AND WHENCE THEY ARE PRESENTLY ALL FOUR RECALLED HOME

"MANY STORIES, delightsome ladies, apt to give beginning to so glad a day as this will be, offer themselves unto me to be related; whereof one is the most pleasing to my mind, for that thereby, beside the happy issue which is to mark this day's discourses, you may understand how holy, how puissant and how full of all good is the power of Love, which many, unknowing what they say, condemn and vilify with great unright; and this, an I err not, must needs be exceeding pleasing to you, for that I believe you all to be in love.

There was, then, in the island of Cyprus, (as we have read aforetime in the ancient histories of the Cypriots,) a very noble gentleman, by name Aristippus, who was rich beyond any other of the country in all temporal things and might have held himself the happiest man alive, had not fortune made him woeful in one only thing, to wit, that amongst his other children he had a son who overpassed all the other youths of his age in stature and goodliness of body, but was a hopeless dullard and well nigh an idiot. His true name was Galesus, but for that neither by toil of teacher nor blandishment nor beating of his father nor study nor endeavour of whatsoever other had it been found possible to put into his head any inkling of letters or good breeding and that he had a rough voice and an uncouth and manners more befitting a beast than a man, he was of well nigh all by way of mockery called Cimon, which in their tongue signified as much as brute beast in ours. His father brooked his wastrel life with the most grievous concern and having presently given over all hope of him, he bade him begone to his country house[1] and there abide with his husbandmen, so he might not still have before him the cause of his chagrin; the which was very agreeable to Cimon, for that the manners and usages of clowns and churls were much more to his liking than those of the townsfolk.

Cimon, then, betaking himself to the country and there employing himself in the things that pertained thereto, it chanced one day, awhile after noon, as he passed from one farm to another, with his staff on his shoulder, that he entered a very fair coppice which was in those parts and which was then all in leaf, for that it was the month of May. Passing therethrough, he happened (even as his fortune guided him thither) upon a little mead compassed about with very high trees, in one corner whereof was a very clear and cool spring, beside which he saw a very fair damsel asleep upon the green grass, with so thin a garment upon her body that it hid well nigh nothing of her snowy flesh. She was covered only from the waist down with a very white and light coverlet; and at her feet slept on like wise two women and a man, her servants. When Cimon espied the young lady, he halted and leaning upon his staff, fell, without saying a word, to gazing most intently upon her with the utmost admiration, no otherwise than as he had never yet seen a woman's form, whilst in his rude breast, wherein for a thousand lessonings no least impression of civil pleasance had availed to penetrate, he felt a thought awaken which intimated to his gross and material spirit that this maiden was the fairest thing that had been ever seen of any living soul. Thence he proceeded to consider her various parts,—commending her hair, which he accounted of gold, her brow, her nose, her mouth, her throat and her arms, and above all her breast, as yet but little upraised,—and grown of a sudden from a churl a judge of beauty, he ardently desired in himself to see the eyes, which, weighed down with deep sleep, she kept closed. To this end, he had it several times in mind to awaken her; but, for that she seemed to him beyond measure fairer than the other women aforetime seen of him, he misdoubted him she must be some goddess. Now he had wit enough to account things divine worthy of more reverence than those mundane; wherefore he forbore, waiting for her to awake of herself; and albeit the delay seemed overlong to him, yet, taken as he was with an unwonted pleasure, he knew not how to tear himself away.

It befell, then, that, after a long while, the damsel, whose name was Iphigenia, came to herself, before any of her people, and opening her eyes, saw Cimon (who, what for his fashion and uncouthness and his father's wealth and nobility, was known in a manner to every one in the country) standing before her, leant on his staff, marvelled exceedingly and said, 'Cimon, what goest thou seeking in this wood at this hour?' He made her no answer, but, seeing her eyes open, began to look steadfastly upon them, himseeming there proceeded thence a sweetness which fulfilled him with a pleasure such as he had never before felt. The young lady, seeing this, began to misdoubt her lest his so fixed looking upon her should move his rusticity to somewhat that might turn to her shame; wherefore, calling her women, she rose up, saying, 'Cimon, abide with God.' To which he replied, 'I will begone with thee'; and albeit the young lady, who was still in fear of him, would have declined his company, she could not win to rid herself of him till he had accompanied her to her own house.

Thence he repaired to his father's house [in the city,] and declared to him that he would on no wise consent to return to the country; the which was irksome enough to Aristippus and his kinsfolk; nevertheless they let him be, awaiting to see what might be the cause of his change of mind. Love's arrow having, then, through Iphigenia's beauty, penetrated into Cimon's heart, whereinto no teaching had ever availed to win an entrance, in a very brief time, proceeding from one idea to another, he made his father marvel and all his kinsfolk and every other that knew him. In the first place he besought his father that he would cause him go bedecked with clothes and every other thing, even as his brothers, the which Aristippus right gladly did. Then, consorting with young men of condition and learning the fashions and carriage that behoved unto gentlemen and especially unto lovers, he first, to the utmost wonderment of every one, in a very brief space of time, not only learned the first [elements of] letters, but became very eminent among the students of philosophy, and after (the love which he bore Iphigenia being the cause of all this) he not only reduced his rude and rustical manner of speech to seemliness and civility, but became a past master of song and sound[2] and exceeding expert and doughty in riding and martial exercises, both by land and by sea. In short, not to go recounting every particular of his merits, the fourth year was not accomplished from the day of his first falling in love, ere he was grown the sprightliest and most accomplished gentleman of all the young men in the island of Cyprus, ay, and the best endowed with every particular excellence. What, then, charming ladies, shall we say of Cimon? Certes, none other thing than that the lofty virtues implanted by heaven in his generous soul had been bounden with exceeding strong bonds of jealous fortune and shut in some straitest corner of his heart, all which bonds Love, as a mightier than fortune, broke and burst in sunder and in its quality of awakener and quickener of drowsed and sluggish wits, urged forth into broad daylight the virtues aforesaid, which had till then been overdarkened with a barbarous obscurity, thus manifestly discovering from how mean a room it can avail to uplift those souls that are subject unto it and to what an eminence it can conduct them with its beams.

Although Cimon, loving Iphigenia as he did, might exceed in certain things, as young men in love very often do, nevertheless Aristippus, considering that Love had turned him from a dunce into a man, not only patiently bore with the extravagances into which it might whiles lead him, but encouraged him to ensue its every pleasure. But Cimon, (who refused to be called Galesus, remembering that Iphigenia had called him by the former name,) seeking to put an honourable term to his desire, once and again caused essay Cipseus, Iphigenia's father, so he should give him his daughter to wife; but Cipseus still answered that he had promised her to Pasimondas, a young nobleman of Rhodes, to whom he had no mind to fail of his word. The time coming the covenanted nuptials of Iphigenia and the bridegroom having sent for her, Cimon said to himself, 'Now, O Iphigenia, is the time to prove how much thou art beloved of me. By thee am I become a man and so I may but have thee, I doubt not to become more glorious than any god; and for certain I will or have thee or die.'

Accordingly, having secretly recruited certain young noblemen who were his friends and let privily equip a ship with everything apt for naval battle, he put out to sea and awaited the vessel wherein Iphigenia was to be transported to her husband in Rhodes. The bride, after much honour done of her father to the bridegroom's friends, took ship with the latter, who turned their prow towards Rhodes and departed. On the following day, Cimon, who slept not, came out upon them with his ship and cried out, in a loud voice, from the prow, to those who were on board Iphigenia's vessel, saying, 'Stay, strike your sails or look to be beaten and sunken in the sea.' Cimon's adversaries had gotten up their arms on deck and made ready to defend themselves; whereupon he, after speaking the words aforesaid, took a grappling-iron and casting it upon the poop of the Rhodians, who were making off at the top of their speed, made it fast by main force to the prow of his own ship. Then, bold as a lion, he leapt on board their ship, without waiting for any to follow him, as if he held them all for nought, and Love spurring him, he fell upon his enemies with marvellous might, cutlass in hand, striking now this one and now that and hewing them down like sheep.

The Rhodians, seeing this, cast down their arms and all as with one voice confessed themselves prisoners; whereupon quoth Cimon to them, 'Young men, it was neither lust of rapine nor hate that I had against you made me depart Cyprus to assail you, arms in hand, in mid sea. That which moved me thereunto was the desire of a thing which to have gotten is a very grave matter to me and to you a very light one to yield me in peace; it is, to wit, Iphigenia, whom I loved over all else and whom, availing not to have of her father on friendly and peaceful wise, Love hath constrained me to win from you as an enemy and by force of arms. Wherefor I mean to be to her that which your friend Pasimondas should have been. Give her to me, then, and begone and God's grace go with you.'

The Rhodians, more by force constrained than of freewill, surrendered Iphigenia, weeping, to Cimon, who, seeing her in tears, said to her, 'Noble Lady, be not disconsolate; I am thy Cimon, who by long love have far better deserved to have thee than Pasimondas by plighted faith.' Thereupon he caused carry her aboard his own ship and returning to his companions, let the Rhodians go, without touching aught else of theirs. Then, glad beyond any man alive to have gotten so dear a prey, after devoting some time to comforting the weeping lady, he took counsel with his comrades not to return to Cyprus at that present; wherefore, of one accord, they turned the ship's head towards Crete, where well nigh every one, and especially Cimon, had kinsfolk, old and new, and friends in plenty and where they doubted not to be in safety with Iphigenia. But fortune the unstable, which had cheerfully enough vouchsafed unto Cimon the acquisition of the lady, suddenly changed the inexpressible joyance of the enamoured youth into sad and bitter mourning; for it was not four full told hours since he had left the Rhodians when the night (which Cimon looked to be more delightsome than any he had ever known) came on and with it a very troublous and tempestuous shift of weather, which filled all the sky with clouds and the sea with ravening winds, by reason whereof none could see what to do or whither to steer, nor could any even keep the deck to do any office.

How sore concerned was Cimon for this it needeth not to ask; himseemed the gods had vouchsafed him his desire but to make death the more grievous to him, whereof, without that, he had before recked little. His comrades lamented on like wise, but Iphigenia bewailed herself over all, weeping sore and fearing every stroke of the waves; and in her chagrin she bitterly cursed Cimon's love and blamed his presumption, avouching that the tempest had arisen for none other thing but that the gods chose not that he, who would fain against their will have her to wife, should avail to enjoy his presumptuous desire, but, seeing her first die, should after himself perish miserably.

Amidst such lamentations and others yet more grievous, the wind waxing hourly fiercer and the seamen knowing not what to do, they came, without witting whither they went or availing to change their course, near to the island of Rhodes, and unknowing that it was Rhodes, they used their every endeavour to get to land thereon, an it were possible, for the saving of their lives. In this fortune was favourable to them and brought them into a little bight of the sea, where the Rhodians whom Cimon had let go had a little before arrived with their ship; nor did they perceive that they had struck the island of Rhodes till the dawn broke and made the sky somewhat clearer, when they found themselves maybe a bowshot distant from the ship left of them the day before. At this Cimon was beyond measure chagrined and fearing lest that should betide them which did in very deed ensue, bade use every endeavour to issue thence and let fortune after carry them whither it should please her, for that they could be nowhere in worse case than there. Accordingly, they made the utmost efforts to put to sea, but in vain; for the wind blew so mightily against them that not only could they not avail to issue from the little harbour, but whether they would or no, it drove them ashore.

No sooner were they come thither than they were recognized by the Rhodian sailors, who had landed from their ship, and one of them ran nimbly to a village hard by, whither the young Rhodian gentlemen had betaken themselves, and told the latter that, as luck would have it,[3] Cimon and Iphigenia were come thither aboard their ship, driven, like themselves, by stress of weather. They, hearing this, were greatly rejoiced and repairing in all haste to the sea-shore, with a number of the villagers, took Cimon, together with Iphigenia and all his company, who had now landed and taken counsel together to flee into some neighbouring wood, and carried them to the village. The news coming to Pasimondas, he made his complaint to the senate of the island and according as he had ordered it with them, Lysimachus, in whom the chief magistracy of the Rhodians was for that year vested, coming thither from the city with a great company of men-at-arms, haled Cimon and all his men to prison. On such wise did the wretched and lovelorn Cimon lose his Iphigenia, scantwhile before won of him, without having taken of her more than a kiss or two; whilst she herself was received by many noble ladies of

Rhodes and comforted as well for the chagrin had of her seizure as for the fatigue suffered by reason of the troubled sea; and with them she abode against the day appointed for her nuptials.

As for Cimon and his companions, their lives were granted them, in consideration of the liberty given by them to the young Rhodians the day before,—albeit Pasimondas used his utmost endeavour to procure them to be put to death,—and they were condemned to perpetual prison, wherein, as may well be believed, they abode woebegone and without hope of any relief. However, whilst Pasimondas, as most he might, hastened the preparations for his coming nuptials, fortune, as if repenting her of the sudden injury done to Cimon, brought about a new circumstance for his deliverance, the which was on this wise. Pasimondas had a brother called Ormisdas, less in years, but not in merit, than himself, who had been long in treaty for the hand of a fair and noble damsel of the city, by name Cassandra, whom Lysimachus ardently loved, and the match had sundry times been broken off by divers untoward accidents. Now Pasimondas, being about to celebrate his own nuptials with the utmost splendour, bethought himself that it were excellently well done if he could procure Ormisdas likewise to take wife on the same occasion, not to resort afresh to expense and festival making. Accordingly, he took up again the parleys with Cassandra's parents and brought them to a successful issue; wherefore he and his brother agreed, in concert with them, that Ormisdas should take Cassandra to wife on the same day whenas himself took Iphigenia.

Lysimachus hearing this, it was beyond measure displeasing to him, for that he saw himself bereaved of the hope which he cherished, that, an Ormisdas took her not, he should certainly have her. However, like a wise man, he kept his chagrin hidden and fell to considering on what wise he might avail to hinder this having effect, but could see no way possible save the carrying her off. This seemed easy to him to compass for the office which he held, but he accounted the deed far more dishonourable than if he had not held the office in question. Ultimately, however, after long deliberation, honour gave place to love and he determined, come what might of it, to carry off Cassandra. Then, bethinking himself of the company he must have and the course he must hold to do this, he remembered him of Cimon, whom he had in prison with his comrades, and concluded that he might have no better or trustier companion than Cimon in this affair.

Accordingly, that same night he had him privily into his chamber and proceeded to bespeak him on this wise: 'Cimon, like as the gods are very excellent and bountiful givers of things to men, even so are they most sagacious provers of their virtues, and those, whom they find resolute and constant under all circumstances, they hold deserving, as the most worthy, of the highest recompenses. They have been minded to have more certain proof of thy worth than could be shown by thee within the limits of thy father's house, whom I know to be abundantly endowed with riches; wherefore, first, with the poignant instigations of love they brought thee from a senseless animal to be a man, and after with foul fortune and at this present with prison dour, they would fain try if thy spirit change not from that which it was, whenas thou wast scantwhile glad of the gotten prize. If that[4] be the same as it was erst, they never yet vouchsafed thee aught so gladsome as that which they are presently prepared to bestow on thee and which, so thou mayst recover thy wonted powers and resume thy whilom spirit, I purpose to discover to thee.

Pasimondas, rejoicing in thy misadventure and a diligent promoter of thy death, bestirreth himself as most he may to celebrate his nuptials with thine Iphigenia, so therein he may enjoy the prize which fortune first blithely conceded thee and after, growing troubled, took from thee of a sudden. How much this must grieve thee, an thou love as I believe, I know by myself, to whom Ormisdas his brother prepareth in one same day to do a like injury in the person of Cassandra, whom I love over all else. To escape so great an unright and annoy of fortune, I see no way left open of her to us, save the valour of our souls and the might of our right hands, wherein it behoveth us take our swords and make us a way to the carrying off of our two mistresses, thee for the second and me for the first time. If, then, it be dear to thee to have again —I will not say thy liberty, whereof methinketh thou reckest little without thy lady, but—thy mistress, the gods have put her in thy hands, an thou be willing to second me in my emprize.'

All Cimon's lost spirit was requickened in him by these words and he replied, without overmuch consideration, 'Lysimachus, thou canst have no stouter or trustier comrade than myself in such an enterprise, an that be to ensue thereof for me which thou avouchest; wherefore do thou command me that which thou deemest should be done of me, and thou shalt find thyself wonder-puissantly seconded.' Then said Lysimachus, 'On the third day from this the new-married wives will for the first time enter their husbands' houses, whereinto thou with thy companions armed and I with certain of my friends, in whom I put great trust, will make our way towards nightfall and snatching up our mistresses out of the midst of the guests, will carry them off to a ship, which I have caused secretly equip, slaying whosoever shall presume to offer opposition.' The devise pleased Cimon and he abode quiet in prison until the appointed time.

The wedding-day being come, great and magnificent was the pomp of the festival and every part of the two brothers' house was full of mirth and merrymaking; whereupon Lysimachus, having made ready everything needful, divided Cimon and his companions, together with his own friends, all armed under their clothes, into three parties and having first kindled them to his purpose with many words, secretly despatched one party to the harbour, so none might hinder their going aboard the ship, whenas need should be. Then, coming with the other twain, whenas it seemed to him time, to Pasimondas his house, he left one party of them at the door, so as none might shut them up therewithin or forbid them the issue, and with Cimon and the rest went up by the stairs. Coming to the saloon where the new-wedded brides were seated orderly at meat with many other ladies, they rushed in upon them and overthrowing the tables, took each his mistress and putting them in the hands of their comrades, bade straightway carry them to the ship that was in waiting. The brides fell a-weeping and shrieking, as did likewise the other ladies and the servants, and the whole house was of a sudden full of clamour and lamentation.

Cimon and Lysimachus and their companions, drawing their swords, made for the stairs, without any opposition, all giving way to them, and as they descended, Pasimondas presented himself before them, with a great cudgel in his hand, being drawn thither by the outcry; but Cimon dealt him a swashing blow on the head and cleaving it sheer in sunder, laid him dead at his feet. The wretched Ormisdas, running to his brother's aid, was on like wise slain by one of Cimon's strokes, and divers others who sought to draw nigh them were in like manner wounded and beaten off by the companions of the latter and Lysimachus, who, leaving the house full of blood and clamour and weeping and woe, drew together and made their way to the ship with their prizes, unhindered of any. Here they embarked with their mistresses and all their companions, the shore being now full of armed folk come to the rescue of the ladies, and thrusting the oars into the water, made off, rejoicing, about their business. Coming presently to Crete, they were there joyfully received by many, both friends and kinsfolk, and espousing their mistresses with great pomp, gave themselves up to the glad enjoyment of their purchase. Loud and long were the clamours and differences in Cyprus and in Rhodes by reason of their doings; but, ultimately, their friends and kinsfolk, interposing in one and the other place, found means so to adjust matters that, after some exile, Cimon joyfully returned to Cyprus with Iphigenia, whilst Lysimachus on like wise returned to Rhodes with Cassandra, and each lived long and happily with his mistress in his own country."

1. Or farm (*villa*).
2. *i.e.* of music, vocal and instrumental.
3. *Per fortuna.* This may also be rendered "by tempest," *fortuna* being a name for a squall or hurricane, which Boccaccio uses elsewhere in the same sense.
4. *i.e.* thy spirit.

❧ 2 ❧

THE SECOND STORY

COSTANZA LOVETH MARTUCCIO GOMITO AND
HEARING THAT HE IS DEAD, EMBARKETH FOR
DESPAIR ALONE IN A BOAT, WHICH IS CARRIED BY
THE WIND TO SUSA. FINDING HER LOVER ALIVE AT
TUNIS, SHE DISCOVERETH HERSELF TO HIM AND HE,
BEING GREAT IN FAVOUR WITH THE KING FOR
COUNSELS GIVEN, ESPOUSETH HER AND
RETURNETH RICH WITH HER TO LIPARI

THE QUEEN, seeing Pamfilo's story at an end, after she had much commended it, enjoined Emilia to follow on, telling another, and she accordingly began thus: "Every one must naturally delight in those things wherein he seeth rewards ensue according to the affections;[1] and for that love in the long run deserveth rather happiness than affliction, I shall, intreating of the present theme, obey the queen with much greater pleasure to myself than I did the king in that of yesterday.

You must know, then, dainty dames, that near unto Sicily is an islet called Lipari, wherein, no great while agone, was a very fair damsel called Costanza, born of a very considerable family there. It chanced that a young man of the same island, called Martuccio Gomito, who was very agreeable and well bred and of approved worth[2] in his craft,[3] fell in love with her; and she in like manner so burned for him that she was never easy save whenas she saw him. Martuccio, wishing to have her to wife, caused demand her of her father, who answered that he was poor and that therefore he would not give her to him. The young man, enraged to see himself rejected for poverty, in concert with certain of his friends and kinsmen, equipped a light ship and swore never to return to Lipari, except rich. Accordingly, he departed thence and turning corsair, fell to cruising off the coast of Barbary and plundering all who were weaker than himself; wherein fortune was favourable enough to him, had he known how to set bounds to his wishes; but, it sufficing him not to have waxed very rich, he and his comrades, in a brief space of time, it befell that, whilst they sought to grow overrich, he was, after a long defence, taken and plundered with all his companions by certain ships of the Saracens, who, after scuttling the vessel and sacking the greater part of the crew, carried Martuccio to Tunis, where he was put in prison and long kept in misery.

The news was brought to Lipari, not by one or by two, but by many and divers persons, that he and all on board the bark had been drowned; whereupon the girl, who had been beyond measure woebegone for her lover's departure, hearing that he was dead with the others, wept sore and resolved in herself to live no longer; but, her heart suffering her not to slay herself by violence, she determined to give a new occasion[4] to her death.[5] Accordingly, she issued secretly forth of her father's house one night and betaking herself to the harbour, happened upon a fishing smack, a little aloof from the other ships, which, for that its owners had but then landed therefrom, she found furnished with mast and sail and oars. In this she hastily embarked and rowed herself out to sea; then, being somewhat skilled in the mariner's art, as the women of that island mostly are, she made sail and casting the oars and rudder adrift, committed herself altogether to the mercy of the waves, conceiving that it must needs happen that the wind would either overturn a boat without lading or steersman or drive it upon some rock and break it up, whereby she could not, even if she would, escape, but must of necessity be drowned. Accordingly, wrapping her head in a mantle, she laid herself, weeping, in the bottom of the boat.

But it befell altogether otherwise than as she conceived, for that, the wind being northerly and very light and there being well nigh no sea, the boat rode it out in safety and brought her on the morrow, about vespers, to a beach near a town called Susa, a good hundred miles beyond Tunis. The girl, who, for aught that might happen, had never lifted nor meant to lift her head, felt nothing of being ashore more than at sea;[6] but, as chance would have it, there was on the beach, whenas the bark struck upon it, a poor woman in act to take up from the sun the nets of the fishermen her masters, who, seeing the bark, marvelled how it should be left to strike full sail upon the land. Thinking that the fishermen aboard were asleep, she went up to the bark and seeing none therein but the damsel aforesaid, who slept fast, called her many times and having at last aroused her and knowing her by her habit for a Christian, asked her in Latin how she came there in that bark all alone. The girl, hearing her speak Latin, misdoubted her a shift of wind must have driven her back to Lipari and starting suddenly to her feet, looked about her, but knew not the country, and seeing herself on land, asked the good woman where she was; to which she answered, 'Daughter mine, thou art near unto Susa in Barbary.' The girl, hearing this, was woeful for that God had not chosen to vouchsafe her the death she sought, and being in fear of shame and knowing not what to do, she seated herself at the foot of her bark and fell a-weeping.

The good woman, seeing this, took pity upon her and brought her, by dint of entreaty, into a little hut of hers and there so humoured her that she told her how she came thither; whereupon, seeing that she was fasting, she set before her her own dry bread and somewhat of fish and water and so besought her that she ate a little. Costanza after asked her who she was that she spoke Latin thus; to which she answered that she was from Trapani and was called Carapresa and served certain Christian fishermen there. The girl, hearing the name of Carapresa, albeit she was exceeding woebegone and knew not what reason moved her thereunto, took it unto herself for a good augury to have heard this name[7] and began to hope, without knowing what, and somewhat to abate of her wish to die. Then, without discovering who or whence she was, she earnestly besought the good woman to have pity, for the love of God, on her youth and give her some counsel how she might escape any affront being offered her.

Carapresa, like a good woman as she was, hearing this, left her in her hut, whilst she hastily gathered up her nets; then, returning to her, she wrapped her from head to foot in her own mantle and carried her to Susa, where she said to her, 'Costanza, I will bring thee into the house of a very good Saracen lady, whom I serve oftentimes in her occasions and who is old and pitiful. I will commend thee to her as most I may and I am very certain that she will gladly receive thee and use thee as a daughter; and do thou, abiding with her, study thine utmost, in serving her, to gain her favour, against God send thee better fortune.' And as she said, so she did. The lady, who was well stricken in years, hearing the woman's story, looked the girl in the face and fell a-weeping; then taking her by the hand, she kissed her on the forehead and carried her into her house, where she and sundry other women abode, without any man, and wrought all with their hands at various crafts, doing divers works of silk and palm-fibre and leather.

Costanza soon learned to do some of these and falling to working with the rest, became in such favour with the lady and the others that it was a marvellous thing; nor was it long before, with their teaching, she learnt their language.

What while she abode thus at Susa, being now mourned at home for lost and dead, it befell that, one Mariabdela[8] being King of Tunis, a certain youth of great family and much puissance in Granada, avouching that that kingdom belonged to himself, levied a great multitude of folk and came upon King Mariabdela, to oust him from the kingship. This came to the ears of Martuccio Gomito in prison and he knowing the Barbary language excellent well and hearing that the king was making great efforts for his defence, said to one of those who had him and his fellows in keeping, 'An I might have speech of the king, my heart assureth me that I could give him a counsel, by which he should gain this his war.' The keeper reported these words to his chief, and he carried them incontinent to the king, who bade fetch Martuccio and asked him what might be his counsel; whereto he made answer on this wise, 'My lord, if, what time I have otherwhiles frequented these your dominions, I have noted aright the order you keep in your battles, meseemeth you wage them more with archers than with aught else; wherefore, if a means could be found whereby your adversary's bowmen should lack of arrows, whilst your own had abundance thereof, methinketh your battle would be won.' 'Without doubt,' answered the king, 'and this might be compassed, I should deem myself assured of victory.' Whereupon, 'My lord,' quoth Martuccio, 'an you will, this may very well be done, and you shall hear how. You must let make strings for your archers' bows much thinner than those which are everywhere commonly used and after let make arrows, the notches whereof shall not serve but for these thin strings. This must be so secretly done that your adversary should know nought thereof; else would he find a remedy therefor; and the reason for which I counsel you thus is this. After your enemy's archers and your own shall have shot all their arrows, you know that, the battle lasting, it will behove your foes to gather up the arrows shot by your men and the latter in like manner to gather theirs; but the enemy will not be able to make use of your arrows, by reason of the strait notches which will not take their thick strings, whereas the contrary will betide your men of the enemy's arrows, for that the thin strings will excellently well take the wide-notched arrows; and so your men will have abundance of ammunition, whilst the others will suffer default thereof.'

The king, who was a wise prince, was pleased with Martuccio's counsel and punctually following it, found himself thereby to have won his war. Wherefore Martuccio became in high favour with him and rose in consequence to great and rich estate. The report of these things spread over the land and it came presently to Costanza's ears that Martuccio Gomito, whom she had long deemed dead, was alive, whereupon the love of him, that was now grown cool in her heart, broke out of a sudden into fresh flame and waxed greater than ever, whilst dead hope revived in her. Therewithal she altogether discovered her every adventure to the good lady, with whom she dwelt, and told her that she would fain go to Tunis, so she might satisfy her eyes of that whereof her ears had made them desireful, through the reports received. The old lady greatly commended her purpose and taking ship with her, carried her, as if she had been her mother, to Tunis, where they were honourably entertained in the house of a kinswoman of hers. There she despatched Carapresa, who had come with them, to see what she could learn of Martuccio, and she, finding him alive and in great estate and reporting this to the old gentlewoman, it pleased the latter to will to be she who should signify unto Martuccio that his Costanza was come thither to him; wherefore, betaking herself one day whereas he was, she said to him, 'Martuccio, there is come to my house a servant of thine from Lipari, who would fain speak with thee privily there; wherefore, not to trust to others, I have myself, at his desire, come to give thee notice thereof.' He thanked her and followed her to her house, where when

Costanza saw him, she was like to die of gladness and unable to contain herself, ran straightway with open arms to throw herself on his neck; then, embracing him, without availing to say aught, she fell a-weeping tenderly, both for compassion of their past ill fortunes and for present gladness.

Martuccio, seeing his mistress, abode awhile dumb for amazement, then said sighing, 'O my Costanza, art thou then yet alive? It is long since I heard that thou wast lost; nor in our country was aught known of thee.' So saying, he embraced her, weeping, and kissed her tenderly. Costanza then related to him all that had befallen her and the honourable treatment which she had received from the gentlewoman with whom she dwelt; and Martuccio, after much discourse, taking leave of her, repaired to the king his master and told him all, to wit, his own adventures and those of the damsel, adding that, with his leave, he meant to take her to wife, according to our law. The king marvelled at these things and sending for the damsel and hearing from her that it was even as Martuccio had avouched, said to her, 'Then hast thou right well earned him to husband.' Then, letting bring very great and magnificent gifts, he gave part thereof to her and part to Martuccio, granting them leave to do one with the other that which was most pleasing unto each of them; whereupon Martuccio, having entreated the gentlewoman who had harboured Costanza with the utmost honour and thanked her for that which she had done to serve her and bestowed on her such gifts as sorted with her quality, commended her to God and took leave of her, he and his mistress, not without many tears from the latter. Then, with the king's leave, they embarked with Carapresa on board a little ship and returned with a fair wind to Lipari, where so great was the rejoicing that it might never be told. There Martuccio took Costanza to wife and held great and goodly nuptials; after which they long in peace and repose had enjoyment of their loves."

---

1. Syn. inclinations (*affezioni*). This is a somewhat obscure passage, owing to the vagueness of the word *affezioni* (syn. *affetti*) in this position, and may be rendered, with about equal probability, in more than one way.
2. Or "eminent" (*valoroso*), *i.e.* in modern parlance, "a man of merit and talent."
3. *Valoroso nel suo mestiere*. It does not appear that Martuccio was a craftsman and it is possible, therefore, that Boccaccio intended the word *mestiere* to be taken in the sense (to me unknown) of "condition" or "estate," in which case the passage would read, "a man of worth for (*i.e.* as far as comported with) his [mean] estate"; and this seems a probable reading.
4. Lit. necessity (*necessità*).
5. *i.e.* to use a new (or strange) fashion of exposing herself to an inevitable death (*nuova necessità dare alla sua morte*).
6. *i.e.* knew not whether she was ashore or afloat, so absorbed was she in her despair.
7. Or "augured well from the hearing of the name." *Carapresa* signifies "a dear or precious prize, gain or capture."
8. This name is apparently a distortion of the Arabic *Amir Abdullah*.

THE THIRD STORY

PIETRO BOCCAMAZZA, FLEEING WITH AGNOLELLA, FALLETH AMONG THIEVES; THE GIRL ESCAPETH THROUGH A WOOD AND IS LED [BY FORTUNE] TO A CASTLE, WHILST PIETRO IS TAKEN BY THE THIEVES, BUT PRESENTLY, ESCAPING FROM THEIR HANDS, WINNETH, AFTER DIVERS ADVENTURES, TO THE CASTLE WHERE HIS MISTRESS IS AND ESPOUSING HER, RETURNETH WITH HER TO ROME

THERE WAS none among all the company but commended Emilia's story, which the queen seeing to be finished, turned to Elisa and bade her follow on. Accordingly, studious to obey, she began: "There occurreth to my mind, charming ladies, an ill night passed by a pair of indiscreet young lovers; but, for that many happy days ensued thereon, it pleaseth me to tell the story, as one that conformeth to our proposition.

There was, a little while agone, at Rome,—once the head, as it is nowadays the tail of the world,[1]—a youth, called Pietro Boccamazza, of a very worshipful family among those of the city, who fell in love with a very fair and lovesome damsel called Agnolella, the daughter of one Gigliuozzo Saullo, a plebeian, but very dear to the Romans, and loving her, he contrived so to do that the girl began to love him no less than he loved her; whereupon, constrained by fervent love and himseeming he might no longer brook the cruel pain that the desire he had of her gave him, he demanded her in marriage; which no sooner did his kinsfolk know than they all repaired to him and chid him sore for that which he would have done; and on the other hand they gave Gigliuozzo to understand that he should make no account of Pietro's words, for that, an he did this, they would never have him for friend or kinsman. Pietro seeing that way barred whereby alone he deemed he might avail to win to his desire, was like to die of chagrin, and had Gigliuozzo consented, he would have taken his daughter to wife, in despite of all his kindred. However, he determined, an it liked the girl, to contrive to give effect to their wishes, and having assured himself, by means of an intermediary, that this was agreeable to her, he agreed with her that she should flee with him from Rome.

Accordingly, having taken order for this, Pietro arose very early one morning and taking horse with the damsel, set out for Anagni, where he had certain friends in whom he trusted greatly. They had no leisure to make a wedding of it, for that they feared to be followed, but rode on, devising of their love and now and again kissing one another. It chanced that, when they came mayhap eight miles from Rome, the way not being overwell known to Pietro, they took a path to the left, whereas they should have kept to the right; and scarce had they ridden more than two miles farther when they found themselves near a little castle, wherefrom, as soon as they were seen, there issued suddenly a dozen footmen. The girl, espying these, whenas they were already close upon them, cried out, saying, 'Pietro, let us begone, for we are attacked'; then, turning her rouncey's head, as best she knew, towards a great wood hard by, she clapped her spurs fast to his flank and held on to the saddlebow, whereupon the nag, feeling himself goaded, bore her into the wood at a gallop.

Pietro, who went gazing more at her face than at the road, not having become so quickly aware as she of the new comers, was overtaken and seized by them, whilst he still looked, without yet perceiving them, to see whence they should come. They made him alight from his hackney and enquired who he was, which he having told, they proceeded to take counsel together and said, 'This fellow is of the friends of our enemies; what else should we do but take from him these clothes and this nag and string him up to one of yonder oaks, to spite the Orsini?' They all fell in with this counsel and bade Pietro put off his clothes, which as he was in act to do, foreboding him by this of the ill fate which awaited him, it chanced that an ambush of good five-and-twenty footmen started suddenly out upon the others, crying, 'Kill! Kill!' The rogues, taken by surprise, let Pietro be and turned to stand upon their defence, but, seeing themselves greatly outnumbered by their assailants, betook themselves to flight, whilst the others pursued them.

Pietro, seeing this, hurriedly caught up his gear and springing on his hackney, addressed himself, as best he might, to flee by the way he had seen his mistress take; but finding her not and seeing neither road nor footpath in the wood neither perceiving any horse's hoof marks, he was the woefullest man alive; and as soon as himseemed he was safe and out of reach of those who had taken him, as well as of the others by whom they had been assailed, he began to drive hither and thither about the wood, weeping and calling; but none answered him and he dared not turn back and knew not where he might come, an he went forward, more by token that he was in fear of the wild beasts that use to harbour in the woods, at once for himself and for his mistress, whom he looked momently to see strangled of some bear or some wolf. On this wise, then, did the unlucky Pietro range all day about the wood, crying and calling, whiles going backward, when as he thought to go forward, until, what with shouting and weeping and fear and long fasting, he was so spent that he could no more and seeing the night come and knowing not what other course to take, he dismounted from his hackney and tied the latter to a great oak, into which he climbed, so he might not be devoured of the wild beasts in the night. A little after the moon rose and the night being very clear and bright, he abode there on wake, sighing and weeping and cursing his ill luck, for that he durst not go to sleep, lest he should fall, albeit, had he had more commodity thereof, grief and the concern in which he was for his mistress would not have suffered him to sleep.

Meanwhile, the damsel, fleeing, as we have before said, and knowing not whither to betake herself, save whereas it seemed good to her hackney to carry her, fared on so far into the wood that she could not see where she had entered, and went wandering all day about that desert place, no otherwise than as Pietro had done, now pausing [to hearken] and now going on, weeping the while and calling and making moan of her illhap. At last, seeing that Pietro came not and it being now eventide, she happened on a little path, into which her hackney turned, and following it, after she had ridden some two or more miles she saw a little house afar off. Thither she made her way as quickliest she might and found there a good man sore stricken in years and a woman, his wife alike old, who, seeing her alone, said to her, 'Daughter, what dost thou alone at this hour in these parts?' The damsel replied, weeping, that she had lost her company in the wood and enquired how near she was to Anagni. 'Daughter mine,' answered the good man, 'this is not the way to go to Anagni; it is more than a dozen miles hence.' Quoth the girl, 'And how far is it hence to any habitations where I may have a lodging for the night?' To which the good man answered, 'There is none anywhere so near that thou mayst come thither by daylight.' Then said the damsel, 'Since I can go no otherwhere, will it please you harbour me here to-night for the love of God?' 'Young lady,' replied the old man, 'thou art very welcome to abide with us this night; algates, we must warn you that there are many ill companies, both of friends and of foes that come and go about these parts both by day and by night, who many a time do us sore annoy and great mischief; and if, by ill chance, thou being here, there come any of them and seeing thee, fair and young as thou art, should offer to do thee affront and shame, we could not avail to succour thee therefrom. We deem it well to apprise thee of this, so that, an it betide, thou mayst not be able to complain of us.'

The girl, seeing that it was late, albeit the old man's words affrighted her, said, 'An it please God, He will keep both you and me from that annoy; and even if it befall me, it were a much less evil to be maltreated of men than to be mangled of the wild beasts in the woods.' So saying, she alighted from the rouncey and entered the poor man's house, where she supped with him on such poor fare as they had and after, all clad as she was, cast herself, together with them, on a little bed of theirs. She gave not over sighing and bewailing her own mishap and that of Pietro all night, knowing not if she might hope other than ill of him; and when it drew near unto morning, she heard a great trampling of folk approaching, whereupon she arose and betaking herself to a great courtyard, that lay behind the little house, saw in a corner a great heap of hay, in which she hid herself, so she might not be so quickly found, if those folk should come thither. Hardly had she made an end of hiding herself when these, who were a great company of ill knaves, came to the door of the little house and causing open to them, entered and found Agnolella's hackney yet all saddled and bridled; whereupon they asked who was there and the good man, not seeing the girl, answered, 'None is here save ourselves; but this rouncey, from whomsoever it may have escaped, came hither yestereve and we brought it into the house, lest the wolves should eat it.' 'Then,' said the captain of the troop, 'since it hath none other master, it is fair prize for us.'

Thereupon they all dispersed about the little house and some went into the courtyard, where, laying down their lances and targets, it chanced that one of them, knowing not what else to do, cast his lance into the hay and came very near to slay the hidden girl and she to discover herself, for that the lance passed so close to her left breast that the steel tore a part of her dress, wherefore she was like to utter a great cry, fearing to be wounded; but, remembering where she was, she abode still, all fear-stricken. Presently, the rogues, having dressed the kids and other meat they had with them and eaten and drunken, went off, some hither and some thither, about their affairs, and carried with them the girl's hackney. When they had gone some distance, the good man asked his wife, 'What befell of our young woman, who came thither yestereve? I have seen nothing of her since we arose.' The good wife replied that she knew not and went looking for her, whereupon the girl, hearing that the rogues were gone, came forth of the hay, to the no small contentment of her host, who, rejoiced to see that she had not fallen into their hands, said to her, it now growing day, 'Now that the day cometh, we will, an it please thee, accompany thee to a castle five miles hence, where thou wilt be in safety; but needs must thou go afoot, for yonder ill folk, that now departed hence, have carried off thy rouncey.' The girl concerned herself little about the nag, but besought them for God's sake to bring her to the castle in question, whereupon they set out and came thither about half tierce.

Now this castle belonged to one of the Orsini family, by name Lionello di Campodifiore, and there by chance was his wife, a very pious and good lady, who, seeing the girl, knew her forthright and received her with joy and would fain know orderly how she came thither. Agnolella told her all and the lady, who knew Pietro on like wise, as being a friend of her husband's, was grieved for the ill chance that had betided and hearing where he had been taken, doubted not but he was dead; wherefore she said to Agnolella, 'Since thou knowest not what is come of Pietro, thou shalt abide here till such time as I shall have a commodity to send thee safe to Rome.'

Meanwhile Pietro abode, as woebegone as could be, in the oak, and towards the season of the first sleep, he saw a good score of wolves appear, which came all about his hackney, as soon as they saw him. The horse, scenting them, tugged at his bridle, till he broke it, and would have fled, but being surrounded and unable to escape, he defended himself a great while with his teeth and his hoofs. At last, however, he was brought down and strangled and quickly disembowelled by the wolves, which took all their fill of his flesh and having devoured him, made off, without leaving aught but the bones, whereat Pietro, to whom it seemed he had in the rouncey a companion and a support in his troubles, was sore dismayed and misdoubted he should never avail to win forth of the wood. However, towards daybreak, being perished with cold in the oak and looking still all about him, he caught sight of a great fire before him, mayhap a mile off, wherefore, as soon as it was grown broad day, he came down from the oak, not without fear, and making for the fire, fared on till he came to the place, where he found shepherds eating and making merry about it, by whom he was received for compassion.

After he had eaten and warmed himself, he acquainted them with his misadventure and telling them how he came thither alone, asked them if there was in those parts a village or castle, to which he might betake himself. The shepherds answered that some three miles thence there was a castle belonging to Lionello di Campodifiore, whose lady was presently there; whereat Pietro was much rejoiced and besought them that one of them should accompany him to the castle, which two of them readily did. There he found some who knew him and was in act to enquire for a means of having search made about the forest for the damsel, when he was bidden to the lady's presence and incontinent repaired to her. Never was joy like unto his, when he saw Agnolella with her, and he was all consumed with desire to embrace her, but forbore of respect for the lady, and if he was glad, the girl's joy was no less great. The gentle lady, having welcomed him and made much of him and heard from him what had betided him, chid him amain of that which he would have done against the will of his kinsfolk; but, seeing that he was e'en resolved upon this and that it was agreeable to the girl also, she said in herself, 'Why do I weary myself in vain? These two love and know each other and both are friends of my husband. Their desire is an honourable one and meseemeth it is pleasing to God, since the one of them hath scaped the gibbet and the other the lance-thrust and both the wild beasts of the wood; wherefore be it as they will.' Then, turning to the lovers, she said to them, 'If you have it still at heart to be man and wife, it is my pleasure also; be it so, and let the nuptials be celebrated here at Lionello's expense. I will engage after to make peace between you and your families.' Accordingly, they were married then and there, to the great contentment of Pietro and the yet greater satisfaction of Agnolella, and the gentle lady made them honourable nuptials, in so far as might be in the mountains. There, with the utmost delight, they enjoyed the first-fruits of their love and a few days after, they took horse with the lady and returned, under good escort, to Rome, where she found Pietro's kinsfolk sore incensed at that which he had done, but contrived to make his peace with them, and he lived with his Agnolella in all peace and pleasure to a good old age."

---

1. Clement V. early in the fourteenth century removed the Papal See to Avignon, where it continued to be during the reigns of the five succeeding Popes, Rome being in the meantime abandoned by the Papal Court, till Gregory XI, in the year 1376 again took up his residence at the latter city. It is apparently to this circumstance that Boccaccio alludes in the text.

✣ 4 ✣

THE FOURTH STORY

RICCIARDO MANARDI, BEING FOUND BY MESSER LIZIO DA VALBONA WITH HIS DAUGHTER, ESPOUSETH HER AND ABIDETH IN PEACE WITH HER FATHER

ELISA HOLDING her peace and hearkening to the praises bestowed by the ladies her companions upon her story, the Queen charged Filostrato tell one of his own, whereupon he began, laughing, "I have been so often rated by so many of you ladies for having imposed on you matter for woeful discourse and such as tended to make you weep, that methinketh I am beholden, an I would in some measure requite you that annoy, to relate somewhat whereby I may make you laugh a little; and I mean therefore to tell you, in a very short story, of a love that, after no worse hindrance than sundry sighs and a brief fright, mingled with shame, came to a happy issue.

It is, then, noble ladies, no great while ago since there lived in Romagna a gentleman of great worth and good breeding, called Messer Lizio da Valbona, to whom, well nigh in his old age, it chanced there was born of his wife, Madam Giacomina by name, a daughter, who grew up fair and agreeable beyond any other of the country; and for that she was the only child that remained to her father and mother, they loved and tendered her exceeding dear and guarded her with marvellous diligence, looking to make some great alliance by her. Now there was a young man of the Manardi of Brettinoro, comely and lusty of his person, by name Ricciardo, who much frequented Messer Lizio's house and conversed amain with him and of whom the latter and his lady took no more account than they would have taken of a son of theirs. Now, this Ricciardo, looking once and again upon the young lady and seeing her very fair and sprightly and commendable of manners and fashions, fell desperately in love with her, but was very careful to keep his love secret. The damsel presently became aware thereof and without anywise seeking to shun the stroke, began on like wise to love him; whereat Ricciardo was mightily rejoiced. He had many a time a mind to speak to her, but kept silence of misdoubtance; however, one day, taking courage and opportunity, he said to her, 'I prithee, Caterina, cause me not die of love.' To which she straightway made answer, 'Would God thou wouldst not cause *me* die!'

This answer added much courage and pleasure to Ricciardo and he said to her, 'Never shall aught that may be agreeable to thee miscarry[1] for me; but it resteth with thee to find a means of saving thy life and mine.' 'Ricciardo,' answered she, 'thou seest how straitly I am guarded;

240

wherefore, for my part, I cannot see how thou mayst avail to come at me; but, if thou canst see aught that I may do without shame to myself, tell it me and I will do it.' Ricciardo, having bethought himself of sundry things, answered promptly, 'My sweet Caterina, I can see no way, except that thou lie or make shift to come upon the gallery that adjoineth thy father's garden, where an I knew that thou wouldst be anights, I would without fail contrive to come to thee, how high soever it may be.' 'If thou have the heart to come thither,' rejoined Caterina, 'methinketh I can well enough win to be there.' Ricciardo assented and they kissed each other once only in haste and went their ways.

Next day, it being then near the end of May, the girl began to complain before her mother that she had not been able to sleep that night for the excessive heat. Quoth the lady, 'Of what heat dost thou speak, daughter? Nay, it was nowise hot.' 'Mother mine,' answered Caterina, 'you should say "To my seeming," and belike you would say sooth; but you should consider how much hotter are young girls than ladies in years.' 'Daughter mine,' rejoined the lady, 'that is true; but I cannot make it cold and hot at my pleasure, as belike thou wouldst have me do. We must put up with the weather, such as the seasons make it; maybe this next night will be cooler and thou wilt sleep better.' 'God grant it may be so!' cried Caterina. 'But it is not usual for the nights to go cooling, as it groweth towards summer.' 'Then what wouldst thou have done?' asked the mother; and she answered, 'An it please my father and you, I would fain have a little bed made in the gallery, that is beside his chamber and over his garden, and there sleep. There I should hear the nightingale sing and having a cooler place to lie in, I should fare much better than in your chamber.' Quoth the mother, 'Daughter, comfort thyself; I will tell thy father, and as he will, so will we do.'

Messer Lizio hearing all this from his wife, said, for that he was an old man and maybe therefore somewhat cross-grained, 'What nightingale is this to whose song she would sleep? I will yet make her sleep to the chirp of the crickets.' Caterina, coming to know this, more of despite than for the heat, not only slept not that night, but suffered not her mother to sleep, still complaining of the great heat. Accordingly, next morning, the latter repaired to her husband and said to him, 'Sir, you have little tenderness for yonder girl; what mattereth it to you if she lie in the gallery? She could get no rest all night for the heat. Besides, can you wonder at her having a mind to hear the nightingale sing, seeing she is but a child? Young folk are curious of things like themselves. Messer Lizio, hearing this, said, 'Go to, make her a bed there, such as you think fit, and bind it about with some curtain or other, and there let her lie and hear the nightingale sing to her heart's content.'

The girl, learning this, straightway let make a bed in the gallery and meaning to lie there that same night, watched till she saw Ricciardo and made him a signal appointed between them, by which he understood what was to be done. Messer Lizio, hearing the girl gone to bed, locked a door that led from his chamber into the gallery and betook himself likewise to sleep. As for Ricciardo, as soon as he heard all quiet on every hand, he mounted a wall, with the aid of a ladder, and thence, laying hold of certain toothings of another wall, he made his way, with great toil and danger, if he had fallen, up to the gallery, where he was quietly received by the girl with the utmost joy. Then, after many kisses, they went to bed together and took delight and pleasure one of another well nigh all that night, making the nightingale sing many a time. The nights being short and the delight great and it being now, though they thought it not, near day, they fell asleep without any covering, so overheated were they what with the weather and what with their sport, Caterina having her right arm entwined about Ricciardo's neck and holding him with the left hand by that thing which you ladies think most shame to name among men.

As they slept on this wise, without awaking, the day came on and Messer Lizio arose and remembering him that his daughter lay in the gallery, opened the door softly, saying in himself, 'Let us see how the nightingale hath made Caterina sleep this night.' Then, going in, he softly lifted up the serge, wherewith the bed was curtained about, and saw his daughter and Ricciardo lying asleep, naked and uncovered, embraced as it hath before been set out; whereupon, having recognized Ricciardo, he went out again and repairing to his wife's chamber, called to her, saying, 'Quick, wife, get thee up and come see, for that thy daughter hath been so curious of the nightingale that she hath e'en taken it and hath it in hand.' 'How can that be?' quoth she; and he answered, 'Thou shalt see it, an thou come quickly.' Accordingly, she made haste to dress herself and quietly followed her husband to the bed, where, the curtain being drawn, Madam Giacomina might plainly see how her daughter had taken and held the nightingale, which she had so longed to hear sing; whereat the lady, holding herself sore deceived of Ricciardo, would have cried out and railed at him; but Messer Lizio said to her, 'Wife, as thou holdest my love dear, look thou say not a word, for, verily, since she hath gotten it, it shall be hers. Ricciardo is young and rich and gently born; he cannot make us other than a good son-in-law. An he would part from me on good terms, needs must he first marry her, so it will be found that he hath put the nightingale in his own cage and not in that of another.'

The lady was comforted to see that her husband was not angered at the matter and considering that her daughter had passed a good night and rested well and had caught the nightingale, to boot, she held her tongue. Nor had they abidden long after these words when Ricciardo awoke and seeing that it was broad day, gave himself over for lost and called Caterina, saying, 'Alack, my soul, how shall we do, for the day is come and hath caught me here?' Whereupon Messer Lizio came forward and lifting the curtain, answered, 'We shall do well.' When Ricciardo saw him, himseemed the heart was torn out of his body and sitting up in bed, he said, 'My lord, I crave your pardon for God's sake. I acknowledged to have deserved death, as a disloyal and wicked man; wherefore do you with me as best pleaseth you; but, I prithee, an it may be, have mercy on my life and let me not die.' 'Ricciardo,' answered Messer Lizio, 'the love that I bore thee and the faith I had in thee merited not this return; yet, since thus it is and youth hath carried thee away into such a fault, do thou, to save thyself from death and me from shame, take Caterina to thy lawful wife, so that, like as this night she hath been thine, she may e'en be thine so long as she shall live. On this wise thou mayst gain my pardon and thine own safety; but, an thou choose not to do this, commend thy soul to God.'

Whilst these words were saying, Caterina let go the nightingale and covering herself, fell to weeping sore and beseeching her father to pardon Ricciardo, whilst on the other hand she entreated her lover to do as Messer Lizio wished, so they might long pass such nights together in security. But there needed not overmany prayers, for that, on the one hand, shame of the fault committed and desire to make amends for it, and on the other, the fear of death and the wish to escape,—to say nothing of his ardent love and longing to possess the thing beloved,— made Ricciardo freely and without hesitation avouch himself ready to do that which pleased Messer Lizio; whereupon the latter borrowed of Madam Giacomina one of her rings and there, without budging, Ricciardo in their presence took Caterina to his wife. This done, Messer Lizio and his lady departed, saying, 'Now rest yourselves, for belike you have more need thereof than of rising.' They being gone, the young folk clipped each other anew and not having run more than half a dozen courses overnight, they ran other twain ere they arose and so made an end of the first day's tilting. Then they arose and Ricciardo having had more orderly conference with Messer Lizio, a few days after, as it beseemed, he married the damsel over again, in the presence of their friends and kinsfolk, and brought her with great pomp to his own house.

There he held goodly and honourable nuptials and after went long nightingale-fowling with her to his heart's content, in peace and solace, both by night and by day."

---

1. Lit. stand (*stare*), *i.e.* abide undone.

✦ 5 ✦

THE FIFTH STORY

GUIDOTTO DA CREMONA LEAVETH TO GIACOMINO DA PAVIA A DAUGHTER OF HIS AND DIETH. GIANNOLE DI SEVERINO AND MINGHINO DI MINGOLE FALL IN LOVE WITH THE GIRL AT FAENZA AND COME TO BLOWS ON HER ACCOUNT. ULTIMATELY SHE IS PROVED TO BE GIANNOLE'S SISTER AND IS GIVEN TO MINGHINO TO WIFE

ALL THE LADIES, hearkening to the story of the nightingale, had laughed so much that, though Filostrato had made an end of telling, they could not yet give over laughing. But, after they had laughed awhile, the queen said to Filostrato, "Assuredly, if thou afflictedest us ladies yesterday, thou hast so tickled us to-day that none of us can deservedly complain of thee." Then, addressing herself to Neifile, she charged her tell, and she blithely began to speak thus: "Since Filostrato, discoursing, hath entered into Romagna, it pleaseth me on like wise to go ranging awhile therein with mine own story.

I say, then, that there dwelt once in the city of Fano two Lombards, whereof the one was called Guidotto da Cremona and the other Giacomino da Pavia, both men advanced in years, who had in their youth been well nigh always soldiers and engaged in deeds of arms. Guidotto, being at the point of death and having nor son nor other kinsmen nor friend in whom he trusted more than in Giacomino, left him a little daughter he had, of maybe ten years of age, and all that he possessed in the world, and after having bespoken him at length of his affairs, he died. In those days it befell that the city of Faenza, which had been long in war and ill case, was restored to somewhat better estate and permission to sojourn there was freely conceded to all who had a mind to return thither; wherefore Giacomino, who had abidden there otherwhile and had a liking for the place, returned thither with all his good and carried with him the girl left him by Guidotto, whom he loved and entreated as his own child.

The latter grew up and became as fair a damsel as any in the city, ay, and as virtuous and well bred as she was fair; wherefore she began to be courted of many, but especially two very agreeable young men of equal worth and condition vowed her a very great love, insomuch that for jealousy they came to hold each other in hate out of measure. They were called, the one Giannole di Severino and the other Minghino di Mingole; nor was there either of them but would gladly have taken the young lady, who was now fifteen years old, to wife, had it been suffered of his kinsfolk; wherefore, seeing her denied to them on honourable wise, each cast about to get her for himself as best he might. Now Giacomino had in his house an old serving-wench and a serving-man, Crivello by name, a very merry and obliging person, with whom Giannole clapped up a great acquaintance and to whom, whenas himseemed time, he discovered his passion, praying him to be favourable to him in his endeavour to obtain his desire and promising him great things an he did this; whereto quoth Crivello, 'Look you, I can do nought for thee in this matter other than that, when next Giacomino goeth abroad to supper, I will bring thee whereas she may be; for that, an I offered to say a word to her in thy favour, she would never stop to listen to me. If this like thee, I promise it to thee and will do it; and do thou after, an thou know how, that which thou deemest shall best serve thy purpose.' Giannole answered that he desired nothing more and they abode on this understanding. Meanwhile Minghino, on his part, had suborned the maidservant and so wrought with her that she had several times carried messages to the girl and had well night inflamed her with love of him; besides which she had promised him to bring him in company with her, so soon as Giacomino should chance to go abroad of an evening for whatever cause.

Not long after this it chanced that, by Crivello's contrivance, Giacomino went to sup with a friend of his, whereupon Crivello gave Giannole to know thereof and appointed with him that, whenas he made a certain signal, he should come and would find the door open. The maid, on her side, knowing nothing of all this, let Minghino know that Giacomino was to sup abroad and bade him abide near the house, so that, whenas he saw a signal which she should make he might come and enter therein. The evening come, the two lovers, knowing nothing of each other's designs, but each misdoubting of his rival, came, with sundry companions armed, to enter into possession. Minghino, with his troop took up his quarters in the house of a friend of his, a neighbour of the young lady's; whilst Giannole and his friends stationed themselves at a little distance from the house. Meanwhile, Crivello and the maid, Giacomino being gone, studied each to send the other away. Quoth he to her, 'Why dost thou not get thee to bed? Why goest thou still wandering about the house?' 'And thou,' retorted she, 'why goest thou not for thy master? What awaitest thou here, now that thou hast supped?' And so neither could make other avoid the place; but Crivello, seeing the hour come that he had appointed with Giannole said in himself, 'What reck I of her? An she abide not quiet, she is like to smart for it.'

Accordingly, giving the appointed signal, he went to open the door, whereupon Giannole, coming up in haste with two companions, entered and finding the young lady in the saloon, laid hands on her to carry her off. The girl began to struggle and make a great outcry, as likewise did the maid, which Minghino hearing, he ran thither with his companions and seeing the young lady being presently dragged out at the door, they pulled out their swords and cried all, 'Ho, traitors, ye are dead men! The thing shall not go thus. What is this violence?' So saying, they fell to hewing at them, whilst the neighbors, issuing forth at the clamour with lights and arms, began to blame Giannole's behaviour and to second Minghino; wherefore, after long contention, the latter rescued the young lady from his rival and restored her to Giacomino's house. But, before the fray was over, up came the town-captain's officers and arrested many of them; and amongst the rest Minghino and Giannole and Crivello were taken and carried off to prison. After matters were grown quiet again, Giacomino returned home and was sore chagrined at that which had happened; but, enquiring how it had come about and finding that the girl was nowise at fault, he was somewhat appeased and determined in himself to marry her as quickliest he might, so the like should not again betide.

Next morning, the kinsfolk of the two young men, hearing the truth of the case and knowing the ill that might ensue thereof for the imprisoned youths, should Giacomino choose to do that which he reasonably might, repaired to him and prayed him with soft words to have regard, not so much to the affront which he had suffered from the little sense of the young men as to the love and goodwill which they believed he bore to themselves who thus besought him, submitting themselves and the young men who had done the mischief to any amends it should please him take. Giacomino, who had in his time seen many things and was a man of sense, answered briefly, 'Gentlemen, were I in mine own country, as I am in yours, I hold myself so much your friend that neither in this nor in otherwhat would I do aught save insomuch as it should please you; besides, I am the more bounden to comply with your wishes in this matter, inasmuch as you have therein offended against yourselves, for that the girl in question is not, as belike many suppose, of Cremona nor of Pavia; nay, she is a Faentine,[1] albeit neither I nor she nor he of whom I had her might ever learn whose daughter she was; wherefore, concerning that whereof you pray me, so much shall be done by me as you yourselves shall enjoin me.'

The gentlemen, hearing this, marvelled and returning thanks to Giacomino for his gracious answer, prayed him that it would please him tell them how she came to his hands and how he knew her to be a Faentine; whereto quoth he, 'Guidotto da Cremona, who was my friend and comrade, told me, on his deathbed, that, when this city was taken by the Emperor Frederick and everything given up to pillage, he entered with his companions into a house and found it full of booty, but deserted by its inhabitants, save only this girl, who was then some two years old or thereabouts and who, seeing him mount the stairs, called him "father"; whereupon, taking compassion upon her, he carried her off with him to Fano, together with all that was in the house, and dying there, left her to me with what he had, charging me marry her in due time and give her to her dowry that which had been hers. Since she hath come to marriageable age, I have not yet found an occasion of marrying her to my liking, though I would gladly do it, rather than that another mischance like that of yesternight should betide me on her account.'

Now among the others there was a certain Guiglielmino da Medicina, who had been with Guidotto in that affair[2] and knew very well whose house it was that he had plundered, and he, seeing the person in question[3] there among the rest, accosted him, saying, 'Bernabuccio, hearest thou what Giacomino saith?' 'Ay do I,' answered Bernabuccio, 'and I was presently in thought thereof, more by token that I mind me to have lost a little daughter of the age whereof Giacomino speaketh in those very troubles.' Quoth Guiglielmino, 'This is she for certain, for that I was once in company with Guidotto, when I heard him tell where he had done the plundering and knew it to be thy house that he had sacked; wherefore do thou bethink thee if thou mayst credibly recognize her by any token and let make search therefor; for thou wilt assuredly find that she is thy daughter.'

Accordingly, Bernabuccio bethought himself and remembered that she should have a little cross-shaped scar over her left ear, proceeding from a tumour, which he had caused cut for her no great while before that occurrence; whereupon, without further delay, he accosted Giacomino, who was still there, and besought him to carry him to his house and let him see the damsel. To this he readily consented and carrying him thither, let bring the girl before him. When Bernabuccio set eyes on her, himseemed he saw the very face of her mother, who was yet a handsome lady; nevertheless, not contenting himself with this, he told Giacomino that he would fain of his favour have leave to raise her hair a little above her left ear, to which the other consented. Accordingly, going up to the girl, who stood shamefast, he lifted up her hair with his right hand and found the cross; whereupon, knowing her to be indeed his daughter, he fell to weeping tenderly and embracing her, notwithstanding her resistance; then, turning to Giacomino, 'Brother mine,' quoth he, 'this is my daughter; it was my house Guidotto plundered and this girl was, in the sudden alarm, forgotten there of my wife and her mother; and until now we believed that she had perished with the house, which was burned me that same day.'

The girl, hearing this, and seeing him to be a man in years, gave credence to his words and submitting herself to his embraces, as moved by some occult instinct, fell a-weeping tenderly with him. Bernabuccio presently sent for her mother and other her kinswomen and for her sisters and brothers and presented her to them all, recounting the matter to them; then, after a thousand embraces, he carried her home to his house with the utmost rejoicing, to the great satisfaction of Giacomino. The town-captain, who was a man of worth, learning this and knowing that Giannole, whom he had in prison, was Bernabuccio's son and therefore the lady's own brother, determined indulgently to overpass the offence committed by him and released with him Minghino and Crivello and the others who were implicated in the affair. Moreover, he interceded with Bernabuccio and Giacomino concerning these matters and making peace between the two young men, gave the girl, whose name was Agnesa, to Minghino to wife, to the great contentment of all their kinsfolk; whereupon Minghino, mightily rejoiced, made a great and goodly wedding and carrying her home, lived with her many years after in peace and weal."

---

1. *i.e.* a native of Faenza (*Faentina*).
2. *A questo fatto, i.e.* at the storm of Faenza.
3. *i.e.* the owner of the plundered house.

༄ 6 ༄

THE SIXTH STORY

GIANNI DI PROCIDA BEING FOUND WITH A YOUNG LADY, WHOM HE LOVED AND WHO HAD BEEN GIVEN TO KING FREDERICK OF SICILY, IS BOUND WITH HER TO A STAKE TO BE BURNT; BUT, BEING RECOGNIZED BY RUGGIERI DELL' ORIA, ESCAPETH AND BECOMETH HER HUSBAND

NEIFILE'S STORY, which had much pleased the ladies, being ended, the queen bade Pampinea address herself to tell another, and she accordingly, raising her bright face, began: "Exceeding great, charming ladies, is the might of Love and exposeth lovers to sore travails, ay, and to excessive and unforeseen perils, as may be gathered from many a thing that hath been related both to-day and otherwhiles; nevertheless, it pleaseth me yet again to demonstrate it to you with a story of an enamoured youth.

Ischia is an island very near Naples, and therein, among others, was once a very fair and sprightly damsel, by name Restituta, who was the daughter of a gentleman of the island called Marino Bolgaro and whom a youth named Gianni, a native of a little island near Ischia, called Procida, loved more than his life, as she on like wise loved him. Not only did he come by day from Procida to see her, but oftentimes anights, not finding a boat, he had swum from Procida to Ischia, at the least to look upon the walls of her house, an he might no otherwise. During the continuance of this so ardent love, it befell that the girl, being all alone one summer day on the sea-shore, chanced, as she went from rock to rock, loosening shell-fish from the stones with a knife, upon a place hidden among the cliffs, where, at once for shade and for the commodity of a spring of very cool water that was there, certain young men of Sicily, coming from Naples, had taken up their quarters with a pinnace they had. They, seeing that she was alone and very handsome and was yet unaware of them, took counsel together to seize her and carry her off and put their resolve into execution. Accordingly, they took her, for all she made a great outcry, and carrying her aboard the pinnace, made the best of their way to Calabria, where they fell to disputing of whose she should be. Brief, each would fain have her; wherefore, being unable to agree among themselves and fearing to come to worse and to mar their affairs for her, they took counsel together to present her to Frederick, King of Sicily, who was then a young man and delighted in such toys. Accordingly, coming to Palermo, they made gift of the damsel to the king, who, seeing her to be fair, held her dear; but, for that he was presently somewhat infirm of his person, he commanded that, against he should be stronger, she should be lodged in a very goodly pavilion, belonging to a garden of his he called La Cuba, and there tended; and so it was done.

Great was the outcry in Ischia for the ravishment of the damsel and what most chagrined them was that they could not learn who they were that had carried her off; but Gianni, whom the thing concerned more than any other, not looking to get any news of this in Ischia and learning in what direction the ravishers had gone, equipped another pinnace and embarking therein, as quickliest as he might, scoured all the coast from La Minerva to La Scalea in Calabria, enquiring everywhere for news of the girl. Being told at La Scalea that she had been carried off to Palermo by some Sicilian sailors, he betook himself thither, as quickliest he might, and there, after much search, finding that she had been presented to the king and was by him kept under ward at La Cuba, he was sore chagrined and lost well nigh all hope, not only of ever having her again, but even of seeing her. Nevertheless, detained by love, having sent away his pinnace and seeing that he was known of none there, he abode behind and passing often by La Cuba, he chanced one day to catch sight of her at a window and she saw him, to the great contentment of them both.

Gianni, seeing the place lonely, approached as most he might and bespeaking her, was instructed by her how he must do, an he would thereafterward have further speech of her. He then took leave of her, having first particularly examined the ordinance of the place in every part, and waited till a good part of the night was past, when he returned thither and clambering up in places where a woodpecker had scarce found a foothold, he made his way into the garden. There he found a long pole and setting it against the window which his mistress had shown him, climbed up thereby lightly enough. The damsel, herseeming she had already lost her honour, for the preservation whereof she had in times past been somewhat coy to him, thinking that she could give herself to none more worthily than to him and doubting not to be able to induce him to carry her off, had resolved in herself to comply with him in every his desire; wherefore she had left the window open, so he might enter forthright. Accordingly, Gianni, finding it open, softly made his way into the chamber and laid himself beside the girl, who slept not and who, before they came to otherwhat, discovered to him all her intent, instantly beseeching him to take her thence and carry her away. Gianni answered that nothing could be so pleasing to him as this and promised that he would without fail, as soon as he should have taken his leave of her, put the matter in train on such wise that he might carry her away with him, the first time he returned thither. Then, embracing each other with exceeding pleasure, they took that delight beyond which Love can afford no greater, and after reiterating it again and again, they fell asleep, without perceiving it, in each other's arms.

Meanwhile, the king, who had at first sight been greatly taken with the damsel, calling her to mind and feeling himself well of body, determined, albeit it was nigh upon day, to go and abide with her awhile. Accordingly, he betook himself privily to La Cuba with certain of his servants and entering the pavilion, caused softly open the chamber wherein he knew the girl slept. Then, with a great lighted flambeau before him, he entered therein and looking upon the bed, saw her and Gianni lying asleep and naked in each other's arms; whereas he was of a sudden furiously incensed and flamed up into such a passion of wrath that it lacked of little but he had, without saying a word, slain them both then and there with a dagger he had by his side. However, esteeming it a very base thing of any man, much more a king, to slay two naked folk in their sleep, he contained himself and determined to put them to death in public and by fire; wherefore, turning to one only companion he had with him, he said to him, 'How deemest thou of this vile woman, on whom I had set my hope?' And after he asked him if he knew the young man who had dared enter his house to do him such an affront and such an outrage; but he answered that he remembered not ever to have seen him. The king then departed the chamber, full of rage, and commanded that the two lovers should be taken and bound, naked as they were, and that, as soon as it was broad day, they should be carried to Palermo and there bound to a stake, back to back, in the public place, where they should be kept till the hour of tierce, so they might be seen of all, and after burnt, even as they had deserved; and this said, he returned to his palace at Palermo, exceeding wroth.

The king gone, there fell many upon the two lovers and not only awakened them, but forthright without any pity took them and bound them; which when they saw, it may lightly be conceived if they were woeful and feared for their lives and wept and made moan. According to the king's commandment, they were carried to Palermo and bound to a stake in the public place, whilst the faggots and the fire were made ready before their eyes, to burn them at the hour appointed. Thither straightway flocked all the townsfolk, both men and women, to see the two lovers; the men all pressed to look upon the damsel and like as they praised her for fair and well made in every part of her body, even so, on the other hand, the women, who all ran to gaze upon the young man, supremely commended him for handsome and well shapen. But the wretched lovers, both sore ashamed, stood with bowed heads and bewailed their sorry fortune, hourly expecting the cruel death by fire.

Whilst they were thus kept against the appointed hour, the default of them committed, being bruited about everywhere, came to the ears of Ruggieri dell' Oria, a man of inestimable worth and then the king's admiral, whereupon he repaired to the place where they were bound and considering first the girl, commended her amain for beauty, then, turning to look upon the young man, knew him without much difficulty and drawing nearer to him, asked him if he were not Gianni di Procida. The youth, raising his eyes and recognizing the admiral, answered, 'My lord, I was indeed he of whom you ask; but I am about to be no more.' The admiral then asked him what had brought him to that pass, and he answered, 'Love and the king's anger.' The admiral caused him tell his story more at large and having heard everything from him as it had happened, was about to depart, when Gianni called him back and said to him, 'For God's sake, my lord, an it may be, get me one favour of him who maketh me to abide thus.' 'What is that?' asked Ruggieri; and Gianni said, 'I see I must die, and that speedily, and I ask, therefore, by way of favour,—as I am bound with my back to this damsel, whom I have loved more than my life, even as she hath loved me, and she with her back to me,—that we may be turned about with our faces one to the other, so that, dying, I may look upon her face and get me gone, comforted.' 'With all my heart,' answered Ruggieri, laughing; 'I will do on such wise that thou shalt yet see her till thou grow weary of her sight.'

Then, taking leave of him, he charged those who were appointed to carry the sentence into execution that they should proceed no farther therein, without other commandment of the king, and straightway betook himself to the latter, to whom, albeit he saw him sore incensed, he spared not to speak his mind, saying, 'King, in what have the two young folk offended against thee, whom thou hast commanded to be burned yonder in the public place?' The king told him and Ruggieri went on, 'The offence committed by them deserveth it indeed, but not from thee; for, like as defaults merit punishment, even so do good offices merit recompense, let alone grace and clemency. Knowest thou who these are thou wouldst have burnt?' The king answered no, and Ruggieri continued, 'Then I will have thee know them, so thou mayst see how discreetly[1] thou sufferest thyself to be carried away by the transports of passion. The young man is the son of Landolfo di Procida, own brother to Messer Gian di Procida,[2] by whose means thou art king and lord of this island, and the damsel is the daughter of Marino Bolgaro, to whose influence thou owest it that thine officers have not been driven forth of Ischia. Moreover, they are lovers who have long loved one another and constrained of love, rather than of will to do despite to thine authority, have done this sin, if that can be called sin which young folk do for love. Wherefore, then, wilt thou put them to death, whenas thou shouldst rather honour them with the greatest favours and boons at thy commandment?'

The king, hearing this and certifying himself that Ruggieri spoke sooth, not only forbore from proceeding to do worse, but repented him of that which he had done, wherefore he commanded incontinent that the two lovers should be loosed from the stake and brought before him; which was forthright done. Therewith, having fully acquainted himself with their case, he concluded that it behoved him requite them the injury he had done them with gifts and honour; wherefore he let clothe them anew on sumptuous wise and finding them of one accord, caused Gianni to take the damsel to wife. Then, making them magnificent presents, he sent them back, rejoicing, to their own country, where they were received with the utmost joyance and delight."

---

1. Iron., meaning "with how little discretion."
2. Gianni (Giovanni) di Procida was a Sicilian noble, to whose efforts in stirring up the island to revolt against Charles of Anjou was mainly due the popular rising known as the Sicilian Vespers (a.d. 1283) which expelled the French usurper from Sicily and transferred the crown to the house of Arragon. The Frederick (a.d. 1296-1337) named in the text was the fourth prince of the latter dynasty.

THE SEVENTH STORY

TEODORO, BEING ENAMOURED OF VIOLANTE, DAUGHTER OF MESSER AMERIGO HIS LORD, GETTETH HER WITH CHILD AND IS CONDEMNED TO BE HANGED; BUT, BEING RECOGNIZED AND DELIVERED BY HIS FATHER, AS THEY ARE LEADING HIM TO THE GALLOWS, SCOURGING HIM THE WHILE, HE TAKETH VIOLANTE TO WIFE

THE LADIES, who abode all fearful in suspense to know if the lovers should be burnt, hearing of their escape, praised God and were glad; whereupon the queen, seeing that Pampinea had made an end of her story, imposed on Lauretta the charge of following on, who blithely proceeded to say: "Fairest ladies, in the days when good King William[1] ruled over Sicily, there was in that island a gentleman hight Messer Amerigo Abate of Trapani, who, among other worldly goods, was very well furnished with children; wherefore, having occasion for servants and there coming thither from the Levant certain galleys of Genoese corsairs, who had, in their cruises off the coast of Armenia, taken many boys, he bought some of these latter, deeming them Turks, and amongst them one, Teodoro by name, of nobler mien and better bearing than the rest, who seemed all mere shepherds. Teodoro, although entreated as a slave, was brought up in the house with Messer Amerigo's children and conforming more to his own nature than to the accidents of fortune, approved himself so accomplished and well-bred and so commended himself to Messer Amerigo that he set him free and still believing him to be a Turk, caused baptize him and call him Pietro and made him chief over all his affairs, trusting greatly in him.

As Messer Amerigo's children grew up, there grew up with them a daughter of his, called Violante, a fair and dainty damsel, who, her father tarrying overmuch to marry her, became by chance enamoured of Pietro and loving him and holding his manners and fashions in great esteem, was yet ashamed to discover this to him. But Love spared her that pains, for that Pietro, having once and again looked upon her by stealth, had become so passionately enamoured of her that he never knew ease save whenas he saw her; but he was sore afraid lest any should become aware thereof, himseeming that in this he did other than well. The young lady, who took pleasure in looking upon him, soon perceived this and to give him more assurance, showed herself exceeding well pleased therewith, as indeed she was. On this wise they abode a great while, daring not to say aught to one another, much as each desired it; but, whilst both, alike enamoured, languished enkindled in the flames of love, fortune, as if it had determined of will aforethought that this should be, furnished them with an occasion of doing away the timorousness that baulked them.

Messer Amerigo had, about a mile from Trapani, a very goodly place,[2] to which his lady was wont ofttimes to resort by way of pastime with her daughter and other women and ladies. Thither accordingly they betook themselves one day of great heat, carrying Pietro with them, and there abiding, it befell, as whiles we see it happen in summer time, that the sky became of a sudden overcast with dark clouds, wherefore the lady set out with her company to return to Trapani, so they might not be there overtaken of the foul weather, and fared on as fast as they might. But Pietro and Violante, being young, outwent her mother and the rest by a great way, urged belike, no less by love than by fear of the weather, and they being already so far in advance that they were hardly to be seen, it chanced that, of a sudden, after many thunderclaps, a very heavy and thick shower of hail began to fall, wherefrom the lady and her company fled into the house of a husbandman.

Pietro and the young lady, having no readier shelter, took refuge in a little old hut, well nigh all in ruins, wherein none dwelt, and there huddled together under a small piece of roof, that yet remained whole. The scantness of the cover constrained them to press close one to other, and this touching was the means of somewhat emboldening their minds to discover the amorous desires that consumed them both; and Pietro first began to say, 'Would God this hail might never give over, so but I might abide as I am!' 'Indeed,' answered the girl, 'that were dear to me also.' From these words they came to taking each other by the hands and pressing them and from that to clipping and after to kissing, it hailing still the while; and in short, not to recount every particular, the weather mended not before they had known the utmost delights of love and had taken order to have their pleasure secretly one of the other. The storm ended, they fared on to the gate of the city, which was near at hand, and there awaiting the lady, returned home with her.

Thereafter, with very discreet and secret ordinance, they foregathered again and again in the same place, to the great contentment of them both, and the work went on so briskly that the young lady became with child, which was sore unwelcome both to the one and the other; wherefore she used many arts to rid herself, contrary to the course of nature, of her burden, but could nowise avail to accomplish it. Therewithal, Pietro, fearing for his life, bethought himself to flee and told her, to which she answered, 'An thou depart, I will without fail kill myself.' Whereupon quoth Pietro, who loved her exceedingly, 'Lady mine, how wilt thou have me abide here? Thy pregnancy will discover our default and it will lightly be pardoned unto thee; but I, poor wretch, it will be must needs bear the penalty of thy sin and mine own.' 'Pietro,' replied she, 'my sin must indeed be discovered; but be assured that thine will never be known, an thou tell not thyself.' Then said he, 'Since thou promisest me this, I will remain; but look thou keep thy promise to me.'

After awhile, the young lady, who had as most she might, concealed her being with child, seeing that, for the waxing of her body, she might no longer dissemble it, one day discovered her case to her mother, beseeching her with many tears to save her; whereupon the lady, beyond measure woeful, gave her hard words galore and would know of her how the thing had come about. Violante, in order that no harm might come to Pietro, told her a story of her own devising, disguising the truth in other forms. The lady believed it and to conceal her daughter's default, sent her away to a country house of theirs. There, the time of her delivery coming and the girl crying out, as women use to do, what while her mother never dreamed that Messer Amerigo, who was well nigh never wont to do so, should come thither, it chanced that he passed, on his return from hawking, by the chamber where his daughter lay and marvelling at the outcry she made, suddenly entered the chamber and demanded what was to do. The lady, seeing her husband come unawares, started up all woebegone and told him that which had befallen the girl. But he, less easy of belief than his wife had been, declared that it could not be true that she knew not by whom she was with child and would altogether know who he was, adding that, by confessing it, she might regain his favour; else must she make ready to die without mercy.

The lady did her utmost to persuade her husband to abide content with that which she had said; but to no purpose. He flew out into a passion and running, with his naked sword in his hand, at his daughter, who, what while her mother held her father in parley, had given birth to a male child, said, 'Either do thou discover by whom the child was begotten, or thou shalt die without delay.' The girl, fearing death, broke her promise to Pietro and discovered all that had passed between him and her; which when the gentleman heard, he fell into a fury of anger and hardly withheld himself from slaying her.

However, after he had said to her that which his rage dictated to him, he took horse again and returning to Trapani, recounted the affront that Pietro had done him to a certain Messer Currado, who was captain there for the king. The latter caused forthright seize Pietro, who was off his guard, and put him to the torture, whereupon he confessed all and being a few days after sentenced by the captain to be flogged through the city and after strung up by the neck, Messer Amerigo (whose wrath had not been done away by the having brought Pietro to death,) in order that one and the same hour should rid the earth of the two lovers and their child, put poison in a hanap with wine and delivering it, together with a naked poniard, to a serving-man of his, said to him, 'Carry these two things to Violante and bid her, on my part, forthright take which she will of these two deaths, poison or steel; else will I have her burned alive, even as she hath deserved, in the presence of as many townsfolk as be here. This done, thou shalt take the child, a few days agone born of her, and dash its head against the wall and after cast it to the dogs to eat.' This barbarous sentence passed by the cruel father upon his daughter and his grandchild, the servant, who was more disposed to ill than to good, went off upon his errand.

Meanwhile, Pietro, as he was carried to the gallows by the officers, being scourged of them the while, passed, according as it pleased those who led the company, before a hostelry wherein were three noblemen of Armenia, who had been sent by the king of that country ambassadors to Rome, to treat with the Pope of certain matters of great moment, concerning a crusade that was about to be undertaken, and who had lighted down there to take some days' rest and refreshment. They had been much honoured by the noblemen of Trapani and especially by Messer Amerigo, and hearing those pass who led Pietro, they came to a window to see. Now Pietro was all naked to the waist, with his hands bounden behind his back, and one of the three ambassadors, a man of great age and authority, named Fineo, espied on his breast a great vermeil spot, not painted, but naturally imprinted on his skin, after the fashion of what women here call *roses*. Seeing this, there suddenly recurred to his memory a son of his who had been carried off by corsairs fifteen years agone upon the coast of Lazistan and of whom he had never since been able to learn any news; and considering the age of the poor wretch who was scourged, he bethought himself that, if his son were alive, he must be of such an age as Pietro appeared to him. Wherefore he began to suspect by that token that it must be he and bethought himself that, were he indeed his son, he should still remember him of his name and that of his father and of the Armenian tongue. Accordingly, as he drew near, he called out, saying, 'Ho, Teodoro!' Pietro, hearing this, straightway lifted up his head and Fineo, speaking in Armenian, said to him, 'What countryman art thou and whose son?' The sergeants who had him in charge halted with him, of respect for the nobleman, so that Pietro answered, saying, 'I was of Armenia and son to one Fineo and was brought hither, as a little child, by I know not what folk.'

Fineo, hearing this, knew him for certain to be the son whom he had lost, wherefore he came down, weeping, with his companions, and ran to embrace him among all the sergeants; then, casting over his shoulders a mantle of the richest silk, which he had on his own back, he besought the officer who was escorting him to execution to be pleased to wait there till such time as commandment should come to him to carry the prisoner back; to which he answered that he would well. Now Fineo had already learned the reason for which Pietro was being led to death, report having noised it abroad everywhere; wherefore he straightway betook himself, with his companions and their retinue, to Messer Currado and bespoke him thus: 'Sir, he whom you have doomed to die, as a slave, is a free man and my son and is ready to take to wife her whom it is said he hath bereft of her maidenhead; wherefore may it please you to defer the execution till such time as it may be learned if she will have him to husband, so, in case she be willing, you may not be found to have done contrary to the law.' Messer Currado, hearing that the condemned man was Fineo's son, marvelled and confessing that which the latter said to be true, was somewhat ashamed of the unright of fortune and straightway caused carry Pietro home; then, sending for Messer Amerigo, he acquainted him with these things.

Messer Amerigo, who by this believed his daughter and grandson to be dead, was the woefullest man in the world for that which he had done, seeing that all might very well have been set right, so but Violante were yet alive. Nevertheless, he despatched a runner whereas his daughter was, to the intent that, in case his commandment had not been done, it should not be carried into effect. The messenger found the servant sent by Messer Amerigo rating the lady, before whom he had laid the poniard and the poison, for that she made not her election as speedily [as he desired], and would have constrained her to take the one or the other. But, hearing his lord's commandment, he let her be and returning to Messer Amerigo, told him how the case stood, to the great satisfaction of the latter, who, betaking himself whereas Fineo was, excused himself, well nigh with tears, as best he knew, of that which had passed, craving pardon therefor and evouching that, an Teodoro would have his daughter to wife, he was exceeding well pleased to give her to him. Fineo gladly received his excuses and answered, 'It is my intent that my son shall take your daughter to wife; and if he will not, let the sentence passed upon him take its course.'

Accordingly, being thus agreed, they both repaired whereas Teodoro abode yet all fearful of death, albeit he was rejoiced to have found his father again, and questioned him of his mind concerning this thing. When he heard that, an he would, he might have Violante to wife, such was his joy that himseemed he had won from hell to heaven at one bound, and he answered that this would be to him the utmost of favours, so but it pleased both of them. Thereupon they sent to know the mind of the young lady, who, whereas she abode in expectation of death, the woefullest woman alive, hearing that which had betided and was like to betide Teodoro, after much parley, began to lend some faith to their words and taking a little comfort, answered that, were she to ensue her own wishes in the matter, no greater happiness could betide her than to be the wife of Teodoro; algates, she would do that which her father should command her.

Accordingly, all parties being of accord, the two lovers were married with the utmost magnificence, to the exceeding satisfaction of all the townsfolk; and the young lady, heartening herself and letting rear her little son, became ere long fairer than ever. Then, being risen from childbed, she went out to meet Fineo, whose return was expected from Rome, and paid him reverence as to a father; whereupon he, exceeding well pleased to have so fair a daughter-in-law, caused celebrate their nuptials with the utmost pomp and rejoicing and receiving her as a daughter, ever after held her such. And after some days, taking ship with his son and her and his little grandson, he carried them with him into Lazistan, where the two lovers abode in peace and happiness, so long as life endured unto them."

---

1. William II. (a.d. 1166-1189), the last (legitimate) king of the Norman dynasty in Sicily, called the Good, to distinguish him from his father, William the Bad.
2. Apparently a pleasure-garden, without a house attached in which they might have taken shelter from the rain.

🌿 8 🌿

THE EIGHTH STORY

NASTAGIO DEGLI ONESTI, FALLING IN LOVE WITH A
LADY OF THE TRAVERSARI FAMILY, SPENDETH HIS
SUBSTANCE WITHOUT BEING BELOVED IN RETURN,
AND BETAKING HIMSELF, AT THE INSTANCE OF HIS
KINSFOLK, TO CHIASSI, HE THERE SEETH A
HORSEMAN GIVE CHASE TO A DAMSEL AND SLAY HER
AND CAUSE HER BE DEVOURED OF TWO DOGS.
THEREWITHAL HE BIDDETH HIS KINSFOLK AND THE
LADY WHOM HE LOVETH TO A DINNER, WHERE HIS
MISTRESS SEETH THE SAME DAMSEL TORN IN PIECES
AND FEARING A LIKE FATE, TAKETH NASTAGIO TO
HUSBAND

NO SOONER WAS Lauretta silent than Filomena, by the queen's commandment, began thus: "Lovesome ladies, even as pity is in us commended, so also is cruelty rigorously avenged by Divine justice; the which that I may prove to you and so engage you altogether to purge yourselves therefrom, it pleaseth me tell you a story no less pitiful than delectable.

In Ravenna, a very ancient city of Romagna, there were aforetime many noblemen and gentlemen, and amongst the rest a young man called Nastagio degli Onesti, who had, by the death of his father and an uncle of his, been left rich beyond all estimation and who, as it happeneth often with young men, being without a wife, fell in love with a daughter of Messer Paolo Traversari, a young lady of much greater family than his own, hoping by his fashions to bring her to love him in return. But these, though great and goodly and commendable, not only profited him nothing; nay, it seemed they did him harm, so cruel and obdurate and intractable did the beloved damsel show herself to him, being grown belike, whether for her singular beauty or the nobility of her birth, so proud and disdainful that neither he nor aught that pleased him pleased her. This was so grievous to Nastagio to bear that many a time, for chagrin, being weary of complaining, he had it in his thought to kill himself, but held his hand therefrom; and again and again he took it to heart to let her be altogether or have her, an he might, in hatred, even as she had him. But in vain did he take such a resolve, for that, the more hope failed him, the more it seemed his love redoubled. Accordingly, he persisted both in loving and in spending without stint or measure, till it seemed to certain of his friends and kinsfolk that he was like to consume both himself and his substance; wherefore they besought him again and again and counselled him depart Ravenna and go sojourn awhile in some other place, for that, so doing, he would abate both his passion and his expenditure. Nastagio long made light of this counsel, but, at last, being importuned of them and able no longer to say no, he promised to do as they would have him and let make great preparations, as he would go into France or Spain or some other far place. Then, taking horse in company with many of his friends, he rode out of Ravenna and betook himself to a place called Chiassi, some three miles

257

from the city, where, sending for tents and pavilions, he told those who had accompanied him thither that he meant to abide and that they might return to Ravenna. Accordingly, having encamped there, he proceeded to lead the goodliest and most magnificent life that was aye, inviting now these, now those others, to supper and to dinner, as he was used.

It chanced one day, he being come thus well nigh to the beginning of May and the weather being very fair, that, having entered into thought of his cruel mistress, he bade all his servants leave him to himself, so he might muse more at his leisure, and wandered on, step by step, lost in melancholy thought, till he came [unwillingly] into the pine-wood. The fifth hour of the day was well nigh past and he had gone a good half mile into the wood, remembering him neither of eating nor of aught else, when himseemed of a sudden he heard a terrible great wailing and loud cries uttered by a woman; whereupon, his dulcet meditation being broken, he raised his head to see what was to do and marvelled to find himself among the pines; then, looking before him, he saw a very fair damsel come running, naked through a thicket all thronged with underwood and briers, towards the place where he was, weeping and crying sore for mercy and all dishevelled and torn by the bushes and the brambles. At her heels ran two huge and fierce mastiffs, which followed hard upon her and ofttimes bit her cruelly, whenas they overtook her; and after them he saw come riding upon a black courser a knight arrayed in sad-coloured armour, with a very wrathful aspect and a tuck in his hand, threatening her with death in foul and fearsome words.

This sight filled Nastagio's mind at once with terror and amazement and after stirred him to compassion of the ill-fortuned lady, wherefrom arose a desire to deliver her, an but he might, from such anguish and death. Finding himself without arms, he ran to take the branch of a tree for a club, armed wherewith, he advanced to meet the dogs and the knight. When the latter saw this, he cried out to him from afar off, saying, 'Nastagio, meddle not; suffer the dogs and myself to do that which this wicked woman hath merited.' As he spoke, the dogs, laying fast hold of the damsel by the flanks, brought her to a stand and the knight, coming up, lighted down from his horse; whereupon Nastagio drew near unto him and said, 'I know not who thou mayst be, that knowest me so well; but this much I say to see that it is a great felony for an armed knight to seek to slay a naked woman and to set the dogs on her, as she were a wild beast; certes, I will defend her as most I may.'

'Nastagio,' answered the knight, 'I was of one same city with thyself and thou wast yet a little child when I, who hight Messer Guido degli Anastagi, was yet more passionately enamoured of this woman than thou art presently of yonder one of the Traversari and my ill fortune for her hard-heartedness and barbarity came to such a pass that one day I slew myself in despair with this tuck thou seest in my hand and was doomed to eternal punishment. Nor was it long ere she, who was beyond measure rejoiced at my death, died also and for the sin of her cruelty and of the delight had of her in my torments (whereof she repented her not, as one who thought not to have sinned therein, but rather to have merited reward,) was and is on like wise condemned to the pains of hell. Wherein no sooner was she descended than it was decreed unto her and to me, for penance thereof,[1] that she should flee before me and that I, who once loved her so dear, should pursue her, not as a beloved mistress, but as a mortal enemy, and that, as often as I overtook her, I should slay her with this tuck, wherewith I slew myself, and ripping open her loins, tear from her body, as thou shalt presently see, that hard and cold heart, wherein nor love nor pity might ever avail to enter, together with the other entrails, and give them to the dogs to eat. Nor is it a great while after ere, as God's justice and puissance will it, she riseth up again, as she had not been dead, and beginneth anew her woeful flight, whilst the dogs and I again pursue her. And every Friday it betideth that I come up with her here at this hour and wreak on her the slaughter that thou shalt see; and think not that we rest the other days; nay, I overtake her in other places, wherein she thought and wrought cruelly against me. Thus, being as thou seest, from her lover grown her foe, it behoveth me pursue her on this wise as many years as she was cruel to me months. Wherefore leave me to carry the justice of God into effect and seek not to oppose that which thou mayst not avail to hinder.'

Nastagio, hearing these words, drew back, grown all adread, with not an hair on his body but stood on end, and looking upon the wretched damsel, began fearfully to await that which the knight should do. The latter, having made an end of his discourse, ran, tuck in hand, as he were a ravening dog, at the damsel, who, fallen on her knees and held fast by the two mastiffs, cried him mercy, and smiting her with all his might amiddleward the breast, pierced her through and through. No sooner had she received this stroke than she fell grovelling on the ground, still weeping and crying out; whereupon the knight, clapping his hand to his hunting-knife, ripped open her loins and tearing forth her heart and all that was thereabout, cast them to the two mastiffs, who devoured them incontinent, as being sore anhungred. Nor was it long ere, as if none of these things had been, the damsel of a sudden rose to her feet and began to flee towards the sea, with the dogs after her, still rending her; and in a little while they had gone so far that Nastagio could see them no more. The latter, seeing these things, abode a great while between pity and fear, and presently it occurred to his mind that this might much avail him, seeing that it befell every Friday; wherefore, marking the place, he returned to his servants and after, whenas it seemed to him fit, he sent for sundry of his kinsmen and friends and said to them, 'You have long urged me leave loving this mine enemy and put an end to my expenditure, and I am ready to do it, provided you will obtain me a favour; the which is this, that on the coming Friday you make shift to have Messer Paolo Traversari and his wife and daughter and all their kinswomen and what other ladies soever it shall please you here to dinner with me. That for which I wish this, you shall see then.' This seemed to them a little thing enough to do, wherefore, returning to Ravenna, they in due time invited those whom Nastagio would have to dine with him, and albeit it was no easy matter to bring thither the young lady whom he loved, natheless she went with the other ladies. Meanwhile, Nastagio let make ready a magnificent banquet and caused set the tables under the pines round about the place where he had witnessed the slaughter of the cruel lady.

The time come, he seated the gentlemen and the ladies at table and so ordered it that his mistress should be placed right over against the spot where the thing should befall. Accordingly, hardly was the last dish come when the despairful outcry of the hunted damsel began to be heard of all, whereat each of the company marvelled and enquired what was to do, but none could say; whereupon all started to their feet and looking what this might be, they saw the woeful damsel and the knight and the dogs; nor was it long ere they were all there among them. Great was the clamor against both dogs and knight, and many rushed forward to succour the damsel; but the knight, bespeaking them as he had bespoken Nastagio, not only made them draw back, but filled them all with terror and amazement. Then did he as he had done before, whereat all the ladies that were there (and there were many present who had been kinswomen both to the woeful damsel and to the knight and who remembered them both of his love and of his death) wept as piteously as if they had seen this done to themselves.

The thing carried to its end and the damsel and the knight gone, the adventure set those who had seen it upon many and various discourses; but of those who were the most affrighted was the cruel damsel beloved of Nastagio, who had distinctly seen and heard the whole matter and understood that these things concerned her more than any other who was there, remembering her of the cruelty she had still used towards Nastagio; wherefore herseemed she fled already before her enraged lover and had the mastiffs at her heels. Such was the terror awakened in her thereby that,—so this might not betide her,—no sooner did she find an opportunity (which was afforded her that same evening) than, turning her hatred into love, she despatched to Nastagio a trusty chamberwoman of hers, who besought him that it should please him to go to her, for that she was ready to do all that should be his pleasure. He answered that this was exceeding agreeable to him, but that, so it pleased her, he desired to have his pleasure of her with honour, to wit, by taking her to wife. The damsel, who knew that it rested with none other than herself that she had not been his wife, made answer to him that it liked her well; then, playing the messenger herself, she told her father and mother that she was content to be Nastagio's wife, whereat they were mightily rejoiced, and he, espousing her on the ensuing Sunday and celebrating his nuptials, lived with her long and happily. Nor was this affright the cause of that good only; nay, all the ladies of Ravenna became so fearful by reason thereof, that ever after they were much more amenable than they had before been to the desires of the men."

---

1. *i.e.* of her sin.

✣ 9 ✣

THE NINTH STORY

FEDERIGO DEGLI ALBERIGHI LOVETH AND IS NOT LOVED. HE WASTETH HIS SUBSTANCE IN PRODIGAL HOSPITALITY TILL THERE IS LEFT HIM BUT ONE SOLE FALCON, WHICH, HAVING NOUGHT ELSE, HE GIVETH HIS MISTRESS TO EAT, ON HER COMING TO HIS HOUSE; AND SHE, LEARNING THIS, CHANGETH HER MIND AND TAKING HIM TO HUSBAND, MAKETH HIM RICH AGAIN

FILOMENA HAVING CEASED SPEAKING, the queen, seeing that none remained to tell save only herself and Dioneo, whose privilege entitled him to speak last, said, with blithe aspect, "It pertaineth now to me to tell and I, dearest ladies, will willingly do it, relating a story like in part to the foregoing, to the intent that not only may you know how much the love of you[1] can avail in gentle hearts, but that you may learn to be yourselves, whenas it behoveth, bestowers of your guerdons, without always suffering fortune to be your guide, which most times, as it chanceth, giveth not discreetly, but out of all measure.

You must know, then, that Coppo di Borghese Domenichi, who was of our days and maybe is yet a man of great worship and authority in our city and illustrious and worthy of eternal renown, much more for his fashions and his merit than for the nobility of his blood, being grown full of years, delighted oftentimes to discourse with his neighbours and others of things past, the which he knew how to do better and more orderly and with more memory and elegance of speech than any other man. Amongst other fine things of his, he was used to tell that there was once in Florence a young man called Federigo, son of Messer Filippo Alberighi and renowned for deeds of arms and courtesy over every other bachelor in Tuscany, who, as betideth most gentlemen, became enamoured of a gentlewoman named Madam Giovanna, in her day held one of the fairest and sprightliest ladies that were in Florence; and to win her love, he held jousts and tourneyings and made entertainments and gave gifts and spent his substance without any stint; but she, being no less virtuous than fair, recked nought of these things done for her nor of him who did them. Federigo spending thus far beyond his means and gaining nought, his wealth, as lightly happeneth, in course of time came to an end and he abode poor, nor was aught left him but a poor little farm, on whose returns he lived very meagrely, and to boot a falcon he had, one of the best in the world. Wherefore, being more in love than ever and himseeming he might no longer make such a figure in the city as he would fain do, he took up his abode at Campi, where his farm was, and there bore his poverty with patience, hawking whenas he might and asking of no one.

Federigo being thus come to extremity, it befell one day that Madam Giovanna's husband fell sick and seeing himself nigh upon death, made his will, wherein, being very rich, he left a son of his, now well grown, his heir, after which, having much loved Madam Giovanna, he substituted her to his heir, in case his son should die without lawful issue, and died. Madam Giovanna, being thus left a widow, betook herself that summer, as is the usance of our ladies, into the country with her son to an estate of hers very near that of Federigo; wherefore it befell that the lad made acquaintance with the latter and began to take delight in hawks and hounds, and having many a time seen his falcon flown and being strangely taken therewith, longed sore to have it, but dared not ask it of him, seeing it so dear to him. The thing standing thus, it came to pass that the lad fell sick, whereat his mother was sore concerned, as one who had none but him and loved him with all her might, and abode about him all day, comforting him without cease; and many a time she asked him if there were aught he desired, beseeching him tell it her, for an it might be gotten, she would contrive that he should have it. The lad, having heard these offers many times repeated, said, 'Mother mine, an you could procure me to have Federigo's falcon, methinketh I should soon be whole.'

The lady hearing this, bethought herself awhile and began to consider how she should do. She knew that Federigo had long loved her and had never gotten of her so much as a glance of the eye; wherefore quoth she in herself, 'How shall I send or go to him to seek of him this falcon, which is, by all I hear, the best that ever flew and which, to boot, maintaineth him in the world? And how can I be so graceless as to offer to take this from a gentleman who hath none other pleasure left?' Perplexed with this thought and knowing not what to say, for all she was very certain of getting the bird, if she asked for it, she made no reply to her son, but abode silent. However, at last, the love of her son so got the better of her that she resolved in herself to satisfy him, come what might, and not to send, but to go herself for the falcon and fetch it to him. Accordingly she said to him, 'My son, take comfort and bethink thyself to grow well again, for I promise thee that the first thing I do to-morrow morning I will go for it and fetch it to thee.' The boy was rejoiced at this and showed some amendment that same day.

Next morning, the lady, taking another lady to bear her company, repaired, by way of diversion, to Federigo's little house and enquired for the latter, who, for that it was no weather for hawking nor had been for some days past, was then in a garden he had, overlooking the doing of certain little matters of his, and hearing that Madam Giovanna asked for him at the door, ran thither, rejoicing and marvelling exceedingly. She, seeing him come, rose and going with womanly graciousness to meet him, answered his respectful salutation with 'Give you good day, Federigo!' then went on to say, 'I am come to make thee amends for that which thou hast suffered through me, in loving me more than should have behooved thee; and the amends in question is this that I purpose to dine with thee this morning familiarly, I and this lady my companion.' 'Madam,' answered Federigo humbly, 'I remember me not to have ever received any ill at your hands, but on the contrary so much good that, if ever I was worth aught, it came about through your worth and the love I bore you; and assuredly, albeit you have come to a poor host, this your gracious visit is far more precious to me than it would be an it were given me to spend over again as much as that which I have spent aforetime.' So saying, he shamefastly received her into his house and thence brought her into his garden, where, having none else to bear her company, he said to her, 'Madam, since there is none else here, this good woman, wife of yonder husbandman, will bear you company, whilst I go see the table laid.'

Never till that moment, extreme as was his poverty, had he been so dolorously sensible of the straits to which he had brought himself for the lack of those riches he had spent on such disorderly wise. But that morning, finding he had nothing wherewithal he might honourably entertain the lady, for love of whom he had aforetime entertained folk without number, he was made perforce aware of his default and ran hither and thither, perplexed beyond measure, like a man beside himself, inwardly cursing his ill fortune, but found neither money nor aught he might pawn. It was now growing late and he having a great desire to entertain the gentle lady with somewhat, yet choosing not to have recourse to his own labourer, much less any one else, his eye fell on his good falcon, which he saw on his perch in his little saloon; whereupon, having no other resource, he took the bird and finding him fat, deemed him a dish worthy of such a lady. Accordingly, without more ado, he wrung the hawk's neck and hastily caused a little maid of his pluck it and truss it and after put it on the spit and roast it diligently. Then, the table laid and covered with very white cloths, whereof he had yet some store, he returned with a blithe countenance to the lady in the garden and told her that dinner was ready, such as it was in his power to provide. Accordingly, the lady and her friend, arising, betook themselves to table and in company with Federigo, who served them with the utmost diligence, ate the good falcon, unknowing what they did.

Presently, after they had risen from table and had abidden with him awhile in cheerful discourse, the lady, thinking it time to tell that wherefor she was come, turned to Federigo and courteously bespoke him, saying, 'Federigo, I doubt not a jot but that, when thou hearest that which is the especial occasion of my coming hither, thou wilt marvel at my presumption, remembering thee of thy past life and of my virtue, which latter belike thou reputedst cruelty and hardness of heart; but, if thou hadst or hadst had children, by whom thou mightest know how potent is the love one beareth them, meseemeth certain that thou wouldst in part hold me excused. But, although thou hast none, I, who have one child, cannot therefore escape the common laws to which other mothers are subject and whose enforcements it behoveth me ensue, need must I, against my will and contrary to all right and seemliness, ask of thee a boon, which I know is supremely dear to thee (and that with good reason, for that thy sorry fortune hath left thee none other delight, none other diversion, none other solace), to wit, thy falcon, whereof my boy is so sore enamoured that, an I carry it not to him, I fear me his present disorder will be so aggravated that there may presently ensue thereof somewhat whereby I shall lose him. Wherefore I conjure thee,—not by the love thou bearest me and whereto thou art nowise beholden, but by thine own nobility, which in doing courtesy hath approved itself greater than in any other,—that it please thee give it to me, so by the gift I may say I have kept my son alive and thus made him for ever thy debtor.'

Federigo, hearing what the lady asked and knowing that he could not oblige her, for that he had given her the falcon to eat, fell a-weeping in her presence, ere he could answer a word. The lady at first believed that his tears arose from grief at having to part from his good falcon and was like to say that she would not have it. However, she contained herself and awaited what Federigo should reply, who, after weeping awhile, made answer thus: 'Madam, since it pleased God that I should set my love on you, I have in many things reputed fortune contrary to me and have complained of her; but all the ill turns she hath done me have been a light matter in comparison with that which she doth me at this present and for which I can never more be reconciled to her, considering that you are come hither to my poor house, whereas you deigned not to come what while I was rich, and seek of me a little boon, the which she hath so wrought that I cannot grant you; and why this cannot be I will tell you briefly. When I heard that you, of your favour, were minded to dine with me, I deemed it a light thing and a seemly, having regard to your worth and the nobility of your station, to honour you, as far as in me lay, with some choicer victual than that which is commonly set before other folk; wherefore, remembering me of the falcon which you ask of me and of his excellence, I judged him a dish worthy of you. This very morning, then, you have had him roasted upon the trencher, and indeed I had accounted him excellently well bestowed; but now, seeing that you would fain have had him on other wise, it is so great a grief to me that I cannot oblige you therein that methinketh I shall never forgive myself therefor.' So saying, in witness of this, he let cast before her the falcon's feathers and feet and beak.

The lady, seeing and hearing this, first blamed him for having, to give a woman to eat, slain such a falcon, and after inwardly much commended the greatness of his soul, which poverty had not availed nor might anywise avail to abate. Then, being put out of all hope of having the falcon and fallen therefore in doubt of her son's recovery, she took her leave and returned, all disconsolate, to the latter, who, before many days had passed, whether for chagrin that he could not have the bird or for that his disorder was e'en fated to bring him to that pass, departed this life, to the inexpressible grief of his mother. After she had abidden awhile full of tears and affliction, being left very rich and yet young, she was more than once urged by her brothers to marry again, and albeit she would fain not have done so, yet, finding herself importuned and calling to mind Federigo's worth and his last magnificence, to wit, the having slain such a falcon for her entertainment, she said to them, 'I would gladly, an it liked you, abide as I am; but, since it is your pleasure that I take a [second] husband, certes I will never take any other, an I have not Federigo degli Alberighi.' Whereupon her brothers, making mock of her, said 'Silly woman that thou art, what is this thou sayest? How canst thou choose him, seeing he hath nothing in the world?' 'Brothers mine,' answered she, 'I know very well that it is as you say; but I would liefer have a man that lacketh of riches than riches that lack of a man.' Her brethren, hearing her mind and knowing Federigo for a man of great merit, poor though he was, gave her, with all her wealth, to him, even as she would; and he, seeing himself married to a lady of such worth and one whom he had loved so dear and exceeding rich, to boot, became a better husband of his substance and ended his days with her in joy and solace."

---

1. Syn. your charms (*la vostra vaghezza*).

✿ IO ✿

THE TENTH STORY

PIETRO DI VINCIOLO GOETH TO SUP ABROAD,
WHEREUPON HIS WIFE LETTETH FETCH HER A
YOUTH TO KEEP HER COMPANY, AND HER HUSBAND
RETURNING, UNLOOKED FOR, SHE HIDETH HER
GALLANT UNDER A HEN-COOP. PIETRO TELLETH
HER HOW THERE HAD BEEN FOUND IN THE HOUSE
OF ONE ARCOLANO, WITH WHOM HE WAS TO HAVE
SUPPED, A YOUNG MAN BROUGHT IN BY HIS WIFE,
AND SHE BLAMETH THE LATTER. PRESENTLY, AN ASS,
BY MISCHANCE, SETTETH FOOT ON THE FINGERS OF
HIM WHO IS UNDER THE COOP AND HE ROARETH
OUT, WHEREUPON PIETRO RUNNETH THITHER AND
ESPYING HIM, DISCOVERETH HIS WIFE'S UNFAITH,
BUT ULTIMATELY COMETH TO AN ACCORD WITH HER
FOR HIS OWN LEWD ENDS

THE QUEEN'S story come to an end and all having praised God for that He had rewarded Federigo according to his desert, Dioneo, who never waited for commandment, began on this wise: "I know not whether to say if it be a casual vice, grown up in mankind through perversity of manners and usances, or a defect inherent in our nature, that we laugh rather at things ill than at good works, especially when they concern us not. Wherefore, seeing that the pains I have otherwhiles taken and am now about to take aim at none other end than to rid you of melancholy and afford you occasion for laughter and merriment,—albeit the matter of my present story may be in part not altogether seemly, nevertheless, lovesome lasses, for that it may afford diversion, I will e'en tell it you, and do you, hearkening thereunto, as you are wont to do, whenas you enter into gardens, where, putting out your dainty hands, you cull the roses and leave the thorns be. On this wise must you do with my story, leaving the naughty man of whom I shall tell you to his infamy and ill-luck go with him, what while you laugh merrily at the amorous devices of his wife, having compassion, whenas need is, of the mischances of others.

There was, then, in Perugia, no great while agone, a rich man called Pietro di Vinciolo, who, belike more to beguile others and to abate the general suspect in which he was had of all the Perugians, than for any desire of his own, took him a wife, and fortune in this was so far conformable to his inclination that the wife he took was a thickset, red-haired, hot-complexioned wench, who would liefer have had two husbands than one, whereas she happened upon one who had a mind far more disposed to otherwhat than to her. Becoming, in process of time, aware of this and seeing herself fair and fresh and feeling herself buxom and lusty, she began by being sore incensed thereat and came once and again to unseemly words thereof with her husband, with whom she was well nigh always at variance. Then, seeing that this might result rather in her own exhaustion than in the amendment of her husband's depravity, she said in herself, 'Yonder caitiff forsaketh me to go of his ribaldries on pattens through the dry, and I will study to carry others on shipboard through the wet. I took him to husband and brought him a fine great dowry, knowing him to be a man and supposing him desireful of that whereunto men are and should be fain; and had I not believed that he would play the part of a man, I had never taken him. He knew that I was a woman; why, then, did he take me to wife, if women were not to his mind? This is not to be suffered. Were I minded to renounce the world, I should have made myself a nun; but, if, choosing to live in the world, as I do, I look for delight or pleasure from yonder fellow, I may belike grow old, expecting in vain, and whenas I shall be old, I shall in vain repent and bemoan myself of having wasted my youth, which latter he himself is a very good teacher and demonstrator how I should solace, showing me by example how I should delect myself with that wherein he delighteth, more by token that this were commendable in me, whereas in him it is exceeding blameworthy, seeing that I should offend against the laws alone, whereas he offendeth against both law and nature.'

Accordingly, the good lady, having thus bethought herself and belike more than once, to give effect privily to these considerations, clapped up an acquaintance with an old woman who showed like Saint Verdiana, that giveth the serpents to eat, and still went to every pardoning, beads in hand, nor ever talked of aught but the lives of the Holy Fathers or of the wounds of St. Francis and was of well nigh all reputed a saint, and whenas it seemed to her time, frankly discovered to her her intent. 'Daughter mine,' replied the beldam, 'God who knoweth all knoweth that thou wilt do exceeding well, and if for nought else, yet shouldst thou do it, thou and every other young woman, not to lose the time of your youth, for that to whoso hath understanding, there is no grief like that of having lost one's time. And what a devil are we women good for, once we are old, save to keep the ashes about the fire-pot? If none else knoweth it and can bear witness thereof, that do and can I; for, now that I am old, I recognize without avail, but not without very sore and bitter remorse of mind, the time that I let slip, and albeit I lost it not altogether (for that I would not have thee deem me a ninny), still I did not what I might have done; whereof whenas I remember me, seeing myself fashioned as thou seest me at this present, so that thou wouldst find none to give me fire to my tinder,[1] God knoweth what chagrin I feel. With men it is not so; they are born apt for a thousand things, not for this alone, and most part of them are of much more account old than young; but women are born into the world for nothing but to do this and bear children, and it is for this that they are prized; the which, if from nought else, thou mayst apprehend from this, that we women are still ready for the sport; more by token that one woman would tire out many men at the game, whereas many men cannot tire one woman; and for that we are born unto this, I tell thee again that thou wilt do exceeding well to return thy husband a loaf for his bannock, so thy soul may have no cause to reproach thy flesh in thine old age. Each one hath of this world just so much as he taketh to himself thereof, and especially is this the case with women, whom it behoveth, much more than men, make use of their time, whilst they have it; for thou mayst see how, when we grow old, nor husband nor other will look at us; nay, they send us off to the kitchen to tell tales to the cat and count the pots and pans; and what is worse, they tag rhymes on us and say,

"Tidbits for wenches young;
Gags[2] for the old wife's tongue."

And many another thing to the like purpose. And that I may hold thee no longer in parley, I tell thee in fine that thou couldst not have discovered thy mind to any one in the world who can be more useful to thee than I, for that there is no man so high and mighty but I dare tell him what behoveth, nor any so dour or churlish but I know how to supple him aright and bring him to what I will. Wherefore do thou but show me who pleaseth thee and after leave me do; but one thing I commend to thee, daughter mine, and that is, that thou be mindful of me, for that I am a poor body and would have thee henceforth a sharer in all my pardonings and in all the paternosters I shall say, so God may make them light and candles for thy dead.'[3]

WITH THIS SHE made an end of her discourse, and the young lady came to an understanding with her that, whenas she chanced to spy a certain young spark who passed often through that quarter and whose every feature she set out to her, she should know what she had to do; then, giving her a piece of salt meat, she dismissed her with God's blessing; nor had many days passed ere the old woman brought her him of whom she had bespoken her privily into her chamber, and a little while after, another and another, according as they chanced to take the lady's fancy, who stinted not to indulge herself in this as often as occasion offered, though still fearful of her husband. It chanced one evening that, her husband being to sup abroad with a friend of his, Ercolano by name, she charged the old woman bring her a youth, who was one of the goodliest and most agreeable of all Perugia, which she promptly did; but hardly had the lady seated herself at table to sup with her gallant, when, behold, Pietro called out at the door to have it opened to him. She, hearing this, gave herself up for lost, but yet desiring, an she might, to conceal the youth and not having the presence of mind to send him away or hide him elsewhere, made him take refuge under a hen-coop, that was in a shed adjoining the chamber where they were at supper, and cast over him the sacking of a pallet-bed that she had that day let empty.

This done, she made haste to open to her husband, to whom quoth she, as soon as he entered the house, 'You have very soon despatched this supper of yours!' 'We have not so much as tasted it,' replied he; and she said, 'How was that?' Quoth he, 'I will tell thee. Scarce were we seated at table, Ercolano and his wife and I, when we heard some one sneeze hard by, whereof we took no note the first time nor the second; but, he who sneezed sneezing yet a third time and a fourth and a fifth and many other times, it made us all marvel; whereupon Ercolano, who was somewhat vexed with his wife for that she had kept us a great while standing at the door, without opening to us, said, as if in a rage, "What meaneth this? Who is it sneezeth thus?" And rising from table, made for a stair that stood near at hand and under which, hard by the stairfoot, was a closure of planks, wherein to bestow all manner things, as we see those do every day who set their houses in order. Himseeming it was from this that came the noise of sneezing, he opened a little door that was therein and no sooner had he done this than there issued forth thereof the frightfullest stench of sulphur that might be. Somewhat of this smell had already reached us and we complaining thereof, the lady had said, "It is because I was but now in act to bleach my veils with sulphur and after set the pan, over which I had spread them to catch the fumes, under the stair, so that it yet smoketh thereof."

As soon as the smoke was somewhat spent, Ercolano looked into the cupboard and there espied him who had sneezed and who was yet in act to sneeze, for that the fumes of the sulphur constrained him thereto, and indeed they had by this time so straitened his breast that, had he abidden a while longer, he had never sneezed nor done aught else again. Ercolano, seeing him, cried out, "Now, wife, I see why, whenas we came hither awhile ago, we were kept so long at the door, without its being opened to us; but may I never again have aught that shall please me, an I pay thee not for this!" The lady, hearing this and seeing that her sin was discovered, stayed not to make any excuse, but started up from table and made off I know not whither. Ercolano, without remarking his wife's flight, again and again bade him who sneezed come forth; but the latter, who was now at the last gasp, offered not to stir, for all that he could say; whereupon, taking him by one foot, he haled him forth of his hiding-place and ran for a knife to kill him; but I, fearing the police on mine own account, arose and suffered him not to slay him or do him any hurt; nay, crying out and defending him, I gave the alarm to certain of the neighbours, who ran thither and taking the now half-dead youth, carried him forth the house I know not whither. Wherefore, our supper being disturbed by these things, I have not only not despatched it, nay, I have, as I said, not even tasted it.'

The lady, hearing this, knew that there were other women as wise as herself, albeit illhap bytimes betided some of them thereof, and would fain have defended Ercolano's wife with words; but herseeming that, by blaming others' defaults, she might make freer way for her own, she began to say, 'Here be fine doings! A holy and virtuous lady indeed she must be! She, to whom, as I am an honest woman, I would have confessed myself, so spiritually minded meseemed she was! And the worst of it is that she, being presently an old woman, setteth a mighty fine example to the young. Accursed by the hour she came into the world and she also, who suffereth herself to live, perfidious and vile woman that she must be, the general reproach and shame of all the ladies of this city, who, casting to the winds her honour and the faith plighted to her husband and the world's esteem, is not ashamed to dishonour him, and herself with him, for another man, him who is such a man and so worshipful a citizen and who used her so well! So God save me, there should be no mercy had of such women as she; they should be put to death; they should be cast alive into the fire and burned to ashes.' Then, bethinking her of her gallant, whom she had hard by under the coop, she began to exhort Pietro to betake himself to bed, for that it was time; but he, having more mind to eat than to sleep, enquired if there was aught for supper. 'Supper, quotha!' answered the lady. 'Truly, we are much used to get supper, whenas thou art abroad! A fine thing, indeed! Dost thou take me for Ercolano's wife? Alack, why dost thou not go to sleep for to-night? How far better thou wilt do!' Now it chanced that, certain husbandmen of Pietro's being come that evening with sundry matters from the farm and having put up their asses, without watering them, in a little stable adjoining the shed, one of the latter, being sore athirst, slipped his head out of the halter and making his way out of the stable, went smelling to everything, so haply he might find some water, and going thus, he came presently full on the hen-coop, under which was the young man. The latter having, for that it behoved him abide on all fours, put out the fingers of one hand on the ground beyond the coop, such was his luck, or rather let us say, his ill luck, that the ass set his hoof on them, whereupon the youth, feeling an exceeding great pain, set up a terrible outcry. Pietro, hearing this, marvelled and perceived that the noise came from within the house; wherefore he went out into the shed and hearing the other still clamouring, for that the ass had not lifted up his hoof from his fingers, but still trod hard upon them, said, 'Who is there?' Then, running to the hen-coop, he raised it and espied the young man, who, beside the pain he suffered from his fingers that were crushed by the ass's hoof, was all a-trembling for fear lest Pietro should do him a mischief.

The latter, knowing him for one whom he had long pursued for his lewd ends, asked him what he did there, whereto he answered him nothing, but prayed him for the love of God do him no harm. Quoth Pietro, 'Arise and fear not that I will do thee any hurt; but tell me how thou comest here and for what purpose.' The youth told him all, whereupon Pietro, no less rejoiced to have found him than his wife was woeful, taking him by the hand, carried him into the chamber, where the lady awaited him with the greatest affright in the world, and seating himself overagainst her, said, 'But now thou cursedst Ercolano's wife and avouchedst that she should be burnt and that she was the disgrace of all you women; why didst thou not speak of thyself? Or, an thou choosedst not to speak of thyself, how could thy conscience suffer thee to speak thus of her, knowing thyself to have done even as did she? Certes, none other thing moved thee thereunto save that you women are all made thus and look to cover your own doings with others' defaults; would fire might come from heaven to burn you all up, perverse generation that you are!'

The lady, seeing that, in the first heat of the discovery, he had done her no harm other than in words and herseeming she saw that he was all agog with joy for that he held so goodly a stripling by the hand, took heart and said, 'Of this much, indeed, I am mighty well assured, that thou wouldst have fire come from heaven to burn us women all up, being, as thou art, as fain to us as a dog to cudgels; but, by Christ His cross, thou shalt not get thy wish. However, I would fain have a little discourse with thee, so I may know of what thou complainest. Certes, it were a fine thing an thou shouldst seek to even me with Ercolano's wife, who is a beat-breast, a smell-sin,[4] and hath of her husband what she will and is of him held dear as a wife should be, the which is not the case with me. For, grant that I am well clad and shod of thee, thou knowest but too well how I fare for the rest and how long it is since thou hast lain with me; and I had liefer go barefoot and rags to my back and be well used of thee abed than have all these things, being used as I am of thee. For understand plainly, Pietro; I am a woman like other women and have a mind unto that which other women desire; so that, an I procure me thereof, not having it from thee, thou hast no call to missay of me therefor; at the least, I do thee this much honour that I have not to do with horseboys and scald-heads.'

PIETRO PERCEIVED that words were not like to fail her for all that night; wherefore, as one who recked little of her, 'Wife,' said he, 'no more for the present; I will content thee aright of this matter; but thou wilt do us a great courtesy to let us have somewhat to sup withal, for that meseemeth this lad, like myself, hath not yet supped.' 'Certes, no,' answered the lady, 'he hath not yet supped; for we were sitting down to table, when thou camest in thine ill hour.' 'Go, then,' rejoined Pietro, 'contrive that we may sup, and after I will order this matter on such wise that thou shalt have no cause to complain.' The lady, finding that her husband was satisfied, arose and caused straightway reset the table; then, letting bring the supper she had prepared, she supped merrily in company with her caitiff of a husband and the young man. After supper, what Pietro devised for the satisfaction of all three hath escaped my mind; but this much I know that on the following morning the youth was escorted back to the public place, not altogether certain which he had the more been that night, wife or husband. Wherefore, dear my ladies, this will I say to you, 'Whoso doth it to you, do you it to him'; and if you cannot presently, keep it in mind till such time as you can, so he may get as good as he giveth."

DIONEO HAVING MADE an end of his story, which had been less laughed at by the ladies [than usual], more for shamefastness than for the little delight they took therein, the queen, seeing the end of her sovranty come, rose to her feet and putting off the laurel crown, set it blithely on Elisa's head, saying, "With you, madam, henceforth it resteth to command." Elisa, accepting the honour, did even as it had been done before her, in that, having first, to the satisfaction of the company, taken order with the seneschal for that whereof there was need for the time of her governance, she said, "We have many a time heard how, by dint of smart sayings and ready repartees and prompt advisements, many have availed with an apt retort[5] to take the edge off other folks' teeth or to fend off imminent perils; and, for that the matter is goodly and may be useful,[6] I will that to-morrow, with God's aid, it be discoursed within these terms, to wit, OF WHOSO, BEING ASSAILED WITH SOME JIBING SPEECH, HATH VINDICATED HIMSELF

OR HATH WITH SOME READY REPLY OR ADVISEMENT ESCAPED LOSS, PERIL OR SHAME."

This was much commended of all, whereupon the queen, rising to her feet, dismissed them all until supper time. The honourable company, seeing her risen, stood up all and each, according to the wonted fashion, applied himself to that which was most agreeable to him. But, the crickets having now given over singing, the queen let call every one and they betook themselves to supper, which being despatched with merry cheer, they all gave themselves to singing and making music, and Emilia having, at the queen's commandment, set up a dance, Dioneo was bidden sing a song, whereupon he straightway struck up with "Mistress Aldruda, come lift up your fud-a, for I bring you, I bring you, good tidings." Whereat all the ladies fell a-laughing and especially the queen, who bade him leave that and sing another. Quoth Dioneo, "Madam, had I a tabret, I would sing 'Come truss your coats, I prithee, Mistress Burdock,' or 'Under the olive the grass is'; or will you have me say 'The waves of the sea do great evil to me'? But I have no tabret, so look which you will of these others. Will it please you have 'Come forth unto us, so it may be cut down, like a May in the midst of the meadows'?" "Nay," answered the queen; "give us another." "Then," said Dioneo, "shall I sing, 'Mistress Simona, embarrel, embarrel! It is not the month of October'?" Quoth the queen, laughing, "Ill luck to thee, sing us a goodly one, an thou wilt, for we will none of these." "Nay, madam," rejoined Dioneo, "fash not yourself; but which then like you better? I know more than a thousand. Will you have 'This my shell an I prick it not well,' or 'Fair and softly, husband mine' or 'I'll buy me a cock, a cock of an hundred pounds sterling'?"[7] Therewithal the queen, somewhat provoked, though all the other ladies laughed, said, "Dioneo, leave jesting and sing us a goodly one; else shalt thou prove how I can be angry." Hearing this, he gave over his quips and cranks and forthright fell a-singing after this fashion:

O Love, the amorous light
That beameth from yon fair one's lovely eyes
Hath made me thine and hers in servant-guise.

The splendour of her lovely eyes, it wrought
That first thy flames were kindled in my breast,
Passing thereto through mine;
Yea, and thy virtue first unto my thought
Her visage fair it was made manifest,
Which picturing, I twine
And lay before her shrine
All virtues, that to her I sacrifice,
Become the new occasion of my sighs.

Thus, dear my lord, thy vassal am I grown
And of thy might obediently await
Grace for my lowliness;
Yet wot I not if wholly there be known
The high desire that in my breast thou'st set
And my sheer faith, no less,
Of her who doth possess
My heart so that from none beneath the skies,
Save her alone, peace would I take or prize.

Wherefore I pray thee, sweet my lord and sire,
Discover it to her and cause her taste
Some scantling of thy heat
To-me-ward, —for thou seest that in the fire,
Loving, I languish and for torment waste
By inches at her feet, —
And eke in season meet
Commend me to her favour on such wise
As I would plead for thee, should need arise.[8]

Dioneo, by his silence, showing that his song was ended, the queen let sing many others, having natheless much commended his. Then, somedele of the night being spent and the queen feeling the heat of the day to be now overcome of the coolness of the night, she bade each at his pleasure betake himself to rest against the ensuing day.

---

1. *i.e.* she was grown so repulsively ugly in her old age, that no one cared to do her even so trifling a service as giving her a spark in tinder to light her fire withal.
2. Or chokebits (*stranguglioni*).
3. *i.e.* that they may serve to purchase remission from purgatory for the souls of her dead relatives, instead of the burning of candles and tapers, which is held by the Roman Catholic Church to have that effect.
4. *i.e.* a hypocritical sham devotee, covering a lewd life with an appearance of sanctity.
5. Lit. a due or deserved bite (*debito morso*). I mention this to show the connection with teeth.
6. An ellipsis of a kind common in Boccaccio and indeed in all the old Italian writers, meaning "it may be useful to enlarge upon the subject in question."
7. The songs proposed by Dioneo are all apparently of a light, if not a wanton, character and "not fit to be sung before ladies."
8. This singularly naïve give-and-take fashion of asking a favour of a God recalls the old Scotch epitaph cited by Mr. George Macdonald:
   Here lie I Martin Elginbrodde:
   Hae mercy o' my soul, Lord God;
   As I wad do, were I Lord God
   And ye were Martin Elginbrodde.

DAY THE SIXTH

Here Beginneth the Sixth Day of the Decameron
Wherein Under the Governance of Elisa Is
Discoursed of Whoso Being Assailed With Some
Jibing Speech Hath Vindicated Himself or Hath
With Some Ready Reply or Advisement Escaped
Loss, Peril or Shame

The moon, being now in the middest heaven, had lost its radiance and every part of our world was bright with the new coming light, when, the queen arising and letting call her company, they all with slow step fared forth and rambled over the dewy grass to a little distance from the fair hill, holding various discourse of one thing and another and debating of the more or less goodliness of the stories told, what while they renewed their laughter at the various adventures related therein, till such time as the sun mounting high and beginning to wax hot, it seemed well to them all to turn homeward. Wherefore, reversing their steps, they returned to the palace and there, by the queen's commandment, the tables being already laid and everything strewn with sweet-scented herbs and fair flowers, they addressed themselves to eat, ere the heat should grow greater. This being joyously accomplished, ere they did otherwhat, they sang divers goodly and pleasant canzonets, after which some went to sleep, whilst some sat down to play at chess and other some at tables and Dioneo fell to singing, in concert with Lauretta, of Troilus and Cressida. Then, the hour come for their reassembling after the wonted fashion,[1] they all, being summoned on the part of the queen, seated themselves, as of their usance, about the fountain; but, as she was about to call for the first story, there befell a thing that had not yet befallen there, to wit, that a great clamour was heard by her and by all, made by the wenches and serving-men in the kitchen.

The seneschal, being called and questioned who it was that cried thus and what might be the occasion of the turmoil, answered that the clamour was between Licisca and Tindaro, but that he knew not the cause thereof, being but then come thither to make them bide quiet, whenas he had been summoned on her part. The queen bade him incontinent fetch thither the two offenders and they being come, enquired what was the cause of their clamour; whereto Tindaro offering to reply, Licisca, who was well in years and somewhat overmasterful, being heated with the outcry she had made, turned to him with an angry air and said, "Mark this brute of a man who dareth to speak before me, whereas I am! Let me speak." Then, turning again to the queen, "Madam," quoth she, "this fellow would teach me, forsooth, to know Sicofante's wife and neither more nor less than as if I had not been familiar with her, would fain give me to believe that, the first night her husband lay with her, Squire Maul[2] made his entry into Black Hill[3] by force and with effusion of blood; and I say that it is not true; nay, he entered there in peace and to the great contentment of those within. Marry, this fellow is simple enough to believe wenches to be such ninnies that they stand to lose their time, abiding the commodity of their fathers and brothers, who six times out of seven tarry three or four years more than they should to marry them. Well would they fare, forsooth, were they to wait so long! By Christ His faith (and I should know what I say, when I swear thus) I have not a single gossip who went a maid to her husband; and as for the wives, I know full well how many and what tricks they play their husbands; and this blockhead would teach me to know women, as if I had been born yesterday."

What while Licisca spoke, the ladies kept up such a laughing that you might have drawn all their teeth; and the queen imposed silence upon her a good half dozen times, but to no purpose; she stinted not till she had said her say. When she had at last made an end of her talk, the queen turned to Dioneo and said, laughing, "Dioneo, this is a matter for thy jurisdiction; wherefore, when we shall have made an end of our stories, thou shalt proceed to give final judgment thereon." Whereto he answered promptly, "Madam, the judgment is already given, without hearing more of the matter; and I say that Licisca is in the right and opine that it is even as she saith and that Tindaro is an ass." Licisca, hearing this, fell a-laughing and turning to Tindaro, said, "I told thee so; begone and God go with thee; thinkest thou thou knowest better than I, thou whose eyes are not yet dry?[4] Gramercy, I have not lived here below for nothing, no, not I!" And had not the queen with an angry air imposed silence on her and sent her and Tindaro away, bidding her make no more words or clamour, an she would not be flogged, they had had nought to do all that day but attend to her. When they were gone, the queen called on Filomena to make a beginning with the day's stories and she blithely began thus:

---

1. Lit. for their returning to consistory (*del dovere a concistoro tornare*).
2. *Messer Mazza, i.e.* veretrum.
3. *Monte Nero, i.e.* vas muliebre.
4. *i.e.* who are yet a child, in modern parlance, "Thou whose lips are yet wet with thy mother's milk."

THE FIRST STORY

A GENTLEMAN ENGAGETH TO MADAM ORETTA TO CARRY HER A-HORSEBACK WITH A STORY, BUT, TELLING IT DISORDERLY, IS PRAYED BY HER TO SET HER DOWN AGAIN

"Young ladies, like as stars, in the clear nights, are the ornaments of the heavens and the flowers and the leaf-clad shrubs, in the Spring, of the green fields and the hillsides, even so are praiseworthy manners and goodly discourse adorned by sprightly sallies, the which, for that they are brief, beseem women yet better than men, inasmuch as much speaking is more forbidden to the former than to the latter. Yet, true it is, whatever the cause, whether it be the meanness of our[1] understanding or some particular grudge borne by heaven to our times, that there be nowadays few or no women left who know how to say a witty word in due season or who, an it be said to them, know how to apprehend it as it behoveth; the which is a general reproach to our whole sex. However, for that enough hath been said aforetime on the subject by Pampinea,[2] I purpose to say no more thereof; but, to give you to understand how much goodliness there is in witty sayings, when spoken in due season, it pleaseth me to recount to you the courteous fashion in which a lady imposed silence upon a gentleman.

As many of you ladies may either know by sight or have heard tell, there was not long since in our city a noble and well-bred and well-spoken gentlewoman, whose worth merited not that her name be left unsaid. She was called, then, Madam Oretta and was the wife of Messer Geri Spina. She chanced to be, as we are, in the country, going from place to place, by way of diversion, with a company of ladies and gentlemen, whom she had that day entertained to dinner at her house, and the way being belike somewhat long from the place whence they set out to that whither they were all purposed to go afoot, one of the gentlemen said to her, 'Madam Oretta, an you will, I will carry you a-horseback great part of the way we have to go with one of the finest stories in the world.' 'Nay, sir,' answered the lady, 'I pray you instantly thereof; indeed, it will be most agreeable to me.' Master cavalier, who maybe fared no better, sword at side than tale on tongue, hearing this, began a story of his, which of itself was in truth very goodly; but he, now thrice or four or even half a dozen times repeating one same word, anon turning back and whiles saying, 'I said not aright,' and often erring in the names and putting one for another, marred it cruelly, more by token that he delivered himself exceedingly ill, having regard to the quality of the persons and the nature of the incidents of his tale. By reason whereof, Madam Oretta, hearkening to him, was many a time taken with a sweat and failing of the heart, as she were sick and near her end, and at last, being unable to brook the thing any more and seeing the gentleman engaged in an imbroglio from which he was not like to extricate himself, she said to him pleasantly, 'Sir, this horse of yours hath too hard a trot; wherefore I pray you be pleased to set me down.' The gentleman, who, as it chanced, understood a hint better than he told a story, took the jest in good part and turning it off with a laugh, fell to discoursing of other matters and left unfinished the story that he had begun and conducted so ill."

---

1. *i.e.* women's.
2. See ante Introduction to the last story of the First Day.

THE SECOND STORY

CISTI THE BAKER WITH A WORD OF HIS FASHION MAKETH MESSER GERI SPINA SENSIBLE OF AN INDISCREET REQUEST OF HIS

MADAM ORETTA'S saying was greatly commended of all, ladies and men, and the queen bidding Pampinea follow on, she began thus: "Fair ladies, I know not of mine own motion to resolve me which is the more at fault, whether nature in fitting to a noble soul a mean body or fortune in imposing a mean condition upon a body endowed with a noble soul, as in one our townsman Cisti and in many another we may have seen it happen; which Cisti being gifted with a very lofty spirit, fortune made him a baker. And for this, certes, I should curse both nature and fortune like, did I not know the one to be most discreet and the other to have a thousand eyes, albeit fools picture her blind; and I imagine, therefore, that, being exceeding well-advised, they do that which is oftentimes done of human beings, who, uncertain of future events, bury their most precious things, against their occasions, in the meanest places of their houses, as being the least suspect, and thence bring them forth in their greatest needs, the mean place having the while kept them more surely than would the goodly chamber. And so, meseemeth, do the governors of the world hide oftentimes their most precious things under the shadow of crafts and conditions reputed most mean, to the end that, bringing them forth therefrom in time of need, their lustre may show the brighter. Which how Cisti the baker made manifest, though in but a trifling matter, restoring to Messer Geri Spina (whom the story but now told of Madam Oretta, who was his wife, hath recalled to my memory) the eyes of the understanding, it pleaseth me to show you in a very short story.

I must tell you, then, that Pope Boniface, with whom Messer Geri Spina was in very great favour, having despatched to Florence certain of his gentlemen on an embassy concerning sundry important matters of his, they lighted down at the house of Messer Geri and he treating the pope's affairs in company with them, it chanced, whatever might have been the occasion thereof, that he and they passed well nigh every morning afoot before Santa Maria Ughi, where Cisti the baker had his bakehouse and plied his craft in person. Now, albeit fortune had appointed Cisti a humble enough condition, she had so far at the least been kind to him therein that he was grown very rich and without ever choosing to abandon it for any other, lived very splendidly, having, amongst his other good things, the best wines, white and red, that were to be found in Florence or in the neighbouring country. Seeing Messer Geri and the pope's ambassadors pass every morning before his door and the heat being great, he bethought himself that it were a great courtesy to give them to drink of his good white wine; but, having regard to his own condition and that of Messer Geri, he deemed it not a seemly thing to presume to invite them, but determined to bear himself on such wise as should lead Messer Geri to invite himself.

Accordingly, having still on his body a very white doublet and an apron fresh from the wash, which bespoke him rather a miller than a baker, he let set before his door, every morning, towards the time when he looked for Messer Geri and the ambassadors to pass, a new tinned pail of fair water and a small pitcher of new Bolognese ware, full of his good white wine, together with two beakers, which seemed of silver, so bright they were, and seated himself there, against they should pass, when, after clearing his throat once or twice, he fell to drinking of that his wine with such a relish that he had made a dead man's mouth water for it. Messer Geri, having seen him do thus one and two mornings, said on the third, 'How now, Cisti? Is it good?' Whereupon he started to his feet and said, 'Ay is it, Sir; but how good I cannot give you to understand, except you taste thereof.' Messer Geri, in whom either the nature of the weather or belike the relish with which he saw Cisti drink had begotten a thirst, turned to the ambassadors and said, smiling, 'Gentlemen, we shall do well to taste this honest man's wine; belike it is such that we shall not repent thereof.' Accordingly, he made with them towards Cisti, who let bring a goodly settle out of his bakehouse and praying them sit, said to their serving-men, who pressed forward to rinse the beakers, 'Stand back, friends, and leave this office to me, for that I know no less well how to skink than to wield the baking-peel; and look you not to taste a drop thereof.' So saying, he with his own hands washed out four new and goodly beakers and letting bring a little pitcher of his good wine, busied himself with giving Messer Geri and his companions to drink, to whom the wine seemed the best they had drunken that great while; wherefore they commended it greatly, and well nigh every morning, whilst the ambassadors abode there, Messer Geri went thither to drink in company with them.

After awhile, their business being despatched and they about to depart, Messer Geri made them a magnificent banquet, whereto he bade a number of the most worshipful citizens and amongst the rest, Cisti, who would, however, on no condition go thither; whereupon Messer Geri bade one of his serving-men go fetch a flask of the baker's wine and give each guest a half beaker thereof with the first course. The servant, despiteful most like for that he had never availed to drink of the wine, took a great flagon, which when Cisti saw, 'My son,' said he, 'Messer Geri sent thee not to me.' The man avouched again and again that he had, but, getting none other answer, returned to Messer Geri and reported it to him. Quoth he, 'Go back to him and tell him that I do indeed send thee to him; and if he still make thee the same answer, ask him to whom I send thee, [an it be not to him.]' Accordingly, the servant went back to the baker and said to him, 'Cisti, for certain Messer Geri sendeth me to thee and none other.' 'For certain, my son,' answered the baker, 'he doth it not.' 'Then,' said the man, 'to whom doth he send me?' 'To the Arno,' replied Cisti; which answer when the servant reported to Messer Geri, the eyes of his understanding were of a sudden opened and he said to the man, 'Let me see what flask thou carriedst thither.'

When he saw the great flagon aforesaid, he said, 'Cisti saith sooth,' and giving the man a sharp reproof, made him take a sortable flask, which when Cisti saw, 'Now,' quoth he, 'I know full well that he sendeth thee to me,' and cheerfully filled it unto him. Then, that same day, he let fill a little cask with the like wine and causing carry it softly to Messer Geri's house, went presently thither and finding him there, said to him, 'Sir. I would not have you think that the great flagon of this morning frightened me; nay, but, meseeming that which I have of these past days shown you with my little pitchers had escaped your mind, to wit, that this is no household wine,[1] I wished to recall it to you. But, now, for that I purpose no longer to be your steward thereof, I have sent it all to you; henceforward do with it as it pleaseth you.' Messer Geri set great store by Cisti's present and rendering him such thanks as he deemed sortable, ever after held him for a man of great worth and for friend."

---

1. Lit. Family wine (*vin da famiglia*), *i.e.* no wine for servants' or general drinking, but a choice vintage, to be reserved for special occasions.

✣ 3 ✣

THE THIRD STORY

MADAM NONNA DE' PULCI, WITH A READY RETORT TO
A NOT ALTOGETHER SEEMLY PLEASANTRY,
IMPOSETH SILENCE ON THE BISHOP OF FLORENCE

PAMPINEA HAVING MADE an end of her story and both Cisti's reply and his liberality having been much commended of all, it pleased the queen that the next story should be told by Lauretta, who blithely began as follows, "Jocund ladies, first Pampinea and now Filomena have spoken truly enough touching our little worth and the excellence of pithy sayings, whereto that there may be no need now to return, I would fain remind you, over and above that which hath been said on the subject, that the nature of smart sayings is such that they should bite upon the hearer, not as the dog, but as the sheep biteth; for that, an a trait bit like a dog, it were not a trait, but an affront. The right mean in this was excellently well hit both by Madam Oretta's speech and Cisti's reply. It is true that, if a smart thing be said by way of retort, and the answerer biteth like a dog, having been bitten on like wise, meseemeth he is not to be blamed as he would have been, had this not been the case; wherefore it behoveth us look how and with whom, no less than when and where, we bandy jests; to which considerations, a prelate of ours, taking too little heed, received at least as sharp a bite as he thought to give, as I shall show you in a little story.

Messer Antonio d'Orso, a learned and worthy prelate, being Bishop of Florence, there came thither a Catalan gentleman, called Messer Dego della Ratta, marshal for King Robert, who, being a man of a very fine person and a great amorist, took a liking to one among other Florentine ladies, a very fair lady and granddaughter to a brother of the said bishop, and hearing that her husband, albeit a man of good family, was very sordid and miserly, agreed with him to give him five hundred gold florins, so he would suffer him lie a night with his wife. Accordingly, he let gild so many silver poplins,[1] a coin which was then current, and having lain with the lady, though against her will, gave them to the husband. The thing after coming to be known everywhere, the sordid wretch of a husband reaped both loss and scorn, but the bishop, like a discreet man as he was, affected to know nothing of the matter. Wherefore, he and the marshal consorting much together, it chanced, as they rode side by side with each other, one St. John's Day, viewing the ladies on either side of the way where the mantle is run for,[2] the prelate espied a young lady,—of whom this present pestilence hath bereft us and whom all you ladies must have known, Madam Nonna de' Pulci by name, cousin to Messer Alessio Rinucci, a fresh and fair young woman, both well-spoken and high-spirited, then not long before married in Porta San Piero,—and pointed her out to the marshal; then, being near her, he laid his hand on the latter's shoulder and said to her, 'Nonna, how deemest thou of this gallant? Thinkest thou thou couldst make a conquest of him?' It seemed to the lady that those words somewhat trenched upon her honour and were like to sully it in the eyes of those (and there were many there) who heard them; wherefore, not thinking to purge away the soil, but to return blow for blow, she promptly answered, 'Maybe, sir, he would not make a conquest of me; but, in any case, I should want good money.' The marshal and the bishop, hearing this, felt themselves alike touched to the quick by her speech, the one as the author of the cheat put upon the bishop's brother's granddaughter and the other as having suffered the affront in the person of his kinswoman, and made off, shamefast and silent, without looking at one another or saying aught more to her that day. Thus, then, the young lady having been bitten, it was not forbidden her to bite her biter with a retort."

---

1. A silver coin of about the size and value of our silver penny, which, when gilded, would pass muster well enough for a gold florin, unless closely examined.
2. *Il palio*, a race anciently run at Florence on St. John's Day, as that of the Barberi at Rome during the Carnival.

❦ 4 ❧

THE FOURTH STORY

CHICHIBIO, COOK TO CURRADO GIANFIGLIAZZI,
WITH A READY WORD SPOKEN TO SAVE HIMSELF,
TURNETH HIS MASTER'S ANGER INTO LAUGHTER
AND ESCAPETH THE PUNISHMENT THREATENED HIM
BY THE LATTER

LAURETTA BEING silent and Nonna having been mightily commended of all, the queen charged Neifile to follow on, and she said, "Although, lovesome ladies, a ready wit doth often furnish folk with words both prompt and useful and goodly, according to the circumstances, yet fortune whiles cometh to the help of the fearful and putteth of a sudden into their mouths such answers as might never of malice aforethought be found of the speaker, as I purpose to show you by my story.

Currado Gianfigliazzi, as each of you ladies may have both heard and seen, hath still been a noble citizen of our city, liberal and magnificent, and leading a knightly life, hath ever, letting be for the present his weightier doings, taken delight in hawks and hounds. Having one day with a falcon of his brought down a crane and finding it young and fat, he sent it to a good cook he had, a Venetian hight Chichibio, bidding him roast it for supper and dress it well. Chichibio, who looked the new-caught gull he was, trussed the crane and setting it to the fire, proceeded to cook it diligently. When it was all but done and gave out a very savoury smell, it chanced that a wench of the neighbourhood, Brunetta by name, of whom Chichibio was sore enamoured, entered the kitchen and smelling the crane and seeing it, instantly besought him to give her a thigh thereof. He answered her, singing, and said, 'Thou shalt not have it from me, Mistress Brunetta, thou shalt not have it from me.' Whereat she, being vexed, said to him, 'By God His faith, an thou give it me not, thou shalt never have of me aught that shall pleasure thee.' In brief, many were the words between them and at last, Chichibio, not to anger his mistress, cut off one of the thighs of the crane and gave it her.

The bird being after set before Messer Currado and certain stranger guests of his, lacking a thigh, and the former marvelling thereat, he let call Chichibio and asked him what was come of the other thigh; whereto the liar of a Venetian answered without hesitation, 'Sir, cranes have but one thigh and one leg.' 'What a devil?' cried Currado in a rage. 'They have but one thigh and one leg? Have I never seen a crane before?' 'Sir,' replied Chichibio, 'it is as I tell you, and whenas it pleaseth you, I will cause you see it in the quick.' Currado, out of regard for the strangers he had with him, chose not to make more words of the matter, but said, 'Since thou sayst thou wilt cause me see it in the quick, a thing I never yet saw or heard tell of, I desire to

282

see it to-morrow morning, in which case I shall be content; but I swear to thee, by Christ His body, that, an it be otherwise, I will have thee served on such wise that thou shalt still have cause to remember my name to thy sorrow so long as thou livest.' There was an end of the talk for that night; but, next morning, as soon as it was day, Currado, whose anger was nothing abated for sleep, arose, still full of wrath, and bade bring the horses; then, mounting Chichibio upon a rouncey, he carried him off towards a watercourse, on whose banks cranes were still to be seen at break of day, saying, 'We shall soon see who lied yestereve, thou or I.'

Chichibio, seeing that his master's wrath yet endured and that needs must be made good his lie and knowing not how he should avail thereunto, rode after Currado in the greatest fright that might be, and fain would he have fled, so but he might. But, seeing no way of escape, he looked now before him and now behind and now on either side and took all he saw for cranes standing on two feet. Presently, coming near to the river, he chanced to catch sight, before any other, of a round dozen of cranes on the bank, all perched on one leg, as they use to do, when they sleep; whereupon he straightway showed them to Currado, saying, 'Now, sir, if you look at those that stand yonder, you may very well see that I told you the truth yesternight, to wit, that cranes have but one thigh and one leg.' Currado, seeing them, answered, 'Wait and I will show thee that they have two,' and going somewhat nearer to them, he cried out, 'Ho! Ho!' At this the cranes, putting down the other leg, all, after some steps, took to flight; whereupon Currado said to him, 'How sayst thou now, malapert knave that thou art? Deemest thou they have two legs?' Chichibio, all confounded and knowing not whether he stood on his head or his heels,[1] answered, 'Ay, sir; but you did not cry, "Ho! Ho!" to yesternight's crane; had you cried thus, it would have put out the other thigh and the other leg, even as did those yonder.' This reply so tickled Currado that all his wrath was changed into mirth and laughter and he said, 'Chichibio, thou art in the right; indeed, I should have done it.' Thus, then, with his prompt and comical answer did Chichibio avert ill luck and made his peace with his master."

---

1. Lit. knowing not whence himself came.

❧ 5 ❧

THE FIFTH STORY

MESSER FORESE DA RABATTA AND MASTER GIOTTO THE PAINTER COMING FROM MUGELLO, EACH JESTINGLY RALLIETH THE OTHER ON HIS SCURVY FAVOUR

NEIFILE BEING silent and the ladies having taken much pleasure in Chichibio's reply, Pamfilo, by the queen's desire, spoke thus: "Dearest ladies, it chanceth often that, like as fortune whiles hideth very great treasures of worth and virtue under mean conditions, as hath been a little before shown by Pampinea, even so, under the sorriest of human forms are marvellous wits found to have been lodged by nature; and this very plainly appeared in two townsmen of ours, of whom I purpose briefly to entertain you. For that the one, who was called Messer Forese da Rabatta, though little of person and misshapen, with a flat camoys face, that had been an eyesore on the shoulders of the foulest cadger in Florence, was yet of such excellence in the interpretation of the laws, that he was of many men of worth reputed a very treasury of civil right; whilst the other, whose name was Giotto, had so excellent a genius that there was nothing of all which Nature, mother and mover of all things, presenteth unto us by the ceaseless revolution of the heavens, but he with pencil and pen and brush depicted it and that so closely that not like, nay, but rather the thing itself it seemed, insomuch that men's visual sense is found to have been oftentimes deceived in things of his fashion, taking that for real which was but depictured. Wherefore, he having brought back to the light this art, which had for many an age lain buried under the errors of certain folk who painted more to divert the eyes of the ignorant than to please the understanding of the judicious, he may deservedly be styled one of the chief glories of Florence, the more so that he bore the honours he had gained with the utmost humility and although, while he lived, chief over all else in his art, he still refused to be called master, which title, though rejected by him, shone so much the more gloriously in him as it was with greater eagerness greedily usurped by those who knew less than he, or by his disciples. Yet, great as was his skill, he was not therefore anywise goodlier of person or better favoured than Messer Forese. But, to come to my story:

I must tell you that Messer Forese and Giotto had each his country house at Mugello and the former, having gone to visit his estates, at that season of the summer when the Courts hold holiday, and returning thence on a sorry cart-horse, chanced to fall in with the aforesaid Giotto, who had been on the same errand and was then on his way back to Florence nowise better equipped than himself in horse and accoutrements. Accordingly, they joined company and fared on softly, like old men as they were. Presently, it chanced, as we often see it happen in summer time, that a sudden shower overtook them, from which, as quickliest they might, they took shelter in the house of a husbandman, a friend and acquaintance of both of them. After awhile, the rain showing no sign of giving over and they wishing to reach Florence by daylight, they borrowed of their host two old homespun cloaks and two hats, rusty with age, for that there were no better to be had, and set out again upon their way.

When they had gone awhile and were all drenched and bemired with the splashing that their hackneys kept up with their hoofs—things which use not to add worship to any one's looks,—the weather began to clear a little and the two wayfarers, who had long fared on in silence, fell to conversing together. Messer Forese, as he rode, hearkening to Giotto, who was a very fine talker, fell to considering his companion from head to foot and seeing him everywise so ill accoutred and in such scurvy case, burst out laughing and without taking any thought to his own plight, said to him, 'How sayst thou, Giotto? An there encountered us here a stranger who had never seen thee, thinkest thou he would believe thee to be, as thou art, the finest painter in the world?' 'Ay, sir,' answered Giotto forthright, 'methinketh he might e'en believe it whenas, looking upon you, he should believe that you knew your A B C.' Messer Forese, hearing this, was sensible of his error and saw himself paid with money such as the wares he had sold."[1]

---

1. Or, as we should say, "in his own coin."

✣ 6 ✤

THE SIXTH STORY

MICHELE SCALZA PROVETH TO CERTAIN YOUNG MEN THAT THE CADGERS OF FLORENCE ARE THE BEST GENTLEMEN OF THE WORLD OR THE MAREMMA AND WINNETH A SUPPER

THE LADIES yet laughed at Giotto's prompt retort, when the queen charged Fiammetta follow on and she proceeded to speak thus: "Young ladies, the mention by Pamfilo of the cadgers of Florence, whom peradventure you know not as doth he, hath brought to my mind a story, wherein, without deviating from our appointed theme, it is demonstrated how great is their nobility; and it pleaseth me, therefore, to relate it.

It is no great while since there was in our city a young man called Michele Scalza, who was the merriest and most agreeable man in the world and he had still the rarest stories in hand, wherefore the young Florentines were exceeding glad to have his company whenas they made a party of pleasure amongst themselves. It chanced one day, he being with certain folk at Monte Ughi, that the question was started among them of who were the best and oldest gentlemen of Florence. Some said the Uberti, others the Lamberti, and one this family and another that, according as it occurred to his mind; which Scalza hearing, he fell a-laughing and said, 'Go to, addlepates that you are! You know not what you say. The best gentlemen and the oldest, not only of Florence, but of all the world or the Maremma,[1] are the Cadgers,[2] a matter upon which all the phisopholers and every one who knoweth them, as I do, are of accord; and lest you should understand it of others, I speak of the Cadgers your neighbors of Santa Maria Maggiore.'

When the young men, who looked for him to say otherwhat, heard this, they all made mock of him and said, 'Thou gullest us, as if we knew not the Cadgers, even as thou dost.' 'By the Evangels,' replied Scalza, 'I gull you not; nay, I speak the truth, and if there be any here who will lay a supper thereon, to be given to the winner and half a dozen companions of his choosing, I will willingly hold the wager; and I will do yet more for you, for I will abide by the judgment of whomsoever you will.' Quoth one of them, called Neri Mannini, 'I am ready to try to win the supper in question'; whereupon, having agreed together to take Piero di Fiorentino, in whose house they were, to judge, they betook themselves to him, followed by all the rest, who looked to see Scalza lose and to make merry over his discomfiture, and recounted to him all that had passed. Piero, who was a discreet young man, having first heard Neri's argument, turned to Scalza and said to him, 'And thou, how canst thou prove this that thou affirmest?'

'How, sayest thou?' answered Scalza. 'Nay, I will prove it by such reasoning that not only thou, but he who denieth it, shall acknowledge that I speak sooth. You know that, the ancienter men are, the nobler they are; and so was it said but now among these. Now the Cadgers are more ancient than any one else, so that they are nobler; and showing you how they are the most ancient, I shall undoubtedly have won the wager. You must know, then, that the Cadgers were made by God the Lord in the days when He first began to learn to draw; but the rest of mankind were made after He knew how to draw. And to assure yourselves that in this I say sooth, do but consider the Cadgers in comparison with other folk; whereas you see all the rest of mankind with faces well composed and duly proportioned, you may see the Cadgers, this with a visnomy very long and strait and with a face out of all measure broad; one hath too long and another too short a nose and a third hath a chin jutting out and turned upward and huge jawbones that show as they were those of an ass, whilst some there be who have one eye bigger than the other and other some who have one set lower than the other, like the faces that children used to make, whenas they first begin to learn to draw. Wherefore, as I have already said, it is abundantly apparent that God the Lord made them, what time He was learning to draw; so that they are more ancient and consequently nobler than the rest of mankind.' At this, both Piero, who was the judge, and Neri, who had wagered the supper, and all the rest, hearing Scalza's comical argument and remembering themselves,[3] fell all a-laughing and affirmed that he was in the right and had won the supper, for that the Cadgers were assuredly the noblest and most ancient gentlemen that were to be found not in Florence alone, but in the world or the Maremma. Wherefore it was very justly said of Pamfilo, seeking to show the foulness of Messer Forese's visnomy, that it would have showed notably ugly on one of the Cadgers."

---

1. A commentator notes that the adjunction to the world of the Maremma (cf. Elijer Goff, "The Irish Question has for some centuries been enjoyed by *the universe and other parts*") produces a risible effect and gives the reader to understand that Scalza broaches the question only by way of a joke. The same may be said of the jesting inversion of the word philosophers (phisopholers, Fisofoli) in the next line.
2. *Baronci*, the Florentine name for what we should call professional beggars, "mumpers, chanters and Abrahammen," called *Bari* and *Barocci* in other parts of Italy. This story has been a prodigious stumbling-block to former translators, not one of whom appears to have had the slightest idea of Boccaccio's meaning.
3. *i.e.* of the comical fashion of the Cadgers.

❦ 7 ❦

THE SEVENTH STORY

MADAM FILIPPA, BEING FOUND BY HER HUSBAND
WITH A LOVER OF HERS AND BROUGHT TO JUSTICE,
DELIVERETH HERSELF WITH A PROMPT AND
PLEASANT ANSWER AND CAUSETH MODIFY THE
STATUTE

FIAMMETTA WAS NOW silent and all laughed yet at the novel argument used by Scalza for the ennoblement over all of the Cadgers, when the queen enjoined Filostrato to tell and he accordingly began to say, "It is everywise a fine thing, noble ladies, to know how to speak well, but I hold it yet goodlier to know how to do it whereas necessity requireth it, even as a gentlewoman, of whom I purpose to entertain you, knew well how to do on such wise that not only did she afford her hearers matter for mirth and laughter, but did herself loose from the toils of an ignominious death, as you shall presently hear.

There was, then, aforetime, in the city of Prato, a statute in truth no less blameworthy than cruel, which, without making any distinction, ordained that any woman found by her husband in adultery with any her lover should be burnt, even as she who should be discovered to have sold her favours for money. What while this statute was in force, it befell that a noble and beautiful lady, by name Madam Filippa, who was of a singularly amorous complexion, was one night found by Rinaldo de' Pugliesi her husband, in her own chamber in the arms of Lazzerino de' Guazzagliotri, a noble and handsome youth of that city, whom she loved even as herself. Rinaldo, seeing this, was sore enraged and scarce contained himself from falling upon them and slaying them; and but that he feared for himself, an he should ensue the promptings of his anger, he had certainly done it. However, he forbore from this, but could not refrain from seeking of the law of Prato that which it was not permitted him to accomplish with his own hand, to wit, the death of his wife. Having, therefore, very sufficient evidence to prove the lady's default, no sooner was the day come than, without taking other counsel, he lodged an accusation against her and caused summon her before the provost.

Madam Filippa, being great of heart, as women commonly are who are verily in love, resolved, although counselled to the contrary by many of her friends and kinsfolk, to appear, choosing rather, confessing the truth, to die with an undaunted spirit, than, meanly fleeing, to live an outlaw in exile and confess herself unworthy of such a lover as he in whose arms she had been the foregoing night. Wherefore, presenting herself before the provost, attended by a great company of men and ladies and exhorted of all to deny the charge, she demanded, with a firm voice and an assured air, what he would with her. The magistrate, looking upon her and seeing her very fair and commendable of carriage and according as her words testified, of a lofty spirit, began to have compassion of her, fearing lest she should confess somewhat wherefore it should behoove him, for his own honour's sake, condemn her to die. However, having no choice but to question her of that which was laid to her charge, he said to her, 'Madam, as you see, here is Rinaldo your husband, who complaineth of you, avouching himself to have found you in adultery with another man and demanding that I should punish you therefor by putting you to death, according to the tenor of a statute which here obtaineth; but this I cannot do, except you confess it; wherefore look well what you answer and tell me if that be true whereof your husband impeacheth you.'

The lady, no wise dismayed, replied very cheerfully, 'Sir, true it is that Rinaldo is my husband and that he found me last night in the arms of Lazzarino, wherein, for the great and perfect love I bear him, I have many a time been; nor am I anywise minded to deny this. But, as I am assured you know, laws should be common to all and made with the consent of those whom they concern; and this is not the case with this statute, which is binding only upon us unhappy women, who might far better than men avail to satisfy many; more by token that, when it was made, not only did no woman yield consent thereunto, but none of us was even cited to do so; wherefore it may justly be styled naught. However, an you choose, to the prejudice of my body and of your own soul, to be the executor of this unrighteous law, it resteth with you to do so; but, ere you proceed to adjudge aught, I pray you do me one slight favour, to wit, that you question my husband if at all times and as often as it pleased him, without ever saying him nay, I have or not vouchsafed him entire commodity of myself.'

Rinaldo, without waiting to be questioned of the provost, straightway made answer that undoubtedly the lady had, at his every request, accorded him his every pleasure of herself; whereupon, 'Then, my lord provost,' straightway rejoined she, 'if he have still taken of me that which was needful and pleasing to him, what, I ask you, was or am I to do with that which remaineth over and above his requirements? Should I cast it to the dogs? Was it not far better to gratify withal a gentleman who loveth me more than himself, than to leave it waste or spoil?' Now well nigh all the people of Prato had flocked thither to the trial of such a matter and of so fair and famous a lady, and hearing so comical a question, they all, after much laughter, cried out as with one voice that she was in the right of it and that she said well. Moreover, ere they departed thence, at the instance of the provost, they modified the cruel statute and left it to apply to those women only who should for money make default to their husbands. Thereupon Rinaldo, having taken nought but shame by so fond an emprise, departed the court, and the lady returned in triumph to her own house, joyful and free and in a manner raised up out of the fire."

8

THE EIGHTH STORY

FRESCO EXHORTETH HIS NIECE NOT TO MIRROR HERSELF IN THE GLASS, IF, AS SHE SAITH, IT IRKETH HER TO SEE DISAGREEABLE FOLK

THE STORY TOLD by Filostrato at first touched the hearts of the listening ladies with some little shamefastness and they gave token thereof by a modest redness that appeared upon their faces; but, after looking one at another, they hearkened thereto, tittering the while and scarce able to abstain from laughing. As soon as he was come to the end thereof, the queen turned to Emilia and bade her follow on, whereupon, sighing no otherwise than as she had been aroused from a dream, she began, "Lovesome lasses, for that long thought hath held me far from here, I shall, to obey our queen content myself with [relating] a story belike much slighter than that which I might have bethought myself to tell, had my mind been present here, recounting to you the silly default of a damsel, corrected by an uncle of hers with a jocular retort, had she been woman enough to have apprehended it.

A certain Fresco da Celatico, then, had a niece familiarly called Ciesca,[1] who, having a comely face and person (though none of those angelical beauties that we have often seen aforetime), set so much store by herself and accounted herself so noble that she had gotten a habit of carping at both men and women and everything she saw, without anywise taking thought to herself, who was so much more fashous, froward and humoursome than any other of her sex that nothing could be done to her liking. Beside all this, she was so prideful that, had she been of the blood royal of France, it had been overweening; and when she went abroad, she gave herself so many airs that she did nought but make wry faces, as if there came to her a stench from whomsoever she saw or met. But, letting be many other vexatious and tiresome fashions of hers, it chanced one day that she came back to the house, where Fresco was, and seating herself near him, all full of airs and grimaces, did nothing but puff and blow; whereupon quoth he, 'What meaneth this, Ciesca, that, to-day being a holiday, thou comest home so early?' To which she answered, all like to die away with affectation, 'It is true I have come back soon, for that I believe there were never in this city so many disagreeable and tiresome people, both men and women, as there are to-day; there passeth none about the streets but is hateful to me as ill-chance, and I do not believe there is a woman in the world to whom it is more irksome to see disagreeable folk than it is to me; wherefore I have returned thus early, not to see them.' 'My lass,' rejoined Fresco, to whom his niece's airs and graces were mighty displeasing, 'if disagreeable folk be so distasteful to thee as thou sayest, never mirror thyself in the glass, so thou wouldst live merry.' But she, emptier than a reed, albeit herseemed she was a match for Solomon in wit, apprehended Fresco's true speech no better than a block; nay, she said that she chose to mirror herself in the glass like other women; and so she abode in her folly and therein abideth yet."

---

1. An abbreviation of Francesca.

ૐ 9 ૐ

THE NINTH STORY

GUIDO CAVALCANTI WITH A PITHY SPEECH
COURTEOUSLY FLOUTETH CERTAIN FLORENTINE
GENTLEMEN WHO HAD TAKEN HIM BY SURPRISE

THE QUEEN, seeing Emilia delivered of her story and that it rested with none other than herself to tell, saving him who was privileged to speak last, began thus, "Although, sprightly ladies, you have this day taken out of my mouth at the least two stories, whereof I had purposed to relate one, I have yet one left to tell, the end whereof compriseth a saying of such a fashion that none, peradventure, of such pertinence, hath yet been cited to us.

You must know, then, that there were in our city, of times past, many goodly and commendable usances, whereof none is left there nowadays, thanks to the avarice that hath waxed therein with wealth and hath banished them all. Among these there was a custom to the effect that the gentlemen of the various quarters of Florence assembled together in divers places about the town and formed themselves into companies of a certain number, having a care to admit thereinto such only as might aptly bear the expense, whereof to-day the one and to-morrow the other, and so all in turn, hold open house, each his day, for the whole company. At these banquets they often entertained both stranger gentlemen, whenas there came any thither, and those of the city; and on like wise, once at the least in the year, they clad themselves alike and rode in procession through the city on the most notable days and whiles they held passes of arms, especially on the chief holidays or whenas some glad news of victory or the like came to the city.

Amongst these companies was one of Messer Betto Brunelleschi, whereinto the latter and his companions had studied amain to draw Guido, son of Messer Cavalcante de' Cavalcanti, and not without cause; for that, besides being one of the best logicians in the world and an excellent natural philosopher (of which things, indeed, they recked little), he was very sprightly and well-bred and a mighty well-spoken man and knew better than any other to do everything that he would and that pertained unto a gentleman, more by token that he was very rich and knew wonder-well how to entertain whomsoever he deemed deserving of honour. But Messer Betto had never been able to win and to have him, and he and his companions believed that this betided for that Guido, being whiles engaged in abstract speculations, became much distraught from mankind; and for that he inclined somewhat to the opinion of the Epicureans,

292

it was reported among the common folk that these his speculations consisted only in seeking if it might be discovered that God was not.

It chanced one day that Guido set out from Orto San Michele and came by way of the Corso degli Ademari, the which was oftentimes his road, to San Giovanni, round about which there were at that present divers great marble tombs (which are nowadays at Santa Reparata) and many others. As he was between the columns of porphyry there and the tombs in question and the door of the church, which was shut, Messer Betto and his company, coming a-horseback along the Piazza di Santa Reparata, espied him among the tombs and said, 'Let us go plague him.' Accordingly, spurring their horses, they charged all down upon him in sport and coming upon him ere he was aware of them, said to him, 'Guido, thou refusest to be of our company; but, harkye, whenas thou shalt have found that God is not, what wilt thou have accomplished?' Guido, seeing himself hemmed in by them, answered promptly, 'Gentlemen, you may say what you will to me in your own house'; then, laying his hand on one of the great tombs aforesaid and being very nimble of body, he took a spring and alighting on the other side, made off, having thus rid himself of them.

The gentlemen abode looking one upon another and fell a-saying that he was a crack-brain and that this that he had answered them amounted to nought seeing that there where they were they had no more to do than all the other citizens, nor Guido himself less than any of themselves. But Messer Betto turned to them and said, 'It is you who are the crackbrains, if you have not apprehended him. He hath courteously and in a few words given us the sharpest rebuke in the world; for that, an you consider aright, these tombs are the houses of the dead, seeing they are laid and abide therein, and these, saith he, are our house, meaning thus to show us that we and other foolish and unlettered men are, compared with him and other men of learning, worse than dead folk; wherefore, being here, we are in our own house.' Thereupon each understood what Guido had meant to say and was abashed nor ever plagued him more, but held Messer Betto thenceforward a gentleman of a subtle wit and an understanding."

🪸 10 🪸

THE TENTH STORY

FRA CIPOLLA PROMISETH CERTAIN COUNTRY FOLK TO SHOW THEM ONE OF THE ANGEL GABRIEL'S FEATHERS AND FINDING COALS IN PLACE THEREOF, AVOUCHETH THESE LATTER TO BE OF THOSE WHICH ROASTED ST. LAWRENCE

EACH OF THE company being now quit of his[1] story, Dioneo perceived that it rested with him to tell; whereupon, without awaiting more formal commandment, he began on this wise, silence having first been imposed on those who commended Guido's pregnant retort: "Charming ladies, albeit I am privileged to speak of that which most liketh me, I purpose not to-day to depart from the matter whereof you have all very aptly spoken; but, ensuing in your footsteps, I mean to show you how cunningly a friar of the order of St. Anthony, by name Fra Cipolla, contrived with a sudden shift to extricate himself from a snare[2] which had been set for him by two young men; nor should it irk you if, for the complete telling of the story, I enlarge somewhat in speaking, an you consider the sun, which is yet amiddleward in the sky.

Certaldo, as you may have heard, is a burgh of Val d' Elsa situate in our country, which, small though it be, was once inhabited by gentlemen and men of substance; and thither, for that he found good pasture there, one of the friars of the order of St. Anthony was long used to resort once a year, to get in the alms bestowed by simpletons upon him and his brethren. His name was Fra Cipolla and he was gladly seen there, no less belike, for his name's sake[3] than for other reasons, seeing that these parts produce onions that are famous throughout all Tuscany. This Fra Cipolla was little of person, red-haired and merry of countenance, the jolliest rascal in the world, and to boot, for all he was no scholar, he was so fine a talker and so ready of wit that those who knew him not would not only have esteemed him a great rhetorician, but had avouched him to be Tully himself or may be Quintilian; and he was gossip or friend or well-wisher[4] to well nigh every one in the country.

One August among others he betook himself thither according to his wont, and on a Sunday morning, all the goodmen and goodwives of the villages around being come to hear mass at the parish church, he came forward, whenas it seemed to him time, and said, 'Gentlemen and ladies, it is, as you know, your usance to send every year to the poor of our lord Baron St. Anthony of your corn and of your oats, this little and that much, according to his means and his devoutness, to the intent that the blessed St. Anthony may keep watch over your beeves and asses and swine and sheep; and besides this, you use to pay, especially such of you as are inscribed into our company, that small due which is payable once a year. To collect these I have

294

been sent by my superior, to wit, my lord abbot; wherefore, with the blessing of God, you shall, after none, whenas you hear the bells ring, come hither without the church, where I will make preachment to you after the wonted fashion and you shall kiss the cross; moreover, for that I know you all to be great devotees of our lord St. Anthony, I will, as an especial favour show you a very holy and goodly relic, which I myself brought aforetime from the holy lands beyond seas; and that is one of the Angel Gabriel's feathers, which remained in the Virgin Mary's chamber, whenas he came to announce to her in Nazareth.' This said, he broke off and went on with his mass.

Now, when he said this, there were in the church, among many others, two roguish young fellows, hight one Giovanni del Bragioniera and the other Biagio Pizzini, who, after laughing with one another awhile over Fra Cipolla's relic, took counsel together, for all they were great friends and cronies of his, to play him some trick in the matter of the feather in question. Accordingly, having learned that he was to dine that morning with a friend of his in the burgh, they went down into the street as soon as they knew him to be at table, and betook themselves to the inn where he had alighted, purposing that Biagio should hold his servant in parley, whilst Giovanni should search his baggage for the feather aforesaid, whatever it might be, and carry it off, to see what he should say to the people of the matter.

Fra Cipolla had a servant, whom some called Guccio[5] Balena,[6] others Guccio Imbratta[7] and yet others Guccia Porco[8] and who was such a scurvy knave that Lipo Topo[9] never wrought his like, inasmuch as his master used oftentimes to jest of him with his cronies and say, 'My servant hath in him nine defaults, such that, were one of them in Solomon or Aristotle or Seneca, it would suffice to mar all their worth, all their wit and all their sanctity. Consider, then, what a man he must be, who hath all nine of them and in whom there is neither worth nor wit nor sanctity.' Being questioned whiles what were these nine defaults and having put them into doggerel rhyme, he would answer, 'I will tell you. He's a liar, a sloven, a slugabed; disobedient, neglectful, ill bred; o'erweening, foul-spoken, a dunderhead; beside which he hath divers other peccadilloes, whereof it booteth not to speak. But what is most laughable of all his fashions is that, wherever he goeth, he is still for taking a wife and hiring a house; for, having a big black greasy beard, him-seemeth he is so exceeding handsome and agreeable that he conceiteth himself all the women who see him fall in love with him, and if you let him alone, he would run after them all till he lost his girdle.[10] Sooth to say, he is of great assistance to me, for that none can ever seek to speak with me so secretly but he must needs hear his share; and if it chance that I be questioned of aught, he is so fearful lest I should not know how to answer, that he straightway answereth for me both Ay and No, as he judgeth sortable.'

Now Fra Cipolla, in leaving him at the inn, had bidden him look well that none touched his gear, and more particularly his saddle-bags, for that therein were the sacred things. But Guccio, who was fonder of the kitchen than the nightingale of the green boughs, especially if he scented some serving-wench there, and who had seen in that of the inn a gross fat cookmaid, undersized and ill-made, with a pair of paps that showed like two manure-baskets and a face like a cadger's, all sweaty, greasy and smoky, leaving Fra Cipolla's chamber and all his gear to care for themselves, swooped down upon the kitchen, even as the vulture swoopeth upon carrion, and seating himself by the fire, for all it was August, entered into discourse with the wench in question, whose name was Nuta, telling her that he was by rights a gentleman and had more than nine millions of florins, beside that which he had to give others, which was rather more than less, and that he could do and say God only knew what. Moreover, without regard to his bonnet, whereon was grease enough to have seasoned the caldron of Altopascio,[11] and his doublet all torn and pieced and enamelled with filth about the collar and under the armpits, with more spots and patches of divers colours than ever had Turkey or India stuffs, and his shoes all broken and hose unsewn, he told her, as he had been the Sieur de Châtillon,[12] that he meant to clothe her and trick her out anew and deliver her from the wretchedness of abiding with others,[13] and bring her to hope of better fortune, if without any great wealth in possession, and many other things, which, for all he delivered them very earnestly, all turned to wind and came to nought, as did most of his enterprises.

The two young men, accordingly, found Guccio busy about Nuta, whereat they were well pleased, for that it spared them half their pains, and entering Fra Cipolla's chamber, which they found open, the first thing that came under their examination was the saddle-bags wherein was the feather. In these they found, enveloped in a great taffetas wrapper, a little casket and opening this latter, discovered therein a parrot's tail-feather, which they concluded must be that which the friar had promised to show the people of Certaldo. And certes he might lightly cause it to be believed in those days, for that the refinements of Egypt had not yet made their way save into a small part of Tuscany, as they have since done in very great abundance, to the undoing of all Italy; and wherever they may have been some little known, in those parts they were well nigh altogether unknown of the inhabitants; nay the rude honesty of the ancients yet enduring there, not only had they never set eyes on a parrot, but were far from having ever heard tell of such a bird. The young men, then, rejoiced at finding the feather, laid hands on it and not to leave the casket empty, filled it with some coals they saw in a corner of the room and shut it again. Then, putting all things in order as they had found them, they made off in high glee with the feather, without having been seen, and began to await what Fra Cipolli should say, when he found the coals in place thereof.

The simple men and women who were in the church, hearing that they were to see the Angel Gabriel's feather after none, returned home, as soon as mass was over, and neighbor telling it to neighbor and gossip to gossip, no sooner had they all dined than so many men and women flocked to the burgh that it would scarce hold them, all looking eagerly to see the aforesaid feather. Fra Cipolla, having well dined and after slept awhile, arose a little after none and hearing of the great multitude of country folk come to see the feather, sent to bid Guccio Imbratta come thither with the bells and bring his saddle-bags. Guccio, tearing himself with difficulty away from the kitchen and Nuta, betook himself with the things required to the appointed place, whither coming, out of breath, for that the water he had drunken had made his belly swell amain, he repaired, by his master's commandment, to the church door and fell to ringing the bells lustily.

When all the people were assembled there, Fra Cipolla, without observing that aught of his had been meddled with, began his preachment and said many words anent his affairs; after which, thinking to come to the showing of the Angel Gabriel's feather, he first recited the Confiteor with the utmost solemnity and let kindle a pair of flambeaux; then, pulling off his bonnet, he delicately unfolded the taffetas wrapper and brought out the casket. Having first pronounced certain ejaculations in praise and commendation of the Angel Gabriel and of his relic, he opened the casket and seeing it full of coals, suspected not Guccio Balena of having played him this trick, for that he knew him not to be man enough; nor did he curse him for having kept ill watch lest others should do it, but silently cursed himself for having committed to him the care of his gear, knowing him, as he did, to be negligent, disobedient, careless and forgetful.

Nevertheless, without changing colour, he raised his eyes and hands to heaven and said, so as to be heard of all, 'O God, praised be still thy puissance!' Then, shutting the casket and turning to the people, 'Gentlemen and ladies,' quoth he, 'you must know that, whilst I was yet very young, I was dispatched by my superior to those parts where the sun riseth and it was expressly commanded me that I should seek till I found the Privileges of Porcellana, which, though they cost nothing to seal, are much more useful to others than to us. On this errand I set out from Venice and passed through Borgo de' Greci,[14] whence, riding through the kingdom of Algarve and Baldacca,[15] I came to Parione,[16] and from there, not without thirst, I came after awhile into Sardinia. But what booteth it to set out to you in detail all the lands explored by me? Passing the straits of San Giorgio,[17] I came into Truffia[18] and Buffia,[19] countries much inhabited and with great populations, and thence into the land of Menzogna,[20] where I found great plenty of our brethren and of friars of other religious orders, who all went about those parts, shunning unease for the love of God, recking little of others' travail, whenas they saw their own advantage to ensue, and spending none other money than such as was uncoined.[21] Thence I passed into the land of the Abruzzi, where the men and women go in clogs over the mountains, clothing the swine in their own guts;[22] and a little farther I found folk who carried bread on sticks and wine in bags. From this I came to the Mountains of the Bachi, where all the waters run down hill; and in brief, I made my way so far inward that I won at last even to India Pastinaca,[23] where I swear to you, by the habit I wear on my back, that I saw hedge-bills[24] fly, a thing incredible to whoso hath not seen it. But of this Maso del Saggio will confirm me, whom I found there a great merchant, cracking walnuts and selling the shells by retail.

Being unable to find that which I went seeking, for that thence one goeth thither by water, I turned back and arrived in those holy countries, where, in summer-years, cold bread is worth four farthings a loaf and the hot goeth for nothing. There I found the venerable father my lord Blamemenot Anitpleaseyou, the very worshipful Patriarch of Jerusalem, who, for reverence of the habit I have still worn of my lord Baron St. Anthony, would have me see all the holy relics that he had about him and which were so many that, an I sought to recount them all to you, I should not come to an end thereof in several miles. However, not to leave you disconsolate, I will tell you some thereof. First, he showed me the finger of the Holy Ghost, as whole and sound as ever it was, and the forelock of the seraph that appeared to St. Francis and one of the nails of the Cherubim and one of the ribs of the Verbum Caro[25] Get-thee-to-the-windows and some of the vestments of the Holy Catholic Faith and divers rays of the star that appeared to the Three Wise Men in the East and a vial of the sweat of St. Michael, whenas he fought with the devil, and the jawbone of the death of St. Lazarus and others. And for that I made him a free gift of the Steeps[26] of Monte Morello in the vernacular and of some chapters of the Caprezio,[27] which he had long gone seeking, he made me a sharer in his holy relics and gave me one of the teeth of the Holy Rood and somewhat of the sound of the bells of Solomon's Temple in a vial and the feather of the Angel Gabriel, whereof I have already bespoken you, and one of the pattens of St. Gherardo da Villa Magna, which not long since at Florence I gave to Gherardo di Bonsi, who hath a particular devotion for that saint; and he gave me also of the coals wherewith the most blessed martyr St. Lawrence was roasted; all which things I devoutly brought home with me and yet have. True it is that my superior hath never suffered me to show them till such time as he should be certified if they were the very things or not. But now that, by certain miracles performed by them and by letters received from the patriarch, he hath been made certain of this, he hath granted me leave to show them; and I, fearing to trust them to others, still carry them with me.

Now I carry the Angel Gabriel's feather, so it may not be marred, in one casket, and the coals wherewith St. Lawrence was roasted in another, the which are so like one to other, that it hath often happened to me to take one for the other, and so hath it betided me at this present, for that, thinking to bring hither the casket wherein was the feather, I have brought that wherein are the coals. The which I hold not to have been an error; nay, meseemeth certain that it was God's will and that He Himself placed the casket with the coals in my hands, especially now I mind me that the feast of St. Lawrence is but two days hence; wherefore God, willing that, by showing you the coals wherewith he was roasted, I should rekindle in your hearts the devotion it behoveth you have for him, caused me take, not the feather, as I purposed, but the blessed coals extinguished by the sweat of that most holy body. So, O my blessed children, put off your bonnets and draw near devoutly to behold them; but first I would have you knew that whoso is scored with these coals, in the form of the sign of the cross, may rest assured, for the whole year to come, that fire shall not touch him but he shall feel it.'

Having thus spoken, he opened the casket, chanting the while a canticle in praise of St. Lawrence, and showed the coals, which after the simple multitude had awhile beheld with reverent admiration, they all crowded about Fra Cipolla and making him better offerings than they were used, besought him to touch them withal. Accordingly, taking the coals in hand, he fell to making the biggest crosses for which he could find room upon their white smocks and doublets and upon the veils of the women, avouching that how much soever the coals diminished in making these crosses, they after grew again in the casket, as he had many a time proved. On this wise he crossed all the people of Certaldo, to his no small profit, and thus, by his ready wit and presence of mind, he baffled those who, by taking the feather from him, had thought to baffle him and who, being present at his preachment and hearing the rare shift employed by him and from how far he had taken it and with what words, had so laughed that they thought to have cracked their jaws. Then, after the common folk had departed, they went up to him and with all the mirth in the world discovered to him that which they had done and after restored him his feather, which next year stood him in as good stead as the coals had done that day."

THIS STORY AFFORDED unto all the company alike the utmost pleasure and solace, and it was much laughed of all at Fra Cipolla, and particularly of his pilgrimage and the relics seen and brought back by him. The queen, seeing the story and likewise her sovantry at an end, rose to her feet and put off the crown, which she set laughingly on Dioneo's head, saying, "It is time, Dioneo, that thou prove awhile what manner charge it is to have ladies to govern and guide; be thou, then, king and rule on such wise that, in the end, we may have reason to give ourselves joy of thy governance." Dioneo took the crown and answered, laughing, "You may often enough have seen much better kings than I, I mean chess-kings; but, an you obey me as a king should in truth be obeyed, I will cause you enjoy that without which assuredly no entertainment is ever complete in its gladness. But let that talk be; I will rule as best I know."

Then, sending for the seneschal, according to the wonted usance, he orderly enjoined him of that which he should do during the continuance of his seignory and after said, "Noble ladies, it hath in divers manners been devised of human industry[28] and of the various chances [of fortune,] insomuch that, had not Dame Licisca come hither a while agone and found me matter with her prate for our morrow's relations, I misdoubt me I should have been long at pains to find a subject of discourse. As you heard, she avouched that she had not a single gossip who had come to her husband a maid and added that she knew right well how many and what manner tricks married women yet played their husbands. But, letting be the first part, which is a childish matter, methinketh the second should be an agreeable subject for discourse; wherefore I will and ordain it that, since Licisca hath given us occasion therefor, it be discoursed to-morrow OF THE TRICKS WHICH, OR FOR LOVE OR FOR THEIR OWN PRESERVATION, WOMEN HAVE HERETOFORE PLAYED THEIR HUSBANDS, WITH OR WITHOUT THE LATTER'S COGNIZANCE THEREOF."

It seemed to some of the ladies that to discourse of such a matter would ill beseem them and they prayed him, therefore, to change the theme proposed; wherefore answered he, "Ladies, I am no less cognizant than yourselves of that which I have ordained, and that which you would fain allege to me availed not to deter me from ordaining it, considering that the times are such that, provided men and women are careful to eschew unseemly actions, all liberty of discourse is permitted. Know you not that, for the malignity of the season, the judges have forsaken the tribunals, that the laws, as well Divine as human, are silent and full licence is conceded unto every one for the preservation of his life? Wherefore, if your modesty allow itself some little freedom in discourse, not with intent to ensue it with aught of unseemly in deeds, but to afford yourselves and others diversion, I see not with what plausible reason any can blame you in the future. Moreover, your company, from the first day of our assembling until this present, hath been most decorous, nor, for aught that hath been said here, doth it appear to me that its honour hath anywise been sullied. Again, who is there knoweth not your virtue? Which, not to say mirthful discourse, but even fear of death I do not believe could avail to shake. And to tell you the truth, whosoever should hear that you shrank from devising bytimes of these toys would be apt to suspect that you were guilty in the matter and were therefore unwilling to discourse thereof. To say nothing of the fine honour you would do me in that, I having been obedient unto all, you now, having made me your king, seek to lay down the law to me, and not to discourse of the subject which I propose. Put off, then, this misdoubtance, apter to mean minds than to yours, and good luck to you, let each of you bethink herself of some goodly story to tell." When the ladies heard this, they said it should be as he pleased; whereupon he gave them all leave to do their several pleasures until supper-time.

The sun was yet high, for that the discoursement[29] had been brief; wherefor Dioneo having addressed himself to play at tables with the other young men, Elisa called the other ladies apart and said to them, "Since we have been here, I have still wished to carry you to a place very near at hand, whither methinketh none of you hath ever been and which is called the Ladies' Valley, but have never yet found an occasion of bringing you thither unto to-day; wherefore, as the sun is yet high, I doubt not but, an it please you come thither, you will be exceeding well pleased to have been there." They answered that they were ready and calling one of their maids, set out upon their way, without letting the young men know aught thereof; nor had they gone much more than a mile, when they came to the Ladies' Valley. They entered therein by a very strait way, on one side whereof ran a very clear streamlet, and saw it as fair and as delectable, especially at that season whenas the heat was great, as most might be conceived. According to that which one of them after told me, the plain that was in the valley was as round as if it had been traced with the compass, albeit it seemed the work of nature and not of art, and was in circuit a little more than half a mile, encompassed about with six little hills not over-high, on the summit of each of which stood a palace builded in guise of a goodly castle. The sides of these hills went sloping gradually downward to the plain on such wise as we see in amphitheatres, the degrees descend in ordered succession from the highest to the lowest, still contracting their circuit; and of these slopes those which looked toward the south were all full of vines and olives and almonds and cherries and figs and many another kind of fruit-bearing trees, without a span thereof being wasted; whilst those which faced the North Star[30] were all covered with thickets of dwarf oaks and ashes and other trees as green and straight as might be. The middle plain, which had no other inlet than that whereby the ladies were come thither, was full of firs and cypresses and laurels and various sorts of pines, as well arrayed and ordered as if the best artist in that kind had planted them; and between these little or no sun, even at its highest, made its way to the ground, which was all one meadow of very fine grass, thick-sown with flowers purpurine and others. Moreover, that which afforded no less delight than otherwhat was a little stream, which ran down from a valley that divided two of the hills aforesaid and falling over cliffs of live rock, made a murmur very delectable to hear, what while it showed from afar, as it broke over the stones, like so much quicksilver jetting out, under pressure of somewhat, into fine spray. As it came down into the little plain, it was there received into a fair channel and ran very swiftly into the middest thereof, where it formed a lakelet, such as the townsfolk made whiles, by way of fishpond, in their gardens, whenas they have a commodity thereof. This lakelet was no deeper than a man's stature, breast high, and its waters being exceeding clear and altogether untroubled with any admixture, it showed its bottom to be of a very fine gravel, the grains whereof whoso had nought else to do might, an he would, have availed to number; nor, looking into the water, was the bottom alone to be seen, nay, but so many fish fleeting hither and thither that, over and above the pleasure thereof, it was a marvel to behold; nor was it enclosed with other banks than the very soil of the meadow, which was the goodlier thereabout in so much as it received the more of its moisture. The water that abounded over and above the capacity of the lake was received into another channel, whereby, issuing forth of the little valley, it ran off into the lower parts.

Hither then came the young ladies and after they had gazed all about and much commended the place, they took counsel together to bathe, for that the heat was great and that they saw the lakelet before them and were in no fear of being seen. Accordingly, bidding their serving maid abide over against the way whereby one entered there and look if any should come and give them notice thereof, they stripped themselves naked, all seven, and entered the lake, which hid their white bodies no otherwise than as a thin glass would do with a vermeil rose. Then, they being therein and no troubling of the water ensuing thereof, they fell, as best they might, to faring hither and thither in pursuit of the fish, which had uneath where to hide themselves, and seeking to take them with the naked hand. After they had abidden awhile in such joyous pastime and had taken some of the fish, they came forth of the lakelet and clad themselves anew. Then, unable to commend the place more than they had already done and themseeming time to turn homeward, they set out, with soft step, upon their way, discoursing much of the goodliness of the valley.

They reached the palace betimes and there found the young men yet at play where they had left them; to whom quoth Pampinea, laughing. "We have e'en stolen a march on you to-day." "How?" asked Dioneo. "Do you begin to do deeds ere you come to say words?"[31] "Ay, my lord," answered she and related to him at large whence they came and how the place was fashioned and how far distant thence and that which they had done. The king, hearing tell of the goodliness of the place and desirous of seeing it, caused straightway order the supper, which being dispatched to the general satisfaction, the three young men, leaving the ladies, betook themselves with their servants to the valley and having viewed it in every part, for that none of them had ever been there before, extolled it for one of the goodliest things in the world. Then, for that it grew late, after they had bathed and donned their clothes, they returned home, where they found the ladies dancing a round, to the accompaniment of a song sung by Fiammetta.

The dance ended, they entered with them into a discourse of the Ladies' Valley and said much in praise and commendation thereof. Moreover, the king, sending for the seneschal, bade him look that the dinner be made ready there on the following morning and have sundry beds carried thither, in case any should have a mind to lie or sleep there for nooning; after which he let bring lights and wine and confections and the company having somedele refreshed themselves, he commanded that all should address themselves to dancing. Then, Pamfilo having, at his commandment, set up a dance, the king turned to Elisa and said courteously to her, "Fair damsel, thou has to-day done me the honour of the crown and I purpose this evening to do thee that of the song; wherefore look thou sing such an one as most liketh thee." Elisa answered, smiling, that she would well and with dulcet voice began on this wise:

Love, from thy clutches could I but win free,
Hardly, methinks, again
Shall any other hook take hold on me.
I entered in thy wars a youngling maid,
Thinking thy strife was utmost peace and sweet,
And all my weapons on the ground I laid,
As one secure, undoubting of defeat;
But thou, false tyrant, with rapacious heat,
Didst fall on me amain
With all the grapnels of thine armoury.

Then, wound about and fettered with thy chains,
To him, who for my death in evil hour
Was born, thou gav'st me, bounden, full of pains
And bitter tears; and syne within his power
He hath me and his rule's so harsh and dour
No sighs can move the swain
Nor all my wasting plaints to set me free.

My prayers, the wild winds bear them all away;
He hearkeneth unto none and none will hear;
Wherefore each hour my torment waxeth aye;
I cannot die, albeit life irks me drear.
Ah, Lord, have pity on my heavy cheer;
Do that I seek in vain
And give him bounden in thy chains to me.

An this thou wilt not, at the least undo
The bonds erewhen of hope that knitted were;
Alack, O Lord, thereof to thee I sue,
For, an thou do it, yet to waxen fair
Again I trust, as was my use whilere,
And being quit of pain
Myself with white flowers and with red besee.

Elisa ended her song with a very plaintive sigh, and albeit all marvelled at the words thereof, yet was there none who might conceive what it was that caused her sing thus. But the king, who was in a merry mood, calling for Tindaro, bade him bring out his bagpipes, to the sound whereof he let dance many dances; after which, a great part of the night being now past, he bade each go sleep.

---

1. "Or her."
2. Lit. to avoid or elude a scorn (*fuggire uno scorno*).
3. *Cipolla* means onion.
4. The term "well-wisher" (*benivogliente*), when understood in relation to a woman, is generally equivalent (at least with the older Italian writers) to "lover." See ante, passim.
5. Diminutive of contempt of Arrigo, contracted from Arriguccio, *i.e.* mean little Arrigo.
6. *i.e.* Whale.
7. *i.e.* Dirt.

8. *i.e.* Hog.

9. A painter of Boccaccio's time, of whom little or nothing seems to be known.

10. *Perpendo lo coreggia.* The exact meaning of this passage is not clear. The commentators make sundry random shots at it, but, as usual, only succeed in making confusion worse confounded. It may perhaps be rendered, "till his wind failed him."

11. Said by the commentators to have been an abbey, where they made cheese-soup for all comers twice a week; hence "the caldron of Altopascio" became a proverb; but *quære* is not the name Altopascio (high feeding) a fancy one?

12. It does not appear to which member of this great house Boccaccio here alludes, but the Châtillons were always rich and magnificent gentlemen, from Gaucher de Châtillon, who followed Philip Augustus to the third crusade, to the great Admiral de Coligny.

13. Sic (*star con altrui*); but "being in the service of or dependent upon others" seems to be the probable meaning.

14. Apparently the Neapolitan town of that name.

15. The name of a famous tavern in Florence (*Florio*).

16. *Quære* a place in Florence? One of the commentators, with characteristic carelessness, states that the places mentioned in the preachment of Fra Cipolla (an amusing specimen of the patter-sermon of the mendicant friar of the middle ages, that ecclesiastical Cheap Jack of his day) are all names of streets or places of Florence, a statement which, it is evident to the most cursory reader, is altogether inaccurate.

17. Apparently the island of that name near Venice.

18. *i.e.* Nonsense-land.

19. *i.e.* Land of Tricks or Cozenage.

20. *i.e.* Falsehood, Lie-land.

21. *i.e.* paying their way with fine words, instead of coin.

22. *i.e.* making sausages of them.

23. *Bachi*, drones or maggots. *Pastinaca* means "parsnip" and is a meaningless addition of Fra Cipolla's fashion.

24. A play of words upon the primary meaning (winged things) of the word *pennate*, hedge-bills.

25. *i.e.* The Word [made] flesh. Get-thee-to-the-windows is only a patter tag.

26. Or Slopes or Coasts (*piaggie*).

27. ?

28. *Industria* in the old sense of ingenuity, skilful procurement, etc.

29. *i.e.* the tale-telling.

30. Lit. the northern chariot (*carro di tramontana*); *quære* the Great Bear?

31. Alluding to the subject fixed for the next day's discourse, as who should say, "Have you begun already to play tricks upon us men in very deed, ere you tell about them in words?"

DAY THE SEVENTH

Here Beginneth the Seventh Day of the Decameron
Wherein Under the Governance of Dioneo Is
Discoursed of the Tricks Which or for Love or for
Their Own Preservation Women Have Heretofore
Played Their Husbands With or Without the
Latter's Cognizance Thereof

Every star was already fled from the parts of the East, save only that which we style Lucifer and which shone yet in the whitening dawn, when the seneschal, arising, betook himself, with a great baggage-train, to the Ladies' Valley, there to order everything, according to commandment had of his lord. The king, whom the noise of the packers and of the beasts had awakened, tarried not long after his departure to rise and being risen, caused arouse all the ladies and likewise the young men; nor had the rays of the sun yet well broken forth, when they all entered upon the road. Never yet had the nightingales and the other birds seemed to them to sing so blithely as they did that morning, what while, accompanied by their carols, they repaired to the Ladies' Valley, where they were received by many more, which seemed to them to make merry for their coming. There, going round about the place and reviewing it all anew, it appeared to them so much fairer than on the foregoing day as the season of the day was more sorted to its goodliness. Then, after they had broken their fast with good wine and confections, not to be behindhand with the birds in the matter of song, they fell a-singing and the valley with them, still echoing those same songs which they did sing, whereto all the birds, as if they would not be outdone, added new and dulcet notes. Presently, the dinner-hour being come and the tables spread hard by the fair lakelet under the thickset laurels and other goodly trees, they seated themselves there, as it pleased the king, and eating, watched the fish swim in vast shoals about the lake, which gave bytimes occasion for talk as well as observation. When they had made an end of dining and the meats and tables were removed, they fell anew to singing more blithely than ever; after which, beds having been spread in various places about the little valley and all enclosed about by the discreet seneschal with curtains and canopies of French serge, whoso would might with the king's permission, go sleep; whilst those who had no mind to sleep might at their will take pleasure of their other wonted pastimes. But, after awhile, all being now arisen and the hour come when they should assemble together for story-telling, carpets were, at the king's commandment, spread upon the grass, not far from the place where they had eaten, and all having seated themselves thereon hard by the lake, the king bade Emilia begin; whereupon she blithely proceeded to speak, smiling, thus:

THE FIRST STORY

GIANNI LOTTERINGHI HEARETH KNOCK AT HIS DOOR BY NIGHT AND AWAKENETH HIS WIFE, WHO GIVETH HIM TO BELIEVE THAT IT IS A PHANTOM; WHEREUPON THEY GO TO EXORCISE IT WITH A CERTAIN ORISON AND THE KNOCKING CEASETH

"MY LORD, it had been very agreeable to me, were such your pleasure, that other than I should have given a beginning to so goodly a matter as is that whereof we are to speak; but, since it pleaseth you that I give all the other ladies assurance by my example, I will gladly do it. Moreover, dearest ladies, I will study to tell a thing that may be useful to you in time to come, for that, if you others are as fearful as I, and especially of phantoms, (though what manner of thing they may be God knoweth I know not, nor ever found I any woman who knew it, albeit all are alike adread of them,) you may, by noting well my story, learn a holy and goodly orison of great virtue for the conjuring them away, should they come to you.

There was once in Florence, in the quarter of San Brancazio, a wool-comber called Gianni Lotteringhi, a man more fortunate in his craft than wise in other things, for that, savoring of the simpleton, he was very often made captain of the Laudsingers[1] of Santa Maria Novella and had the governance of their confraternity, and he many a time had other little offices of the same kind, upon which he much valued himself. This betided him for that, being a man of substance, he gave many a good pittance to the clergy, who, getting of him often, this a pair of hose, that a gown and another a scapulary, taught him in return store of goodly orisons and gave him the paternoster in the vulgar tongue, the Song of Saint Alexis, the Lamentations of Saint Bernard, the Canticles of Madam Matilda and the like trumpery, all which he held very dear and kept very diligently for his soul's health. Now he had a very fair and lovesome lady to wife, by name Mistress Tessa, who was the daughter of Mannuccio dalla Cuculia and was exceeding discreet and well advised. She, knowing her husband's simplicity and being enamoured of Federigo di Neri Pegolotti, a brisk and handsome youth, and he of her, took order with a serving-maid of hers that he should come speak with her at a very goodly country house which her husband had at Camerata, where she sojourned all the summer and whither Gianni came whiles to sup and sleep, returning in the morning to his shop and bytimes to his Laudsingers.

Federigo, who desired this beyond measure, taking his opportunity, repaired thither on the day appointed him towards vespers and Gianni not coming thither that evening, supped and lay the night in all ease and delight with the lady, who, being in his arms, taught him that night a good half dozen of her husband's lauds. Then, neither she nor Federigo purposing that this should be the last, as it had been the first time [of their foregathering], they took order together on this wise, so it should not be needful to send the maid for him each time, to wit, that every day, as he came and went to and from a place he had a little farther on, he should keep his eye on a vineyard that adjoined the house, where he would see an ass's skull set up on one of the vine poles, which whenas he saw with the muzzle turned towards Florence, he should without fail and in all assurance betake himself to her that evening after dark; and if he found the door shut he should knock softly thrice and she would open to him; but that, whenas he saw the ass's muzzle turned towards Fiesole, he should not come, for that Gianni would be there; and doing on this wise, they foregathered many a time.

But once, amongst other times, it chanced that, Federigo being one night to sup with Mistress Tessa and she having let cook two fat capons, Gianni, who was not expected there that night, came thither very late, whereat the lady was much chagrined and having supped with her husband on a piece of salt pork, which she had let boil apart, caused the maid wrap the two boiled capons in a white napkin and carry them, together with good store of new-laid eggs and a flask of good wine, into a garden she had, whither she could go, without passing through the house, and where she was wont to sup whiles with her lover, bidding her lay them at the foot of a peach-tree that grew beside a lawn there. But such was her trouble and annoy that she remembered not to bid the maid wait till Federigo should come and tell him that Gianni was there and that he should take the viands from the garden; wherefore, she and Gianni betaking themselves to bed and the maid likewise, it was not long before Federigo came to the door and knocked softly once. The door was so near to the bedchamber that Gianni heard it incontinent, as also did the lady; but she made a show of being asleep, so her husband might have no suspicion of her. After waiting a little, Federigo knocked a second time, whereupon Gianni, marvelling, nudged his wife somewhat and said, 'Tessa, hearest thou what I hear? Meseemeth there is a knocking at our door.'

The lady, who had heard it much better than he, made a show of awaking and said, 'Eh? How sayst thou?' 'I say,' answered Gianni, 'that meseemeth there is a knocking at our door.' 'Knocking!' cried she. 'Alack, Gianni mine, knowst thou not what it is? It is a phantom, that hath these last few nights given me the greatest fright that ever was, insomuch that, whenas I hear it, I put my head under the clothes and dare not bring it out again until it is broad day.' Quoth Gianni, 'Go to, wife; have no fear, if it be so; for I said the *Te Lucis* and the *Intemerata* and such and such other pious orisons, before we lay down, and crossed the bed from side to side, in the name of the Father, the Son and the Holy Ghost, so that we have no need to fear, for that, what power soever it have, it cannot avail to harm us.'

The lady, fearing lest Federigo should perchance suspect otherwhat and be angered with her, determined at all hazards to arise and let him know that Gianni was there; wherefore quoth she to her husband, 'That is all very well; thou sayst thy words, thou; but, for my part, I shall never hold myself safe nor secure, except we exorcise it, since thou art here.' 'And how is it to be exorcised?' asked he; and she, 'I know full well how to exorcise it; for, the other day, when I went to the Pardon at Fiesole, a certain anchoress (the very holiest of creatures, Gianni mine, God only can say how holy she is,) seeing me thus fearful, taught me a pious and effectual orison and told me that she had made trial of it several times, ere she became a recluse, and that it had always availed her. God knoweth I should never have dared go alone to make proof of it; but, now that thou art here, I would have us go exorcise the phantom.'

Gianni answered that he would well and accordingly they both arose and went softly to the door, without which Federigo, who now began to misdoubt him of somewhat, was yet in waiting. When they came thither, the lady said to Gianni, 'Do thou spit, whenas I shall bid thee.' And he answered, 'Good.' Then she began the conjuration and said, 'Phantom, phantom that goest by night, with tail upright[2] thou cam'st to us; now get thee gone with tail upright. Begone into the garden to the foot of the great peach tree; there shalt thou find an anointed twice-anointed one[3] and an hundred turds of my sitting hen;[4] set thy mouth to the flagon and get thee gone again and do thou no hurt to my Gianni nor to me.' Then to her husband, 'Spit, Gianni,' quoth she, and he spat. Federigo, who heard all this from without and was now quit of jealousy, had, for all his vexation, so great a mind to laugh that he was like to burst, and when Gianni spat, he said under his breath '[Would it were] thy teeth!'

The lady, having thrice conjured the phantom on this wise, returned to bed with her husband, whilst Federigo, who had not supped, looking to sup with her, and had right well apprehended the words of the conjuration, betook himself to the garden and finding the capons and wine and eggs at the foot of the great peach-tree, carried them off to his house and there supped at his ease; and after, when he next foregathered with the lady, he had a hearty laugh with her anent the conjuration aforesaid. Some say indeed that the lady had actually turned the ass's skull towards Fiesole, but that a husbandman, passing through the vineyard, had given it a blow with a stick and caused it spin round and it had become turned towards Florence, wherefore Federigo, thinking himself summoned, had come thither, and that the lady had made the conjuration on this wise: 'Phantom, phantom, get thee gone in God's name; for it was not I turned the ass's head; but another it was, God put him to shame! and I am here with my Gianni in bed'; whereupon he went away and abode without supper or lodging. But a neighbour of mine, a very ancient lady, telleth me that, according to that which she heard, when a child, both the one and the other were true; but that the latter happened, not to Gianni Lotteringhi, but to one Gianni di Nello, who abode at Porta San Piero and was no less exquisite a ninny than the other. Wherefore, dear my ladies, it abideth at your election to take whether of the two orisons most pleaseth you, except you will have both. They have great virtue in such cases, as you have had proof in the story you have heard; get them, therefore, by heart and they may yet avail you."

---

1. See ante n. 161.
2. *i.e.* pene arrecto.
3. *i.e.* a fattened capon well larded.
4. *i.e.* eggs.

❦ 2 ❦

THE SECOND STORY

PERONELLA HIDETH A LOVER OF HERS IN A VAT,
UPON HER HUSBAND'S UNLOOKED FOR RETURN, AND
HEARING FROM THE LATTER THAT HE HATH SOLD
THE VAT, AVOUCHETH HERSELF TO HAVE SOLD IT TO
ONE WHO IS PRESENTLY THEREWITHIN, TO SEE IF IT
BE SOUND; WHEREUPON THE GALLANT, JUMPING
OUT OF THE VAT, CAUSETH THE HUSBAND SCRAPE IT
OUT FOR HIM AND AFTER CARRY IT HOME TO HIS
HOUSE

EMILIA'S STORY was received with loud laughter and the conjuration commended of all as goodly and excellent; and this come to an end, the king bade Filostrato follow on, who accordingly began, "Dearest ladies, so many are the tricks that men, and particularly husbands, play you, that, if some woman chance whiles to put a cheat upon her husband, you should not only be blithe that this hath happened and take pleasure in coming to know it or hearing it told of any, but should yourselves go telling it everywhere, so men may understand that, if they are knowing, women, on their part, are no less so! the which cannot be other than useful unto you, for that, when one knoweth that another is on the alert, he setteth himself not overlightly to cozen him. Who, then, can doubt but that which we shall say to-day concerning this matter, coming to be known of men, may be exceeding effectual in restraining them from cozening you ladies, whenas they find that you likewise know how to cozen, an you will? I purpose, therefore, to tell you the trick which, on the spur of the moment, a young woman, albeit she was of mean condition, played her husband for her own preservation.

In Naples no great while agone there was a poor man who took to wife a fair and lovesome damsel called Peronella, and albeit he with his craft, which was that of a mason, and she by spinning, earned but a slender pittance, they ordered their life as best they might. It chanced one day that a young gallant of the neighbourhood saw this Peronella and she pleasing him mightily, he fell in love with her and importuned her one way and another till he became familiar with her and they took order with each other on this wise, so they might be together; to wit, seeing that her husband arose every morning betimes to go to work or to find work, they agreed that the young man should be whereas he might see him go out, and that, as soon as he was gone,—the street where she abode, which was called Avorio, being very solitary,—he should come to her house. On this wise they did many times; but one morning, the good man having gone out and Giannello Strignario (for so was the lover named) having entered the house and being with Peronella, it chanced that, after awhile, the husband returned home, whereas it was his wont to be abroad all day, and finding the door locked within, knocked and after fell a-saying in himself, 'O my God, praised be Thou ever! For, though Thou hast made me poor, at least Thou hast comforted me with a good and honest damsel to wife. See how she locked the door within as soon as I was gone out, so none might enter to do her any annoy.'

Peronella, knowing her husband by his way of knocking, said to her lover, 'Alack, Giannello mine, I am a dead woman! For here is my husband, whom God confound, come back and I know not what this meaneth, for never yet came he back hither at this hour; belike he saw thee whenas thou enteredst here. But, for the love of God, however the case may be, get thee into yonder vat, whilst I go open to him, and we shall see what is the meaning of his returning home so early this morning.' Accordingly, Giannello betook himself in all haste into the vat, whilst Peronella, going to the door, opened to her husband and said to him, with an angry air, 'What is to do now, that thou returnest home so soon this morning? Meseemeth thou hast a mind to do nought to-day, that I see thee come back, tools in hand; and if thou do thus, on what are we to live? Whence shall we get bread? Thinkest thou I will suffer thee pawn my gown and my other poor clothes? I, who do nothing but spin day and night, till the flesh is come apart from my nails, so I may at the least have so much oil as will keep our lamp burning! Husband, husband, there is not a neighbour's wife of ours but marvelleth thereat and maketh mock of me for the pains I give myself and all that I endure; and thou, thou returnest home to me, with thy hands a-dangle, whenas thou shouldst be at work.'

So saying, she fell a-weeping and went on to say, 'Alack, woe is me, unhappy woman that I am! In what an ill hour was I born, at what an ill moment did I come hither! I who might have had a young man of such worth and would none of him, so I might come to this fellow here, who taketh no thought to her whom he hath brought home! Other women give themselves a good time with their lovers, for there is none [I know] but hath two and some three, and they enjoy themselves and show their husbands the moon for the sun. But I, wretch that I am! because I am good and occupy myself not with such toys, I suffer ill and ill hap. I know not why I do not take me a lover, as do other women. Understand well, husband mine, that had I a mind to do ill, I could soon enough find the wherewithal, for there be store of brisk young fellows who love me and wish me well and have sent to me, proffering money galore or dresses and jewels, at my choice; but my heart would never suffer me to do it, for that I was no mother's daughter of that ilk; and here thou comest home to me, whenas thou shouldst be at work.'

'Good lack, wife,' answered the husband, 'fret not thyself, for God's sake; thou shouldst be assured that I know what manner of woman thou art, and indeed this morning I have in part had proof thereof. It is true that I went out to go to work; but it seemeth thou knowest not, as I myself knew not, that this is the Feast-day of San Galeone and there is no work doing; that is why I am come back at this hour; but none the less I have provided and found a means how we shall have bread for more than a month, for I have sold yonder man thou seest here with me the vat which, as thou knowest, hath this long while cumbered the house; and he is to give me five lily-florins[1] for it.' Quoth Peronella, 'So much the more cause have I to complain; thou, who art a man and goest about and should be versed in the things of the world, thou hast sold a vat for five florins, whilst I, a poor silly woman who hath scarce ever been without the door, seeing the hindrance it gave us in the house, have sold it for seven to an honest man, who entered it but now, as thou camest back, to see if it were sound!' When the husband heard this, he was more than satisfied and said to him who had come for the vat, 'Good man, begone in peace; for thou hearest that my wife hath sold the vat for seven florins, whereas thou wast to give me but five for it.' 'Good,' replied the other and went his way; whereupon quoth Peronella to her husband, 'Since thou art here, come up and settle with him thyself.' Giannello, who abode with his ears pricked up to hear if it behoved him fear or be on his guard against aught, hearing his mistress's words, straightway scrambled out of the vat and cried out, as if he had heard nothing of the husband's return, 'Where art thou, good wife?' whereupon the goodman, coming up, answered, 'Here am I; what wouldst thou have?' 'Who art thou?' asked Giannello. 'I want the woman with whom I made the bargain for this vat.' Quoth the other, 'You may deal with me in all assurance, for I am her husband.' Then said Giannello, 'The vat appeareth to me sound enough; but meseemeth you have kept dregs or the like therein, for it is all overcrusted with I know not what that is so hard and dry that I cannot remove aught thereof with my nails; wherefore I will not take it, except I first see it clean.' 'Nay,' answered Peronella, 'the bargain shall not fall through for that; my husband will clean it all out.' 'Ay will I,' rejoined the latter, and laying down his tools, put off his coat; then, calling for a light and a scraper, he entered the vat and fell to scraping. Peronella, as if she had a mind to see what he did, thrust her head and one of her arms, shoulder and all, in at the mouth of the vat, which was not overbig, and fell to saying, 'Scrape here' and 'There' and 'There also' and 'See, here is a little left.'

Whilst she was thus engaged in directing her husband and showing him where to scrape, Giannello, who had scarce yet that morning done his full desire, when they were interrupted by the mason's coming, seeing that he could not as he would, bethought himself to accomplish it as he might; wherefore, boarding her, as she held the mouth of the vat all closed up, on such wise as in the ample plains the unbridled stallions, afire with love, assail the mares of Parthia, he satisfied his juvenile ardour, the which enterprise was brought to perfection well nigh at the same moment as the scraping of the vat; whereupon he dismounted and Peronella withdrawing her head from the mouth of the vat, the husband came forth thereof. Then said she to her gallant, 'Take this light, good man, and look if it be clean to thy mind.' Giannello looked in and said that it was well and that he was satisfied and giving the husband seven florins, caused carry the vat to his own house."

---

1. So called from the figure of a lily stamped on the coin; cf. our rose-nobles.

﹖ 3 ﹖

THE THIRD STORY

FRA RINALDO LIETH WITH HIS GOSSIP AND BEING FOUND OF HER HUSBAND CLOSETED WITH HER IN HER CHAMBER, THEY GIVE HIM TO BELIEVE THAT HE WAS IN ACT TO CONJURE WORMS FROM HIS GODSON

FILOSTRATO HAD NOT KNOWN to speak so obscurely of the mares of Parthia but that the roguish ladies laughed thereat, making believe to laugh at otherwhat. But, when the king saw that his story was ended, he bade Elisa tell, who accordingly, with obedient readiness, began, "Charming ladies, Emilia's conjuration of the phantom hath brought to my memory the story of another conjuration, which latter, though it be not so goodly as hers, nevertheless, for that none other bearing upon our subject occurreth to me at this present, I will proceed to relate.

You must know that there was once in Siena a very agreeable young man and of a worshipful family, by name Rinaldo, who was passionately enamored of a very beautiful lady, a neighbour of his and the wife of a rich man, and flattered himself that, could he but find means to speak with her unsuspected, he might avail to have of her all that he should desire. Seeing none other way and the lady being great with child, he bethought himself to become her gossip and accordingly, clapping up an acquaintance with her husband, he offered him, on such wise as appeared to him most seemly, to be godfather to his child. His offer was accepted and he being now become Madam Agnesa's gossip and having a somewhat more colourable excuse for speaking with her, he took courage and gave her in so many words to know that of his intent which she had indeed long before gathered from his looks; but little did this profit him, although the lady was nothing displeased to have heard him.

Not long after, whatever might have been the reason, it came to pass that Rinaldo turned friar and whether or not he found the pasturage to his liking, he persevered in that way of life; and albeit, in the days of his becoming a monk, he had for awhile laid on one side the love he bore his gossip, together with sundry other vanities of his, yet, in process of time, without quitting the monk's habit, he resumed them[1] and began to delight in making a show and wearing fine stuffs and being dainty and elegant in all his fashions and making canzonets and sonnets and ballads and in singing and all manner other things of the like sort. But what say I of our Fra Rinaldo, of whom we speak? What monks are there that do not thus? Alack, shame that they are of the corrupt world, they blush not to appear fat and ruddy in the face, dainty in their garb and in all that pertaineth unto them, and strut along, not like doves, but like very

GIOVANNI BOCCACCIO

turkey-cocks, with crest erect and breast puffed out; and what is worse (to say nothing of having their cells full of gallipots crammed with electuaries and unguents, of boxes full of various confections, of phials and flagons of distilled waters and oils, of pitchers brimming with Malmsey and Cyprus and other wines of price, insomuch that they seem to the beholder not friars' cells, but rather apothecaries' or perfumers' shops) they think no shame that folk should know them to be gouty, conceiving that others see not nor know that strict fasting, coarse viands and spare and sober living make men lean and slender and for the most part sound of body, and that if indeed some sicken thereof, at least they sicken not of the gout, whereto it is used to give, for medicine, chastity and everything else that pertaineth to the natural way of living of an honest friar. Yet they persuade themselves that others know not that, —let alone the scant and sober living,—long vigils, praying and discipline should make men pale and mortified and that neither St. Dominic nor St. Francis, far from having four gowns for one, clad themselves in cloth dyed in grain nor in other fine stuffs, but in garments of coarse wool and undyed, to keep out the cold and not to make a show. For which things, as well as for the souls of the simpletons who nourish them, there is need that God provide.

Fra Rinaldo, then, having returned to his former appetites, began to pay frequent visits to his gossip and waxing in assurance, proceeded to solicit her with more than his former instancy to that which he desired of her. The good lady, seeing herself hard pressed and Fra Rinaldo seeming to her belike goodlier than she had thought him aforetime, being one day sore importuned of him, had recourse to that argument which all women use who have a mind to yield that which is asked of them and said, 'How now, Fra Rinaldo? Do monks such things?' 'Madam,' answered he, 'when as I shall have this gown off my back,—and I can put it off mighty easily,—I shall appear to you a man fashioned like other men and not a monk.' The lady pulled a demure face and said, 'Alack, wretched me! You are my gossip; how can I do this? It were sadly ill, and I have heard many a time that it is a very great sin; but, certes, were it not for this, I would do that which you wish.' Quoth Fra Rinaldo, 'You are a simpleton, if you forbear for this; I do not say that it is not a sin, but God pardoneth greater than this to whoso repenteth. But tell me, who is more akin to your child, I who held him at baptism or your husband who begat him?' 'My husband is more akin to him,' answered the lady; whereupon, 'You say sooth,' rejoined the friar. 'And doth not your husband lie with you?' 'Ay doth he,' replied she. 'Then,' said Fra Rinaldo, 'I, who am less akin to your child than is your husband, may lie with you even as doth he.' The lady, who knew no logic and needed little persuasion, either believed or made a show of believing that the friar spoke the truth and answered, 'Who might avail to answer your learned words?' And after, notwithstanding the gossipship, she resigned herself to do his pleasure; nor did they content themselves with one bout, but foregathered many and many a time, having the more commodity thereof under cover of the gossipship, for that there was less suspicion.

But once, amongst other times, it befell that Fra Rinaldo, coming to the lady's house and finding none with her but a little maid of hers, who was very pretty and agreeable, despatched his comrade with the latter to the pigeon-loft, to teach her her Paternoster, and entered with the lady, who had her child in her hand, into her bedchamber, where they locked themselves in and fell to taking their pleasure upon a daybed that was there. As they were thus engaged, it chanced that the husband came home and making for the bedchamber-door, unperceived of any, knocked and called to the lady, who, hearing this, said to the friar, 'I am a dead woman, for here is my husband, and now he will certainly perceive what is the reason of our familiarity.' Now Rinaldo was stripped to his waistcoat, to wit, he had put off his gown and his scapulary, and hearing this, answered, 'You say sooth; were I but dressed, there might be some means; but, if you open to him and he find me thus, there can be no excuse for us.' The lady, seized with a sudden idea, said, 'Harkye, dress yourself and when you are dressed, take your godchild in your arms and hearken well to that which I shall say to him, so your words may after accord with mine, and leave me do.' Then, to the good man, who had not yet left knocking, 'I come to thee,' quoth she and rising, opened the chamber-door and said, with a good countenance, 'Husband mine, I must tell thee that Fra Rinaldo, our gossip, is come hither and it was God sent him to us; for, certes, but for his coming, we should to-day have lost our child.'

The good simple man, hearing this, was like to swoon and said, 'How so?' 'O husband mine,' answered Agnesa, 'there took him but now of a sudden a fainting-fit, that methought he was dead, and I knew not what to do or say; but just then Fra Rinaldo our gossip came in and taking him in his arms, said, "Gossip, these be worms he hath in his body, the which draw near to his heart and would infallibly kill him; but have no fear, for I will conjure them and make them all die; and ere I go hence, you shall see the child whole again as ever you saw him." And for that we had need of thee to repeat certain orisons and that the maid could not find thee, he caused his comrade say them in the highest room of our house, whilst he and I came hither and locked ourselves in, so none should hinder us, for that none other than the child's mother might be present at such an office. Indeed, he hath the child yet in his arms and methinketh he waiteth but for his comrade to have made an end of saying the orisons and it will be done, for that the boy is already altogether restored to himself.' The good simple man, believing all this, was so straitened with concern for his child that it never entered his mind to suspect the cheat put upon him by his wife; but, heaving a great sigh, he said, 'I will go see him.' 'Nay,' answered she, 'thou wouldst mar that which hath been done. Wait; I will go see an thou mayst come in and call thee.'

Meanwhile, Fra Rinaldo, who had heard everything and had dressed himself at his leisure, took the child in his arms and called out, as soon as he had ordered matters to his mind, saying, 'Harkye, gossip, hear I not my gossip your husband there?' 'Ay, sir,' answered the simpleton; whereupon, 'Then,' said the other, 'come hither.' The cuckold went to him and Fra Rinaldo said to him, 'Take your son by the grace of God whole and well, whereas I deemed but now you would not see him alive at vespers; and look you let make a waxen image of his bigness and set it up, to the praise and glory of God, before the statue of our lord St. Ambrose, through whose intercession He hath vouchsafed to restore him unto you.' The child, seeing his father, ran to him and caressed him, as little children used to do, whilst the latter, taking him, weeping, in his arms, no otherwise than as he had brought him forth of the grave, fell to kissing him and returning thanks to his gossip for that he had made him whole.

Meanwhile, Fra Rinaldo's comrade, who had by this taught the serving-wench not one, but maybe more than four paternosters, and had given her a little purse of white thread, which he had from a nun, and made her his devotee, hearing the cuckold call at his wife's chamber-door, had softly betaken himself to a place whence he could, himself unseen, both see and hear what should betide and presently, seeing that all had passed off well, came down and entering the chamber, said, 'Fra Rinaldo, I have despatched all four of the orisons which you bade me say.' 'Brother mine,' answered the friar, 'thou hast a good wind and hast done well; I, for my part, had said but two thereof, when my gossip came; but God the Lord, what with thy pains and mine, hath shown us such favour that the child is healed.' Therewithal the cuckold let bring good wines and confections and entertained his gossip and the latter's comrade with that whereof they had more need than of aught else. Then, attending them to the door, he commended them to God and letting make the waxen image without delay, he sent to hang it up with the others[2] before the statue of St. Ambrose, but not that of Milan."[3]

1. *i.e.* the discarded vanities aforesaid.
2. *i.e.* the other ex votos.
3. There is apparently some satirical allusion here, which I cannot undertake to explain.

❦ 4 ❧

THE FOURTH STORY

TOFANO ONE NIGHT SHUTTETH HIS WIFE OUT OF DOORS, WHO, AVAILING NOT TO RE-ENTER BY DINT OF ENTREATIES, FEIGNETH TO CAST HERSELF INTO A WELL AND CASTETH THEREIN A GREAT STONE. TOFANO COMETH FORTH OF THE HOUSE AND RUNNETH THITHER, WHEREUPON SHE SLIPPETH IN AND LOCKING HIM OUT, BAWLETH REPROACHES AT HIM FROM THE WINDOW

THE KING no sooner perceived Elisa's story to be ended than, turning without delay to Lauretta, he signified to her his pleasure that she should tell; whereupon she, without hesitation, began thus, "O Love, how great and how various is thy might! How many thy resources and thy devices! What philosopher, what craftsman[1] could ever have availed or might avail to teach those shifts, those feints, those subterfuges which thou on the spur of the moment suggestest to whoso ensueth in thy traces! Certes, all others' teaching is halting compared with thine, as may very well have been apprehended by the devices which have already been set forth and to which, lovesome ladies, I will add one practised by a woman of a simple wit enough and such as I know none but Love could have taught her.

There was once, then, in Arezzo, a rich man called Tofano and he was given to wife a very fair lady, by name Madam Ghita, of whom, without knowing why, he quickly waxed jealous. The lady, becoming aware of this, was despited thereat and questioned him once and again of the reason of his jealousy; but he was able to assign her none, save such as were general and naught; wherefore it occurred to her mind to cause him die of the disease whereof he stood without reason in fear. Accordingly, perceiving that a young man, who was much to her taste, sighed for her, she proceeded discreetly to come to an understanding with him and things being so far advanced between them that there lacked but with deeds to give effect to words, she cast about for a means of bringing this also to pass; wherefore, having already remarked, amongst her husband's other ill usances, that he delighted in drinking, she began not only to commend this to him, but would often artfully incite him thereto. This became so much his wont that, well nigh whensoever it pleased her, she led him to drink even to intoxication, and putting him to bed whenas she saw him well drunken, she a first time foregathered with her lover, with whom many a time thereafter she continued to do so in all security. Indeed, she grew to put such trust in her husband's drunkenness that not only did she make bold to bring her gallant into the house, but went whiles to pass a great part of the night with him in his own house, which was not very far distant.

The enamoured lady continuing on this wise, it befell that the wretched husband came to perceive that she, whilst encouraging him to drink, natheless herself drank never; wherefore

315

suspicion took him that it might be as in truth it was, to wit, that she made him drunken, so she might after do her pleasure what while he slept, and wishing to make proof of this, an it were so, he one evening, not having drunken that day, feigned himself, both in words and fashions, the drunkenest man that was aye. The lady, believing this and judging that he needed no more drink, put him to bed in all haste and this done, betook herself, as she was used to do whiles, to the house of her lover, where she abode till midnight. As for Tofano, no sooner did he know the lady to have left the house than he straightway arose and going to the doors, locked them from within; after which he posted himself at the window, so he might see her return and show her that he had gotten wind of her fashions; and there he abode till such time as she came back. The lady, returning home and finding herself locked out, was beyond measure woeful and began to essay an she might avail to open the door by force, which, after Tofano had awhile suffered, 'Wife,' quoth he, 'thou weariest thyself in vain, for thou canst nowise come in here again. Go, get thee back whereas thou hast been till now and be assured that thou shalt never return thither till such time as I shall have done thee, in respect of this affair, such honour as beseemeth thee in the presence of thy kinsfolk and of the neighbours.'

The lady fell to beseeching him for the love of God that it would please him open to her, for that she came not whence he supposed, but from keeping vigil with a she-neighbour of hers, for that the nights were long and she could not sleep them all out nor watch at home alone. However, prayers profited her nought, for that her brute of a husband was minded to have all the Aretines[2] know their shame, whereas none as yet knew it; wherefore, seeing that prayers availed her not, she had recourse to threats and said, 'An thou open not to me, I will make thee the woefullest man alive.' 'And what canst thou do to me?' asked Tofano, and Mistress Tessa, whose wits Love had already whetted with his counsels, replied, 'Rather than brook the shame which thou wouldst wrongfully cause me suffer, I will cast myself into this well that is herenigh, where when I am found dead, there is none will believe otherwise than that thou, for very drunkenness, hast cast me therein; wherefore it will behove thee flee and lose all thou hast and abide in banishment or have thy head cut off for my murderer, as thou wilt in truth have been.'

Tofano was nowise moved by these words from his besotted intent; wherefore quoth she to him, 'Harkye now, I can no longer brook this thy fashery, God pardon it thee! Look thou cause lay up[3] this distaff of mine that I leave here.' So saying, the night being so dark that one might scarce see other by the way, she went up to the well and taking a great stone that lay thereby, cried out, 'God pardon me!' and let it drop into the water. The stone, striking the water, made a very great noise, which when Tofano heard, he verily believed that she had cast herself in; wherefore, snatching up the bucket and the rope, he rushed out of the house and ran to the well to succour her. The lady, who had hidden herself near the door, no sooner saw him run to the well than she slipped into the house and locked herself in; then, getting her to the window, 'You should water your wine, whenas you drink it,' quoth she, 'and not after and by night.' Tofano, hearing this, knew himself to have been fooled and returned to the door, but could get no admission and proceeded to bid her open to him; but she left speaking softly, as she had done till then, and began, well nigh at a scream, to say, 'By Christ His Cross, tiresome sot that thou art, thou shalt not enter here to-night; I cannot brook these thy fashions any longer; needs must I let every one see what manner of man thou art and at what hour thou comest home anights.' Tofano, on his side, flying into a rage, began to rail at her and bawl; whereupon the neighbours, hearing the clamour, arose, both men and women, and coming to the windows, asked what was to do. The lady answered, weeping, 'It is this wretch of a man, who still returneth to me of an evening, drunken, or falleth asleep about the taverns and after cometh home at this hour; the which I have long suffered, but, it availing me not and I being unable to put up with it longer, I have bethought me to shame him therefor by locking him out of doors, to see and he will mend himself thereof.'

Tofano, on the other hand, told them, like an ass as he was, how the case stood and threatened her sore; but she said to the neighbours, 'Look you now what a man he is! What would you say, were I in the street, as he is, and he in the house, as am I? By God His faith, I doubt me you would believe he said sooth. By this you may judge of his wits; he saith I have done just what methinketh he hath himself done. He thought to fear me by casting I know not what into the well; but would God he had cast himself there in good sooth and drowned himself, so he might have well watered the wine which he hath drunken to excess.' The neighbours, both men and women, all fell to blaming Tofano, holding him at fault, and chid him for that which he said against the lady; and in a short time the report was so noised abroad from neighbour to neighbour that it reached the ears of the lady's kinsfolk, who came thither and hearing the thing from one and another of the neighbours, took Tofano and gave him such a drubbing that they broke every bone in his body. Then, entering the house, they took the lady's gear and carried her off home with them, threatening Tofano with worse. The latter, finding himself in ill case and seeing that his jealousy had brought him to a sorry pass, for that he still loved his wife heartily,[4] procured certain friends to intercede for him and so wrought that he made his peace with the lady and had her home again with him, promising her that he would never be jealous again. Moreover, he gave her leave to do her every pleasure, provided she wrought so discreetly that he should know nothing thereof; and on this wise, like a crack-brained churl as he was, he made peace after suffering damage. So long live Love and death to war and all its company!"

---

1. Syn. professor of the liberal arts (*artista*).
2. *i.e.* inhabitants of Arezzo.
3. *Riporre*, possibly a mistake for *riportare*, to fetch back.
4. Lit. wished her all his weal.

✺ 5 ✺

THE FIFTH STORY

A JEALOUS HUSBAND, IN THE GUISE OF A PRIEST, CONFESSETH HIS WIFE, WHO GIVETH HIM TO BELIEVE THAT SHE LOVETH A PRIEST, WHO COMETH TO HER EVERY NIGHT; AND WHILST THE HUSBAND SECRETLY KEEPETH WATCH AT THE DOOR FOR THE LATTER, THE LADY BRINGETH IN A LOVER OF HERS BY THE ROOF AND LIETH WITH HIM

LAURETTA HAVING MADE an end of her story and all having commended the lady for that she had done aright and even as befitted her wretch of a husband, the king, to lose no time, turned to Fiammetta and courteously imposed on her the burden of the story-telling; whereupon she began thus, "Most noble ladies, the foregoing story moveth me to tell you, on like wise, of a jealous husband, accounting, as I do, all that their wives do unto such,—particularly whenas they are jealous without cause,—to be well done and holding that, if the makers of the laws had considered everything, they should have appointed none other penalty unto women who offend in this than that which they appoint unto whoso offendeth against other in self-defence; for that jealous men are plotters against the lives of young women and most diligent procurers of their deaths. Wives abide all the week mewed up at home, occupying themselves with domestic offices and the occasions of their families and households, and after they would fain, like every one else, have some solace and some rest on holidays and be at leisure to take some diversion even as do the tillers of the fields, the artisans of the towns and the administrators of the laws, according to the example of God himself, who rested from all His labours the seventh day, and to the intent of the laws, both human and Divine, which, looking to the honour of God and the common weal of all, have distinguished working days from those of repose. But to this jealous men will on no wise consent; nay, those days which are gladsome for all other women they make wretcheder and more doleful than the others to their wives, keeping them yet closelier straitened and confined; and what a misery and a languishment this is for the poor creatures those only know who have proved it. Wherefore, to conclude, I say that what a woman doth to a husband who is jealous without cause should certes not be condemned, but rather commended.

There was, then, in Arimino a merchant, very rich both in lands and monies, who, having to wife a very fair lady, became beyond measure jealous of her; nor had he other cause for this save that, as he loved her exceedingly and held her very fair and saw that she studied with all her might to please him, even so he imagined that every man loved her and that she appeared fair to all and eke that she studied to please others as she did himself, which was the reasoning of a man of nought and one of little sense. Being grown thus jealous, he kept such strict watch over her and held her in such constraint that belike many there be of those who are condemned to capital punishment who are less straitly guarded of their gaolers; for, far from being at liberty to go to weddings or entertainments or to church or indeed anywise to set foot without the house, she dared not even stand at the window nor look abroad on any occasion; wherefore her life was most wretched and she brooked this annoy with the more impatience as she felt herself the less to blame. Accordingly, seeing herself unjustly suspected of her husband, she determined, for her own solacement, to find a means (an she but might) of doing on such wise that he should have reason for his ill usage of her. And for that she might not station herself at the window and so had no opportunity of showing herself favourable to the suit of any one who might take note of her, as he passed along her street, and pay his court to her,—knowing that in the adjoining house there was a certain young man both handsome and agreeable,—she bethought herself to look if there were any hole in the wall that parted the two houses and therethrough to spy once and again till such time as she should see the youth aforesaid and find an occasion of speaking with him and bestowing on him her love, so he would accept thereof, purposing, if a means could be found, to foregather with him bytimes and on this wise while away her sorry life till such time as the demon [of jealousy] should take leave of her husband.

Accordingly, she went spying about the walls of the house, now in one part and now in another, whenas her husband was abroad, and happened at last upon a very privy place where the wall was somewhat opened by a fissure and looking therethrough, albeit she could ill discover what was on the other side, algates she perceived that the opening gave upon a bedchamber there and said in herself, 'Should this be the chamber of Filippo,' to wit, the youth her neighbour, 'I were half sped.' Then, causing secretly enquire of this by a maid of hers, who had pity upon her, she found that the young man did indeed sleep in that chamber all alone; wherefore, by dint of often visiting the crevice and dropping pebbles and such small matters, whenas she perceived him to be there, she wrought on such wise that he came to the opening, to see what was to do; whereupon she called to him softly. He, knowing her voice, answered her, and she, profiting by the occasion, discovered to him in brief all her mind; whereat the youth was mightily content and made shift to enlarge the hole from his side on such wise that none could perceive it; and therethrough they many a time bespoke one another and touched hands, but could go no farther, for the jealous vigilance of the husband.

After awhile, the Feast of the Nativity drawing near, the lady told her husband that, an it pleased him, she would fain go to church on Christmas morning and confess and take the sacrament, as other Christians did. Quoth he, 'And what sin hast thou committed that thou wouldst confess?' 'How?' answered the lady. 'Thinkest thou that I am a saint, because thou keepest me mewed up? Thou must know well enough that I commit sins like all others that live in this world; but I will not tell them to thee, for that thou art not a priest.' The jealous wretch took suspicion at these words and determined to seek to know what sins she had committed; wherefore, having bethought himself of a means whereby he might gain his end, he answered that he was content, but that he would have her go to no other church than their parish chapel and that thither she must go betimes in the morning and confess herself either to their chaplain or to such priest as the latter should appoint her and to none other and presently return home. Herseemed she half apprehended his meaning; but without saying otherwhat, she answered that she would do as he said.

Accordingly, Christmas Day come, the lady arose at daybreak and attiring herself, repaired to the church appointed her of her husband, who, on his part, betook himself to the same place and reached it before her. Having already taken order with the chaplain of that which he had a mind to do, he hastily donned one of the latter's gowns, with a great flapped cowl, such as we see priests wear, and drawing the hood a little over his face, seated himself in the choir. The lady, entering the chapel, enquired for the chaplain, who came and hearing from her that she would fain confess, said that he could not hear her, but would send her one of his brethren. Accordingly, going away, he sent her the jealous man, in an ill hour for the latter, who came up with a very grave air, and albeit the day was not over bright and he had drawn the cowl far over his eyes, knew not so well to disguise himself but he was readily recognized by the lady, who, seeing this, said in herself, 'Praised be God! From a jealous man he is turned priest; but no matter; I will e'en give him what he goeth seeking.'

Accordingly, feigning not to know him, she seated herself at his feet. My lord Jealousy had put some pebbles in his mouth, to impede his speech somewhat, so his wife might not know him by his voice, himseeming he was in every other particular so thoroughly disguised that he was nowise fearful of being recognized by her. To come to the confession, the lady told him, amongst other things, (having first declared herself to be married,) that she was enamoured of a priest, who came every night to lie with her. When the jealous man heard this, himseemed he had gotten a knife-thrust in the heart, and had not desire constrained him to know more, he had abandoned the confession and gone away. Standing fast, then, he asked the lady, 'How! Doth not your husband lie with you?' 'Ay doth he, sir,' replied she. 'How, then,' asked the jealous man, 'can the priest also lie with you?' 'Sir,' answered she, 'by what art he doth it I know not, but there is not a door in the house so fast locked but it openeth so soon as he toucheth it; and he telleth me that, whenas he cometh to the door of my chamber, before opening it, he pronounceth certain words, by virtue whereof my husband incontinent falleth asleep, and so soon as he perceiveth him to be fast, he openeth the door and cometh in and lieth with me; and this never faileth.' Quoth the mock priest, 'Madam, this is ill done, and it behoveth you altogether to refrain therefrom.' 'Sir,' answered the lady, 'methinketh I could never do that, for that I love him too well.' 'Then,' said the other, 'I cannot shrive you.' Quoth she, 'I am grieved for that; but I came not hither to tell you lies; an I thought I could do it, I would tell you so.' 'In truth, madam,' replied the husband, 'I am concerned for you, for that I see you lose your soul at this game; but, to do you service, I will well to take the pains of putting up my special orisons to God in your name, the which maybe shall profit you, and I will send you bytimes a little clerk of mine, to whom you shall say if they have profited you or not; and if they have profited you, we will proceed farther.' 'Sir,' answered the lady, 'whatever you do, send none to me at home, for, should my husband come to know of it, he is so terribly jealous that nothing in the world would get it out of his head that your messenger came hither for nought[1] but ill, and I should have no peace with him this year to come.' Quoth the other, 'Madam, have no fear of that, for I will certainly contrive it on such wise that you shall never hear a word of the matter from him.' Then said she, 'So but you can engage to do that, I am content.' Then, having made her confession and gotten her penance, she rose to her feet and went off to hear mass; whilst the jealous man, (ill luck go with him!) withdrew, bursting with rage, to put off his priest's habit, and returned home, impatient to find a means of surprising the priest with his wife, so he might play the one and the other an ill turn.

Presently the lady came back from church and saw plainly enough from her husband's looks that she had given him an ill Christmas; albeit he studied, as most he might, to conceal that which he had done and what himseemed he had learned. Then, being inwardly resolved to lie in wait near the street-door that night and watch for the priest's coming, he said to the lady, 'Needs must I sup and lie abroad to-night, wherefore look thou lock the street-door fast, as well as that of the midstair and that of thy chamber, and get thee to bed, whenas it seemeth good to thee.' The lady answered, 'It is well,' and betaking herself, as soon as she had leisure, to the hole in the wall, she made the wonted signal, which when Filippo heard, he came to her forthright. She told him how she had done that morning and what her husband had said to her after dinner and added, 'I am certain he will not leave the house, but will set himself to watch the door; wherefore do thou find means to come hither to me to-night by the roof, so we may lie together.' The young man was mightily rejoiced at this and answered, 'Madam, leave me do.'

Accordingly, the night come, the jealous man took his arms and hid himself by stealth in a room on the ground floor, whilst the lady, whenas it seemed to her time,—having caused lock all the doors and in particular that of the midstair, so he might not avail to come up,—summoned the young man, who came to her from his side by a very privy way. Thereupon they went to bed and gave themselves a good time, taking their pleasure one of the other till daybreak, when the young man returned to his own house. Meanwhile, the jealous man stood to his arms well nigh all night beside the street-door, sorry and supperless and dying of cold, and waited for the priest to come till near upon day, when, unable to watch any longer, he returned to the ground floor room and there fell asleep. Towards tierce he awoke and the street door being now open, he made a show of returning from otherwhere and went up into his house and dined. A little after, he sent a lad, as he were the priest's clerkling that had confessed her, to the lady to ask if she wot of were come thither again. She knew the messenger well enough and answered that he had not come thither that night and that if he did thus, he might haply pass out of her mind, albeit she wished it not. What more should I tell you? The jealous man abode on the watch night after night, looking to catch the priest at his entering in, and the lady still had a merry life with her lover the while.

At length the cuckold, able to contain himself no longer, asked his wife, with an angry air, what she had said to the priest the morning she had confessed herself to him. She answered that she would not tell him, for that it was neither a just thing nor a seemly; whereupon, 'Vile woman that thou art!' cried he. 'In despite of thee I know what thou saidst to him, and needs must I know the priest of whom thou art so mightily enamoured and who, by means of his conjurations, lieth with thee every night; else will I slit thy weasand.' She replied that it was not true that she was enamoured of any priest. 'How?' cried the husband, 'Saidst thou not thus and thus to the priest who confessed thee?' And she, 'Thou couldst not have reported it better, not to say if he had told it thee, but if thou hadst been present; ay, I did tell him this.' 'Then,' rejoined the jealous man, 'tell me who is this priest, and that quickly.'

The lady fell a-smiling and answered, 'It rejoiceth me mightily to see a wise man led by the nose by a woman, even as one leadeth a ram by the horns to the shambles, albeit thou art no longer wise nor hast been since the hour when, unknowing why, thou sufferedst the malignant spirit of jealousy to enter thy breast; and the sillier and more besotted thou art, so much the less is my glory thereof. Deemest thou, husband mine, I am as blind of the eyes of the body as thou of those of the mind? Certes, no; I perceived at first sight who was the priest that confessed me and know that thou wast he; but I had it at heart to give thee that which thou wentest seeking, and in sooth I have done it. Wert thou as wise as thou thinkest to be, thou wouldst not have essayed by this means to learn the secrets of thy good wife, but wouldst, without taking vain suspicion, have recognized that which she confessed to thee to be the very truth, without her having sinned in aught. I told thee that I loved a priest, and wast not thou, whom I am much to blame to love as I do, become a priest? I told thee that no door of my house could abide locked, whenas he had a mind to lie with me; and what door in the house was ever kept against thee, whenas thou wouldst come whereas I might be? I told thee that the priest lay with me every night, and when was it that thou layest not with me? And whenassoever thou sentest thy clerk to me, which was thou knowest, as often as thou layest from me, I sent thee word that the priest had not been with me. What other than a crack-brain like thee, who has suffered thyself to be blinded by thy jealousy, had failed to understand these things? Thou hast abidden in the house, keeping watch anights, and thoughtest to have given me to believe that thou wast gone abroad to sup and sleep. Bethink thee henceforth and become a man again, as thou wast wont to be; and make not thyself a laughing stock to whoso knoweth thy fashions, as do I, and leave this unconscionable watching that thou keepest; for I swear to God that, an the fancy took me to make thee wear the horns, I would engage, haddest thou an hundred eyes, as thou hast but two, to do my pleasure on such wise that thou shouldst not be ware thereof.'

The jealous wretch, who thought to have very adroitly surprised his wife's secrets, hearing this, avouched himself befooled and without answering otherwhat, held the lady for virtuous and discreet; and whenas it behoved him to be jealous, he altogether divested himself of his jealousy, even as he had put it on, what time he had no need thereof. Wherefore the discreet lady, being in a manner licensed to do her pleasures, thenceforward no longer caused her lover to come to her by the roof, as go the cats, but e'en brought him in at the door, and dealing advisedly, many a day thereafter gave herself a good time and led a merry life with him."

---

1. Boccaccio writes carelessly "for *aught*" (*altro*), which makes nonsense of the passage.

❧ 6 ❧

THE SIXTH STORY

MADAM ISABELLA, BEING IN COMPANY WITH LEONETTO HER LOVER, IS VISITED BY ONE MESSER LAMBERTUCCIO, OF WHOM SHE IS BELOVED; HER HUSBAND RETURNING, [UNEXPECTED,] SHE SENDETH LAMBERTUCCIO FORTH OF THE HOUSE, WHINGER IN HAND, AND THE HUSBAND AFTER ESCORTETH LEONETTO HOME

THE COMPANY WERE wonder-well pleased with Fiammetta's story, all affirming that the lady had done excellently well and as it behoved unto such a brute of a man, and after it was ended, the king bade Pampinea follow on, who proceeded to say, "There are many who, speaking ignorantly, avouch that love bereaveth folk of their senses and causeth whoso loveth to become witless. Meseemeth this is a foolish opinion, as hath indeed been well enough shown by the things already related, and I purpose yet again to demonstrate it.

In our city, which aboundeth in all good things, there was once a young lady both gently born and very fair, who was the wife of a very worthy and notable gentleman; and as it happeneth often that folk cannot for ever brook one same food, but desire bytimes to vary their diet, this lady, her husband not altogether satisfying her, became enamoured of a young man called Leonetto and very well bred and agreeable, for all he was of no great extraction. He on like wise fell in love with her, and as you know that seldom doth that which both parties desire abide without effect, it was no great while before accomplishment was given to their loves. Now it chanced that, she being a fair and engaging lady, a gentleman called Messer Lambertuccio became sore enamoured of her, whom, for that he seemed to her a disagreeable man and a tiresome, she could not for aught in the world bring herself to love. However, after soliciting her amain with messages and it availing him nought, he sent to her threatening her, for that he was a notable man, to dishonour her, an she did not his pleasure; wherefore she, fearful and knowing his character, submitted herself to do his will.

It chanced one day that the lady, whose name was Madam Isabella, being gone, as is our custom in summer-time, to abide at a very goodly estate she had in the country and her husband having ridden somewhither to pass some days abroad, she sent for Leonetto to come and be with her, whereat he was mightily rejoiced and betook himself thither incontinent. Meanwhile Messer Lambertuccio, hearing that her husband was gone abroad, took horse and repairing, all alone, to her house, knocked at the door. The lady's waiting-woman, seeing him, came straight to her mistress, who was closeted with Leonetto, and called to her, saying, 'Madam, Messer Lambertuccio is below, all alone.' The lady, hearing this, was the woefullest woman in the world, but, as she stood in great fear of Messer Lambertuccio, she besought

Leonetto not to take it ill to hide himself awhile behind the curtains of her bed till such time as the other should be gone. Accordingly, Leonetto, who feared him no less than did the lady, hid himself there and she bade the maid go open to Messer Lambertuccio, which being done, he lighted down in the courtyard and making his palfrey fast to a staple there, went up into the house. The lady put on a cheerful countenance and coming to the head of the stair, received him with as good a grace as she might and asked him what brought him thither; whereupon he caught her in his arms and clipped her and kissed her, saying, 'My soul, I understood that your husband was abroad and am come accordingly to be with you awhile.' After these words, they entered a bedchamber, where they locked themselves in, and Messer Lambertuccio fell to taking delight of her.

As they were thus engaged, it befell, altogether out of the lady's expectation, that her husband returned, whom when the maid saw near the house, she ran in haste to the lady's chamber and said, 'Madam, here is my lord come back; methinketh he is already below in the courtyard.' When the lady heard this, bethinking her that she had two men in the house and knowing that there was no hiding Messer Lambertuccio, by reason of his palfrey which was in the courtyard, she gave herself up for lost. Nevertheless, taking a sudden resolution, she sprang hastily down from the bed and said to Messer Lambertuccio, 'Sir, an you wish me anywise well and would save me from death, do that which I shall bid you. Take your hanger naked in your hand and go down the stair with an angry air and all disordered and begone, saying, "I vow to God that I will take him elsewhere." And should my husband offer to detain you or question you of aught, do you say no otherwhat than that which I have told you, but take horse and look you abide not with him on any account.' The gentleman answered that he would well, and accordingly, drawing his hanger, he did as she had enjoined him, with a face all afire what with the swink he had furnished and with anger at the husband's return. The latter was by this dismounted in the courtyard and marvelled to see the palfrey there; then, offering to go up into the house, he saw Messer Lambertuccio come down and wondering both at his words and his air, said, 'What is this, sir?' Messer Lambertuccio putting his foot in the stirrup and mounting to horse, said nought but, 'Cock's body, I shall find him again otherwhere,' and made off.

The gentleman, going up, found his wife at the stairhead, all disordered and fearful, and said to her, 'What is all this? Whom goeth Messer Lambertuccio threatening thus in such a fury?' The lady, withdrawing towards the chamber where Leonetto was, so he might hear her, answered, 'Sir, never had I the like of this fright. There came fleeing hither but now a young man, whom I know not, followed by Messer Lambertuccio, hanger in hand, and finding by chance the door of this chamber open, said to me, all trembling, "For God's sake, madam, help me, that I be not slain in your arms." I rose to my feet and was about to question him who he was and what ailed him, when, behold, in rushed Messer Lambertuccio, saying, "Where art thou, traitor?" I set myself before the chamber-door and hindered him from entering; and he was in so far courteous that, after many words, seeing it pleased me not that he should enter there, he went his way down, as you have seen.' Quoth the husband, 'Wife, thou didst well, it were too great a reproach to us, had a man been slain in our house, and Messer Lambertuccio did exceeding unmannerly to follow a person who had taken refuge here.'

Then he asked where the young man was, and the lady answered, 'Indeed sir, I know not where he hath hidden himself.' Then said the husband 'Where art thou? Come forth in safety.' Whereupon Leonetto, who had heard everything, came forth all trembling for fear, (as indeed he had had a great fright,) of the place where he had hidden himself, and the gentleman said to him, 'What hast thou to do with Messer Lambertuccio?' 'Sir,' answered he, 'I have nothing in the world to do with him, wherefore methinketh assuredly he is either not in his right wits or he hath mistaken me for another; for that no sooner did he set eyes on me in the road not far from this house than he forthright clapped his hand to his hanger and said, "Traitor, thou art a dead man!" I stayed not to ask why, but took to my heels as best I might and made my way hither, where, thanks to God and to this gentlewoman, I have escaped.' Quoth the husband, 'Go to; have no fears; I will bring thee to thine own house safe and sound, and thou canst after seek out what thou hast to do with him.' Accordingly, when they had supped, he mounted him a-horseback and carrying him back to Florence, left him in his own house. As for Leonetto, that same evening, according as he had been lessoned of the lady, he privily bespoke Messer Lambertuccio and took such order with him, albeit there was much talk of the matter thereafterward, the husband never for all that became aware of the cheat that had been put on him by his wife."

7

THE SEVENTH STORY

LODOVICO DISCOVERETH TO MADAM BEATRICE THE
LOVE HE BEARETH HER, WHEREUPON SHE SENDETH
EGANO HER HUSBAND INTO THE GARDEN, IN HER
OWN FAVOUR, AND LIETH MEANWHILE WITH
LODOVICO, WHO, PRESENTLY ARISING, GOETH AND
CUDGELLETH EGANO IN THE GARDEN

MADAM ISABELLA'S presence of mind, as related by Pampinea, was held admirable by all the company; but, whilst they yet marvelled thereat, Filomena, whom the king had appointed to follow on, said, "Lovesome ladies, and I mistake not, methinketh I can tell you no less goodly a story on the same subject, and that forthright.

You must know, then, that there was once in Paris a Florentine gentleman, who was for poverty turned merchant and had thriven so well in commerce that he was grown thereby very rich. He had by his lady one only son, whom he had named Lodovico, and for that he might concern himself with his father's nobility and not with trade, he had willed not to place him in any warehouse, but had sent him to be with other gentlemen in the service of the King of France, where he learned store of goodly manners and other fine things. During his sojourn there, it befell that certain gentlemen, who were returned from visiting the Holy Sepulchre, coming in upon a conversation between certain young men, of whom Lodovico was one, and hearing them discourse among themselves of the fair ladies of France and England and other parts of the world, one of them began to say that assuredly, in all the lands he had traversed and for all the ladies he had seen, he had never beheld the like for beauty of Madam Beatrice, the wife of Messer Egano de' Gulluzzi of Bologna; to which all his companions, who had with him seen her at Bologna, agreed.

Lodovico, who had never yet been enamoured of any woman, hearkening to this, was fired with such longing to see her that he could hold his thought to nothing else and being altogether resolved to journey to Bologna for that purpose and there, if she pleased him, to abide awhile, he feigned to his father that he had a mind to go visit the Holy Sepulchre, the which with great difficulty he obtained of him. Accordingly, taking the name of Anichino, he set out for Bologna, and on the day following [his arrival,] as fortune would have it, he saw the lady in question at an entertainment, where she seemed to him fairer far than he had imagined her; wherefore, falling most ardently enamoured of her, he resolved never to depart Bologna till he should have gained her love. Then, devising in himself what course he should take to this end, he bethought himself, leaving be all other means, that, an he might but avail to become one of her husband's servants, whereof he entertained many, he might peradventure compass that which he desired.

Accordingly, having sold his horses and disposed as best might be of his servants, bidding them make a show of knowing him not, he entered into discourse with his host and told him that he would fain engage for a servant with some gentleman of condition, could such an one be found. Quoth the host, 'Thou art the right serving-man to please a gentleman of this city, by name Egano, who keepeth many and will have them all well looking, as thou art. I will bespeak him of the matter.' As he said, so he did, and ere he took leave of Egano, he had brought Anichino to an accord with him, to the exceeding satisfaction of the latter, who, abiding with Egano and having abundant opportunity of seeing his lady often, proceeded to serve him so well and so much to his liking that he set such store by him that he could do nothing without him and committed to him the governance, not of himself alone, but of all his affairs.

It chanced one day that, Egano being gone a-fowling and having left Anichino at home, Madam Beatrice (who was not yet become aware of his love for her, albeit, considering him and his fashions, she had ofttimes much commended him to herself and he pleased her,) fell to playing chess with him and he, desiring to please her, very adroitly contrived to let himself be beaten, whereat the lady was marvellously rejoiced. Presently, all her women having gone away from seeing them play and left them playing alone, Anichino heaved a great sigh, whereupon she looked at him and said, 'What aileth thee, Anichino? Doth it irk thee that I should beat thee?' 'Madam,' answered he, 'a far greater thing than that was the cause of my sighing.' Quoth the lady, 'Prithee, as thou wishest me well, tell it me.' When Anichino heard himself conjured, 'as thou wishest me well,' by her whom he loved over all else, he heaved a sigh yet heavier than the first; wherefore the lady besought him anew that it would please him tell her the cause of his sighing. 'Madam,' replied Anichino, 'I am sore fearful lest it displease you, if I tell it you, and moreover I misdoubt me you will tell it again to others.' Whereto rejoined she, 'Certes, it will not displease me, and thou mayst be assured that, whatsoever thou sayest to me I will never tell to any, save whenas it shall please thee.' Quoth he, 'Since you promise me this, I will e'en tell it you.' Then, with tears in his eyes, he told her who he was and what he had heard of her and when and how he was become enamoured of her and why he had taken service with her husband and after humbly besought her that it would please her have compassion on him and comply with him in that his secret and so fervent desire, and in case she willed not to do this, that she should suffer him to love her, leaving him be in that his then present guise.

O singular blandness of the Bolognese blood! How art thou still to be commended in such circumstance! Never wast thou desirous of tears or sighs; still wast thou compliant unto prayers and amenable unto amorous desires! Had I words worthy to commend thee, my voice should never weary of singing thy praises. The gentle lady, what while Anichino spoke, kept her eyes fixed on him and giving full credence to his words, received, by the prevalence of his prayers, the love of him with such might into her heart that she also fell a-sighing and presently answered, 'Sweet my Anichino, be of good courage; neither presents nor promises nor solicitations of nobleman or gentleman or other (for I have been and am yet courted of many) have ever availed to move my heart to love any one of them; but thou, in this small space of time that thy words have lasted, hast made me far more thine than mine own. Methinketh thou hast right well earned my love, wherefore I give it thee and promise thee that I will cause thee have enjoyment thereof ere this next night be altogether spent. And that this may have effect, look thou come to my chamber about midnight. I will leave the door open; thou knowest which side the bed I lie; do thou come thither and if I sleep, touch me so I may awake, and I will ease thee of this so long desire that thou hast had. And that thou mayst believe this that I say, I will e'en give thee a kiss by way of arles.' Accordingly, throwing her arms about his neck, she kissed him amorously and he on like wise kissed her. These things said, he left her and went to do certain occasions of his, awaiting with the greatest gladness in the world the coming of the night.

Presently, Egano returned from fowling and being weary, betook himself to bed, as soon as he had supper, and after him the lady, who left the chamber-door open, as she had promised. Thither, at the appointed hour, came Anichino and softly entering the chamber, shut the door again from within; then, going up to the bed on the side where the lady lay, he put his hand to her breast and found her awake. As soon as she felt him come, she took his hand in both her own and held it fast; then, turning herself about in the bed, she did on such wise that Egano, who was asleep, awoke; whereupon quoth she to him, 'I would not say aught to thee yestereve, for that meseemed thou was weary; but tell me, Egano, so God save thee, whom holdest thou thy best and trustiest servant and him who most loveth thee of those whom thou hast in the house?' 'Wife,' answered Egano, 'what is this whereof thou askest me? Knowest thou it not? I have not nor had aye any in whom I so trusted and whom I loved as I love and trust in Anichino. But why dost thou ask me thereof?'

Anichino, seeing Egano awake and hearing talk of himself, was sore afraid lest the lady had a mind to cozen him and offered again and again to draw his hand away, so he might begone; but she held it so fast that he could not win free. Then said she to Egano, 'I will tell thee. I also believed till to-day that he was even such as thou sayest and that he was more loyal to thee than any other, but he hath undeceived me; for that, what while thou wentest a-fowling to-day, he abode here, and whenas it seemed to him time, he was not ashamed to solicit me to yield myself to his pleasures, and I, so I might make thee touch and see this thing and that it might not behove me certify thee thereof with too many proofs, replied that I would well and that this very night, after midnight, I would go into our garden and there await him at the foot of the pine. Now for my part I mean not to go thither; but thou, an thou have a mind to know thy servant's fidelity, thou mayst lightly do it by donning a gown and a veil of mine and going down yonder to wait and see if he will come thither, as I am assured he will.' Egano hearing this, answered, 'Certes, needs must I go see,' and rising, donned one of the lady's gowns, as best he knew in the dark; then, covering his head with a veil, he betook himself to the garden and proceeded to await Anichino at the foot of the pine.

As for the lady, as soon as she knew him gone forth of the chamber, she arose and locked the door from within, whilst Anichino, (who had had the greatest fright he had ever known and had enforced himself as most he might to escape from the lady's hands, cursing her and her love and himself who had trusted in her an hundred thousand times,) seeing this that she had done in the end, was the joyfullest man that was aye. Then, she having returned to bed, he, at her bidding, put off his clothes and coming to bed to her, they took delight and pleasure together a pretty while; after which, herseeming he should not abide longer, she caused him arise and dress himself and said to him, 'Sweetheart, do thou take a stout cudgel and get thee to the garden and there, feigning to have solicited me to try me, rate Egano, as he were I, and ring me a good peal of bells on his back with the cudgel, for that thereof will ensue to us marvellous pleasance and delight.' Anichino accordingly repaired to the garden, with a sallow-stick in his hand, and Egano, seeing him draw near the pine, rose up and came to meet him, as he would receive him with the utmost joy; whereupon quoth Anichino, 'Ah, wicked woman, art thou then come hither, and thinkest thou I would do my lord such a wrong? A thousand times ill come to thee!' Then, raising the cudgel, he began to lay on to him.

Egano, hearing this and seeing the cudgel, took to his heels, without saying a word, whilst Anichino still followed after him, saying, 'Go to, God give thee an ill year, vile woman that thou art! I will certainly tell it to Egano to-morrow morning.' Egano made his way back to the chamber as quickliest he might, having gotten sundry good clouts, and being questioned of the lady if Anichino had come to the garden, 'Would God he had not!' answered he. 'For that, taking me for thee, he hath cudgelled me to a mummy and given me the soundest rating that was aye bestowed upon lewd woman. Certes, I marvelled sore at him that he should have said these words to thee, with intent to do aught that might be a shame to me; but, for that he saw thee so blithe and gamesome, he had a mind to try thee.' Then said the lady, 'Praised be God that he hath tried me with words and thee with deeds! Methinketh he may say that I suffered his words more patiently than thou his deeds. But, since he is so loyal to thee, it behoveth thee hold him dear and do him honour.' 'Certes,' answered Egano, 'thou sayst sooth'; and reasoning by this, he concluded that he had the truest wife and the trustiest servant that ever gentleman had; by reason whereof, albeit both he and the lady made merry more than once with Anichino over this adventure, the latter and his mistress had leisure enough of that which belike, but for this, they would not have had, to wit, to do that which afforded them pleasance and delight, that while it pleased Anichino abide with Egano in Bologna."

❧ 8 ❧

THE EIGHTH STORY

A MAN WAXETH JEALOUS OF HIS WIFE, WHO BINDETH
A PIECE OF PACKTHREAD TO HER GREAT TOE
ANIGHTS, SO SHE MAY HAVE NOTICE OF HER LOVER'S
COMING. ONE NIGHT HER HUSBAND BECOMETH
AWARE OF THIS DEVICE AND WHAT WHILE HE
PURSUETH THE LOVER, THE LADY PUTTETH
ANOTHER WOMAN TO BED IN HER ROOM. THIS
LATTER THE HUSBAND BEATETH AND CUTTETH OFF
HER HAIR, THEN FETCHETH HIS WIFE'S BROTHERS,
WHO, FINDING HIS STORY [SEEMINGLY] UNTRUE,
GIVE HIM HARD WORDS

It SEEMED to them all that Madam Beatrice had been extraordinarily ingenious in cozening her husband and all agreed that Anichino's fright must have been very great, whenas, being the while held fast by the lady, he heard her say that he had required her of love. But the king, seeing Filomena silent, turned to Neifile and said to her, "Do you tell"; whereupon she, smiling first a little, began, "Fair ladies, I have a hard task before me if I desire to pleasure you with a goodly story, as those of you have done, who have already told; but, with God's aid, I trust to discharge myself thereof well enough.

You must know, then, that there was once in our city a very rich merchant called Arriguccio Berlinghieri, who, foolishly thinking, as merchants yet do every day, to ennoble himself by marriage, took to wife a young gentlewoman ill sorting with himself, by name Madam Sismonda, who, for that he, merchant-like, was much abroad and sojourned little with her, fell in love with a young man called Ruberto, who had long courted her, and clapped up a lover's privacy with him. Using belike over-little discretion in her dealings with her lover, for that they were supremely delightsome to her, it chanced that, whether Arriguccio scented aught of the matter or how else soever it happened, the latter became the most jealous man alive and leaving be his going about and all his other concerns, applied himself well nigh altogether to the keeping good watch over his wife; nor would he ever fall asleep, except he first felt her come into the bed; by reason whereof the lady suffered the utmost chagrin, for that on no wise might she avail to be with her Ruberto.

However, after pondering many devices for finding a means to foregather with him and being to boot continually solicited thereof by him, it presently occurred to her to do on this wise; to wit, having many a time observed that Arriguccio tarried long to fall asleep, but after slept very soundly, she determined to cause Ruberto come about midnight to the door of the house and to go open to him and abide with him what while her husband slept fast. And that she might know when he should be come, she bethought herself to hang a twine out of the window of her bedchamber, which looked upon the street, on such wise that none might perceive it, one end whereof should well nigh reach the ground, whilst she carried the other end along the floor of the room to the bed and hid it under the clothes, meaning to make it fast to her great toe, whenas she should be abed. Accordingly, she sent to acquaint Ruberto with this and charged him, when he came, to pull the twine, whereupon, if her husband slept, she would let it go and come to open to him; but, if he slept not, she would hold it fast and draw it to herself, so he should not wait. The device pleased Ruberto and going thither frequently, he was whiles able to foregather with her and whiles not.

On this wise they continued to do till, one night, the lady being asleep, it chanced that her husband stretched out his foot in bed and felt the twine, whereupon he put his hand to it and finding it made fast to his wife's toe, said in himself, 'This should be some trick'; and presently perceiving that the twine led out of window, he held it for certain. Accordingly, he cut it softly from the lady's toe and making it fast to his own, abode on the watch to see what this might mean. He had not waited long before up came Ruberto and pulled at the twine, as of his wont; whereupon Arriguccio started up; but, he not having made the twine well fast to his toe and Ruberto pulling hard, it came loose in the latter's hand, whereby he understood that he was to wait and did so. As for Arriguccio, he arose in haste and taking his arms, ran to the door, to see who this might be and do him a mischief, for, albeit a merchant, he was a stout fellow and a strong. When he came to the door, he opened it not softly as the lady was used to do, which when Ruberto, who was await, observed, he guessed how the case stood, to wit, that it was Arriguccio who opened the door, and accordingly made off in haste and the other after him. At last, having fled a great way and Arriguccio stinting not from following him, Ruberto, being also armed, drew his sword and turned upon his pursuer, whereupon they fell to blows, the one attacking and the other defending himself.

Meanwhile, the lady, awaking, as Arriguccio opened the chamber-door, and finding the twine cut from her toe, knew incontinent that her device was discovered, whereupon, perceiving that her husband had run after her lover, she arose in haste and foreseeing what might happen, called her maid, who knew all, and conjured her to such purpose that she prevailed with her to take her own place in the bed, beseeching her patiently to endure, without discovering herself, whatsoever buffets Arriguccio might deal her, for that she would requite her therefor on such wise that she should have no cause to complain; after which she did out the light that burnt in the chamber and going forth thereof, hid herself in another part of the house and there began to await what should betide.

Meanwhile, the people of the quarter, aroused by the noise of the affray between Arriguccio and Ruberto, arose and fell a-railing at them; whereupon the husband, fearing to be known, let the youth go, without having availed to learn who he was or to do him any hurt, and returned to his house, full of rage and despite. There, coming into the chamber, he cried out angrily, saying, 'Where art thou, vile woman? Thou hast done out the light, so I may not find thee; but thou art mistaken.' Then, coming to the bedside, he seized upon the maid, thinking to take his wife, and laid on to her so lustily with cuffs and kicks, as long as he could wag his hands and feet, that he bruised all her face, ending by cutting off her hair, still giving her the while the hardest words that were ever said to worthless woman. The maid wept sore, as indeed she had good cause to do, and albeit she said whiles, 'Alas, mercy, for God's sake!' and 'Oh, no more!' her voice was so broken with sobs and Arriguccio was so hindered with his rage that he never discerned it to be that of another woman than his wife.

Having, then, as we have said, beaten her to good purpose and cut off her hair, he said to her, 'Wicked woman that thou art, I mean not to touch thee otherwise, but shall now go fetch thy brothers and acquaint them with thy fine doings and after bid them come for thee and deal with thee as they shall deem may do them honour and carry thee away; for assuredly in this house thou shalt abide no longer.' So saying, he departed the chamber and locking the door

331

from without, went away all alone. As soon as Madam Sismonda, who had heard all, was certified of her husband's departure, she opened the door and rekindling the light, found her maid all bruised and weeping sore; whereupon she comforted her as best she might and carried her back to her own chamber, where she after caused privily tend her and care for her and so rewarded her of Arriguccio's own monies that she avouched herself content. No sooner had she done this than she hastened to make the bed in her own chamber and all restablished it and set it in such order as if none had lain there that night; after which she dressed and tired herself, as if she had not yet gone to bed; then, lighting a lamp, she took her clothes and seated herself at the stairhead, where she proceeded to sew and await the issue of the affair.

Meanwhile Arriguccio betook himself in all haste to the house of his wife's brothers and there knocked so long and so loudly that he was heard and it was opened to him. The lady's three brothers and her mother, hearing that it was Arriguccio, rose all and letting kindle lights, came to him and asked what he went seeking at that hour and alone. Whereupon, beginning from the twine he had found tied to wife's toe, he recounted to them all that he had discovered and done, and to give them entire proof of the truth of his story, he put into their hands the hair he thought to have cut from his wife's head, ending by requiring them to come for her and do with her that which they should judge pertinent to their honour, for that he meant to keep her no longer in his house. The lady's brothers, hearing this and holding it for certain, were sore incensed against her and letting kindle torches, set out to accompany Arriguccio to his house, meaning to do her a mischief; which their mother seeing, she followed after them, weeping and entreating now the one, now the other not to be in such haste to believe these things of their sister, without seeing or knowing more of the matter, for that her husband might have been angered with her for some other cause and have maltreated her and might now allege this in his own excuse, adding that she marvelled exceedingly how this [whereof he accused her] could have happened, for that she knew her daughter well, as having reared her from a little child, with many other words to the like purpose.

When they came to Arriguccio's house, they entered and proceeded to mount the stair, whereupon Madam Sismonda, hearing them come, said, 'Who is there?' To which one of her brothers answered, 'Thou shalt soon know who it is, vile woman that thou art!' 'God aid us!' cried she. 'What meaneth this?' Then, rising to her feet, 'Brothers mine,' quoth she, 'you are welcome; but what go you all three seeking at this hour?' The brothers,—seeing her seated sewing, with no sign of beating on her face, whereas Arriguccio avouched that he had beaten her to a mummy,—began to marvel and curbing the violence of their anger, demanded of her how that had been whereof Arriguccio accused her, threatening her sore, and she told them not all. Quoth she, 'I know not what you would have me say nor of what Arriguccio can have complained to you of me.' Arriguccio, seeing her thus, eyed her as if he had lost his wits, remembering that he had dealt her belike a thousand buffets on the face and scratched her and done her all the ill in the world, and now he beheld her as if nothing of all this had been.

Her brothers told her briefly what they had heard from Arriguccio, twine and beating and all, whereupon she turned to him and said, 'Alack, husband mine, what is this I hear? Why wilt thou make me pass, to thine own great shame, for an ill woman, where as I am none, and thyself for a cruel and wicked man, which thou art not? When wast thou in this house to-night till now, let alone with me? When didst thou beat me? For my part, I have no remembrance of it.' 'How, vile woman that thou art!' cried he. 'Did we not go to bed together here? Did I not return hither, after running after thy lover? Did I not deal thee a thousand buffets and cut off thy hair?' 'Thou wentest not to bed in this house to-night,' replied Sismonda. 'But let that pass, for I can give no proof thereof other than mine own true words, and let us come to that which thou sayest, to wit, that thou didst beat me and cut off my hair. Me thou hast never beaten, and do all who are here and thou thyself take note of me, if I have any mark of beating in any part of my person. Indeed, I should not counsel thee make so bold as to lay a hand on me, for, by Christ His Cross, I would mar thy face for thee! Neither didst thou cut off my hair, for aught that I felt or saw; but haply thou didst it on such wise that I perceived it not; let me see if I have it shorn or no.' Then, putting off her veil from her head, she showed that she had her hair unshorn and whole.

Her mother and brothers, seeing and hearing all this, turned upon her husband and said to him, 'What meanest thou, Arriguccio? This is not that so far which thou camest to tell us thou hadst done, and we know not how thou wilt make good the rest.' Arriguccio stood as one in a trance and would have spoken; but, seeing that it was not as he thought he could show, he dared say nothing; whereupon the lady, turning to her brothers, said to them, 'Brothers mine, I see he hath gone seeking to have me do what I have never yet chosen to do, to wit, that I should acquaint you with his lewdness and his vile fashions, and I will do it. I firmly believe that this he hath told you hath verily befallen him and that he hath done as he saith; and you shall hear how. This worthy man, to whom in an ill hour for me you gave me to wife, who calleth himself a merchant and would be thought a man of credit, this fellow, forsooth, who should be more temperate than a monk and chaster than a maid, there be few nights but he goeth fuddling himself about the taverns, foregathering now with this lewd woman and now with that and keeping me waiting for him, on such wise as you find me, half the night and whiles even till morning. I doubt not but that, having well drunken, he went to bed with some trull of his and waking, found the twine on her foot and after did all these his fine feats whereof he telleth, winding up by returning to her and beating her and cutting off her hair; and not being yet well come to himself, he fancied (and I doubt not yet fancieth) that he did all this to me; and if you look him well in the face, you will see he is yet half fuddled. Algates, whatsoever he may have said of me, I will not have you take it to yourselves except as a drunken man's talk, and since I forgive him, do you also pardon him.'

Her mother, hearing this, began to make an outcry and say, 'By Christ His Cross, daughter mine, it shall not pass thus! Nay, he should rather be slain for a thankless, ill-conditioned dog, who was never worthy to have a girl of thy fashion to wife. Marry, a fine thing, forsooth! He could have used thee no worse, had he picked thee up out of the dirt! Devil take him if thou shalt abide at the mercy of the spite of a paltry little merchant of asses' dung! They come to us out of their pigstyes in the country, clad in homespun frieze, with their bag-breeches and pen in arse, and as soon as they have gotten a leash of groats, they must e'en have the daughters of gentlemen and right ladies to wife and bear arms and say, "I am of such a family" and "Those of my house did thus and thus." Would God my sons had followed my counsel in the matter, for that they might have stablished thee so worshipfully in the family of the Counts Guidi, with a crust of bread to thy dowry! But they must needs give thee to this fine jewel of fellow, who, whereas thou art the best girl in Florence and the modestest, is not ashamed to knock us up in the middle of the night, to tell us that thou art a strumpet, as if we knew thee not. But, by God His faith, an they would be ruled by me, he should get such a trouncing therefor that he should stink for it!' Then, turning to the lady's brothers, 'My sons,' said she, 'I told you this could not be. Have you heard how your fine brother-in-law here entreateth your sister? Four-farthing[1] huckster that he is! Were I in your shoes, he having said what he hath of her and doing that which he doth, I would never hold myself content nor appeased till I had rid the earth of him; and were I a man, as I am a woman, I would trouble none other than myself to despatch his business. Confound him for a sorry drunken beast, that hath no shame!'

The young men, seeing and hearing all this, turned upon Arriguccio and gave him the soundest rating ever losel got; and ultimately they said to him. 'We pardon thee this as to a drunken man; but, as thou tenderest thy life, look henceforward we hear no more news of this kind, for, if aught of the like come ever again to our ears, we will pay thee at once for this and for that.' So saying, they went their ways, leaving Arriguccio all aghast, as it were he had taken leave of his wits, unknowing in himself whether that which he had done had really been or whether he had dreamed it; wherefore he made no more words thereof, but left his wife in peace. Thus the lady, by her ready wit, not only escaped the imminent peril [that threatened her,] but opened herself a way to do her every pleasure in time to come, without evermore having any fear of her husband."

---

1. Or, in modern parlance, "twopennny-halfpenny."

9

THE NINTH STORY

LYDIA, WIFE OF NICOSTRATUS, LOVETH PYRRHUS, WHO, SO HE MAY BELIEVE IT, REQUIRETH OF HER THREE THINGS, ALL WHICH SHE DOTH. MOREOVER, SHE SOLACETH HERSELF WITH HIM IN THE PRESENCE OF NICOSTRATUS AND MAKETH THE LATTER BELIEVE THAT THAT WHICH HE HATH SEEN IS NOT REAL

NEIFILE'S STORY so pleased the ladies that they could neither give over to laugh at nor to talk of it, albeit the king, having bidden Pamfilo tell his story, had several times imposed silence upon them. However, after they had held their peace, Pamfilo began thus: "I do not believe, worshipful ladies, that there is anything, how hard and doubtful soever it be, that whoso loveth passionately will not dare to do; the which, albeit it hath already been demonstrated in many stories, methinketh, nevertheless, I shall be able yet more plainly to show forth to you in one which I purpose to tell you and wherein you shall hear of a lady, who was in her actions much more favoured of fortune than well-advised of reason; wherefore I would not counsel any one to adventure herself in the footsteps of her of whom I am to tell, for that fortune is not always well disposed nor are all men in the world equally blind.

In Argos, city of Achia far more famous for its kings of past time than great in itself, there was once a nobleman called Nicostratus, to whom, when already neighbouring on old age, fortune awarded a lady of great family to wife, whose name was Lydia and who was no less high-spirited than fair. Nicostratus, like a nobleman and a man of wealth as he was, kept many servants and hounds and hawks and took the utmost delight in the chase. Among his other servants he had a young man called Pyrrhus, who was sprightly and well bred and comely of his person and adroit in all that he had a mind to do, and him he loved and trusted over all else. Of this Pyrrhus Lydia became so sore enamoured that neither by day nor by night could she have her thought otherwhere than with him; but he, whether it was that he perceived not her liking for him or that he would none of it, appeared to reck nothing thereof, by reason whereof the lady suffered intolerable chagrin in herself and being altogether resolved to give him to know of her passion, called a chamberwoman of hers, Lusca by name, in whom she much trusted, and said to her, 'Lusca, the favours thou hast had of me should make thee faithful and obedient; wherefore look thou none ever know that which I shall presently say to thee, save he to whom I shall charge thee tell it. As thou seest, Lusca, I am a young and lusty lady, abundantly endowed with all those things which any woman can desire; in brief, I can complain of but one thing, to wit, that my husband's years are overmany, an they be measured by mine own, wherefore I fare but ill in the matter of that thing wherein young women take most pleasure, and none the less desiring it, as other women do, I have this long while determined in myself, since fortune hath been thus little my friend in giving me so old a husband, that I will not be so much mine own enemy as not to contrive to find means for my pleasures and my weal; which that I may have as complete in this as in other things, I have bethought myself to will that our Pyrrhus, as being worthier thereof than any other, should furnish them with his embracements; nay, I have vowed him so great a love that I never feel myself at ease save whenas I see him or think of him, and except I foregather with him without delay, methinketh I shall certainly die thereof. Wherefore, if my life be dear to thee, thou wilt, on such wise as shall seem best to thee, signify to him any love and beseech him, on my part, to be pleased to come to me, whenas thou shalt go for him.'

The chamberwoman replied that she would well and taking Pyrrhus apart, whenas first it seemed to her time and place, she did her lady's errand to him as best she knew. Pyrrhus, hearing this, was sore amazed thereat, as one who had never anywise perceived aught of the matter, and misdoubted him the lady had let say this to him to try him; wherefore he answered roughly and hastily, 'Lusca, I cannot believe that these words come from my lady; wherefore, have a care what thou sayst; or, if they do indeed come from her, I do not believe that she caused thee say them with intent, and even if she did so, my lord doth me more honour than I deserve and I would not for my life do him such an outrage; wherefore look thou bespeak me no more of such things.' Lusca, nowise daunted by his austere speech, said to him, 'Pyrrhus, I will e'en bespeak thee both of this and of everything else wherewithal my lady shall charge me when and as often as she shall bid me, whether it cause thee pleasure or annoy; but thou art an ass.' Then, somewhat despited at his words, she returned to her mistress, who, hearing what Pyrrhus had said, wished for death, but, some days after, she again bespoke the chamberwoman of the matter and said to her, 'Lusca, thou knowest that the oak falleth not for the first stroke; wherefore meseemeth well that thou return anew to him who so strangely willeth to abide loyal to my prejudice, and taking a sortable occasion, throughly discover to him my passion and do thine every endeavour that the thing may have effect; for that, an it fall through thus, I shall assuredly die of it. Moreover, he will think to have been befooled, and whereas we seek to have his love, hate will ensue thereof.'

The maid comforted her and going in quest of Pyrrhus found him merry and well-disposed and said to him, 'Pyrrhus I showed thee, a few days agone, in what a fire my lady and thine abideth for the love she beareth thee, and now anew I certify thee thereof, for that, an thou persist in the rigour thou showedst the other day, thou mayst be assured that she will not live long; wherefore I prithee be pleased to satisfy her of her desire, and if thou yet abide fast in thine obstinacy, whereas I have still accounted thee mighty discreet, I shall hold thee a blockhead. What can be a greater glory for thee than that such a lady, so fair and so noble, should love thee over all else? Besides, how greatly shouldst thou acknowledge thyself beholden unto Fortune, seeing that she proffereth thee a thing of such worth and so conformable to the desires of thy youth and to boot, such a resource for thy necessities! Which of thy peers knowest thou who fareth better by way of delight than thou mayst fare, an thou be wise? What other couldst thou find who may fare so well in the matter of arms and horses and apparel and monies as thou mayst do, so thou wilt but vouchsafe thy love to this lady? Open, then, thy mind to my words and return to thy senses; bethink thee that once, and no oftener, it is wont to betide that fortune cometh unto a man with smiling face and open arms, who an he know not then to welcome, if after he find himself poor and beggarly, he hath himself and not her to blame. Besides, there is no call to use that loyalty between servants and masters that behoveth between friends and kinsfolk; nay, servants should use their masters, in so far as they may, like as themselves are used of them. Thinkest thou, an thou hadst a fair wife or mother or daughter or sister, who pleased Nicostratus, that he would go questing after this loyalty that thou wouldst fain observe towards him in respect of this lady? Thou are a fool, if thou think thus; for thou mayst hold it for certain that, if blandishments and prayers sufficed him not, he would not scruple to use force in the matter, whatsoever thou mightest deem thereof. Let us, then, entreat them and their affairs even as they entreat us and ours. Profit by the favour of fortune and drive her not away, but welcome her with open arms and meet her halfway, for assuredly, and thou do it not, thou wilt yet (leave alone the death that will without fail ensue thereof to thy lady) repent thee thereof so many a time thou wilt be fain to die therefor.'

Pyrrhus, who had again and again pondered the words that Lusca had said to him, had determined, and she should return to him, to make her another guess answer and altogether to submit himself to comply with the lady's wishes, so but he might be certified that it was not a trick to try him, and accordingly answered, 'Harkye, Lusca; all that thou sayst to me I allow to be true; but, on the other hand, I know my lord for very discreet and well-advised, and as he committeth all his affairs to my hands, I am sore adread lest Lydia, with his counsel and by his wish, do this to try me; wherefore, an it please her for mine assurance do three things that I shall ask, she shall for certain thereafterward command me nought but I will do it forthright. And the three things I desire are these: first, that in Nicostratus his presence she slay his good hawk; secondly, that she send me a lock of her husband's beard and lastly, one of his best teeth.' These conditions seemed hard unto Lusca and to the lady harder yet; however, Love, who is an excellent comforter[1] and a past master in shifts and devices, made her resolve to do his pleasure and accordingly she sent him word by her chamberwoman that she would punctually do what he required and that quickly, and that over and above this, for that he deemed Nicostratus so well-advised, she would solace herself with him in her husband's presence and make the latter believe that it was not true.

Pyrrhus, accordingly, began to await what the lady should do, and Nicostratus having, a few days after, made, as he oftentimes used to do, a great dinner to certain gentlemen, Madam Lydia, whenas the tables were cleared away, came forth of her chamber, clad in green samite and richly bedecked, and entered the saloon where the guests were. There, in the sight of Pyrrhus and of all the rest, she went up to the perch, whereon was the hawk that Nicostratus held so dear, and cast it loose, as she would set it on her hand; then, taking it by the jesses, she dashed it against the wall and killed it; whereupon Nicostratus cried out at her, saying, 'Alack, wife, what hast thou done?' She answered him nothing, but, turning to the gentlemen who had eaten with him, she said to them, 'Gentlemen, I should ill know how to avenge myself on a king who did me a despite, an I dared not take my wreak of a hawk. You must know that this bird hath long robbed me of all the time which should of men be accorded to the pleasuring of the ladies; for that no sooner is the day risen than Nicostratus is up and drest and away he goeth a-horseback, with his hawk on his fist, to the open plains, to see him fly, whilst I, such as you see me, abide in bed alone and ill-content; wherefore I have many a time had a mind to do that which I have now done, nor hath aught hindered me therefrom but that I waited to do it in the presence of gentlemen who would be just judges in my quarrel, as methinketh you will be.' The gentlemen, hearing this and believing her affection for Nicostratus to be no otherwise than as her words denoted, turned all to the latter, who was angered, and said, laughing, 'Ecod, how well hath the lady done to avenge herself of her wrong by the death of the hawk!' Then, with divers of pleasantries upon the subject (the lady being now gone back to her chamber), they turned Nicostratus his annoy into laughter; whilst Pyrrhus, seeing all this, said in himself, 'The lady hath given a noble beginning to my happy loves; God grant she persevere!'

Lydia having thus slain the hawk, not many days were passed when, being in her chamber with Nicostratus, she fell to toying and frolicking with him, and he, pulling her somedele by the hair, by way of sport, gave her occasion to accomplish the second thing required of her by Pyrrhus. Accordingly, taking him of a sudden by a lock of his beard, she tugged so hard at it, laughing the while, that she plucked it clean out of his chin; whereof he complaining, 'How now?' quoth she. 'What aileth thee to pull such a face? Is it because I have plucked out maybe half a dozen hairs of thy beard? Thou feltest not that which I suffered, whenas thou pulledst me now by the hair.' On this wise continuing their disport from one word to another, she privily kept the lock of hair that she had plucked from his beard and sent it that same day to her lover.

Anent the last of the three things required by Pyrrhus she was harder put to it for a device; nevertheless, being of a surpassing wit and Love making her yet quicker of invention, she soon bethought herself what means she should use to give it accomplishment. Nicostratus had two boys given him of their father, to the intent that, being of gentle birth, they might learn somewhat of manners and good breeding in his house, of whom, whenas he was at meat, one carved before him and the other gave him to drink. Lydia called them both and giving them to believe that they stank at the mouth, enjoined them that, whenas they served Nicostratus, they should still hold their heads backward as most they might nor ever tell this to any. The boys, believing that which she said, proceeded to do as she had lessoned them, and she after a while said to her husband one day, 'Hast thou noted that which yonder boys do, whenas they serve thee?' 'Ay have I,' replied Nicostratus; 'and indeed I had it in mind to ask them why they did it.' Quoth the lady, 'Do it not, for I can tell thee the reason; and I have kept it silent from thee this long while, not to cause thee annoy; but, now I perceive that others begin to be aware thereof, it skilleth not to hide it from thee longer. This betideth thee for none other what than that thou stinkest terribly at the mouth, and I know not what can be the cause thereof; for that it used not to be thus. Now this is a very unseemly thing for thee who hast to do with gentlemen, and needs must we see for a means of curing it.' Whereupon said he, 'What can this be? Can I have some rotten tooth in my head?' 'Maybe ay,' answered Lydia and carried him to a window, where she made him open his mouth, and after she had viewed it in every part, 'O Nicostratus,' cried she, 'how canst thou have put up with it so long? Thou hast a tooth on this side which meseemth is not only decayed, but altogether rotten, and assuredly, and thou keep it much longer in thy mouth, it will mar thee those which be on either side; wherefore I counsel thee have it drawn, ere the thing go farther.' 'Since it seemeth good to thee,' answered he, 'I will well; let a surgeon be sent for without more delay, who shall draw it for me.' 'God forbid,' rejoined the lady, 'that a surgeon come hither for that! Methinketh it lieth on such wise that I myself, without any surgeon, can very well draw it for thee; more by token that these same surgeons are so barbarous in doing such offices that my heart would on no account suffer me to see or know thee in the hands of any one of them; for, an it irk thee overmuch, I will at least loose thee incontinent, which a surgeon would not do.'

Accordingly, she let fetch the proper instruments and sent every one forth of the chamber, except only Lusca; after which, locking herself in, she made Nicostratus lie down on a table and thrusting the pincers into his mouth, what while the maid held him fast, she pulled out one of his teeth by main force, albeit he roared out lustily for the pain. Then, keeping to herself that which she had drawn, she brought out a frightfully decayed tooth she had ready in her hand and showed it to her husband, half dead as he was for pain, saying, 'See what thou hast had in thy mouth all this while.' Nicostratus believed what she said and now that the tooth was out, for all he had suffered the most grievous pain and made sore complaint thereof, him seemed he was cured; and presently, having comforted himself with one thing and another and the pain being abated, he went forth of the chamber; whereupon his wife took the tooth and straightway despatched it to her gallant, who, being now certified of her love, professed himself ready to do her every pleasure.

The lady, albeit every hour seemed to her a thousand till she should be with him, desiring to give him farther assurance and wishful to perform that which she had promised him, made a show one day of being ailing and being visited after dinner by Nicostratus, with no one in his company but Pyrrhus, she prayed them, by way of allaying her unease, to help her go into the garden. Accordingly, Nicostratus taking her on one side and Pyrrhus on the other, they carried her into the garden and set her down on a grassplot, at the foot of a fine pear-tree; where, after they had sat awhile, the lady, who had already given her gallant to know what he had to do, said, 'Pyrrhus, I have a great desire to eat of yonder pears; do thou climb up and throw us down some of them.' Pyrrhus straightway climbed up into the tree and fell to throwing down of the pears, which as he did, he began to say, 'How now, my lord! What is this you do? And you, madam, are you not ashamed to suffer it in my presence? Think you I am blind? But now you were sore disordered; how cometh it you have so quickly recovered that you do such things? An you have a mind unto this, you have store of goodly chambers; why go you not do it in one of these? It were more seemly than in my presence.'

The lady turned to her husband and said, 'What saith Pyrrhus? Doth he rave?' 'No, madam,' answered the young man, 'I rave not. Think you I cannot see?' As for Nicostratus, he marvelled sore and said, 'Verily, Pyrrhus, methinketh thou dreamest.' 'My lord,' replied Pyrrhus, 'I dream not a jot, neither do you dream; nay, you bestir yourselves on such wise that were this tree to do likewise, there would not be a pear left on it.' Quoth the lady, 'What may this be? Can it be that this he saith appeareth to him to be true? So God save me, and I were whole as I was aforetime, I would climb up into the tree, to see what marvels are those which this fellow saith he seeth.' Meanwhile Pyrrhus from the top of the pear-tree still said the same thing and kept up the pretence; whereupon Nicostratus bade him come down. Accordingly he came down and his master said to him, 'Now, what sayst thou thou sawest?' 'Methinketh,' answered he, 'you take me for a lackwit or a loggerhead. Since I must needs say it, I saw you a-top of your lady, and after, as I came down, I saw you arise and seat yourself where you presently are.' 'Assuredly,' said Nicostratus, 'thou dotest; for we have not stirred a jot, save as thou seest, since thou climbest up into the pear-tree.' Whereupon quoth Pyrrhus, 'What booteth it to make words of the matter? I certainly saw you; and if I did see you, it was a-top of your own.'

Nicostratus waxed momently more and more astonished, insomuch that he said, 'Needs must I see if this pear-tree is enchanted and if whoso is thereon seeth marvels.' Thereupon he climbed up into the tree and no sooner was he come to the top than the lady and Pyrrhus fell to solacing themselves together; which when Nicostratus saw, he began to cry out, saying, 'Ah, vile woman that thou art, what is this thou dost? And thou, Pyrrhus, in whom I most trusted?' So saying, he proceeded to descend the tree, whilst the lovers said, 'We are sitting here'; then, seeing him come down, they reseated themselves whereas he had left them. As soon as he was down and saw his wife and Pyrrhus where he had left them, he fell a-railing at them; whereupon quoth Pyrrhus, 'Now, verily, Nicostratus, I acknowledged that, as you said before, I must have seen falsely what while I was in the pear-tree, nor do I know it otherwise than by this, that I see and know yourself to have seen falsely in the like case. And that I speak the truth nought else should be needful to certify you but that you have regard to the circumstances of the case and consider if it be possible that your lady, who is the most virtuous of women and discreeter than any other of her sex, could, an she had a mind to outrage you on such wise, bring herself to do it before your very eyes. I speak not of myself, who would rather suffer myself to be torn limb-meal than so much as think of such a thing, much more come to do it in your presence. Wherefore the fault of this misseeing must needs proceed from the pear-tree, for that all the world had not made me believe but that you were in act to have carnal knowledge

339

of your lady here, had I not heard you say that it appeared to yourself that I did what I know most certainly I never thought, much less did.'

Thereupon the lady, feigning to be mightily incensed, rose to her feet and said, 'Ill luck betide thee, dost thou hold me so little of wit that, an I had a mind to such filthy fashions as thou wouldst have us believe thou sawest, I should come to do them before thy very eyes? Thou mayst be assured of this that, if ever the fancy took me thereof, I should not come hither; marry, methinketh I should have sense enough to contrive it in one of our chambers, on such wise and after such a fashion that it would seem to me an extraordinary thing if ever thou camest to know of it.' Nicostratus, himseeming that what the lady and Pyrrhus said was true, to wit, that they would never have ventured upon such an act there before himself, gave over words and reproaches and fell to discoursing of the strangeness of the fact and the miracle of the sight, which was thus changed unto whoso climbed up into the pear-tree. But his wife, feigning herself chagrined for the ill thought he had shown of her, said, 'Verily, this pear-tree shall never again, if I can help it, do me nor any other lady the like of this shame; wherefore do thou run, Pyrrhus, and fetch a hatchet and at one stroke avenge both thyself and me by cutting it down; albeit it were better yet lay it about Nicostratus his cosard, who, without any consideration, suffered the eyes of his understanding to be so quickly blinded, whenas, however certain that which thou[2] saidst might seem to those[3] which thou hast in thy head, thou shouldst for nought in the world in the judgment of thy mind have believed or allowed that such a thing could be.'

Pyrrhus very readily fetched the hatchet and cut down the tree, which when the lady saw fallen, she said to Nicostratus, 'Since I see the enemy of mine honour overthrown, my anger is past,' and graciously forgave her husband, who besought her thereof, charging him that it should never again happen to him to presume such a thing of her, who loved him better than herself. Accordingly, the wretched husband, thus befooled, returned with her and her lover to the palace, where many a time thereafterward Pyrrhus took delight and pleasance more at ease of Lydia and she of him. God grant us as much!"

---

1. Syn. encourager, helper, auxiliary (*confortatore*).
2. This sudden change from the third to the second person, in speaking of Nicostratus, is a characteristic example of Boccaccio's constant abuse of the figure enallage in his dialogues.
3. *i.e.* those eyes.

10

DAY THE SEVENTH

TWO SIENNESE LOVE A LADY, WHO IS GOSSIP TO ONE OF THEM; THE LATTER DIETH AND RETURNING TO HIS COMPANION, ACCORDING TO PROMISE MADE HIM, RELATETH TO HIM HOW FOLK FARE IN THE OTHER WORLD

IT NOW RESTED ONLY with the king to tell and he accordingly, as soon as he saw the ladies quieted, who lamented the cutting down of the unoffending pear-tree, began, "It is a very manifest thing that every just king should be the first to observe the laws made by him, and an he do otherwise, he must be adjudged a slave deserving of punishment and not a king, into which offence and under which reproach I, who am your king, am in a manner constrained to fall. True it is that yesterday I laid down the law for to-day's discourses, purposing not this day to make use of my privilege, but, submitting myself to the same obligation as you, to discourse of that whereof you have all discoursed. However, not only hath that story been told which I had thought to tell, but so many other and far finer things have been said upon the matter that, for my part, ransack my memory as I will, I can call nothing to mind and must avouch myself unable to say aught anent such a subject that may compare with those stories which have already been told. Wherefore, it behoving me transgress against the law made by myself, I declare myself in advance ready, as one deserving of punishment, to submit to any forfeit which may be imposed on me, and so have recourse to my wonted privilege. Accordingly, dearest ladies, I say that Elisa's story of Fra Rinaldo and his gossip and eke the simplicity of the Siennese have such efficacy that they induce me, letting be the cheats put upon foolish husbands by their wily wives, to tell you a slight story of them,[1] which though it have in it no little of that which must not be believed, will natheless in part, at least, be pleasing to hear.

There were, then, in Siena two young men of the people, whereof one was called Tingoccio Mini and the other Meuccio di Tura; they abode at Porta Salaja and consorted well nigh never save one with the other. To all appearance they loved each exceedingly and resorting, as men do, to churches and preachings, they had many a time heard tell of the happiness and of the misery that are, according to their deserts, allotted in the next world to the souls of those who die; of which things desiring to have certain news and finding no way thereto, they promised one another that whichever of them died first should, an he might, return to him who abode on life and give him tidings of that which he would fain know; and this they confirmed with an oath. Having come to this accord and companying still together, as hath been said, it chanced that Tingoccio became godfather to a child which one Ambruogio Anselmini, abiding at Campo

Reggi, had had of his wife, Mistress Mita by name, and from time to time visiting, together with Meuccio, his gossip who was a very fair and lovesome lady, he became, notwithstanding the gossipship, enamoured of her. Meuccio, on like wise, hearing her mightily commended of his friend and being himself much pleased with her, fell in love with her, and each hid his love from the other, but not for one same reason. Tingoccio was careful not to discover it to Meuccio, on account of the naughty deed which himseemed he did to love his gossip and which he had been ashamed that any should know. Meuccio, on the other hand, kept himself therefrom,[2] for that he had already perceived that the lady pleased Tingoccio; whereupon he said in himself, 'If I discover this to him, he will wax jealous of me and being able, as her gossip, to bespeak her at his every pleasure, he will, inasmuch as he may, bring me in ill savour with her, and so I shall never have of her aught that may please me.'

Things being at this pass, it befell that Tingoccio, having more leisure of discovering his every desire to the lady, contrived with acts and words so to do that he had his will of her, of which Meuccio soon became aware and albeit it sore misliked him, yet, hoping some time or other to compass his desire, he feigned ignorance thereof, so Tingoccio might not have cause or occasion to do him an ill turn or hinder him in any of his affairs. The two friends loving thus, the one more happily than the other, it befell that Tingoccio, finding the soil of his gossip's demesne soft and eath to till, so delved and laboured there that there overcame him thereof a malady, which after some days waxed so heavy upon him that, being unable to brook it, he departed this life. The third day after his death (for that belike he had not before been able) he came by night, according to the promise made, into Meuccio's chamber and called the latter, who slept fast. Meuccio awoke and said, 'Who art thou?' Whereto he answered, 'I am Tingoccio, who, according to the promise which I made thee, am come back to thee to give thee news of the other world.'

Meuccio was somewhat affrighted at seeing him; nevertheless, taking heart, 'Thou art welcome, brother mine,' quoth he, and presently asked him if he were lost. 'Things are lost that are not to be found,' replied Tingoccio; 'and how should I be here, if I were lost?' 'Alack,' cried Meuccio, 'I say not so; nay, I ask thee if thou art among the damned souls in the avenging fire of hell.' Whereto quoth Tingoccio, 'As for that, no; but I am, notwithstanding, in very grievous and anguishful torment for the sins committed by me.' Meuccio then particularly enquired of him what punishments were awarded in the other world for each of the sins that folk use to commit here below, and he told him them all. After this Meuccio asked if there were aught he might do for him in this world, whereto Tingoccio replied that there was, to wit, that he should let say for him masses and orisons and do alms in his name, for that these things were mightily profitable to those who abode yonder. Meuccio said that he would well and Tingoccio offering to take leave of him, he remembered himself of the latter's amour with his gossip and raising his head, said, 'Now that I bethink me, Tingoccio, what punishment is given thee over yonder anent thy gossip, with whom thou layest, whenas thou wast here below?' 'Brother mine,' answered Tingoccio, 'whenas I came yonder, there was one who it seemed knew all my sins by heart and bade me betake myself to a certain place, where I bemoaned my offences in exceeding sore punishment and where I found many companions condemned to the same penance as myself. Being among them and remembering me of that which I had done whilere with my gossip, I looked for a much sorer punishment on account thereof than that which had presently been given me and went all shivering for fear, albeit I was in a great fire and an exceeding hot; which one who was by my side perceiving, he said to me, "What aileth thee more than all the others who are here that thou shiverest, being in the fire?" "Marry," said I, "my friend, I am sore in fear of the sentence I expect for a grievous sin I wrought aforetime." The other asked me what sin this was, and I answered, "It was that I lay with a gossip of mine, and that with such a vengeance that it cost me my life"; whereupon quoth he, making merry over my fear, "Go to, fool; have no fear. Here is no manner of account taken of gossips." Which when I heard, I was altogether reassured.' This said and the day drawing near, 'Meuccio,' quoth he, 'abide with God, for I may no longer be with thee,' and was suddenly gone. Meuccio, hearing that no account was taken of gossips in the world to come, began to make mock of his own simplicity, for that whiles he had spared several of them; wherefore, laying by his ignorance, he became wiser in that respect for the future. Which things if Fra Rinaldo had known, he had not needed to go a-syllogizing,[3] whenas he converted his good gossip to his pleasure."

ZEPHYR WAS NOW ARISEN, for the sun that drew near unto the setting, when the king, having made an end of his story and there being none other left to tell, put off the crown from his own head and set it on that of Lauretta, saying, "Madam, with yourself[4] I crown you queen of our company; do you then, from this time forth, as sovereign lady, command that which you may deem shall be for the pleasure and solacement of all." This said, he reseated himself, whereupon Lauretta, become queen, let call the seneschal and bade him look that the tables be set in the pleasant valley somewhat earlier than of wont, so they might return to the palace at their leisure; after which she instructed him what he should do what while her sovranty lasted. Then, turning to the company, she said, "Dioneo willed yesterday that we should discourse to-day of the tricks that women play their husbands and but that I am loath to show myself of the tribe of snappish curs, which are fain incontinent to avenge themselves of any affront done them, I would say that to-morrow's discourse should be of the tricks that men play their wives. But, letting that be, I ordain that each bethink himself to tell OF THE TRICKS THAT ALL DAY LONG WOMEN PLAY MEN OR MEN WOMEN OR MEN ONE ANOTHER; and I doubt not but that in this[5] there will be no less of pleasant discourse than there hath been to-day." So saying, she rose to her feet and dismissed the company till supper-time.

Accordingly, they all, ladies and men alike, arose and some began to go barefoot through the clear water, whilst others went a-pleasuring upon the greensward among the straight and goodly trees. Dioneo and Fiammetta sang together a great while of Arcite and Palemon, and on this wise, taking various and divers delights, they passed the time with the utmost satisfaction until the hour of supper; which being come, they seated themselves at table beside the lakelet and there, to the song of a thousand birds, still refreshed by a gentle breeze, that came from the little hills around, and untroubled of any fly, they supped in peace and cheer. Then, the tables being removed and the sun being yet half-vespers[6] high, after they had gone awhile round about the pleasant valley, they wended their way again, even as it pleased their queen, with slow steps towards their wonted dwelling-place, and jesting and chattering a thousand things, as well of those whereof it had been that day discoursed as of others, they came near upon nightfall to the fair palace, where having with the coolest of wines and confections done away the fatigues of the little journey, they presently fell to dancing about the fair fountain, carolling[7] now to the sound of Tindaro's bagpipe and anon to that of other instruments. But, after awhile, the queen bade Filomena sing a song, whereupon she began thus:

> *Alack, my life forlorn!*
> *Will't ever chance I may once more regain*
> *Th' estate whence sorry fortune hath me torn?*
>
> *Certes, I know not, such a wish of fire*

343

I carry in my thought
To find me where, alas! I was whilere.
O dear my treasure, thou my sole desire,
That holdst my heart distraught.
Tell it me, thou; for whom I know nor dare
To ask it otherwhere.
Ah, dear my lord, oh, cause me hope again,
So I may comfort me my spright wayworn.

What was the charm I cannot rightly tell
That kindled in me such
A flame of love that rest nor day nor night
I find; for, by some strong unwonted spell,
Hearing and touch
And seeing each new fires in me did light,
Wherein I burn outright;
Nor other than thyself can soothe my pain
Nor call my senses back, by love o'erborne.

O tell me if and when, then, it shall be
That I shall find thee e'er
Whereas I kissed those eyes that did me slay.
O dear my good, my soul, ah, tell it me,
When thou wilt come back there,
And saying "Quickly," comfort my dismay
Somedele. Short be the stay
Until thou come, and long mayst thou remain!
I'm so love-struck, I reck not of men's scorn.

If once again I chance to hold thee aye,
I will not be so fond
As erst I was to suffer thee to fly;
Nay, fast I'll hold thee, hap of it what may,
And having thee in bond,
Of thy sweet mouth my lust I'll satisfy.
Now of nought else will I
Discourse. Quick, to thy bosom come me strain;
The sheer thought bids me sing like lark at morn.

This song caused all the company conclude that a new and pleasing love held Filomena in bonds, and as by the words it appeared that she had tasted more thereof than sight alone, she was envied of this by certain who were there and who held her therefor so much the happier. But, after her song was ended, the queen, remembering her that the ensuing day was Friday, thus graciously bespoke all, "You know, noble ladies and you also, young men, that to-morrow is the day consecrated to the passion of our Lord, the which, an you remember aright, what time Neifile was queen, we celebrated devoutly and therein gave pause to our delightsome discoursements, and on like wise we did with the following Saturday. Wherefore, being minded to follow the good example given us by Neifile, I hold it seemly that to-morrow and the next day we abstain, even as we did a week agone, from our pleasant story-telling, recalling to memory that which on those days befell whilere for the salvation of our souls." The queen's pious speech was pleasing unto all and a good part of the night being now past, they all, dismissed by her, betook them to repose.

---

1. *i.e.* the Siennese.
2. *i.e.* from discovering to his friend his liking for the lady.
3. Or, in modern parlance, logic-chopping (*sillogizzando*).
4. *i.e.* with that whereof you bear the name, *i.e.* laurel (*laurea*).
5. Or "on this subject" (*in questo*).
6. *Quære*, "half-complines," *i.e.* half-past seven p.m. "Half-vespers" would be half-past four, which seems too early.
7. *Carolando*, *i.e.* dancing in a round and singing the while, the original meaning of our word "carol."

DAY THE EIGHTH

Here Beginneth the Eighth Day of the Decameron
Wherein Under the Governance of Lauretta Is
Discoursed of the Tricks That All Day Long
Women Play Men or Men Women or Men One
Another

Already on the Sunday morning the rays of the rising light appeared on the summits of the higher mountains and every shadow having departed, things might manifestly be discerned, when the queen, arising with her company, went wandering first through the dewy grass and after, towards half-tierce,[1] visiting a little neighboring church, heard there divine service; then, returning home, they ate with mirth and joyance and after sang and danced awhile till the queen dismissed them, so whoso would might go rest himself. But, whenas the sun had passed the meridian, they all seated themselves, according as it pleased the queen, near the fair fountain, for the wonted story-telling, and Neifile, by her commandment, began thus:

---

1. *i.e.* half-past seven a.m.

THE FIRST STORY

GULFARDO BORROWETH OF GUASPARRUOLO CERTAIN MONIES, FOR WHICH HE HATH AGREED WITH HIS WIFE THAT HE SHALL LIE WITH HER, AND ACCORDINGLY GIVETH THEM TO HER; THEN, IN HER PRESENCE, HE TELLETH GUASPARRUOLO THAT HE GAVE THEM TO HER, AND SHE CONFESSETH IT TO BE TRUE

"SINCE GOD HATH SO ORDERED it that I am to give a beginning to the present day's discourses, with my story, I am content, and therefore, lovesome ladies, seeing that much hath been said of the tricks played by women upon men, it is my pleasure to relate one played by a man upon a woman, not that I mean therein to blame that which the man did or to deny that it served the woman aright, nay, rather to commend the man and blame the woman and to show that men also know how to cozen those who put faith in them, even as themselves are cozened by those in whom they believe. Indeed, to speak more precisely, that whereof I have to tell should not be called cozenage; nay, it should rather be styled a just requital; for that, albeit a woman should still be virtuous and guard her chastity as her life nor on any account suffer herself be persuaded to sully it, yet, seeing that, by reason of our frailty, this is not always possible as fully as should be, I affirm that she who consenteth to her own dishonour for a price is worthy of the fire, whereas she who yieldeth for Love's sake, knowing his exceeding great puissance, meriteth forgiveness from a judge not too severe, even as, a few days agone, Filostrato showed it to have been observed towards Madam Filippa at Prato.

There was, then, aforetime at Milan a German, by name Gulfardo, in the pay of the state, a stout fellow of his person and very loyal to those in whose service he engaged himself, which is seldom the case with Germans; and for that he was a very punctual repayer of such loans as were made him, he might always find many merchants ready to lend him any quantity of money at little usance. During his sojourn in Milan, he set his heart upon a very fair lady called Madam Ambruogia, the wife of a rich merchant, by name Guasparruolo Cagastraccio, who was much his acquaintance and friend, and loving her very discreetly, so that neither her husband nor any other suspected it, he sent one day to speak with her, praying her that it would please her vouchsafe him her favours and protesting that he, on his part, was ready to do whatsoever she should command him. The lady, after many parleys, came to this conclusion, that she was ready to do that which Gulfardo wished, provided two things should ensue thereof; one, that this should never be by him discovered to any and the other, that, as she had need of two hundred gold florins for some occasion of hers, he, who was a rich man, should give them to her; after which she would still be at his service.

Gulfardo, hearing this and indignant at the sordidness of her whom he had accounted a lady of worth, was like to exchange his fervent love for hatred and thinking to cheat her, sent back to her, saying that he would very willingly do this and all else in his power that might please her and that therefore she should e'en send him word when she would have him go to her, for that he would carry her the money, nor should any ever hear aught of the matter, save a comrade of his in whom he trusted greatly and who still bore him company in whatsoever he did. The lady, or rather, I should say, the vile woman, hearing this, was well pleased and sent to him, saying that Guasparruolo her husband was to go to Genoa for his occasions a few days hence and that she would presently let him know of this and send for him. Meanwhile, Gulfardo, taking his opportunity, repaired to Guasparruolo and said to him, 'I have present occasion for two hundred gold florins, the which I would have thee lend me at that same usance whereat thou art wont to lend me other monies.' The other replied that he would well and straightway counted out to him the money.

A few days thereafterward Guasparruolo went to Genoa, even as the lady had said, whereupon she sent to Gulfardo to come to her and bring the two hundred gold florins. Accordingly, he took his comrade and repaired to the lady's house, where finding her expecting him, the first thing he did was to put into her hands the two hundred gold florins, in his friend's presence, saying to her, 'Madam, take these monies and give them to your husband, whenas he shall be returned.' The lady took them, never guessing why he said thus, but supposing that he did it so his comrade should not perceive that he gave them to her by way of price, and answered, 'With all my heart; but I would fain see how many they are.' Accordingly, she turned them out upon the table and finding them full two hundred, laid them up, mighty content in herself; then, returning to Gulfardo and carrying him into her chamber, she satisfied him of her person not that night only, but many others before her husband returned from Genoa.

As soon as the latter came back, Gulfardo, having spied out a time when he was in company with his wife, betook himself to him, together with his comrade aforesaid, and said to him, in the lady's presence, 'Guasparruolo, I had no occasion for the monies, to wit, the two hundred gold florins, thou lentest me the other day, for that I could not compass the business for which I borrowed them. Accordingly, I brought them presently back to thy lady here and gave them to her; wherefore look thou cancel my account.' Guasparruolo, turning to his wife, asked her if she had the monies, and she, seeing the witness present, knew not how to deny, but said, 'Ay, I had them and had not yet remembered me to tell thee.' Whereupon quoth Guasparruolo, 'Gulfardo, I am satisfied; get you gone and God go with you: I will settle your account aright.' Gulfardo gone, the lady, finding herself cozened, gave her husband the dishonourable price of her baseness; and on this wise the crafty lover enjoyed his sordid mistress without cost."

THE SECOND STORY

THE PARISH PRIEST OF VARLUNGO LIETH WITH MISTRESS BELCOLORE AND LEAVETH HER A CLOAK OF HIS IN PLEDGE; THEN, BORROWING A MORTAR OF HER, HE SENDETH IT BACK TO HER, DEMANDING IN RETURN THE CLOAK LEFT BY WAY OF TOKEN, WHICH THE GOOD WOMAN GRUDGINGLY GIVETH HIM BACK

MEN AND LADIES alike commended that which Gulfardo had done to the sordid Milanese lady, and the queen, turning to Pamfilo, smilingly charged him follow on; whereupon quoth he, "Fair ladies, it occurreth to me to tell you a little story against those who continually offend against us, without being open to retaliation on our part, to wit, the clergy, who have proclaimed a crusade against our wives and who, whenas they avail to get one of the latter under them, conceive themselves to have gained forgiveness of fault and pardon of penalty no otherwise than as they had brought the Soldan bound from Alexandria to Avignon.[1] Whereof the wretched laymen cannot return them the like, albeit they wreak their ire upon the priests' mothers and sisters, doxies and daughters, assailing them with no less ardour than the former do their wives. Wherefore I purpose to recount to you a village love-affair, more laughable for its conclusion than long in words, wherefrom you may yet gather, by way of fruit, that priests are not always to be believed in everything.

You must know, then, that there was once at Varlungo,—a village very near here, as each of you ladies either knoweth or may have heard,—a worthy priest and a lusty of his person in the service of the ladies, who, albeit he knew not overwell how to read, natheless regaled his parishioners with store of good and pious saws at the elmfoot on Sundays and visited their women, whenas they went abroad anywhither, more diligently than any priest who had been there aforetime, carrying them fairings and holy water and a stray candle-end or so, whiles even to their houses. Now it chanced that, among other his she-parishioners who were most to his liking, one pleased him over all, by name Mistress Belcolore, the wife of a husbandman who styled himself Bentivegna del Mazzo, a jolly, buxom country wench, brown-favoured and tight-made, as apt at turning the mill[2] as any woman alive. Moreover, it was she who knew how to play the tabret and sing 'The water runneth to the ravine' and lead up the haye and the round, when need was, with a fine muckender in her hand and a quaint, better than any woman of her neighbourhood; by reason of which things my lord priest became so sore enamoured of her that he was like to lose his wits therefor and would prowl about all day long to get a sight of her. Whenas he espied her in church of a Sunday morning, he would say a Kyrie and a Sanctus, studying to show himself a past master in descant, that it seemed as it were an ass a-braying;

whereas, when he saw her not there, he passed that part of the service over lightly enough. But yet he made shift to do on such wise that neither Bentivegna nor any of his neighbours suspected aught; and the better to gain Mistress Belcolore's goodwill, he made her presents from time to time, sending her whiles a clove of garlic, which he had the finest of all the countryside in a garden he tilled with his own hands, and otherwhiles a punnet of peascods or a bunch of chives or scallions, and whenas he saw his opportunity, he would ogle her askance and cast a friendly gibe at her; but she, putting on the prude, made a show of not observing it and passed on with a demure air; wherefore my lord priest could not come by his will of her.

It chanced one day that as he sauntered about the quarter on the stroke of noon, he encountered Bentivegna del Mazzo, driving an ass laden with gear, and accosting him, asked whither he went. 'Faith, sir,' answered the husbandman, 'to tell you the truth, I am going to town about a business of mine and am carrying these things to Squire Bonaccorri da Ginestreto, so he may help me in I know not what whereof the police-court judge hath summoned me by his proctor for a peremptory attendance.' The priest was rejoiced to hear this and said, 'Thou dost well, my son; go now with my benison and return speedily; and shouldst thou chance to see Lapuccio or Naldino, forget not to bid them bring me those straps they wot of for my flails.' Bentivegna answered that it should be done and went his way towards Florence, whereupon the priest bethought himself that now was his time to go try his luck with Belcolore. Accordingly, he let not the grass grow under his feet, but set off forthright and stayed not till he came to her house and entering in, said, 'God send us all well! Who is within there?' Belcolore, who was gone up into the hay-loft, hearing him, said, 'Marry, sir, you are welcome; but what do you gadding it abroad in this heat?' 'So God give me good luck,' answered he, 'I came to abide with thee awhile, for that I met thy man going to town.'

Belcolore came down and taking a seat, fell to picking over cabbage-seed which her husband had threshed out a while before; whereupon quoth the priest to her, 'Well, Belcolore, wilt thou still cause me die for thee on this wise?' She laughed and answered, 'What is it I do to you?' Quoth he, 'Thou dost nought to me, but thou sufferest me not do to thee that which I would fain do and which God commandeth.' 'Alack!' cried Belcolore, 'Go to, go to. Do priests do such things?' 'Ay do we,' replied he, 'as well as other men; and why not? And I tell thee more, we do far and away better work and knowest thou why? Because we grind with a full head of water. But in good sooth it shall be shrewdly to thy profit, an thou wilt but abide quiet and let me do.' 'And what might this "shrewdly to my profit" be?' asked she. 'For all you priests are stingier than the devil.' Quoth he, 'I know not; ask thou. Wilt have a pair of shoes or a head-lace or a fine stammel waistband or what thou wilt?' 'Pshaw!' cried Belcolore. 'I have enough and to spare of such things; but an you wish me so well, why do you not render me a service, and I will do what you will?' Quoth the priest, 'Say what thou wilt have of me, and I will do it willingly.' Then said she, 'Needs must I go to Florence, come Saturday, to carry back the wool I have spun and get my spinning-wheel mended; and an you will lend me five crowns, which I know you have by you, I can take my watchet gown out of pawn and my Sunday girdle[3] that I brought my husband, for you see I cannot go to church nor to any decent place, because I have them not; and after I will still do what you would have me.' 'So God give me a good year,' replied the priest, 'I have them not about me; but believe me, ere Saturday come, I will contrive that thou shalt have them, and that very willingly.' 'Ay,' said Belcolore, 'you are all like this, great promisers, and after perform nothing to any. Think you to do with me as you did with Biliuzza, who went off with the ghittern-player?[4] Cock's faith, then, you shall not, for that she is turned a common drab only for that. If you have them not about you, go for them.' 'Alack,' cried the priest, 'put me not upon going all the way home. Thou seest that I have the luck just now to find thee alone, but maybe, when I return, there will be some one or other here to hinder us; and I know not when I shall find so good an opportunity again.' Quoth she, 'It is well; an you choose to go, go; if not, go without.'

The priest, seeing that she was not in the humour to do his pleasure without a *salvum me fac,* whereas he would fain have done it *sine custodiâ,* said, 'Harkye, thou believest not that I will bring thee the money; but, so thou mayst credit me, I will leave thee this my blue-cloth cloak.' Belcolore raised her eyes and said, 'Eh what! That cloak? What is it worth?' 'Worth?' answered the priest. 'I would have thee know that it is cloth of Douay, nay, Threeay, and there be some of our folk here who hold it for Fouray.[5] It is scarce a fortnight since it cost me seven crowns of hard money to Lotto the broker, and according to what Buglietto telleth me (and thou knowest he is a judge of this kind of cloth), I had it good five shillings overcheap.' 'Indeed!' quoth Belcolore. 'So God be mine aid, I had never thought it. But give it me first of all.' My lord priest, who had his arbalest ready cocked, pulled off the cloak and gave it her; and she, after she had laid it up, said, 'Come, sir, let us go into the barn, for no one ever cometh there.' And so they did. There the priest gave her the heartiest busses in the world and making her sib to God Almighty,[6] solaced himself with her a great while; after which he took leave of her and returned to the parsonage in his cassock, as it were he came from officiating at a wedding.

There, bethinking himself that all the candle-ends he got by way of offertory in all the year were not worth the half of five crowns, him seemed he had done ill and repenting him of having left the cloak, he fell to considering how he might have it again without cost. Being shrewd enough in a small way, he soon hit upon a device and it succeeded to his wish; for that on the morrow, it being a holiday, he sent a neighbour's lad of his to Mistress Belcolore's house, with a message praying her be pleased to lend him her stone mortar, for that Binguccio dal Poggio and Nuto Buglietti were to dine with him that morning and he had a mind to make sauce. She sent it to him and towards dinner-time, the priest, having spied out when Bentivegna and his wife were at meat together, called his clerk and said to him, 'Carry this mortar back to Belcolore and say to her, 'His reverence biddeth you gramercy and prayeth you send him back the cloak that the boy left you by way of token.' The clerk accordingly repaired to her house and there, finding her at table with Bentivegna, set down the mortar and did the priest's errand. Belcolore, hearing require the cloak again, would have answered; but her husband said, with an angry air, 'Takest thou a pledge of his reverence? I vow to Christ, I have a mind to give thee a good clout over the head! Go, give it quickly back to him, pox take thee! And in future, let him ask what he will of ours, (ay, though he should seek our ass,) look that it be not denied him.' Belcolore rose, grumbling, and pulling the cloak out of the chest, gave it to the clerk, saying, 'Tell her reverence from me, Belcolore saith, she voweth to God you shall never again pound sauce in her mortar; you have done her no such fine honour of this bout.'

The clerk made off with the cloak and did her message to the priest, who said, laughing, 'Tell her, when thou seest her, that, an she will not lend me her mortar, I will not lend her my pestle; and so we shall be quits.' Bentivegna concluded that his wife had said this, because he had chidden her, and took no heed thereof; but Belcolore bore the priest a grudge and held him at arm's length till vintage-time; when, he having threatened to cause her go into the mouth of Lucifer the great devil, for very fear she made her peace with him over must and roast chestnuts and they after made merry together time and again. In lieu of the five crowns, the priest let put new parchment to her tabret and string thereto a cast of hawk's bells, and with this she was fain to be content."

---

1. Where the papal court then was.
2. Or, as La Fontaine would say, "aussi bien faite pour armer un lit."
3. Or apron.

4. *Se n'andò col ceteratojo*; a proverbial expression of similar meaning to our "was whistled down the wind," *i.e.* was lightly dismissed without provision, like a cast-off hawk.
5. A play of words upon the Italian equivalent of the French word Douay (*Duagio, i.e. Twoay, Treagio, Quattragio*) invented by the roguish priest to impose upon the simple goodwife.
6. Or in modern parlance, "making her a connection by marriage of etc.," Boccaccio feigning priests to be members of the Holy Family, by virtue of their office.

🎕 3 🎕

THE THIRD STORY

CALANDRINO, BRUNO AND BUFFALMACCO GO
COASTING ALONG THE MUGNONE IN SEARCH OF THE
HELIOTROPE AND CALANDRINO THINKETH TO HAVE
FOUND IT. ACCORDINGLY HE RETURNETH HOME,
LADEN WITH STONES, AND HIS WIFE CHIDETH HIM;
WHEREUPON, FLYING OUT INTO A RAGE, HE
BEATETH HER AND RECOUNTETH TO HIS
COMPANIONS THAT WHICH THEY KNOW BETTER
THAN HE

PAMFILO HAVING MADE an end of his story, at which the ladies had laughed so much that they laugh yet, the queen bade Elisa follow on, who, still laughing, began, "I know not, charming ladies, if with a little story of mine, no less true than pleasant, I shall succeed in making you laugh as much as Pamfilo hath done with his; but I will do my endeavor thereof.

In our city, then, which hath ever abounded in various fashions and strange folk, there was once, no great while since, a painter called Calandrino, a simple-witted man and of strange usances. He companied most of his time with other two painters, called the one Bruno and the other Buffalmacco, both very merry men, but otherwise well-advised and shrewd, who consorted with Calandrino for that they ofttimes had great diversion of his fashions and his simplicity. There was then also in Florence a young man of a mighty pleasant humor and marvellously adroit in all he had a mind to do, astute and plausible, who was called Maso del Saggio, and who, hearing certain traits of Calandrino's simplicity, determined to amuse himself at his expense by putting off some cheat on him or causing him believe some strange thing. He chanced one day to come upon him in the church of San Giovanni and seeing him intent upon the carved work and paintings of the pyx, which is upon the altar of the said church and which had then not long been placed there, he judged the place and time opportune for carrying his intent into execution. Accordingly, acquainting a friend of his with that which he purposed to do, they both drew near unto the place where Calandrino sat alone and feigning not to see him, fell a-discoursing together of the virtues of divers stones, whereof Maso spoke as authoritatively as if he had been a great and famous lapidary.

Calandrino gave ear to their talk and presently, seeing that it was no secret, he rose to his feet and joined himself to them, to the no small satisfaction of Maso, who, pursuing his discourse, was asked by Calandrino where these wonder-working stones were to be found. Maso replied that the most of them were found in Berlinzone, a city of the Basques, in a country called Bengodi,[1] where the vines are tied up with sausages and a goose is to be had for a farthing[2] and a gosling into the bargain, and that there was a mountain all of grated Parmesan cheese, whereon abode folk who did nothing but make maccaroni and ravioli[3] and cook them in capon-broth, after which they threw them down thence and whoso got most thereof had

355

most; and that hard by ran a rivulet of vernage,[4] the best ever was drunk, without a drop of water therein. 'Marry,' cried Calandrino, 'that were a fine country; but tell me, what is done with the capons that they boil for broth?' Quoth Maso, 'The Basques eat them all.' Then said Calandrino, 'Wast thou ever there?' 'Was I ever there, quotha!' replied Maso. 'If I have been there once I have been there a thousand times.' 'And how many miles is it distant hence?' asked Calandrino; and Maso, 'How many? a million or more; you might count them all night and not know.' 'Then,' said Calandrino, 'it must be farther off than the Abruzzi?' 'Ay, indeed,' answered Maso; 'it is a trifle farther.'

Calandrino, like a simpleton as he was, hearing Maso tell all this with an assured air and without laughing, gave such credence thereto as can be given to whatsoever verity is most manifest and so, holding it for truth, said, 'That is overfar for my money; though, were it nearer, I tell thee aright I would go thither with thee once upon a time, if but to see the maccaroni come tumbling headlong down and take my fill thereof. But tell me, God keep thee merry, is there none of those wonder-working stones to be found in these parts?' 'Ay is there,' answered Maso; 'there be two kinds of stones of very great virtue found here; the first are the grits of Settignano and Montisci, by virtue whereof, when they are wrought into millstones, flour is made; wherefore it is said in those parts that grace cometh from God and millstones from Montisci; but there is such great plenty of these grits that they are as little prized with us as emeralds with the folk over yonder, where they have mountains of them bigger than Mount Morello, which shine in the middle of the night, I warrant thee. And thou must know that whoso should cause set fine and perfect millstones, before they are pierced, in rings and carry them to the Soldan might have for them what he would. The other is what we lapidaries call Heliotrope, a stone of exceeding great virtue, for that whoso hath it about him is not seen of any other person whereas he is not, what while he holdeth it.' Quoth Calandrino, 'These be indeed great virtues; but where is this second stone found?' To which Maso replied that it was commonly found in the Mugnone. 'What bigness is this stone,' asked Calandrino, 'and what is its colour?' Quoth Maso, 'It is of various sizes, some more and some less; but all are well nigh black of colour.'

Calandrino noted all this in himself and feigning to have otherwhat to do, took leave of Maso, inwardly determined to go seek the stone in question, but bethought himself not to do it without the knowledge of Bruno and Buffalmacco, whom he most particularly affected. Accordingly he addressed himself to seek for them, so they might, without delay and before any else, set about the search, and spent all the rest of the morning seeking them. At last, when it was past none, he remembered him that they were awork in the Ladies' Convent at Faenza and leaving all his other business, he betook himself thither well nigh at a run, notwithstanding the great heat. As soon as he saw them, he called them and bespoke them thus: 'Comrades, an you will hearken to me, we may become the richest men in all Florence, for that I have learned from a man worthy of belief that in the Mugnone is to be found a stone, which whoso carrieth about him is not seen of any; wherefore meseemeth we were best go thither in quest thereof without delay, ere any forestall us. We shall certainly find it, for that I know it well, and when we have gotten it, what have we to do but put it in our poke and getting us to the moneychangers' tables, which you know stand still laden with groats and florins, take as much as we will thereof? None will see us, and so may we grow rich of a sudden, without having to smear walls all day long, snail-fashion.'

Bruno and Buffalmacco, hearing this, fell a-laughing in their sleeves and eyeing each other askance, made a show of exceeding wonderment and praised Calandrino's counsel, but Bruno asked how the stone in question was called. Calandrino, who was a clod-pated fellow, had already forgotten the name, wherefore quoth he, 'What have we to do with the name, since we know the virtue of the stone? Meseemeth we were best go about the quest without more ado.'

'Well, then,' said Bruno, 'how is it fashioned?' 'It is of all fashions,' replied Calandrino; 'but all are well nigh black; wherefore meseemeth that what we have to do is to gather up all the black stones we see, till we happen upon the right. So let us lose no time, but get us gone.' Quoth Bruno, 'Wait awhile,' and turning to his comrade, said, 'Methinketh Calandrino saith well; but meseemeth this is no season for the search, for that the sun is high and shineth full upon the Mugnone, where it hath dried all the stones, so that certain of those that be there appear presently white, which of a morning, ere the sun have dried them, show black; more by token that, to-day being a working day, there be many folk, on one occasion or another abroad along the banks, who, seeing us, may guess what we are about and maybe do likewise, whereby the stone may come to their hands and we shall have lost the trot for the amble. Meseemeth (an you be of the same way of thinking) that this is a business to be undertaken of a morning, whenas the black may be the better known from the white, and of a holiday, when there will be none there to see us.'

Buffalmacco commended Bruno's counsel and Calandrino fell in therewith; wherefore they agreed to go seek for the stone all three on the following Sunday morning, and Calandrino besought them over all else not to say a word of the matter to any one alive, for that it had been imparted to him in confidence, and after told them that which he had heard tell of the land of Bengodi, affirming with an oath that it was as he said. As soon as he had taken his leave, the two others agreed with each other what they should do in the matter and Calandrino impatiently awaited the Sunday morning, which being come, he arose at break of day and called his friends, with whom he sallied forth of the city by the San Gallo gate and descending into the bed of the Mugnone, began to go searching down stream for the stone. Calandrino, as the eagerest of the three, went on before, skipping nimbly hither and thither, and whenever he espied any black stone, he pounced upon it and picking it up, thrust it into his bosom. His comrades followed after him picking up now one stone and now another; but Calandrino had not gone far before he had his bosom full of stones; wherefore, gathering up the skirts of his grown, which was not cut Flanders fashion,[5] he tucked them well into his surcingle all round and made an ample lap thereof. However, it was no great while ere he had filled it, and making a lap on like wise of his mantle, soon filled this also with stones. Presently, the two others seeing that he had gotten his load and that dinner-time drew nigh, quoth Bruno to Buffalmacco, in accordance with the plan concerted between them, 'Where is Calandrino?' Buffalmacco, who saw him hard by, turned about and looking now here and now there, answered, 'I know not; but he was before us but now.' 'But now, quotha!' cried Bruno. 'I warrant you he is presently at home at dinner and hath left us to play the fool here, seeking black stones down the Mugnone.' 'Egad,' rejoined Buffalmacco 'he hath done well to make mock of us and leave us here, since we were fools enough to credit him. Marry, who but we had been simple enough to believe that a stone of such virtue was to be found in the Mugnone?'

Calandrino, hearing this, concluded that the heliotrope had fallen into his hands and that by virtue thereof they saw him not, albeit he was present with them, and rejoiced beyond measure at such a piece of good luck, answered them not a word, but determined to return; wherefore, turning back, he set off homeward. Buffalmacco, seeing this, said to Bruno, 'What shall we do? Why do we not get us gone?' Whereto Bruno answered, 'Let us begone; but I vow to God that Calandrino shall never again serve me thus, and were I presently near him as I have been all the morning, I would give him such a clout on the shins with this stone that he should have cause to remember this trick for maybe a month to come.' To say this and to let fly at Calandrino's shins with the stone were one and the same thing; and the latter, feeling the pain, lifted up his leg and began to puff and blow, but yet held his peace and fared on. Presently Buffalmacco took one of the flints he had picked up and said to Bruno, 'Look at this fine flint;

here should go for Calandrino's loins!' So saying, he let fly and dealt him a sore rap in the small of the back with the stone. Brief, on this wise, now with one word and now with another, they went pelting him up the Mugnone till they came to the San Gallo gate, where they threw down the stones they had gathered and halted awhile at the custom house.

The officers, forewarned by them, feigned not to see Calandrino and let him pass, laughing heartily at the jest, whilst he, without stopping, made straight for his house, which was near the Canto alla Macina, and fortune so far favoured the cheat that none accosted him, as he came up the stream and after through the city, as, indeed, he met with few, for that well nigh every one was at dinner. Accordingly, he reached his house, thus laden, and as chance would have it, his wife, a fair and virtuous lady, by name Mistress Tessa, was at the stairhead. Seeing him come and somewhat provoked at his long tarriance, she began to rail at him, saying, 'Devil take the man! Wilt thou never think to come home betimes? All the folk have already dined whenas thou comest back to dinner.' Calandrino, hearing this and finding that he was seen, was overwhelmed with chagrin and vexation and cried out, 'Alack, wicked woman that thou art, wast thou there? Thou hast undone me; but, by God His faith, I will pay thee therefor!' Therewithal he ran up to a little saloon he had and there disburdened himself of the mass of stones he had brought home; then, running in a fury at his wife, he laid hold of her by the hair and throwing her down at his feet, cuffed and kicked her in every part as long as he could wag his arms and legs, without leaving a hair on her head or a bone in her body that was not beaten to a mash, nor did it avail her aught to cry him mercy with clasped hands.

Meanwhile Bruno and Buffalmacco, after laughing awhile with the keepers of the gate, proceeded with slow step to follow Calandrino afar off and presently coming to the door of his house, heard the cruel beating he was in act to give his wife; whereupon, making a show of having but then come back, they called Calandrino, who came to the window, all asweat and red with anger and vexation, and prayed them come up to him. Accordingly, they went up, making believe to be somewhat vexed, and seeing the room full of stones and the lady, all torn and dishevelled and black and blue in the face for bruises, weeping piteously in one corner of the room, whilst Calandrino sat in another, untrussed and panting like one forspent, eyed them awhile, then said, 'What is this, Calandrino? Art thou for building, that we see all these stones here? And Mistress Tessa, what aileth her? It seemeth thou hast beaten her. What is all this ado?' Calandrino, outwearied with the weight of the stones and the fury with which he had beaten his wife, no less than with chagrin for the luck which himseemed he had lost, could not muster breath to give them aught but broken words in reply; wherefore, as he delayed to answer, Buffalmacco went on, 'Harkye, Calandrino, whatever other cause for anger thou mightest have had, thou shouldst not have fooled us as thou hast done, in that, after thou hadst carried us off to seek with thee for the wonder-working stone, thou leftest us in the Mugnone, like a couple of gulls, and madest off home, without saying so much as God be with you or devil; the which we take exceeding ill; but assuredly this shall be the last trick thou shalt ever play us.'

Therewithal, Calandrino enforcing himself,[6] answered, 'Comrades, be not angered; the case standeth otherwise than as you deem. I (unlucky wretch that I am!) had found the stone in question, and you shall hear if I tell truth. When first you questioned one another of me, I was less than half a score yards distant from you; but, seeing that you made off and saw me not, I went on before you and came back hither, still keeping a little in front of you.' Then, beginning from the beginning, he recounted to them all that they had said and done, first and last, and showed them how the stones had served his back and shins; after which, 'And I may tell you,' continued he, 'that, whenas I entered in at the gate, with all these stones about me which you see here, there was nothing said to me, albeit you know how vexatious and tiresome these gatekeepers use to be in wanting to see everything; more by token that I met by the way several of my friends and gossips, who are still wont to accost me and invite me to drink; but none of them said a word to me, no, nor half a word, as those who saw me not. At last, being come home hither, this accursed devil of a woman presented herself before me, for that, as you know, women cause everything lose its virtue, wherefore I, who might else have called myself the luckiest man in Florence, am become the most unlucky. For this I have beaten her as long as I could wag my fists and I know not what hindereth me from slitting her weasand, accursed be the hour when first I saw her and when she came to me in this house.' Then, flaming out into fresh anger, he offered to rise and beat her anew.

Bruno and Buffalmacco, hearing all this, made believe to marvel exceedingly and often confirmed that which Calandrino said, albeit they had the while so great a mind to laugh that they were like to burst; but, seeing him start up in a rage to beat his wife again, they rose upon him and withheld him, avouching that the lady was nowise at fault, but that he had only himself to blame for that which had happened, since he knew that women caused things to lose their virtue and had not bidden her beware of appearing before him that day, and that God had bereft him of foresight to provide against this, either for that the adventure was not to be his or because he had had it in mind to cozen his comrades, to whom he should have discovered the matter, as soon as he perceived that he had found the stone. Brief, after many words, they made peace, not without much ado, between him and the woebegone lady and went their ways, leaving him disconsolate, with the house full of stones."

---

1. *i.e.* Good cheer.
2. A play upon the double meaning of *a denajo*, which signifies also "for money."
3. A kind of rissole made of eggs, sweet herbs and cheese.
4. *Vernaccia*, a kind of rich white wine like Malmsey.
5. *i.e.* not strait-cut.
6. *Sforzandosi*, *i.e.* recovering his wind with an effort.

THE FOURTH STORY

THE RECTOR OF FIESOLE LOVETH A WIDOW LADY, BUT IS NOT LOVED BY HER AND THINKING TO LIE WITH HER, LIETH WITH A SERVING-WENCH OF HERS, WHILST THE LADY'S BROTHERS CAUSE THE BISHOP FIND HIM IN THIS CASE

ELISA BEING COME to the end of her story, which she had related to the no small pleasure of all the company, the queen turned to Emilia, and signified to her her wish that she should follow after with her story, whereupon she promptly began thus: "I have not forgotten, noble ladies, that it hath already been shown, in sundry of the foregoing stories, how much we women are exposed to the importunities of the priests and friars and clergy of every kind; but, seeing that so much cannot be said thereof but that yet more will remain to say, I purpose, to boot, to tell you a story of a rector, who, maugre all the world, would e'en have a gentlewoman wish him well,[1] whether she would or not; whereupon she, like a very discreet woman as she was, used him as he deserved.

As all of you know, Fiesole, whose hill we can see hence, was once a very great and ancient city, nor, albeit it is nowadays all undone, hath it ever ceased to be, as it is yet, the seat of a bishop. Near the cathedral church there a widow lady of noble birth, by name Madam Piccarda, had an estate, where, for that she was not overwell to do, she abode the most part of the year in a house of hers that was not very big, and with her, two brothers of hers, very courteous and worthy youths. It chanced that, the lady frequenting the cathedral church and being yet very young and fair and agreeable, the rector of the church became so sore enamoured of her that he could think of nothing else, and after awhile, making bold to discover his mind to her, he prayed her accept of his love and love him as he loved her. Now he was already old in years, but very young in wit, malapert and arrogant and presumptuous in the extreme, with manners and fashions full of conceit and ill grace, and withal so froward and ill-conditioned that there was none who wished him well; and if any had scant regard for him, it was the lady in question, who not only wished him no whit of good, but hated him worse than the megrims; wherefore, like a discreet woman as she was, she answered him, 'Sir, that you love me should be mighty pleasing to me, who am bound to love you and will gladly do so; but between your love and mine nothing unseemly should ever befall. You are my spiritual father and a priest and are presently well stricken in years, all which things should make you both modest and chaste; whilst I, on the other hand, am no girl, nor do these amorous toys beseem my present condition, for that I am a widow and you well know what discretion is required in widows;

wherefore I pray you hold me excused, for that I shall never love you after the fashion whereof you require me; nor do I wish to be thus loved of you.'

The rector could get of her no other answer for that time, but, nowise daunted or disheartened by the first rebuff, solicited her again and again with the most overweening importunity, both by letter and message, nay, even by word of mouth, whenas he saw her come into the church. Wherefor, herseeming that this was too great and too grievous an annoy, she cast about to rid herself of him after such a fashion as he deserved, since she could no otherwise, but would do nought ere she had taken counsel with her brothers. Accordingly, she acquainted them with the rector's behaviour towards her and that which she purposed to do, and having therein full license from them, went a few days after to the church, as was her wont. As soon as the rector saw her, he came up to her and with his usual assurance, accosted her familiarly. The lady received him with a cheerful countenance and withdrawing apart with him, after he had said many words to her in his wonted style, she heaved a great sigh and said, 'Sir, I have heard that there is no fortalice so strong but that, being every day assaulted, it cometh at last to be taken, and this I can very well see to have happened to myself; for that you have so closely beset me with soft words and with one complaisance and another, that you have made me break my resolve, and I am now disposed, since I please you thus, to consent to be yours.' 'Gramercy, madam,' answered the rector, overjoyed, 'to tell you the truth, I have often wondered how you could hold out so long, considering that never did the like betide me with any woman; nay, I have said whiles, "Were women of silver, they would not be worth a farthing, for that not one of them would stand the hammer." But let that pass for the present. When and where can we be together?' Whereto quoth the lady, 'Sweet my lord, as for the when, it may be what time soever most pleaseth us, for that I have no husband to whom it behoveth me render an account of my nights; but for the where I know not how to contrive.' 'How?' cried the priest. 'Why, in your house to be sure.' 'Sir,' answered the lady, 'you know I have two young brothers, who come and go about the house with their companions day and night, and my house is not overbig; wherefore it may not be there, except one chose to abide there mute-fashion, without saying a word or making the least sound, and be in the dark, after the manner of the blind. An you be content to do this, it might be, for they meddle not with my bedchamber; but their own is so close to mine that one cannot whisper the least word, without its being heard.' 'Madam,' answered the rector, 'this shall not hinder us for a night or two, against I bethink me where we may foregather more at ease.' Quoth she, 'Sir, let that rest with you; but of one thing I pray you, that this abide secret, so no word be ever known thereof.' 'Madam,' replied he, 'have no fear for that; but, an it may be, make shift that we shall foregather this evening.' 'With all my heart,' said the lady; and appointing him how and when he should come, she took leave of him and returned home.

Now she had a serving-wench, who was not overyoung, but had the foulest and worst-favoured visnomy was ever seen; for she had a nose flattened sore, a mouth all awry, thick lips and great ill-set teeth; moreover, she inclined to squint, nor was ever without sore eyes, and had a green and yellow complexion, which gave her the air of having passed the summer not at Fiesole, but at Sinigaglia.[2] Besides all this, she was hipshot and a thought crooked on the right side. Her name was Ciuta, but, for that she had such a dog's visnomy of her own, she was called of every one Ciutazza;[3] and for all she was misshapen of her person, she was not without a spice of roguishness. The lady called her and said to her, 'Harkye, Ciutazza, an thou wilt do me a service this night. I will give thee a fine new shift.' Ciutazza, hearing speak of the shift, answered, 'Madam, so you give me a shift, I will cast myself into the fire, let alone otherwhat.' 'Well, then,' said her mistress, 'I would have thee lie to-night with a man in my bed and load him with caresses, but take good care not to say a word, lest thou be heard by my brothers, who, as thou knowest, sleep in the next room; and after I will give thee the shift.' Quoth Ciutazza, 'With all my heart. I will lie with half a dozen men, if need be, let alone one.' Accordingly, at nightfall, my lord the rector made his appearance, according to agreement, whilst the two young men, by the lady's appointment, were in their bedchamber and took good care to make themselves heard; wherefore he entered the lady's chamber in silence and darkness and betook himself, as she had bidden him, straight to the bed, whither on her part came Ciutazza, who had been well lessoned by the lady of that which she had to do. My lord rector, thinking he had his mistress beside him, caught Ciutazza in his arms and fell to kissing her, without saying a word, and she him; whereupon he proceeded to solace himself with her, taking, as he thought, possession of the long-desired good.

The lady, having done this, charged her brothers carry the rest of the plot into execution, wherefore, stealing softly out of the chamber, they made for the great square and fortune was more favorable to them than they themselves asked in that which they had a mind to do, inasmuch as, the heat being great, the bishop had enquired for the two young gentlemen, so he might go a-pleasuring to their house and drink with them. But, seeing them coming, he acquainted them with his wish and returned with them to their house, where, entering a cool little courtyard of theirs, in which were many flambeaux alight, he drank with great pleasure of an excellent wine of theirs. When he had drunken, the young men said to him, 'My lord, since you have done us so much favour as to deign to visit this our poor house, whereto we came to invite you, we would have you be pleased to view a small matter with which we would fain show you.' The bishop answered that he would well; whereupon one of the young men, taking a lighted flambeau in his hand, made for the chamber where my lord rector lay with Ciutazza, followed by the bishop and all the rest. The rector, to arrive the quicklier at his journey's end, had hastened to take horse and had already ridden more than three miles before they came thither; wherefore, being somewhat weary, he had, notwithstanding the heat, fallen asleep with Ciutazza in his arms. Accordingly, when the young man entered the chamber, light in hand, and after him the bishop and all the others, he was shown to the prelate in this plight; whereupon he awoke and seeing the light and the folk about him, was sore abashed and hid his head for fear under the bed-clothes. The bishop gave him a sound rating and made him put out his head and see with whom he had lain; whereupon the rector, understanding the trick that had been played him of the lady, what with this and what with the disgrace himseemed he had gotten, became of a sudden the woefullest man that was aye. Then, having, by the bishop's commandment, reclad himself, he was despatched to his house under good guard, to suffer sore penance for the sin he had committed. The bishop presently enquiring how it came to pass that he had gone thither to lie with Ciutazza, the young men orderly related everything to him, which having heard, he greatly commended both the lady and her brothers for that, without choosing to imbrue their hands in the blood of a priest, they had entreated him as he deserved. As for the rector, he caused him bewail his offence forty days' space; but love and despite made him rue it for more than nine-and-forty,[4] more by token that, for a great while after, he could never go abroad but the children would point at him and say, 'See, there is he who lay with Ciutazza'; the which was so sore an annoy to him that he was like to go mad therefor. On such wise did the worthy lady rid herself of the importunity of the malapert rector and Ciutazza gained the shift and a merry night."

---

1. *i.e.* love him, grant him her favours. See ante, passim.
2. *i.e.* in the malaria district.
3. *i.e.* great ugly Ciuta.
4. *Quarantanove*, a proverbial expression for an indefinite number.

�֍ 5 ֎

THE FIFTH STORY

THREE YOUNG MEN PULL THE BREECHES OFF A MARCHEGAN JUDGE IN FLORENCE, WHAT WHILE HE IS ON THE BENCH, ADMINISTERING JUSTICE

EMILIA HAVING MADE an end of her story and the widow lady having been commended of all, the queen looked to Filostrato and said, "It is now thy turn to tell." He answered promptly that he was ready and began, "Delightsome ladies, the mention by Elisa a little before of a certain young man, to wit, Maso del Saggio, hath caused me leave a story I purposed to tell you, so I may relate to you one of him and certain companions of his, which, if (albeit it is nowise unseemly) it offer certain expressions which you think shame to use, is natheless so laughable that I will e'en tell it.

As you may all have heard, there come oftentimes to our city governors from the Marches of Ancona, who are commonly mean-spirited folk and so paltry and sordid of life that their every fashion seemeth nought other than a lousy cadger's trick; and of this innate paltriness and avarice, they bring with them judges and notaries, who seem men taken from the plough-tail or the cobbler's stall rather than from the schools of law. Now, one of these being come hither for Provost, among the many judges whom he brought with him was one who styled himself Messer Niccola da San Lepidio and who had more the air of a tinker than of aught else, and he was set with other judges to hear criminal causes. As it oft happeneth that, for all the townsfolk have nought in the world to do at the courts of law, yet bytimes they go thither, it befell that Maso del Saggio went thither one morning, in quest of a friend of his, and chancing to cast his eyes whereas this said Messer Niccola sat, himseemed that here was a rare outlandish kind of wild fowl. Accordingly, he went on to examine him from head to foot, and albeit he saw him with the miniver bonnet on his head all black with smoke and grease and a paltry inkhorn at his girdle, a gown longer than his mantle and store of other things all foreign to a man of good breeding and manners, yet of all these the most notable, to his thinking, was a pair of breeches, the backside whereof, as the judge sat, with his clothes standing open in front for straitness, he perceived came halfway down his legs. Thereupon, without tarrying longer to look upon him, he left him with whom he went seeking and beginning a new quest, presently found two comrades of his, called one Ribi and the other Matteuzzo, men much of the same mad humour as himself, and said to them, 'As you tender me, come with me to the law courts, for I wish to show you the rarest scarecrow you ever saw.'

Accordingly, carrying them to the court house, he showed them the aforesaid judge and his breeches, whereat they fell a-laughing, as soon as they caught sight of him afar off; then, drawing nearer to the platform whereon my lord judge sat, they saw that one might lightly pass thereunder and that, moreover, the boards under his feet were so broken that one might with great ease thrust his hand and arm between them; whereupon quoth Maso to his comrades, 'Needs must we pull him off those breeches of his altogether, for that it may very well be done.' Each of the others had already seen how;[1] wherefore, having agreed among themselves what they should say and do, they returned thither next morning, when, the court being very full of folk, Matteuzzo, without being seen of any, crept under the bench and posted himself immediately beneath the judge's feet. Meanwhile, Maso came up to my lord judge on one side and taking him by the skirt of his gown, whilst Ribi did the like on the other side, began to say, 'My lord, my lord, I pray you for God's sake, ere yonder scurvy thief on the other side of you go elsewhere, make him restore me a pair of saddle-bags whereof he hath saith indeed he did it not; but I saw him, not a month ago, in act to have them resoled.' Ribi on his side cried out with all his might, 'Believe him not, my lord; he is an arrant knave, and for that he knoweth I am come to lay a complaint against him for a pair of saddle-bags whereof he hath robbed me, he cometh now with his story of the boothose, which I have had in my house this many a day. An you believe me not, I can bring you to witness my next-door neighbor Trecca and Grassa the tripewoman and one who goeth gathering the sweepings from Santa Masia at Verjaza, who saw him when he came back from the country.'

Maso on the other hand suffered not Ribi to speak, but bawled his loudest, whereupon the other but shouted the more. The judge stood up and leaned towards them, so he might the better apprehend what they had to say, wherefore Matteuzzo, watching his opportunity, thrust his hand between the crack of the boards and laying hold of Messer Niccola's galligaskins by the breech, tugged at them amain. The breeches came down incontinent, for that the judge was lean and lank of the crupper; whereupon, feeling this and knowing not what it might be, he would have sat down again and pulled his skirts forward to cover himself; but Maso on the one side and Ribi on the other still held him fast and cried out, 'My lord, you do ill not to do me justice and to seek to avoid hearing me and get you gone otherwhere; there be no writs granted in this city for such small matters as this.' So saying, they held him fast by the clothes on such wise that all who were in the court perceived that his breeches had been pulled down. However, Matteuzzo, after he had held them awhile, let them go and coming forth from under the platform, made off out of the court and went his way without being seen; whereupon quoth Ribi, himseeming he had done enough, 'I vow to God I will appeal to the syndicate!' Whilst Maso, on his part, let go the mantle and said, 'Nay, I will e'en come hither again and again until such time as I find you not hindered as you seem to be this morning.' So saying, they both made off as quickliest they might, each on his own side, whilst my lord judge pulled up his breeches in every one's presence, as if he were arisen from sleep; then, perceiving how the case stood, he enquired whither they were gone who were at difference anent the boothose and the saddle-bags; but they were not to be found, whereupon he began to swear by Cock's bowels that need must he know and learn if it were the wont at Florence to pull down the judges' breeches, whenas they sat on the judicial bench. The Provost, on his part, hearing of this, made a great stir; but, his friends having shown him that this had only been done to give him notice that the Florentines right well understood how, whereas he should have brought judges, he had brought them sorry patches, to have them better cheap, he thought it best to hold his peace, and so the thing went no farther for the nonce."

1. *i.e.* how they might do this.

❧ 6 ❧

THE SIXTH STORY

BRUNO AND BUFFALMACCO, HAVING STOLEN A PIG
FROM CALANDRINO, MAKE HIM TRY THE ORDEAL
WITH GINGER BOLUSES AND SACK AND GIVE HIM
(INSTEAD OF THE GINGER) TWO DOG-BALLS
COMPOUNDED WITH ALOES, WHEREBY IT APPEARETH
THAT HE HIMSELF HATH HAD THE PIG AND THEY
MAKE HIM PAY BLACKMAIL, AN HE WOULD NOT HAVE
THEM TELL HIS WIFE

NO SOONER HAD Filostrato despatched his story, which had given rise to many a laugh, than the queen bade Filomena follow on, whereupon she began: "Gracious ladies, even as Filostrato was led by the mention of Maso to tell the story which you have just heard from him, so neither more nor less am I moved by that of Calandrino and his friends to tell you another of them, which methinketh will please you.

Who Calandrino, Bruno and Buffalmacco were I need not explain to you, for that you have already heard it well enough; wherefore, to proceed with my story, I must tell you that Calandrino owned a little farm at no great distance from Florence, that he had had to his wife's dowry. From this farm, amongst other things that he got thence, he had every year a pig, and it was his wont still to betake himself thither, he and his wife, and kill the pig and have it salted on the spot. It chanced one year that, his wife being somewhat ailing, he went himself to kill the pig, which Bruno and Buffalmacco hearing and knowing that his wife was not gone to the farm with him, they repaired to a priest, very great friend of theirs and a neighbor of Calandrino, to sojourn some days with him. Now Calandrino had that very morning killed the pig and seeing them with the priest, called to them saying, 'You are welcome. I would fain have you see what a good husband[1] I am.' Then carrying them into the house, he showed them the pig, which they seeing to be a very fine one and understanding from Calandrino that he meant to salt it down for his family, 'Good lack,' quoth Bruno to him, 'what a ninny thou art! Sell it and let us make merry with the price, and tell thy wife that it hath been stolen from thee.' 'Nay, answered Calandrino, 'she would never believe it and would drive me out of the house. Spare your pains, for I will never do it.' And many were the words, but they availed nothing.

Calandrino invited them to supper, but with so ill a grace that they refused to sup there and took their leave of him; whereupon quoth Bruno and Buffalmacco, 'What sayest thou to stealing yonder pig from him to-night?' 'Marry,' replied the other, 'how can we do it?' Quoth Bruno, 'I can see how well enough, an he remove it not from where it was but now.' 'Then,' rejoined his companion, 'let us do it. Why should we not? And after we will make merry over it with the parson here.' The priest answered that he would well, and Bruno said, 'Here must some little art be used. Thou knowest, Buffalmacco, how niggardly Calandrino is and how gladly he drinketh when others pay; let us go and carry him to the tavern, where the priest shall make believe to pay the whole scot in our honor nor suffer him to pay aught. Calandrino will soon grow fuddled and then we can manage it lightly enough, for that he is alone in the house.' As he said, so they did and Calandrino seeing that the priest suffered none to pay, gave himself up to drinking and took in a good load, albeit it needed no great matter to make him drunk. It was pretty late at night when they left the tavern and Calandrino, without troubling himself about supper, went straight home, where, thinking to have shut the door, he left it open and betook himself to bed. Buffalmacco and Bruno went off to sup with the priest and after supper repaired quietly to Calandrino's house, carrying with them certain implements wherewithal to break in whereas Bruno had appointed it; but, finding the door open, they entered and unhooking the pig, carried it off to the priest's house, where they laid it up and betook themselves to sleep.

On the morrow, Calandrino, having slept off the fumes of the wine, arose in the morning and going down, missed his pig and saw the door open; whereupon he questioned this one and that if they knew who had taken it and getting no news of it, began to make a great outcry, saying, 'Woe is me, miserable wretch that I am!' for that the pig had been stolen from him. As soon as Bruno and Buffalmacco were risen, they repaired to Calandrino's house, to hear what he would say anent the pig, and he no sooner saw them than he called out to them, well nigh weeping, and said, 'Woe's me, comrades mine; my pig hath been stolen from me!' Whereupon Bruno came up to him and said softly, 'It is a marvel that thou hast been wise for once.' 'Alack,' replied Calandrino, 'indeed I say sooth.' 'That's the thing to say,' quoth Bruno. 'Make a great outcry, so it may well appear that it is e'en as thou sayst.' Therewithal Calandrino bawled out yet loudlier, saying, 'Cock's body, I tell thee it hath been stolen from me in good earnest!' 'Good, good,' replied Bruno; 'that's the way to speak; cry out lustily, make thyself well heard, so it may seem true.' Quoth Calandrino, 'Thou wouldst make me give my soul to the Fiend! I tell thee and thou believest me not. May I be strung up by the neck an it have not been stolen from me!' 'Good lack!' cried Bruno. 'How can that be? I saw it here but yesterday. Thinkest thou to make me believe that it hath flown away?' Quoth Calandrino, 'It is as I tell thee.' 'Good lack,' repeated Bruno, 'can it be?' 'Certes,' replied Calandrino, 'it is so, more by token that I am undone and know not how I shall return home. My wife will never believe me; or even if she do, I shall have no peace with her this year to come.' Quoth Bruno, 'So God save me, this is ill done, if it be true; but thou knowest, Calandrino, I lessoned thee yesterday to say thus and I would not have thee at once cozen thy wife and us.' Therewithal Calandrino fell to crying out and saying, 'Alack, why will you drive me to desperation and make me blaspheme God and the Saints? I tell you the pig was stolen from me yesternight.'

Then said Buffalmacco, 'If it be so indeed, we must cast about for a means of having it again, an we may contrive it.' 'But what means,' asked Calandrino, 'can we find?' Quoth Buffalmacco, 'We may be sure that there hath come none from the Indies to rob thee of thy pig; the thief must have been some one of thy neighbors. An thou canst make shift to assemble them, I know how to work the ordeal by bread and cheese and we will presently see for certain who hath had it.' 'Ay,' put in Bruno, 'thou wouldst make a fine thing of bread and cheese with such gentry as we have about here, for one of them I am certain hath had the pig, and he would smoke the trap and would not come.' 'How, then, shall we do?' asked Buffalmacco, and Bruno said, 'We must e'en do it with ginger boluses and good vernage[2] and invite them to drink. They will suspect nothing and come, and the ginger boluses can be blessed even as the bread and cheese.' Quoth Buffalmacco, 'Indeed, thou sayst sooth. What sayst thou, Calandrino? Shall's do 't?' 'Nay,' replied the gull, 'I pray you thereof for the love of God; for, did I but know who hath had it, I should hold myself half consoled.' 'Marry, then,' said Bruno, 'I am ready to go to Florence, to oblige thee, for the things aforesaid, so thou wilt give me the money.' Now Calandrino had maybe forty shillings, which he gave him, and Bruno accordingly repaired to Florence to a friend of his, a druggist, of whom he bought a pound of fine ginger boluses and caused compound a couple of dogballs with fresh confect of hepatic aloes; after which he let cover these latter with sugar, like the others, and set thereon a privy mark by which he might very well know them, so he should not mistake them nor change them. Then, buying a flask of good vernage, he returned to Calandrino in the country and said to him, 'Do thou to-morrow morning invite those whom thou suspectest to drink with thee; it is a holiday and all will willingly come. Meanwhile, Buffalmacco and I will to-night make the conjuration over the pills and bring them to thee to-morrow morning at home; and for the love of thee I will administer them myself and do and say that which is to be said and done.'

Calandrino did as he said and assembled on the following morning a goodly company of such young Florentines as were presently about the village and of husbandmen; whereupon Bruno and Buffalmacco came with a box of pills and the flask of wine and made the folk stand in a ring. Then said Bruno, 'Gentlemen, needs must I tell you the reason wherefore you are here, so that, if aught betide that please you not, you may have no cause to complain of me. Calandrino here was robbed yesternight of a fine pig, nor can he find who hath had it; and for that none other than some one of us who are here can have stolen it from him, he proffereth each of you, that he may discover who hath had it, one of these pills to eat and a draught of wine. Now you must know that he who hath had the pig will not be able to swallow the pill; nay, it will seem to him more bitter than poison and he will spit it out; wherefore, rather than that shame be done him in the presence of so many, he were better tell it to the parson by way of confession and I will proceed no farther with this matter.'

All who were there declared that they would willingly eat of the pills, whereupon Bruno ranged them in order and set Calandrino among them; then, beginning at one end of the line, he proceeded to give each his bolus, and whenas he came over against Calandrino, he took one of the dogballs and put it into his hand. Calandrino clapped it incontinent into his mouth and began to chew it; but no sooner did his tongue taste the aloes, than he spat it out again, being unable to brook the bitterness. Meanwhile, each was looking other in the face, to see who should spit out his bolus, and whilst Bruno, not having made an end of serving them out, went on to do so, feigning to pay no heed to Calandrino's doing, he heard say behind him, 'How now, Calandrino? What meaneth this?' Whereupon he turned suddenly round and seeing that Calandrino had spat out his bolus, said, 'Stay, maybe somewhat else hath caused him spit it out. Take another of them.' Then, taking the other dogball, he thrust it into Calandrino's mouth and went on to finish giving out the rest. If the first ball seemed bitter to Calandrino, the second was bitterer yet; but, being ashamed to spit it out, he kept it awhile in his mouth, chewing it and shedding tears that seemed hazel-nuts so big they were, till at last, unable to hold out longer, he cast it forth, like as he had the first. Meanwhile Buffalmacco and Bruno gave the company to drink, and all, seeing this, declared that Calandrino had certainly stolen the pig from himself; nay, there were those there who rated him roundly.

After they were all gone, and the two rogues left alone with Calandrino, Buffalmacco said to him, 'I still had it for certain that it was thou tookst the pig thyself and wouldst fain make us believe that it had been stolen from thee, to escape giving us one poor while to drink of the monies thou hadst for it.' Calandrino, who was not yet quit of the bitter taste of the aloes, began to swear that he had not had it, and Buffalmacco said, 'But in good earnest, comrade, what gottest thou for it? Was it six florins?' Calandrino, hearing this, began to wax desperate, and Bruno said, 'Harkye, Calandrino, there was such an one in the company that ate and drank with us, who told me that thou hast a wench over yonder, whom thou keepest for thy pleasure and to whom thou givest whatsoever thou canst scrape together, and that he held it for certain that thou hadst sent her the pig. Thou hast learned of late to play pranks of this kind; thou carriedst us off t'other day down the Mugnone, picking up black stones, and whenas thou hadst gotten us aboard ship without biscuit,[3] thou madest off and wouldst after have us believe that thou hadst found the magic stone; and now on like wise thou thinkest, by dint of oaths, to make us believe that the pig, which thou hast given away or more like sold, hath been stolen from thee. But we are used to thy tricks and know them; thou shalt not avail to play us any more of them, and to be plain with thee, since we have been at pains to make the conjuration, we mean that thou shalt give us two pairs of capons; else will we tell Mistress Tessa everything.' Calandrino, seeing that he was not believed and himseeming he had had vexation enough, without having his wife's scolding into the bargain, gave them two pairs of capons, which they carried off to Florence, after they had salted the pig, leaving Calandrino to digest the loss and the flouting as best he might."

---

1. *i.e.* in the old sense of "manager" (*massajo*).
2. *i.e.* white wine.
3. *i.e.* embarked on a bootless quest.

THE SEVENTH STORY

A SCHOLAR LOVETH A WIDOW LADY, WHO, BEING ENAMOURED OF ANOTHER, CAUSETH HIM SPEND ONE WINTER'S NIGHT IN THE SNOW AWAITING HER, AND HE AFTER CONTRIVETH, BY HIS SLEIGHT, TO HAVE HER ABIDE NAKED, ALL ONE MID-JULY DAY, ON THE SUMMIT OF A TOWER, EXPOSED TO FLIES AND GADS AND SUN

THE LADIES LAUGHED amain at the unhappy Calandrino and would have laughed yet more, but that it irked them to see him fleeced of the capons, to boot, by those who had already robbed him of the pig. But, as soon as the end of the story was come, the queen charged Pampinea tell hers, and she promptly began thus: "It chanceth oft, dearest ladies, that craft is put to scorn by craft and it is therefore a sign of little wit to delight in making mock of others. We have, for several stories, laughed amain at tricks that have been played upon folk and whereof no vengeance is recorded to have been taken; but I purpose now to cause you have some compassion of a just retribution wreaked upon a townswoman of ours, on whose head her own cheat recoiled and was retorted well nigh unto death; and the hearing of this will not be without profit unto you, for that henceforward you will the better keep yourselves from making mock of others, and in this you will show great good sense.

Not many years ago there was in Florence, a young lady, by name Elena, fair of favour and haughty of humour, of very gentle lineage and endowed with sufficient abundance of the goods of fortune, who, being widowed of her husband, chose never to marry again, for that she was enamoured of a handsome and agreeable youth of her own choice, and with the aid of a maid of hers, in whom she put great trust, being quit of every other care, she often with marvellous delight gave herself a good time with him. In these days it chanced that a young gentleman of our city, by name Rinieri, having long studied in Paris, not for the sake of after selling his knowledge by retail, as many do, but to know the nature of things and their causes, the which excellently becometh a gentleman, returned thence to Florence and there lived citizen-fashion, much honoured as well for his nobility as for his learning. But, as it chanceth often that those, who have the most experience of things profound, are the soonest snared of love, even so it befell this Rinieri; for, having one day repaired, by way of diversion, to an entertainment, there presented herself before his eyes the aforesaid Elena, clad all in black, as our widows go, and full, to his judgment, of such beauty and pleasantness as himseemed he had never beheld in any other woman; and in his heart he deemed that he might call himself blest whom God should vouchsafe to hold her naked in his arms. Then, furtively considering her once and again and knowing that great things and precious were not to be acquired without travail, he altogether determined in himself to devote all his pains and all his diligence to the pleasing her, to the end that thereby he might gain her love and so avail to have his fill of her.

The young lady, (who kept not her eyes fixed upon the nether world, but, conceiting herself as much and more than as much as she was, moved them artfully hither and thither, gazing all about, and was quick to note who delighted to look upon her,) soon became aware of Rinieri and said, laughing, in herself, 'I have not come hither in vain to-day; for, an I mistake not, I have caught a woodcock by the bill.' Accordingly, she fell to ogling him from time to time with the tail of her eye and studied, inasmuch as she might, to let him see that she took note of him, thinking that the more men she allured and ensnared with her charms, so much the more of price would her beauty be, especially to him on whom she had bestowed it, together with her love. The learned scholar, laying aside philosophical speculations, turned all his thoughts to her and thinking to please her, enquired where she lived and proceeded to pass to and fro before her house, colouring his comings and goings with various pretexts, whilst the lady, idly glorying in this, for the reason already set out, made believe to take great pleasure in seeing him. Accordingly, he found means to clap up an acquaintance with her maid and discovering to her his love, prayed her make interest for him with her mistress, so he might avail to have her favour. The maid promised freely and told the lady, who hearkened with the heartiest laughter in the world and said, 'Seest thou where yonder man cometh to lose the wit he hath brought back from Paris? Marry, we will give him that which he goeth seeking. An he bespeak thee again, do thou tell him that I love him far more than he loveth me; but that it behoveth me look to mine honour, so I may hold up my head with the other ladies; whereof and he be as wise as folk say, he will hold me so much the dearer.' Alack, poor silly soul, she knew not aright, ladies mine, what it is to try conclusions with scholars. The maid went in search of Rinieri and finding him, did that which had been enjoined her of her mistress, whereat he was overjoyed and proceeded to use more urgent entreaties, writing letters and sending presents, all of which were accepted, but he got nothing but vague and general answers; and on this wise she held him in play a great while.

At last, to show her lover, to whom she had discovered everything and who was whiles somewhat vexed with her for this and had conceived some jealousy of Rinieri, that he did wrong to suspect her thereof, she despatched to the scholar, now grown very pressing, her maid, who told him, on her mistress's part, that she had never yet had an opportunity to do aught that might pleasure him since he had certified her of his love, but that on the occasion of the festival of the Nativity she hoped to be able to be with him; wherefore, an it liked him, he was on the evening of the feast to come by night to her courtyard, whither she would go for him as first she might. At this the scholar was the gladdest man alive and betook himself at the appointed time to his mistress's house, where he was carried by the maid into a courtyard and being there locked in, proceeded to wait the lady's coming. The latter had that evening sent for her lover and after she had supped merrily with him, she told him that which she purposed to do that night, adding, 'And thou mayst see for thyself what and how great is the love I have borne and bear him of whom thou hast taken a jealousy.' The lover heard these words with great satisfaction and was impatient to see by the fact that which the lady gave him to understand with words.

It had by chance snowed hard during the day and everything was covered with snow, wherefore the scholar had not long abidden in the courtyard before he began to feel colder than he could have wished; but, looking to recruit himself speedily, he was fain to endure it with patience. Presently, the lady said to her lover, 'Let us go look from a lattice what yonder fellow, of whom thou art waxed jealous, doth and hear what he shall answer the maid, whom I have sent to parley with him.' Accordingly, they betook themselves to a lattice and thence, seeing, without being seen, they heard the maid from another lattice bespeak the scholar and say, 'Rinieri, my lady is the woefullest woman that was aye, for that there is one of her brothers come hither to-night, who hath talked much with her and after must needs sup with her, nor is yet gone away; but methinketh he will soon be gone; wherefore she hath not been able to come to thee, but will soon come now and prayeth thee not to take the waiting in ill part.' Rinieri, believing this to be true, replied, 'Tell my lady to give herself no concern for me till such time as she can at her commodity come to me, but bid her do this as quickliest she may.' The maid turned back into the house and betook herself to bed, whilst the lady said to her gallant, 'Well, how sayst thou? Thinkest thou that, an I wished him such weal as thou fearest, I would suffer him stand a-freezing down yonder?' So saying, she betook herself to bed with her lover, who was now in part satisfied, and there they abode a great while in joyance and liesse, laughing and making mock of the wretched scholar, who fared to and fro the while in the courtyard, making shift to warm himself with exercise, nor had whereas he might seat himself or shelter from the night-damp. He cursed her brother's long stay with the lady and took everything he heard for the opening of a door to him by her, but hoped in vain.

The lady, having solaced herself with her lover till near upon midnight, said to him, 'How deemest thou, my soul, of our scholar? Whether seemeth to thee the greater, his wit or the love I bear him? Will the cold which I presently cause him suffer do away from thy mind the doubts which my pleasantries aroused therein the other day?' Whereto he replied, 'Heart of my body, yes, I know right well that, like as thou art my good and my peace and my delight and all my hope, even so am I thine.' 'Then,' rejoined she, 'kiss me a thousand times, so I may see if thou say sooth.' Whereupon he clipped her fast in his arms and kissed her not a thousand, but more than an hundred thousand times. Then, after they had abidden awhile in such discourse, the lady said, 'Marry, let us arise a little and go see if the fire is anydele spent, wherein this my new lover wrote me that he burnt all day long.' Accordingly, they arose and getting them to the accustomed lattice, looked out into the courtyard, where they saw the scholar dancing a right merry jig on the snow, so fast and brisk that never had they seen the like, to the sound of the chattering of the teeth that he made for excess of cold; whereupon quoth the lady, 'How sayst thou, sweet my hope? Seemeth to thee that I know how to make folk jig it without sound of trump or bagpipe?' Whereto he answered, laughing, 'Ay dost thou, my chief delight.' Quoth the lady, 'I will that we go down to the door; thou shalt abide quiet, whilst I bespeak him, and we shall hear what he will say; belike we shall have no less diversion thereof than we had from seeing him.'

Accordingly, they softly opened the chamber and stole down to the door, where, without opening it anydele, the lady called to the scholar in a low voice by a little hole that was there. Rinieri hearing himself called, praised God, taking it oversoon for granted that he was to be presently admitted, and coming up to the door, said, 'Here am I, madam; open for God's sake, for I die of cold.' 'O ay,' replied the lady, 'I know thou art a chilly one; is then the cold so exceeding great, because, forsooth, there is a little snow about? I wot the nights are much colder in Paris. I cannot open to thee yet, for that accursed brother of mine, who came to sup with me to-night, is not yet gone; but he will soon begone and I will come incontinent to open to thee. I have but now very hardly stolen away from him, that I might come to exhort thee not to wax weary of waiting.' 'Alack, madam,' cried the scholar, 'I pray you for God's sake open to me, so I may abide within under cover, for that this little while past there is come on the thickest snow in the world and it yet snoweth, and I will wait for you as long as it shall please you.' 'Woe's me, sweet my treasure,' replied the lady, 'that cannot I; for this door maketh so great a noise, whenas it is opened, that it would lightly be heard of my brother, if I should open to thee; but I will go bid him begone, so I may after come back and open to thee.' 'Then go quickly,' rejoined he; 'and I prithee let make a good fire, so I may warm me as soon as I come in, for that I am grown so cold I can scarce feel myself.' Quoth the lady, 'That should not be possible, an that be true which thou hast many a time written me, to wit, that thou burnest for the love of me. Now, I must go, wait and be of good heart.' Then, with her lover, who had heard all this with the utmost pleasure, she went back to bed, and that night they slept little, nay, they spent it well nigh all in dalliance and delight and in making mock of Rinieri.

Meanwhile, the unhappy scholar (now well nigh grown a stork, so sore did his teeth chatter,) perceiving at last that he was befooled, essayed again and again to open the door and sought an he might not avail to issue thence by another way; but, finding no means thereunto, he fell a-ranging to and fro like a lion, cursing the foulness of the weather and the lady's malignity and the length of the night, together with his own credulity; wherefore, being sore despited against his mistress, the long and ardent love he had borne her was suddenly changed to fierce and bitter hatred and he revolved in himself many and various things, so he might find a means of revenge, the which he now desired far more eagerly than he had before desired to be with the lady. At last, after much long tarriance, the night drew near unto day and the dawn began to appear; whereupon the maid, who had been lessoned by the lady, coming down, opened the courtyard door and feigning to have compassion of Rinieri, said, 'Bad luck may he have who came hither yestereve! He hath kept us all night upon thorns and hath caused thee freeze; but knowest thou what? Bear it with patience, for that which could not be to-night shall be another time. Indeed, I know nought could have happened that had been so displeasing to my lady.'

The despiteful scholar, like a wise man as he was, who knew that threats are but arms for the threatened, locked up in his breast that which untempered will would fain have vented and said in a low voice, without anywise showing himself vexed, 'In truth I have had the worst night I ever had; but I have well apprehended that the lady is nowise to blame for this, inasmuch as she herself of her compassion for me, came down hither to excuse herself and to hearten me; and as thou sayest, that which hath not been to-night shall be another time. Commend me to her and God be with thee.' Therewithal, well nigh stark with cold, he made his way, as best he might, back to his house, where, being drowsed to death, he cast himself upon his bed to sleep and awoke well nigh crippled of his arms and legs; wherefore, sending for sundry physicians and acquainting them with the cold he had suffered, he caused take order for his cure. The leaches, plying him with prompt and very potent remedies, hardly, after some time, availed to recover him of the shrinking of the sinews and cause them relax; and but that he was young and that the warm season came on, he had overmuch to suffer. However, being restored to health and lustihead, he kept his hate to himself and feigned himself more than ever enamoured of his widow.

Now it befell, after a certain space of time, that fortune furnished him with an occasion of satisfying his desire [for vengeance], for that the youth beloved of the widow being, without any regard for the love she bore him, fallen enamoured of another lady, would have nor little nor much to say to her nor do aught to pleasure her, wherefore she pined in tears and bitterness. But her maid, who had great compassion of her, finding no way of rousing her mistress from the chagrin into which the loss of her lover had cast her and seeing the scholar pass along the street, after the wonted manner, entered into a fond conceit, to wit, that the lady's lover might be brought by some necromantic operation or other to love her as he had been wont to do and that the scholar should be a past master in this manner of thing, and told her thought to her mistress. The latter, little wise, without considering that, had the scholar been acquainted with the black art, he would have practised it for himself, lent her mind to her

maid's words and bade her forthright learn from him if he would do it and give him all
assurance that, in requital thereof, she would do whatsoever pleased him. The maid did her
errand well and diligently, which when the scholar heard, he was overjoyed and said in
himself, 'Praised be Thou, my God! The time is come when with Thine aid I may avail to make
yonder wicked woman pay the penalty of the harm she did me in requital of the great love I
bore her.' Then to the maid, 'Tell my lady,' quoth he, 'that she need be in no concern for this, for
that, were her lover in the Indies, I would speedily cause him come to her and crave pardon of
that which he hath done to displeasure her; but the means she must take to this end I purpose
to impart to herself, when and where it shall most please her. So say to her and hearten her on
my part.'

The maid carried his answer to her mistress and it was agreed that they should foregather at
Santa Lucia del Prato, whither, accordingly, the lady, and the scholar being come and speaking
together alone, she, remembering her not that she had aforetime brought him well nigh to
death's door, openly discovered to him her case and that which she desired and besought him
to succour her. 'Madam,' answered he, 'it is true that amongst the other things I learned at Paris
was necromancy, whereof for certain I know that which is extant thereof; but for that the thing
is supremely displeasing unto God, I had sworn never to practise it either for myself or for
others. Nevertheless, the love I bear you is of such potency that I know not how I may deny
you aught that you would have me do; wherefore, though it should behove me for this alone go
to the devil's stead, I am yet ready to do it, since it is your pleasure. But I must forewarn you
that the thing is more uneath to do than you perchance imagine, especially whenas a woman
would recall a man to loving her or a man a woman, for that this cannot be done save by the
very person unto whom it pertaineth; and it behoveth that whoso doth it be of an assured
mind, seeing it must be done anights and in solitary places without company; which things I
know not how you are disposed to do.' The lady, more enamoured than discreet, replied, 'Love
spurreth me on such wise that there is nothing I would not do to have again him who hath
wrongfully forsaken me. Algates, an it please you, show me in what I must approve myself
assured of mind.' 'Madam,' replied the scholar, who had a patch of ill hair to his tail,[1] 'I must
make an image of pewter in his name whom you desire to get again, which whenas I shall send
you, it will behove you seven times bathe yourself therewith, all naked, in a running stream, at
the hour of the first sleep, what time the moon is far on the wane. Thereafter, naked as you are,
you must get you up into a tree or to the top of some uninhabited house and turning to the
north, with the image in your hand, seven times running say certain words which I shall give
you written; which when you shall have done, there will come to you two of the fairest damsels
you ever beheld, who will salute you and ask you courteously what you would have done. Do
you well and throughly discover to them your desires and look it betide you not to name one
for another. As soon as you have told them, they will depart and you may then come down to
the place where you shall have left your clothes and re-clothe yourself and return home; and for
certain, ere it be the middle of the ensuing night, your lover will come, weeping, to crave you
pardon and mercy; and know that from that time forth he will never again leave you for any
other.'

The lady, hearing all this and lending entire faith thereto, was half comforted, herseeming
she already had her lover again in her arms, and said, 'Never fear; I will very well do these
things, and I have therefor the finest commodity in the world; for I have, towards the upper
end of the Val d'Arno, a farm, which is very near the river-bank, and it is now July, so that
bathing will be pleasant; more by token that I mind me there is, not far from the stream, a little
uninhabited tower, save that the shepherds climb up bytimes, by a ladder of chestnut-wood
that is there, to a sollar at the top, to look for their strayed beasts: otherwise it is a very solitary

out-of-the-way[2] place. Thither will I betake myself and there I hope to do that which you shall enjoin me the best in the world.' The scholar, who very well knew both the place and the tower mentioned by the lady, was rejoiced to be certified of her intent and said, 'Madam, I was never in these part and therefore know neither the farm nor the tower; but, an it be as you say, nothing in the world can be better. Wherefore, whenas it shall be time, I will send you the image and the conjuration; but I pray you instantly, whenas you shall have gotten your desire and shall know I have served you well, that you be mindful of me and remember to keep your promise to me.' She answered that she would without fail do it and taking leave of him, returned to her house; whilst the scholar, rejoiced for that himseemed his desire was like to have effect, made an image with certain talismanic characters of his own devising, and wrote a rigmarole of his fashion, by way of conjuration; the which, whenas it seemed to him time, he despatched to the lady and sent to tell her that she must that very night, without more tarriance, do that which he had enjoined her; after which he secretly betook himself, with a servant of his, to the house of one of his friends who abode very near the tower, so he might give effect to his design.

The lady, on her part, set out with her maid and repaired to her farm, where, as soon as the night was come, she made a show of going to bed and sent the maid away to sleep, but towards the hour of the first sleep, she issued quietly forth of the house and betook herself to the bank of the Arno hard by the tower, where, looking first well all about and seeing nor hearing any, she put off her clothes and hiding them under a bush, bathed seven times with the image; after which, naked as she was, she made for the tower, image in hand. The scholar, who had, at the coming on of the night, hidden himself with his servant among the willows and other trees near the tower and had witnessed all this, seeing her, as she passed thus naked close to him, overcome the darkness of the night with the whiteness of her body and after considering her breast and the other parts of her person and seeing them fair, bethought himself what they should become in a little while and felt some compassion of her; whilst, on the other hand, the pricks of the flesh assailed him of a sudden and caused that stand on end which erst lay prone, inciting him to issue forth of his ambush and go take her and do his will of her. Between the one and the other he was like to be overcome; but, calling to mind who he was and what the injury he had suffered and wherefore and at whose hands and he being thereby rekindled in despite and compassion and carnal appetite banished, he abode firm in his purpose and let her go.

The lady, going up on to the tower and turning to the north, began to repeat the words given her by the scholar, who, coming quietly into the tower awhile after, little by little removed the ladder, which led to the sollar where she was, and after awaited that which she should do and say. Meanwhile, the lady, having seven times said her conjuration, began to look for the two damsels and so long was her waiting (more by token that she felt it cooler than she could have wished) that she saw the dawn appear; whereupon, woeful that it had not befallen as the scholar had told her, she said in herself, 'I fear me yonder man hath had a mind to give me a night such as that which I gave him; but, an that be his intent, he hath ill known to avenge himself, for that this night hath not been as long by a third as was his, forbye that the cold was of anothergates sort.' Then, so the day might not surprise her there, she proceeded to seek to go down from the tower, but found the ladder gone; whereupon her courage forsook her, as it were the world had failed beneath her feet, and she fell down aswoon upon the platform of the tower. As soon as her sense returned to her, she fell to weeping piteously and bemoaning herself, and perceiving but too well that this must have been the scholar's doing, she went on to blame herself for having affronted others and after for having overmuch trusted in him whom she had good reason to believe her enemy; and on this wise she abode a great while. Then, looking if there were no way of descending and seeing none, she fell again to her lamentation and gave herself up to bitter thought, saying in herself, 'Alas, unhappy woman! What will be said of thy brothers and kinsfolk and neighbours and generally of all the people of Florence, when it shall be known that thou has been found here naked? Thy repute, that hath hitherto been so great, will be known to have been false; and shouldst thou seek to frame lying excuses for thyself, (if indeed there are any to be found) the accursed scholar, who knoweth all thine affairs, will not suffer thee lie. Oh wretched woman, that wilt at one stroke have lost the youth so ill-fatedly beloved and thine own honour!'

Therewithal she fell into such a passion of woe that she was like to cast herself down from the tower to the ground; but, the sun being now risen and she drawing near to one side of the walls of the tower, to look if any boy should pass with cattle, whom she might send for her maid, it chanced that the scholar, who had slept awhile at the foot of a bush, awaking, saw her and she him; whereupon quoth he to her, 'Good day, madam; are the damsels come yet?' The lady, seeing and hearing him, began afresh to weep sore and besought him to come within the tower, so she might speak with him. In this he was courteous enough to comply with her and she laying herself prone on the platform and showing only her head at the opening, said, weeping, 'Assuredly, Rinieri, if I gave thee an ill night, thou hast well avenged thyself of me, for that, albeit it is July, I have thought to freeze this night, naked as I am, more by token that I have so sore bewept both the trick I put upon thee and mine own folly in believing thee that it is a wonder I have any eyes left in my head. Wherefore I entreat thee, not for the love of me, whom thou hast no call to love, but for the love of thyself, who are a gentleman, that thou be content, for vengeance of the injury I did thee, with that which thou hast already done and cause fetch me my clothes and suffer me come down hence, nor seek to take from me that which thou couldst not after restore me, an thou wouldst, to wit, my honour; for, if I took from thee the being with me that night, I can render thee many nights for that one, whenassoever it liketh thee. Let this, then, suffice and let it content thee, as a man of honour, to have availed to avenge thyself and to have caused me confess it. Seek not to use thy strength against a woman; no glory is it for an eagle to have overcome a dove, wherefore, for the love of God and thine own honour, have pity on me.'

The scholar, with stern mind revolving in himself the injury suffered and seeing her weep and beseech, felt at once both pleasure and annoy; pleasure in the revenge which he had desired more than aught else, and annoy he felt, for that his humanity moved him to compassion of the unhappy woman. However, humanity availing not to overcome the fierceness of his appetite [for vengeance], 'Madam Elena,' answered he, 'if my prayers (which, it is true, I knew not to bathe with tears nor to make honeyed, as thou presently knowest to proffer thine,) had availed, the night when I was dying of cold in thy snow-filled courtyard, to procure me to be put of thee but a little under cover, it were a light matter to me to hearken now unto thine; but, if thou be presently so much more concerned for thine honour than in the past and it be grievous to thee to abide up there naked, address these thy prayers to him in whose arms thou didst not scruple, that night which thou thyself recallest, to abide naked, hearing me the while go about thy courtyard, chattering with my teeth and trampling the snow, and get thee succour of him; cause him fetch thee thy clothes and set thee the ladder, whereby thou mayest descend, and study to inform him with tenderness for thine honour, the which thou hast not scrupled both now and a thousand other times to imperil for him. Why dost thou not call him to come help thee? To whom pertaineth it more than unto him? Thou art his; and what should he regard or succour, an he regard not neither succour thee? Call him, silly woman that thou art, and prove if the love thou bearest him and thy wits and his together can avail to deliver thee from my folly, whereof, dallying with him the while, thou questionedst aforetime whether himseemed the greater, my folly or the love thou borest him.[3] Thou canst not now be lavish to me of that which I desire not, nor couldst thou deny it to me, an I desired it; keep thy nights for thy lover, an it chance that thou come off hence alive; be they thine and his. I had overmuch of one of them and it sufficeth me to have been once befooled. Again, using thy craft and wiliness in speech, thou studiest, by extolling me, to gain my goodwill and callest me a gentleman and a man of honour, thinking thus to cajole me into playing the magnanimous and forebearing to punish thee for thy wickedness; but thy blandishments shall not now darken me the eyes of the understanding, as did thy disloyal promises whilere. I know myself, nor did I learn so much of myself what while I sojourned at Paris as thou taughtest me in one single night of thine. But, granted I were indeed magnanimous, thou art none of those towards whom magnanimity should be shown; the issue of punishment, as likewise of vengeance, in the case of wild beasts such as thou art, behoveth to be death, whereas for human beings that should suffice whereof thou speakest. Wherefore, albeit I am no eagle, knowing thee to be no dove, but a venomous serpent, I mean to pursue thee, as an immemorial enemy, with every hate and all my might, albeit this that I do to thee can scarce properly be styled vengeance, but rather chastisement, inasmuch as vengeance should overpass the offence and this will not attain thereto; for that, an I sought to avenge myself, considering to what a pass thou broughtest my soul, thy life, should I take it from thee, would not suffice me, no, nor the lives of an hundred others such as thou, since, slaying thee, I should but slay a vile, wicked and worthless trull of a woman. And what a devil more account (setting aside this thy scantling of fair favour,[4] which a few years will mar, filling it with wrinkles,) art thou than whatsoever other sorry serving-drab? Whereas it was no fault of thine that thou failedst of causing the death of a man of honour, as thou styledst me but now, whose life may yet in one day be of more service to the world than an hundred thousand of thy like could be what while the world endureth. I will teach thee, then, by means of this annoy that thou sufferest, what it is to flout men of sense, and particularly scholars, and will give thee cause never more, an thou comest off alive, to fall into such a folly. But, an thou have so great a wish to descend, why dost thou not cast thyself down? On this wise, with God's help, thou wilt, by breaking thy neck, at once deliver thyself from the torment, wherein it seemeth to thee thou art, and make me the joyfullest man in the world. Now, I have no more to say to thee. I knew to contrive on such wise that I caused thee go up thither; do thou now contrive to come down thence, even as thou knewest to befool me.'

What while the scholar spoke thus, the wretched lady wept without ceasing and the time lapsed by, the sun still rising high and higher; but, when she saw that he was silent, she said, 'Alack, cruel man, if the accursed night was so grievous to thee and if my default seem to thee so heinous a thing that neither my young beauty nor my bitter tears and humble prayers may avail to move thee to any pity, at least let this act of mine alone some little move thee and abate the rigour of thy rancour, to wit, that I but now trusted in thee and discovered to thee mine every secret, opening withal to thy desire a way whereby thou mightest avail to make me cognizant of my sin; more by token that, except I had trusted in thee, thou hadst had no means of availing to take of me that vengeance, which thou seemest to have so ardently desired. For God's sake, leave thine anger and pardon me henceforth; I am ready, so thou wilt but forgive me and bring me down hence, altogether to renounce yonder faithless youth and to have thee alone to lover and lord, albeit thou decriest my beauty, avouching it short-lived and little worth; natheless, whatever it be, compared with that of other women, yet this I know, that, if for nought else, it is to be prized for that it is the desire and pastime and delight of men's youth, and thou art not old. And albeit I am cruelly entreated of thee, I cannot believe withal that thou wouldst fain see me die so unseemly a death as were the casting myself down from this tower, as in desperation, before thine eyes, wherein, an thou was not a liar as thou are since become, I was erst so pleasing. Alack, have ruth on me for God's sake and pity's! The sun beginneth to wax hot, and like as the overmuch cold irked me this night, even so doth the heat begin to do me sore annoy.'

The scholar, who held her in parley for his diversion, answered, 'Madam, thou hast not presently trusted thine honour in my hands for any love that thou borest me, but to regain him whom thou hast lost, wherefore it meriteth but greater severity, and if thou think that this way alone was apt and opportune unto the vengeance desired of me, thou thinkest foolishly; I had a thousand others; nay, whilst feigning to love thee, I had spread a thousand snares about thy feet, and it would not have been long, had this not chanced, ere thou must of necessity have fallen into one of them, nor couldst thou have fallen into any but it had caused thee greater torment and shame than this present, the which I took, not to ease thee, but to be the quicklier satisfied. And though all else should have failed me, the pen had still been left me, wherewithal I would have written such and so many things of thee and after such a fashion that, whenas thou camest (as thou wouldst have come) to know of them, thou wouldst a thousand times a day have wished thyself never born. The power of the pen is far greater than they imagine who have not proved it with experience. I swear to God (so may He gladden me to the end of this vengeance that I take of thee, even as He hath made me glad thereof in the beginning!) that I would have written such things of thee, that, being ashamed, not to say before other folk, but before thine own self, thou shouldst have put out thine own eyes, not to see thyself in the glass; wherefore let not the little rivulet twit the sea with having caused it wax. Of thy love or that thou be mine, I reck not, as I have already said, a jot; be thou e'en his, an thou may, whose thou wast erst and whom, as I once hated, so at this present I love, having regard unto that which he hath wrought towards thee of late. You women go falling enamoured of young springalds and covet their love, for that you see them somewhat fresher of colour and blacker of beard and they go erect and jaunty and dance and joust, all which things they have had who are somewhat more in years, ay, and these know that which those have yet to learn. Moreover, you hold them better cavaliers and deem that they fare more miles in a day than men of riper age. Certes, I confess that they jumble a wench's furbelows more briskly; but those more in years, being men of experience, know better where the fleas stick, and little meat and savoury is far and away rather to be chosen than much and insipid, more by token that hard trotting undoth and wearieth folk, how young soever they be, whereas easy going, though belike it bring one somewhat later to the inn, at the least carrieth him thither unfatigued. You women perceive not, animals without understanding that you are, how much ill lieth hid under this scantling of fair seeming. Young fellows are not content with one woman; nay, as many as they see, so many do they covet and of so many themseemeth they are worthy; wherefore their love cannot be stable, and of this thou mayst presently of thine own experience bear very true witness. Themseemeth they are worthy to be worshipped and caressed of their mistresses and they have no greater glory than to vaunt them of those whom they have had; the which default of theirs hath aforetime cast many a woman into the arms of the monks, who tell no tales. Albeit thou sayst that never did any know of thine amours, save thy maid and myself, thou knowest it ill and believest awry, an thou think thus. His[5] quarter talketh well nigh of nothing else, and thine likewise; but most times the last to whose ears such things come is he to whom they pertain. Young men, to boot, despoil you, whereas it is given you[6] of men of riper years. Since, then, thou hast ill chosen, be thou his to whom thou gavest thyself and leave me, of whom thou madest mock, to others, for that I have found a mistress of much more account than thou, who hath been wise enough to know me better than thou didst. And that thou mayst carry into the other world greater assurance of the desire of mine eyes than meseemeth thou gatherest from my words, do but cast thyself down forthright and thy soul, being, as I doubt not it will be, straightway received into the arms of the devil, will be able to see if mine eyes be troubled or not at seeing thee fall headlong. But, as medoubteth thou wilt not consent to do me so much pleasure, I counsel thee, if the sun begin to scorch thee, remember thee of the cold thou madest me suffer, which an thou mingle with the heat aforesaid, thou wilt without fail feel the sun attempered.'

The disconsolate lady, seeing that the scholar's words tended to a cruel end, fell again to weeping and said, 'Harkye, since nothing I can say availeth to move thee to pity of me, let the love move thee, which thou bearest that lady whom thou hast found wiser than I and of whom thou sayst thou art beloved, and for the love of her pardon me and fetch me my clothes, so I may dress myself, and cause me descend hence.' Therewith the scholar began to laugh and seeing that tierce was now passed by a good hour, replied, 'Marry, I know not how to say thee nay, since thou conjurest me by such a lady; tell me where thy clothes are and I will go for them and help thee come down from up yonder.' The lady, believing this, was somewhat comforted and showed him where she had laid her clothes; whereupon he went forth of the tower and bidding his servant not depart thence, but abide near at hand and watch as most he might that none should enter there till such time as he should return, went off to his friend's house, where he dined at his ease and after, whenas himseemed time, betook himself to sleep; whilst the lady, left upon the tower, albeit some little heartened with fond hope, natheless beyond measure woebegone, sat up and creeping close to that part of the wall where there was a little shade, fell a-waiting, in company of very bitter thoughts. There she abode, now hoping and now despairing of the scholar's return with her clothes, and passing from one thought to another, she presently fell asleep, as one who was overcome of dolour and who had slept no whit the past night.

The sun, which was exceeding hot, being now risen to the meridian, beat full and straight upon her tender and delicate body and upon her head, which was all uncovered, with such force that not only did it burn her flesh, wherever it touched it, but cracked and opened it all over little by little, and such was the pain of the burning that it constrained her to awake, albeit she slept fast. Feeling herself on the roast and moving somewhat, it seemed as if all her scorched skin cracked and clove asunder for the motion, as we see happen with a scorched sheepskin, if any stretch it, and to boot her head irked her so sore that it seemed it would burst, which was no wonder. And the platform of the tower was so burning hot that she could find no restingplace there either for her feet or for otherwhat; wherefore, without standing fast, she still removed now hither and now thither, weeping. Moreover, there being not a breath of wind, the flies and gads flocked thither in swarms and settling upon her cracked flesh, stung her so cruelly that each prick seemed to her a pike-stab; wherefore she stinted not to fling her hands about, still cursing herself, her life, her lover and the scholar.

Being thus by the inexpressible heat of the sun, by the flies and the gads and likewise by hunger, but much more by thirst, and by a thousand irksome thoughts, to boot, tortured and stung and pierced to the quick, she started to her feet and addressed herself to look if she might see or hear any one near at hand, resolved, whatever might betide thereof, to call him and crave aid. But of this resource also had her unfriendly fortune deprived her. The husbandmen were all departed from the fields for the heat, more by token that none had come that day to work thereingh, they being all engaged in threshing out their sheaves beside their houses; wherefore she heard nought but crickets and saw the Arno, which latter sight, provoking in her desire of its waters, abated not her thirst, but rather increased it. In several places also she saw thickets and shady places and houses here and there, which were all alike to her an anguish for desire of them. What more shall we say of the ill-starred lady? The sun overhead and the heat of the platform underfoot and the stings of the flies and gads on every side had so entreated her that, whereas with her whiteness she had overcome the darkness of the foregoing night, she was presently grown red as ruddle,[7] and all bescabbed as she was with blood, had seemed to whoso saw her the foulest thing in the world.

As she abode on this wise, without aught of hope or counsel,[8] expecting death more than otherwhat, it being now past half none, the scholar, arising from sleep and remembering him of his mistress, returned to the tower, to see what was come of her, and sent his servant, who was yet fasting, to eat. The lady, hearing him, came, all weak and anguishful as she was for the grievous annoy she had suffered, overagainst the trap-door and seating herself there, began, weeping, to say, 'Indeed, Rinieri, thou hast beyond measure avenged thyself, for, if I made thee freeze in my courtyard by night, thou hast made me roast, nay burn, on this tower by day and die of hunger and thirst to boot; wherefore I pray thee by the One only God that thou come up hither and since my heart suffereth me not give myself death with mine own hands, give it me thou, for that I desire it more than aught else, such and so great are the torments I endure. Or, an thou wilt not do me that favour, let bring me, at the least, a cup of water, so I may wet my mouth, whereunto my tears suffice not; so sore is the drouth and the burning that I have therein.'

The scholar knew her weakness by her voice and eke saw, in part, her body all burnt up of the sun; wherefore and for her humble prayers there overcame him a little compassion of her; but none the less he answered, 'Wicked woman, thou shalt not die by my hands; nay, by thine own shalt thou die, an thou have a mind thereto; and thou shalt have of me as much water for the allaying of thy heat as I had fire of thee for the comforting of my cold. This much I sore regret that, whereas it behoved me heal the infirmity of my cold with the heat of stinking dung, that of thy heat will be healed with the coolth of odoriferous rose-water; and whereas I was like to lose both limbs and life, thou, flayed by this heat, wilt abide fair none otherwise than doth the snake, casting its old skin.' 'Alack, wretch that I am,' cried the lady, 'God give beauties on such wise acquired to those who wish me ill! But thou, that are more cruel than any wild beast, how couldst thou have the heart to torture me after this fashion? What more could I expect from thee or any other, if I had done all thy kinsfolk to death with the cruellest torments? Certes, meknoweth not what greater cruelty could be wreaked upon a traitor who had brought a whole city to slaughter than that whereto thou hast exposed me in causing me to be roasted of the sun and devoured of the flies and withal denying me a cup of water, whenas to murderers condemned of justice is oftentimes, as they go to their death, given to drink of wine, so but they ask it. Nay, since I see thee abide firm in thy savage cruelty and that my sufferance availeth not anywise to move thee, I will resign myself with patience to receive death, so God, whom I beseech to look with equitable eyes upon this thy dealing, may have mercy upon my soul.'

So saying, she dragged herself painfully to the midward of the platform, despairing to escape alive from so fierce a heat; and not once, but a thousand times, over and above her other torments, she thought to swoon for thirst, still weeping and bemoaning her illhap. However, it being now vespers and it seeming to the scholar he had done enough, he caused his servant take up the unhappy lady's clothes and wrap them in his cloak; then, betaking himself to her house, he found her maid seated before the door, sad and disconsolate and unknowing what to do, and said to her, 'Good woman, what is come of thy mistress?' 'Sir,' replied she, 'I know not. I thought to find her this morning in the bed whither meseemed I saw her betake herself yesternight; but I can find her neither there nor otherwhere and know not what is come of her; wherefore I suffer the utmost concern. But you, sir, can you not tell me aught of her?' Quoth he, 'Would I had had thee together with her whereas I have had her, so I might have punished thee of thy default, like as I have punished her for hers! But assuredly thou shalt not escape from my hands, ere I have so paid thee for thy dealings that thou shalt never more make mock of any man, without remembering thee of me.' Then to his servant, 'Give her the clothes,' quoth he, 'and bid her go to her mistress, an she will.' The man did his bidding and gave the clothes to the maid, who, knowing them and hearing what Rinieri said, was sore afraid lest they should have slain her mistress and scarce refrained from crying out; then, the scholar being done, she set out with the clothes for the tower, weeping the while.

Now it chanced that one of the lady's husbandmen had that day lost two of his swine and going in search of them, came, a little after the scholar's departure, to the tower. As he went spying about everywhere if he should see his hogs, he heard the piteous lamentation made of the miserable lady and climbing up as most he might, cried out, 'Who maketh moan there aloft?' The lady knew her husbandman's voice and calling him by name, said to him, 'For God's sake, fetch me my maid and contrive so she may come up hither to me.' Whereupon quoth the man, recognizing her, 'Alack, madam, who hath brought you up yonder? Your maid hath gone seeking you all day; but who had ever thought you could be here?' Then, taking the ladder-poles, he set them up in their place and addressed himself to bind the cross-staves thereto with withy bands.[9] Meanwhile, up came the maid, who no sooner entered the tower than, unable any longer to hold her tongue, she fell to crying out, buffeting herself the while with her hands, 'Alack, sweet my lady, where are you?' The lady, hearing her, answered as loudliest she might, 'O sister mine, I am here aloft. Weep not, but fetch me my clothes quickly.' When the maid heard her speak, she was in a manner all recomforted and with the husbandman's aid, mounting the ladder, which was now well nigh repaired, reached the sollar, where, whenas she saw her lady lying naked on the ground, all forspent and wan, more as she were a half-burnt log than a human being, she thrust her nails into her own face and fell a-weeping over her, no otherwise than as she had been dead.

The lady besought her for God's sake be silent and help her dress herself, and learning from her that none knew where she had been save those who had carried her the clothes and the husbandman there present, was somewhat comforted and prayed them for God's sake never to say aught of the matter to any one. Then, after much parley, the husbandman, taking the lady in his arms, for that she could not walk, brought her safely without the tower; but the unlucky maid, who had remained behind, descending less circumspectly, made a slip of the foot and falling from the ladder to the ground, broke her thigh, whereupon she fell a-roaring for the pain, that it seemed a lion. The husbandman, setting the lady down on a plot of grass, went to see what ailed the maid and finding her with her thigh broken, carried her also to the grass-plat and laid her beside her mistress, who, seeing this befallen in addition to her other troubles and that she had broken her thigh by whom she looked to have been succoured more than by any else, was beyond measure woebegone and fell a-weeping afresh and so piteously that not only could the husbandman not avail to comfort her, but himself fell a-weeping like wise. But presently, the sun being now low, he repaired, at the instance of the disconsolate lady, lest the night should overtake them there, to his own house, and there called his wife and two brothers of his, who returned to the tower with a plank and setting the maid thereon, carried her home, whilst he himself, having comforted the lady with a little cold water and kind words, took her up in his arms and brought her to her own chamber.

His wife gave her a wine-sop to eat and after, undressing her, put her to bed; and they contrived that night to have her and her maid carried to Florence. There, the lady, who had shifts and devices great plenty, framed a story of her fashion, altogether out of conformity with that which had passed, and gave her brothers and sisters and every one else to believe that this had befallen herself and her maid by dint of diabolical bewitchments. Physicians were quickly at hand, who, not without putting her to very great anguish and vexation, recovered the lady of a sore fever, after she had once and again left her skin sticking to the sheets, and on like wise healed the maid of her broken thigh. Wherefore, forgetting her lover, from that time forth she discreetly forbore both from making mock of others and from loving, whilst the scholar, hearing that the maid had broken her thigh, held himself fully avenged and passed on, content, without saying otherwhat thereof. Thus, then, did it befall the foolish young lady of her pranks, for that she thought to fool it with a scholar as she would have done with another, unknowing that scholars,—I will not say all, but the most part of them,—know where the devil keepeth his tail. Wherefore, ladies, beware of making mock of folk, and especially of scholars."

---

1. A proverbial way of saying that he bore malice and was vindictive.
2. Lit. out of hand (*fuor di mano*).
3. Boccaccio here misquotes himself. See earlier, where the lady says to her lover, "Whether seemeth to thee the greater, his wit or the love I bear him?" This is only one of the numberless instances of negligence and inconsistency which occur in the Decameron and which make it evident to the student that it must have passed into the hands of the public without the final revision and correction by the author, that *limæ labor* without which no book is complete and which is especially necessary in the case of such a work as the present, where Boccaccio figures as the virtual creator of Italian prose.
4. Lit. face, aspect (*viso*).
5. *i.e.* thy lover's.
6. *V'è donato, i.e.* young lovers look to receive gifts of their mistresses, whilst those of more mature age bestow them.
7. Lit. red as rabies (*rabbia*). Some commentators suppose that Boccaccio meant to write *robbia*, madder.
8. *i.e.* resource (*consiglio*). See ante, passim.
9. Boccaccio appears to have forgotten to mention that Rinieri had broken the rounds of the ladder, when he withdrew it, apparently to place an additional obstacle in the way of the lady's escape.

❧ 8 ❧

THE EIGHTH STORY

TWO MEN CONSORTING TOGETHER, ONE LIETH
WITH THE WIFE OF HIS COMRADE, WHO, BECOMING
AWARE THEREOF, DOTH WITH HER ON SUCH WISE
THAT THE OTHER IS SHUT UP IN A CHEST, UPON
WHICH HE LIETH WITH HIS WIFE, HE BEING INSIDE
THE WHILE

ELENA'S TROUBLES had been irksome and grievous to the ladies to hear; natheless, for that they deemed them in part justly befallen her, they passed them over with more moderate compassion, albeit they held the scholar to have been terribly stern and obdurate, nay, cruel. But, Pampinea being now come to the end of her story, the queen charged Fiammetta follow on, who, nothing loath to obey, said, "Charming ladies, for that meseemeth the severity of the offended scholar hath somedele distressed you, I deem it well to solace your ruffled spirits with somewhat more diverting; wherefore I purpose to tell you a little story of a young man who received an injury in a milder spirit and avenged it after a more moderate fashion, by which you may understand that, whenas a man goeth about to avenge an injury suffered, it should suffice him to give as good as he hath gotten, without seeking to do hurt overpassing the behoof of the feud.

You must know, then, that there were once in Siena, as I have understood aforetime, two young men in easy enough case and of good city families, whereof one was named Spinelloccio Tanena and the other Zeppa di Mino, and they were next-door neighbours in Camollia.[1] These two young men still companied together and loved each other, to all appearance, as they had been brothers, or better; and each of them had a very fair wife. It chanced that Spinelloccio, by dint of much frequenting Zeppa's house, both when the latter was at home and when he was abroad, grew so private with his wife that he ended by lying with her, and on this wise they abode a pretty while, before any became aware thereof. However, at last, one day, Zeppa being at home, unknown to his wife, Spinelloccio came to call him and the lady said that he was abroad; whereupon the other came straightway up into the house and finding her in the saloon and seeing none else there, he took her in his arms and fell to kissing her and she him. Zeppa, who saw this, made no sign, but abode hidden to see in what the game should result and presently saw his wife and Spinelloccio betake themselves, thus embraced, to a chamber and there lock themselves in; whereat he was sore angered. But, knowing that his injury would not become less for making an outcry nor for otherwhat, nay, that shame would but wax therefor, he set himself to think what revenge he should take thereof, so his soul might abide content, without the thing being known all about, and himseeming, after long consideration, he had found the means, he abode hidden so long as Spinelloccio remained with his wife.

As soon as the other was gone away, he entered the chamber and there finding the lady, who had not yet made an end of adjusting her head-veils, which Spinelloccio had plucked down in dallying with her, said to her, 'Wife, what dost thou?' Quoth she, 'Seest thou not?' And Zeppa answered, 'Ay, indeed, I have seen more than I could wish.' So saying, he taxed her with that which had passed and she, in sore affright, confessed to him, after much parley, that which she could not aptly deny of her familiarity with Spinelloccio. Then she began to crave him pardon, weeping, and Zeppa said to her, 'Harkye, wife, thou hast done ill, and if thou wilt have me pardon it to thee, bethink thee punctually to do that which I shall enjoin thee, which is this; I will have thee bid Spinelloccio find an occasion to part company with me to-morrow morning, towards tierce, and come hither to thee. When he is here I will come back and so soon as thou hearest me, do thou make him enter this chest here and lock him therein. Then, when thou shalt have done this, I will tell thee what else thou shalt do; and have thou no fear of doing this, for that I promise thee I will do him no manner of hurt.' The lady, to satisfy him, promised to do his bidding, and so she did.

The morrow come and Zeppa and Spinelloccio being together towards tierce, the latter, who had promised the lady to be with her at that hour, said to the former, 'I am to dine this morning with a friend, whom I would not keep waiting for me; wherefore God be with thee.' Quoth Zeppa, 'It is not dinner-time yet awhile'; but Spinelloccio answered, 'No matter; I am to speak with him also of an affair of mine, so that needs must I be there betimes.' Accordingly, taking leave of him, he fetched a compass and making for Zeppa's house, entered a chamber with the latter's wife. He had not been there long ere Zeppa returned, whom when the lady heard, feigning to be mightily affrighted, she made him take refuge in the chest, as her husband had bidden her, and locking him therein, went forth of the chamber. Zeppa, coming up, said, 'Wife, is it dinner-time?' 'Ay,' answered she, 'forthright.' Quoth he, 'Spinelloccio is gone to dine this morning with a friend of his and hath left his wife alone; get thee to the window and call her and bid her come dine with us.' The lady, fearing for herself and grown therefor mighty obedient, did as he bade her and Spinelloccio's wife, being much pressed by her and hearing that her own husband was to dine abroad, came hither.

Zeppa made much of her and whispering his wife begone into the kitchen, took her familiarly by the hand and carried her into the chamber, wherein no sooner were they come than, turning back, he locked the door within. When the lady saw him do this, she said, 'Alack, Zeppa, what meaneth this? Have you then brought me hither for this? Is this the love you bear Spinelloccio and the loyal companionship you practise towards him?' Whereupon quoth Zeppa, drawing near to the chest wherein was her husband locked up and holding her fast, 'Madam, ere thou complainest, hearken to that which I have to say to thee. I have loved and love Spinelloccio as a brother, and yesterday, albeit he knoweth it not, I found that the trust I had in him was come to this, that he lieth with my wife even as with thee. Now, for that I love him, I purpose not to take vengeance of him, save on such wise as the offence hath been; he hath had my wife and I mean to have thee. An thou wilt not, needs must I take him here and for that I mean not to let this affront go unpunished, I will play him such a turn that neither thou nor he shall ever again be glad.' The lady, hearing this and believing what Zeppa said, after many affirmations made her of him, replied, 'Zeppa mine, since this vengeance is to fall on me, I am content, so but thou wilt contrive, notwithstanding what we are to do, that I may abide at peace with thy wife, even as I intend to abide with her, notwithstanding this that she hath done to me.' 'Assuredly,' rejoined Zeppa, 'I will do it; and to boot, I will give thee a precious and fine jewel as none other thou hast.' So saying, he embraced her; then, laying her flat on the chest, there to his heart's content, he solaced himself with her, and she with him.

Spinelloccio, hearing from within the chest all that Zeppa said his wife's answer and feeling the morrisdance[2] that was toward over his head, was at first so sore despited that himseemed he should die; and but that he stood in fear of Zeppa, he had rated his wife finely, shut up as he was. However, bethinking himself that the offence had begun with him and that Zeppa was in his right to do as he did and had indeed borne himself towards him humanely and like a comrade, he presently resolved in himself to be, an he would, more than ever his friend. Zeppa, having been with the lady so long as it pleased him, dismounted from the chest, and she asking for the promised jewel, he opened the chamber-door and called his wife, who said nought else than 'Madam, you have given me a loaf for my bannock'; and this she said laughing. To her quoth Zeppa, 'Open this chest.' Accordingly she opened it and therein Zeppa showed the lady her husband, saying, 'Here is the jewel I promised thee.' It were hard to say which was the more abashed of the twain, Spinelloccio, seeing Zeppa and knowing that he knew what he had done, or his wife, seeing her husband and knowing that he had both heard and felt that which she had done over his head. But Spinelloccio, coming forth of the chest, said, without more parley, 'Zeppa, we are quits; wherefore it is well, as thou saidst but now to my wife, that we be still friends as we were, and that, since there is nothing unshared between us two but our wives, we have these also in common.' Zeppa was content and they all four dined together in the utmost possible harmony; and thenceforward each of the two ladies had two husbands and each of the latter two wives, without ever having any strife or grudge anent the matter."

---

1. *Quære*, the street of that name?
2. *Danza trivigiana*, lit. Trevisan dance, O.E. the shaking of the sheets.

✢ 9 ✢

THE NINTH STORY

MASTER SIMONE THE PHYSICIAN, HAVING BEEN
INDUCED BY BRUNO AND BUFFALMACCO TO REPAIR
TO A CERTAIN PLACE BY NIGHT, THERE TO BE MADE
A MEMBER OF A COMPANY THAT GOETH A-ROVING, IS
CAST BY BUFFALMACCO INTO A TRENCH FULL OF
ORDURE AND THERE LEFT

AFTER THE LADIES had chatted awhile over the community of wives practised by the two Siennese, the queen, with whom alone it rested to tell, so she would not do Dioneo an unright, began on this wise: "Right well, lovesome ladies, did Spinelloccio deserve the cheat put upon him by Zeppa; wherefore meseemeth he is not severely to be blamed (as Pampinea sought awhile ago to show), who putteth a cheat on those who go seeking it or deserve it. Now Spinelloccio deserved it, and I mean to tell you of one who went seeking it for himself. Those who tricked him, I hold not to be blameworthy, but rather commendable, and he to whom it was done was a physician, who, having set out for Bologna a sheepshead, returned to Florence all covered with miniver.[1]

As we see daily, our townsmen return hither from Bologna, this a judge, that a physician and a third a notary, tricked out with robes long and large and scarlets and minivers and store of other fine paraphernalia, and make a mighty brave show, to which how far the effects conform we may still see all day long. Among the rest a certain Master Simone da Villa, richer in inherited goods than in learning, returned hither, no great while since, a doctor of medicine, according to his own account, clad all in scarlet[2] and with a great miniver hood, and took a house in the street which we call nowadays the Via del Cocomero. This said Master Simone, being thus newly returned, as hath been said, had, amongst other his notable customs, a trick of asking whosoever was with him who was no matter what man he saw pass in the street, and as if of the doings and fashions of men he should compound the medicines he gave his patients, he took note of all and laid them all up in his memory. Amongst others on whom it occurred to him more particularly to cast his eyes were two painters of whom it hath already twice to-day been discoursed, namely, Bruno and Buffalmacco, who were neighbours of his and still went in company. Himseeming they recked less of the world and lived more merrily than other folk, as was indeed the case, he questioned divers persons of their condition and hearing from all that they were poor men and painters, he took it into his head that it might not be they lived so blithely of their poverty, but concluded, for that he had heard they were shrewd fellows, that they must needs derive very great profits from some source unknown to the general; wherefore he was taken with a desire to clap up an acquaintance, an he might, with them both, or at least with one of them, and succeeded in making friends with Bruno. The latter, perceiving, after he had been with him a few times, that the physician was a very jackass, began to give himself the finest time in the world with him and to be hugely diverted with his extraordinary humours, whilst Master Simone in like manner took a marvellous delight in his company.

After a while, having sundry times bidden him to dinner and thinking himself entitled in consequence to discourse familiarly with him, he discovered to him the wonderment that he felt at him and Buffalmacco, how, being poor men, they lived so merrily, and besought him to apprise him how they did. Bruno, hearing this talk from the physician and himseeing the question was one of his wonted witless impertinences, fell a-laughing in his sleeve, and bethinking himself to answer him according as his folly deserved, said, 'Doctor, there are not many whom I would tell how we do; but you I shall not scruple to tell, for that you are a friend and I know you will not repeat it to any. It is true we live, my friend and I, as merrily and as well as it appeareth to you, nay, more so, albeit neither of our craft nor of revenues we derive from any possessions might we have enough to pay for the very water we consume. Yet I would not, for all that, have you think that we go steal; nay, we go a-roving, and thence, without hurt unto any, we get us all to which we have a mind or for which we have occasion; hence the merry life you see us lead.'

The physician, hearing this and believing it, without knowing what it was, marvelled exceedingly and forthright conceiving an ardent desire to know what manner of thing this going a-roving might be, besought him very urgently to tell him, affirming that he would assuredly never discover it to any. 'Alack, doctor,' cried Bruno, 'what is this you ask me? This you would know is too great a secret and a thing to undo me and drive me from the world, nay, to bring me into the mouth of the Lucifer of San Gallo,[3] should any come to know it. But so great is the love I bear your right worshipful pumpkinheadship of Legnaja[4] and the confidence I have in you that I can deny you nothing you would have; wherefore I will tell it you, on condition that you swear to me by the cross at Montesone, never, as you have promised, to tell it to any one.

The physician declared that he would never repeat what he should tell him, and Bruno said, 'You must know, then, honey doctor mine, that not long since there was in this city a great master in necromancy, who was called Michael Scott, for that he was of Scotland, and who received the greatest hospitality from many gentlemen, of whom few are nowadays alive; wherefore, being minded to depart hence, he left them, at their instant prayers, two of his ablest disciples, whom he enjoined still to hold themselves in readiness to satisfy every wish of the gentlemen who had so worshipfully entertained him. These two, then, freely served the aforesaid gentlemen in certain amours of theirs and other small matters, and afterward, the city and the usages of the folk pleasing them, they determined to abide there always. Accordingly, they contracted great and strait friendship with certain of the townfolk, regarding not who they were, whether gentle or simple, rich or poor, but solely if they were men comfortable to their own usances; and to pleasure these who were thus become their friends, they founded a company of maybe five-and-twenty men, who should foregather twice at the least in the month in some place appointed of them, where being assembled, each should tell them his desire, which they would forthright accomplish unto him for that night. Buffalmacco and I, having an especial friendship and intimacy with these two, were put of them on the roll of the aforesaid company and are still thereof. And I may tell you that, what time it chanceth that we assemble together, it is a marvellous thing to see the hangings about the saloon where we eat and the tables spread on royal wise and the multitude of noble and goodly servants, as well female as male, at the pleasure of each one who is of the company, and the basons and ewers and flagons and goblets and the vessels of gold and silver, wherein we eat and drink, more by token of the

387

many and various viands that are set before us, each in its season, according to that which each one desireth. I could never avail to set out to you what and how many are the sweet sounds of innumerable instruments and the songs full of melody that are heard there; nor might I tell you how much wax is burned at these suppers nor what and how many are the confections that are consumed there nor how costly are the wines that are drunken. But I would not have you believe, good saltless pumpkinhead mine, that we abide there in this habit and with these clothes that you see us wear every day; nay, there is none of us of so little account but would seem to you an emperor, so richly are we adorned with vestments of price and fine things. But, over all the other pleasures that be there is that of fair ladies, who, so one but will it, are incontinent brought thither from the four quarters of the world. There might you see the Sovereign Lady of the Rascal-Roughs, the Queen of the Basques, the wife of the Soldan, the Empress of the Usbeg Tartars, the Driggledraggletail of Norroway, the Moll-a-green of Flapdoodleland and the Madkate of Woolgathergreen. But why need I enumerate them to you? There be all the queens in the world, even, I may say, to the Sirreverence of Prester John, who hath his horns amiddleward his arse; see you now? There, after we have drunken and eaten confections and walked a dance or two, each lady betaketh herself to her bedchamber with him at whose instance she hath been brought thither. And you must know that these bedchambers are a very paradise to behold, so goodly they are; ay, and they are no less odoriferous than are the spice-boxes of your shop, whenas you let bray cummin-seed, and therein are beds that would seem to you goodlier than that of the Doge of Venice, and in these they betake themselves to rest. Marry, what a working of the treadles, what a hauling-to of the battens to make the cloth close, these weaveresses keep up, I will e'en leave you to imagine; but of those who fare best, to my seeming, are Buffalmacco and myself, for that he most times letteth come thither the Queen of France for himself, whilst I send for her of England, the which are two of the fairest ladies in the world, and we have known so to do that they have none other eye in their head than us.[5] Wherefore you may judge for yourself if we can and should live and go more merrily than other men, seeing we have the love of two such queens, more by token that, whenas we would have a thousand or two thousand florins of them, we get them not. This, then, we commonly style going a-roving, for that, like as the rovers take every man's good, even so do we, save that we are in this much different from them that they never restore that which they take, whereas we return it again, whenas we have used it. Now, worthy doctor mine, you have heard what it is we call going a-roving; but how strictly this requireth to be kept secret you can see for yourself, and therefore I say no more to you nor pray you thereof.'

The physician, whose science reached no farther belike than the curing children of the scald-head, gave as much credit to Bruno's story as had been due to the most manifest truth and was inflamed with as great desire to be received into that company as might be kindled in any for the most desirable thing in the world; wherefore he made answer to him that assuredly it was no marvel if they went merry and hardly constrained himself to defer requesting him to bring him to be there until such time as, having done him further hospitality, he might with more confidence proffer his request to him. Accordingly, reserving this unto a more favourable season, he proceeded to keep straiter usance with Bruno, having him morning and evening to eat with him and showing him an inordinate affection; and indeed so great and so constant was this their commerce that it seemed as if the physician could not nor knew how to live without the painter. The latter, finding himself in good case, so he might not appear ungrateful for the hospitality shown him, had painted Master Simone a picture of Lent in his saloon, besides an Agnus Dei at the entering in of his chamber and a chamber-pot over the street-door, so those who had occasion for his advice might know how to distinguish him from the others; and in a little gallery he had, he had depictured him the battle of the rats and the cats, which appeared to the physician a very fine thing. Moreover, he said whiles to him, whenas he had not supper with him overnight, 'I was at the society yesternight and being a trifle tired of the Queen of England, I caused fetch me the Dolladoxy of the Grand Cham of Tartary.' 'What meaneth Dolladoxy?' asked Master Simone. 'I do not understand these names.' 'Marry, doctor mine,' replied Bruno, 'I marvel not thereat, for I have right well heard that Porcograsso and Vannacena[6] say nought thereof.' Quoth the physician. 'Thou meanest Ipocrasso and Avicenna.' 'I' faith,' answered Bruno, 'I know not; I understand your names as ill as you do mine; but Dolladoxy in the Grand Cham's lingo meaneth as much as to say Empress in our tongue. Egad, you would think her a plaguy fine woman! I dare well say she would make you forget your drugs and your clysters and all your plasters.'

On this wise he bespoke him at one time and another, to enkindle him the more, till one night, what while it chanced my lord doctor held the light to Bruno, who was in act to paint the battle of the rats and the cats, the former, himseeming he had now well taken him with his hospitalities, determined to open his mind to him, and accordingly, they being alone together, he said to him, 'God knoweth, Bruno, there is no one alive for whom I would do everything as I would for thee; indeed, shouldst thou bid me go hence to Peretola, methinketh it would take little to make me go thither; wherefore I would not have thee marvel if I require thee of somewhat familiarly and with confidence. As thou knowest, it is no great while since thou bespokest me of the fashions of your merry company, wherefore so great a longing hath taken me to be one of you that never did I desire aught so much. Nor is this my desire without cause, as thou shalt see, if ever it chance that I be of your company; for I give thee leave to make mock of me an I cause not come thither the finest serving-wench thou ever setst eyes on. I saw her but last year at Cacavincigli and wish her all my weal;[7] and by the body of Christ, I had e'en given her half a score Bolognese groats, so she would but have consented to me; but she would not. Wherefore, as most I may, I prithee teach me what I must do to avail to be of your company and do thou also do and contrive so I may be thereof. Indeed, you will have in me a good and loyal comrade, ay, and a worshipful. Thou seest, to begin with, what a fine man I am and how well I am set up on my legs. Ay, and I have a face as it were a rose, more by token that I am a doctor of medicine, such as I believe you have none among you. Moreover, I know many fine things and goodly canzonets; marry, I will sing you one.' And incontinent he fell a-singing.

Bruno had so great a mind to laugh that he was like to burst; however he contained himself and the physician, having made an end of his song, said, 'How deemedst thou thereof?' 'Certes,' answered Bruno, 'there's no Jew's harp but would lose with you, so archigothically do you caterwarble it.' Quoth Master Simone, 'I tell thee thou wouldst never have believed it, hadst thou not heard me.' 'Certes,' replied Bruno, 'you say sooth!' and the physician went on, 'I know store of others; but let that be for the present. Such as thou seest me, my father was a gentleman, albeit he abode in the country, and I myself come by my mother of the Vallecchio family. Moreover, as thou mayst have seen, I have the finest books and gowns of any physician in Florence. Cock's faith, I have a gown that stood me, all reckoned, in nigh upon an hundred pounds of doits, more than half a score years ago; wherefore I pray thee as most I may, to bring me to be of your company, and by Cock's faith, an thou do it, thou mayst be as ill as thou wilt, for I will never take a farthing of thee for my services.'

Bruno, hearing this and the physician seeming to him a greater numskull than ever, said, 'Doctor, hold the light a thought more this way and take patience till I have made these rats their tails, and after I will answer you.' The tails being finished, Bruno made believe that the physician's request was exceeding irksome to him and said, 'Doctor mine, these be great things you would do for me and I acknowledge it; nevertheless, that which you ask of me, little as it may be for the greatness of your brain, is yet to me a very grave matter, nor know I any one in

GIOVANNI BOCCACCIO

the world for whom, it being in my power, I would do it, an I did it not for you, both because I love you as it behoveth and on account of your words, which are seasoned with so much wit that they would draw the straps out of a pair of boots, much more me from my purpose; for the more I consort with you, the wiser you appear to me. And I may tell you this, to boot, that, though I had none other reason, yet do I wish you well, for that I see you enamoured of so fair a creature as is she of whom you speak. But this much I will say to you; I have no such power in this matter as you suppose and cannot therefore do for you that which were behoving; however, an you will promise me, upon your solemn and surbated[8] faith, to keep it me secret, I will tell you the means you must use and meseemeth certain that, with such fine books and other gear as you tell me you have, you will gain your end.'

Quoth the doctor, 'Say on in all assurance; I see thou art not yet well acquainted with me and knowest not how I can keep a secret. There be few things indeed that Messer Guasparruolo da Saliceto did, whenas he was judge of the Provostry at Forlimpopoli, but he sent to tell me, for that he found me so good a secret-keeper.[9] And wilt thou judge an I say sooth? I was the first man whom he told that he was to marry Bergamina: seest thou now?' 'Marry, then,' rejoined Bruno, 'all is well; if such a man trusted in you, I may well do so. The course you must take is on this wise. You must know that we still have to this our company a captain and two counsellors, who are changed from six months to six months, and without fail, at the first of the month, Buffalmacco will be captain and I shall be counsellor; for so it is settled. Now whoso is captain can do much by way of procuring whomsoever he will to be admitted into the company; wherefore meseemeth you should seek, inasmuch as you may, to gain Buffalmacco's friendship and do him honour. He is a man, seeing you so wise, to fall in love with you incontinent, and whenas with your wit and with these fine things you have you shall have somedele ingratiated yourself with him, you can make your request to him; he will not know how to say you nay. I have already bespoken him of you and he wisheth you all the weal in the world; and whenas you shall have done this, leave me do with him.' Quoth the physician, 'That which thou counsellest liketh me well. Indeed, an he be a man who delighteth in men of learning and talketh but with me a little, I will engage to make him go still seeking my company, for that, as for wit, I have so much thereof that I could stock a city withal and yet abide exceeding wise.'

This being settled, Bruno imparted the whole matter to Buffalmacco, wherefore it seemed to the latter a thousand years till they should come to do that which this arch-zany went seeking. The physician, who longed beyond measure to go a-roving, rested not till he made friends with Buffalmacco, which he easily succeeded in doing, and therewithal he fell to giving him, and Bruno with him, the finest suppers and dinners in the world. The two painters, like the accommodating gentlemen they were, were nothing loath to engage with him and having once tasted the excellent wines and fat capons and other good things galore, with which he plied them, stuck very close to him and ended by quartering themselves upon him, without awaiting overmuch invitation, still declaring that they would not do this for another. Presently, whenas it seemed to him time, the physician made the same request to Buffalmacco as he had made Bruno aforetime; whereupon Buffalmacco feigned himself sore chagrined and made a great outcry against Bruno, saying, 'I vow to the High God of Pasignano that I can scarce withhold myself from giving thee such a clout over the head as should cause thy nose drop to thy heels, traitor that thou art; for none other than thou hath discovered these matters to the doctor.'

Master Simone did his utmost to excuse Bruno, saying and swearing that he had learned the thing from another quarter, and after many of his wise words, he succeeded in pacifying Buffalmacco; whereupon the latter turned to him and said, 'Doctor mine, it is very evident that you have been at Bologna and have brought back a close mouth to these parts; and I tell you moreover that you have not learnt your A B C on the apple as many blockheads are fain to do; nay, you have learned it aright on the pumpkin, that is so long;[10] and if I mistake not, you were baptized on a Sunday.[11] And albeit Bruno hath told me that you told me that you studied medicine there, meseemeth you studied rather to learn to catch men, the which you, with your wit and your fine talk, know better to do than any man I ever set eyes on.' Here the physician took the words out of his mouth and breaking in, said to Bruno, 'What a thing it is to talk and consort with learned men! Who would so have quickly apprehended every particular of my intelligence as hath this worthy man? Thou didst not half so speedily become aware of my value as he; but, at the least, that which I told thee, whenas thou saidst to me that Buffalmacco delighted in learned men, seemeth it to thee I have done it?' 'Ay hast thou,' replied Bruno, 'and better.'

Then said the doctor to Buffalmacco, 'Thou wouldst have told another tale, hadst thou seen me at Bologna, where there was none, great or small, doctor or scholar, but wished me all the weal in the world, so well did I know to content them all with my discourse and my wit. And what is more, I never said a word there, but I made every one laugh, so hugely did I please them; and whenas I departed thence, they all set up the greatest lament in the world and would all have had me remain there; nay, to such a pass came it for that I should abide there, that they would have left it to me alone to lecture on medicine to as many students as were there; but I would not, for that I was e'en minded to come hither to certain very great heritages which I have here and which have still been in my family; and so I did.' Quoth Bruno to Buffalmacco, 'How deemest thou? Thou believedst me not, whenas I told it thee. By the Evangels, there is not a leach in these parts who is versed in asses' water to compare with this one, and assuredly thou wouldst not find another of him from here to Paris gates. Marry, hold yourself henceforth [if you can,] from doing that which he will.' Quoth Master Simone, 'Bruno saith sooth; but I am not understood here. You Florentines are somewhat dull of wit; but I would have you see me among the doctors, as I am used to be.' 'Verily, doctor,' said Buffalmacco, 'you are far wiser than I could ever have believed; wherefore to speak to you as it should be spoken to scholars such as you are, I tell you, cut-and-slash fashion,[12] I will without fail procure you to be of our company.'

After this promise the physician redoubled in his hospitalities to the two rogues, who enjoyed themselves [at his expense,] what while they crammed him with the greatest extravagances in the world and fooled him to the top of his bent, promising him to give him to mistress the Countess of Jakes,[13] who was the fairest creature to be found in all the back-settlements of the human generation. The physician enquired who this countess was, whereto quoth Buffalmacco, 'Good my seed-pumpkin, she is a very great lady and there be few houses in the world wherein she hath not some jurisdiction. To say nothing of others, the Minor Friars themselves render her tribute, to the sound of kettle-drums.[14] And I can assure you that, whenas she goeth abroad, she maketh herself well felt,[15] albeit she abideth for the most part shut up. Natheless, it is no great while since she passed by your door, one night that she repaired to the Arno, to wash her feet and take the air a little; but her most continual abiding-place is in Draughthouseland.[16] There go ofttimes about store of her serjeants, who all in token of her supremacy, bear the staff and the plummet, and of her barons many are everywhere to be seen, such as Sirreverence of the Gate, Goodman Turd, Hardcake,[17] Squitterbreech and others, who methinketh are your familiars, albeit you call them not presently to mind. In the soft arms, then, of this great lady, leaving be her of Cacavincigli, we will, an expectation cheat us not, bestow you.'

The physician, who had been born and bred at Bologna, understood not their canting terms and accordingly avouched himself well pleased with the lady in question. Not long after this talk, the painters brought him news that he was accepted to member of the company and the day being come before the night appointed for their assembly, he had them both to dinner. When they had dined, he asked them what means it behoved him take to come thither; whereupon quoth Buffalmacco, 'Look you, doctor, it behoveth you have plenty of assurance; for that, an you be not mighty resolute, you may chance to suffer hindrance and do us very great hurt; and in what it behoveth you to approve yourself very stout-hearted you shall hear. You must find means to be this evening, at the season of the first sleep, on one of the raised tombs which have been lately made without Santa Maria Novella, with one of your finest gowns on your back, so you may make an honourable figure for your first appearance before the company and also because, according to what was told us (we were not there after) the Countess is minded, for that you are a man of gentle birth, to make you a Knight of the Bath at her own proper costs and charges; and there you must wait till there cometh for you he whom we shall send. And so you may be apprised of everything, there will come for you a black horned beast, not overbig, which will go capering about the piazza before you and making a great whistling and bounding, to terrify you; but, when he seeth that you are not to be daunted, he will come up to you quietly. Then do you, without any fear, come down from the tomb and mount the beast, naming neither God nor the Saints; and as soon as you are settled on his back, you must cross your hands upon your breast, in the attitude of obeisance, and touch him no more. He will then set off softly and bring you to us; but if you call upon God or the Saints or show fear, I must tell you that he may chance to cast you off or strike you into some place where you are like to stink for it; wherefore, an your heart misgive you and unless you can make sure of being mighty resolute, come not thither, for you would but do us a mischief, without doing yourself any good.'[18]

Quoth the physician, 'I see you know me not yet; maybe you judge of me by my gloves and long gown. If you knew what I did aforetimes at Bologna anights, when I went a-wenching whiles with my comrades, you would marvel. Cock's faith, there was such and such a night when, one of them refusing to come with us, (more by token that she was a scurvy little baggage, no higher than my fist,) I dealt her, to begin with, good store of cuffs, then, taking her up bodily, I dare say I carried her a crossbowshot and wrought so that needs must she come with us. Another time I remember me that, without any other in my company than a serving-man of mine, I passed yonder alongside the Cemetery of the Minor Friars, a little after the Ave Maria, albeit there had been a woman buried there that very day, and felt no whit of fear; wherefore misdoubt you not of this, for I am but too stout of heart and lusty. Moreover, I tell you that, to do you credit at my coming thither, I will don my gown of scarlet, wherein I was admitted doctor, and we shall see if the company rejoice not at my sight and an I be not made captain out of hand. You shall e'en see how the thing will go, once I am there, since, without having yet set eyes on me, this countess hath fallen so enamoured of me that she is minded to make me a Knight of the Bath. It may be knighthood will not sit so ill on me nor shall I be at a loss to carry it off with worship! Marry, only leave me do.' 'You say very well,' answered Buffalmacco; 'but look you leave us not in the lurch and not come or not be found at the trysting-place, whenas we shall send for you; and this I say for that the weather is cold and you gentlemen doctors are very careful of yourselves thereanent.' 'God forbid!' cried Master Simone. 'I am none of your chilly ones. I reck not of the cold; seldom or never, whenas I rise of a night for my bodily occasions, as a man will bytimes, do I put me on more than my fur gown over my doublet. Wherefore I will certainly be there.'

Thereupon they took leave of him and whenas it began to grow towards night, Master Simone contrived to make some excuse or other to his wife and secretly got out his fine gown; then, whenas it seemed to him time, he donned it and betook himself to Santa Maria Novella, where he mounted one of the aforesaid tombs and huddling himself up on the marble, for that the cold was great, he proceeded to wait the coming of the beast. Meanwhile Buffalmacco, who was tall and robust of his person, made shift to have one of those masks that were wont to be used for certain games which are not held nowadays, and donning a black fur pelisse, inside out, arrayed himself therein on such wise that he seemed a very bear, save that his mask had a devil's face and was horned. Thus accoutred, he betook himself to the new Piazza of Santa Maria, Bruno following him to see how the thing should go. As soon as he perceived that the physician was there, he fell a-capering and caracoling and made a terrible great blustering about the piazza, whistling and howling and bellowing as he were possessed of the devil. When Master Simone, who was more fearful than a woman, heard and saw this, every hair of his body stood on end and he fell a-trembling all over, and it was now he had liefer been at home than there. Nevertheless, since he was e'en there, he enforced himself to take heart, so overcome was he with desire to see the marvels whereof the painters had told him.

After Buffalmacco had raged about awhile, as hath been said, he made a show of growing pacified and coming up to the tomb whereon was the physician, stood stock-still. Master Simone, who was all a-tremble for fear, knew not what to do, whether to mount or abide where he was. However, at last, fearing that the beast should do him a mischief, an he mounted him not, he did away the first fear with the second and coming down from the tomb, mounted on his back, saying softly, 'God aid me!' Then he settled himself as best he might and still trembling in every limb, crossed his hands upon his breast, as it had been enjoined him; whereupon Buffalmacco set off at an amble towards Santa Maria della Scala and going on all fours, brought him hard by the Nunnery of Ripole. In those days there were dykes in that quarter, wherein the tillers of the neighbouring lands let empty the jakes, to manure their fields withal; whereto whenas Buffalmacco came nigh, he went up to the brink of one of them and taking the opportunity, laid hold of one of the physician's legs and jerking him off his back, pitched him clean in, head foremost. Then he fell a-snorting and snarling and capering and raged about awhile; after which he made off alongside Santa Maria della Scala till he came to Allhallows Fields. There he found Bruno, who had taken to flight, for that he was unable to restrain his laughter; and with him, after they had made merry together at Master Simone's expense, he addressed himself to see from afar what the bemoiled physician should do.

My lord leech, finding himself in that abominable place, struggled to arise and strove as best he might to win forth thereof; and after falling in again and again, now here and now there, and swallowing some drachms of the filth, he at last succeeded in making his way out of the dyke, in the woefullest of plights, bewrayed from head to foot and leaving his bonnet behind him. Then, having wiped himself as best he might with his hands and knowing not what other course to take, he returned home and knocked till it was opened to him. Hardly was he entered, stinking as he did, and the door shut again ere up came Bruno and Buffalmacco, to hear how he should be received of his wife, and standing hearkening, they heard the lady give him the foulest rating was ever given poor devil, saying, 'Good lack, what a pickle thou art in! Thou hast been gallanting it to some other woman and must needs seek to cut a figure with thy gown of scarlet! What, was not I enough for thee? Why, man alive, I could suffice to a whole people, let alone thee. Would God they had choked thee, like as they cast thee whereas thou deservedst to be thrown! Here's a fine physician for you, to have a wife of his own and go a-gadding anights after other folk's womankind!' And with these and many other words of the same fashion she gave not over tormenting him till midnight, what while the physician let wash himself from head to foot.

Next morning up came Bruno and Buffalmacco, who had painted all their flesh under their clothes with livid blotches, such as beatings use to make, and entering the physician's house, found him already arisen. Accordingly they went in to him and found the whole place full of stench, for that they had not yet been able so to clean everything that it should not stink there. Master Simone, seeing them enter, came to meet them and bade God give them good day; whereto the two rogues, as they had agreed beforehand, replied with an angry air, saying, 'That say we not to you; nay, rather, we pray God give you so many ill years that you may die a dog's death, as the most disloyal man and the vilest traitor alive; for it was no thanks to you that, whereas we studied to do you pleasure and worship, we were not slain like dogs. As it is, thanks to your disloyalty, we have gotten so many buffets this past night that an ass would go to Rome for less, without reckoning that we have gone in danger of being expelled the company into which we had taken order for having you received. An you believe us not, look at our bodies and see how they have fared.' Then, opening their clothes in front, they showed him, by an uncertain light, their breasts all painted and covered them up again in haste.

The physician would have excused himself and told of his mishaps and how and where he had been cast; but Buffalmacco said, 'Would he had thrown you off the bridge into the Arno! Why did you call on God and the Saints? Were you not forewarned of this?' 'By God His faith,' replied the physician, 'I did it not.' 'How?' cried Buffalmacco. 'You did not call on them? Egad, you did it again and again; for our messenger told us that you shook like a reed and knew not where you were. Marry, for the nonce you have befooled us finely; but never again shall any one serve us thus, and we will yet do you such honour thereof as you merit.' The physician fell to craving pardon and conjuring them for God's sake not to dishonour him and studied to appease them with the best words he could command. And if aforetime he had entreated them with honour, from that time forth he honoured them yet more and made much of them, entertaining them with banquets and otherwhat, for fear lest they should publish his shame. Thus, then, as you have heard, is sense taught to whoso hath learned no great store thereof at Bologna."

---

1. *i.e.* with the doctor's hood of miniver.
2. The colour of the doctors' robes of that time.
3. The commentators note here that on the church door of San Gallo was depicted an especially frightful Lucifer, with many mouths.
4. Legnaja is said to be famous for big pumpkins.
5. *i.e.* they think of and cherish us alone, holding us as dear as their very eyes.
6. *i.e.* Fat-hog and Get-thee-to-supper, burlesque perversions of the names Ipocrasso (Hippocrates) and Avicenna.
7. *i.e.* love her beyond anything in the world. For former instances of this idiomatic expression, see ante, passim.
8. Syn. cauterized (*calterita*), a nonsensical word employed by Bruno for the purpose of mystifying the credulous physician.
9. Syn. secretary, confidant (*segretaro*).
10. A play of words upon *mela* (apple) and *mellone* (pumpkin). *Mellone* is strictly a water-melon; but I have rendered it "pumpkin," to preserve the English idiom, "pumpkinhead" being our equivalent for the Italian "melon," used in the sense of dullard, noodle.
11. According to the commentators, "baptized on a Sunday" anciently signified a simpleton, because salt (which is constantly used by the Italian classical writers as a synonym for wit or sense) was not sold on Sundays.
12. Syn. confusedly (*frastagliatamente*).
13. *La Contessa di Civillari, i.e.* the public sewers. Civillari, according to the commentators, was the name of an alley in Florence, where all the ordure and filth of the neighbourhood was deposited and stored in trenches for manure.
14. *Nacchere*, syn. a loud crack of wind.
15. Syn. smelt (*sentito*).
16. *Laterina, i.e.* Latrina.
17. Lit. Broom-handle (*Manico della Scopa*).
18. Lit. "do *yourself* a mischief, without doing *us* any good"; but the sequel shows that the contrary is meant, as in the text.

❧ 10 ❧

THE TENTH STORY

A CERTAIN WOMAN OF SICILY ARTFULLY DESPOILETH A MERCHANT OF THAT WHICH HE HAD BROUGHT TO PALERMO; BUT HE, MAKING BELIEVE TO HAVE RETURNED THITHER WITH MUCH GREATER PLENTY OF MERCHANDISE THAN BEFORE, BORROWETH MONEY OF HER AND LEAVETH HER WATER AND TOW IN PAYMENT

How MUCH THE queen's story in divers places made the ladies laugh, it needed not to ask; suffice it to say that there was none of them to whose eyes the tears had not come a dozen times for excess of laughter: but, after it had an end, Dioneo, knowing that it was come to his turn to tell, said, "Gracious ladies, it is a manifest thing that sleights and devices are the more pleasing, the subtler the trickster who is thereby artfully outwitted. Wherefore, albeit you have related very fine stories, I mean to tell you one, which should please you more than any other that hath been told upon the same subject, inasmuch as she who was cheated was a greater mistress of the art of cheating others than was any of the men or women who were cozened by those of whom you have told.

There used to be, and belike is yet, a custom, in all maritime places which have a port, that all merchants who come thither with merchandise, having unloaded it, should carry it all into a warehouse, which is in many places called a customhouse, kept by the commonalty or by the lord of the place. There they give unto those who are deputed to that end a note in writing of all their merchandise and the value thereof, and they thereupon make over to each merchant a storehouse, wherein he layeth up his goods under lock and key. Moreover, the said officers enter in the book of the Customs, to each merchant's credit, all his merchandise, causing themselves after he paid their dues of the merchants, whether for all his said merchandise or for such part thereof as he withdraweth from the customhouse. By this book of the Customs the brokers mostly inform themselves of the quality and the quantity of the goods that are in bond there and also who are the merchants that own them; and with these latter, as occasion serveth them, they treat of exchanges and barters and sales and other transactions. This usance, amongst many other places, was current at Palermo in Sicily, where likewise there were and are yet many women, very fair of their person, but sworn enemies to honesty, who would be and are by those who know them not held great ladies and passing virtuous and who, being given not to shave, but altogether to flay men, no sooner espy a merchant there than they inform themselves by the book of the Customs of that which he hath there and how much he can do;[1] after which by their lovesome and engaging fashions and with the most dulcet words, they study to allure the said merchants and draw them into the snare of their love; and many an one

395

have they aforetime lured thereinto, from whom they have wiled great part of their merchandise; nay, many have they despoiled of all, and of these there be some who have left goods and ship and flesh and bones in their hands, so sweetly hath the barberess known to ply the razor.

It chanced, not long since, that there came thither, sent by his masters, one of our young Florentines, by name Niccolo da Cignano, though more commonly called Salabaetto, with as many woollen cloths, left on his hands from the Salerno fair, as might be worth some five hundred gold florins, which having given the customhouse officers the invoice thereof, he laid up in a magazine and began, without showing overmuch haste to dispose of them, to go bytimes a-pleasuring about the city. He being of a fair complexion and yellow-haired and withal very sprightly and personable, it chanced that one of these same barberesses, who styled herself Madam Biancofiore, having heard somewhat of his affairs, cast her eyes on him; which he perceiving and taking her for some great lady, concluded that he pleased her for his good looks and bethought himself to order this amour with the utmost secrecy; wherefore, without saying aught thereof to any, he fell to passing and repassing before her house. She, noting this, after she had for some days well enkindled him with her eyes, making believe to languish for him, privily despatched to him one of her women, who was a past mistress in the procuring art and who, after much parley, told him, well nigh with tears in her eyes, that he had so taken her mistress with his comeliness and his pleasing fashions that she could find no rest day or night; wherefore, whenas it pleased him, she desired, more than aught else, to avail to foregather with him privily in a bagnio; then, pulling a ring from her pouch, she gave it to him on the part of her mistress. Salabaetto, hearing this, was the joyfullest man that was aye and taking the ring, rubbed it against his eyes and kissed it; after which he set it on his finger and replied to the good woman that, if Madam Biancofiore loved him, she was well requited it, for that he loved her more than his proper life and was ready to go whereassoever it should please her and at any hour. The messenger returned to her mistress with this answer and it was appointed Salabaetto out of hand at what bagnio he should expect her on the ensuing day after vespers.

Accordingly, without saying aught of the matter to any, he punctually repaired thither at the hour appointed him and found the bagnio taken by the lady; nor had he waited long ere there came two slave-girls laden with gear and bearing on their heads, the one a fine large mattress of cotton wool and the other a great basket full of gear. The mattress they set on a bedstead in one of the chambers of the bagnio and spread thereon a pair of very fine sheets, laced with silk, together with a counterpane of snow-white Cyprus buckram[2] and two pillows wonder-curiously wrought.[3] Then, putting off their clothes they entered the bath and swept it all and washed it excellent well. Nor was it long ere the lady herself came thither, with other two slave-girls, and accosted Salabaetto with the utmost joy; then, as first she had commodity, after she had both clipped and kissed him amain, heaving the heaviest sighs in the world, she said to him, 'I know not who could have brought me to this pass, other than thou; thou hast kindled a fire in my vitals, little dog of a Tuscan!' Then, at her instance, they entered the bath, both naked, and with them two of the slave-girls; and there, without letting any else lay a finger on him, she with her own hands washed Salabaetto all wonder-well with musk and clove-scented soap; after which she let herself be washed and rubbed of the slave-girls. This done, the latter brought two very white and fine sheets, whence came so great a scent of roses that everything there seemed roses, in one of which they wrapped Salabaetto and in the other the lady and taking them in their arms, carried them both to the bed prepared for them. There, whenas they had left sweating, the slave-girls did them loose from the sheets wherein they were wrapped and they abode naked in the others, whilst the girls brought out of the basket wonder-goodly casting-bottles of silver, full of sweet waters, rose and jessamine and orange and citron-flower scented, and sprinkled them all therewith; after which boxes of succades and wines of great price were produced and they refreshed themselves awhile.

It seemed to Salabaetto as he were in Paradise and he cast a thousand glances at the lady, who was certes very handsome, himseeming each hour was an hundred years till the slave-girls should begone and he should find himself in her arms. Presently, at her commandment, the girls departed the chamber, leaving a flambeau alight there; whereupon she embraced Salabaetto and he her, and they abode together a great while, to the exceeding pleasure of the Florentine, to whom it seemed she was all afire for love of him. Whenas it seemed to her time to rise, she called the slave-girls and they clad themselves; then they recruited themselves somedele with a second collation of wine and sweetmeats and washed their hands and faces with odoriferous waters; after which, being about to depart, the lady said to Salabaetto, 'So it be agreeable to thee, it were doing me a very great favour an thou camest this evening to sup and lie the night with me.' Salabaetto, who was by this time altogether captivated by her beauty and the artful pleasantness of her fashions and firmly believed himself to be loved of her as he were the heart out of her body, replied, 'Madam, your every pleasure is supremely agreeable to me, wherefore both to-night and at all times I mean to do that which shall please you and that which shall be commanded me of you.'

Accordingly the lady returned to her house, where she caused well bedeck her bedchamber with her dresses and gear and letting make ready a splendid supper, awaited Salabaetto, who, as soon as it was grown somewhat dark, betook himself thither and being received with open arms, supped with all cheer and commodity of service. Thereafter they betook themselves into the bedchamber, where he smelt a marvellous fragrance of aloes-wood and saw the bed very richly adorned with Cyprian singing-birds[4] and store of fine dresses upon the pegs, all which things together and each of itself made him conclude that this must be some great and rich lady. And although he had heard some whispers to the contrary anent her manner of life, he would not anywise believe it; or, if he e'en gave so much credit thereto as to allow that she might erst have cozened others, for nothing in the world could he have believed that this might possibly happen to himself. He lay that night with her in the utmost delight, still waxing more enamoured, and in the morning she girt him on a quaint and goodly girdle of silver, with a fine purse thereto, saying, 'Sweet my Salabaetto, I commend myself to thy remembrance, and like as my person is at thy pleasure, even so is all that is here and all that dependeth upon me at thy service and commandment.' Salabaetto, rejoiced, embraced and kissed her; then, going forth of her house, he betook himself whereas the other merchants were used to resort.

On this wise consorting with her at one time and another, without its costing him aught in the world, and growing every hour more entangled, it befell that he sold his stuffs for ready money and made a good profit thereby; of which the lady incontinent heard, not from him, but from others, and Salabaetto being come one night to visit her, she fell to prattling and wantoning with him, kissing and clipping him and feigning herself so enamoured of him that it seemed she must die of love in his arms. Moreover, she would fain have given him two very fine hanaps of silver that she had; but he would not take them, for that he had had of her, at one time and another, what was worth a good thirty gold florins, without availing to have her take of him so much as a groat's worth. At last, whenas she had well enkindled him by showing herself so enamoured and freehanded, one of her slave-girls called her, as she had ordained beforehand; whereupon she left the chamber and coming back, after awhile, in tears cast herself face downward on the bed and fell to making the woefullest lamentation ever woman made. Salabaetto, marvelling at this, caught her in his arms and fell a-weeping with her and saying, 'Alack, heart of my body, what aileth thee thus suddenly? What is the cause of this grief? For God's sake, tell it me, my soul.' The lady, after letting herself be long entreated, answered,

'Woe's me, sweet my lord, I know not what to say or to do; I have but now received letters from Messina and my brother writeth me that, should I sell or pawn all that is here,[5] I must without fail send him a thousand gold florins within eight days from this time, else will his head be cut off; and I know not how I shall do to get this sum so suddenly. Had I but fifteen days' grace, I would find a means of procuring it from a certain quarter whence I am to have much more, or I would sell one of our farms; but, as this may not be, I had liefer be dead than that this ill news should have come to me.'

So saying, she made a show of being sore afflicted and stinted not from weeping; whereupon quoth Salabaetto, whom the flames of love had bereft of great part of his wonted good sense, so that he believed her tears to be true and her words truer yet, 'Madam, I cannot oblige you with a thousand florins, but five hundred I can very well advance you, since you believe you will be able to return them to me within a fortnight from this time; and this is of your good fortune that I chanced but yesterday to sell my stuffs; for, had it not been so, I could not have lent you a groat.' 'Alack,' cried the lady, 'hast thou then been straitened for lack of money? Marry, why didst thou not require me thereof? Though I have not a thousand, I had an hundred and even two hundred to give thee. Thou hast deprived me of all heart to accept of thee the service thou profferest me.' Salabaetto was more than ever taken with these words and said, 'Madam, I would not have you refrain on that account, for, had I had such an occasion therefor as you presently have, I would assuredly have asked you.' 'Alack, Salabaetto mine,' replied the lady, 'now know I aright that thine is a true and perfect love for me, since, without waiting to be required, thou freely succoureth me, in such a strait, with so great a sum of money. Certes, I was all thine without this, but with this I shall be far more so; nor shall I ever forget that I owe thee my brother's life. But God knoweth I take it sore unwillingly, seeing that thou art a merchant and that with money merchants transact all their affairs; however, since need constraineth me, and I have certain assurance of speedily restoring it to thee, I will e'en take it; and for the rest, an I find no readier means, I will pawn all these my possessions.' So saying, she let herself fall, weeping, on Salabaetto's neck. He fell to comforting her and after abiding the night with her, he, next morning, to approve himself her most liberal servant, without waiting to be asked by her, carried her five hundred right gold florins, which she received with tears in her eyes, but laughter in her heart, Salabaetto contenting himself with her simple promise.

As soon as the lady had the money, the signs began to change, and whereas before he had free access to her whenassoever it pleased him, reasons now began to crop up, whereby it betided him not to win admission there once out of seven times, nor was he received with the same countenance nor the same caresses and rejoicings as before. And the term at which he was to have had his monies again being, not to say come, but past by a month or two and he requiring them, words were given him in payment. Thereupon his eyes were opened to the wicked woman's arts and his own lack of wit, wherefore, feeling that he could say nought of her beyond that which might please her concerning the matter, since he had neither script nor other evidence thereof, and being ashamed to complain to any, as well for that he had been forewarned thereof as for fear of the scoffs which he might reasonably expect for his folly, he was beyond measure woeful and inwardly bewailed his credulity.

At last, having had divers letters from his masters, requiring him to change[6] the monies in question and remit them to them, he determined to depart, lest, an he did it not, his default should be discovered there, and accordingly, going aboard a little ship, he betook himself, not to Pisa, as he should have done, but to Naples. There at that time was our gossip Pietro dello Canigiano, treasurer to the Empress of Constantinople, a man of great understanding and subtle wit and a fast friend of Salabaetto and his family; and to him, as to a very discreet man, the disconsolate Florentine recounted that which he had done and the mischance that had befallen him, requiring him of aid and counsel, so he might contrive to gain his living there, and avouching his intention nevermore to return to Florence. Canigiano was concerned for this and said, 'Ill hast thou done and ill hast thou carried thyself; thou hast disobeyed thy masters and hast, at one cast, spent a great sum of money in wantonness; but, since it is done, we must look for otherwhat.'[7] Accordingly, like a shrewd man as he was, he speedily bethought himself what was to be done and told it to Salabaetto, who was pleased with the device and set about putting it in execution. He had some money and Canigiano having lent him other some, he made up a number of bales well packed and corded; then, buying a score of oil-casks and filling them, he embarked the whole and returned to Palermo, where, having given the customhouse officers the bill of lading and the value of the casks and let enter everything to his account, he laid the whole up in the magazines, saying that he meant not to touch them till such time as certain other merchandise which he expected should be come.

Biancofiore, getting wind of this and hearing that the merchandise he had presently brought with him was worth good two thousand florins, without reckoning what he looked for, which was valued at more than three thousand, bethought herself that she had flown at too small game and determined to restore him the five hundred florins, so she might avail to have the greater part of the five thousand. Accordingly, she sent for him and Salabaetto, grown cunning, went to her; whereupon, making believe to know nothing of that which he had brought with him, she received him with a great show of fondness and said to him, 'Harkye, if thou wast vexed with me, for that I repaid thee not thy monies on the very day....' Salabaetto fell a-laughing and answered; 'In truth, madam, it did somewhat displease me, seeing I would have torn out my very heart to give it you, an I thought to pleasure you withal; but I will have you hear how I am vexed with you. Such and so great is the love I bear you, that I have sold the most part of my possessions and have presently brought hither merchandise to the value of more than two thousand florins and expect from the westward as much more as will be worth over three thousand, with which I mean to stock me a warehouse in this city and take up my sojourn here, so I may still be near you, meseeming I fare better of your love than ever lover of his lady.'

'Look you, Salabaetto,' answered the lady, 'every commodity of thine is mighty pleasing to me, as that of him whom I love more than my life, and it pleaseth me amain that thou art returned hither with intent to sojourn here, for that I hope yet to have good time galore with thee; but I would fain excuse myself somedele to thee for that, whenas thou wast about to depart, thou wouldst bytimes have come hither and couldst not, and whiles thou camest and wast not so gladly seen as thou wast used to be, more by token that I returned thee not thy monies at the time promised. Thou must know that I was then in very great concern and sore affliction, and whoso is in such case, how much soever he may love another, cannot always show him so cheerful a countenance or pay him such attention as he might wish. Moreover, thou must know that it is mighty uneasy for a woman to avail to find a thousand gold florins; all day long we are put off with lies and that which is promised us is not performed unto us; wherefore needs must we in our turn lie unto others. Hence cometh it, and not of my default, that I gave thee not back thy monies. However, I had them a little after thy departure, and had I known whither to send them, thou mayst be assured that I would have remitted them to thee; but, not knowing this, I kept them for thee.' Then, letting fetch a purse wherein were the very monies he had brought her, she put it into his hand, saying, 'Count them if there be five hundred.' Never was Salabaetto so glad; he counted them and finding them five hundred, put them up and said, 'Madam, I am assured that you say sooth; but you have done enough [to convince me of your love for me,] and I tell you that, for this and for the love I bear you, you could never require me, for any your occasion, of whatsoever sum I might command, but I would oblige you therewith; and whenas I am established here, you may put this to the proof.'

Having again on this wise renewed his loves with her in words, he fell again to using amically with her, whilst she made much of him and showed him the greatest goodwill and honour in the world, feigning the utmost love for him. But he, having a mind to return her cheat for cheat, being one day sent for by her to sup and sleep with her, went thither so chapfallen and so woebegone that it seemed as he would die. Biancofiore, embracing him and kissing him, began to question him of what ailed him to be thus melancholy, and he, after letting himself be importuned a good while, answered, 'I am a ruined man, for that the ship, wherein is the merchandise I expected, hath been taken by the corsairs of Monaco and held to ransom in ten thousand gold florins, whereof it falleth to me to pay a thousand, and I have not a farthing, for that the five hundred pieces thou returnedst to me I sent incontinent to Naples to lay out in cloths to be brought hither; and should I go about at this present to sell the merchandise I have here, I should scarce get a penny for two pennyworth, for that it is no time for selling. Nor am I yet so well known that I could find any here to help me to this, wherefore I know not what to do or to say; for, if I send not the monies speedily, the merchandise will be carried off to Monaco and I shall never again have aught thereof.'

The lady was mightily concerned at this, fearing to lose him altogether, and considering how she should do, so he might not go to Monaco, said, 'God knoweth I am sore concerned for the love of thee; but what availeth it to afflict oneself thus? If I had the monies, God knoweth I would lend them to thee incontinent; but I have them not. True, there is a certain person here who obliged me the other day with the five hundred florins that I lacked; but he will have heavy usance for his monies; nay, he requireth no less than thirty in the hundred, and if thou wilt borrow of him, needs must he be made secure with a good pledge. For my part, I am ready to engage for thee all these my goods and my person, to boot, for as much as he will lend thereon; but how wilt thou assure him of the rest?' Salabaetto readily apprehended the reason that moved her to do him this service and divined that it was she herself who was to lend him the money; wherewith he was well pleased and thanking her, answered that he would not be put off for exorbitant usance, need constraining him. Moreover, he said that he would give assurance of the merchandise he had in the customhouse, letting inscribe it to him who should lend him the money; but that needs must be kept the key of the magazines, as well that he might be able to show his wares, an it were required of him, as that nothing might be touched or changed or tampered withal.

The lady answered that it was well said and that this was good enough assurance; wherefore, as soon as the day was come, she sent for a broker, in whom she trusted greatly, and taking order with him of the matter, gave him a thousand gold florins, which he lent to Salabaetto, letting inscribe in his own name at the customhouse that which the latter had there; then, having made their writings and counter-writings together and being come to an accord,[8] they occupied themselves with their other affairs. Salabaetto, as soonest he might, embarked, with the fifteen hundred gold florins, on board a little ship and returned to Pietro dello Canigiano at Naples, whence he remitted to his masters, who had despatched him with the stuffs, a good and entire account thereof. Then, having repaid Pietro and every other to whom he owed aught, he made merry several days with Canigiano over the cheat he had put upon the Sicilian trickstress; after which, resolved to be no more a merchant, he betook himself to Ferrara.

Meanwhile, Biancofiore, finding that Salabaetto had left Palermo, began to marvel and wax misdoubtful and after having awaited him good two months, seeing that he came not, she caused the broker force open the magazines. Trying first the casks, which she believed to be filled with oil, she found them full of seawater, save that there was in each maybe a runlet of oil at the top near the bunghole. Then, undoing the bales, she found them all full of tow, with the exception of two, which were stuffs; and in brief, with all that was there, there was not more than two hundred florins' worth. Wherefore Biancofiore, confessing herself outwitted, long lamented the five hundred florins repaid and yet more the thousand lent, saying often, 'Who with a Tuscan hath to do, Must nor be blind nor see askew.' On this wise, having gotten nothing for her pains but loss and scorn, she found, to her cost, that some folk know as much as others."

No sooner had Dioneo made an end of his story than Lauretta, knowing the term to be come beyond which she was not to reign and having commended Canigiano's counsel (which was approved good by its effect) and Salabaetto's shrewdness (which was no less commendable) in carrying it into execution, lifted the laurel from her own head and set it on that of Emilia, saying, with womanly grace, "Madam, I know not how pleasant a queen we shall have of you; but, at the least, we shall have a fair one. Look, then, that your actions be conformable to your beauties." So saying, she returned to her seat, whilst Emilia, a thought abashed, not so much at being made queen as to see herself publicly commended of that which women use most to covet, waxed such in face as are the new-blown roses in the dawning. However, after she had kept her eyes awhile lowered, till the redness had given place, she took order with the seneschal of that which concerned the general entertainment and presently said, "Delightsome ladies, it is common, after oxen have toiled some part of the day, confined under the yoke, to see them loosed and eased thereof and freely suffered to go a-pasturing, where most it liketh them, about the woods; and it is manifest also that leafy gardens, embowered with various plants, are not less, but much more fair than groves wherein one seeth only oaks. Wherefore, seeing how many days we have discoursed, under the restraint of a fixed law, I opine that, as well unto us as to those whom need constraineth to labour for their daily bread, it is not only useful, but necessary, to play the truant awhile and wandering thus afield, to regain strength to enter anew under the yoke. Wherefore, for that which is to be related to-morrow, ensuing your delectable usance of discourse, I purpose not to restrict you to any special subject, but will have each discourse according as it pleaseth him, holding it for certain that the variety of the things which will be said will afford us no less entertainment than to have discoursed of one alone; and having done thus, whoso shall come after me in the sovranty may, as stronger than I, avail with greater assurance to restrict us within the limits of the wonted laws." So saying, she set every one at liberty till supper-time.

All commended the queen of that which she had said, holding it sagely spoken, and rising to their feet, addressed themselves, this to one kind of diversion and that to another, the ladies to weaving garlands and to gambolling and the young men to gaming and singing. On this wise they passed the time until the supper-hour, which being come, they supped with mirth and good cheer about the fair fountain and after diverted themselves with singing and dancing according to the wonted usance. At last, the queen, to ensue the fashion of her predecessors, commanded Pamfilo to sing a song, notwithstanding those which sundry of the company had already sung of their freewill; and he readily began thus:

> Such is thy pleasure, Love
> And such the allegresse I feel thereby
> That happy, burning in thy fire, am I.
>
> The abounding gladness in my heart that glows,

For the high joy and dear
Whereto thou hast me led,
Unable to contain there, overflows
And in my face's cheer
Displays my happihead;
For being enamouréd
In such a worship-worthy place and high
Makes eath to me the burning I aby.

I cannot with my finger what I feel
Limn, Love, nor do I know
My bliss in song to vent;
Nay, though I knew it, needs must I conceal,
For, once divulged, I trow
'Twould turn to dreariment.
Yet am I so content,
All speech were halt and feeble, did I try
The least thereof with words to signify.

Who might conceive it that these arms of mine
Should anywise attain
Whereas I've held them aye,
Or that my face should reach so fair a shrine
As that, of favour fain
And grace, I've won to? Nay,
Such fortune ne'er a day
Believed me were; whence all afire am I,
Hiding the source of my liesse thereby.

This was the end of Pamfilo's song, whereto albeit it had been completely responded of all, there was none but noted the words thereof with more attent solicitude than pertained unto him, studying to divine that which, as he sang, it behoved him to keep hidden from them; and although sundry went imagining various things, nevertheless none happened upon the truth of the case.[9] But the queen, seeing that the song was ended and that both young ladies and men would gladly rest themselves, commanded that all should betake themselves to bed.

---

1. *i.e.* what he is worth.
2. *Bucherame.* The word "buckram" was anciently applied to the finest linen cloth, as is apparently the case here; see Ducange, voce *Boquerannus*, and Florio, voce *Bucherame*.
3. *i.e.* in needlework.
4. "It was the custom in those days to attach to the bedposts sundry small instruments in the form of birds, which, by means of certain mechanical devices, gave forth sounds modulated like the song of actual birds."—*Fanfani.*
5. Syn. that which belongeth to us (*ciò che ci è,*) *ci,* as I have before noted, signifying both "here" and "us," dative and accusative.
6. *i.e.* procure bills of exchange for.
7. *i.e.* we must see what is to be done.
8. *i.e.* having executed and exchanged the necessary legal documents for the proper carrying out of the transaction and completed the matter to their mutual satisfaction.
9. The song sung by Pamfilo (under which name, as I have before pointed out, the author appears to represent himself) apparently alludes to Boccaccio's amours with the Princess Maria of Naples (Fiammetta), by whom his passion was returned in kind.

DAY THE NINTH

Here Beginneth the Ninth Day of the Decameron
Wherein Under the Governance of Emilia Each
Discourseth According As It Pleaseth Him and of
That Which Is Most to His Liking

The light, from whose resplendence the night fleeth, had already changed all the eighth heaven[1] from azure to watchet-colour[2] and the flowerets began to lift their heads along the meads, when Emilia, uprising, let call the ladies her comrades and on like wise the young men, who, being come, fared forth, ensuing the slow steps of the queen, and betook themselves to a coppice but little distant from the palace. Therein entering, they saw the animals, wild goats and deer and others, as if assured of security from the hunters by reason of the prevailing pestilence, stand awaiting them no otherwise than as they were grown without fear or tame, and diverted themselves awhile with them, drawing near, now to this one and now to that, as if they would fain lay hands on them, and making them run and skip. But, the sun now waxing high, they deemed it well to turn back. They were all garlanded with oak leaves, with their hands full of flowers and sweet-scented herbs, and whoso encountered them had said no otherwhat than "Or these shall not be overcome of death or it will slay them merry." On this wise, then, they fared on, step by step, singing and chatting and laughing, till they came to the palace, where they found everything orderly disposed and their servants full of mirth and joyous cheer. There having rested awhile, they went not to dinner till half a dozen canzonets, each merrier than other, had been carolled by the young men and the ladies; then, water being given to their hands, the seneschal seated them all at table, according to the queen's pleasure, and the viands being brought, they all ate blithely. Rising thence, they gave themselves awhile to dancing and music-making, and after, by the queen's commandment, whoso would betook himself to rest. But presently, the wonted hour being come, all in the accustomed place assembled to discourse, whereupon the queen, looking at Filomena, bade her give commencement to the stories of that day, and she, smiling, began on this wise:

---

1. According to the Ptolemaic system, the earth is encompassed by eight celestial zones or heavens; the first or highest, above which is the empyrean, (otherwise called the ninth heaven,) is that of the Moon, the second that of Mercury, the third that of Venus, the fourth that of the Sun, the fifth that of Mars, the sixth that of Jupiter, the seventh that of Saturn and the eighth or lowest that of the fixed stars and of the Earth.

2. *D'azzurrino in color cilestro.* This is one of the many passages in which Boccaccio has imitated Dante (cf. Purgatorio, c. xxvi. II. 4-6, "... il sole.... Che già, raggiando, tutto l'occidente Mutava in bianco aspetto di cilestro,") and also one of the innumerable instances in which former translators (who all agree in making the advent of the light change the colour of the sky from azure to a darker colour, instead of, as Boccaccio intended, to watchet, *i.e.* a paler or greyish blue,) have misrendered the text, for sheer ignorance of the author's meaning.

THE FIRST STORY

MADAM FRANCESCA, BEING COURTED BY ONE
RINUCCIO PALERMINI AND ONE ALESSANDRO
CHIARMONTESI AND LOVING NEITHER THE ONE NOR
THE OTHER, ADROITLY RIDDETH HERSELF OF BOTH
BY CAUSING ONE ENTER FOR DEAD INTO A
SEPULCHRE AND THE OTHER BRING HIM FORTH
THEREOF FOR DEAD, ON SUCH WISE THAT THEY
CANNOT AVAIL TO ACCOMPLISH THE CONDITION
IMPOSED

"Since it is your pleasure, madam, I am well pleased to be she who shall run the first ring in this open and free field of story-telling, wherein your magnificence hath set us; the which an I do well, I doubt not but that those who shall come after will do well and better. Many a time, charming ladies, hath it been shown in our discourses what and how great is the power of love; natheless, for that medeemeth not it hath been fully spoken thereof (no, nor would be, though we should speak of nothing else for a year to come,) and that not only doth love bring lovers into divers dangers of death, but causeth them even to enter for dead into the abiding-places of the dead, it is my pleasure to relate to you a story thereof, over and above those which have been told, whereby not only will you apprehend the puissance of love, but will know the wit used by a worthy lady in ridding herself of two who loved her against her will.

You must know, then, that there was once in the city of Pistoia a very fair widow lady, of whom two of our townsmen, called the one Rinuccio Palermini and the other Alessandro Chiarmontesi, there abiding by reason of banishment from Florence, were, without knowing one of other, passionately enamoured, having by chance fallen in love with her and doing privily each his utmost endeavour to win her favour. The gentlewoman in question, whose name was Madam Francesca de' Lazzari, being still importuned of the one and the other with messages and entreaties, to which she had whiles somewhat unwisely given ear, and desiring, but in vain, discreetly to retract, bethought herself how she might avail to rid herself of their importunity by requiring them of a service, which, albeit it was possible, she conceived that neither of them would render her, to the intent that, they not doing that which she required, she might have a fair and colourable occasion of refusing to hearken more to their messages; and the device which occurred to her was on this wise.

There had died that very day at Pistoia, one, who, albeit his ancestors were gentlemen, was reputed the worst man that was, not only in Pistoia, but in all the world; more by token that he was in his lifetime so misshapen and of so monstrous a favour that whoso knew him not, seeing him for the first time, had been affeared of him; and he had been buried in a tomb without the church of the Minor Friars. This circumstance she bethought herself would in part be very apt to her purpose and accordingly she said to a maid of hers, 'Thou knowest the annoy and the vexation I suffer all day long by the messages of yonder two Florentines, Rinuccio and Alessandro. Now I am not disposed to gratify [either of] them with my love, and to rid myself of them, I have bethought myself, for the great proffers that they make, to seek to make proof of them in somewhat which I am certain they will not do; so shall I do away from me this their importunity, and thou shalt see how. Thou knowest that Scannadio,[1] for so was the wicked man called of whom we have already spoken, 'was this morning buried in the burial-place of the Minor Brethren, Scannadio, of whom, whenas they saw him alive, let alone dead, the doughtiest men of this city went in fear; wherefore go thou privily first to Alessandro and bespeak him, saying, "Madam Francesca giveth thee to know that now is the time come whenas thou mayst have her love, which thou hast so much desired, and be with her, an thou wilt, on this wise. This night, for a reason which thou shalt know after, the body of Scannadio, who was this morning buried, is to be brought to her house by a kinsman of hers, and she, being in great fear of him, dead though he be, would fain not have him there; wherefore she prayeth thee that it please thee, by way of doing her a great service, go this evening, at the time of the first sleep, to the tomb wherein he is buried, and donning the dead man's clothes, abide as thou wert he until such time as they shall come for thee. Then, without moving or speaking, thou must suffer thyself be taken up out of the tomb and carried to her house, where she will receive thee, and thou mayst after abide with her and depart at thy leisure, leaving to her the care of the rest." An he say that he will do it, well and good; but, should he refuse, bid him on my part, never more show himself whereas I may be and look, as he valueth his life, that he send me no more letters or messages. Then shalt thou betake thee to Rinuccio Palermini and say to him, "Madam Francesca saith that she is ready to do thine every pleasure, an thou wilt render her a great service, to wit, that to-night, towards the middle hour, thou get thee to the tomb wherein Scannadio was this morning buried and take him up softly thence and bring him to her at her house, without saying a word of aught thou mayst hear or feel. There shalt thou learn what she would with him and have of her thy pleasure; but, an it please thee not to do this, she chargeth thee never more send her writ nor message."'

The maid betook herself to the two lovers and did her errand punctually to each, saying as it had been enjoined her; whereto each made answer that, an it pleased her, they would go, not only into a tomb, but into hell itself. The maid carried their reply to the lady and she waited to see if they would be mad enough to do it. The night come, whenas it was the season of the first sleep, Alessandro Chiarmontesi, having stripped himself to his doublet, went forth of his house to take Scannadio's place in the tomb; but, by the way, there came a very frightful thought into his head and he fell a-saying in himself, 'Good lack, what a fool I am! Whither go I? How know I but yonder woman's kinsfolk, having maybe perceived that I love her and believing that which is not, have caused me do this, so they may slaughter me in yonder tomb? An it should happen thus, I should suffer for it nor would aught in the world be ever known thereof to their detriment. Or what know I but maybe some enemy of mine hath procured me this, whom she belike loveth and seeketh to oblige therein?' Then said he, 'But, grant that neither of these things be and that her kinsfolk are e'en for carrying me to her house, I must believe that they want not Scannadio's body to hold it in their arms or to put it in hers; nay, it is rather to be conceived that they mean to do it some mischief, as the body of one who maybe disobliged them in somewhat aforetime. She saith that I am not to say a word for aught that I may feel. But, should they put out mine eyes or draw my teeth or lop off my hands or play me any other such trick, how shall I do? How could I abide quiet? And if I speak, they will know me and mayhap do me a mischief, or, though they do me no hurt, yet shall I have accomplished nothing, for that they will not leave me with the lady; whereupon she will say that I have broken her commandment and will never do aught to pleasure me.' So saying, he had well nigh returned home; but, nevertheless, his great love urged him on with counter arguments of such potency that they brought him to the tomb, which he opened and entering therein, stripped Scannadio of his clothes; then, donning them and shutting the tomb upon himself, he laid himself in the dead man's place. Thereupon he began to call to mind what manner of man the latter had been and remembering him of all the things whereof he had aforetime heard tell as having befallen by night, not to say in the sepulchres of the dead, but even otherwhere, his every hair began to stand on end and himseemed each moment as if Scannadio should rise upright and butcher him then and there. However, aided by his ardent love, he got the better of these and the other fearful thoughts that beset him and abiding as he were the dead man, he fell to awaiting that which should betide him.

Meanwhile, Rinuccio, midnight being now at hand, departed his house, to do that which had been enjoined him of his mistress, and as he went, he entered into many and various thoughts of the things which might possibly betide him; as, to wit, that he might fall into the hands of the police, with Scannadio's body on his shoulders, and be doomed to the fire as a sorcerer, and that he should, an the thing came to be known, incur the ill-will of his kinsfolk, and other like thoughts, whereby he was like to have been deterred. But after, bethinking himself again, 'Alack,' quoth he, 'shall I deny this gentlewoman, whom I have so loved and love, the first thing she requireth of me, especially as I am thereby to gain her favour? God forbid, though I were certainly to die thereof, but I should set myself to do that which I have promised!' Accordingly, he went on and presently coming to the sepulchre, opened it easily; which Alessandro hearing, abode still, albeit he was in great fear. Rinuccio, entering in and thinking to take Scannadio's body, laid hold of Alessandro's feet and drew him forth of the tomb; then, hoisting him on his shoulders, he made off towards the lady's house.

Going thus and taking no manner of heed to his burden, he jolted it many a time now against one corner and now another of certain benches that were beside the way, more by token that the night was so cloudy and so dark he could not see whither he went. He was already well nigh at the door of the gentlewoman, who had posted herself at the window with her maid, to see if he would bring Alessandro, and was ready armed with an excuse to send them both away, when it chanced that the officers of the watch, who were ambushed in the street and abode silently on the watch to lay hands upon a certain outlaw, hearing the scuffling that Rinuccio made with his feet, suddenly put out a light, to see what was to do and whither to go, and rattled their targets and halberds, crying, 'Who goeth there?' Rinuccio, seeing this and having scant time for deliberation, let fall his burden and made off as fast as his legs would carry him; whereupon Alessandro arose in haste and made off in his turn, for all he was hampered with the dead man's clothes, which were very long. The lady, by the light of the lantern put out by the police, had plainly recognized Rinuccio, with Alessandro on his shoulders, and perceiving the latter to be clad in Scannadio's clothes, marvelled amain at the exceeding hardihood of both; but, for all her wonderment, she laughed heartily to see Alessandro cast down on the ground and to see him after take to flight. Then, rejoiced at this accident and praising God that He had rid her of the annoy of these twain, she turned back into the house and betook herself to her chamber, avouching to her maid that without doubt they both loved her greatly, since, as it appeared, they had done that which she had enjoined them.

Meanwhile Rinuccio, woeful and cursing his ill fortune, for all that returned not home, but, as soon as the watch had departed the neighbourhood, he came back whereas he had dropped Alessandro and groped about, to see if he could find him again, so he might make an end of his service; but, finding him not and concluding that the police had carried him off, he returned to his own house, woebegone, whilst Alessandro, unknowing what else to do, made off home on like wise, chagrined at such a misadventure and without having recognized him who had borne him thither. On the morrow, Scannadio's tomb being found open and his body not to be seen, for that Alessandro had rolled it to the bottom of the vault, all Pistoia was busy with various conjectures anent the matter, and the simpler sort concluded that he had been carried off by the devils. Nevertheless, each of the two lovers signified to the lady that which he had done and what had befallen and excusing himself withal for not having full accomplished her commandment, claimed her favour and her love; but she, making believe to credit neither of this, rid herself of them with a curt response to the effect that she would never consent to do aught for them, since they had not done that which she had required of them."

---

1. *Scannadio* signifies "Murder-God" and was no doubt a nickname bestowed upon the dead man, on account of his wicked and reprobate way of life.

THE SECOND STORY

AN ABBESS, ARISING IN HASTE AND IN THE DARK TO
FIND ONE OF HER NUNS, WHO HAD BEEN
DENOUNCED TO HER, IN BED WITH HER LOVER AND
THINKING TO COVER HER HEAD WITH HER COIF,
DONNETH INSTEAD THEREOF THE BREECHES OF A
PRIEST WHO IS ABED WITH HER; THE WHICH THE
ACCUSED NUN OBSERVING AND MAKING HER AWARE
THEREOF, SHE IS ACQUITTED AND HATH LEISURE TO
BE WITH HER LOVER

FILOMENA WAS NOW silent and the lady's address in ridding herself of those whom she chose not to love having been commended of all, whilst, on the other hand, the presumptuous hardihood of the two gallants was held of them to be not love, but madness, the queen said gaily to Elisa, "Elisa, follow on." Accordingly, she promptly began, "Adroitly, indeed, dearest ladies, did Madam Francesca contrive to rid herself of her annoy, as hath been told; but a young nun, fortune aiding her, delivered herself with an apt speech from an imminent peril. As you know, there be many very dull folk, who set up for teachers and censors of others, but whom, as you may apprehend from my story, fortune bytimes deservedly putteth to shame, as befell the abbess, under whose governance was the nun of whom I have to tell.

You must know, then, that there was once in Lombardy a convent, very famous for sanctity and religion, wherein, amongst the other nuns who were there, was a young lady of noble birth and gifted with marvellous beauty, who was called Isabetta and who, coming one day to the grate to speak with a kinsman of hers, fell in love with a handsome young man who accompanied him. The latter, seeing her very fair and divining her wishes with his eyes, became on like wise enamoured of her, and this love they suffered a great while without fruit, to the no small unease of each. At last, each being solicited by a like desire, the young man hit upon a means of coming at his nun in all secrecy, and she consenting thereto, he visited her, not once, but many times, to the great contentment of both. But, this continuing, it chanced one night that he was, without the knowledge of himself or his mistress, seen of one of the ladies of the convent to take leave of Isabetta and go his ways. The nun communicated her discovery to divers others and they were minded at first to denounce Isabetta to the abbess, who was called Madam Usimbalda and who, in the opinion of the nuns and of whosoever knew her, was a good and pious lady; but, on consideration, they bethought themselves to seek to have the abbess take her with the young man, so there might be no room for denial. Accordingly, they held their peace and kept watch by turns in secret to surprise her.

Now it chanced that Isabetta, suspecting nothing of this nor being on her guard, caused her lover come thither one night, which was forthright known to those who were on the watch for this and who, whenas it seemed to them time, a good part of the night being spent, divided themselves into two parties, whereof one abode on guard at the door of her cell, whilst the other ran to the abbess's chamber and knocking at the door, till she answered, said to her, 'Up, madam; arise quickly, for we have discovered that Isabetta hath a young man in her cell.' Now the abbess was that night in company with a priest, whom she ofttimes let come to her in a chest; but, hearing the nuns' outcry and fearing lest, of their overhaste and eagerness, they should push open the door, she hurriedly arose and dressed herself as best she might in the dark. Thinking to take certain plaited veils, which nuns wear on their heads and call a psalter, she caught up by chance the priest's breeches, and such was her haste that, without remarking what she did, she threw them over her head, in lieu of the psalter, and going forth, hurriedly locked the door after her, saying, 'Where is this accursed one of God?' Then, in company with the others, who were so ardent and so intent upon having Isabetta taken in default that they noted not that which the abbess had on her head, she came to the cell-door and breaking it open, with the aid of the others, entered and found the two lovers abed in each other's arms, who, all confounded at such a surprise, abode fast, unknowing what to do.

The young lady was incontinent seized by the other nuns and haled off, by command of the abbess, to the chapter-house, whilst her gallant dressed himself and abode await to see what should be the issue of the adventure, resolved, if any hurt were offered to his mistress, to do a mischief to as many nuns as he could come at and carry her off. The abbess, sitting in chapter, proceeded, in the presence of all the nuns, who had no eyes but for the culprit, to give the latter the foulest rating that ever woman had, as having by her lewd and filthy practices (an the thing should come to be known without the walls) sullied the sanctity, the honour and the fair fame of the convent; and to this she added very grievous menaces. The young lady, shamefast and fearful, as feeling herself guilty, knew not what to answer and keeping silence, possessed the other nuns with compassion for her. However, after a while, the abbess multiplying words, she chanced to raise her eyes and espied that which the former had on her head and the hose-points that hung down therefrom on either side; whereupon, guessing how the matter stood, she was all reassured and said, 'Madam, God aid you, tie up your coif and after say what you will to me.'

The abbess, taking not her meaning, answered, 'What coif, vile woman that thou art? Hast thou the face to bandy pleasantries at such a time? Thinkest thou this that thou hast done is a jesting matter?' 'Prithee, madam,' answered Isabetta, 'tie up your coif and after say what you will to me.' Thereupon many of the nuns raised their eyes to the abbess's head and she also, putting her hand thereto, perceived, as did the others, why Isabetta spoke thus; wherefore the abbess, becoming aware of her own default and perceiving that it was seen of all, past hope of recoverance, changed her note and proceeding to speak after a fashion altogether different from her beginning, came to the conclusion that it is impossible to withstand the pricks of the flesh, wherefore she said that each should, whenas she might, privily give herself a good time, even as it had been done until that day. Accordingly, setting the young lady free, she went back to sleep with her priest and Isabetta returned to her lover, whom many a time thereafter she let come thither, in despite of those who envied her, whilst those of the others who were loverless pushed their fortunes in secret, as best they knew."

🌂 3 🍂

THE THIRD STORY

MASTER SIMONE, AT THE INSTANCE OF BRUNO AND
BUFFALMACCO AND NELLO, MAKETH CALANDRINO
BELIEVE THAT HE IS WITH CHILD; WHEREFORE HE
GIVETH THEM CAPONS AND MONEY FOR MEDICINES
AND RECOVERETH WITHOUT BRINGING FORTH

AFTER ELISA HAD FINISHED her story and all the ladies had returned thanks to God, who had with a happy issue delivered the young nun from the claws of her envious companions, the queen bade Filostrato follow on, and he, without awaiting further commandment, began, "Fairest ladies, the unmannerly lout of a Marchegan judge, of whom I told you yesterday, took out of my mouth a story of Calandrino and his companions, which I was about to relate; and for that, albeit it hath been much discoursed of him and them, aught that is told of him cannot do otherwise than add to our merriment, I will e'en tell you that which I had then in mind.

It hath already been clearly enough shown who Calandrino was and who were the others of whom I am to speak in this story, wherefore, without further preface, I shall tell you that an aunt of his chanced to die and left him two hundred crowns in small coin; whereupon he fell a-talking of wishing to buy an estate and entered into treaty with all the brokers in Florence, as if he had ten thousand gold florins to expend; but the matter still fell through, when they came to the price of the estate in question. Bruno and Buffalmacco, knowing all this, had told him once and again that he were better spend the money in making merry together with them than go buy land, as if he had had to make pellets;[1] but, far from this, they had never even availed to bring him to give them once to eat. One day, as they were complaining of this, there came up a comrade of theirs, a painter by name Nello, and they all three took counsel together how they might find a means of greasing their gullets at Calandrino's expense; wherefore, without more delay, having agreed among themselves of that which was to do, they watched next morning for his coming forth of his house, nor had he gone far when Nello accosted him, saying, 'Good-day, Calandrino.' Calandrino answered God give him good day and good year, and Nello, halting awhile, fell to looking him in the face; whereupon Calandrino asked him, 'At what lookest thou?' Quoth the painter, 'Hath aught ailed thee this night? Meseemeth thou are not thyself this morning.' Calandrino incontinent began to quake and said, 'Alack, how so? What deemest thou aileth me?' 'Egad,' answered Nello, 'as for that I can't say; but thou seemest to me all changed; belike it is nothing.' So saying, he let him pass, and Calandrino fared on, all misdoubtful, albeit he felt no whit ailing; but Buffalmacco, who was not far off, seeing him quit of Nello, made for him and saluting him, enquired if aught ailed him. Quoth Calandrino, 'I

411

know not; nay, Nello told me but now that I seemed to him all changed. Can it be that aught aileth me?' 'Ay,' rejoined Buffalmacco, 'there must e'en be something or other amiss with thee, for thou appearest half dead.'

By this time it seemed to Calandrino that he had the fevers, when, lo, up came Bruno and the first thing he said was, 'Calandrino, what manner of face is this?' Calandrino, hearing them all in the same tale, held it for certain that he was in an ill way and asked them, all aghast, 'what shall I do?' Quoth Bruno, 'Methinketh thou wert best return home and get thee to bed and cover thyself well and send thy water to Master Simone the doctor, who is, as thou knowest, as our very creature and will tell thee incontinent what thou must do. We will go with thee and if it behoveth to do aught, we will do it.' Accordingly, Nello having joined himself to them, they returned home with Calandrino, who betook himself, all dejected, into the bedchamber and said to his wife, 'Come, cover me well, for I feel myself sore disordered.' Then, laying himself down, he despatched his water by a little maid to Master Simone, who then kept shop in the Old Market, at the sign of the Pumpkin, whilst Bruno said to his comrades, 'Abide you here with him, whilst I go hear what the doctor saith and bring him hither, if need be.' 'Ay, for God's sake, comrade mine,' cried Calandrino, 'go thither and bring me back word how the case standeth, for I feel I know not what within me.'

Accordingly, Bruno posted off to Master Simone and coming thither before the girl who brought the water, acquainted him with the case; wherefore, the maid being come and the physician, having seen the water, he said to her, 'Begone and bid Calandrino keep himself well warm, and I will come to him incontinent and tell him that which aileth him and what he must do.' The maid reported this to her master nor was it long before the physician and Bruno came, whereupon the former, seating himself beside Calandrino, fell to feeling his pulse and presently, the patient's wife being there present, he said, 'Harkye, Calandrino, to speak to thee as a friend, there aileth thee nought but that thou art with child.' When Calandrino heard this, he fell a-roaring for dolour and said, 'Woe's me! Tessa, this is thy doing, for that thou wilt still be uppermost; I told thee how it would be.' The lady, who was a very modest person, hearing her husband speak thus, blushed all red for shamefastness and hanging her head, went out of the room, without answering a word; whilst Calandrino, pursuing his complaint, said, 'Alack, wretch that I am! How shall I do? How shall I bring forth this child? Whence shall he issue? I see plainly I am a dead man, through the mad lust of yonder wife of mine, whom God make as woeful as I would fain be glad! Were I as well as I am not, I would arise and deal her so many and such buffets that I would break every bone in her body; albeit it e'en serveth me right, for that I should never have suffered her get the upper hand; but, for certain, an I come off alive this time, she may die of desire ere she do it again.'

Bruno and Buffalmacco and Nello were like to burst with laughter, hearing Calandrino's words; however, they contained themselves, but Doctor Simple-Simon[2] laughed so immoderately that you might have drawn every tooth in his head. Finally, Calandrino commending himself to the physician and praying him give him aid and counsel in this his strait, the latter said to him, 'Calandrino, I will not have thee lose heart; for, praised be God, we have taken the case so betimes that, in a few days and with a little trouble, I will deliver thee thereof; but it will cost thee some little expense.' 'Alack, doctor mine,' cried Calandrino, 'ay, for the love of God, do it! I have here two hundred crowns, wherewith I was minded to buy me an estate; take them all, if need be, so I be not brought to bed; for I know not how I should do, seeing I hear women make such a terrible outcry, whereas they are about to bear child, for all they have ample commodity therefor, that methinketh, if I had that pain to suffer, I should die ere I came to the bringing forth.' Quoth the doctor, 'Have no fear of that; I will let make thee a certain ptisan of distilled waters, very good and pleasant to drink, which will in three mornings' time carry off everything and leave thee sounder than a fish; but look thou be more discreet for the future and suffer not thyself fall again into these follies. Now for this water it behoveth us have three pairs of fine fat capons, and for other things that are required thereanent, do thou give one of these (thy comrades) five silver crowns, so he may buy them, and let carry everything to my shop; and to-morrow, in God's name, I will send thee the distilled water aforesaid, whereof thou shalt proceed to drink a good beakerful at a time.' 'Doctor mine,' replied Calandrino, 'I put myself in your hands'; and giving Bruno five crowns and money for three pairs of capons, he besought him to oblige him by taking the pains to buy these things.

The physician then took his leave and letting make a little clary,[3] despatched it to Calandrino, whilst Bruno, buying the capons and other things necessary for making good cheer, ate them in company with his comrades and Master Simone. Calandrino drank of his clary three mornings, after which the doctor came to him, together with his comrades, and feeling his pulse, said to him, 'Calandrino, thou art certainly cured; wherefore henceforth thou mayst safely go about thine every business nor abide longer at home for this.' Accordingly, Calandrino arose, overjoyed, and went about his occasions, mightily extolling, as often as he happened to speak with any one, the fine cure that Master Simone had wrought of him, in that he had unbegotten him with child in three days' time, without any pain; whilst Bruno and Buffalmacco and Nello abode well pleased at having contrived with this device to overreach his niggardliness, albeit Dame Tessa, smoking the cheat, rated her husband amain thereanent."

---

1. *i.e.* balls for a pellet bow, usually made out of clay. Bruno and Buffalmacco were punning upon the double meaning, land and earth (or clay), of the word *terra*.
2. *Scimmione* (lit. ape), a contemptuous distortion of *Simone*.
3. *Chiarea*. According to the commentators, the composition of this drink is unknown, but that of clary, a sort of hippocras or spiced wine *clear-strained* (whence the name), offers no difficulty to the student of old English literature.

☙ 4 ❧

THE FOURTH STORY

CECCO FORTARRIGO GAMETH AWAY AT
BUONCONVENTO ALL HIS GOOD AND THE MONIES
OF CECCO ANGIOLIERI [HIS MASTER;] MOREOVER,
RUNNING AFTER THE LATTER, IN HIS SHIRT, AND
AVOUCHING THAT HE HATH ROBBED HIM, HE
CAUSETH HIM BE TAKEN OF THE COUNTRYFOLK;
THEN, DONNING ANGIOLIERI'S CLOTHES AND
MOUNTING HIS PALFREY, HE MAKETH OFF AND
LEAVETH THE OTHER IN HIS SHIRT

CALANDRINO'S SPEECH concerning his wife had been hearkened of all the company with the utmost laughter; then, Filostrato being silent, Neifile, as the queen willed it, began, "Noble ladies, were it not uneather for men to show forth unto others their wit and their worth than it is for them to exhibit their folly and their vice, many would weary themselves in vain to put a bridle on their tongues; and this hath right well been made manifest to you by the folly of Calandrino, who had no call, in seeking to be made whole of the ailment in which his simplicity caused him believe, to publish the privy diversions of his wife; and this hath brought to my mind somewhat of contrary purport to itself, to wit, a story of how one man's knavery got the better of another's wit, to the grievous hurt and confusion of the over-reached one, the which it pleaseth me to relate to you.

There were, then, in Siena, not many years ago, two (as far as age went) full-grown men, each of whom was called Cecco. One was the son of Messer Angiolieri and the other of Messer Fortarrigo, and albeit in most other things they sorted ill of fashions one with the other, they were natheless so far of accord in one particular, to wit, that they were both hated of their fathers, that they were by reason thereof grown friends and companied often together. After awhile, Angiolieri, who was both a handsome man and a well-mannered, himseeming he could ill live at Siena of the provision assigned him of his father and hearing that a certain cardinal, a great patron of his, was come into the Marches of Ancona as the Pope's Legate, determined to betake himself to him, thinking thus to better his condition. Accordingly, acquainting his father with his purpose, he took order with him to have at once that which he was to give him in six months, so he might clothe and horse himself and make an honourable figure. As he went seeking some one whom he might carry with him for his service, the thing came to Fortarrigo's knowledge, whereupon he presently repaired to Angiolieri and besought him, as best he knew, to carry him with him, offering himself to be to him lackey and serving-man and all, without any wage beyond his expenses paid. Angiolieri answered that he would nowise take him, not but he knew him to be right well sufficient unto every manner of service, but for that he was a gambler and bytimes a drunkard, to boot. But the other replied that he would without fail keep himself from both of these defaults and affirmed it unto him with oaths galore, adding so many prayers that Angiolieri was prevailed upon and said that he was content.

Accordingly, they both set out one morning and went to dine at Buonconvento, where, after dinner, the heat being great, Angiolieri let make ready a bed at the inn and undressing himself, with Fortarrigo's aid, went to sleep, charging the latter call him at the stroke of none. As soon as his master was asleep, Fortarrigo betook himself to the tavern and there, after drinking awhile, he fell to gaming with certain men, who in a trice won of him some money he had and after, the very clothes he had on his back; whereupon, desirous of retrieving himself, he repaired, in his shirt as he was, to Angiolieri's chamber and seeing him fast asleep, took from his purse what monies he had and returning to play, lost these as he had lost the others. Presently, Angiolieri awoke and arising, dressed himself and enquired for Fortarrigo. The latter was not to be found and Angiolieri, concluding him to be asleep, drunken, somewhere, as was bytimes his wont, determined to leave him be and get himself another servant at Corsignano. Accordingly, he caused put his saddle and his valise on a palfrey he had and thinking to pay the reckoning, so he might get him gone, found himself without a penny; whereupon great was the outcry and all the hostelry was in an uproar, Angiolieri declaring that he had been robbed there and threatening to have the host and all his household carried prisoners to Siena.

At this moment up came Fortarrigo in his shirt, thinking to take his master's clothes, as he had taken his money, and seeing the latter ready to mount, said, 'What is this, Angiolieri? Must we needs be gone already? Good lack, wait awhile; there will be one here forthwith who hath my doublet in pawn for eight-and-thirty shillings; and I am certain that he will render it up for five-and-thirty, money down.' As he spoke, there came one who certified Angiolieri that it was Fortarrigo who had robbed him of his monies, by showing him the sum of those which the latter had lost at play; wherefore he was sore incensed and loaded Fortarrigo with reproaches; and had he not feared others more than he feared God, he had done him a mischief; then, threatening to have him strung up by the neck or outlawed from Siena, he mounted to horse. Fortarrigo, as if he spoke not to him, but to another, said, 'Good lack, Angiolieri, let be for the nonce this talk that skilleth not a straw, and have regard unto this; by redeeming it[1] forthright, we may have it again for five-and-thirty shillings; whereas, if we tarry but till to-morrow, he will not take less than the eight-and-thirty he lent me thereon; and this favour he doth me for that I staked it after his counsel. Marry, why should we not better ourselves by these three shillings?'

Angiolieri, hearing him talk thus, lost all patience (more by token that he saw himself eyed askance by the bystanders, who manifestly believed, not that Fortarrigo had gamed away his monies, but that he had yet monies of Fortarrigo's in hand) and said to him, 'What have I to do with thy doublet? Mayst thou be strung up by the neck, since not only hast thou robbed me and gambled away my money, but hinderest me to boot in my journey, and now thou makest mock of me.' However, Fortarrigo still stood to it, as it were not spoken to him and said, 'Ecod, why wilt thou not better me these three shillings? Thinkest thou I shall not be able to oblige thee therewith another time? Prithee, do it, an thou have any regard for me. Why all this haste? We shall yet reach Torrenieri betimes this evening. Come, find the purse; thou knowest I might ransack all Siena and not find a doublet to suit me so well as this; and to think I should let yonder fellow have it for eight-and-thirty shillings! It is worth yet forty shillings or more, so that thou wouldst worsen me in two ways.'[2]

Angiolieri, beyond measure exasperated to see himself first robbed and now held in parley after this fashion, made him no further answer, but, turning his palfrey's head, took the road to Torrenieri, whilst Fortarrigo, bethinking himself of a subtle piece of knavery, proceeded to trot after him in his shirt good two miles, still requiring him of his doublet. Presently, Angiolieri pricking on amain, to rid his ears of the annoy, Fortarrigo espied some husbandmen in a field, adjoining the highway in advance of him, and cried out to them, saying, 'Stop him, stop him!' Accordingly, they ran up, some with spades and others with mattocks, and presenting themselves in the road before Angiolieri, concluding that he had robbed him who came crying after him in his shirt, stopped and took him. It availed him little to tell them who he was and how the case stood, and Fortarrigo, coming up, said with an angry air, 'I know not what hindereth me from slaying thee, disloyal thief that thou wast to make off with my gear!' Then, turning to the countrymen, 'See, gentlemen,' quoth he, 'in what a plight he left me at the inn, having first gamed away all his own! I may well say by God and by you have I gotten back this much, and thereof I shall still be beholden to you.'

Angiolieri told them his own story, but his words were not heeded; nay, Fortarrigo, with the aid of the countrymen, pulled him off his palfrey and stripping him, clad himself in his clothes; then, mounting to horse, he left him in his shirt and barefoot and returned to Siena, avouching everywhere that he had won the horse and clothes of Angiolieri, whilst the latter, who had thought to go, as a rich man, to the cardinal in the Marches, returned to Buonconvento, poor and in his shirt, nor dared for shamefastness go straight back to Siena, but, some clothes being lent him, he mounted the rouncey that Fortarrigo had ridden and betook himself to his kinsfolk at Corsignano, with whom he abode till such time as he was furnished anew by his father. On this wise Fortarrigo's knavery baffled Angiolieri's fair advisement,[3] albeit his villainy was not left by the latter unpunished in due time and place."

---

1. *i.e.* the doublet.
2. *i.e.* do me a double injury.
3. Syn. goodly design of foresight (*buono avviso*).

𝄞 5 𝄢

THE FIFTH STORY

CALANDRINO FALLETH IN LOVE WITH A WENCH AND BRUNO WRITETH HIM A TALISMAN, WHEREWITH WHEN HE TOUCHETH HER, SHE GOETH WITH HIM; AND HIS WIFE FINDING THEM TOGETHER, THERE BETIDETH HIM GRIEVOUS TROUBLE AND ANNOY

NEIFILE'S short story being finished and the company having passed it over without overmuch talk or laughter, the queen turned to Fiammetta and bade her follow on, to which she replied all blithely that she would well and began, "Gentlest ladies, there is, as methinketh you may know, nothing, how much soever it may have been talked thereof, but will still please, provided whoso is minded to speak of it know duly to choose the time and the place that befit it. Wherefore, having regard to our intent in being here (for that we are here to make merry and divert ourselves and not for otherwhat), meseemeth that everything which may afford mirth and pleasance hath here both due place and due time; and albeit it may have been a thousand times discoursed thereof, it should natheless be none the less pleasing, though one speak of it as much again. Wherefore, notwithstanding it hath been many times spoken among us of the sayings and doings of Calandrino, I will make bold, considering, as Filostrato said awhile ago, that these are all diverting, to tell you yet another story thereof, wherein were I minded to swerve from the fact, I had very well known to disguise and recount it under other names; but, for that, in the telling of a story, to depart from the truth of things betided detracteth greatly from the listener's pleasure, I will e'en tell it you in its true shape, moved by the reason aforesaid.

Niccolo Cornacchini was a townsman of ours and a rich man and had, among his other possessions, a fine estate at Camerata, whereon he let build a magnificent mansion and agreed with Bruno and Buffalmacco to paint it all for him; and they, for that the work was great, joined to themselves Nello and Calandrino and fell to work. Thither, for that there was none of the family in the house, although there were one or two chambers furnished with beds and other things needful and an old serving-woman abode there, as guardian of the place, a son of the said Niccolo, by name Filippo, being young and without a wife, was wont bytimes to bring some wench or other for his diversion and keep her there a day or two and after send her away. It chanced once, among other times, that he brought thither one called Niccolosa, whom a lewd fellow, by name Mangione, kept at his disposal in a house at Camaldoli and let out on hire. She was a woman of a fine person and well clad and for her kind well enough mannered and spoken.

One day at noontide, she having come forth her chamber in a white petticoat, with her hair twisted about her head, and being in act to wash her hands and face at a well that was in the courtyard of the mansion, it chanced that Calandrino came thither for water and saluted her familiarly. She returned him his greeting and fell to eying him, more because he seemed to her an odd sort of fellow than for any fancy she had for him; whereupon he likewise fell a-considering her and himseeming she was handsome, he began to find his occasions for abiding there and returned not to his comrades with the water, but, knowing her not, dared not say aught to her. She, who had noted his looking, glanced at him from time to time, to make game of him, heaving some small matter of sighs the while; wherefore Calandrino fell suddenly over head and ears in love with her and left not the courtyard till she was recalled by Filippo into the chamber. Therewithal he returned to work, but did nought but sigh, which Bruno, who had still an eye to his doings, for that he took great delight in his fashions, remarking, 'What a devil aileth thee, friend Calandrino?' quoth he. 'Thou dost nought but sigh.' 'Comrade,' answered Calandrino, 'had I but some one to help me, I should fare well.' 'How so?' enquired Bruno; and Calandrino replied, 'It must not be told to any; but there is a lass down yonder, fairer than a fairy, who hath fallen so mightily in love with me that 'twould seem to thee a grave matter. I noted it but now, whenas I went for the water.' 'Ecod,' cried Bruno, 'look she be not Filippo's wife.' Quoth Calandrino, 'Methinketh it is she, for that he called her and she went to him in the chamber; but what of that? In matters of this kind I would jockey Christ himself, let alone Filippo; and to tell thee the truth, comrade, she pleaseth me more than I can tell thee.' 'Comrade,' answered Bruno, 'I will spy thee out who she is, and if she be Filippo's wife, I will order thine affairs for thee in a brace of words, for she is a great friend of mine. But how shall we do, so Buffalmacco may not know? I can never get a word with her, but he is with me.' Quoth Calandrino, 'Of Buffalmacco I reck not; but we must beware of Nello, for that he is Tessa's kinsman and would mar us everything.' And Bruno said, 'True.'

Now he knew very well who the wench was, for that he had seen her come and moreover Filippo had told him. Accordingly, Calandrino having left work awhile and gone to get a sight of her, Bruno told Nello and Buffalmacco everything and they took order together in secret what they should do with him in the matter of this his enamourment. When he came back, Bruno said to him softly, 'Hast seen her?' 'Alack, yes,' replied Calandrino; 'she hath slain me.' Quoth Bruno, 'I must go see an it be she I suppose; and if it be so, leave me do.' Accordingly, he went down into the courtyard and finding Filippo and Niccolosa there, told them precisely what manner of man Calandrino was and took order with them of that which each of them should do and say, so they might divert themselves with the lovesick gull and make merry over his passion. Then, returning to Calandrino, he said, 'It is indeed she; wherefore needs must the thing be very discreetly managed, for, should Filippo get wind of it, all the water in the Arno would not wash us. But what wouldst thou have me say to her on thy part, if I should chance to get speech of her?' 'Faith,' answered Calandrino, 'thou shalt tell her, to begin with, that I will her a thousand measures of that good stuff that getteth with child, and after, that I am her servant and if she would have aught.... Thou takest me?' 'Ay,' said Bruno, 'leave me do.'

Presently, supper-time being come, the painters left work and went down into the courtyard, where they found Filippo and Niccolosa and tarried there awhile, to oblige Calandrino. The latter fell to ogling Niccolosa and making the oddest grimaces in the world, such and so many that a blind man would have remarked them. She on her side did everything that she thought apt to inflame him, and Filippo, in accordance with the instructions he had of Bruno, made believe to talk with Buffalmacco and the others and to have no heed of this, whilst taking the utmost diversion in Calandrino's fashions. However, after a while, to the latter's exceeding chagrin, they took their leave and as they returned to Florence, Bruno said to

Calandrino, 'I can tell thee thou makest her melt like ice in the sun. Cock's body, wert thou to fetch thy rebeck and warble thereto some of those amorous ditties of thine, thou wouldst cause her cast herself out of window to come to thee.' Quoth Calandrino, 'Deemest thou, gossip? Deemest thou I should do well to fetch it?' 'Ay, do I,' answered Bruno; and Calandrino went on, 'Thou wouldst not credit me this morning, whenas I told it thee; but, for certain, gossip, methinketh I know better than any man alive to do what I will. Who, other than I, had known to make such a lady so quickly in love with me? Not your trumpeting young braggarts,[1] I warrant you, who are up and down all day long and could not make shift, in a thousand years, to get together three handsful of cherry stones. I would fain have thee see me with the rebeck; 'twould be fine sport for thee. I will have thee to understand once for all that I am no dotard, as thou deemest me, and this she hath right well perceived, she; but I will make her feel it othergates fashion, so once I get my claw into her back; by the very body of Christ, I will lead her such a dance that she will run after me, as the madwoman after her child.' 'Ay,' rejoined Bruno, 'I warrant me thou wilt rummage her; methinketh I see thee, with those teeth of thine that were made for virginal jacks,[2] bite that little vermeil mouth of hers and those her cheeks, that show like two roses, and after eat her all up.'

Calandrino, hearing this, fancied himself already at it and went singing and skipping, so overjoyed that he was like to jump out of his skin. On the morrow, having brought the rebeck, he, to the great diversion of all the company, sang sundry songs thereto; and in brief, he was taken with such an itch for the frequent seeing of her that he wrought not a whit, but ran a thousand times a day, now to the window, now to the door and anon into the courtyard, to get a look at her, whereof she, adroitly carrying out Bruno's instructions, afforded him ample occasion. Bruno, on his side, answered his messages in her name and bytimes brought him others as from her; and whenas she was not there, which was mostly the case, he carried him letters from her, wherein she gave him great hopes of compassing his desire, feigning herself at home with her kinsfolk, where he might not presently see her. On this wise, Bruno, with the aid of Buffalmacco, who had a hand in the matter, kept the game afoot and had the greatest sport in the world with Calandrino's antics, causing him give them bytimes, as at his mistress's request, now an ivory comb, now a purse and anon a knife and such like toys, for which they brought him in return divers paltry counterfeit rings of no value, with which he was vastly delighted; and to boot, they had of him, for their pains, store of dainty collations and other small matters of entertainment, so they might be diligent about his affairs.

On this wise they kept him in play good two months, without getting a step farther, at the end of which time, seeing the work draw to an end and bethinking himself that, an he brought not his amours to an issue in the meantime, he might never have another chance thereof, he began to urge and importune Bruno amain; wherefore, when next the girl came to the mansion, Bruno, having first taken order with her and Filippo of what was to be done, said to Calandrino, 'Harkye, gossip, yonder lady hath promised me a good thousand times to do that which thou wouldst have and yet doth nought thereof, and meseemeth she leadeth thee by the nose; wherefore, since she doth it not as she promiseth, we will an it like thee, make her do it, will she, nill she.' 'Ecod, ay!' answered Calandrino. 'For the love of God let it be done speedily.' Quoth Bruno, 'Will thy heart serve thee to touch her with a script I shall give thee?' 'Ay, sure,' replied Calandrino; and the other, 'Then do thou make shift to bring me a piece of virgin parchment and a live bat, together with three grains of frankincense and a candle that hath been blessed by the priest, and leave me do.' Accordingly, Calandrino lay in wait all the next night with his engines to catch a bat and having at last taken one, carried it to Bruno, with the other things required; whereupon the latter, withdrawing to a chamber, scribbled divers toys of his fashion upon the parchment, in characters of his own devising, and brought it to him, saying, 'Know, Calandrino, that, if thou touch her with this script, she will incontinent follow thee and do what thou wilt. Wherefore, if Filippo should go abroad anywhither to-day, do thou contrive to accost her on some pretext or other and touch her; then betake thyself to the barn yonder, which is the best place here for thy purpose, for that no one ever frequenteth there. Thou wilt find she will come thither, and when she is there, thou knowest well what thou hast to do.' Calandrino was the joyfullest man alive and took the script, saying, 'Gossip, leave me do.'

Now Nello, whom Calandrino mistrusted, had as much diversion of the matter as the others and bore a hand with them in making sport of him: wherefore, of accord with Bruno, he betook himself to Florence to Calandrino's wife and said to her, 'Tessa, thou knowest what a beating Calandrino gave thee without cause the day he came back, laden with stones from the Mugnone; wherefore I mean to have thee avenge thyself on him; and if thou do it not, hold me no more for kinsman or for friend. He hath fallen in love with a woman over yonder, and she is lewd enough to go very often closeting herself with him. A little while agone, they appointed each other to foregather together this very day; wherefore I would have thee come thither and lie in wait for him and chastise him well.' When the lady heard this, it seemed to her no jesting matter, but, starting to her feet, she fell a-saying, 'Alack, common thief that thou art, is it thus that thou usest me? By Christ His Cross, it shall not pass thus, but I will pay thee therefor!' Then, taking her mantle and a little maid to bear her company, she started off at a good round pace for the mansion, together with Nello.

As soon as Bruno saw the latter afar off, he said to Filippo, 'Here cometh our friend'; whereupon the latter, betaking himself whereas Calandrino and the others were at work, said, 'Masters, needs must I go presently to Florence; work with a will.' Then, going away, he hid himself in a place when he could, without being seen, see what Calandrino should do. The latter, as soon as he deemed Filippo somewhat removed, came down into the courtyard and finding Niccolosa there alone, entered into talk with her, whilst she, who knew well enough what she had to do, drew near him and entreated him somewhat more familiarly than of wont. Thereupon he touched her with the script and no sooner had he done so than he turned, without saying a word, and made for the barn, whither she followed him. As soon as she was within, she shut the door and taking him in her arms, threw him down on the straw that was on the floor; then, mounting astride of him and holding him with her hands on his shoulders, without letting him draw near her face, she gazed at him, as he were her utmost desire, and said, 'O sweet my Calandrino, heart of my body, my soul, my treasure, my comfort, how long have I desired to have thee and to be able to hold thee at my wish! Thou hast drawn all the thread out of my shift with thy gentilesse; thou hast tickled my heart with thy rebeck. Can it be true that I hold thee?' Calandrino, who could scarce stir, said, 'For God's sake, sweet my soul, let me buss thee.' 'Marry,' answered she, 'thou art in a mighty hurry. Let me first take my fill of looking upon thee; let me sate mine eyes with that sweet face of thine.'

Now Bruno and Buffalmacco were come to join Filippo and all three heard and saw all this. As Calandrino was now offering to kiss Niccolosa perforce, up came Nello with Dame Tessa and said, as soon as he reached the place, 'I vow to God they are together.' Then, coming up to the door of the barn, the lady, who was all a-fume with rage, dealt it such a push with her hands that she sent it flying, and entering, saw Niccolosa astride of Calandrino. The former, seeing the lady, started up in haste and taking to flight, made off to join Filippo, whilst Dame Tessa fell tooth and nail upon Calandrino, who was still on his back, and clawed all his face; then, clutching him by the hair and haling him hither and thither, 'Thou sorry shitten cur,' quoth she, 'dost thou then use me thus? Besotted dotard that thou art, accursed be the weal I have willed thee! Marry, seemeth it to thee thou hast not enough to do at home, that thou must go wantoning it in other folk's preserves? A fine gallant, i'faith! Dost thou not know thyself, losel that thou art? Dost thou not know thyself, good for nought? Wert thou to be squeezed dry, there would not come as much juice from thee as might suffice for a sauce. Cock's faith, thou canst not say it was Tessa that was presently in act to get thee with child, God make her sorry, who ever she is, for a scurvy trull as she must be to have a mind to so fine a jewel as thou!'

Calandrino, seeing his wife come, abode neither dead nor alive and had not the hardihood to make any defence against her; but, rising, all scratched and flayed and baffled as he was, and picking up his bonnet, he fell to humbly beseeching her leave crying out, an she would not have him cut in pieces, for that she who had been with him was the wife of the master of the house; whereupon quoth she, 'So be it, God give her an ill year.' At this moment, Bruno and Buffalmacco, having laughed their fill at all this, in company with Filippo and Niccolosa, came up, feigning to be attracted by the clamour, and having with no little ado appeased the lady, counselled Calandrino betake himself to Florence and return thither no more, lest Filippo should get wind of the matter and do him a mischief. Accordingly he returned to Florence, chapfallen and woebegone, all flayed and scratched, and never ventured to go thither again; but, being plagued and harassed night and day with his wife's reproaches, he made an end of his fervent love, having given much cause for laughter to his companions, no less than to Niccolosa and Filippo."

---

1. *Giovani di tromba marina.* The sense seems as above; the commentators say that *giovani di tromba marina* is a name given to those youths who go trumpeting about everywhere the favours accorded them by women; but the *tromba marina* is a *stringed* (not a wind) *instrument*, a sort of primitive violoncello with one string.
2. "Your teeth did dance like virginal jacks."—*Ben Jonson.*

❧ 6 ❧

THE SIXTH STORY

TWO YOUNG GENTLEMEN LODGE THE NIGHT WITH
AN INNKEEPER, WHEREOF ONE GOETH TO LIE WITH
THE HOST'S DAUGHTER, WHILST HIS WIFE
UNWITTINGLY COUCHETH WITH THE OTHER; AFTER
WHICH HE WHO LAY WITH THE GIRL GETTETH HIM
TO BED WITH HER FATHER AND TELLETH HIM ALL,
THINKING TO BESPEAK HIS COMRADE. THEREWITHAL
THEY COME TO WORDS, BUT THE WIFE, PERCEIVING
HER MISTAKE, ENTERETH HER DAUGHTER'S BED AND
THENCE WITH CERTAIN WORDS APPEASETH
EVERYTHING

CALANDRINO, who had otherwhiles afforded the company matter for laughter, made them laugh this time also, and whenas the ladies had left devising of his fashions, the queen bade Pamfilo tell, whereupon quoth he, "Laudable ladies, the name of Niccolosa, Calandrino's mistress, hath brought me back to mind a story of another Niccolosa, which it pleaseth me to tell you, for that therein you shall see how a goodwife's ready wit did away a great scandal.

In the plain of Mugnone there was not long since a good man who gave wayfarers to eat and drink for their money, and although he was poor and had but a small house, he bytimes at a pinch gave, not every one, but sundry acquaintances, a night's lodging. He had a wife, a very handsome woman, by whom he had two children, whereof one was a fine buxom lass of some fifteen or sixteen years of age, who was not yet married, and the other a little child, not yet a year old, whom his mother herself suckled. Now a young gentleman of our city, a sprightly and pleasant youth, who was often in those parts, had cast his eyes on the girl and loved her ardently; and she, who gloried greatly in being beloved of a youth of his quality, whilst studying with pleasing fashions to maintain him in her love, became no less enamoured of him, and more than once, by mutual accord, this their love had had the desired effect, but that Pinuccio (for such was the young man's name) feared to bring reproach upon his mistress and himself. However, his ardour waxing from day to day, he could no longer master his desire to foregather with her and bethought himself to find a means of harbouring with her father, doubting not, from his acquaintance with the ordinance of the latter's house, but he might in that event contrive to pass the night in her company, without any being the wiser; and no sooner had he conceived this design than he proceeded without delay to carry it into execution.

Accordingly, in company with a trusty friend of his called Adriano, who knew his love, he late one evening hired a couple of hackneys and set thereon two pairs of saddle-bags, filled belike with straw, with which they set out from Florence and fetching a compass, rode till they came overagainst the plain of Mugnone, it being by this night; then, turning about, as they were on their way back from Romagna, they made for the good man's house and knocked at the door. The host, being very familiar with both of them, promptly opened the door and Pinuccio said to him, 'Look you, thou must needs harbour us this night. We thought to reach Florence before dark, but have not availed to make such haste but that we find ourselves here, as thou seest at this hour.' 'Pinuccio,' answered the host, 'thou well knowest how little commodity I have to lodge such men as you are; however, since the night hath e'en overtaken you here and there is no time for you to go otherwhere, I will gladly harbour you as I may.' The two young men accordingly alighted and entered the inn, where they first eased[1] their hackneys and after supper with the host, having taken good care to bring provision with them.

Now the good man had but one very small bedchamber, wherein were three pallet-beds set as best he knew, two at one end of the room and the third overagainst them at the other end; nor for all that was there so much space left that one could go there otherwise than straitly. The least ill of the three the host let make ready for the two friends and put them to lie there; then, after a while neither of the gentlemen being asleep, though both made a show thereof, he caused his daughter betake herself to bed in one of the two others and lay down himself in the third, with his wife, who set by the bedside the cradle wherein she had her little son. Things being ordered after this fashion and Pinuccio having seen everything, after a while, himseeming that every one was asleep, he arose softly and going to the bed where slept the girl beloved of him, laid himself beside the latter, by whom, for all she did it timorously, he was joyfully received, and with her he proceeded to take of that pleasure which both most desired. Whilst Pinuccio abode thus with his mistress, it chanced that a cat caused certain things fall, which the good wife, awaking, heard; whereupon, fearing lest it were otherwhat, she arose, as she was, in the dark and betook herself whereas she had heard the noise.

Meanwhile, Adriano, without intent aforethought, arose by chance for some natural occasion and going to despatch this, came upon the cradle, whereas it had been set by the good wife, and unable to pass without moving it, took it up and set it down beside his own bed; then, having accomplished that for which he had arisen, he returned and betook himself to bed again, without recking of the cradle. The good wife, having searched and found the thing which had fallen was not what she thought, never troubled herself to kindle a light, to see it, but, chiding the cat, returned to the chamber and groped her way to the bed where her husband lay. Finding the cradle not there, 'Mercy o' me!' quoth she in herself. 'See what I was about to do! As I am a Christian, I had well nigh gone straight to our guest's bed.' Then, going a little farther and finding the cradle, she entered the bed whereby it stood and laid herself down beside Adriano, thinking to couch with her husband. Adriano, who was not yet asleep, feeling this, received her well and joyously and laying her aboard in a trice, clapped on all sail, to the no small contentment of the lady.

Meanwhile, Pinuccio, fearing lest sleep should surprise him with his lass and having taken of her his fill of pleasure, arose from her, to return to his own bed, to sleep, and finding the cradle in his way, took the adjoining bed for that of his host; wherefore, going a little farther, he lay down with the latter, who awoke at his coming. Pinuccio, deeming himself beside Adriano, said, 'I tell thee there never was so sweet a creature as is Niccolosa. Cock's body, I have had with her the rarest sport ever man had with woman, more by token that I have gone upwards of six times into the country, since I left thee.' The host, hearing this talk and being not overwell pleased therewith, said first in himself, 'What a devil doth this fellow here?' Then, more angered than well-advised, 'Pinuccio,' quoth he, 'this hath been a great piece of villainy of thine, and I know not why thou shouldst have used me thus; but, by the body of God, I will pay thee for it!!' Pinuccio, who was not the wisest lad in the world, seeing his mistake, addressed not himself to mend it as best he might, but said, 'Of what wilt thou pay me? What canst thou do to me?' Therewithal the hostess, who thought herself with her husband, said to Adriano, 'Good lack, hark to our guests how they are at I know not what words together!'

Quoth Adriano, laughing, 'Leave them do, God land them in an ill year! They drank overmuch yesternight.'

The good wife, herseeming she had heard her husband scold and hearing Adriano speak, incontinent perceived where and with whom she had been; whereupon, like a wise woman as she was, she arose forthright, without saying a word, and taking her little son's cradle, carried it at a guess, for that there was no jot of light to be seen in the chamber, to the side of the bed where her daughter slept and lay down with the latter; then, as if she had been aroused by her husband's clamour, she called him and enquired what was to do between himself and Pinuccio. He answered, 'Hearest thou not what he saith he hath done this night unto Niccolosa?' 'Marry,' quoth she, 'he lieth in his throat, for he was never abed with Niccolosa, seeing that I have lain here all night; more by token that I have not been able to sleep a wink; and thou art an ass to believe him. You men drink so much of an evening that you do nothing but dream all night and fare hither and thither, without knowing it, and fancy you do wonders. 'Tis a thousand pities you don't break your necks. But what doth Pinuccio yonder? Why bideth he not in his own bed?' Adriano, on his part, seeing how adroitly the good wife went about to cover her own shame and that of her daughter, chimed in with, 'Pinuccio, I have told thee an hundred times not to go abroad, for that this thy trick of arising in thy sleep and telling for true the extravagances thou dreamest will bring thee into trouble some day or other. Come back here, God give thee an ill night!'

The host, hearing what his wife and Adriano said, began to believe in good earnest that Pinuccio was dreaming; and accordingly, taking him by the shoulders, he fell to shaking and calling him, saying, 'Pinuccio, awake; return to thine own bed.' Pinuccio having apprehended all that had been said began to wander off into other extravagances, after the fashion of a man a-dream; whereat the host set up the heartiest laughter in the world. At last, he made believe to awake for stress of shaking, and calling to Adriano, said, 'Is it already day, that thou callest me?' 'Ay,' answered the other, 'come hither.' Accordingly, Pinuccio, dissembling and making a show of being sleepy-eyed, arose at last from beside the host and went back to bed with Adriano. The day come and they being risen, the host fell to laughing and mocking at Pinuccio and his dreams; and so they passed from one jest to another, till the young men, having saddled their rounceys and strapped on their valises and drunken with the host, remounted to horse and rode away to Florence, no less content with the manner in which the thing had betided than with the effect itself thereof. Thereafter Pinuccio found other means of foregathering with Niccolosa, who vowed to her mother that he had certainly dreamt the thing; wherefore the goodwife, remembering her of Adriano's embracements, inwardly avouched herself alone to have waked."

---

1. *Adagiarono, i.e.* unsaddled and stabled and fed them.

7

THE SEVENTH STORY

TALANO DI MOLESE DREAMETH THAT A WOLF
MANGLETH ALL HIS WIFE'S NECK AND FACE AND
BIDDETH HER BEWARE THEREOF; BUT SHE PAYETH
NO HEED TO HIS WARNING AND IT BEFALLETH HER
EVEN AS HE HAD DREAMED

PAMFILO'S STORY being ended and the goodwife's presence of mind having been commended of all, the queen bade Pampinea tell hers and she thereupon began, "It hath been otherwhile discoursed among us, charming ladies, of the truths foreshown by dreams, the which many of our sex scoff at; wherefore, notwithstanding that which hath been said thereof, I shall not scruple to tell you, in a very few words, that which no great while ago befell a she-neighbour of mine for not giving credit to a dream of herself seen by her husband.

I know not if you were acquainted with Talano di Molese, a very worshipful man, who took to wife a young lady called Margarita, fair over all others, but so humoursome, ill-conditioned and froward that she would do nought of other folk's judgment, nor could others do aught to her liking; the which, irksome as it was to Talano to endure, natheless, as he could no otherwise, needs must he put up with. It chanced one night that, being with this Margarita of his at an estate he had in the country, himseemed in his sleep he saw his wife go walking in a very fair wood which they had not far from their house, and as she went, himseemed there came forth of a thicket a great and fierce wolf, which sprang straight at her throat and pulling her to the ground, enforced himself to carry her off, whilst she screamed for aid; and after, she winning free of his fangs, it seemed he had marred all her throat and face. Accordingly, when he arose in the morning, he said to the lady, 'Wife, albeit thy frowardness hath never suffered me to have a good day with thee, yet it would grieve me should ill betide thee; wherefore, an thou wilt hearken to my counsel, thou wilt not go forth the house to-day'; and being asked of her why, he orderly recounted to her his dream.

The lady shook her head and said, 'Who willeth thee ill, dreameth thee ill. Thou feignest thyself mighty careful of me; but thou dreamest of me that which thou wouldst fain see come to pass; and thou mayst be assured that I will be careful both to-day and always not to gladden thee with this or other mischance of mine.' Quoth Talano, 'I knew thou wouldst say thus; for that such thanks still hath he who combeth a scald-head; but, believe as thou listeth, I for my part tell it to thee for good, and once more I counsel thee abide at home to-day or at least beware of going into our wood.' 'Good,' answered the lady, 'I will do it'; and after fell a-saying to herself, 'Sawest thou how artfully yonder man thinketh to have feared me from going to our

425

wood to-day? Doubtless he hath given some trull or other tryst there and would not have me find him with her. Marry, it were fine eating for him with blind folk and I should be a right simpleton an I saw not his drift and if I believed him! But certes he shall not have his will; nay, though I abide there all day, needs must I see what traffic is this that he hath in hand to-day.'

Accordingly, her husband being gone out at one door, she went out at the other and betook herself as most secretly she might straight to the wood and hid herself in the thickest part thereof, standing attent and looking now here and now there, an she should see any one come. As she abode on this wise, without any thought of danger, behold, there sallied forth of a thick coppice hard by a terrible great wolf, and scarce could she say, 'Lord, aid me!' when it flew at her throat and laying fast hold of her, proceeded to carry her off, as she were a lambkin. She could neither cry nor aid herself on other wise, so sore was her gullet straitened; wherefore the wolf, carrying her off, would assuredly have throttled her, had he not encountered certain shepherds, who shouted at him and constrained him to loose her. The shepherds knew her and carried her home, in a piteous plight, where, after long tending by the physicians, she was healed, yet not so wholly but she had all her throat and a part of her face marred on such wise that, whereas before she was fair, she ever after appeared misfeatured and very foul of favour; wherefore, being ashamed to appear whereas she might be seen, she many a time bitterly repented her of her frowardness and her perverse denial to put faith, in a matter which cost her nothing, in her husband's true dream."

8

THE EIGHTH STORY

BIONDELLO CHEATETH CIACCO OF A DINNER, WHEREOF THE OTHER CRAFTILY AVENGETH HIMSELF, PROCURING HIM TO BE SHAMEFULLY BEATEN

THE MERRY COMPANY with one accord avouched that which Talano had seen in sleep to have been no dream, but a vision, so punctually, without there failing aught thereof, had it come to pass. But, all being silent the queen charged Lauretta follow on, who said, "Like as those, most discreet ladies, who have to-day foregone me in speech, have been well nigh all moved to discourse by something already said, even so the stern vengeance wreaked by the scholar, of whom Pampinea told us yesterday, moveth me to tell of a piece of revenge, which, without being so barbarous as the former, was nevertheless grievous unto him who brooked it.

I must tell you, then, that there was once in Florence a man whom all called Ciacco,[1] as great a glutton as ever lived. His means sufficing him not to support the expense that his gluttony required and he being, for the rest, a very well-mannered man and full of goodly and pleasant sayings, he addressed himself to be, not altogether a buffoon, but a spunger[2] and to company with those who were rich and delighted to eat of good things; and with these he went often to dine and sup, albeit he was not always bidden. There was likewise at Florence, in those days, a man called Biondello, a little dapper fellow of his person, very quaint of his dress and sprucer than a fly, with his coif on his head and his yellow periwig still drest to a nicety, without a hair awry, who plied the same trade as Ciacco. Going one morning in Lent whereas they sell the fish and cheapening two very fine lampreys for Messer Vieri de' Cerchj, he was seen by Ciacco, who accosted him and said, 'What meaneth this?' Whereto Biondello made answer, 'Yestereve there were sent unto Messer Corso Donati three lampreys, much finer than these, and a sturgeon; to which sufficing him not for a dinner he is minded to give certain gentlemen, he would have me buy these other two. Wilt thou not come thither, thou?' Quoth Ciacco, 'Thou knowest well that I shall be there.'

. Accordingly, whenas it seemed to him time, he betook himself to Messer Corso's house, where he found him with sundry neighbours of his, not yet gone to dinner, and being asked of him what he went doing, answered, 'Sir, I am come to dine with you and your company.' Quoth Messer Corso, 'Thou art welcome; and as it is time, let us to table.' Thereupon they seated themselves at table and had, to begin with, chickpease and pickled tunny, and after a dish of fried fish from the Arno, and no more, Ciacco, perceiving the cheat that Biondello had put upon him, was inwardly no little angered thereat and resolved to pay him for it; nor had many days passed ere he again encountered the other, who had by this time made many folk merry with the trick he had played him. Biondello, seeing him, saluted him and asked him, laughing, how he had found Messer Corso's lampreys; to which Ciacco answered, 'That shalt thou know much better than I, ere eight days be past.'

Then, without wasting time over the matter, he took leave of Biondello and agreeing for a price with a shrewd huckster, carried him near to the Cavicciuoli Gallery and showing him a gentleman there, called Messer Filippo Argenti, a big burly rawboned fellow and the most despiteful, choleric and humoursome man alive, gave him a great glass flagon and said to him, 'Go to yonder gentleman with this flask in hand and say to him, "Sir Biondello sendeth me to you and prayeth you be pleased to rubify him this flask with your good red wine, for that he would fain make merry somedele with his minions." But take good care he lay not his hands on thee; else will he give thee an ill morrow and thou wilt have marred my plans.' 'Have I aught else to say,' asked the huckster; and Ciacco answered, 'No; do but go and say this and after come back to me here with the flask and I will pay thee.' The huckster accordingly set off and did his errand to Messer Filippo, who, hearing the message and being lightly ruffled, concluded that Biondello, whom he knew, had a mind to make mock of him, and waxing all red in the face, said, 'What "rubify me" and what "minions" be these? God land thee and him an ill year!' Then, starting to his feet, he put out his hand to lay hold of the huckster; but the latter, who was on his guard, promptly took to his heels and returning by another way to Ciacco, who had seen all that had passed, told him what Messer Filippo had said to him. Ciacco, well pleased, paid him and rested not till he found Biondello, to whom quoth he, 'Hast thou been late at the Cavicciuoli Gallery?' 'Nay,' answered the other. 'Why dost thou ask me?' 'Because,' replied Ciacco, 'I must tell thee that Messer Filippo enquireth for thee; I know not what he would have.' 'Good,' rejoined Biondello; 'I am going that way and will speak with him.' Accordingly, he made off, and Ciacco followed him, to see how the thing should pass.

Meanwhile Messer Filippo, having failed to come at the huckster, abode sore disordered and was inwardly all a-fume with rage, being unable to make anything in the world of the huckster's words, if not that Biondello, at whosesoever instance, was minded to make mock of him. As he fretted himself thus, up came Biondello, whom no sooner did he espy than he made for him and dealt him a sore buffet in the face. 'Alack, sir,' cried Biondello, 'what is this?' Whereupon Messer Filippo, clutching him by the hair and tearing his coif, cast his bonnet to the ground and said, laying on to him amain the while, 'Knave that thou art, thou shalt soon see what it is! What is this thou sendest to say to me with thy "rubify me" and thy "minions"? Deemest thou me a child, to be flouted on this wise?' So saying, he battered his whole face with his fists, which were like very iron, nor left him a hair on his head unruffled; then, rolling him in the mire, he tore all the clothes off his back; and to this he applied himself with such a will that Biondello could not avail to say a word to him nor ask why he served him thus. He had heard him indeed speak of 'rubify me' and 'minions,' but knew not what this meant.

At last, Messer Filippo having beaten him soundly, the bystanders, whereof many had by this time gathered about them, dragged him, with the utmost difficulty, out of the other's clutches, all bruised and battered as he was, and told him why the gentleman had done this, blaming him for that which he had sent to say to him and telling him that he should by that time have known Messer Filippo better and that he was not a man to jest withal. Biondello, all in tears protested his innocence, declaring that he had never sent to Messer Filippo for wine, and as soon as he was somewhat recovered, he returned home, sick and sorry, divining that this must have been Ciacco's doing. When, after many days, the bruises being gone, he began to go abroad again, it chanced that Ciacco encountered him and asked him, laughing, 'Harkye,

Biondello, how deemest thou of Messer Filippo's wine?' 'Even as thou of Messer Corso's lampreys,' replied the other; and Ciacco said, 'The thing resteth with thee henceforth. Whenever thou goest about to give me to eat as thou didst, I will give thee in return to drink after t'other day's fashion.' Biondello, knowing full well that it was easier to wish Ciacco ill than to put it in practise, besought God of his peace[3] and thenceforth was careful to affront him no more."

---

1. *i.e.* hog.
2. Lit. a backbiter (*morditore*).
3. *i.e.* conjured him by God to make peace with him.

9

THE NINTH STORY

TWO YOUNG MEN SEEK COUNSEL OF SOLOMON, ONE
HOW HE MAY BE LOVED AND THE OTHER HOW HE
MAY AMEND HIS FROWARD WIFE, AND IN ANSWER HE
BIDDETH THE ONE LOVE AND THE OTHER GET HIM
TO GOOSEBRIDGE

NONE OTHER THAN the queen remaining to tell, so she would maintain Dioneo his privilege, she, after the ladies had laughed at the unlucky Biondello, began blithely to speak thus: "Lovesome ladies, if the ordinance of created things be considered with a whole mind, it will lightly enough be seen that the general multitude of women are by nature, by custom and by law subjected unto men and that it behoveth them order and govern themselves according to the discretion of these latter; wherefore each woman, who would have quiet and ease and solace with those men to whom she pertaineth, should be humble, patient and obedient, besides being virtuous, which latter is the supreme and especial treasure of every wise woman. Nay, though the laws, which in all things regard the general weal, and usance or (let us say) custom, whose puissance is both great and worship-worth, taught us not this, nature very manifestly showeth it unto us, inasmuch as she hath made us women tender and delicate of body and timid and fearful of spirit and hath given us little bodily strength, sweet voices and soft and graceful movements, all things testifying that we have need of the governance of others. Now, those who have need to be helped and governed, all reason requireth that they be obedient and submissive and reverent to their governors; and whom have we to governors and helpers, if not men? To men, therefore, it behoveth us submit ourselves, honouring them supremely; and whoso departeth from this, I hold her deserving, not only of grave reprehension, but of severe punishment. To these considerations I was lead, though not for the first time, by that which Pampinea told us a while ago of Talano's froward wife, upon whom God sent that chastisement which her husband had not known to give her; wherefore, as I have already said, all those women who depart from being loving, compliant and amenable, as nature, usance and law will it, are, in my judgment, worthy of stern and severe chastisement. It pleaseth me, therefore, to recount to you a counsel given by Solomon, as a salutary medicine for curing women who are thus made of that malady; which counsel let none, who meriteth not such treatment, repute to have been said for her, albeit men have a byword which saith, 'Good horse and bad horse both the spur need still, And women need the stick, both good and ill.' Which words, an one seek to interpret them by way of pleasantry, all women will lightly allow to be true; nay, but considering them morally,[1] I say that the same must be conceded of them; for that women are all naturally unstable and prone [to frailty,] wherefore, to correct the iniquity of those who allow themselves too far to overpass the limits appointed them, there needeth the stick which punisheth them, and to support the virtue of others who suffer not themselves to transgress, there needeth the stick which sustaineth and affeareth them. But, to leave be preaching for the nonce and come to that which I have it in mind to tell.

You must know that, the high renown of Solomon's miraculous wisdom being bruited abroad well nigh throughout the whole world, no less than the liberality with which he dispensed it unto whoso would fain be certified thereof by experience, there flocked many to him from divers parts of the world for counsel in their straitest and most urgent occasions. Amongst others who thus resorted to him was a young man, Melisso by name, a gentleman of noble birth and great wealth, who set out from the city of Lajazzo,[2] whence he was and where he dwelt; and as he journeyed towards Jerusalem, it chanced that, coming forth of Antioch, he rode for some distance with a young man called Giosefo, who held the same course as himself. As the custom is of wayfarers, he entered into discourse with him and having learned from him what and whence he was, he asked him whither he went and upon what occasion; to which Giosefo replied that he was on his way to Solomon, to have counsel of him what course he should take with a wife he had, the most froward and perverse woman alive, whom neither with prayers nor with blandishments nor on any other wise could he avail to correct of her waywardness. Then he in his turn questioned Melisso whence he was and whither he went and on what errand, and he answered, 'I am of Lajazzo, and like as thou hast a grievance, even so have I one; I am young and rich and spend my substance in keeping open house and entertaining my fellow-townsmen, and yet, strange to say, I cannot for all that find one who wisheth me well; wherefore I go whither thou goest, to have counsel how I may win to be beloved.'

Accordingly, they joined company and journeyed till they came to Jerusalem, where, by the introduction of one of Solomon's barons, they were admitted to the presence of the king, to whom Melisso briefly set forth his occasion. Solomon answered him, 'Love'; and this said, Melisso was straightway put forth and Giosefo told that for which he was there. Solomon made him no other answer than 'Get thee to Goosebridge'; which said, Giosefo was on like wise removed, without delay, from the king's presence and finding Melisso awaiting him without, told him that which he had had for answer. Thereupon, pondering Solomon's words and availing to apprehend therefrom neither significance nor profit whatsoever for their occasions, they set out to return home, as deeming themselves flouted. After journeying for some days, they came to a river, over which was a fine bridge, and a caravan of pack-mules and sumpter-horses being in act to pass, it behoved them tarry till such time as these should be crossed over. Presently, the beasts having well nigh all crossed, it chanced that one of the mules took umbrage, as oftentimes we see them do, and would by no means pass on; whereupon a muleteer, taking a stick, began to beat it at first moderately enough to make it go on; but the mule shied now to this and now to that side of the road and whiles turned back altogether, but would on no wise pass on; whereupon the man, incensed beyond measure, fell to dealing it with the stick the heaviest blows in the world, now on the head, now on the flanks and anon on the crupper, but all to no purpose.

Melisso and Giosefo stood watching this and said often to the muleteer, 'Alack, wretch that thou art, what dost thou? Wilt thou kill the beast? Why studiest thou not to manage him by fair means and gentle dealing? He will come quicklier than for cudgeling him as thou dost.' To which the man answered, 'You know your horses and I know my mule; leave me do with him.'

So saying, he fell again to cudgelling him and belaboured him to such purpose on one side and on the other, that the mule passed on and the muleteer won the bout. Then, the two young men being now about to depart, Giosefo asked a poor man, who sat at the bridge-head, how the place was called, and he answered, 'Sir, this is called Goosebridge.' When Giosefo heard this, he straightway called to mind Solomon's words and said to Melisso, 'Marry, I tell thee, comrade, that the counsel given me by Solomon may well prove good and true, for I perceive very plainly that I knew not how to beat my wife; but this muleteer hath shown me what I have to do.'

Accordingly, they fared on and came, after some days, to Antioch, where Giosefo kept Melisso with him, that he might rest himself a day or two, and being scurvily enough received of his wife, he bade her prepare supper according as Melisso should ordain; whereof the latter, seeing that it was his friend's pleasure, acquitted himself in a few words. The lady, as her usance had been in the past, did not as Melisso had ordained, but well nigh altogether the contrary; which Giosefo seeing, he was vexed and said, 'Was it not told thee on what wise thou shouldst prepare the supper?' The lady, turning round haughtily, answered, 'What meaneth this? Good lack, why dost thou not sup, an thou have a mind to sup? An if it were told me otherwise, it seemed good to me to do thus. If it please thee, so be it; if not, leave it be.' Melisso marvelled at the lady's answer and blamed her exceedingly; whilst Giosefo, hearing this, said, 'Wife, thou art still what thou wast wont to be; but, trust me, I will make thee change thy fashion.' Then turning to Melisso, 'Friend,' said he, 'we shall soon see what manner of counsel was Solomon's; but I prithee let it not irk thee to stand to see it and hold that which I shall do for a sport. And that thou mayest not hinder me, bethink thee of the answer the muleteer made us, when we pitied his mule.' Quoth Melisso, 'I am in thy house, where I purpose not to depart from thy good pleasure.'

Giosefo then took a round stick, made of a young oak, and repaired a chamber, whither the lady, having arisen from table for despite, had betaken herself, grumbling; then, laying hold of her by the hair, he threw her down at his feet and proceeded to give her a sore beating with the stick. The lady at first cried out and after fell to threats; but, seeing that Giosefo for all that stinted not and being by this time all bruised, she began to cry him mercy for God's sake and besought him not to kill her, declaring that she would never more depart from his pleasure. Nevertheless, he held not his hand; nay, he continued to baste her more furiously than ever on all her seams, belabouring her amain now on the ribs, now on the haunches and now about the shoulder, nor stinted till he was weary and there was not a place left unbruised on the good lady's back. This done, he returned to his friend and said to him, 'To-morrow we shall see what will be the issue of the counsel to go to Goosebridge.' Then, after he had rested awhile and they had washed their hands, he supped with Melisso and in due season they betook themselves to bed.

Meanwhile the wretched lady arose with great pain from the ground and casting herself on the bed, there rested as best she might until the morning, when she arose betimes and let ask Giosefo what he would have dressed for dinner. The latter, making merry over this with Melisso, appointed it in due course, and after, whenas it was time, returning, they found everything excellently well done and in accordance with the ordinance given; wherefore they mightily commended the counsel at first so ill apprehended of them. After some days, Melisso took leave of Giosefo and returning to his own house, told one, who was a man of understanding, the answer he had had from Solomon; whereupon quoth the other, 'He could have given thee no truer nor better counsel. Thou knowest thou lovest no one, and the honours and services thou renderest others, thou dost not for love that thou bearest them, but for pomp and ostentation. Love, then, as Solomon bade thee, and thou shalt be loved.' On this wise, then, was the froward wife corrected and the young man, loving, was beloved."

---

1. *i.e.* from a serious or moral point of view.
2. Apparently Laodicea (*hod.* Eskihissar) in Anatolia, from which a traveller, taking the direct land route, would necessarily pass Antioch (*hod.* Antakhia) on his way to Jerusalem.

❧ 10 ❧

THE TENTH STORY

DOM GIANNI, AT THE INSTANCE OF HIS GOSSIP
PIETRO, PERFORMETH A CONJURATION FOR THE
PURPOSE OF CAUSING THE LATTER'S WIFE TO
BECOME A MARE; BUT, WHENAS HE COMETH TO PUT
ON THE TAIL, PIETRO MARRETH THE WHOLE
CONJURATION, SAYING THAT HE WILL NOT HAVE
A TAIL

THE QUEEN'S story made the young men laugh and gave rise to some murmurs on the part of the ladies; then, as soon as the latter were quiet, Dioneo began to speak thus, "Sprightly ladies, a black crow amongst a multitude of white doves addeth more beauty than would a snow-white swan, and in like manner among many sages one less wise is not only an augmentation of splendour and goodliness to their maturity, but eke a source of diversion and solace. Wherefore, you ladies being all exceeding discreet and modest, I, who savour somewhat of the scatterbrain, should be dearer to you, causing, as I do, your worth to shine the brightlier for my default, than if with my greater merit I made this of yours wax dimmer; and consequently, I should have larger license to show you myself such as I am and should more patiently be suffered of you, in saying that which I shall say, than if I were wiser. I will, therefore, tell you a story not overlong, whereby you may apprehend how diligently it behoveth to observe the conditions imposed by those who do aught by means of enchantment and how slight a default thereof sufficeth to mar everything done by the magician.

A year or two agone there was at Barletta a priest called Dom Gianni di Barolo, who, for that he had but a poor cure, took to eking out his livelihood by hawking merchandise hither and thither about the fairs of Apulia with a mare of his and buying and selling. In the course of his travels he contracted a strait friendship with one who styled himself Pietro da Tresanti and plied the same trade with the aid of an ass he had. In token of friendship and affection, he called him still Gossip Pietro, after the Apulian fashion, and whenassoever he visited Barletta, he carried him to his parsonage and there lodged him with himself and entertained him to the best of his power. Gossip Pietro, on his part, albeit he was very poor and had but a sorry little house at Tresanti, scarce sufficing for himself and a young and buxom wife he had and his ass, as often as Dom Gianni came to Tresanti, carried him home with him and entertained him as best he might, in requital of the hospitality received from him at Barletta. Nevertheless, in the matter of lodging, having but one sorry little bed, in which he slept with his handsome wife, he could not entertain him as he would, but, Dom Gianni's mare being lodged with Pietro's ass in a little stable he had, needs must the priest himself lie by her side on a truss of straw.

The goodwife, knowing the hospitality which the latter did her husband at Barletta, would more than once, whenas the priest came thither, have gone to lie with a neighbor of hers, by name Zita Caraprese, [daughter] of Giudice Leo, so he might sleep in the bed with her husband, and had many a time proposed it to Dom Gianni, but he would never hear of it; and once, amongst other times, he said to her, 'Gossip Gemmata, fret not thyself for me; I fare very well, for that, whenas it pleaseth me, I cause this mare of mine become a handsome wench and couch with her, and after, when I will, I change her into a mare again; wherefore I care not to part from her.'

The young woman marvelled, but believed his tale and told her husband, saying, 'If he is so much thy friend as thou sayest, why dost thou not make him teach thee his charm, so thou mayst avail to make of me a mare and do thine affairs with the ass and the mare? So should we gain two for one; and when we were back at home, thou couldst make me a woman again, as I am.' Pietro, who was somewhat dull of wit, believed what she said and falling in with her counsel, began, as best he knew, to importune Dom Gianni to teach him the trick. The latter did his best to cure him of that folly, but availing not thereto, he said, 'Harkye, since you will e'en have it so, we will arise to-morrow morning before day, as of our wont, and I will show you how it is done. To tell thee the truth, the uneathest part of the matter is the putting on of the tail, as thou shalt see.'

Accordingly, whenas it drew near unto day, Goodman Pietro and Gossip Gemmata, who had scarce slept that night, with such impatience did they await the accomplishment of the matter, arose and called Dom Gianni, who, arising in his shirt, betook himself to Pietro's little chamber and said to him, 'I know none in the world, except you, for whom I would do this; wherefore since it pleaseth you, I will e'en do it; but needs must you do as I shall bid you, an you would have the thing succeed.' They answered that they would do that which he should say; whereupon, taking the light, he put it into Pietro's hand and said to him, 'Mark how I shall do and keep well in mind that which I shall say. Above all, have a care, an thou wouldst not mar everything, that, whatsoever thou hearest or seest, thou say not a single word, and pray God that the tail may stick fast.' Pietro took the light, promising to do exactly as he said, whereupon Dom Gianni let strip Gemmata naked as she was born and caused her stand on all fours, mare-fashion, enjoining herself likewise not to utter a word for aught that should betide. Then, passing his hand over her face and her head, he proceeded to say, 'Be this a fine mare's head,' and touching her hair, said, 'Be this a fine mare's mane'; after which he touched her arms, saying, 'Be these fine mare's legs and feet,' and coming presently to her breast and finding it round and firm, such an one awoke that was not called and started up on end,[1] whereupon quoth he, 'Be this a fine mare's chest.' And on like wise he did with her back and belly and crupper and thighs and legs. Ultimately, nothing remaining to do but the tail, he pulled up his shirt and taking the dibble with which he planted men, he thrust it hastily into the furrow made therefor and said, 'And be this a fine mare's tail.'

Pietro, who had thitherto watched everything intently, seeing this last proceeding and himseeming it was ill done, said, 'Ho there, Dom Gianni, I won't have a tail there, I won't have a tail there!' The radical moisture, wherewith all plants are made fast, was by this come, and Dom Gianni drew it forth, saying, 'Alack, gossip Pietro, what hast thou done? Did I not bid thee say not a word for aught that thou shouldst see? The mare was all made; but thou hast marred everything by talking, nor is there any means of doing it over again henceforth.' Quoth Pietro, 'Marry, I did not want that tail there. Why did you not say to me, "Make it thou"? More by token that you were for setting it too low.' 'Because,' answered Dom Gianni, 'thou hadst not known for the first time to set it on so well as I.' The young woman, hearing all this, stood up and said to her husband, in all good faith, 'Dolt that thou art, why hast thou marred thine affairs and mine? What mare sawest thou ever without a tail? So God aid me, thou art poor, but

435

it would serve thee right, wert thou much poorer.' Then, there being now, by reason of the words that Pietro had spoken, no longer any means of making a mare of the young woman, she donned her clothes, woebegone and disconsolate, and Pietro, continuing to ply his old trade with an ass, as he was used, betook himself, in company with Dom Gianni, to the Bitonto fair, nor ever again required him of such a service."

HOW MUCH THE company laughed at this story, which was better understood of the ladies than Dioneo willed, let her who shall yet laugh thereat imagine for herself. But, the day's stories being now ended and the sun beginning to abate of its heat, the queen, knowing the end of her seignory to be come, rose to her feet and putting off the crown, set it on the head of Pamfilo, whom alone it remained to honour after such a fashion, and said, smiling, "My lord, there devolveth on thee a great burden, inasmuch as with thee it resteth, thou being the last, to make amends for my default and that of those who have foregone me in the dignity which thou presently holdest; whereof God lend thee grace, even as He hath vouchsafed it unto me to make thee king." Pamfilo blithely received the honour done him and answered, "Your merit and that of my other subjects will do on such wise that I shall be adjudged deserving of commendation, even as the others have been." Then, having, according to the usance of his predecessors, taken order with the seneschal of the things that were needful, he turned to the expectant ladies and said to them, "Lovesome ladies, it was the pleasure of Emilia, who hath this day been our queen, to give you, for the purpose of affording some rest to your powers, license to discourse of that which should most please you; wherefore, you being now rested, I hold it well to return to the wonted ordinance, and accordingly I will that each of you bethink herself to discourse to-morrow of this, to wit, OF WHOSO HATH ANYWISE WROUGHT GENEROUSLY OR MAGNIFICENTLY IN MATTERS OF LOVE OR OTHERWHAT. The telling and doing of these things will doubtless fire your well-disposed minds to do worthily; so will our life, which may not be other than brief in this mortal body, be made perpetual in laudatory renown; a thing which all, who serve not the belly only, as do the beasts, should not only desire, but with all diligence seek and endeavour after."

The theme pleased the joyous company, who having all, with the new king's license, arisen from session, gave themselves to their wonted diversions, according to that unto which each was most drawn by desire; and on this wise they did until the hour of supper, whereunto they came joyously and were served with diligence and fair ordinance. Supper at an end, they arose to the wonted dances, and after they had sung a thousand canzonets, more diverting of words than masterly of music, the king bade Neifile sing one in her own name; whereupon, with clear and blithesome voice, she cheerfully and without delay began thus:

> A youngling maid am I and full of glee,
> Am fain to carol in the new-blown May,
> Love and sweet thoughts-a-mercy, blithe and free.
>
> I go about the meads, considering
> The vermeil flowers and golden and the white,
> Roses thorn-set and lilies snowy-bright,
> And one and all I fare a-likening
> Unto his face who hath with love-liking
> Ta'en and will hold me ever, having aye
> None other wish than as his pleasures be;

Whereof when one I find me that doth show,
Unto my seeming, likest him, full fain
I cull and kiss and talk with it amain
And all my heart to it, as best I know,
Discover, with its store of wish and woe,
Then it with others in a wreath I lay,
Bound with my hair so golden-bright of blee.

Ay, and that pleasure which the eye doth prove,
By nature, of the flower's view, like delight
Doth give me as I saw the very wight
Who hath inflamed me of his dulcet love,
And what its scent thereover and above
Worketh in me, no words indeed can say;
But sighs thereof bear witness true for me,

The which from out my bosom day nor night
Ne'er, as with other ladies, fierce and wild,
Storm up; nay, thence they issue warm and mild
And straight betake them to my loved one's sight,
Who, hearing, moveth of himself, delight
To give me; ay, and when I'm like to say
"Ah come, lest I despair," still cometh he.

Neifile's canzonet was much commended both of the king and of the other ladies; after which, for that a great part of the night was now spent, the king commanded that all should betake themselves to rest until the day.

---

1. *i.e.* arrectus est penis ejus.

DAY THE TENTH

Here Beginneth the Tenth and Last Day of the
Decameron Wherein Under the Governance of
Pamfilo Is Discoursed of Whoso Hath Anywise
Wrought Generously or Magnificently in Matters of
Love or Otherwhat

Certain cloudlets in the West were yet vermeil, what time those of the East were already at their
marges grown lucent like unto very gold, when Pamfilo, arising, let call his comrades and the
ladies, who being all come, he took counsel with them of whither they should go for their
diversion and fared forth with slow step, accompanied by Filomena and Fiammetta, whilst all
the others followed after. On this wise, devising and telling and answering many things of their
future life together, they went a great while a-pleasuring; then, having made a pretty long
circuit and the sun beginning to wax overhot, they returned to the palace. There they let rinse
the beakers in the clear fountain and whoso would drank somewhat; after which they went
frolicking among the pleasant shades of the garden until the eating-hour. Then, having eaten
and slept, as of their wont, they assembled whereas it pleased the king and there he called upon
Neifile for the first discourse, who blithely began thus:

THE FIRST STORY

A KNIGHT IN THE KING'S SERVICE OF SPAIN THINKING HIMSELF ILL GUERDONED, THE KING BY VERY CERTAIN PROOF SHOWETH HIM THAT THIS IS NOT HIS FAULT, BUT THAT OF HIS OWN PERVERSE FORTUNE, AND AFTER LARGESSETH HIM MAGNIFICENTLY

"NEEDS, honourable ladies, must I repute it a singular favour to myself that our king hath preferred me unto such an honour as it is to be the first to tell of magnificence, the which, even as the sun is the glory and adornment of all the heaven, is the light and lustre of every other virtue. I will, therefore, tell you a little story thereof, quaint and pleasant enough to my thinking, which to recall can certes be none other than useful.

You must know, then, that, among the other gallant gentlemen who have from time immemorial graced our city, there was one (and maybe the most of worth) by name Messer Ruggieri de' Figiovanni, who, being both rich and high-spirited and seeing that, in view of the way of living and of the usages of Tuscany, he might, if he tarried there, avail to display little or nothing of his merit, resolved to seek service awhile with Alfonso, King of Spain, the renown of whose valiance transcended that of every other prince of his time; wherefore he betook himself, very honourably furnished with arms and horses and followers, to Alfonso in Spain and was by him graciously received. Accordingly, he took up his abode there and living splendidly and doing marvellous deeds of arms, he very soon made himself known for a man of worth and valour.

When he had sojourned there a pretty while and had taken particular note of the king's fashions, himseemed he bestowed castles and cities and baronies now upon one and now upon another with little enough discretion, as giving them to those who were unworthy thereof, and for that to him, who held himself for that which he was, nothing was given, he conceived that his repute would be much abated by reason thereof; wherefore he determined to depart and craved leave of the king. The latter granted him the leave he sought and gave him one of the best and finest mules that ever was ridden, the which, for the long journey he had to make, was very acceptable to Messer Ruggieri. Moreover, he charged a discreet servant of his that he should study, by such means as seemed to him best, to ride with Messer Ruggieri on such wise that he should not appear to have been sent by the king, and note everything he should say of him, so as he might avail to repeat it to him, and that on the ensuing morning he should command him return to the court. Accordingly, the servant, lying in wait for Messer Ruggieri's departure, accosted him, as he came forth the city, and very aptly joined company with him, giving him to understand that he also was bound for Italy. Messer Ruggieri, then, fared on, riding the mule given him by the king and devising of one thing and another with the latter's servant, till hard upon tierce, when he said, 'Methinketh it were well done to let our beasts stale.' Accordingly, they put them up in a stable and they all staled, except the mule; then they rode on again, whilst the squire still took note of the gentleman's words, and came presently to a river, where, as they watered their cattle, the mule staled in the stream; which Messer Ruggieri seeing, 'Marry,' quoth he, 'God confound thee, beast, for that thou art made after the same fashion as the prince who gave thee to me!' The squire noted these words and albeit he took store of many others, as he journeyed with him all that day, he heard him say nought else but what was to the highest praise of the king.

Next morning, they being mounted and Ruggieri offering to ride towards Tuscany, the squire imparted to him the king's commandment, whereupon he incontinent turned back. When he arrived at court, the king, learning what he had said of the mule, let call him to himself and receiving him with a cheerful favour, asked him why he had likened him to his mule, or rather why he had likened the mule to him. 'My lord,' replied Ruggieri frankly, 'I likened her to you for that, like as you give whereas it behoveth not and give not whereas it behoveth, even so she staled not whereas it behoved, but staled whereas it behoved not.' Then said the king, 'Messer Ruggieri, if I have not given to you, as I have given unto many who are of no account in comparison with you, it happened not because I knew you not for a most valiant cavalier and worthy of every great gift; nay, but it is your fortune, which hath not suffered me guerdon you according to your deserts, that hath sinned in this, and not I; and that I may say sooth I will manifestly prove to you.' 'My lord,' replied Ruggieri, 'I was not chagrined because I have gotten no largesse of you, for that I desire not to be richer than I am, but because you have on no wise borne witness to my merit. Natheless, I hold your excuse for good and honourable and am ready to see that which it shall please you show me, albeit I believe you without proof.' The king then carried him into a great hall of his, where, as he had ordered it beforehand, were two great locked coffers, and said to him, in presence of many, 'Messer Ruggieri, in one of these coffers is my crown, the royal sceptre and the orb, together with many goodly girdles and ouches and rings of mine, and in fine every precious jewel I have; and the other is full of earth. Take, then, one and be that which you shall take yours; and you may thus see whether of the twain hath been ungrateful to your worth, myself of your ill fortune.'

Messer Ruggieri, seeing that it was the king's pleasure, took one of the coffers, which, being opened by Alfonso's commandment, was found to be that which was full of earth; whereupon quoth the king, laughing, 'Now can you see, Messer Ruggieri, that this that I tell you of your fortune is true; but certes your worth meriteth that I should oppose myself to her might. I know you have no mind to turn Spaniard and therefore I will bestow upon you neither castle nor city in these parts; but this coffer, of which fortune deprived you, I will in her despite shall be yours, so you may carry it off to your own country and justly glorify yourself of your worth in the sight of your countrymen by the witness of my gifts.' Messer Ruggieri accordingly took the coffer and having rendered the king those thanks which sorted with such a gift, joyfully returned therewith to Tuscany."

THE SECOND STORY

GHINO DI TACCO TAKETH THE ABBOT OF CLUNY AND HAVING CURED HIM OF THE STOMACH-COMPLAINT, LETTETH HIM GO; WHEREUPON THE ABBOT, RETURNING TO THE COURT OF ROME, RECONCILETH HIM WITH POPE BONIFACE AND MAKETH HIM A PRIOR OF THE HOSPITALLERS

THE MAGNIFICENCE SHOWN by King Alfonso to the Florentine cavalier having been duly commended, the king, who had been mightily pleased therewith, enjoined Elisa to follow on, and she straightway began thus: "Dainty dames, it cannot be denied that for a king to be munificent and to have shown his munificence to him who had served him is a great and a praiseworthy thing; but what shall we say if a churchman be related to have practised marvellous magnanimity towards one, whom if he had used as an enemy, he had of none been blamed therefor? Certes, we can say none otherwise than that the king's magnificence was a virtue, whilst that of the churchman was a miracle, inasmuch as the clergy are all exceeding niggardly, nay, far more so than women, and sworn enemies of all manner of liberality; and albeit all men naturally hunger after vengeance for affronts received, we see churchmen, for all they preach patience and especially commend the remission of offences, pursue it more eagerly than other folk. This, then, to wit, how a churchman was magnanimous, you may manifestly learn from the following story of mine.

Ghino di Tacco, a man very famous for his cruelty and his robberies, being expelled Siena and at feud with the Counts of Santa Fiore, raised Radicofani against the Church of Rome and taking up his sojourn there, caused his swashbucklers despoil whosoever passed through the surrounding country. Now, Boniface the Eighth being pope in Rome, there came to court the Abbot of Cluny, who is believed to be one of the richest prelates in the world, and having there marred his stomach, he was advised by the physicians to repair to the baths of Siena and he would without fail be cured. Accordingly, having gotten the pope's leave, he set out on his way thither in great pomp of gear and baggage and horses and servitors, unrecking of Ghino's [ill] report. The latter, hearing of his coming, spread his nets and hemmed him and all his household and gear about in a strait place, without letting a single footboy escape. This done, he despatched to the abbot one, the most sufficient, of his men, well accompanied, who in his name very lovingly prayed him be pleased to light down and sojourn with the aforesaid Ghino in his castle. The abbot, hearing this, answered furiously that he would nowise do it, having nought to do with Ghino, but that he would fare on and would fain see who should forbid his passage. Whereto quoth the messenger on humble wise, 'Sir, you are come into parts where,

443

barring God His might, there is nothing to fear for us and where excommunications and interdicts are all excommunicated; wherefore, may it please you, you were best comply with Ghino in this.'

During this parley, the whole place had been encompassed about with men-at-arms; wherefore the abbot, seeing himself taken with his men, betook himself, sore against his will, to the castle, in company with the ambassador, and with him all his household and gear, and alighting there, was, by Ghino's orders, lodged all alone in a very dark and mean little chamber in one of the pavilions, whilst every one else was well enough accommodated, according to his quality, about the castle and the horses and all the gear put in safety, without aught thereof being touched. This done, Ghino betook himself to the abbot and said to him, 'Sir, Ghino, whose guest you are, sendeth to you, praying you acquaint him whither you are bound and on what occasion.' The abbot, like a wise man, had by this laid by his pride and told him whither he went and why. Ghino, hearing this, took his leave and bethought himself to go about to cure him without baths. Accordingly, he let keep a great fire still burning in the little room and causing guard the place well, returned not to the abbot till the following morning, when he brought him, in a very white napkin, two slices of toasted bread and a great beaker of his own Corniglia vernage[1] and bespoke him thus, 'Sir, when Ghino was young, he studied medicine and saith that he learned there was no better remedy for the stomach-complaint than that which he purposeth to apply to you and of which these things that I bring you are the beginning; wherefore do you take them and refresh yourself.'

The abbot, whose hunger was greater than his desire to bandy words, ate the bread and drank the wine, though he did it with an ill will, and after made many haughty speeches, asking and counselling of many things and demanding in particular to see Ghino. The latter, hearing this talk, let part of it pass as idle and answered the rest very courteously, avouching that Ghino would visit him as quickliest he might. This said, he took his leave of him and returned not until the ensuing day, when he brought him as much toasted bread and as much malmsey; and so he kept him several days, till such time as he perceived that he had eaten some dried beans, which he had of intent aforethought brought secretly thither and left there; whereupon he asked him, on Ghino's part, how he found himself about the stomach. The abbot answered, 'Meseemeth I should fare well, were I but out of his hands; and after that, I have no greater desire than to eat, so well have his remedies cured me.' Thereupon Ghino caused the abbot's own people array him a goodly chamber with his own gear and let make ready a magnificent banquet, to which he bade the prelate's whole household, together with many folk of the burgh. Next morning, he betook himself to the abbot and said to him, 'Sir, since you feel yourself well, it is time to leave the infirmary.' Then, taking him by the hand, he brought him to the chamber prepared for him and leaving him there in company of his own people, occupied himself with caring that the banquet should be a magnificent one.

The abbot solaced himself awhile with his men and told them what his life had been since his capture, whilst they, on the other hand, avouched themselves all to have been wonder-well entreated of Ghino. The eating-hour come, the abbot and the rest were well and orderly served with goodly viands and fine wines, without Ghino yet letting himself be known of the prelate; but, after the latter had abidden some days on this wise, the outlaw, having let bring all his gear into one saloon and all his horses, down to the sorriest rouncey, into a courtyard that was under the windows thereof, betook himself to him and asked him how he did and if he deemed himself strong enough to take horse. The abbot answered that he was strong enough and quite recovered of his stomach-complaint and that he should fare perfectly well, once he should be out of Ghino's hands. Ghino then brought him into the saloon, wherein was his gear and all his train, and carrying him to a window, whence he might see all his horses, said, 'My lord abbot, you must know that it was the being a gentleman and expelled from his house and poor and having many and puissant enemies, and not evilness of mind, that brought Ghino di Tacco (who is none other than myself) to be, for the defence of his life and his nobility, a highway-robber and an enemy of the court of Rome. Nevertheless, for that you seem to me a worthy gentleman, I purpose not, now that I have cured you of your stomach-complaint, to use you as I would another, from whom, he being in my hands as you are, I would take for myself such part of his goods as seemed well to me; nay, it is my intent that you, having regard to my need, shall appoint to me such part of your good as you yourself will. It is all here before you in its entirety and your horses you may from this window see in the courtyard; take, therefore, both part and all, as it pleaseth you, and from this time forth be it at your pleasure to go or to stay.'

The abbot marvelled to hear such generous words from a highway-robber and was exceeding well pleased therewith, insomuch that, his anger and despite being of a sudden fallen, nay, changed into goodwill, he became Ghino's hearty friend and ran to embrace him, saying, 'I vow to God that, to gain the friendship of a man such as I presently judge thee to be, I would gladly consent to suffer a far greater affront than that which meseemed but now thou hadst done me. Accursed be fortune that constrained thee to so damnable a trade!' Then, letting take of his many goods but a very few necessary things, and the like of his horses, he left all the rest to Ghino and returned to Rome. The pope had had news of the taking of the abbot and albeit it had given him sore concern, he asked him, when he saw him, how the baths had profited him; whereto he replied, smiling, 'Holy Father, I found a worthy physician nearer than at the baths, who hath excellently well cured me'; and told him how, whereat the pope laughed, and the abbot, following on his speech and moved by a magnanimous spirit, craved a boon of him. The pope, thinking he would demand otherwhat, freely offered to do that which he should ask; and the abbot said, 'Holy Father, that which I mean to ask of you is that you restore your favour to Ghino di Tacco, my physician, for that, of all the men of worth and high account whom I ever knew, he is certes one of the most deserving; and for this ill that he doth, I hold it much more fortune's fault than his; the which[2] if you change by bestowing on him somewhat whereby he may live according to his condition, I doubt not anywise but you will, in brief space of time, deem of him even as I do.' The pope, who was great of soul and a lover of men of worth, hearing this, replied that he would gladly do it, an Ghino were indeed of such account as the abbot avouched, and bade the latter cause him come thither in all security. Accordingly, Ghino, at the abbot's instance, came to court, upon that assurance, nor had he been long about the pope's person ere the latter reputed him a man of worth and taking him into favour, bestowed on him a grand priory of those of the Hospitallers, having first let make him a knight of that order; which office he held whilst he lived, still approving himself a loyal friend and servant of Holy Church and of the Abbot of Cluny."

---

1. See n. 371.
2. *i.e.* fortune.

❧ 3 ❧

THE THIRD STORY

MITHRIDANES, ENVYING NATHAN HIS HOSPITALITY
AND GENEROSITY AND GOING TO KILL HIM,
FALLETH IN WITH HIMSELF, WITHOUT KNOWING
HIM, AND IS BY HIM INSTRUCTED OF THE COURSE HE
SHALL TAKE TO ACCOMPLISH HIS PURPOSE; BY MEANS
WHEREOF HE FINDETH HIM, AS HE HIMSELF HAD
ORDERED IT, IN A COPPICE AND RECOGNIZING HIM,
IS ASHAMED AND BECOMETH HIS FRIEND

THEMSEEMED all they had heard what was like unto a miracle, to wit, that a churchman should have wrought anywhat magnificently; but, as soon as the ladies had left discoursing thereof, the king bade Filostrato proceed, who forthright began, "Noble ladies, great was the magnificence of the King of Spain and that of the Abbot of Cluny a thing belike never yet heard of; but maybe it will seem to you no less marvellous a thing to hear how a man, that he might do generosity to another who thirsted for his blood, nay, for the very breath of his nostrils, privily bethought himself to give them to him, ay, and would have done it, had the other willed to take them, even as I purpose to show you in a little story of mine.

It is a very certain thing (if credit may be given to the report of divers Genoese and others who have been in those countries) that there was aforetime in the parts of Cattajo[1] a man of noble lineage and rich beyond compare, called Nathan, who, having an estate adjoining a highway whereby as of necessity passed all who sought to go from the Ponant to the Levant or from the Levant to the Ponant, and being a man of great and generous soul and desirous that it should be known by his works, assembled a great multitude of artificers and let build there, in a little space of time, one of the fairest and greatest and richest palaces that had ever been seen, the which he caused excellently well furnished with all that was apt unto the reception and entertainment of gentlemen. Then, having a great and goodly household, he there received and honourably entertained, with joyance and good cheer, whosoever came and went; and in this praiseworthy usance he persevered insomuch that not only the Levant, but well nigh all the Ponant, knew him by report. He was already full of years nor was therefore grown weary of the practice of hospitality, when it chanced that his fame reached the ears of a young man of a country not far from his own, by name Mithridanes, who, knowing himself no less rich than Nathan and waxing envious of his renown and his virtues, bethought himself to eclipse or shadow them with greater liberality. Accordingly, letting build a palace like unto that of Nathan, he proceeded to do the most unbounded courtesies[2] that ever any did whosoever came or went about those parts, and in a short time he became without doubt very famous.

It chanced one day that, as he abode all alone in the midcourt of his palace, there came in, by one of the gates, a poor woman, who sought of him an alms and had it; then, coming in again to

446

him by the second, she had of him another alms, and so on for twelve times in succession; but, whenas she returned for the thirteenth time, he said to her, 'Good woman, thou art very diligent in this thine asking,' and natheless gave her an alms. The old crone, hearing these words, exclaimed, 'O liberality of Nathan, how marvellous art thou! For that, entering in by each of the two-and-thirty gates which his palace hath, and asking of him an alms, never, for all that he showed, was I recognized of him, and still I had it; whilst here, having as yet come in but at thirteen gates, I have been both recognized and chidden.' So saying, she went her ways and returned thither no more. Mithridanes, hearing the old woman's words, flamed up into a furious rage, as he who held that which he heard of Nathan's fame a diminishment of his own, and fell to saying, 'Alack, woe is me! When shall I attain to Nathan's liberality in great things, let alone overpass it, as I seek to do, seeing that I cannot approach him in the smallest? Verily, I weary myself in vain, an I remove him not from the earth; wherefore, since eld carrieth him not off, needs must I with mine own hands do it without delay.'

Accordingly, rising upon that motion, he took horse with a small company, without communicating his design to any, and came after three days whereas Nathan abode. He arrived there at eventide and bidding his followers make a show of not being with him and provide themselves with lodging, against they should hear farther from him, abode alone at no great distance from the fair palace, where he found Nathan all unattended, as he went walking for his diversion, without any pomp of apparel, and knowing him not, asked him if he could inform him where Nathan dwelt. 'My son,' answered the latter cheerfully, 'there is none in these parts who is better able than I to show thee that; wherefore, whenas it pleaseth thee, I will carry thee thither.' Mithridanes rejoined that this would be very acceptable to him, but that, an it might be, he would fain be neither seen nor known of Nathan; and the latter said, 'That also will I do, since it pleaseth thee.' Mithridanes accordingly dismounted and repaired to the goodly palace, in company with Nathan, who quickly engaged him in most pleasant discourse. There he caused one of his servants take the young man's horse and putting his mouth to his ear, charged him take order with all those of the house, so none should tell the youth that he was Nathan; and so was it done. Moreover, he lodged him in a very goodly chamber, where none saw him, save those whom he had deputed to this service, and let entertain him with the utmost honour, himself bearing him company.

After Mithridanes had abidden with him awhile on this wise, he asked him (albeit he held him in reverence as a father) who he was; to which Nathan answered, 'I am an unworthy servant of Nathan, who have grown old with him from my childhood, nor hath he ever advanced me to otherwhat than that which thou seest me; wherefore, albeit every one else is mighty well pleased with him, I for my part have little cause to thank him.' These words afforded Mithridanes some hope of availing with more certitude and more safety to give effect to his perverse design, and Nathan very courteously asking him who he was and what occasion brought him into those parts and proffering him his advice and assistance insomuch as lay in his power, he hesitated awhile to reply, but, presently, resolving to trust himself to him, he with a long circuit of words[3] required him first of secrecy and after of aid and counsel and entirely discovered to him who he was and wherefore and on what motion he came. Nathan, hearing his discourse and his cruel design, was inwardly all disordered; but nevertheless, without much hesitation, he answered him with an undaunted mind and a firm countenance, saying, 'Mithridanes, thy father was a noble man and thou showest thyself minded not to degenerate from him, in having entered upon so high an emprise as this thou hast undertaken, to wit, to be liberal unto all; and greatly do I commend the jealousy thou bearest unto Nathan's virtues, for that, were there many such,[4] the world, that is most wretched, would soon become good. The design that thou hast discovered to me I will without fail keep secret; but for the accomplishment thereof I can rather give thee useful counsel than great help; the which is this. Thou mayst from here see a coppice, maybe half a mile hence, wherein Nathan well nigh every morning walketh all alone, taking his pleasure there a pretty long while; and there it will be a light matter to thee to find him and do thy will of him. If thou slay him, thou must, so thou mayst return home without hindrance, get thee gone, not by that way thou camest, but by that which thou wilt see issue forth of the coppice on the left hand, for that, albeit it is somewhat wilder, it is nearer to thy country and safer for thee.'

Mithridanes, having received this information and Nathan having taken leave of him, privily let his companions, who had, like himself, taken up their sojourn in the palace, know where they should look for him on the morrow; and the new day came, Nathan, whose intent was nowise at variance with the counsel he had given Mithridanes nor was anywise changed, betook himself alone to the coppice, there to die. Meanwhile, Mithridanes arose and taking his bow and his sword, for other arms he had not, mounted to horse and made for the coppice, where he saw Nathan from afar go walking all alone. Being resolved, ere he attacked him, to seek to see him and hear him speak, he ran towards him and seizing him by the fillet he had about his head, said, 'Old man, thou art dead.' Whereto Nathan answered no otherwhat than, 'Then have I merited it.' Mithridanes, hearing his voice and looking him in the face, knew him forthright for him who had so lovingly received him and familiarly companied with him and faithfully counselled him; whereupon his fury incontinent subsided and his rage was changed into shame. Accordingly, casting away the sword, which he had already pulled out to smite him, and lighting down from his horse, he ran, weeping, to throw himself at Nathan's feet and said to him, 'Now, dearest father, do I manifestly recognize your liberality, considering with what secrecy you are come hither to give me your life, whereof, without any reason, I showed myself desirous, and that to yourself; but God, more careful of mine honour than I myself, hath, in the extremest hour of need, opened the eyes of my understanding, which vile envy had closed. Wherefore, the readier you have been to comply with me, so much the more do I confess myself beholden to do penance for my default. Take, then, of me the vengeance which you deem conformable to my sin.'

Nathan raised Mithridanes to his feet and tenderly embraced and kissed him, saying, 'My son, it needeth not that thou shouldst ask nor that I should grant forgiveness of thine emprise, whatever thou choosest to style it, whether wicked or otherwise; for that thou pursuedst it, not of hatred, but to win to be held better. Live, then, secure from me and be assured that there is no man alive who loveth thee as I do, having regard to the loftiness of thy soul, which hath given itself, not to the amassing of monies, as do the covetous, but to the expenditure of those that have been amassed. Neither be thou ashamed of having sought to slay me, so though mightest become famous, nor think that I marvel thereat. The greatest emperors and the most illustrious kings have, with well nigh none other art than that of slaying, not one man, as thou wouldst have done, but an infinite multitude of men, and burning countries and razing cities, enlarged their realms and consequently their fame; wherefore, an thou wouldst, to make thyself more famous, have slain me only, thou diddest no new nor extraordinary thing, but one much used.'

Mithridanes, without holding himself excused of his perverse design, commended the honourable excuse found by Nathan and came, in course of converse with him, to say that he marvelled beyond measure how he could have brought himself to meet his death and have gone so far as even to give him means and counsel to that end; whereto quoth Nathan, 'Mithridanes, I would not have thee marvel at my resolution nor at the counsel I gave thee, for that, since I have been mine own master and have addressed myself to do that same thing which thou hast undertaken to do, there came never any to my house but I contented him, so far as in me lay, of that which was required of me by him. Thou camest hither, desirous of my life; wherefore, learning that thou soughtest it, I straightway determined to give it thee, so thou mightest not be the only one to depart hence without his wish; and in order that thou mightest have thy desire, I gave thee such counsel as I thought apt to enable thee to have my life and not lose thine own; and therefore I tell thee once more and pray thee, an it please thee, take it and satisfy thyself thereof. I know not how I may better bestow it. These fourscore years have I occupied it and used it about my pleasures and my diversions, and I know that in the course of nature, according as it fareth with other men and with things in general, it can now be left me but a little while longer; wherefore I hold it far better to bestow it by way of gift, like as I have still given and expended my [other] treasures, than to seek to keep it until such times as it shall be taken from me by nature against my will. To give an hundred years is no great boon; how much less, then, is it to give the six or eight I have yet to abide here? Take it, then, an it like thee. Prithee, then, take it, an thou have a mind thereto; for that never yet, what while I have lived here, have I found any who hath desired it, nor know I when I may find any such, an thou, who demandest it, take it not. And even should I chance to find any one, I know that, the longer I keep it, the less worth will it be; therefore, ere it wax sorrier, take it, I beseech thee.'

Mithridanes was sore abashed and replied, 'God forbid I should, let alone take and sever from you a thing of such price as your life, but even desire to do so, as but late I did,—your life, whose years far from seeking to lessen, I would willingly add thereto of mine own!' Whereto Nathan straightway rejoined, 'And art thou indeed willing, it being in thy power to do it, to add of thy years unto mine and in so doing, to cause me do for thee that which I never yet did for any man, to wit, take of thy good, I who never yet took aught of others?' 'Ay am I,' answered Mithridanes in haste. 'Then,' said Nathan, 'thou must do as I shall bid thee. Thou shalt take up thine abode, young as thou art, here in my house and bear the name of Nathan, whilst I will betake myself to thy house and let still call myself Mithridanes.' Quoth Mithridanes, 'An I knew how to do as well as you have done and do, I would, without hesitation, take that which you proffer me; but, since meseemeth very certain that my actions would be a diminishment of Nathan's fame and as I purpose not to mar in another that which I know not how to order in myself, I will not take it.' These and many other courteous discourses having passed between them, they returned, at Nathan's instance, to the latter's palace, where he entertained Mithridanes with the utmost honour sundry days, heartening him in his great and noble purpose with all manner of wit and wisdom. Then, Mithridanes desiring to return to his own house with his company, he dismissed him, having throughly given him to know that he might never avail to outdo him in liberality."

---

1. *Cattajo*. This word is usually translated Cathay, *i.e.* China; but *semble* Boccaccio meant rather the Dalmatian province of Cattaro, which would better answer the description in the text, Nathan's estate being described as adjoining a highway leading from the Ponant (or Western shores of the Mediterranean) to the Levant (or Eastern shores), *e.g.* the road from Cattaro on the Adriatic to Salonica on the Ægean. Cathay (China) seems, from the circumstances of the case, out of the question, as is also the Italian town called Cattaio, near Padua.
2. *i.e.* to show the most extravagant hospitality.
3. Or as we should say, "After much beating about the bush."
4. *i.e.* jealousies.

THE FOURTH STORY

MESSER GENTILE DE' CARISENDI, COMING FROM
MODONA, TAKETH FORTH OF THE SEPULCHRE A LADY
WHOM HE LOVETH AND WHO HATH BEEN BURIED
FOR DEAD. THE LADY, RESTORED TO LIFE, BEARETH A
MALE CHILD AND MESSER GENTILE RESTORETH HER
AND HER SON TO NICCOLUCCIO CACCIANIMICO, HER
HUSBAND

It seemed to all a marvellous thing that a man should be lavish of his own blood and they declared Nathan's liberality to have verily transcended that of the King of Spain and the Abbot of Cluny. But, after enough to one and the other effect had been said thereof, the king, looking towards Lauretta, signed to her that he would have her tell, whereupon she straightway began, "Young ladies, magnificent and goodly are the things that have been recounted, nor meseemeth is there aught left unto us who have yet to tell, wherethrough we may range a story-telling, so throughly have they all[1] been occupied with the loftiness of the magnificences related, except we have recourse to the affairs of love, which latter afford a great abundance of matter for discourse on every subject; wherefore, at once on this account and for that the theme is one to which our age must needs especially incline us, it pleaseth me to relate to you an act of magnanimity done by a lover, which, all things considered, will peradventure appear to you nowise inferior to any of those already set forth, if it be true that treasures are lavished, enmities forgotten and life itself, nay, what is far more, honour and renown, exposed to a thousand perils, so we may avail to possess the thing beloved.

There was, then, in Bologna, a very noble city of Lombardy, a gentleman very notable for virtue and nobility of blood, called Messer Gentile Carisendi, who, being young, became enamoured of a noble lady called Madam Catalina, the wife of one Niccoluccio Caccianimico; and for that he was ill repaid of his love by the lady, being named provost of Modona, he betook himself thither, as in despair of her. Meanwhile, Niccoluccio being absent from Bologna and the lady having, for that she was with child, gone to abide at a country house she had maybe three miles distant from the city, she was suddenly seized with a grievous fit of sickness,[2] which overcame her with such violence that it extinguished in her all sign of life, so that she was even adjudged dead of divers physicians; and for that her nearest kinswomen declared themselves to have had it from herself that she had not been so long pregnant that the child could be fully formed, without giving themselves farther concern, they buried her, such as she was, after much lamentation, in one of the vaults of a neighbouring church.

The thing was forthright signified by a friend of his to Messer Gentile, who, poor as he had still been of her favour, grieved sore therefor and ultimately said in himself, 'Harkye, Madam

Catalina, thou art dead, thou of whom, what while thou livedst, I could never avail to have so much as a look; wherefore, now thou canst not defend thyself, needs must I take of thee a kiss or two, all dead as thou art.' This said, he took order so his going should be secret and it being presently night, he mounted to horse with one of his servants and rode, without halting, till he came whereas the lady was buried and opened the sepulchre with all despatch. Then, entering therein, he laid himself beside her and putting his face to hers, kissed her again and again with many tears. But presently,—as we see men's appetites never abide content within any limit, but still desire farther, and especially those of lovers,—having bethought himself to tarry there no longer, he said, 'Marry, now that I am here, why should I not touch her somedele on the breast? I may never touch her more, nor have I ever yet done so.' Accordingly, overcome with this desire, he put his hand into her bosom and holding it there awhile, himseemed he felt her heart beat somewhat. Thereupon, putting aside all fear, he sought more diligently and found that she was certainly not dead, scant and feeble as he deemed the life [that lingered in her;] wherefore, with the help of his servant, he brought her forth of the tomb, as softliest he might, and setting her before him on his horse, carried her privily to his house in Bologna.

There was his mother, a worthy and discreet gentlewoman, and she, after she had heard everything at large from her son, moved to compassion, quietly addressed herself by means of hot baths and great fires to recall the strayed life to the lady, who, coming presently to herself, heaved a great sigh and said, 'Ah me, where am I?' To which the good lady replied, 'Be of good comfort; thou art in safety.' Madam Catalina, collecting herself, looked about her and knew not aright where she was; but, seeing Messer Gentile before her, she was filled with wonderment and besought his mother to tell her how she came thither; whereupon Messer Gentile related to her everything in order. At this she was sore afflicted, but presently rendered him such thanks as she might and after conjured him, by the love he had erst borne her and of his courtesy, that she might not in his house suffer at his hands aught that should be anywise contrary to her honour and that of her husband and that, as soon as the day should be come, he would suffer her return to her own house. 'Madam,' answered Messer Gentile, 'whatsoever may have been my desire of time past, I purpose not, either at this present or ever henceforth, (since God hath vouchsafed me this grace that He hath restored you to me from death to life, and that by means of the love I have hitherto borne you,) to use you either here or elsewhere otherwise than as a dear sister; but this my service that I have done you to-night meriteth some recompense; wherefore I would have you deny me not a favour that I shall ask you.'

The lady very graciously replied that she was ready to do his desire, so but she might and it were honourable. Then said he, 'Madam, your kinsfolk and all the Bolognese believe and hold you for certain to be dead, wherefore there is no one who looketh for you more at home, and therefore I would have you of your favour be pleased to abide quietly here with my mother till such time as I shall return from Modona, which will be soon. And the reason for which I require you of this is that I purpose to make a dear and solemn present of you to your husband in the presence of the most notable citizens of this place.' The lady, confessing herself beholden to the gentleman and that his request was an honourable one, determined to do as he asked, how much soever she desired to gladden her kinsfolk of her life,[3] and so she promised it to him upon her faith. Hardly had she made an end of her reply, when she felt the time of her delivery to be come and not long after, being lovingly tended of Messer Gentile's mother, she gave birth to a goodly male child, which manifold redoubled his gladness and her own. Messer Gentile took order that all things needful should be forthcoming and that she should be tended as she were his proper wife and presently returned in secret to Modona. There, having served the term of his office and being about to return to Bologna, he took order for the holding of a great and goodly banquet at his house on the morning he was to enter the city, and thereto he bade many gentlemen of the place, amongst whom was Niccoluccio Caccianimico. Accordingly, when he returned and dismounted, he found them all awaiting him, as likewise the lady, fairer and sounder than ever, and her little son in good case, and with inexpressible joy seating his guests at table, he let serve them magnificently with various meats.

Whenas the repast was near its end, having first told the lady what he meant to do and taken order with her of the course that she should hold, he began to speak thus: 'Gentlemen, I remember to have heard whiles that there is in Persia a custom and to my thinking a pleasant one, to wit, that, whenas any is minded supremely to honour a friend of his, he biddeth him to his house and there showeth him the thing, be it wife or mistress or daughter or whatsoever else, he holdeth most dear, avouching that, like as he showeth him this, even so, an he might, would he yet more willingly show him his very heart; which custom I purpose to observe in Bologna. You, of your favour, have honoured my banquet with your presence, and I in turn mean to honour you, after the Persian fashion, by showing you the most precious thing I have or may ever have in the world. But, ere I proceed to do this, I pray you tell me what you deem of a doubt[4] which I shall broach to you and which is this. A certain person hath in his house a very faithful and good servant, who falleth grievously sick, whereupon the former, without awaiting the sick man's end, letteth carry him into the middle street and hath no more heed of him. Cometh a stranger, who, moved to compassion of the sick man, carrieth him off to his own house and with great diligence and expense bringeth him again to his former health. Now I would fain know whether, if he keep him and make use of his services, his former master can in equity complain of or blame the second, if, he demanding him again, the latter refuse to restore him.'

The gentlemen, after various discourse among themselves, concurring all in one opinion, committed the response to Niccoluccio Caccianimico, for that he was a goodly and eloquent speaker; whereupon the latter, having first commended the Persian usage, declared that he and all the rest were of opinion that the first master had no longer any right in his servant, since he had, in such a circumstance, not only abandoned him, but cast him away, and that, for the kind offices done him by the second, themseemed the servant was justly become his; wherefore, in keeping him, he did the first no hurt, no violence, no unright whatsoever. The other guests at table (and there were men there of worth and worship) said all of one accord that they held to that which had been answered by Niccoluccio; and Messer Gentile, well pleased with this response and that Niccoluccio had made it, avouched himself also to be of the same opinion. Then said he, 'It is now time that I honour you according to promise,' and calling two of his servants, despatched them to the lady, whom he had let magnificently dress and adorn, praying her be pleased to come gladden the company with her presence. Accordingly, she took her little son, who was very handsome, in her arms and coming into the banqueting-hall, attended by two serving-men seated herself, as Messer Gentile willed it, by the side of a gentleman of high standing. Then said he, 'Gentlemen, this is the thing which I hold and purpose to hold dearer than any other; look if it seem to you that I have reason to do so.'

The guests, having paid her the utmost honour, commending her amain and declaring to Messer Gentile that he might well hold her dear, fell to looking upon her; and there were many there who had avouched her to be herself,[5] had they not held her for dead. But Niccoluccio gazed upon her above all and unable to contain himself, asked her, (Messer Gentile having withdrawn awhile,) as one who burned to know who she was, if she were a Bolognese lady or a foreigner. The lady, seeing herself questioned of her husband, hardly restrained herself from answering; but yet, to observe the appointed ordinance, she held her peace. Another asked her if the child was hers and a third if she were Messer Gentile's wife or anywise akin to him; but she made them no reply. Presently, Messer Gentile coming up, one of his guests said to him,

'Sir, this is a fair creature of yours, but she seemeth to us mute; is she so?' 'Gentlemen,' replied he, 'her not having spoken at this present is no small proof of her virtue.' And the other said, 'Tell us, then, who she is.' Quoth Messer Gentile, 'That will I gladly, so but you will promise me that none, for aught that I shall say, will budge from his place till such time as I shall have made an end of my story.'

All promised this and the tables being presently removed, Messer Gentile, seating himself beside the lady, said, 'Gentlemen, this lady is that loyal and faithful servant, of whom I questioned you awhile agone and who, being held little dear of her folk and so, as a thing without worth and no longer useful, cast out into the midward of the street, was by me taken up; yea, by my solicitude and of my handiwork I brought her forth of the jaws of death, and God, having regard to my good intent, hath caused her, by my means, from a frightful corpse become thus beautiful. But, that you may more manifestly apprehend how this betided me, I will briefly declare it to you.' Then, beginning from his falling enamoured of her, he particularly related to them that which had passed until that time, to the great wonderment of the hearers, and added, 'By reason of which things, an you, and especially Niccoluccio, have not changed counsel since awhile ago, the lady is fairly mine, nor can any with just title demand her again of me.' To this none made answer; nay, all awaited that which he should say farther; whilst Niccoluccio and the lady and certain of the others who were there wept for compassion.[6]

Then Messer Gentile, rising to his feet and taking the little child in his arms and the lady by the hand, made for Niccoluccio and said to him, 'Rise up, gossip; I do not restore thee thy wife, whom thy kinsfolk and hers cast away; nay, but I will well bestow on thee this lady my gossip, with this her little son, who I am assured, was begotten of thee and whom I held at baptism and named Gentile; and I pray thee that she be none the less dear to thee for that she hath abidden near upon three months in my house; for I swear to thee,—by that God who belike caused me aforetime fall in love with her, to the intent that my love might be, as in effect it hath been, the occasion of her deliverance,—that never, whether with father or mother or with thee, hath she lived more chastely than she hath done with my mother in my house.' So saying, he turned to the lady and said to her, 'Madam, from this time forth I absolve you of every promise made me and leave you free [to return] to Niccoluccio.'[7] Then, giving the lady and the child into Niccoluccio's arms, he returned to his seat. Niccoluccio received them with the utmost eagerness, so much the more rejoiced as he was the farther removed from hope thereof, and thanked Messer Gentile, as best he might and knew; whilst the others, who all wept for compassion, commended the latter amain of this; yea, and he was commended of whosoever heard it. The lady was received in her house with marvellous rejoicing and long beheld with amazement by the Bolognese, as one raised from the dead; whilst Messer Gentile ever after abode a friend of Niccoluccio and of his kinsfolk and those of the lady.

What, then, gentle ladies, will you say [of this case]? Is, think you, a king's having given away his sceptre and his crown or an abbot's having, without cost to himself, reconciled an evildoer with the pope or an old man's having proffered his weasand to the enemy's knife to be evened with this deed of Messer Gentile, who, being young and ardent and himseeming he had a just title to that which the heedlessness of others had cast away and he of his good fortune had taken up, not only honourably tempered his ardour, but, having in his possession that which he was still wont with all his thoughts to covet and to seek to steal away, freely restored it [to its owner]? Certes, meseemeth none of the magnificences already recounted can compare with this."

---

1. *i.e.* all sections of the given theme.

2. Lit. accident (*accidente*).
3. *i.e.* with news of her life.
4. *Dubbio, i.e.* a doubtful case or question.
5. *i.e.* who would have recognized her as Madam Catalina.
6. *Compassione, i.e.* emotion.
7. Lit. I leave you free *of* Niccoluccio (*libera vi lascio di Niccoluccio*).

THE FIFTH STORY

MADAM DIANORA REQUIRETH OF MESSER ANSALDO A GARDEN AS FAIR IN JANUARY AS IN MAY, AND HE BY BINDING HIMSELF [TO PAY A GREAT SUM OF MONEY] TO A NIGROMANCER, GIVETH IT TO HER. HER HUSBAND GRANTETH HER LEAVE TO DO MESSER ANSALDO'S PLEASURE, BUT HE, HEARING OF THE FORMER'S GENEROSITY, ABSOLVETH HER OF HER PROMISE, WHEREUPON THE NIGROMANCER, IN HIS TURN, ACQUITTETH MESSER ANSALDO OF HIS BOND, WITHOUT WILLING AUGHT OF HIS

MESSER GENTILE HAVING by each of the merry company been extolled to the very skies with the highest praise, the king charged Emilia follow on, who confidently, as if eager to speak, began as follows: "Dainty dames, none can with reason deny that Messer Gentile wrought magnificently; but, if it be sought to say that his magnanimity might not be overpassed, it will not belike be uneath to show that more is possible, as I purpose to set out to you in a little story of mine.

In Friuli, a country, though cold, glad with goodly mountains and store of rivers and clear springs, is a city called Udine, wherein was aforetime a fair and noble lady called Madam Dianora, the wife of a wealthy gentleman named Gilberto, who was very debonair and easy of composition. The lady's charm procured her to be passionately loved of a noble and great baron by name Messer Ansaldo Gradense, a man of high condition and everywhere renowned for prowess and courtesy. He loved her fervently and did all that lay in his power to be beloved of her, to which end he frequently solicited her with messages, but wearied himself in vain. At last, his importunities being irksome to the lady and she seeing that, for all she denied him everything he sought of her, he stinted not therefor to love and solicit her, she determined to seek to rid herself of him by means of an extraordinary and in her judgment an impossible demand; wherefore she said one day to a woman, who came often to her on his part, 'Good woman, thou hast many times avouched to me that Messer Ansaldo loveth me over all things and hast proffered me marvellous great gifts on his part, which I would have him keep to himself, seeing that never thereby might I be prevailed upon to love him or comply with his wishes; but, an I could be certified that he loveth me in very deed as much as thou sayest, I might doubtless bring myself to love him and do that which he willeth; wherefore, an he choose to certify me of this with that which I shall require of him, I shall be ready to do his commandments.' Quoth the good woman, 'And what is that, madam, which you would have him do?' 'That which I desire,' replied the lady, 'is this; I will have, for this coming month of January, a garden, near this city, full of green grass and flowers and trees in full leaf, no otherwise than as it were May; the which if he contrive not, let him never more send me thee nor any other, for that, an he importune me more, so surely as I have hitherto kept his pursuit hidden from my husband and my kinsfolk, I will study to rid myself of him by complaining to them.'

The gentleman, hearing the demand and the offer of his mistress, for all it seemed to him a hard thing and in a manner impossible to do and he knew it to be required of the lady for none otherwhat than to bereave him of all hope, determined nevertheless to essay whatsoever might be done thereof and sent into various parts about the world, enquiring if there were any to be found who would give him aid and counsel in the matter. At last, he happened upon one who offered, so he were well guerdoned, to do the thing by nigromantic art, and having agreed with him for a great sum of money, he joyfully awaited the appointed time, which come and the cold being extreme and everything full of snow and ice, the learned man, the night before the calends of January, so wrought by his arts in a very goodly meadow adjoining the city, that it appeared in the morning (according to the testimony of those who saw it) one of the goodliest gardens was ever seen of any, with grass and trees and fruits of every kind. Messer Ansaldo, after viewing this with the utmost gladness, let cull of the finest fruits and the fairest flowers that were there and caused privily present them to his mistress, bidding her come and see the garden required by her, so thereby she might know how he loved her and after, remembering her of the promise made him and sealed with an oath, bethink herself, as a loyal lady, to accomplish it to him.

The lady, seeing the fruits and flowers and having already from many heard tell of the miraculous garden, began to repent of her promise. Natheless, curious, for all her repentance, of seeing strange things, she went with many other ladies of the city to view the garden and having with no little wonderment commended it amain, returned home, the woefullest woman alive, bethinking her of that to which she was bounden thereby. Such was her chagrin that she availed not so well to dissemble it but needs must it appear, and her husband, perceiving it, was urgent to know the reason. The lady, for shamefastness, kept silence thereof a great while; but at last, constrained to speak, she orderly discovered to him everything; which Gilberto, hearing, was at the first sore incensed, but presently, considering the purity of the lady's intent and chasing away anger with better counsel, he said, 'Dianora, it is not the part of a discreet nor of a virtuous woman to give ear unto any message of this sort nor to compound with any for her chastity under whatsoever condition. Words received into the heart by the channel of the ears have more potency than many conceive and well nigh every thing becometh possible to lovers. Thou didst ill, then, first to hearken and after to enter into terms of composition; but, for that I know the purity of thine intent, I will, to absolve thee of the bond of the promise, concede thee that which peradventure none other would do, being thereto the more induced by fear of the nigromancer, whom Messer Ansaldo, an thou cheat him, will maybe cause make us woeful. I will, then, that thou go to him and study to have thyself absolved of this thy promise, preserving thy chastity, if thou mayst anywise contrive it; but, an it may not be otherwise, thou shalt, for this once, yield him thy body, but not thy soul.'

The lady, hearing her husband's speech, wept and denied herself willing to receive such a favour from him; but, for all her much denial, he would e'en have it be so. Accordingly, next morning, at daybreak, the lady, without overmuch adorning herself, repaired to Messer Ansaldo's house, with two of her serving-men before and a chamberwoman after her. Ansaldo, hearing that his mistress was come to him, marvelled sore and letting call the nigromancer, said to him, 'I will have thee see what a treasure thy skill hath gotten me.' Then, going to meet her, he received her with decency and reverence, without ensuing any disorderly appetite, and they entered all[1] into a goodly chamber, wherein was a great fire. There he caused set her a seat and said, 'Madam, I prithee, if the long love I have borne you merit any recompense, let it not irk you to discover to me the true cause which hath brought you hither at such an hour and in such company.' The lady, shamefast and well nigh with tears in her eyes, answered, 'Sir, neither love that I bear you nor plighted faith bringeth me hither, but the commandment of my husband, who, having more regard to the travails of your disorderly passion than to his honour and mine own, hath caused me come hither; and by his behest I am for this once disposed to do your every pleasure.' If Messer Ansaldo had marvelled at the sight of the lady, far more did he marvel, when he heard her words, and moved by Gilberto's generosity, his heat began to change to compassion and he said, 'God forbid, madam, an it be as you say, that I should be a marrer of his honour who hath compassion of my love; wherefore you shall, what while it is your pleasure to abide here, be no otherwise entreated than as you were my sister; and whenas it shall be agreeable to you, you are free to depart, so but you will render your husband, on my part, those thanks which you shall deem befitting unto courtesy such as his hath been and have me ever, in time to come, for brother and for servant.'

The lady, hearing these words, was the joyfullest woman in the world and answered, saying, 'Nothing, having regard to your fashions, could ever make me believe that aught should ensue to me of my coming other than this that I see you do in the matter; whereof I shall still be beholden to you.' Then, taking leave, she returned, under honourable escort, to Messer Gilberto and told him that which had passed, of which there came about a very strait and loyal friendship between him and Messer Ansaldo. Moreover, the nigromancer, to whom the gentleman was for giving the promised guerdon, seeing Gilberto's generosity towards his wife's lover and that of the latter towards the lady, said, 'God forbid, since I have seen Gilberto liberal of his honour and you of your love, that I should not on like wise be liberal of my hire; wherefore, knowing it[2] will stand you in good stead, I intend that it shall be yours.' At this the gentleman was ashamed and studied to make him take or all or part; but, seeing that he wearied himself in vain and it pleasing the nigromancer (who had, after three days, done away his garden) to depart, he commended him to God and having extinguished from his heart his lustful love for the lady, he abode fired with honourable affection for her. How say you now, lovesome ladies? Shall we prefer [Gentile's resignation of] the in a manner dead lady and of his love already cooled for hope forspent, before the generosity of Messer Ansaldo, whose love was more ardent than ever and who was in a manner fired with new hope, holding in his hands the prey so long pursued? Meseemeth it were folly to pretend that this generosity can be evened with that."

---

1. *i.e.* Ansaldo, Dianora and the nigromancer.
2. *i.e.* the money promised him by way of recompense.

✤ 6 ✤

THE SIXTH STORY

KING CHARLES THE OLD, THE VICTORIOUS, FALLETH
ENAMOURED OF A YOUNG GIRL, BUT AFTER,
ASHAMED OF HIS FOND THOUGHT, HONOURABLY
MARRIETH BOTH HER AND HER SISTER

IT WERE over longsome fully to recount the various discourse that had place among the ladies of who used the greatest generosity, Gilberto or Messer Ansaldo or the nigromancer, in Madam Dianora's affairs; but, after the king had suffered them debate awhile, he looked at Fiammetta and bade her, telling a story, put an end to their contention; whereupon she, without hesitation, began as follows: "Illustrious ladies, I was ever of opinion that, in companies such as ours, it should still be discoursed so much at large that the overstraitness[1] of intent of the things said be not unto any matter for debate, the which is far more sortable among students in the schools than among us [women,] who scarce suffice unto the distaff and the spindle. Wherefore, seeing that you are presently at cross-purposes by reason of the things already said, I, who had in mind a thing maybe somewhat doubtful [of meaning,] will leave that be and tell you a story, treating nowise of a man of little account, but of a valiant king, who therein wrought knightly, in nothing attainting his honour.

Each one of you must many a time have heard tell of King Charles the Old or First, by whose magnanimous emprise, and after by the glorious victory gained by him over King Manfred, the Ghibellines were expelled from Florence and the Guelphs returned thither. In consequence of this a certain gentleman, called Messer Neri degli Uberti, departing the city with all his household and much monies and being minded to take refuge no otherwhere than under the hand of King Charles, betook himself to Castellamare di Stabia.[2] There, belike a crossbowshot removed from the other habitations of the place, among olive-trees and walnuts and chestnuts, wherewith the country aboundeth, he bought him an estate and built thereon a goodly and commodious dwelling-house, with a delightsome garden thereby, amiddleward which, having great plenty of running water, he made, after our country fashion, a goodly and clear fishpond and lightly filled it with good store of fish. Whilst he concerned himself to make his garden goodlier every day, it befell that King Charles repaired to Castellamare, to rest himself awhile in the hot season, and there hearing tell of the beauty of Messer Neri's garden, he desired to behold it. Hearing, moreover, to whom it belonged, he bethought himself that, as the gentleman was of the party adverse to his own, it behoved to deal the more familiarly with him, and accordingly sent to him to say that he purposed to sup with him privily in his garden that evening, he and four companions. This was very agreeable to Messer Neri, and having made magnificent preparation and taken order with his household of that which was to do, he received the king in his fair garden as gladliest he might and knew. The latter, after having viewed and commended all the garden and Messer Neri's house and washed, seated himself at one of the tables, which were set beside the fishpond, and seating Count Guy de Montfort, who was of his company, on one side of him and Messer Neri on the other, commanded other three, who were come thither with them, to serve according to the order appointed of his host. Thereupon there came dainty meats and there were wines of the best and costliest and the ordinance was exceeding goodly and praiseworthy, without noise or annoy whatsoever, the which the king much commended.

Presently, as he sat blithely at meat, enjoying the solitary place, there entered the garden two young damsels of maybe fifteen years of age, with hair like threads of gold, all ringleted and hanging loose, whereon was a light chaplet of pervinck-blossoms. Their faces bespoke them rather angels than otherwhat, so delicately fair they were, and they were clad each upon her skin in a garment of the finest linen and white as snow, the which from the waist upward was very strait and thence hung down in ample folds, pavilionwise, to the feet. She who came first bore on her left shoulder a pair of hand-nets and in her right hand a long pole, and the other had on her left shoulder a frying-pan and under the same arm a faggot of wood, whilst in her left hand she held a trivet and in the other a flask of oil and a lighted flambeau. The king, seeing them, marvelled and in suspense awaited what this should mean. The damsels came forward modestly and blushingly did obeisance to him, then, betaking themselves whereas one went down into the fishpond, she who bore the frying-pan set it down and the other things by it and taking the pole that the other carried, they both entered the water, which came up to their breasts. Meanwhile, one of Messer Neri's servants deftly kindled fire under the trivet and setting the pan thereon, poured therein oil and waited for the damsels to throw him fish. The latter, the one groping with the pole in those parts whereas she knew the fish lay hid and the other standing ready with the net, in a short space of time took fish galore, to the exceeding pleasure of the king, who eyed them attently; then, throwing some thereof to the servant, who put them in the pan, well nigh alive, they proceeded, as they had been lessoned, to take of the finest and cast them on the table before the king and his table-fellows. The fish wriggled about the table, to the marvellous diversion of the king, who took of them in his turn and sportively cast them back to the damsels; and on this wise they frolicked awhile, till such time as the servant had cooked the fish which had been given him and which, Messer Neri having so ordered it, were now set before the king, more as a relish than as any very rare and delectable dish.

The damsels, seeing the fish cooked and having taken enough, came forth of the water, their thin white garments all clinging to their skins and hiding well nigh nought of their delicate bodies, and passing shamefastly before the king, returned to the house. The latter and the count and the others who served had well considered the damsels and each inwardly greatly commended them for fair and well shapen, no less than for agreeable and well mannered. But above all they pleased the king, who had so intently eyed every part of their bodies, as they came forth of the water, that, had any then pricked him, he would not have felt it, and as he called them more particularly to mind, unknowing who they were, he felt a very fervent desire awaken in his heart to please them, whereby he right well perceived himself to be in danger of becoming enamoured, an he took no heed to himself thereagainst; nor knew he indeed whether of the twain it was the more pleased him, so like in all things was the one to the other. After he had abidden awhile in this thought, he turned to Messer Neri and asked him who were the two damsels, to which the gentleman answered, 'My lord, these are my daughters born at a birth, whereof the one is called Ginevra the Fair and the other Isotta the Blonde.' The king commended them greatly and exhorted him to marry them, whereof Messer Neri excused himself, for that he was no more able thereunto. Meanwhile, nothing now remaining to be served of the supper but the fruits, there came the two damsels in very goodly gowns of sendal, with two great silver platters in their hands, full of various fruits, such as the season afforded, and these they set on the table before the king; which done, they withdrew a little apart and fell to singing a canzonet, whereof the words began thus:

Whereas I'm come, O Love,
It might not be, indeed, at length recounted, etc.

This song they carolled on such dulcet wise and so delightsomely that to the king, who beheld and hearkened to them with ravishment, it seemed as if all the hierarchies of the angels were lighted there to sing. The song sung, they fell on their knees and respectfully craved of him leave to depart, who, albeit their departure was grievous to him, yet with a show of blitheness accorded it to them. The supper being now at an end, the king remounted to horse with his company and leaving Messer Neri, returned to the royal lodging, devising of one thing and another. There, holding his passion hidden, but availing not, for whatsoever great affair might supervene, to forget the beauty and grace of Ginevra the Fair, (for love of whom he loved her sister also, who was like unto her,) he became so fast entangled in the amorous snares that he could think of well nigh nought else and feigning other occasions, kept a strait intimacy with Messer Neri and very often visited his fair garden, to see Ginevra.

At last, unable to endure longer and bethinking himself, in default of other means of compassing his desire, to take not one alone, but both of the damsels from their father, he discovered both his passion and his intent to Count Guy, who, for that he was an honourable man, said to him, 'My lord, I marvel greatly at that which you tell me, and that more than would another, inasmuch as meseemeth I have from your childhood to this day known your fashions better than any other; wherefore, meseeming never to have known such a passion in your youth, wherein Love might lightlier have fixed his talons, and seeing you presently hard upon old age, it is so new and so strange to me that you should love by way of enamourment[3] that it seemeth to me well nigh a miracle, and were it my office to reprove you thereof, I know well that which I should say to you thereanent, having in regard that you are yet with your harness on your back in a kingdom newly gained, amidst a people unknown and full of wiles and treasons, and are all occupied with very grave cares and matters of high moment, nor have you yet availed to seat yourself [in security;] and yet, among such and so many affairs, you have made place for the allurements of love. This is not the fashion of a magnanimous king; nay, but rather that of a pusillanimous boy. Moreover, what is far worse, you say that you are resolved to take his two daughters from a gentleman who hath entertained you in his house beyond his means and who, to do you the more honour, hath shown you these twain in a manner naked, thereby attesting how great is the faith he hath in you and that he firmly believeth you to be a king and not a ravening wolf. Again, hath it so soon dropped your memory that it was the violences done of Manfred to women that opened you the entry into this kingdom? What treason was ever wroughten more deserving of eternal punishment than this would be, that you should take from him who hospitably entreateth you his honour and hope and comfort? What would be said of you, an you should do it? You think, maybe, it were a sufficient excuse to say, "I did it for that he is a Ghibelline." Is this of the justice of kings, that they who resort on such wise to their arms should be entreated after such a fashion, be they who they may? Let me tell you, king, that it was an exceedingly great glory to you to have overcome Manfred, but a far greater one it is to overcome one's self; wherefore do you, who have to correct others, conquer yourself and curb this appetite, nor offer with such a blot to mar that which you have so gloriously gained.'

These words stung the king's conscience to the quick and afflicted him the more inasmuch as he knew them for true; wherefore, after sundry heavy sighs, he said, 'Certes, Count, I hold every other enemy, however strong, weak and eath enough to the well-lessoned warrior to overcome in comparison with his own appetites; natheless, great as is the travail and inexpressible as is the might it requireth, your words have so stirred me that needs must I, ere many days be past, cause you see by deed that, like as I know how to conquer others, even so do I know how to overcome myself.' Nor had many days passed after this discourse when the king, having returned to Naples, determined, as well to deprive himself of occasion to do dishonourably as to requite the gentleman the hospitality received from him, to go about (grievous as it was to him to make others possessors of that which he coveted over all for himself) to marry the two young ladies, and that not as Messer Neri's daughters, but as his own. Accordingly, with Messer Neri's accord, he dowered them magnificently and gave Ginevra the Fair to Messer Maffeo da Palizzi and Isotta the Blonde to Messer Guglielmo della Magna, both noble cavaliers and great barons, to whom with inexpressible chagrin consigning them, he betook himself into Apulia, where with continual fatigues he so mortified the fierceness of his appetite that, having burst and broken the chains of love, he abode free of such passion for the rest of his life. There are some belike who will say that it was a little thing for a king to have married two young ladies, and that I will allow; but a great and a very great thing I call it, if we consider that it was a king enamoured who did this and who married to another her whom he loved, without having gotten or taking of his love leaf or flower or fruit. On this wise, then, did this magnanimous king, at once magnificently guerdoning the noble gentleman, laudably honouring the young ladies whom he loved and bravely overcoming himself."

---

1. *i.e.*, nicety, minuteness (*strettezza*).
2. A town on the Bay of Naples, near the ruins of Pompeii.
3. *Per amore amiate* (Fr. aimiez par amour).

7

THE SEVENTH STORY

KING PEDRO OF ARRAGON, COMING TO KNOW THE FERVENT LOVE BORNE HIM BY LISA, COMFORTETH THE LOVE-SICK MAID AND PRESENTLY MARRIETH HER TO A NOBLE YOUNG GENTLEMAN; THEN, KISSING HER ON THE BROW, HE EVER AFTER AVOUCHETH HIMSELF HER KNIGHT

FIAMMETTA HAVING MADE an end of her story and the manful magnanimity of King Charles having been much commended, albeit there was one lady there who, being a Ghibelline, was loath to praise him, Pampinea, by the king's commandment, began thus, "There is no one of understanding, worshipful ladies, but would say that which you say of good King Charles, except she bear him ill-will for otherwhat; but, for that there occurreth to my memory a thing, belike no less commendable than this, done of one his adversary to one of our Florentine damsels, it pleaseth me to relate it to you.

At the time of the expulsion of the French from Sicily, one of our Florentines was an apothecary at Palermo, a very rich man called Bernardo Puccini, who had by his wife an only daughter, a very fair damsel and already apt for marriage. Now King Pedro of Arragon, become lord of the island, held high festival with his barons at Palermo, wherein he tilting after the Catalan fashion, it chanced that Bernardo's daughter, whose name was Lisa, saw him running [at the ring] from a window where she was with other ladies, and he so marvellously pleased her that, looking upon him once and again, she fell passionately in love with him; and the festival ended and she abiding in her father's house, she could think of nothing but of this her illustrious and exalted love. And what most irked her in this was the consciousness of her own mean condition, which scarce suffered her to cherish any hope of a happy issue; natheless, she could not therefor bring herself to leave loving the king, albeit, for fear of greater annoy, she dared not discover her passion. The king had not perceived this thing and recked not of her, wherefor she suffered intolerable chagrin, past all that can be imagined. Thus it befell that, love still waxing in her and melancholy redoubling upon melancholy, the fair maid, unable to endure more, fell sick and wasted visibly away from day to day, like snow in the sun. Her father and mother, sore concerned for this that befell her, studied with assiduous tenderness to hearten her and succoured her in as much as might be with physicians and medicines, but it availed nothing, for that, despairing of her love, she had elected to live no longer.

It chanced one day that, her father offering to do her every pleasure, she bethought herself, and she might aptly, to seek, before she died, to make the king acquainted with her love and her intent, and accordingly she prayed him bring her Minuccio d'Arezzo. Now this Minuccio

462

was in those days held a very quaint and subtle singer and player and was gladly seen of the king; and Bernardo concluded that Lisa had a mind to hear him sing and play awhile. Accordingly, he sent to tell him, and Minuccio, who was a man of a debonair humour, incontinent came to her and having somedele comforted her with kindly speech, softly played her a fit or two on a viol he had with him and after sang her sundry songs, the which were fire and flame unto the damsel's passion, whereas he thought to solace her. Presently she told him that she would fain speak some words with him alone, wherefore, all else having withdrawn, she said to him, 'Minuccio, I have chosen thee to keep me very faithfully a secret of mine, hoping in the first place that thou wilt never discover it to any one, save to him of whom I shall tell thee, and after that thou wilt help me in that which lieth in thy power; and of this I pray thee Thou must know, then, Minuccio mine, that the day our lord King Pedro held the great festival in honour of his exaltation to the throne, it befell me, as he tilted, to espy him at so dour a point[1] that for the love of him there was kindled in my heart a fire that hath brought me to this pass wherein thou seest me, and knowing how ill my love beseemeth to a king, yet availing not, let alone to drive it away, but even to abate it, and it being beyond measure grievous to me to bear, I have as a lesser evil elected to die, as I shall do. True it is that I should begone hence cruelly disconsolate, an he first knew it not; wherefore, unknowing by whom I could more aptly acquaint him with this my resolution than by thyself, I desire to commit it to thee and pray thee that thou refuse not to do it, and whenas thou shalt have done it, that thou give me to know thereof, so that, dying comforted, I may be assoiled of these my pains.' And this said, she stinted, weeping.

Minuccio marvelled at the greatness of the damsel's soul and at her cruel resolve and was sore concerned for her; then, it suddenly occurring to his mind how he might honourably oblige her, he said to her, 'Lisa, I pledge thee my faith, whereof thou mayst live assured that thou wilt never find thyself deceived, and after, commending thee of so high an emprise as it is to have set thy mind upon so great a king, I proffer thee mine aid, by means whereof I hope, an thou wilt but take comfort, so to do that, ere three days be past, I doubt not to bring thee news that will be exceeding grateful to thee; and to lose no time, I mean to go about it forthright.' Lisa, having anew besought him amain thereof and promised him to take comfort, bade him God speed; whereupon Minuccio, taking his leave, betook himself to one Mico da Siena, a mighty good rhymer of those days, and constrained him with prayers to make the following canzonet:

> Bestir thee, Love, and get thee to my Sire
> And tell him all the torments I aby;
> Tell him I'm like to die,
> For fearfulness concealing my desire.
>
> Love, with clasped hands I cry thee mercy, so
> Thou mayst betake thee where my lord doth dwell.
> Say that I love and long for him, for lo,
> My heart he hath inflamed so sadly well;
> Yea, for the fire wherewith I'm all aglow,
> I fear to die nor yet the hour can tell
> When I shall part from pain so fierce and fell
> As that which, longing, for his sake I dree
> In shame and fear; ah me,
> For God's sake, cause him know my torment dire.

Since first enamoured, Love, of him I grew,
Thou hast not given me the heart to dare
So much as one poor once my lord unto
My love and longing plainly to declare,
My lord who maketh me so sore to rue;
Death, dying thus, were hard to me to bear.
Belike, indeed, for he is debonair,
'Twould not displease him, did he know what pain
I feel and didst thou deign
Me daring to make known to him my fire.

Yet, since 'twas not thy pleasure to impart,
Love, such assurance to me that by glance
Or sign or writ I might make known my heart
Unto my lord, for my deliverance
I prithee, sweet my master, of thine art
Get thee to him and give him souvenance
Of that fair day I saw him shield and lance
Bear with the other knights and looking more,
Enamoured fell so sore
My heart thereof doth perish and expire.

These words Minuccio forthwith set to a soft and plaintive air, such as the matter thereof required, and on the third day he betook himself to court, where, King Pedro being yet at meat, he was bidden by him sing somewhat to his viol. Thereupon he fell to singing the song aforesaid on such dulcet wise that all who were in the royal hall appeared men astonied, so still and attent stood they all to hearken, and the king maybe more than the others. Minuccio having made an end of his singing, the king enquired whence came this song that himseemed he had never before heard. 'My lord,' replied the minstrel, 'it is not yet three days since the words were made and the air.' The king asked for whom it had been made; and Minuccio answered, 'I dare not discover it save to you alone.' The king, desirous to hear it, as soon as the tables were removed, sent for Minuccio into his chamber and the latter orderly recounted to him all that he had heard from Lisa; wherewith Don Pedro was exceeding well pleased and much commended the damsel, avouching himself resolved to have compassion of so worthful a young lady and bidding him therefore go comfort her on his part and tell her that he would without fail come to visit her that day towards vespers. Minuccio, overjoyed to be the bearer of such pleasing news, betook himself incontinent, viol and all, to the damsel and bespeaking her in private, recounted to her all that had passed and after sang her the song to his viol; whereat she was so rejoiced and so content that she straightway showed manifest signs of great amendment and longingly awaited the hour of vespers, whenas her lord should come, without any of the household knowing or guessing how the case stood.

Meanwhile, the king, who was a debonair and generous prince, having sundry times taken thought to the things heard from Minuccio and very well knowing the damsel and her beauty, waxed yet more pitiful over her and mounting to horse towards vespers, under colour of going abroad for his diversion, betook himself to the apothecary's house, where, having required a very goodly garden which he had to be opened to him, he alighted therein and presently asked Bernardo what was come of his daughter and if he had yet married her. 'My lord,' replied the apothecary, 'she is not married; nay, she hath been and is yet very sick; albeit it is true that since none she hath mended marvellously.' The king readily apprehended what this amendment meant and said, 'In good sooth, 'twere pity so fair a creature should be yet taken from the world. We would fain go visit her.' Accordingly, a little after, he betook himself with Bernardo and two companions only to her chamber and going up to the bed where the damsel, somedele upraised,[2] awaited him with impatience, took her by the hand and said to her, 'What meaneth this, my mistress? You are young and should comfort other women; yet you suffer yourself to be sick. We would beseech you be pleased, for the love of us, to hearten yourself on such wise that you may speedily be whole again.' The damsel, feeling herself touched of his hands whom she loved over all else, albeit she was somewhat shamefast, felt yet such gladness in her heart as she were in Paradise and answered him, as best she might, saying, 'My lord, my having willed to subject my little strength unto very grievous burdens hath been the cause to me of this mine infirmity, whereof, thanks to your goodness, you shall soon see me quit.' The king alone understood the damsel's covert speech and held her momently of more account; nay, sundry whiles he inwardly cursed fortune, who had made her daughter unto such a man; then, after he had tarried with her awhile and comforted her yet more, he took his leave.

This humanity of the king was greatly commended and attributed for great honour to the apothecary and his daughter, which latter abode as well pleased as ever was woman of her lover, and sustained of better hope, in a few days recovered and became fairer than ever. When she was whole again, the king, having taken counsel with the queen of what return he should make her for so much love, mounting one day to horse with many of his barons, repaired to the apothecary's house and entering the garden, let call Master Bernardo and his daughter; then, the queen presently coming thither with many ladies and having received Lisa among them, they fell to making wonder-merry. After a while, the king and queen called Lisa to them and the former said to her, 'Noble damsel, the much love you have borne us hath gotten you a great honour from us, wherewith we would have you for the love of us be content; to wit, that, since you are apt for marriage, we would have you take him to husband whom we shall bestow on you, purposing, notwithstanding this, to call ourselves still your knight, without desiring aught from you of so much love but one sole kiss.' The damsel, grown all vermeil in the face for shamefastness, making the king's pleasure hers, replied in a low voice on this wise, 'My lord, I am well assured that, were it known that I had fallen enamoured of you, most folk would account me mad therefor, thinking belike that I had forgotten myself and knew not mine own condition nor yet yours; but God, who alone seeth the hearts of mortals, knoweth that, in that same hour whenas first you pleased me, I knew you for a king and myself for the daughter of Bernardo the apothecary and that it ill beseemed me to address the ardour of my soul unto so high a place. But, as you know far better than I, none here below falleth in love according to fitness of election, but according to appetite and inclination, against which law I once and again strove with all my might, till, availing no farther, I loved and love and shall ever love you. But, since first I felt myself taken with love of you, I determined still to make your will mine; wherefore, not only will I gladly obey you in this matter of taking a husband at your hands and holding him dear whom it shall please you to bestow on me, since that will be mine honour and estate, but, should you bid me abide in the fire, it were a delight to me, an I thought thereby to pleasure you. To have you, a king, to knight, you know how far it befitteth me, wherefore to that I make no farther answer; nor shall the kiss be vouchsafed you, which alone of my love you would have, without leave of my lady the queen. Natheless, of such graciousness as hath been yours towards me and that of our lady the queen here God render you for me both thanks and recompense, for I have not the wherewithal.' And with that she was silent.

Her answer much pleased the queen and she seemed to her as discreet as the king had reported her. Don Pedro then let call the girl's father and mother and finding that they were well pleased with that which he purposed to do, summoned a young man, by name Perdicone, who was of gentle birth, but poor, and giving certain rings into his hand, married him, nothing loath, to Lisa; which done, he then and there, over and above many and precious jewels bestowed by the queen and himself upon the damsel, gave him Ceffalu and Calatabellotta, two very rich and goodly fiefs, and said to him, 'These we give thee to the lady's dowry. That which we purpose to do for thyself, thou shalt see in time to come.' This said, he turned to the damsel and saying, 'Now will we take that fruit which we are to have of your love,' took her head in his hands and kissed her on the brow. Perdicone and Lisa's father and mother, well pleased, (as indeed was she herself,) held high festival and joyous nuptials; and according as many avouch, the king very faithfully kept his covenant with the damsel, for that, whilst she lived, he still styled himself her knight nor ever went about any deed of arms but he wore none other favour than that which was sent him of her. It is by doing, then, on this wise that subjects' hearts are gained, that others are incited to do well and that eternal renown is acquired; but this is a mark at which few or none nowadays bend the bow of their understanding, most princes being presently grown cruel and tyrannical."

---

1. *In si forte punto*, or, in modern parlance, at so critical or ill-starred a moment.
2. *Sollevata*, syn. solaced, relieved or (3) agitated, troubled.

❧ 8 ❧

THE EIGHTH STORY

SOPHRONIA, THINKING TO MARRY GISIPPUS,
BECOMETH THE WIFE OF TITUS QUINTIUS FULVUS
AND WITH HIM BETAKETH HERSELF TO ROME,
WHITHER GISIPPUS COMETH IN POOR CASE AND
CONCEIVING HIMSELF SLIGHTED OF TITUS,
DECLARETH, SO HE MAY DIE, TO HAVE SLAIN A MAN.
TITUS, RECOGNIZING HIM, TO SAVE HIM,
AVOUCHETH HIMSELF TO HAVE DONE THE DEED,
AND THE TRUE MURDERER, SEEING THIS,
DISCOVERETH HIMSELF; WHEREUPON THEY ARE ALL
THREE LIBERATED BY OCTAVIANUS AND TITUS,
GIVING GISIPPUS HIS SISTER TO WIFE, HATH ALL HIS
GOOD IN COMMON WITH HIM

PAMPINEA HAVING LEFT SPEAKING and all having commended King Pedro, the Ghibelline lady more than the rest, Fiammetta, by the king's commandment, began thus, "Illustrious ladies, who is there knoweth not that kings, when they will, can do everything great and that it is, to boot, especially required of them that they be magnificent? Whoso, then, having the power, doth that which pertaineth unto him, doth well; but folk should not so much marvel thereat nor exalt him to such a height with supreme praise as it would behove them do with another, of whom, for lack of means, less were required. Wherefore, if you with such words extol the actions of kings and they seem to you fair, I doubt not anywise but those of our peers, whenas they are like unto or greater than those of kings, will please you yet more and be yet highlier commended of you, and I purpose accordingly to recount to you, in a story, the praiseworthy and magnanimous dealings of two citizens and friends with each other.

You must know, then, that at the time when Octavianus Cæsar (not yet styled Augustus) ruled the Roman empire in the office called Triumvirate, there was in Rome a gentleman called Publius Quintius Fulvus,[1] who, having a son of marvellous understanding, by name Titus Quintius Fulvus, sent him to Athens to study philosophy and commended him as most he might to a nobleman there called Chremes, his very old friend, by whom Titus was lodged in his own house, in company of a son of his called Gisippus, and set to study with the latter, under the governance of a philosopher named Aristippus. The two young men, coming to consort together, found each other's usances so conformable that there was born thereof a brotherhood between them and a friendship so great that it was never sundered by other accident than death, and neither of them knew weal nor peace save in so much as they were together. Entering upon their studies and being each alike endowed with the highest understanding, they ascended with equal step and marvellous commendation to the glorious altitudes of philosophy; and in this way of life they continued good three years, to the exceeding contentment of Chremes, who in a manner looked upon the one as no more his son than the other. At the end of this time it befell, even as it befalleth of all things, that Chremes, now an old man, departed this life, whereof the two young men suffered a like sorrow, as for a common father, nor could his friends and kinsfolk discern which of the twain was the more in need of consolation for that which had betided them.

It came to pass, after some months, that the friends and kinsfolk of Gisippus resorted to him and together with Titus exhorted him to take a wife, to which he consenting, they found him a young Athenian lady of marvellous beauty and very noble parentage, whose name was Sophronia and who was maybe fifteen years old. The term of the future nuptials drawing nigh, Gisippus one day besought Titus to go visit her with him, for that he had not yet seen her. Accordingly, they being come into her house and she seated between the twain, Titus proceeded to consider her with the utmost attention, as if to judge of the beauty of his friend's bride, and every part of her pleasing him beyond measure, what while he inwardly commended her charms to the utmost, he fell, without showing any sign thereof, as passionately enamoured of her as ever yet man of woman. After they had been with her awhile, they took their leave and returned home, where Titus, betaking himself alone into his chamber, fell a-thinking of the charming damsel and grew the more enkindled the more he enlarged upon her in thought; which, perceiving, he fell to saying in himself, after many ardent sighs, 'Alack, the wretchedness of thy life, Titus! Where and on what settest thou thy mind and thy love and thy hope? Knowest thou not that it behoveth thee, as well for the kindness received from Chremes and his family as for the entire friendship that is between thee and Gisippus, whose bride she is, to have yonder damsel in such respect as a sister? Whom, then, lovest thou? Whither lettest thou thyself be carried away by delusive love, whither by fallacious hope? Open the eyes of thine understanding and recollect thyself, wretch that thou art; give place to reason, curb thy carnal appetite, temper thine unhallowed desires and direct thy thoughts unto otherwhat; gainstand thy lust in this its beginning and conquer thyself, whilst it is yet time. This thou wouldst have is unseemly, nay, it is dishonourable; this thou art minded to ensue it behoveth thee, even wert thou assured (which thou art not) of obtaining it, to flee from, an thou have regard unto that which true friendship requireth and that which thou oughtest. What, then, wilt thou do, Titus? Thou wilt leave this unseemly love, an thou wouldst do that which behoveth.'

Then, remembering him of Sophronia and going over to the contrary, he denounced all that he had said, saying, 'The laws of love are of greater puissance than any others; they annul even the Divine laws, let alone those of friendship; how often aforetime hath father loved daughter, brother sister, stepmother stepson, things more monstrous than for one friend to love the other's wife, the which hath already a thousand times befallen! Moreover, I am young and youth is altogether subject to the laws of Love; wherefor that which pleaseth Him, needs must it please me. Things honourable pertain unto maturer folk; I can will nought save that which Love willeth. The beauty of yonder damsel deserveth to be loved of all, and if I love her, who am young, who can justly blame me therefor? I love her not because she is Gisippus's; nay, I love her for that I should love her, whosesoever she was. In this fortune sinneth that hath allotted her to Gisippus my friend, rather than to another; and if she must be loved, (as she must, and deservedly, for her beauty,) Gisippus, an he came to know it, should be better pleased that I should love her, I, than another.' Then, from that reasoning he reverted again to the contrary, making mock of himself, and wasted not only that day and the ensuing night in passing from this to that and back again, but many others, insomuch that, losing appetite and sleep therefor, he was constrained for weakness to take to his bed.

Gisippus, having beheld him several days full of melancholy thought and seeing him presently sick, was sore concerned and with every art and all solicitude studied to comfort him, never leaving him and questioning him often and instantly of the cause of his melancholy and his sickness. Titus, after having once and again given him idle tales, which Gisippus knew to be such, by way of answer, finding himself e'en constrained thereunto, with tears and sighs replied to him on this wise, 'Gisippus, had it pleased the Gods, death were far more a-gree to me than to live longer, considering that fortune hath brought me to a pass whereas it behoved me make proof of my virtue and that I have, to my exceeding shame, found this latter overcome; but certes I look thereof to have ere long the reward that befitteth me, to wit, death, and this will be more pleasing to me than to live in remembrance of my baseness, which latter, for that I cannot nor should hide aught from thee, I will, not without sore blushing, discover to thee.' Then, beginning from the beginning, he discovered to him the cause of his melancholy and the conflict of his thoughts and ultimately gave him to know which had gotten the victory and confessed himself perishing for love of Sophronia, declaring that, knowing how much this misbeseemed him, he had for penance thereof resolved himself to die, whereof he trusted speedily to make an end.

Gisippus, hearing this and seeing his tears, abode awhile irresolute, as one who, though more moderately, was himself taken with the charms of the fair damsel, but speedily bethought himself that his friend's life should be dearer to him than Sophronia. Accordingly, solicited to tears by those of his friend, he answered him, weeping, 'Titus, wert thou not in need as thou art of comfort, I should complain of thee to thyself, as of one who hath transgressed against our friendship in having so long kept thy most grievous passion hidden from me; since, albeit it appeared not to thee honourable, nevertheless dishonourable things should not, more than honourable, be hidden from a friend; for that a friend, like as he rejoiceth with his friend in honourable things, even so he studieth to do away the dishonourable from his friend's mind; but for the present I will refrain therefrom and come to that which I perceive to be of greater urgency. That thou lovest Sophronia, who is betrothed to me, I marvel not: nay, I should marvel, indeed, if it were not so, knowing her beauty and the nobility of thy mind, so much the more susceptible of passion as the thing that pleaseth hath the more excellence. And the more reason thou hast to love Sophronia, so much the more unjustly dost thou complain of fortune (albeit thou expressest this not in so many words) in that it hath awarded her to me, it seeming to thee that thy love for her had been honourable, were she other than mine; but tell me, if thou be as well advised as thou usest to be, to whom could fortune have awarded her, whereof thou shouldst have more cause to render it thanks, than of having awarded her to me? Whoso else had had her, how honourable soever thy love had been, had liefer loved her for himself[2] than for thee,[3] a thing which thou shouldst not fear[4] from me, an thou hold me a friend such as I am to thee, for that I mind me not, since we have been friends, to have ever had aught that was not as much thine as mine. Now, were the matter so far advanced that it might not be otherwise, I would do with her as I have done with my other possessions;[5] but it is yet at such a point that I can make her thine alone; and I will do so, for that I know not why my friendship should be dear to thee, if, in respect of a thing that may honourably be done, I knew not of a desire of mine to make thine. True it is that Sophronia is my promised bride and that I loved her much and looked with great joyance for my nuptials with her; but, since thou, being far more understanding than I, with more ardour desirest so dear a thing as she is, live assured that she shall enter my chamber, not as my wife, but as thine. Wherefore leave thought-taking, put away melancholy, call back thy lost health and comfort and allegresse and from this time forth expect with blitheness the reward of thy love, far worthier than was mine.'

When Titus heard Gisippus speak thus, the more the flattering hopes given him of the latter afforded him pleasure, so much the more did just reason inform him with shame, showing him that, the greater was Gisippus his liberality, the more unworthy it appeared of himself to use it;

wherefore, without giving over weeping, he with difficulty replied to him thus, 'Gisippus, thy generous and true friendship very plainly showeth me that which it pertaineth unto mine to do. God forfend that her, whom He hath bestowed upon thee as upon the worthier, I should receive from thee for mine! Had He judged it fitting that she should be mine, nor thou nor others can believe that He would ever have bestowed her on thee. Use, therefore, joyfully, thine election and discreet counsel and His gifts, and leave me to languish in the tears, which, as to one undeserving of such a treasure, He hath prepared unto me and which I will either overcome, and that will be dear to thee, or they will overcome me and I shall be out of pain.' 'Titus,' rejoined Gisippus, 'an our friendship might accord me such license that I should enforce thee to ensue a desire of mine and if it may avail to induce thee to do so, it is in this case that I mean to use it to the utmost, and if thou yield not to my prayers with a good grace, I will, with such violence as it behoveth us use for the weal of our friends, procure that Sophronia shall be thine. I know how great is the might of love and that, not once, but many a time, it hath brought lovers to a miserable death; nay, unto this I see thee so near that thou canst neither turn back nor avail to master thy tears, but, proceeding thus, wouldst pine and die; whereupon I, without any doubt, should speedily follow after. If, then, I loved thee not for otherwhat, thy life is dear to me, so I myself may live. Sophronia, therefore, shall be thine, for that thou couldst not lightly find another woman who would so please thee, and as I shall easily turn my love unto another, I shall thus have contented both thyself and me. I should not, peradventure, be so free to do this, were wives as scarce and as uneath to find as friends; however, as I can very easily find me another wife, but not another friend, I had liefer (I will not say *lose* her, for that I shall not lose her, giving her to thee, but shall transfer her to another and a better self, but) transfer her than lose thee. Wherefore, if my prayers avail aught with thee, I beseech thee put away from thee this affliction and comforting at once thyself and me, address thee with good hope to take that joyance which thy fervent love desireth of the thing beloved.'

Although Titus was ashamed to consent to this, namely, that Sophronia should become his wife, and on this account held out yet awhile, nevertheless, love on the one hand drawing him and Gisippus his exhortations on the other urging him, he said, 'Look you, Gisippus, I know not which I can say I do most, my pleasure or thine, in doing that whereof thou prayest me and which thou tellest me is so pleasing to thee, and since thy generosity is such that it overcometh my just shame, I will e'en do it; but of this thou mayst be assured that I do it as one who knoweth himself to receive of thee, not only the beloved lady, but with her his life. The Gods grant, an it be possible, that I may yet be able to show thee, for thine honour and thy weal, how grateful to me is that which thou, more pitiful for me than I for myself, dost for me!' These things said, 'Titus,' quoth Gisippus, 'in this matter, an we would have it take effect, meseemeth this course is to be held. As thou knowest, Sophronia, after long treaty between my kinsfolk and hers, is become my affianced bride; wherefore, should I now go about to say that I will not have her to wife, a sore scandal would ensue thereof and I should anger both her kinsfolk and mine own. Of this, indeed, I should reck nothing, an I saw that she was thereby to become thine; but I misdoubt me that, an I renounce her at this point, her kinsfolk will straightway give her to another, who belike will not be thyself, and so wilt thou have lost that which I shall not have gained. Wherefore meseemeth well, an thou be content, that I follow on with that which I have begun and bring her home as mine and hold the nuptials, and thou mayst after, as we shall know how to contrive, privily lie with her as with thy wife. Then, in due place and season, we will make manifest the fact, which, if it please them not, will still be done and they must perforce be content, being unable to go back upon it.'

The device pleased Titus; wherefore Gisippus received the lady into his house, as his, (Titus being by this recovered and in good case,) and after holding high festival, the night being come, the ladies left the new-married wife in her husband's bed and went their ways. Now Titus his chamber adjoined that of Gisippus and one might go from the one room into the other; wherefore Gisippus, being in his chamber and having put out all the lights, betook himself stealthily to his friend and bade him go couch with his mistress. Titus, seeing this, was overcome with shame and would fain have repented and refused to go; but Gisippus, who with his whole heart, no less than in words, was minded to do his friend's pleasure, sent him thither, after long contention. Whenas he came into the bed, he took the damsel in his arms and asked her softly, as if in sport, if she chose to be his wife. She, thinking him to be Gisippus, answered, 'Yes'; whereupon he set a goodly and rich ring on her finger, saying, 'And I choose to be thy husband.' Then, the marriage consummated, he took long and amorous pleasance of her, without her or others anywise perceiving that other than Gisippus lay with her.

The marriage of Sophronia and Titus being at this pass, Publius his father departed this life, wherefore it was written him that he should without delay return to Rome, to look to his affairs, and he accordingly took counsel with Gisippus to betake himself thither and carry Sophronia with him; which might not nor should aptly be done without discovering to her how the case stood. Accordingly, one day, calling her into the chamber, they thoroughly discovered to her the fact and thereof Titus certified her by many particulars of that which had passed between them twain. Sophronia, after eying the one and the other somewhat despitefully, fell a-weeping bitterly, complaining of Gisippus his deceit; then, rather than make any words of this in his house, she repaired to that of her father and there acquainted him and her mother with the cheat that had been put upon her and them by Gisippus, avouching herself to be the wife of Titus and not of Gisippus, as they believed. This was exceeding grievous to Sophronia's father, who made long and sore complaint thereof to her kinsfolk and those of Gisippus, and much and great was the talk and the clamour by reason thereof. Gisippus was held in despite both by his own kindred and those of Sophronia and every one declared him worthy not only of blame, but of severe chastisement; whilst he, on the contrary, avouched himself to have done an honourable thing and one for which thanks should be rendered him by Sophronia's kinsfolk, having married her to a better than himself.

Titus, on his part, heard and suffered everything with no little annoy and knowing it to be the usance of the Greeks to press on with clamours and menaces, till such times as they found who should answer them, and then to become not only humble, but abject, he bethought himself that their clamour was no longer to be brooked without reply and having a Roman spirit and an Athenian wit, he adroitly contrived to assemble Gisippus his kinsfolk and those of Sophronia in a temple, wherein entering, accompanied by Gisippus alone, he thus bespoke the expectant folk: 'It is the belief of many philosophers that the actions of mortals are determined and foreordained of the immortal Gods, wherefore some will have it that all that is or shall ever be done is of necessity, albeit there be others who attribute this necessity to that only which is already done. If these opinions be considered with any diligence, it will very manifestly be seen that to blame a thing which cannot be undone is to do no otherwhat than to seek to show oneself wiser than the Gods, who, we must e'en believe, dispose of and govern us and our affairs with unfailing wisdom and without any error; wherefore you may very easily see what fond and brutish overweening it is to presume to find fault with their operations and eke how many and what chains they merit who suffer themselves be so far carried away by hardihood as to do this. Of whom, to my thinking, you are all, if that be true which I understand you have said and still say for that Sophronia is become my wife, whereas you had given her to Gisippus, never considering that it was foreordained from all eternity that she should become not his, but mine, as by the issue is known at this present. But, for that to speak of the secret foreordinance and intention of the Gods appeareth unto many a hard thing and a grievous to apprehend, I am willing to suppose that they concern not themselves with aught of our affairs and to condescend to the counsels[6] of mankind, in speaking whereof, it will behove me to do two things, both very contrary to my usances, the one, somedele to commend myself, and the other, in some measure to blame or disparage others; but, for that I purpose, neither in the one nor in the other, to depart from the truth and that the present matter requireth it, I will e'en do it.

Your complainings, dictated more by rage than by reason, upbraid, revile and condemn Gisippus with continual murmurs or rather clamours, for that, of his counsel, he hath given me to wife her whom you of yours[7] had given him; whereas I hold that he is supremely to be commended therefor, and that for two reasons, the one, for that he hath done that which a friend should do, and the other, for that he hath in this wrought more discreetly than did you. That which the sacred laws of friendship will that one friend should do for the other, it is not my intention at this present to expound, being content to have recalled to you this much only thereof, to wit, that the bonds of friendship are far more stringent than those of blood or of kindred, seeing that the friends we have are such as we choose for ourselves and our kinsfolk such as fortune giveth us; wherefore, if Gisippus loved my life more than your goodwill, I being his friend, as I hold myself, none should marvel thereat. But to come to the second reason, whereanent it more instantly behoveth to show you that he hath been wiser than yourselves, since meseemeth you reck nothing of the foreordinance of the Gods and know yet less of the effects of friendship:—I say, then, that you of your judgment, of your counsel and of your deliberation, gave Sophronia to Gisippus, a young man and a philosopher; Gisippus of his gave her to a young man and a philosopher; your counsel gave her to an Athenian and that of Gisippus to a Roman; your counsel gave her to a youth of noble birth and his to one yet nobler; yours to a rich youth, his to a very rich; yours to a youth who not only loved her not, but scarce knew her, his to one who loved her over his every happiness and more than his very life. And to show you that this I say is true and that Gisippus his action is more commendable than yours, let us consider it, part by part. That I, like Gisippus, am a young man and a philosopher, my favour and my studies may declare, without more discourse thereof. One same age is his and mine and still with equal step have we proceeded studying. True, he is an Athenian and I am a Roman. If it be disputed of the glory of our native cities, I say that I am a citizen of a free city and he of a tributary one; I am of a city mistress of the whole world and he of a city obedient unto mine; I am of a city most illustrious in arms, in empery and in letters, whereas he can only commend his own for letters. Moreover, albeit you see me here on lowly wise enough a student, I am not born of the dregs of the Roman populace; my houses and the public places of Rome are full of antique images of my ancestors and the Roman annals will be found full of many a triumph led by the Quintii up to the Roman Capitol; nor is the glory of our name fallen for age into decay, nay, it presently flourisheth more splendidly than ever. I speak not, for shamefastness, of my riches, bearing in mind that honourable poverty hath ever been the ancient and most ample patrimony of the noble citizens of Rome; but, if this be condemned of the opinion of the vulgar and treasures commended, I am abundantly provided with these latter, not as one covetous, but as beloved of fortune.[8] I know very well that it was and should have been and should be dear unto you to have Gisippus here in Athens to kinsman; but I ought not for any reason to be less dear to you at Rome, considering that in me you would have there an excellent host and an useful and diligent and powerful patron, no less in public occasions than in matters of private need.

Who then, letting be wilfulness and considering with reason, will commend your counsels above those of my Gisippus? Certes, none. Sophronia, then, is well and duly married to Titus Quintius Fulvus, a noble, rich and long-descended citizen of Rome and a friend of Gisippus; wherefore whoso complaineth or maketh moan of this doth not that which he ought neither knoweth that which he doth. Some perchance will say that they complain not of Sophronia being the wife of Titus, but of the manner wherein she became his wife, to wit, in secret and by stealth, without friend or kinsman knowing aught thereof; but this is no marvel nor thing that betideth newly. I willingly leave be those who have aforetime taken husbands against their parents' will and those who have fled with their lovers and have been mistresses before they were wives and those who have discovered themselves to be married rather by pregnancy or child-bearing than with the tongue, yet hath necessity commended it to their kinsfolk; nothing of which hath happened in Sophronia's case; nay, she hath orderly, discreetly and honourably been given by Gisippus to Titus. Others will say that he gave her in marriage to whom it appertained not to do so; but these be all foolish and womanish complaints and proceed from lack of advisement. This is not the first time that fortune hath made use of various means and strange instruments to bring matters to foreordained issues. What have I to care if it be a cordwainer rather than a philosopher, that hath, according to his judgment, despatched an affair of mine, and whether in secret or openly, provided the issue be good? If the cordwainer be indiscreet, all I have to do is to look well that he have no more to do with my affairs and thank him for that which is done. If Gisippus hath married Sophronia well, it is a superfluous folly to go complaining of the manner and of him. If you have no confidence in his judgment, look he have no more of your daughters to marry and thank him for this one.

Nevertheless I would have you to know that I sought not, either by art or by fraud, to impose any stain upon the honour and illustriousness of your blood in the person of Sophronia, and that, albeit I took her secretly to wife, I came not as a ravisher to rob her of her maidenhead nor sought, after the manner of an enemy, whilst shunning your alliance, to have her otherwise than honourably; but, being ardently enkindled by her lovesome beauty and by her worth and knowing that, had I sought her with that ordinance which you will maybe say I should have used, I should not (she being much beloved of you) have had her, for fear lest I should carry her off to Rome, I used the occult means that may now be discovered to you and caused Gisippus, in my person, consent unto that which he himself was not disposed to do. Moreover, ardently as I loved her, I sought her embraces not as a lover, but as a husband, nor, as she herself can truly testify, did I draw near to her till I had first both with the due words and with the ring espoused her, asking her if she would have me for husband, to which she answered ay. If it appear to her that she hath been deceived, it is not I who am to blame therefor, but she, who asked me not who I was. This, then, is the great misdeed, the grievous crime, the sore default committed by Gisippus as a friend and by myself as a lover, to wit, that Sophronia hath secretly become the wife of Titus Quintius, and this it is for which you defame and menace and plot against him. What more could you do, had he bestowed her upon a churl, a losel or a slave? What chains, what prison, what gibbets had sufficed thereunto?

But let that be for the present; the time is come which I looked not for yet, to wit, my father is dead and it behoveth me return to Rome; wherefore, meaning to carry Sophronia with me, I have discovered to you that which I should otherwise belike have yet kept hidden from you and with which, an you be wise, you will cheerfully put up, for that, had I wished to cheat or outrage you, I might have left her to you, scorned and dishonored; but God forfend that such a baseness should ever avail to harbour in a Roman breast! She, then, namely Sophronia, by the consent of the Gods and the operation of the laws of mankind, no less than by the admirable contrivance of my Gisippus and mine own amorous astuteness, is become mine, and this it seemeth that you, holding yourselves belike wiser than the Gods and than the rest of mankind, brutishly condemn, showing your disapproval in two ways both exceedingly noyous to myself, first by detaining Sophronia, over whom you have no right, save in so far as it pleaseth me to allow it, and secondly, by entreating Gisippus, to whom you are justly beholden, as an enemy.

How foolishly you do in both which things I purpose not at this present to make farther manifest to you, but will only counsel you, as a friend, to lay by your despites and altogether leaving your resentments and the rancours that you have conceived, to restore Sophronia to me, so I may joyfully depart your kinsman and live your friend; for of this, whether that which is done please you or please you not, you may be assured that, if you offer to do otherwise, I will take Gisippus from you and if I win to Rome, I will without fail, however ill you may take it, have her again who is justly mine and ever after showing myself your enemy, will cause you know by experience that whereof the despite of Roman souls is capable.'

Titus, having thus spoken, rose to his feet, with a countenance all disordered for anger, and taking Gisippus by the hand, went forth of the temple, shaking his head threateningly and showing that he recked little of as many as were there. The latter, in part reconciled by his reasonings to the alliance and desirous of his friendship and in part terrified by his last words, of one accord determined that it was better to have him for a kinsman, since Gisippus had not willed it, than to have lost the latter to kinsman and gotten the former for an enemy. Accordingly, going in quest of Titus, they told him that they were willing that Sophronia should be his and to have him for a dear kinsman and Gisippus for a dear friend; then, having mutually done each other such honours and courtesies as beseem between kinsmen and friends, they took their leaves and sent Sophronia back to him. She, like a wise woman, making a virtue of necessity, readily transferred to Titus the affection she bore Gisippus and repaired with him to Rome, where she was received with great honour.

Meanwhile, Gisippus abode in Athens, held in little esteem of well nigh all, and no great while after, through certain intestine troubles, was, with all those of his house, expelled from Athens, in poverty and misery, and condemned to perpetual exile. Finding himself in this case and being grown not only poor, but beggarly, he betook himself, as least ill he might, to Rome, to essay if Titus should remember him. There, learning that the latter was alive and high in favour with all the Romans and enquiring for his dwelling-place, he stationed himself before the door and there abode till such time as Titus came, to whom, by reason of the wretched plight wherein he was, he dared not say a word, but studied to cause himself be seen of him, so he might recognize him and let call him to himself; wherefore Titus passed on, [without noting him,] and Gisippus, conceiving that he had seen and shunned him and remembering him of that which himself had done for him aforetime, departed, despiteful and despairing. It being by this night and he fasting and penniless, he wandered on, unknowing whither and more desirous of death than of otherwhat, and presently happened upon a very desert part of the city, where seeing a great cavern, he addressed himself to abide the night there and presently, forspent with long weeping, he fell asleep on the naked earth and ill in case. To this cavern two, who had gone a-thieving together that night, came towards morning, with the booty they had gotten, and falling out over the division, one, who was the stronger, slew the other and went away. Gisippus had seen and heard this and himseemed he had found a way to the death so sore desired of him, without slaying himself; wherefore he abode without stirring, till such time as the Serjeants of the watch, who had by this gotten wind of the deed, came thither and laying furious hands of him, carried him off prisoner. Gisippus, being examined, confessed that he had murdered the man nor had since availed to depart the cavern; whereupon the prætor, who was called Marcus Varro, commanded that he should be put to death upon the cross, as the usance then was.

Now Titus was by chance come at that juncture to the prætorium and looking the wretched condemned man in the face and hearing why he had been doomed to die, suddenly knew him for Gisippus; whereupon, marvelling at his sorry fortune and how he came to be in Rome and desiring most ardently to succour him, but seeing no other means of saving him than to accuse himself and thus excuse him, he thrust forward in haste and cried out, saying, 'Marcus Varro, call back the poor man whom thou hast condemned, for that he is innocent. I have enough offended against the Gods with one crime, in slaying him whom thine officer found this morning dead, without willing presently to wrong them with the death of another innocent.' Varro marvelled and it irked him that all the prætorium should have heard him; but, being unable, for his own honour's sake, to forbear from doing that which the laws commanded, he caused bring back Gisippus and in the presence of Titus said to him, 'How camest thou to be so mad that, without suffering any torture, thou confessedst to that which thou didst not, it being a capital matter? Thou declaredst thyself to be he who slew the man yesternight, and now this man cometh and saith that it was not thou, but he that slew him.'

Gisippus looked and seeing that it was Titus, perceived full well that he did this to save him, as grateful for the service aforetime received from him; wherefore, weeping for pity, 'Varro,' quoth he, 'indeed it was I slew him and Titus his solicitude for my safety is now too late.' Titus on the other hand, said, 'Prætor, do as thou seest, this man is a stranger and was found without arms beside the murdered man, and thou mayst see that his wretchedness giveth him occasion to wish to die; wherefore do thou release him and punish me, who have deserved it.' Varro marvelled at the insistence of these two and beginning now to presume that neither of them might be guilty, was casting about for a means of acquitting them, when, behold, up came a youth called Publius Ambustus, a man of notorious ill life and known to all the Romans for an arrant rogue, who had actually done the murder and knowing neither of the twain to be guilty of that whereof each accused himself, such was the pity that overcame his heart for the innocence of the two friends that, moved by supreme compassion, he came before Varro and said, 'Prætor, my fates impel me to solve the grievous contention of these twain and I know not what God within me spurreth and importuneth me to discover to thee my sin. Know, then, that neither of these men is guilty of that whereof each accuseth himself. I am verily he who slew yonder man this morning towards daybreak and I saw this poor wretch asleep there, what while I was in act to divide the booty gotten with him whom I slew. There is no need for me to excuse Titus; his renown is everywhere manifest and every one knoweth him to be no man of such a condition. Release him, therefore, and take of me that forfeit which the laws impose on me.'

By this Octavianus had notice of the matter and causing all three be brought before him, desired to hear what cause had moved each of them to seek to be the condemned man. Accordingly, each related his own story, whereupon Octavianus released the two friends, for that they were innocent, and pardoned the other for the love of them. Thereupon Titus took his Gisippus and first reproaching him sore for lukewarmness[9] and diffidence, rejoiced in him with marvellous great joy and carried him to his house, where Sophronia with tears of compassion received him as a brother. Then, having awhile recruited him with rest and refreshment and reclothed him and restored him to such a habit as sorted with his worth and quality, he first shared all his treasures and estates in common with him and after gave him to wife a young sister of his, called Fulvia, saying, 'Gisippus, henceforth it resteth with thee whether thou wilt abide here with me or return with everything I have given thee into Achaia.' Gisippus, constrained on the one hand by his banishment from his native land and on the other by the love which he justly bore to the cherished friendship of Titus, consented to become a Roman and accordingly took up his abode in the city, where he with his Fulvia and Titus with his Sophronia lived long and happily, still abiding in one house and waxing more friends (an more they might be) every day.

A most sacred thing, then, is friendship and worthy not only of especial reverence, but to be commended with perpetual praise, as the most discreet mother of magnanimity and honour, the sister of gratitude and charity and the enemy of hatred and avarice, still, without waiting to be entreated, ready virtuously to do unto others that which it would have done to itself. Nowadays its divine effects are very rarely to be seen in any twain, by the fault and to the shame of the wretched cupidity of mankind, which, regarding only its own profit, hath relegated it to perpetual exile, beyond the extremest limits of the earth. What love, what riches, what kinship, what, except friendship, could have made Gisippus feel in his heart the ardour, the tears and the sighs of Titus with such efficacy as to cause him yield up to his friend his betrothed bride, fair and gentle and beloved of him? What laws, what menaces, what fears could have enforced the young arms of Gisippus to abstain, in solitary places and in dark, nay, in his very bed, from the embraces of the fair damsel, she mayhap bytimes inviting him, had friendship not done it? What honours, what rewards, what advancements, what, indeed, but friendship, could have made Gisippus reck not of losing his own kinsfolk and those of Sophronia nor of the unmannerly clamours of the populace nor of scoffs and insults, so that he might pleasure his friend? On the other hand, what, but friendship, could have prompted Titus, whenas he might fairly have feigned not to see, unhesitatingly to compass his own death, that he might deliver Gisippus from the cross to which he had of his own motion procured himself to be condemned? What else could have made Titus, without the least demur, so liberal in sharing his most ample patrimony with Gisippus, whom fortune had bereft of his own? What else could have made him so forward to vouchsafe his sister to his friend, albeit he saw him very poor and reduced to the extreme of misery? Let men, then, covet a multitude of comrades, troops of brethren and children galore and add, by dint of monies, to the number of their servitors, considering not that every one of these, who and whatsoever he may be, is more fearful of every least danger of his own than careful to do away the great[10] from father or brother or master, whereas we see a friend do altogether the contrary."

---

1. Sic, *Publio Quinzio Fulvo*; but *quære* should it not rather be *Publio Quinto Fulvio*, *i.e.* Publius Quintus Fulvius, a form of the name which seems more in accordance with the genius of the Latin language?
2. Or "his" (*a sè*).
3. Or "thine" (*a te*).
4. Lit. "hope" (*sperare*).
5. *i.e.* I would have her in common with thee.
6. Or "arguments" (*consigli*).
7. *i.e.* of your counsel.
8. *i.e.* my riches are not the result of covetous amassing, but of the favours of fortune.
9. Sic (*tiepidezza*); but *semble* "timidity" or "distrustfulness" is meant.
10. *i.e.* perils.

❧ 9 ❧

THE NINTH STORY

SALADIN, IN THE DISGUISE OF A MERCHANT, IS
HONOURABLY ENTERTAINED BY MESSER TORELLO
D'ISTRIA, WHO, PRESENTLY UNDERTAKING THE
[THIRD] CRUSADE, APPOINTETH HIS WIFE A TERM
FOR HER MARRYING AGAIN. HE IS TAKEN [BY THE
SARACENS] AND COMETH, BY HIS SKILL IN TRAINING
HAWKS, UNDER THE NOTICE OF THE SOLDAN, WHO
KNOWETH HIM AGAIN AND DISCOVERING HIMSELF
TO HIM, ENTREATETH HIM WITH THE UTMOST
HONOUR. THEN, TORELLO FALLING SICK FOR
LANGUISHMENT, HE IS BY MAGICAL ART
TRANSPORTED IN ONE NIGHT [FROM ALEXANDRIA]
TO PAVIA, WHERE, BEING RECOGNIZED BY HIS WIFE
AT THE BRIDE-FEAST HELD FOR HER MARRYING
AGAIN, HE RETURNETH WITH HER TO HIS OWN
HOUSE

FILOMENA HAVING MADE an end of her discourse and the magnificent gratitude of Titus having been of all alike commended, the king, reserving the last place unto Dioneo, proceeded to speak thus: "Assuredly, lovesome ladies, Filomena speaketh sooth in that which she saith of friendship and with reason complaineth, in concluding her discourse, of its being so little in favour with mankind. If we were here for the purpose of correcting the defaults of the age or even of reprehending them, I might ensue her words with a discourse at large upon the subject; but, for that we aim at otherwhat, it hath occurred to my mind to set forth to you, in a story belike somewhat overlong, but withal altogether pleasing, one of the magnificences of Saladin, to the end that, if, by reason of our defaults, the friendship of any one may not be throughly acquired, we may, at the least, be led, by the things which you shall hear in my story, to take delight in doing service, in the hope that, whenassoever it may be, reward will ensue to us thereof.

I must tell you, then, that, according to that which divers folk affirm, a general crusade was, in the days of the Emperor Frederick the First, undertaken by the Christians for the recovery of the Holy Land, whereof Saladin, a very noble and valiant prince, who was then Soldan of Babylon, having notice awhile beforehand, he bethought himself to seek in his own person to see the preparations of the Christian princes for the undertaking in question, so he might the better avail to provide himself. Accordingly, having ordered all his affairs in Egypt, he made a show of going a pilgrimage and set out in the disguise of a merchant, attended by two only of his chiefest and sagest officers and three serving-men. After he had visited many Christian countries, it chanced that, as they rode through Lombardy, thinking to pass beyond the mountains,[1] they encountered, about vespers, on the road from Milan to Pavia, a gentleman of the latter place, by name Messer Torello d'Istria, who was on his way, with his servants and dogs and falcons, to sojourn at a goodly country seat he had upon the Tesino, and no sooner set eyes on Saladin and his company than he knew them for gentlemen and strangers; wherefore, the Soldan enquiring of one of his servants how far they were yet distant from Pavia and if he might win thither in time to enter the city, he suffered not the man to reply, but himself answered, 'Gentlemen, you cannot reach Pavia in time to enter therein.' 'Then,' said Saladin, 'may it please you acquaint us (for that we are strangers) where we may best lodge the night.' Quoth Messer Torello, 'That will I willingly do. I had it presently in mind to dispatch one of my men here to the neighborhood of Pavia for somewhat: I will send him with you and he shall bring you to a place where you may lodge conveniently enough.' Then, turning to the discreetest of his men he [privily] enjoined him what he should do and sent him with them, whilst he himself, making for his country house, let order, as best he might, a goodly supper and set the tables in the garden; which done, he posted himself at the door to await his guests.

Meanwhile, the servant, devising with the gentlemen of one thing and another, led them about by certain by-roads and brought them, without their suspecting it, to his lord's residence, where, whenas Messer Torello saw them, he came to meet them afoot and said, smiling, 'Gentlemen, you are very welcome.' Saladin, who was very quick of apprehension, understood that the gentleman had misdoubted him they would not have accepted his invitation, had he bidden them whenas he fell in with them, and had, therefore, brought them by practice to his house, so they might not avail to refuse to pass the night with him, and accordingly, returning his greeting, he said, 'Sir, an one could complain of men of courtesy, we might complain of you, for that (letting be that you have somewhat hindered us from our road) you have, without our having merited your goodwill otherwise than by a mere salutation, constrained us to accept of such noble hospitality as is this of yours.' 'Gentlemen,' answered Messer Torello, who was a discreet and well-spoken man, 'it is but a sorry hospitality that you will receive from us, regard had to that which should behove unto you, an I may judge by that which I apprehend from your carriage and that of your companions; but in truth you could nowhere out of Pavia have found any decent place of entertainment; wherefore, let it not irk you to have gone somedele beside your way, to have a little less unease.' Meanwhile, his servants came round about the travellers and helping them to dismount, eased[2] their horses.

Messer Torello then brought the three stranger gentlemen to the chambers prepared for them, where he let unboot them and refresh them somewhat with very cool wines and entertained them in agreeable discourse till such time as they might sup. Saladin and his companions and servants all knew Latin, wherefore they understood very well and were understood, and it seemed to each of them that this gentleman was the most pleasant and well-mannered man they had ever seen, ay, and the best spoken. It appeared to Messer Torello, on the other hand, that they were men of magnificent fashions and much more of account than he had at first conceived, wherefore he was inwardly chagrined that he could not honour them that evening with companions and with a more considerable entertainment. But for this he bethought himself to make them amends on the morrow, and accordingly, having instructed one of his servants of that which he would have done, he despatched him to Pavia, which was very near at hand and where no gate was ever locked, to his lady, who was exceeding discreet and great-hearted. Then, carrying the gentlemen into the garden, he courteously asked them who they were, to which Saladin answered, 'We are merchants from Cyprus and are bound to Paris on our occasions.' 'Would to God,' cried Messer Torello, 'that this our country produced gentlemen of such a fashion as I see Cyprus doth merchants!' In these and other discourses they abode till it was time to sup, whereupon he left it to them to honour themselves at table,[3] and there, for an improvised supper, they were very well and orderly served; nor had they abidden long after the tables were removed, when Messer Torello, judging them to be weary, put them to sleep in very goodly beds and himself a little after in like manner betook himself to rest.

Meanwhile the servant sent to Pavia did his errand to the lady, who, with no womanly, but with a royal spirit, let call in haste a great number of the friends and servants of Messer Torello and made ready all that behoved unto a magnificent banquet. Moreover, she let bid by torchlight many of the noblest of the townfolk to the banquet and bringing out cloths and silks and furs, caused throughly order that which her husband had sent to bid her do. The day come, Saladin and his companions arose, whereupon Messer Torello took horse with them and sending for his falcons, carried them to a neighbouring ford and there showed them how the latter flew; then, Saladin enquiring for some one who should bring him to Pavia and to the best inn, his host said, 'I will be your guide, for that it behoveth me go thither.' The others, believing this, were content and set out in company with him for the city, which they reached about tierce and thinking to be on their way to the best inn, were carried by Messer Torello to his own house, where a good half-hundred of the most considerable citizens were already come to receive the stranger gentlemen and were straightway about their bridles and stirrups. Saladin and his companions, seeing this, understood but too well what was forward and said, 'Messer Torello, this is not what we asked of you; you have done enough for us this past night, ay, and far more than we are worth; wherefore you might now fitly suffer us fare on our way.' 'Gentlemen,' replied Messer Torello, 'for my yesternight's dealing with you I am more indebted to fortune than to you, which took you on the road at an hour when it behoved you come to my poor house; but of your this morning's visit I shall be beholden to yourselves, and with me all these gentlemen who are about you and to whom an it seem to you courteous to refuse to dine with them, you can do so, if you will.'

Saladin and his companions, overcome, dismounted and being joyfully received by the assembled company, were carried to chambers which had been most sumptuously arrayed for them, where having put off their travelling gear and somewhat refreshed themselves, they repaired to the saloon, where the banquet was splendidly prepared. Water having been given to the hands, they were seated at table with the goodliest and most orderly observance and magnificently served with many viands, insomuch that, were the emperor himself come thither, it had been impossible to do him more honour, and albeit Saladin and his companions were great lords and used to see very great things, natheless, they were mightily wondered at this and it seemed to them of the greatest, having regard to the quality of the gentleman, whom they knew to be only a citizen and not a lord. Dinner ended and the tables removed, they conversed awhile of divers things; then, at Messer Torello's instance, the heat being great, the gentlemen of Pavia all betook themselves to repose, whilst he himself, abiding alone with his three guests, carried them into a chamber and (that no precious thing of his should remain unseen of them) let call thither his noble lady. Accordingly, the latter, who was very fair and tall of her person, came in to them, arrayed in rich apparel and flanked by two little sons of hers, as they were two angels, and saluted them courteously. The strangers, seeing her, rose to their feet and receiving her with worship, caused her sit among them and made much of her two fair children. Therewithal she entered into pleasant discourse with them and presently, Messer Torello having gone out awhile, she asked them courteously whence they were and whither they went; to which they made answer even as they had done to her husband; whereupon quoth she, with a blithe air, 'Then see I that my womanly advisement will be useful; wherefore I pray you, of your especial favour, refuse me not neither disdain a slight present, which I shall cause bring you, but accept it, considering that women, of their little heart, give little things and regarding more the goodwill of the giver than the value of the gift.' Then, letting fetch them each two gowns, one lined with silk and the other with miniver, no wise citizens' clothes nor merchants, but fit for great lords to wear, and three doublets of sendal and linen breeches to match, she said, 'Take these; I have clad my lord in gowns of the like fashion, and the other things, for all they are little worth, may be acceptable to you, considering that you are far from your ladies and the length of the way you have travelled and that which is yet to travel and that merchants are proper men and nice of their persons.'

The Saracens marvelled and manifestly perceived that Messer Torello was minded to leave no particular of hospitality undone them; nay, seeing the magnificence of the unmerchantlike gowns, they misdoubted them they had been recognized of him. However, one of them made answer to the lady, saying, 'Madam, these are very great matters and such as should not lightly be accepted, an your prayers, to which it is impossible to say no, constrained us not thereto.' This done and Messer Torello being now returned, the lady, commending them to God, took leave of them and let furnish their servants with like things such as sorted with their condition. Messer Torello with many prayers prevailed upon them to abide with him all that day; wherefore, after they had slept awhile, they donned their gowns and rode with him somedele about the city; then, the supper-hour come, they supped magnificently with many worshipful companions and in due time betook themselves to rest. On the morrow they arose with day and found, in place of their tired hackneys, three stout and good palfreys, and on likewise fresh and strong horses for their servants, which when Saladin saw, he turned to his companions and said, 'I vow to God that never was there a more accomplished gentleman nor a more courteous and apprehensive than this one, and if the kings of the Christians are kings of such a fashion as this is a gentleman, the Soldan of Babylon can never hope to stand against a single one of them, not to speak of the many whom we see make ready to fall upon him.' Then, knowing that it were in vain to seek to refuse this new gift, they very courteously thanked him therefor and mounted to horse.

Messer Torello, with many companions, brought them a great way without the city, till, grievous as it was to Saladin to part from him, (so much was he by this grown enamoured of him,) natheless, need constraining him to press on, he presently besought him to turn back; whereupon, loath as he was to leave them, 'Gentlemen,' quoth he, 'since it pleaseth you, I will do it; but one thing I will e'en say to you; I know not who you are nor do I ask to know more thereof than it pleaseth you to tell me; but, be you who you may, you will never make me believe that you are merchants, and so I commend you to God.' Saladin, having by this taken leave of all Messer Torello's companions, replied to him, saying, 'Sir, we may yet chance to let you see somewhat of our merchandise, whereby we may confirm your belief;[4] meantime, God be with you.' Thereupon he departed with his followers, firmly resolved, if life should endure to him and the war he looked for undo him not, to do Messer Torello no less honour than that which he had done him, and much did he discourse with his companions of him and of his lady and all his affairs and fashions and dealings, mightily commending everything. Then, after he had, with no little fatigue, visited all the West, he took ship with his companions and returned to Alexandria, where, being now fully informed, he addressed himself to his defence. As for Messer Torello, he returned to Pavia and went long in thought who these might be, but never hit upon the truth, no, nor came near it.

The time being now come for the crusade and great preparations made everywhere, Messer Torello, notwithstanding the tears and entreaties of his wife, was altogether resolved to go thereon and having made his every provision and being about to take horse, he said to his lady, whom he loved over all, 'Wife, as thou seest, I go on this crusade, as well for the honour of my body as for the health of my soul. I commend to thee our affairs and our honour, and for that I am certain of the going, but of the returning, for a thousand chances that may betide, I have no assurance, I will have thee do me a favour, to wit, that whatever befall of me, an thou have not certain news of my life, thou shalt await me a year and a month and a day, ere thou marry again, beginning from this the day of my departure.' The lady, who wept sore, answered, 'Messer Torello, I know not how I shall endure the chagrin wherein you leave me by your departure; but, an my life prove stronger than my grief and aught befall you, you may live and die assured that I shall live and die the wife of Messer Torello and of his memory.' 'Wife,' rejoined Messer Torello, 'I am very certain that, inasmuch as in thee lieth, this that thou promisest me will come to pass; but thou art a young woman and fair and of high family and thy worth is great and everywhere known; wherefore I doubt not but many great and noble gentlemen will, should aught be misdoubted of me,[5] demand thee of thy brethren and kinsfolk; from whose importunities, how much soever thou mightest wish, thou wilt not be able to defend thyself and it will behove thee perforce comply with their wishes; and this is why I ask of thee this term and not a greater one.' Quoth the lady, 'I will do what I may of that which I have told you, and should it nevertheless behove me to do otherwise, I will assuredly obey you in this that you enjoin me; but I pray God that He bring nor you nor me to such an extremity in these days.' This said, she embraced him, weeping, and drawing a ring from her finger, gave it to him, saying, 'And it chance that I die ere I see you again, remember me when you look upon this ring.'

Torello took the ring and mounted to horse; then, bidding all his people adieu, he set out on his journey and came presently with his company to Genoa. There he embarked on board a galleon and coming in a little while to Acre, joined himself to the other army[6] of the Christians, wherein, well nigh out of hand, there began a sore sickness and mortality. During this, whether by Saladin's skill or of his good fortune, well nigh all the remnant of the Christians who had escaped alive were taken by him, without blow stricken, and divided among many cities and imprisoned. Messer Torello was one of those taken and was carried prisoner to Alexandria, where, being unknown and fearing to make himself known, he addressed himself, of necessity constrained, to the training of hawks, of which he was a great master, and by this he came under the notice of Saladin, who took him out of prison and entertained him for his falconer. Messer Torello, who was called by the Soldan by none other name than the Christian, recognized him not nor did Saladin recognize him; nay, all his thoughts were in Pavia and he had more than once essayed to flee, but without avail; wherefore, certain Genoese coming ambassadors to Saladin, to treat for the ransom of sundry of their townsmen, and being about to depart, he bethought himself to write to his lady, giving her to know that he was alive and would return to her as quickliest he might and bidding her await him. Accordingly, he wrote letters to this effect and instantly besought one of the ambassadors, whom he knew, to cause them come to the hands of the Abbot of San Pietro in Ciel d'Oro, who was his uncle.

Things being at this pass with him, it befell one day that, as Saladin was devising with him of his hawks, Messer Torello chanced to smile and made a motion with his mouth, which the former had much noted, what while he was in his house at Pavia. This brought the gentleman to his mind and looking steadfastly upon him, himseemed it was himself; wherefore, leaving the former discourse, 'Harkye, Christian, said he, 'What countryman art thou of the West?' 'My lord,' replied Torello, 'I am a Lombard of a city called Pavia, a poor man and of mean condition.' Saladin, hearing this, was in a manner certified of the truth of his suspicion and said joyfully in himself, 'God hath vouchsafed me an opportunity of showing this man how grateful his courtesy was to me.' Accordingly, without saying otherwhat, he let lay out all his apparel in a chamber and carrying him thither, said to him, 'Look, Christian, if there be any among these gowns that thou hast ever seen.' Torello looked and saw those which his lady had given Saladin; but, natheless, conceiving not that they could possibly be the same, he answered, 'My lord, I know none of them; albeit, in good sooth, these twain do favour certain gowns wherewithal I, together with three merchants who came to my house, was invested aforetime.' Thereupon Saladin, unable to contain himself farther, embraced him tenderly, saying, 'You are Messer Torello d'Istria and I am one of the three merchants to whom your lady gave these gowns; and now is the time come to certify you what manner merchandise mine is, even as I told you, at my parting from you, might chance to betide.' Messer Torello, hearing this, was at once rejoiced and ashamed; rejoiced to have had such a guest and ashamed for that himseemed he had entertained him but scurvily. Then said Saladin, 'Messer Torello, since God hath sent you hither to me, henceforth consider that not I, but you are master here.' Accordingly, after they had mightily rejoiced in each other, he clad him in royal apparel and carrying him into the presence of all his chief barons, commanded, after saying many things in praise of his worth, that he should of all who held his favour dear be honoured as himself, which was thenceforward done of all, but above all of the two gentlemen who had been Saladin's companions in his house.

The sudden height of glory to which Messer Torello thus found himself advanced put his Lombardy affairs somedele out of his mind, more by token that he had good reason to hope that his letters were by this come to his uncle's hands. Now there had died and been buried in the camp or rather in the host, of the Christians, the day they were taken by Saladin, a Provençal gentleman of little account, by name Messer Torello de Dignes, by reason whereof, Messer Torello d'Istria being renowned throughout the army for his magnificence, whosoever heard say, 'Messer Torello is dead,' believed it of Messer Torello d'Istria, not of him of Dignes. The hazard of the capture that ensued thereupon suffered not those who had been thus misled to be undeceived; wherefore many Italians returned with this news, amongst whom were some who scrupled not to avouch that they had seen him dead and had been at the burial. This, coming to be known of his wife and kinsfolk, was the cause of grievous and inexpressible sorrow, not only to them, but to all who had known him. It were longsome to set forth what and how great was the grief and sorrow and lamentation of his lady; but, after having bemoaned herself some months in continual affliction, coming to sorrow less and being sought in marriage with the chiefest men in Lombardy, she began to be presently importuned by her brothers and other her kinsfolk to marry again. After having again and again refused with many tears, needs must she at the last consent perforce to do her kinsfolk's will, on condition that she should abide, without going to a husband, so long as she had promised Messer Torello.

The lady's affairs at Pavia being at this pass and there lacking maybe eight days of the term appointed for her going to her new husband, it chanced that Messer Torello espied one day in Alexandria one whom he had seen embark with the Genoese ambassadors on board the galley that was to carry them back to Genoa, and calling him, asked him what manner voyage they had had and when they had reached Genoa; whereto the other replied, 'Sir, the galleon (as I heard in Crete, where I remained,) made an ill voyage; for that, as she drew near unto Sicily, there arose a furious northerly wind, which drove her on to the Barbary quicksands, nor was any one saved; and amongst the rest two brothers of mine perished there.' Messer Torello, giving credit to his words, which were indeed but too true, and remembering him that the term required by him of his wife ended a few days thence, concluded that nothing could be known at Pavia of his condition and held it for certain that the lady must have married again; wherefore he fell into such a chagrin that he lost [sleep and] appetite and taking to his bed, determined to die. When Saladin, who loved him above all, heard of this, he came to him and having, by dint of many and urgent prayers, learned the cause of his grief and his sickness, upbraided him sore for that he had not before told it to him and after besought him to be comforted, assuring him that, if he would but take heart, he would so contrive that he should be in Pavia at the appointed term and told him how. Messer Torello, putting faith in Saladin's words and having many a time heard say that this was possible and had indeed been often enough done, began to take comfort and pressed Saladin to despatch. The Soldan accordingly charged a nigromancer of his, of whose skill he had aforetime made proof, to cast about for a means whereby Messer Torello should be in one night transported upon a bed to Pavia, to which the magician replied that it should be done, but that, for the gentleman's own weal, he must put him to sleep.

This done, Saladin returned to Messer Torello and finding him altogether resolved to seek at any hazard to be in Pavia at the term appointed, if it were possible, and in default thereof, to die, bespoke him thus; 'Messer Torello, God knoweth that I neither will nor can anywise blame you if you tenderly love your lady and are fearful of her becoming another's, for that, of all the women I ever saw, she it is whose manners, whose fashions and whose demeanour, (leaving be her beauty, which is but a short-lived flower,) appear to me most worthy to be commended and held dear. It had been very grateful to me, since fortune hath sent you hither, that we should have passed together, as equal masters in the governance of this my realm, such time as you and I have to live, and if this was not to be vouchsafed me of God, it being fated that you should take it to heart to seek either to die or to find yourself in Pavia at the appointed term, I should above all have desired to know it in time, that I might have you transported to your house with such honour, such magnificence and in such company as your worth meriteth. However, since this hath not been vouchsafed and you desire to be presently there, I will e'en, as I may, despatch you thither after the fashion whereof I have bespoken you.' 'My lord,' replied Messer Torello, 'your acts, without your words, have given me sufficient proof of your favour, which I have never merited in such supreme degree, and of that which you say, though you had not said it, I shall live and die most assured; but, since I have taken this resolve, I pray you that that which you tell me you will do may be done speedily, for that to-morrow is the last day I am to be looked for.'

Saladin answered that this should without fail be accomplished and accordingly, on the morrow, meaning to send him away that same night, he let make, in a great hall of his palace, a very goodly and rich bed of mattresses, all, according to their usance, of velvet and cloth of gold and caused lay thereon a counterpoint curiously wrought in various figures with great pearls and jewels of great price (the which here in Italy was after esteemed an inestimable treasure) and two pillows such as sorted with a bed of that fashion. This done, he bade invest Messer Torello, who was presently well and strong again, in a gown of the Saracen fashion, the richest and goodliest thing that had ever been seen of any, and wind about his head, after their guise, one of his longest turban-cloths.[7] Then, it growing late, he betook himself with many of his barons to the chamber where Messer Torello was and seating himself, well nigh weeping, by his side, bespoke him thus; 'Messer Torello, the hour draweth near that is to sunder me from you, and since I may not bear you company nor cause you to be accompanied, by reason of the nature of the journey you have to make, which suffereth it not, needs must I take leave of you here in this chamber, to which end I am come hither. Wherefore, ere I commend you to God, I conjure you, by that love and that friendship that is between us, that you remember you of me and if it be possible, ere our times come to an end, that, whenas you have ordered your affairs in Lombardy, you come at the least once to see me, to the end that, what while I am cheered by your sight, I may then supply the default which needs must I presently commit by reason of your haste; and against that betide, let it not irk you to visit me with letters and require me of such things as shall please you; for that of a surety I will more gladly do them for you than for any man alive.'

As for Messer Torello, he could not contain his tears; wherefore, being hindered thereby, he answered, in a few words, that it was impossible his benefits and his nobility should ever escape his mind and that he would without fail do that which he enjoined him, whenas occasion should be afforded him; whereupon Saladin, having tenderly embraced him and kissed him, bade him with many tears God speed and departed the chamber. The other barons then all took leave of him and followed the Soldan into the hall where he had caused make ready the bed. Meanwhile, it waxing late and the nigromant awaiting and pressing for despatch, there came a physician to Messer Torello with a draught and making him believe that he gave it him to fortify him, caused him drink it; nor was it long ere he fell asleep and so, by Saladin's commandment, was carried into the hall and laid upon the bed aforesaid, whereon the Soldan placed a great and goodly crown of great price and inscribed it on such wise that it was after manifestly understood to be sent by him to Messer Torello's lady; after which he put on Torello's finger a ring, wherein was a carbuncle enchased, so resplendent that it seemed a lighted flambeau, the value whereof could scarce be reckoned, and girt him with a sword, whose garniture might not lightly be appraised. Moreover, he let hang a fermail on his breast, wherein were pearls whose like were never seen, together with other precious stones galore, and on his either side he caused set two great basins of gold, full of doubloons, and many strings of pearls and rings and girdles and other things, which it were tedious to recount, round about him. This done, he kissed him once more and bade the nigromant despatch, whereupon, in his presence, the bed was incontinent taken away, Messer Torello and all, and Saladin abode devising of him with his barons.

Meanwhile, Messer Torello had been set down, even as he had requested, in the church of San Pietro in Ciel d'Oro at Pavia, with all the jewels and ornaments aforesaid, and yet slept when, matins having sounded, the sacristan of the church entered, with a light in his hand, and chancing suddenly to espy the rich bed, not only marvelled, but, seized with a terrible fright, turned and fled. The abbot and the monks, seeing him flee, marvelled and questioned him of the cause, which he told them; whereupon quoth the abbot, 'Marry, thou art no child nor art thou new to the church that thou shouldst thus lightly take fright; let us go see who hath played the bugbear with thee.' Accordingly, kindling several lights, the abbot and all his monks entered the church and saw that wonder-rich and goodly bed and thereon the gentleman asleep; and what while, misdoubting and fearful, they gazed upon the noble jewels, without drawing anywise near to the bed, it befell that, the virtue of the draught being spent, Messer Torello awoke and heaved a great sigh, which when the monks saw and heard, they took to flight, abbot and all, affrighted and crying, 'Lord aid us!' Messer Torello opened his eyes and looking about him, plainly perceived himself to be whereas he had asked Saladin to have him carried, at which he was mightily content. Then, sitting up, he particularly examined that which he had about him, and for all he had before known of the magnificence of Saladin, it seemed to him now greater and he knew it more. Nevertheless, without moving farther, seeing the monks flee and divining why, he proceeded to call the abbot by name, praying him be not afraid, for that he was Torello his nephew. The abbot, hearing this, waxed yet more fearful, as holding him as dead many months before; but, after awhile, taking assurance by true arguments and hearing himself called, he made the sign of the cross and went up to him; whereupon quoth Messer Torello, 'How now, father mine, of what are you adread? Godamercy, I am alive and returned hither from beyond seas.'

The abbot, for all he had a great beard and was clad after the Saracen fashion, presently recognized him and altogether reassured, took him by the hand, saying, 'My son, thou art welcome back.' Then he continued, 'Thou must not marvel at our affright, for that there is not a man in these parts but firmly believeth thee to be dead, insomuch that I must tell thee that Madam Adalieta thy wife, overmastered by the prayers and threats of her kinsfolk and against her own will, is married again and is this morning to go to her new husband; ay, and the bride-feast and all that pertaineth unto the nuptial festivities is prepared.' Therewithal Messer Torello arose from off the rich bed and greeting the abbot and the monks with marvellous joyance, prayed them all to speak with none of that his return, against he should have despatched an occasion of his; after which, having caused lay up the costly jewels in safety, he recounted to his uncle all that had befallen him up to that moment. The abbot rejoiced in his happy fortunes and together with him, rendered thanks to God, after which Messer Torello asked him who was his lady's new husband. The abbot told him and Torello said, 'I have a mind, ere folk know of my return, to see what manner countenance is that of my wife in these nuptials; wherefore, albeit it is not the usance of men of your habit to go to entertainments of this kind, I would have you contrive, for the love of me, that we may go thither, you and I.' The abbot replied that he would well and accordingly, as soon as it was day, he sent to the new bridegroom, saying that he would fain be at his nuptials with a friend of his, whereto the gentleman answered that it liked him passing well.

Accordingly, eating-time come, Messer Torello, clad as he was, repaired with his uncle to the bridegroom's house, beheld with wonderment of all who saw him, but recognized of none; and the abbot told every one that he was a Saracen sent ambassador from the Soldan to the King of France. He was, therefore, seated at a table right overagainst his lady, whom he beheld with the utmost pleasure, and himseemed she was troubled in countenance at these new nuptials. She, in her turn, looked whiles upon him, but not of any cognizance that she had of him, for that his great beard and outlandish habit and the firm assurance she had that he was dead hindered her thereof. Presently, whenas it seemed to him time to essay if she remembered her of him, he took the ring she had given him at his parting and calling a lad who served before her, said to him, 'Say to the bride, on my part, that it is the usance in my country, whenas any stranger, such as I am here, eateth at the bride-feast of any new-married lady, like herself, that she, in token that she holdeth him welcome at her table, send him the cup, wherein she drinketh, full of wine, whereof after the stranger hath drunken what he will, the cup being covered again, the bride drinketh the rest.'

The page did his errand to the lady, who, like a well-bred and discreet woman as she was, believing him to be some great gentleman, commanded, to show him that she had his coming in gree, that a great gilded cup, which stood before her, should be washed and filled with wine and carried to the gentleman; and so it was done. Messer Torello, taking her ring in his mouth, contrived in drinking to drop it, unseen of any, into the cup, wherein having left but a little wine, he covered it again and despatched it to the lady. Madam Adalieta, taking the cup and uncovering it, that she might accomplish his usance, set it to her mouth and seeing the ring, considered it awhile, without saying aught; then, knowing it for that which she had given to Messer Torello at parting, she took it up and looking fixedly upon him whom she deemed a stranger, presently recognized him; whereupon, as she were waxen mad, she overthrew the table she had before her and cried out, saying, 'It is my lord, it is indeed Messer Torello!' Then, running to the place where he sat, she cast herself as far forward as she might, without taking thought to her clothes or to aught that was on the table, and clipped him close in her arms nor could, for word or deed of any there, be loosed from his neck till she was bidden of Messer Torello contain herself somewhat, for that time enough would yet be afforded her to embrace him. She accordingly having arisen and the nuptials being by this all troubled, albeit in part more joyous than ever for the recovery of such a gentleman, every one, at Messer Torello's request, abode quiet; whereupon he related to them all that had betided him from the day of his departure up to that moment, concluding that the gentleman, who, deeming him dead, had taken his lady to wife, must not hold it ill if he, being alive, took her again unto himself.

The bridegroom, though somewhat mortified, answered frankly and as a friend that it rested with himself to do what most pleased him of his own. Accordingly, the lady put off the ring and crown had of her new groom and donned the ring which she had taken from the cup and the crown sent her by the Soldan; then, issuing forth of the house where they were, they betook themselves, with all the nuptial train, to Messer Torello's house and there recomforted his disconsolate friends and kindred and all the townsfolk, who regarded his return as well nigh a miracle, with long and joyous festival. As for Messer Torello, after imparting of his precious jewels to him who had had the expense of the nuptials, as well as to the abbot and many others, and signifying his happy repatriation by more than one message to Saladin, whose friend and servant he still professed himself, he lived many years thereafterward with his noble lady and thenceforth, used more hospitality and courtesy than ever. Such then was the issue of the troubles of Messer Torello and his beloved lady and the recompense of their cheerful and ready hospitalities, the which many study to practise, who, albeit they have the wherewithal, do yet so ill contrive it that they make those on whom they bestow their courtesies buy them, ere they have done with them, for more than their worth; wherefore, if no reward ensue to them thereof, neither themselves nor others should marvel thereat."

---

1. *i.e.* to cross the Alps into France.
2. *Adagiarono.*
3. *i.e.* to place themselves according to their several ranks, which were unknown to Torello.
4. Sic (*la vostra credenza raffermeremo*); but the meaning is, "whereby we may amend your unbelief and give you cause to credit our assertion that we are merchants."
5. *i.e.* should any rumour get wind of death.
6. Sic (*all' altro esercito*). The meaning of this does not appear, as no mention has yet been made of two Christian armies. Perhaps we should translate "the rest of the army," *i.e.* such part of the remnant of the Christian host as fled to Acre and shut themselves up there after the disastrous day of Hittin (23 June, 1187). Acre fell on the 29th July, 1187.
7. It may be well to remind the European reader that the turban consists of two parts, *i.e.* a skull-cap and a linen cloth, which is wound round it in various folds and shapes, to form the well-known Eastern head-dress.

THE TENTH STORY

THE MARQUESS OF SALUZZO, CONSTRAINED BY THE PRAYERS OF HIS VASSALS TO MARRY, BUT DETERMINED TO DO IT AFTER HIS OWN FASHION, TAKETH TO WIFE THE DAUGHTER OF A PEASANT AND HATH OF HER TWO CHILDREN, WHOM HE MAKETH BELIEVE TO HER TO PUT TO DEATH; AFTER WHICH, FEIGNING TO BE GROWN WEARY OF HER AND TO HAVE TAKEN ANOTHER WIFE, HE LETTETH BRING HIS OWN DAUGHTER HOME TO HIS HOUSE, AS SHE WERE HIS NEW BRIDE, AND TURNETH HIS WIFE AWAY IN HER SHIFT; BUT, FINDING HER PATIENT UNDER EVERYTHING, HE FETCHETH HER HOME AGAIN, DEARER THAN EVER, AND SHOWING HER HER CHILDREN GROWN GREAT, HONOURETH AND LETTETH HONOUR HER AS MARCHIONESS

THE KING'S long story being ended and having, to all appearance, much pleased all, Dioneo said, laughing, "The good man,[1] who looked that night to abase the phantom's tail upright,[2] had not given a brace of farthings of all the praises that you bestow on Messer Torello." Then, knowing that it rested with him alone to tell, he proceeded: "Gentle ladies mine, it appeareth to me that this day hath been given up to Kings and Soldans and the like folk; wherefore, that I may not remove overfar from you, I purpose to relate to you of a marquess, not an act of magnificence, but a monstrous folly, which, albeit good ensued to him thereof in the end, I counsel not any to imitate, for it was a thousand pities that weal betided him thereof.

It is now a great while agone since the chief of the house among the Marquesses of Saluzzo was a youth called Gualtieri, who, having neither wife nor children, spent his time in nought but hunting and hawking nor had any thought of taking a wife nor of having children; wherein he deserved to be reputed very wise. The thing, however, not pleasing his vassals, they besought him many times to take a wife, so he might not abide without an heir nor they without a lord, and offered themselves to find him one of such a fashion and born of such parents that good hopes might be had of her and he be well content with her; whereto he answered, 'My friends, you constrain me unto that which I was altogether resolved never to do, considering how hard a thing it is to find a wife whose fashions sort well within one's own humour and how great an abundance there is of the contrary sort and how dour a life is his who happeneth upon a woman not well suited unto him. To say that you think, by the manners and fashions of the parents, to know the daughters, wherefrom you argue to give me a wife such as will please me, is a folly, since I know not whence you may avail to know their fathers nor yet the secrets of their mothers; and even did you know them, daughters are often unlike their parents. However, since it e'en pleaseth you to bind me in these chains, I am content to do

487

your desire; but, that I may not have occasion to complain of other than myself, if it prove ill done, I mean to find a wife for myself, certifying you that, whomsoever I may take me, if she be not honoured of you as your lady and mistress, you shall prove, to your cost, how much it irketh me to have at your entreaty taken a wife against mine own will.'

The good honest men replied that they were content, so he would but bring himself to take a wife. Now the fashions of a poor girl, who was of a village near to his house, had long pleased Gualtieri, and himseeming she was fair enough, he judged that he might lead a very comfortable life with her; wherefore, without seeking farther, he determined to marry her and sending for her father, who was a very poor man, agreed with him to take her to wife. This done, he assembled all his friends of the country round and said to them, 'My friends, it hath pleased and pleaseth you that I should dispose me to take a wife and I have resigned myself thereto, more to complease you than of any desire I have for marriage. You know what you promised me, to wit, that you would be content with and honour as your lady and mistress her whom I should take, whosoever she might be; wherefore the time is come when I am to keep my promise to you and when I would have you keep yours to me. I have found a damsel after mine own heart and purpose within some few days hence to marry her and bring her home to my house; wherefore do you bethink yourselves how the bride-feast may be a goodly one and how you may receive her with honour, on such wise that I may avouch myself contented of your promise, even as you will have cause to be of mine.' The good folk all answered joyfully that this liked them well and that, be she who he would, they would hold her for lady and mistress and honour her as such in all things; after which they all addressed themselves to hold fair and high and glad festival and on like wise did Gualtieri, who let make ready very great and goodly nuptials and bade thereto many his friends and kinsfolk and great gentlemen and others of the neighbourhood. Moreover, he let cut and fashion store of rich and goodly apparel, after the measure of a damsel who seemed to him like of her person to the young woman he was purposed to marry, and provided also rings and girdles and a rich and goodly crown and all that behoveth unto a bride.

The day come that he had appointed for the nuptials, Gualtieri towards half tierce mounted to horse, he and all those who were come to do him honour, and having ordered everything needful. 'Gentlemen,' quoth he, 'it is time to go fetch the bride.' Then, setting out with all his company, he rode to the village and betaking himself to the house of the girl's father, found her returning in great haste with water from the spring, so she might after go with other women to see Gualtieri's bride come. When the marquess saw her, he called her by name, to wit, Griselda, and asked her where her father was; to which she answered bashfully, 'My lord, he is within the house.' Thereupon Gualtieri dismounted and bidding all await him, entered the poor house alone, where he found her father, whose name was Giannucolo, and said to him, 'I am come to marry Griselda, but first I would fain know of her somewhat in thy presence.' Accordingly, he asked her if, an he took her to wife, she would still study to please him, nor take umbrage at aught that he should do or say, and if she would be obedient, and many other like things, to all of which she answered ay; whereupon Gualtieri, taking her by the hand, led her forth and in the presence of all his company and of every one else, let strip her naked. Then, sending for the garments which he had let make, he caused forthright clothe and shoe her and would have her set the crown on her hair, all tumbled as it was; after which, all marvelling at this, he said, 'Gentlemen, this is she who I purpose shall be my wife, an she will have me to husband.' Then, turning to her, where she stood, all shamefast and confounded, he said to her, 'Griselda, wilt thou have me to thy husband?' To which she answered, 'Ay, my lord.' Quoth he, 'And I will have thee to my wife'; and espoused her in the presence of all. Then, mounting her on a palfrey, he carried her, honourably accompanied, to his mansion, where the nuptials were celebrated with the utmost splendour and rejoicing, no otherwise than as he had taken to wife the king's daughter of France.

The young wife seemed to have, together with her clothes, changed her mind and her manners. She was, as we have already said, goodly of person and countenance, and even as she was fair, on like wise she became so engaging, so pleasant and so well-mannered that she seemed rather to have been the child of some noble gentleman than the daughter of Giannucolo and a tender of sheep; whereof she made every one marvel who had known her aforetime. Moreover, she was so obedient to her husband and so diligent in his service that he accounted himself the happiest and best contented man in the world; and on like wise she bore herself with such graciousness and such loving kindness towards her husband's subjects that there was none of them but loved and honoured her with his whole heart, praying all for her welfare and prosperity and advancement; and whereas they were used to say that Gualtieri had done as one of little wit to take her to wife, they now with one accord declared that he was the sagest and best-advised man alive, for that none other than he might ever have availed to know her high worth, hidden as it was under poor clothes and a rustic habit. Brief, it was no great while ere she knew so to do that, not only in her husband's marquisate, but everywhere else, she made folk talk of her virtues and her well-doing and turned to the contrary whatsoever had been said against her husband on her account, whenas he married her.

She had not long abidden with Gualtieri ere she conceived with child and in due time bore a daughter, whereat he rejoiced greatly. But, a little after, a new[3] thought having entered his mind, to wit, to seek, by dint of long tribulation and things unendurable, to make trial of her patience, he first goaded her with words, feigning himself troubled and saying that his vassals were exceeding ill content with her, by reason of her mean extraction, especially since they saw that she bore children, and that they did nothing but murmur, being sore chagrined for the birth of her daughter. The lady, hearing this, replied, without anywise changing countenance or showing the least distemperature, 'My lord, do with me that which thou deemest will be most for thine honour and solace, for that I shall be content with all, knowing, as I do, that I am of less account than they[4] and that I was unworthy of this dignity to which thou hast advanced me of thy courtesy.' This reply was mighty agreeable to Gualtieri, for that he saw she was not uplifted into aught of pridefulness for any honour that himself or others had done her; but, a little after, having in general terms told her that his vassals could not brook this girl that had been born of her, he sent to her a serving-man of his, whom he had lessoned and who said to her with a very woeful countenance, 'Madam, an I would not die, needs must I do that which my lord commandeth me. He hath bidden me take this your daughter and....' And said no more. The lady, hearing this and seeing the servant's aspect and remembering her of her husband's words, concluded that he had enjoined him put the child to death; whereupon, without changing countenance, albeit she felt a sore anguish at heart, she straightway took her from the cradle and having kissed and blessed her, laid her in the servant's arms, saying, 'Take her and punctually do that which thy lord hath enjoined thee; but leave her not to be devoured of the beasts and the birds, except he command it thee.' The servant took the child and reported that which the lady had said to Gualtieri, who marvelled at her constancy and despatched him with the child to a kinswoman of his at Bologna, praying her to bring her up and rear her diligently, without ever saying whose daughter she was.

In course of time the lady again conceived and in due season bore a male child, to her husband's great joy; but, that which he had already done sufficing him not, he addressed himself to probe her to the quick with a yet sorer stroke and accordingly said to her one day with a troubled air, 'Wife, since thou hast borne this male child, I have nowise been able to live in peace with these my people, so sore do they murmur that a grandson of Giannucolo should become their lord after me; wherefore I misdoubt me, an I would not be driven forth of my domains, it will behove me do in this case that which I did otherwhen and ultimately put thee away and take another wife.' The lady gave ear to him with a patient mind nor answered otherwhat then, 'My lord, study to content thyself and to satisfy thy pleasure and have no thought of me, for that nothing is dear to me save in so much as I see it please thee.' Not many days after, Gualtieri sent for the son, even as he had sent for the daughter, and making a like show of having him put to death, despatched him to Bologna, there to be brought up, even as he had done with the girl; but the lady made no other countenance nor other words thereof than she had done of the girl; whereat Gualtieri marvelled sore and affirmed in himself that no other woman could have availed to do this that she did; and had he not seen her tender her children with the utmost fondness, what while it pleased him, he had believed that she did this because she recked no more of them; whereas in effect he knew that she did it of her discretion. His vassals, believing that he had caused put the children to death, blamed him sore, accounting him a barbarous man, and had the utmost compassion of his wife, who never answered otherwhat to the ladies who condoled with her for her children thus slain, than that that which pleased him thereof who had begotten them, pleased her also.

At last, several years being passed since the birth of the girl, Gualtieri, deeming it time to make the supreme trial of her endurance, declared, in the presence of his people, that he could no longer endure to have Griselda to wife and that he perceived that he had done ill and boyishly in taking her, wherefore he purposed, as far as in him lay, to make interest with the Pope to grant him a dispensation, so he might put her away and take another wife. For this he was roundly taken to task by many men of worth, but answered them nothing save that needs must it be so. The lady, hearing these things and herseeming she must look to return to her father's house and maybe tend sheep again as she had done aforetime, what while she saw another woman in possession of him to whom she willed all her weal, sorrowed sore in herself; but yet, even as she had borne the other affronts of fortune, so with a firm countenance she addressed herself to bear this also. Gualtieri no great while after let come to him from Rome counterfeit letters of dispensation and gave his vassals to believe that the Pope had thereby licensed him to take another wife and leave Griselda; then, sending for the latter, he said to her, in presence of many, 'Wife, by concession made me of the Pope, I am free to take another wife and put thee away, and accordingly, for that mine ancestors have been great gentlemen and lords of this country, whilst thine have still been husbandmen, I mean that thou be no more my wife, but that thou return to Giannucolo his house with the dowry which thou broughtest me, and I will after bring hither another wife, for that I have found one more sorted to myself.'

The lady, hearing this, contained her tears, contrary to the nature of woman, though not without great unease, and answered, 'My lord, I ever knew my mean estate to be nowise sortable with your nobility, and for that which I have been with you I have still confessed myself indebted to you and to God, nor have I ever made nor held it mine, as given to me, but have still accounted it but as a loan. It pleaseth you to require it again and it must and doth please me to restore it to you. Here is your ring wherewith you espoused me; take it. You bid me carry away with me that dowry which I brought hither, which to do you will need no paymaster and I neither purse nor packhorse, for I have not forgotten that you had me naked, and if you account it seemly that this my body, wherein I have carried children begotten of you, be seen of all, I will begone naked; but I pray you, in requital of my maidenhead, which I brought hither and bear not hence with me, that it please you I may carry away at the least one sole shift over and above my dowry.' Gualtieri, who had more mind to weep than to otherwhat, natheless kept a stern countenance and said, 'So be it; carry away a shift.' As many as stood around besought him to give her a gown, so that she who had been thirteen years and more his

490

wife should not be seen go forth of his house on such mean and shameful wise as it was to depart in her shift; but their prayers all went for nothing; wherefore the lady, having commended them to God, went forth his house in her shift, barefoot and nothing on her head, and returned to her father, followed by the tears and lamentations of all who saw her. Giannucolo, who had never been able to believe it true that Gualtieri should entertain his daughter to wife and went in daily expectation of this event, had kept her the clothes which she had put off the morning that Gualtieri had married her and now brought them to her; whereupon she donned them and addressed herself, as she had been wont to do, to the little offices of her father's house, enduring the cruel onslaught of hostile fortune with a stout heart.

Gualtieri, having done this, gave out to his people that he had chosen a daughter of one of the Counts of Panago and letting make great preparations for the nuptials, sent for Griselda to come to him and said to her, 'I am about to bring home this lady, whom I have newly taken to wife, and mean, at this her first coming, to do her honour. Thou knowest I have no women about me who know how to array me the rooms nor to do a multitude of things that behove unto such a festival; wherefore do thou, who art better versed than any else in these household matters, order that which is to do here and let bid such ladies as it seemeth good to thee and receive them as thou wert mistress here; then, when the nuptials are ended, thou mayst begone back to thy house.' Albeit these words were all daggers to Griselda's heart, who had been unable to lay down the love she bore him as she had laid down her fair fortune, she replied, 'My lord, I am ready and willing.' Then, in her coarse homespun clothes, entering the house, whence she had a little before departed in her shift, she fell to sweeping and ordering the chambers and letting place hangings and cover-cloths about the saloons and make ready the viands, putting her hand to everything, as she were some paltry serving-wench of the house, nor ever gave over till she had arrayed and ordered everything as it behoved. Thereafter, having let invite all the ladies of the country on Gualtieri's part, she awaited the day of the festival, which being come, with a cheerful countenance and the spirit and bearing of a lady of high degree, for all she had mean clothes on her back, she received all the ladies who came thither.

Meanwhile, Gualtieri, who had caused the two children be diligently reared in Bologna by his kinswoman, (who was married to a gentleman of the Panago family,) the girl being now twelve years old and the fairest creature that ever was seen and the boy six, had sent to his kinsman[5] at Bologna, praying him be pleased to come to Saluzzo with his son and daughter and take order to bring with him a goodly and honourable company and bidding him tell every one that he was carrying him the young lady to his wife, without otherwise discovering to any aught of who she was. The gentleman did as the marquess prayed him and setting out, with the girl and boy and a goodly company of gentlefolk, after some days' journey, arrived, about dinner-time, at Saluzzo, where he found all the countryfolk and many others of the neighbourhood awaiting Gualtieri's new bride. The latter, being received by the ladies and come into the saloon where the tables were laid, Griselda came to meet her, clad as she was, and accosted her blithely, saying, 'Welcome and fair welcome to my lady.' Thereupon the ladies (who had urgently, but in vain, besought Gualtieri to suffer Griselda to abide in a chamber or lend her one of the gowns that had been hers, so that she might not go thus before his guests) were seated at table and it was proceeded to serve them. The girl was eyed by every one and all declared that Gualtieri had made a good exchange; and among the rest Griselda commended her amain, both her and her young brother.

Gualtieri perceiving that the strangeness of the case in no wise changed her and being assured that this proceeded not from lack of understanding, for that he knew her to be very quick of wit, himseemed he had now seen fully as much as he desired of his lady's patience and he judged it time to deliver her from the bitterness which he doubted not she kept hidden under her constant countenance; wherefore, calling her to himself, he said to her, smiling, in the presence of every one, 'How deemest thou of our bride?' 'My lord,' answered she, 'I deem exceeding well of her, and if, as I believe, she is as discreet as she is fair, I doubt not a whit but you will live the happiest gentleman in the world with her; but I beseech you, as most I may, that you inflict not on her those pangs which you inflicted whilere on her who was sometime yours; for methinketh she might scarce avail to endure them, both because she is younger and because she hath been delicately reared, whereas the other had been in continual fatigues from a little child.' Thereupon, Gualtieri, seeing she firmly believed that the young lady was to be his wife nor therefore spoke anywise less than well, seated her by his side and said to her, 'Griselda, it is now time that thou reap the fruits of thy long patience and that those who have reputed me cruel and unjust and brutish should know that this which I have done I wrought to an end aforeseen, willing to teach thee to be a wife and to show them how to take and use one and at the same time to beget myself perpetual quiet, what while I had to live with thee; the which, whenas I came to take a wife, I was sore afraid might not betide me, and therefore, to make proof thereof, I probed and afflicted thee after such kind as thou knowest. And meseeming, for that I have never perceived that either in word or in deed hast thou departed from my pleasure, that I have of thee that solace which I desired, I purpose presently to restore thee, at one stroke, that which I took from thee at many and to requite thee with a supreme delight the pangs I have inflicted on thee. Wherefore with a joyful heart take this whom thou deemest my bride and her brother for thy children and mine; for these be they whom thou and many others have long accounted me to have barbarously let put to death; and I am thy husband, who loveth thee over all else, believing I may vaunt me that there is none else who can be so content of his wife as can I.'

So saying, he embraced her and kissed her; then, rising up, he betook himself with Griselda, who wept for joy, whereas the daughter, hearing these things, sat all stupefied, and tenderly embracing her and her brother, undeceived her and many others who were there. Thereupon the ladies arose from table, overjoyed, and withdrew with Griselda into a chamber, where, with happier augury, pulling off her mean attire, they clad her anew in a magnificent dress of her own and brought her again to the saloon, as a gentlewoman, which indeed she appeared, even in rags. There she rejoiced in her children with wonder-great joy, and all being overjoyed at this happy issue, they redoubled in feasting and merrymaking and prolonged the festivities several days, accounting Gualtieri a very wise man, albeit they held the trials which he had made of his lady overharsh, nay, intolerable; but over all they held Griselda most sage. The Count of Panago returned, after some days, to Bologna, and Gualtieri, taking Giannucolo from his labour, placed him in such estate as befitted his father-in-law, so that he lived in honour and great solace and so ended his days; whilst he himself, having nobly married his daughter, lived long and happily with Griselda, honouring her as most might be. What more can here be said save that even in poor cottages there rain down divine spirits from heaven, like as in princely palaces there be those who were worthier to tend swine than to have lordship over men? Who but Griselda could, with a countenance, not only dry,[6] but cheerful, have endured the barbarous and unheard proofs made by Gualtieri? Which latter had not belike been ill requited, had he happened upon one who, when he turned her out of doors in her shift, had let jumble her furbelows of another to such purpose that a fine gown had come of it."

DIONEO'S STORY being finished and the ladies having discoursed amain thereof, some inclining to one side and some to another, this blaming one thing and that commending it, the king, lifting his eyes to heaven and seeing that the sun was now low and the hour of vespers at hand, proceeded, without arising from session, to speak thus, "Charming ladies, as I doubt not you know, the understanding of mortals consisteth not only in having in memory things past and taking cognizance of things present; but in knowing, by means of the one and the other of these, to forecast things future is reputed by men of mark to consist the greatest wisdom. To-morrow, as you know, it will be fifteen days since we departed Florence, to take some diversion for the preservation of our health and of our lives, eschewing the woes and dolours and miseries which, since this pestilential season began, are continually to be seen about our city. This, to my judgment, we have well and honourably done; for that, an I have known to see aright, albeit merry stories and belike incentive to concupiscence have been told here and we have continually eaten and drunken well and danced and sung and made music, all things apt to incite weak minds to things less seemly, I have noted no act, no word, in fine nothing blameworthy, either on your part or on that of us men; nay, meseemeth I have seen and felt here a continual decency, an unbroken concord and a constant fraternal familiarity; the which, at once for your honour and service and for mine own, is, certes, most pleasing to me. Lest, however, for overlong usance aught should grow thereof that might issue in tediousness, and that none may avail to cavil at our overlong tarriance,—each of us, moreover, having had his or her share of the honour that yet resideth in myself,—I hold it meet, an it be your pleasure, that we now return whence we came; more by token that, if you consider aright, our company, already known to several others of the neighbourhood, may multiply after a fashion that will deprive us of our every commodity. Wherefore, if you approve my counsel, I will retain the crown conferred on me until our departure, which I purpose shall be to-morrow morning; but, should you determine otherwise, I have already in mind whom I shall invest withal for the ensuing day."

Much was the debate between the ladies and the young men; but ultimately they all took the king's counsel for useful and seemly and determined to do as he proposed; whereupon, calling the seneschal, he bespoke him of the manner which he should hold on the ensuing morning and after, having dismissed the company until supper-time, he rose to his feet. The ladies and the young men, following his example, gave themselves, this to one kind of diversion and that to another, no otherwise than of their wont; and supper-time come, they betook themselves to table with the utmost pleasure and after fell to singing and carolling and making music. Presently, Lauretta leading up a dance, the king bade Fiammetta sing a song, whereupon she very blithely proceeded to sing thus:

If love came but withouten jealousy,
I know no lady born
So blithe as I were, whosoe'er she be.
If gladsome youthfulness
In a fair lover might content a maid,
Virtue and worth discreet,
Valiance or gentilesse,
Wit and sweet speech and fashions all arrayed
In pleasantness complete,
Certes, I'm she for whose behoof these meet
In one; for, love-o'erborne,
All these in him who is my hope I see.

But for that I perceive

493

That other women are as wise as I,
I tremble for affright
And tending to believe
The worst, in others the desire espy
Of him who steals my spright;
Thus this that is my good and chief delight
Enforceth me, forlorn,
Sigh sore and live in dole and misery.

If I knew fealty such
In him my lord as I know merit there,
I were not jealous, I;
But here is seen so much
Lovers to tempt, how true they be soe'er,
I hold all false; whereby
I'm all disconsolate and fain would die,
Of each with doubting torn
Who eyes him, lest she bear him off from me.

Be, then, each lady prayed
By God that she in this be not intent
'Gainst me to do amiss;
For, sure, if any maid
Should or with words or becks or blandishment
My detriment in this
Seek or procure and if I know't, ywis,
Be all my charms forsworn
But I will make her rue it bitterly.

No sooner had Fiammetta made an end of her song than Dioneo, who was beside her, said, laughing, "Madam, you would do a great courtesy to let all the ladies know who he is, lest you be ousted of his possession through ignorance, since you would be so sore incensed thereat." After this divers other songs were sung and the night being now well nigh half spent, they all, by the king's commandment, betook themselves to repose. As the new day appeared, they arose and the seneschal having already despatched all their gear in advance, they returned, under the guidance of their discreet king, to Florence, where the three young men took leave of the seven ladies and leaving them in Santa Maria Novella, whence they had set out with them, went about their other pleasures, whilst the ladies, whenas it seemed to them time, returned to their houses.

---

1. *i.e.* he who was to have married Madam Adalieta.
2. See the First Story of Day Seven.
3. Or "strange" (*nuovo*); see ante, passim.
4. *i.e.* his vassals.
5. *i.e.* the husband of his kinswoman aforesaid.
6. *i.e.* unwetted with tears.

CONCLUSION OF THE AUTHOR

MOST NOBLE DAMSELS, for whose solace I have addressed myself to so long a labour, I have now, methinketh, with the aid of the Divine favour, (vouchsafed me, as I deem, for your pious prayers and not for my proper merits,) throughly accomplished that which I engaged, at the beginning of this present work, to do; wherefore, returning thanks first to God and after to you, it behoveth to give rest to my pen and to my tired hand. Which ere I accord them, I purpose briefly to reply, as to objections tacitly broached, to certain small matters that may peradventure be alleged by some one of you or by others, since meseemeth very certain that these stories have no especial privilege more than other things; nay, I mind me to have shown, at the beginning of the fourth day, that they have none such. There are, peradventure, some of you who will say that I have used overmuch license in inditing these stories, as well as in making ladies whiles say and very often hearken to things not very seemly either to be said or heard of modest women. This I deny, for that there is nothing so unseemly as to be forbidden unto any one, so but he express it in seemly terms, as meseemeth indeed I have here very aptly done. But let us suppose that it is so (for that I mean not to plead with you, who would overcome me,) I say that many reasons very readily offer themselves in answer why I have done this. Firstly, if there be aught thereof[1] in any of them, the nature of the stories required it, the which, an they be considered with the rational eye of a person of understanding, it will be abundantly manifest that I could not have otherwise recounted, an I would not altogether disfeature them. And if perchance there be therein some tittle, some wordlet or two freer, maybe, than liketh your squeamish hypocritical prudes, who weigh words rather than deeds and study more to appear, than to be, good, I say that it should no more be forbidden me to write them than it is commonly forbidden unto men and women to say all day long *hole* and *peg* and *mortar* and *pestle* and *sausage* and *polony* and all manner like things; without reckoning that no less liberty should be accorded to my pen than is conceded to the brush of the limner, who, without any (or, at the least, any just) reprehension, maketh—let be St. Michael smite the serpent with sword or spear and St. George the dragon, whereas it pleaseth them—but Adam male and Eve female and affixeth to the cross, whiles with one nail and whiles with two, the feet of Him Himself who willed for the salvation of the human race to die upon the rood. Moreover, it is eath

495

enough to see that these things are spoken, not in the church, of the affairs whereof it behoveth to speak with a mind and in terms alike of the chastest (albeit among its histories there are tales enough to be found of anothergates fashion than those written by me), nor yet in the schools of philosophy, where decency is no less required than otherwhere, nor among churchmen or philosophers anywhere, but amidst gardens, in a place of pleasance and diversion and among men and women, though young, yet of mature wit and not to be led astray by stories, at a time when it was not forbidden to the most virtuous to go, for their own preservation, with their breeches on their heads. Again, such as they are, these stories, like everything else, can both harm and profit, according to the disposition of the listener. Who knoweth not that wine, though, according to Cinciglione and Scolajo[2] and many others, an excellent thing for people in health,[3] is hurtful unto whoso hath the fever? Shall we say, then, because it harmeth the fevered, that it is naught? Who knoweth not that fire is most useful, nay, necessary to mortals? Shall we say, because it burneth houses and villages and cities, that it is naught? Arms on like wise assure the welfare of those who desire to live in peace and yet oftentimes slay men, not of any malice of their own, but of the perversity of those who use them wrongfully. Corrupt mind never understood word healthily, and even as seemly words profit not depraved minds, so those which are not altogether seemly avail not to contaminate the well-disposed, any more than mire can sully the rays of the sun or earthly foulness the beauties of the sky. What books, what words, what letters are holier, worthier, more venerable than those of the Divine Scriptures? Yet many there be, who, interpreting them perversely, have brought themselves and others to perdition. Everything in itself is good unto somewhat and ill used, may be in many things harmful; and so say I of my stories. If any be minded to draw therefrom ill counsel or ill practice, they will nowise forbid it him, if perchance they have it in them or be strained and twisted into having it; and who so will have profit and utility thereof, they will not deny it him, nor will they be ever styled or accounted other than useful and seemly, if they be read at those times and to those persons for which and for whom they have been recounted. Whoso hath to say paternosters or to make tarts and puddings for her spiritual director, let her leave them be; they will not run after any to make her read them; albeit your she-saints themselves now and again say and even do fine things.

There be some ladies also who will say that there are some stories here, which had been better away. Granted; but I could not nor should write aught save those actually related, wherefore those who told them should have told them goodly and I would have written them goodly. But, if folk will e'en pretend that I am both the inventor and writer thereof (which I am not), I say that I should not take shame to myself that they were not all alike goodly, for that there is no craftsman living (barring God) who doth everything alike well and completely; witness Charlemagne, who was the first maker of the Paladins, but knew not to make so many thereof that he might avail to form an army of them alone. In the multitude of things, needs must divers qualities thereof be found. No field was ever so well tilled but therein or nettles or thistles or somewhat of briers or other weeds might be found mingled with the better herbs. Besides, having to speak to simple lasses, such as you are for the most part, it had been folly to go seeking and wearying myself to find very choice and exquisite matters, and to use great pains to speak very measuredly. Algates, whoso goeth reading among these, let him leave those which offend and read those which divert. They all, not to lead any one into error, bear branded upon the forefront that which they hold hidden within their bosoms.

Again, I doubt not but there be those who will say that some of them are overlong; to whom I say again that whoso hath overwhat to do doth folly to read these stories, even though they were brief. And albeit a great while is passed from the time when I began to write to this present hour whenas I come to the end of my toils, it hath not therefor escaped my memory that I proffered this my travail to idle women and not to others, and unto whoso readeth to pass away the time, nothing can be overlong, so but it do that for which he useth it. Things brief are far better suited unto students, who study, not to pass away, but usefully to employ time, than to you ladies, who have on your hands all the time that you spend not in the pleasures of love; more by token that, as none of you goeth to Athens or Bologna or Paris to study, it behoveth to speak to you more at large than to those who have had their wits whetted by study. Again, I doubt not a jot but there be yet some of you who will say that the things aforesaid are full of quips and cranks and quodlibets and that it ill beseemeth a man of weight and gravity to have written thus. To these I am bound to render and do render thanks, for that, moved by a virtuous jealousy, they are so tender of my fame; but to their objection I reply on this wise; I confess to being a man of weight and to have been often weighed in my time, wherefore, speaking to those ladies who have not weighed me, I declare that I am not heavy; nay, I am so light that I abide like a nutgall in water, and considering that the preachments made of friars, to rebuke men of their sins, are nowadays for the most part seen full of quips and cranks and gibes, I conceived that these latter would not sit amiss in my stories written to ease women of melancholy. Algates, an they should laugh overmuch on that account, the Lamentations of Jeremiah, the Passion of our Saviour and the Complaint of Mary Magdalen will lightly avail to cure them thereof.

Again, who can doubt but there will to boot be found some to say that I have an ill tongue and a venomous, for that I have in sundry places written the truth anent the friars? To those who shall say thus it must be forgiven, since it is not credible that they are moved by other than just cause, for that the friars are a good sort of folk, who eschew unease for the love of God and who grind with a full head of water and tell no tales, and but that they all savour somewhat of the buck-goat, their commerce would be far more agreeable. Natheless, I confess that the things of this world have no stability and are still on the change, and so may it have befallen of my tongue, the which, not to trust to mine own judgment, (which I eschew as most I may in my affairs,) a she-neighbour of mine told me, not long since, was the best and sweetest in the world; and in good sooth, were this the case, there had been few of the foregoing stories to write. But, for that those who say thus speak despitefully, I will have that which hath been said suffice them for a reply; wherefore, leaving each of you henceforth to say and believe as seemeth good to her, it is time for me to make an end of words, humbly thanking Him who hath, after so long a labour, brought us with His help to the desired end. And you, charming ladies, abide you in peace with His favour, remembering you of me, if perchance it profit any of you aught to have read these stories.

---

1. *i.e.* of overmuch licence.
2. Two noted wine-bidders of the time.
3. Lit. living folk (*viventi*).

Made in the USA
Coppell, TX
08 April 2020

19467265R00293